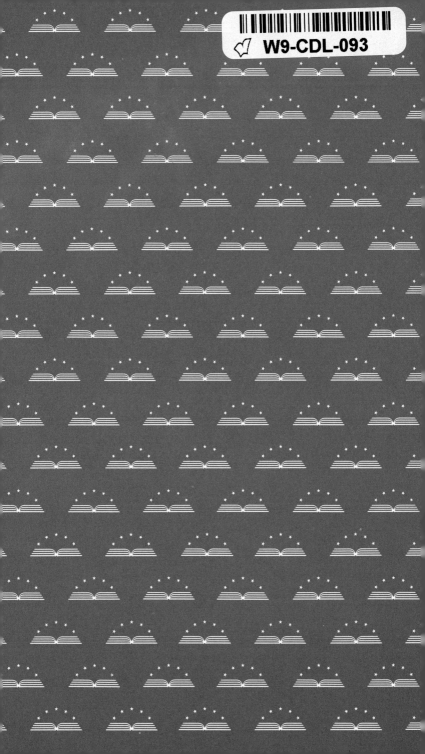

VLADIMIR NABOKOV

VLADIMIR NABOKOV

NOVELS AND MEMOIRS 1941–1951

The Real Life of Sebastian Knight

Bend Sinister

Speak, Memory
An Autobiography Revisited

THE LIBRARY OF AMERICA

The Real Life of Sebastian Knight copyright 1941, 1968 by
Vladimir Nabokov. Published by arrangement with New
Directions Publishing Corp. *Bend Sinister* copyright 1947 by
Vladimir Nabokov; Introduction copyright © 1964 by Vladimir
Nabokov. *Speak, Memory* copyright 1947, 1948, 1949, 1950, 1951 by
Vladimir Nabokov, © 1967 by Vladimir Nabokov. Published by
arrangement with Alfred A. Knopf, Inc.

The paper used in this publication meets the
minimum requirements of the American National Standard for
Information Sciences—Permanence of Paper for Printed
Library Materials, ANSI Z39.48—1984.

Distributed to the trade in the United States
by Penguin Books USA Inc
and in Canada by Penguin Books Canada Ltd.

Library of Congress Catalog Number: 96–15257
For cataloging information, see end of Notes.
ISBN: 1–883011–18–3

First Printing
The Library of America—87

Manufactured in the United States of America

BRIAN BOYD

ADVISED ON TEXTUAL MATTERS AND
WROTE THE NOTES FOR THIS VOLUME

Contents

THE REAL LIFE OF
SEBASTIAN KNIGHT

To Véra

I

SEBASTIAN KNIGHT was born on the thirty-first of December, 1899, in the former capital of my country. An old Russian lady who has for some obscure reason begged me not to divulge her name, happened to show me in Paris the diary she had kept in the past. So uneventful had those years been (apparently) that the collecting of daily details (which is always a poor method of self-preservation) barely surpassed a short description of the day's weather; and it is curious to note in this respect that the personal diaries of sovereigns—no matter what troubles beset their realms—are mainly concerned with the same subject. Luck being what it is when left alone, here I was offered something which I might never have hunted down had it been a chosen quarry. Therefore I am able to state that the morning of Sebastian's birth was a fine windless one, with twelve degrees (Reaumur) below zero . . . this is all, however, that the good lady found worth setting down. On second thought I cannot see any real necessity of complying with her anonymity. That she will ever read this book seems wildly improbable. Her name was and is Olga Olegovna Orlova—an egg-like alliteration which it would have been a pity to withhold.

Her dry account cannot convey to the untravelled reader the implied delights of a winter day such as she describes in St. Petersburg; the pure luxury of a cloudless sky designed not to warm the flesh, but solely to please the eye; the sheen of sledge-cuts on the hard-beaten snow of spacious streets with a tawny tinge about the middle tracks due to a rich mixture of horse-dung; the brightly coloured bunch of toy-balloons hawked by an aproned pedlar; the soft curve of a cupola, its gold dimmed by the bloom of powdery frost; the birch trees in the public gardens, every tiniest twig outlined in white; the rasp and tinkle of winter traffic . . . and by the way how queer it is when you look at an old picture postcard (like the one I have placed on my desk to keep the child of memory amused for a moment) to consider the haphazard way Russian cabs had of turning whenever they liked, anywhere and anyhow, so that instead of the straight, self-conscious stream of modern traffic one sees—on this painted photograph—a dream-wide street with droshkies all awry under incredibly blue skies, which, farther away, melt automatically into a pink flush of mnemonic banality.

I have not been able to obtain a picture of the house where Sebastian was born, but I know it well, for I was born there myself, some six years later. We had the same father: he had married again, soon after divorcing Sebastian's mother. Oddly enough, this second marriage is not mentioned at all in Mr. Goodman's *Tragedy of Sebastian Knight* (which appeared in 1936 and to which I shall have occasion to refer more fully); so that to readers of Goodman's book I am bound to appear non-existent—a bogus relative, a garrulous impostor; but Sebastian himself in his most autobiographical work (*Lost Property*) has some kind words to say about my mother—and I think she deserved them well. Nor is it exact, as suggested in the British press after Sebastian's decease, that his father was killed in the duel he fought in 1913; as a matter of fact he was steadily recovering from the bullet-wound in his chest, when—a full month later—he contracted a cold with which his half-healed lung could not cope.

A fine soldier, a warm-hearted, humorous, high-spirited man, he had in him that rich strain of adventurous restlessness which Sebastian inherited as a writer. Last winter at a literary lunch, in South Kensington, a celebrated old critic, whose brilliancy and learning I have always admired, was heard to remark as the talk fluttered around Sebastian Knight's untimely death: "Poor Knight! he really had two periods, the first—a dull man writing broken English, the second—a broken man writing dull English." A nasty dig, nasty in more ways than one for it is far too easy to talk of a dead author behind the backs of his books. I should like to believe that the jester feels no pride in recalling this particular jest, the more so as he showed far greater restraint when reviewing Sebastian Knight's work a few years ago.

Nevertheless, it must be admitted that in a certain sense, Sebastian's life, though far from being dull, lacked the terrific vigour of his literary style. Every time I open one of his books, I seem to see my father dashing into the room,—that special way he had of flinging open the door and immediately pouncing upon a thing he wanted or a creature he loved. My first impression of him is always a breathless one of suddenly soaring up from the floor, one half of my toy train still dangling from my hand and the crystal pendants of the chandelier dangerously near my head. He would bump me down as suddenly as he had snatched me up, as suddenly as Sebastian's prose sweeps the reader off his feet, to let him drop with a shock into the gleeful bathos of the next wild paragraph. Also some of my father's favourite quips seem to have broken into fantastic flower in such typical Knight stories as *Albinos in Black* or *The Funny Mountain*, his best one perhaps, that beautifully queer tale which always makes me think of a child laughing in its sleep.

It was abroad, in Italy as far as I know, that my father, then a young guardsman on leave, met Virginia Knight. Their first meeting was connected with a fox-hunt in Rome, in the early nineties, but whether this was mentioned by my mother or whether I subconsciously recall seeing some dim snapshot in a family album, I cannot say. He wooed her long. She was the daughter of Edward Knight, a gentleman of means; this is all I know of him, but from the fact that my grandmother, an austere and wilful woman (I remember her fan, her mittens, her cold white fingers) was emphatically opposed to their marriage, and would repeat the legend of her objections even after my father had been married again, I am inclined to deduce that the Knight family (whatever it was) did not quite reach the standard (whatever that standard might have been) which was required by the redheels of the old regime in Russia. I am not sure either whether my father's first marriage did not clash somehow with the traditions of his regiment,—anyway his real military success only began with the Japanese war, which was after his wife had left him.

I was still a child when I lost my father; and it was very much later, in 1922, a few months before my mother's last and fatal operation, that she told me several things which she thought I should know. My father's first marriage had not been happy. A strange woman, a restless reckless being—but not my father's kind of restlessness. His was a constant quest which changed its object only after having attained it. Hers was a half-hearted pursuit, capricious and rambling, now swerving wide off the mark, now forgetting it midway, as one forgets one's umbrella in a taxicab. She was fond of my father after a fashion, a fitful fashion to say the least, and when one day it occurred to her that she might be in love with another (whose name my father never learnt from her lips), she left husband and child as suddenly as a rain-drop starts to slide tipwards down a syringa leaf. That upward jerk of the forsaken leaf, which had been heavy with its bright burden, must have caused my father fierce pain; and I do not like to dwell in mind upon that day in a Paris hotel, with Sebastian aged about four, poorly attended by a puzzled nurse, and my father locked up in his room, "that special kind of hotel room which is so perfectly fit for the staging of the worst tragedies: a dead burnished clock (the waxed moustache of ten minutes to two) under its glass dome on an evil mantelpiece, the French window with its fuddled fly between muslin and pane, and a sample of the hotel's letter paper on the well-used blotting-pad." This is a quotation from *Albinos in Black*, textually in no way connected with that special disaster, but retaining the distant memory of a child's fretfulness on a bleak hotel carpet, with nothing to do and a queer expansion of time, time gone astray, asprawl . . .

War in the Far East allowed my father that happy activity which helped him—if not to forget Virginia—at least to make life worth living again. His vigorous egotism was but a form of manly vitality and as such wholly consistent with an essentially generous nature. Permanent misery, let alone self-destruction, must have seemed to him a mean business, a shameful surrender. When in 1905 he married again, he surely felt satisfaction at having got the upper hand in his dealings with destiny.

Virginia reappeared in 1908. She was an inveterate traveller, always on the move and alike at home in any small pension or expensive hotel, home only meaning to her the comfort of constant change; from her, Sebastian inherited that strange, almost romantic, passion for sleeping-cars and Great European Express Trains, "the soft crackle of polished panels in the blue-shaded night, the long sad sigh of brakes at dimly surmised stations, the upward slide of an embossed leather blind disclosing a platform, a man wheeling luggage, the milky globe of a lamp with a pale moth whirling around it; the clank of an invisible hammer testing wheels; the gliding move into darkness; the passing glimpse of a lone woman touching silver-bright things in her travelling-case on the blue plush of a lighted compartment."

She arrived by the Nord Express on a winter day, without the slightest warning, and sent a curt note asking to see her son. My father was away in the country on a bear-hunt; so my mother quietly took Sebastian to the Hotel d'Europe where Virginia had put up for a single afternoon. There, in the hall, she saw her husband's first wife, a slim, slightly angular woman, with a small quivering face under a huge black hat. She had raised her veil above her lips to kiss the boy, and no sooner had she touched him than she burst into tears, as if Sebastian's warm tender temple was the very source and satiety of her sorrow. Immediately afterwards she put on her gloves and started to tell my mother in bad French a pointless and quite irrelevant story about a Polish woman who had attempted to steal her vanity-bag in the dining-car. Then she thrust into Sebastian's hand a small parcel of sugar-coated violets, gave my mother a nervous smile and followed the porter who was carrying out her luggage. This was all, and next year she died.

It is known from a cousin of hers, H. F. Stainton, that during the last months of her life she roamed all over the South of France, staying for a day or two at small hot provincial towns, rarely visited by tourists—feverish, alone (she had abandoned her lover) and probably very unhappy. One might think she was fleeing from someone or something, as she doubled and re-crossed her tracks; on the other hand, to any one who knew her moods, that hectic dashing might seem but a final exaggeration of her usual restlessness. She died of heart-failure (Lehmann's disease) at the little town of Roque-brune, in the summer of 1909. There was some difficulty in getting the body dispatched to England; her people had died some time before; Mr. Stainton alone attended her burial in London.

My parents lived happily. It was a quiet and tender union, unmarred by the ugly gossip of certain relatives of ours who whispered that my father, although a loving husband, was attracted now and then by other women. One day, about Christmas, 1912, an acquaintance of his, a very charming and thoughtless girl, happened to mention as they walked down the Nevsky, that her sister's fiancé, a certain Palchin, had known his first wife. My father said he remembered the man,—they had met at Biarritz about ten years ago, or was it nine . . .

"Oh, but he knew her later too," said the girl, "you see he confessed to my sister that he had lived with Virginia after you parted . . . Then she dropped him somewhere in Switzerland . . . Funny, nobody knew."

"Well," said my father quietly, "if it has not leaked out before, there is no reason for people to start prattling ten years later."

By a very grim coincidence, on the very next day, a good friend of our family, Captain Belov, casually asked my father whether it was true that his first wife came from Australia,— he, the Captain, had always thought she was English. My father replied that, as far as he knew, her parents had lived for some time in Melbourne, but that she had been born in Kent.

". . . What makes you ask me that?" he added.

The Captain answered evasively that his wife had been at a party or something where somebody had said something . . .

"Some things will have to stop, I'm afraid," said my father.

Next morning he called upon Palchin, who received him with a greater show of geniality than was necessary. He had spent many years abroad, he said, and was glad to meet old friends.

"There is a certain dirty lie being spread," said my father without sitting down, "and I think you know what it is."

"Look here, my dear fellow," said Palchin, "no use my pretending I don't see what you are driving at. I am sorry people have been talking, but really there is no reason to lose our tempers . . . It is nobody's fault that you and I were in the same boat once."

"In that case, Sir," said my father, "my seconds will call on you."

Palchin was a fool and a cad, this much at least I gathered from the story my mother told me (and which in her telling had assumed the vivid direct form I have tried to retain here). But just because Palchin was a fool and a cad, it is hard for me to understand why a man of my father's worth should have risked his life to satisfy—what? Virginia's honour? His own desire of revenge? But just as Virginia's honour had been irredeemably forfeited by the very fact of her flight, so all ideas of vengeance ought to have long lost their bitter lust in the happy years of my father's second marriage. Or was it merely the naming of a name, the seeing of a face, the sudden grotesque sight of an individual stamp upon what had been a tame faceless ghost? And taken all in all was it, this echo of a distant past (and echoes are seldom more than a bark, no matter how pure-voiced the caller), was it worth the ruin of our home and the grief of my mother?

The duel was fought in a snow-storm on the bank of a frozen brook. Two shots were exchanged before my father fell face downwards on a blue-gray army-cloak spread on the snow. Palchin, his hands trembling, lit a cigarette. Captain Belov hailed the coachmen who were humbly waiting some distance away on the snow-swept road. The whole beastly affair had lasted three minutes.

In *Lost Property* Sebastian gives his own impressions of that lugubrious January day. "Neither my stepmother," he writes, "nor any one of the household knew of the pending affair. On the eve, at dinner, my father threw bread-pellets at me across the table: I had been sulking all day because of some fiendish woollies which the doctor had insisted upon my wearing, and he was trying to cheer me up; but I frowned and blushed and turned away. After dinner we sat in his study, he sipping his coffee and listening to my stepmother's account of the noxious way Mademoiselle had of giving my small half-brother sweets after putting him to bed; and I, at the far end of the room, on the sofa, turning the pages of *Chums*: 'Look out for the next instalment of this rattling yarn.' Jokes at the bottom of the large thin pages. 'The guest of honour had been shown over the School: What struck you most?—A pea from a pea-shooter.' Express-trains roaring through the night. The cricket Blue who fielded the knife thrown by a vicious Malay at the cricketer's friend . . . That 'uproarious' serial featuring three boys, one of whom was a contortionist who could make his nose spin, the second a conjuror, the third a ventriloquist . . . A horseman leaping over a racing-car . . .

"Next morning at school, I made a bad mess of the geometrical problem which in our slang we termed 'Pythagoras' Pants.' The morning was so dark that the lights were turned on in the classroom and this always gave me a nasty buzzing in the head. I came home about half past three in the afternoon with that sticky sense of uncleanliness which I always brought back from school and which was now enhanced by ticklish underclothes. My father's orderly was sobbing in the hall."

2

IN HIS SLAPDASH and very misleading book, Mr. Goodman paints in a few ill-chosen sentences a ridiculously wrong picture of Sebastian Knight's childhood. It is one thing to be an author's secretary, it is quite another to set down an author's life; and if such a task is prompted by the desire to get one's book into the market while the flowers on a fresh grave may still be watered with profit, it is still another matter to try to combine commercial haste with exhaustive research, fairness and wisdom. I am not out to damage anybody's reputation. There is no libel in asserting that alone the impetus of a clicking typewriter could enable Mr. Goodman to remark that "a Russian education was forced upon a small boy always conscious of the rich English strain in his blood." This foreign influence, Mr. Goodman goes on, "brought acute suffering to the child, so that in his riper years it was with a shudder that he recalled the bearded moujiks, the ikons, the drone of balalaikas, all of which displaced a healthy English upbringing."

It is hardly worth while pointing out that Mr. Goodman's concept of Russian surroundings is no truer to nature than, say, a Kalmuk's notion of England as a dark place where small boys are flogged to death by red-whiskered schoolmasters. What should be really stressed is the fact that Sebastian was brought up in an atmosphere of intellectual refinement, blending the spiritual grace of a Russian household with the very best treasures of European culture, and that whatever Sebastian's own reaction to his Russian memories, its complex and special nature never sank to the vulgar level suggested by his biographer.

I remember Sebastian as a boy, six years my senior, gloriously messing about with water-colours in the homely aura of a stately kerosene lamp whose pink silk shade seems painted by his own very wet brush, now that it glows in my memory. I see myself, a child of four or five, on tiptoe, straining and fidgeting, trying to get a better glimpse of the paintbox beyond my half-brother's moving elbow; sticky reds and blues, so well-licked and worn that the enamel gleams in their cavities. There is a slight clatter every time Sebastian mixes his colours on the inside of the tin lid, and the water in the glass before him is clouded with magic hues. His dark hair, closely cropped, renders a small birthmark visible above his rose-red diaphanous ear,—I have clambered onto a chair by now—but he continues to pay no attention to me, until with a precarious lunge, I try to dab the bluest cake in the box, and then, with a shove of his shoulder he pushes me away, still not turning, still as silent and distant, as always in regard to me. I remember peering over the banisters and seeing him come up the stairs, after school, dressed in the black regulation uniform with that leather belt I secretly coveted, mounting slowly, slouchingly, lugging his piebald satchel behind him, patting the banisters and now and then pulling himself up over two or three steps at a time. My lips pursed, I squeeze out a white spittal which falls down and down, always missing Sebastian; and this I do not because I want to annoy him, but merely as a wistful and vain attempt to make him notice my existence. I have a vivid recollection, too, of his riding a bicycle with very low handle-bars along a sun-dappled path in the park of our countryplace, spinning on slowly, the pedals motionless, and I trotting behind, trotting a little faster as his sandled foot presses down the pedal; I am doing my best to keep pace with his tick-tick-sizzling back-wheel, but he heeds me not and soon leaves me hopelessly behind, very out of breath and still trotting.

Then later on, when he was sixteen and I ten, he would sometimes help me with my lessons, explaining things in such a rapid impatient way, that nothing ever came of his assistance and after a while he would pocket his pencil and stalk out of the room. At that period he was tall and sallow-complexioned with a dark shadow above his upper lip. His hair was now glossily parted, and he wrote verse in a black copybook which he kept locked up in his drawer.

I once discovered where he kept the key (in a chink of the wall near the white Dutch stove in his room) and I opened that drawer. There was the copybook; also the photograph of a sister of one of his schoolmates; some gold coins; and a small muslin bag of violet sweets. The poems were written in

English. We had had English lessons at home not long before my father's death, and although I never could learn to speak the language fluently, I read and wrote it with comparative ease. I dimly recollect the verse was very romantic, full of dark roses and stars and the call of the sea; but one detail stands out perfectly plain in my memory: the signature under each poem was a little black chess-knight drawn in ink.

I have endeavoured to form a coherent picture of what I saw of my half-brother in those childhood days of mine, between say 1910 (my first year of consciousness) and 1919 (the year he left for England). But the task eludes me. Sebastian's image does not appear as part of my boyhood, thus subject to endless selection and development, nor does it appear as a succession of familiar visions, but it comes to me in a few bright patches, as if he were not a constant member of our family, but some erratic visitor passing across a lighted room and then for a long interval fading into the night. I explain this not so much by the fact that my own childish interests precluded any conscious relation with one who was not young enough to be my companion and not old enough to be my guide, but by Sebastian's constant aloofness, which, although I loved him dearly, never allowed my affection either recognition or food. I could perhaps describe the way he walked, or laughed or sneezed, but all this would be no more than sundry bits of cinema-film cut away by scissors and having nothing in common with the essential drama. And drama there was. Sebastian could never forget his mother, nor could he forget that his father had died for her. That her name was never mentioned in our home added morbid glamour to the remembered charm which suffused his impressionable soul. I do not know whether he could recall with any clarity the time when she was his father's wife; probably he could in a way, as a soft radiance in the background of his life. Nor can I tell what he felt at seeing his mother again when a boy of nine. My mother says he was listless and tongue-tied, afterwards never mentioning that short and pathetically incomplete meeting. In *Lost Property* Sebastian hints at a vaguely bitter feeling towards his happily remarried father, a feeling which changed into one of ecstatic worship when he learnt the reason of his father's fatal duel.

"My discovery of England," writes Sebastian (*Lost Property*), "put new life into my most intimate memories . . . After Cambridge I took a trip to the Continent and spent a quiet fortnight at Monte Carlo. I think there is some Casino place there, where people gamble, but if so, I missed it, as most of my time was taken up by the composition of my first novel—a very pretentious affair which I am glad to say was turned down by almost as many publishers as my next book had readers. One day I went for a long walk and found a place called Roquebrune. It was at Roquebrune that my mother had died thirteen years before. I well remember the day my father told me of her death and the name of the pension where it occurred. The name was 'Les Violettes.' I asked a chauffeur whether he knew of such a house, but he did not. Then I asked a fruit-seller and he showed me the way. I came at last to a pinkish villa roofed with the typical Provence round red tiles, and I noticed a bunch of violets clumsily painted on the gate. So this was the house. I crossed the garden and spoke to the landlady. She said she had only lately taken over the pension from the former owner and knew nothing of the past. I asked her permission to sit awhile in the garden. An old man naked as far down as I could see peered at me from a balcony, but otherwise there was no one about. I sat down on a blue bench under a great eucalyptus, its bark half stripped away, as seems to be always the case with this sort of tree. Then I tried to see the pink house and the tree and the whole complexion of the place as my mother had seen it. I regretted not knowing the exact window of her room. Judging by the villa's name, I felt sure that there had been before her eyes that same bed of purple pansies. Gradually I worked myself into such a state that for a moment the pink and green seemed to shimmer and float as if seen through a veil of mist. My mother, a dim slight figure in a large hat, went slowly up the steps which seemed to dissolve into water. A terrific thump made me regain consciousness. An orange had rolled down out of the paper bag on my lap. I picked it up and left the garden. Some months later in London I happened to meet a cousin of hers. A turn of the conversation led me to mention that I had visited the place where she had died. 'Oh,' he said, 'but it was the other Roquebrune, the one in the Var.' "

It is curious to note that Mr. Goodman, quoting the same passage, is content to comment that "Sebastian Knight was so enamoured of the burlesque side of things and so incapable of caring for their serious core that he managed, without being by nature either callous or cynical, to make fun of intimate emotions, rightly held sacred by the rest of humanity." No wonder this solemn biographer is out of tune with his hero at every point of the story.

For reasons already mentioned I shall not attempt to describe Sebastian's boyhood with anything like the methodical continuity which I would have normally achieved had Sebastian been a character of fiction. Had it been thus I could have hoped to keep the reader instructed and entertained by picturing my hero's smooth development from infancy to youth. But if I should try this with Sebastian the result would be one of those "biographies romancées" which are by far the worst kind of literature yet invented. So let the door be closed leaving but a thin line of taut light underneath, let that lamp go out too in the neighboring room where Sebastian has gone to bed; let the beautiful olivaceous house on the Neva embankment fade out gradually in the gray-blue frosty night, with gently falling snowflakes lingering in the moon-white blaze of the tall street lamp and powdering the mighty limbs of the two bearded corbel figures which support with an Atlas-like effort the oriel of my father's room. My father is dead, Sebastian is asleep, or at least mouse-quiet, in the next room— and I am lying in bed, wide awake, staring into the darkness.

Some twenty years later, I undertook a journey to Lausanne in order to find the old Swiss lady who had been first Sebastian's governess, then mine. She must have been about fifty when she left us in 1914; correspondence between us had long ceased, so I was not at all sure of finding her still alive, in 1936. But I did. There existed, as I discovered, a union of old Swiss women who had been governesses in Russia before the revolution. They "lived in their past," as the very kind gentleman who guided me there explained, spending their last years— and most of these ladies were decrepit and dotty—comparing notes, having petty feuds with one another and reviling the state of affairs in the Switzerland they had discovered after their many years of life in Russia. Their tragedy lay in the fact that during all those years spent in a foreign country they had kept absolutely immune to its influence (even to the extent of not learning the simplest Russian words); somewhat hostile to their surroundings—how often have I heard Mademoiselle bemoan her exile, complain of being slighted and misunderstood, and yearn for her fair native land; but when these poor wandering souls came home, they found themselves complete strangers in a changed country, so that by a queer trick of sentiment—Russia (which to them had really been an unknown abyss, remotely rumbling beyond a lamplit corner of a stuffy back-room with family photographs in mother-of-pearl frames and a water-colour view of Chillon castle), unknown Russia now took on the aspect of a lost paradise, a vast, vague but retrospectively friendly place, peopled with wistful fancies. I found Mademoiselle very deaf and gray, but as voluble as ever, and after the first effusive embraces she started to recall little facts of my childhood which were either hopelessly distorted, or so foreign to my memory that I doubted their past reality. She knew nothing of my mother's death; nor did she know of Sebastian's having died three months ago. Incidentally, she was also ignorant of his having been a great writer. She was very tearful and her tears were very sincere, but it seemed to annoy her somehow that I did not join in the crying. "You were always so self-controlled," she said. I told her I was writing a book about Sebastian and asked her to talk about his childhood. She had come to our house soon after my father's second marriage, but the past in her mind was so blurred and displaced that she talked of my father's first wife ("cette horrible Anglaise") as if she had known her as well as she had my mother ("cette femme admirable"). "My poor little Sebastian," she wailed, "so tender to me, so noble. Ah, how I remember the way he had of flinging his little arms round my neck and saying; 'I hate everybody except you, Zelle, you alone understand my soul.' And that day when I gently smacked his hand,—une toute petite tape—for being rude to your mother,—the expression of his eyes—it made me want to cry—and his voice when he said: 'I am grateful to you, Zelle. It shall never happen again . . .'"

She went on in this fashion for quite a long time, making

me dismally uncomfortable. I managed at last, after several fruitless attempts, to turn the conversation—I was quite hoarse by that time as she had mislaid her ear-trumpet. Then she spoke of her neighbour, a fat little creature still older than she, whom I had met in the passage. "The good woman is quite deaf," she complained, "and a dreadful liar. I know for certain that she only gave lessons to the Princess Demidov's children—never lived there." "Write that book, that beautiful book," she cried as I was leaving, "make it a fairy-tale with Sebastian for prince. The enchanted prince . . . Many a time have I said to him: Sebastian, be careful, women will adore you. And he would reply with a laugh: Well, I'll adore women too . . ."

I squirmed inwardly. She gave me a smacking kiss and patted my hand and was tearful again. I glanced at her misty old eyes, at the dead lustre of her false teeth, at the well-remembered garnet brooch on her bosom . . . We parted. It was raining hard and I felt ashamed and cross at having interrupted my second chapter to make this useless pilgrimage. One impression especially upset me. She had not asked one single thing about Sebastian's later life, not a single question about the way he had died, nothing.

3

In November of 1918 my mother resolved to flee with Sebastian and myself from the dangers of Russia. Revolution was in full swing, frontiers were closed. She got in touch with a man who had made smuggling refugees across the border his profession, and it was settled that for a certain fee, one half of which was paid in advance, he would get us to Finland. We were to leave the train just before the frontier, at a place we could lawfully reach, and then cross over by secret paths, doubly, trebly secret owing to the heavy snowfalls in that silent region. At the starting-point of our train journey, we found ourselves, my mother and I, waiting for Sebastian, who, with the heroic help of Captain Belov, was trundling the luggage from house to station. The train was scheduled to start at 8:40 A.M. Half past and still no Sebastian. Our guide was already in the train and sat quietly reading a newspaper; he had warned my mother that in no circumstance should she talk to him in public, and as the time passed and the train was preparing to leave, a nightmare feeling of numb panic began to come over us. We knew that the man in accordance with the traditions of his profession, would never renew a performance that had misfired at the outset. We knew too that we could not again afford the expenses of flight. The minutes passed and I felt something gurgling desperately in the pit of my stomach. The thought that in a minute or two the train would move off and that we should have to return to a dark cold attic (our house had been nationalised some months ago) was utterly disastrous. On our way to the station we had passed Sebastian and Belov pushing the heavily burdened wheelbarrow through the crunching snow. This picture now stood motionless before my eyes (I was a boy of thirteen and very imaginative) as a charmed thing doomed to its paralysed eternity. My mother, her hands in her sleeves and a wisp of grey hair emerging from beneath her woolen kerchief, walked to and fro, trying to catch the eye of our guide every time she passed by his window. Eight forty-five, eight-fifty . . . The train was late in starting, but at last the whistle blew, a rush of warm white smoke raced its shadow across the brown snow on the platform, and at the same time Sebastian appeared running, the earflaps of his fur cap flying in the wind. The three of us scrambled into the moving train. It took some time before he managed to tell us that Captain Belov had been arrested in the street just as they were passing the house where he had lived before, and that leaving the luggage to its fate, he, Sebastian, had made a desperate dash for the station. A few months later we learned that our poor friend had been shot, together with a score of people in the same batch, shoulder to shoulder with Palchin, who died as bravely as Belov.

In his last published book, *The Doubtful Asphodel* (1936), Sebastian depicts an episodical character who has just escaped from an unnamed country of terror and misery. "What can I tell you of my past, gentlemen [he is saying], I was born in a land where the idea of freedom, the notion of right, the habit of human kindness were things coldly despised and brutally outlawed. Now and then, in the course of history, a hypocrite government would paint the walls of the nation's prison a comelier shade of yellow and loudly proclaim the granting of rights familiar to happier states; but either these rights were solely enjoyed by the jailers or else they contained some secret flaw which made them even more bitter than the decrees of frank tyranny . . . . Every man in the land was a slave, if he was not a bully; since the soul and everything pertaining to it were denied to man, the infliction of physical pain came to be considered as sufficient to govern and guide human nature . . . . From time to time a thing called revolution would occur, turning the slaves into bullies and vice versa . . . . A dark country, a hellish place, gentlemen, and if there is anything of which I am certain in life it is that I shall never exchange the liberty of my exile for the vile parody of home . . ."

Owing to there being in this character's speech a chance reference to "great woods and snow-covered plains," Mr. Goodman promptly assumes that the whole passage tallies with Sebastian Knight's own attitude to Russia. This is a grotesque misconception; it should be quite clear to any unbiased reader that the quoted words refer rather to a fanciful amalgamation of tyrannic iniquities than to any particular nation or historical reality. And if I attach them to that part of my story which deals with Sebastian's escape from revolutionary Russia it is because I want to follow it up immediately with a few sentences borrowed from his most autobiographical work: "I always think," he writes (*Lost Property*), "that one of the purest emotions is that of the banished man pining after the land of his birth. I would have liked to show him straining his memory to the utmost in a continuous effort to keep alive and bright the vision of his past: the blue remembered hills and the happy highways, the hedge with its unofficial rose and the field with its rabbits, the distant spire and the near bluebell . . . But because the theme has already been treated by my betters and also because I have an innate distrust of what I feel easy to express, no sentimental wanderer will ever be allowed to land on the rock of my unfriendly prose."

Whatever the particular conclusion of this passage, it is obvious that only one who has known what it is to leave a dear country could thus be tempted by the picture of nostalgia. I find it impossible to believe that Sebastian, no matter how gruesome the aspect of Russia was at the time of our escape, did not feel the wrench we all experienced. All things considered, it had been his home, and the set of kindly, well-meaning, gentle-mannered people driven to death or exile for the sole crime of their existing, was the set to which he too belonged. His dark youthful broodings, the romantic—and let me add, somewhat artificial—passion for his mother's land, could not, I am sure, exclude real affection for the country where he had been born and bred.

After having tumbled silently into Finland, we lived for a time in Helsingfors. Then our ways parted. My mother acting on the suggestion of an old friend took me to Paris, where I continued my education. And Sebastian went to London and Cambridge. His mother had left him a comfortable income and whatever worries assailed him in later life, they were never monetary. Just before he left, we sat down, the three of us, for the minute of silence according to Russian tradition. I remember the way my mother sat, with her hands in her lap twirling my father's wedding-ring (as she usually did when inactive) which she wore on the same finger as her own and which was so large that she had tied it to her own with black thread. I remember Sebastian's pose too; he was dressed in a dark-blue suit and he sat with his legs crossed, the upper foot gently swinging. I stood up first, then he, then my mother. He had made us promise not to see him to the boat, so it was there, in that whitewashed room, that we said good-bye. My mother made a quick little sign of the cross over his inclined face and a moment later we saw him through the window, getting into the taxi with his bag, in the last hunch-backed attitude of the departing.

We did not hear from him very often, nor were his letters very long. During his three years at Cambridge, he visited us in Paris but twice,—better say once, for the second time was when he came over for my mother's funeral. She and I talked of him fairly frequently, especially in the last years of her life, when she was quite aware of her approaching end. It was she who told me of Sebastian's strange adventure in 1917 of which I then knew nothing, as at the time I had happened to be on a holiday in the Crimea. It appears that Sebastian had developed a friendship with the futurist poet Alexis Pan and his wife Larissa, a weird couple who rented a cottage close to our country estate near Luga. He was a noisy robust little man with a gleam of real talent concealed in the messy obscurity of his verse. But because he did his best to shock people with his monstrous mass of otiose words (he was the inventor of the "submental grunt" as he called it), his main output seems now so nugatory, so false, so old-fashioned (super-modern things have a queer knack of dating much faster than others) that his true value is only remembered by a few scholars who admire the magnificent translations of English poems made by him at the very outset of his literary career,—one of these at least being a very miracle of verbal transfusion: his Russian rendering of Keats's "La Belle Dame Sans Merci."

So one morning in early summer seventeen-year-old Sebastian disappeared, leaving my mother a short note which informed her that he was accompanying Pan and his wife on a journey to the East. At first she took it to be a joke (Sebastian, for all his moodiness, at times devised some piece of ghoulish fun, as when in a crowded tramcar he had the ticket-collector transmit to a girl in the far end of the car a scribbled message which really ran thus: I am only a poor ticket-collector, but I love you); when, however, she called upon the Pans she actually found that they had left. It transpired somewhat later that Pan's idea of a Marcopolian journey consisted in gently working eastwards from one provincial town to another, arranging in every one a "lyrical surprise," that is, renting a hall (or a shed if no hall was available) and holding there a poetical performance whose net profit was supposed to get him, his wife and Sebastian to the next town. It was never made clear in what Sebastian's functions, help or duties lay, or if he was merely supposed to hover around, to fetch things when needed and to be nice to Larissa, who had a quick temper and was not easily soothed. Alexis Pan generally appeared on the stage dressed in a morning coat, perfectly correct but for its being embroidered with huge lotus flowers. A constellation (the Greater Dog) was painted on his bald brow. He delivered his verse in a great booming voice which, coming from so small a man, made one think of a mouse engendering mountains. Next to him on the platform sat Larissa, a large equine woman in a mauve dress, sewing on buttons or patching up a pair of old trousers, the point being that she never did any of these things for her husband in everyday life. Now and then, between two poems, Pan would perform a slow dance— a mixture of Javanese wrist-play and his own rhythmic inventions. After recitals he got gloriously soused—and this was his undoing. The journey to the East ended in Simbirsk with Alexis dead-drunk and penniless in a filthy inn and Larissa and her tantrums locked up at the police-station for having slapped the face of some meddlesome official who had disapproved of her husband's noisy genius. Sebastian came home as nonchalantly as he had left. "Any other boy," added my mother, "would have looked rather sheepish and rightly ashamed of the whole foolish affair," but Sebastian talked of his trip as of some quaint incident of which he had been a dispassionate observer. Why he had joined in that ludicrous show and what in fact had led him to pal with that grotesque couple remained a complete mystery (my mother thought that perhaps he had been ensnared by Larissa but the woman was perfectly plain, elderly and violently in love with her freak of a husband). They dropped out of Sebastian's life soon after. Two or three years later Pan enjoyed a short artificial vogue in Bolshevik surroundings which was due I think to the queer notion (mainly based on a muddle of terms) that there is a natural connection between extreme politics and extreme art. Then, in 1922 or 1923 Alexis Pan committed suicide with the aid of a pair of braces.

"I've always felt," said my mother, "that I never really knew Sebastian, I knew he obtained good marks at school, read an astonishing number of books, was clean in his habits, insisted on taking a cold bath every morning although his lungs were none too strong,—I knew all this and more, but he himself escaped me. And now that he lives in a strange country and writes to us in English I cannot help thinking that he will always remain an enigma,—though the Lord knows how hard I have tried to be kind to the boy."

When Sebastian visited us in Paris at the close of his first University year, I was struck by his foreign appearance. He wore a canary yellow jumper under his tweed coat. His flannel trousers were baggy, and his thick socks sagged, innocent of suspenders. The stripes of his tie were loud and for some odd reason he carried his handkerchief in his sleeve. He smoked his pipe in the street, knocking it out against his heel. He had developed a new way of standing with his back to the fire, his hands deep in his trouser pockets. He spoke Russian gingerly, lapsing into English as soon as the conversation drew out to anything longer than a couple of sentences. He stayed exactly one week.

The next time he came, my mother was no more. We sat together for a long time after the funeral. He awkwardly patted me on the shoulder when the chance sight of her spectacles lying alone on a shelf sent me into shivers of tears which I had managed to restrain until then. He was very kind and helpful in a distant vague way, as if he was thinking of something else all the time. We discussed matters and he suggested my coming to the Riviera and then to England; I had just finished my schooling. I said I preferred pottering on in Paris where I had a number of friends. He did not insist. The question of money was also touched on and he remarked in his queer off-hand way that he could always let me have as much cash as I might require,—I think he used the word "tin," though I am not sure. Next day he left for the South of France. In the morning we went for a short stroll and as it usually happened when we were alone together I was curiously embarrassed, every now and then catching myself painfully digging for a topic of conversation. He was silent too. Just before parting he said: "Well, that's that. If you need anything write me to my London address. I hope your Sore-bone works out as well as my Cambridge. And by the way try and find some subject you like and stick to it—until you find it bores you." There was a slight twinkle in his dark eyes. "Good luck," he said, "cheerio,"—and shook my hand in the limp self-conscious fashion he had acquired in England. Suddenly for no earthly reason I felt immensely sorry for him and longed to say something real, something with wings and a heart, but the birds I wanted settled on my shoulders and head only later when I was alone and not in need of words.

4

Two months had elapsed after Sebastian's death when this book was started. Well do I know how much he would have hated my waxing sentimental, but still I cannot help saying that my life-long affection for him, which somehow or other had always been crushed and thwarted, now leapt into new being with such a blaze of emotional strength—that all my other affairs were turned into flickering silhouettes. During our rare meetings we had never discussed literature, and now when the possibility of any sort of communication between us was barred by the strange habit of human death, I regretted desperately never having told Sebastian how much I delighted in his books. As it is I find myself helplessly wondering whether he had been aware I had ever read them.

But what actually did I know about Sebastian? I might devote a couple of chapters to the little I remembered of his childhood and youth—but what next? As I planned my book it became evident that I would have to undertake an immense amount of research, bringing up his life bit by bit and soldering the fragments with my inner knowledge of his character. Inner knowledge? Yes, this was a thing I possessed, I felt it in every nerve. And the more I pondered on it, the more I perceived that I had yet another tool in my hand: when I imagined actions of his which I heard of only after his death, I knew for certain that in such or such a case I should have acted just as he had. Once I happened to see two brothers, tennis champions, matched against one another; their strokes were totally different, and one of the two was far, far better than the other; but the general rhythm of their motions as they swept all over the court was exactly the same, so that had it been possible to draught both systems two identical designs would have appeared.

I daresay Sebastian and I also had some kind of common rhythm; this might explain the curious "it-has-happened-before-feeling" which seizes me when following the bends of his life. And if, as often was the case with him, the "why's" of his behaviour were as many X's, I often find their meaning disclosed now in a subconscious turn of this or that sentence put down by me. This is not meant to imply that I shared with him any riches of the mind, any facets of talent. Far from it. His genius always seemed to me a miracle utterly independent of any of the definite things we may have both experienced in the similar background of our childhood. I may have seen and remembered what he saw and remembered, but the difference between his power of expression and mine is comparable to that which exists between a Bechstein piano and a baby's rattle. I would never have let him see the least sentence of this book lest he should wince at the way I manage my miserable English. And wince he would. Nor do I dare imagine his reactions had he learnt that before starting on his biography, his half-brother (whose literary experience had amounted till then to one or two chance English translations required by a motor-firm) had decided to take up a "be-an-author" course buoyantly advertised in an English magazine. Yes, I confess to it,—not that I regret it. The gentleman, who for a reasonable fee was supposed to make a successful writer of my person,—really took the utmost pains to teach me to be coy and graceful, forcible and crisp, and if I proved a hopeless pupil—although he was far too kind to admit it,—it was because from the very start I had been hypnotised by the perfect glory of a short story which he sent me as a sample of what his pupils could do and sell. It contained among other things a wicked Chinaman who snarled, a brave girl with hazel eyes and a big quiet fellow whose knuckles turned white when someone really annoyed him. I would now refrain from mentioning this rather eerie business did it not disclose how unprepared I was for my task and to what wild extremities my diffidence drove me. When at last I did take pen in hand, I had composed myself to face the inevitable which is but another way of saying I was ready to try and do my best.

There is still another little moral lurking behind this affair. If Sebastian had followed the same kind of correspondence course just for the fun of the thing, just to see what would have happened (he appreciated such amusements), he would have turned out an incalculably more hopeless pupil than I.

Told to write like Mr. Everyman he would have written like none. I cannot even copy his manner because the manner of his prose was the manner of his thinking and that was a dazzling succession of gaps; and you cannot ape a gap because you are bound to fill it in somehow or other—and blot it out in the process. But when in Sebastian's books I find some detail of mood or impression which makes me remember at once, say, a certain effect of lighting in a definite place which we two had noticed, unknown to one another, then I feel that in spite of the toe of his talent being beyond my reach we did possess certain psychological affinities which will help me out.

The tool was there, it must now be put to use. My first duty after Sebastian's death was to go through his belongings. He had left everything to me and I had a letter from him instructing me to burn certain of his papers. It was so obscurely worded that at first I thought it might refer to rough drafts or discarded manuscripts, but I soon found out that except for a few odd pages dispersed among other papers, he himself had destroyed them long ago, for he belonged to that rare type of writer who knows that nothing ought to remain except the perfect achievement: the printed book; that its actual existence is inconsistent with that of its spectre, the uncouth manuscript flaunting its imperfections like a revengeful ghost carrying its own head under its arm; and that for this reason the litter of the workshop, no matter its sentimental or commercial value, must never subsist.

When for the first time in my life I visited Sebastian's small flat in London at 36 Oak Park Gardens, I had an empty feeling of having postponed an appointment until too late. Three rooms, a cold fireplace, silence. During the last years of his life he had not lived there very much, nor had he died there. Half a dozen suits, mostly old, were hanging in the wardrobe, and for a second I had an odd impression of Sebastian's body being stiffly multiplied in a succession of square-shouldered forms. I had seen him once in that brown coat; I touched its sleeve, but it was limp and irresponsive to that faint call of memory. There were shoes too, which had walked many miles and had now reached the end of their journey. Folded shirts lying on their backs. What could all these quiet things tell me of Sebastian? His bed. A small old oil-painting, a little cracked (muddy road, rainbow, beautiful puddles) on the ivory white of the wall above. The eye-spot of his awakening.

As I looked about me, all things in that bedroom seemed to have just jumped back in the nick of time as if caught unawares, and now were gradually returning my gaze, trying to see whether I had noticed their guilty start. This was particularly the case with the low, white-robed arm-chair near the bed; I wondered what it had stolen. Then by groping in the recesses of its reluctant folds I found something hard: it turned out to be a Brazil nut, and the armchair again folding its arms resumed its inscrutable expression (which might have been one of contemptuous dignity).

The bathroom. The glass shelf, bare save for an empty talc-powder tin with violets figured between its shoulders, standing there alone, reflected in the mirror like a coloured advertisement.

Then I examined the two main rooms. The dining-room was curiously impersonal, like all places where people eat,— perhaps because food is our chief link with the common chaos of matter rolling about us. There was, it is true, a cigarette end in a glass ashtray, but it had been left there by a certain Mr. McMath, house-agent.

The study. From here one got a view of the back-garden or park, the fading sky, a couple of elms, not oaks, in spite of the street-name's promise. A leather divan sprawling at one end of the room. Bookshelves densely peopled. The writing-desk. There was almost nothing on it: a red pencil, a box of paper clips—it looked sullen and distant, but the lamp on its western edge was adorable. I found its pulse and the opal globe melted into light: that magic moon had seen Sebastian's white moving hand. Now I was really getting down to business. I took the key that had been bequeathed me and unlocked the drawers.

First of all I dislodged the two bundles of letters on which Sebastian had scribbled: to be destroyed. One was folded in such a fashion that I could not get a glimpse of the writing: the note-paper was egg-shell blue with a dark-blue rim. The other packet consisted of a medley of note-paper crisscrossed in a bold feminine scrawl. I guessed whose it was. For a wild instant I struggled with the temptation to examine closer both bundles. I am sorry to say the better man won. But as I was burning them in the grate one sheet of the blue became loose, curving backwards under the torturing flame, and before the crumpling blackness had crept over it, a few words appeared in full radiance, then swooned and all was over.

I sank down in an armchair and mused for some moments. The words I had seen were Russian words, part of a Russian sentence,—quite insignificant in themselves, really (not that I might have expected from the flame of chance the slick intent of a novelist's plot). The literal English translation would be "thy manner always to find" . . . —and it was not the sense that struck me, but the mere fact of its being in my language. I had not the vaguest inkling as to who she might be, that Russian woman whose letters Sebastian had kept in close proximity to those of Clare Bishop—and somehow it perplexed and bothered me. From my chair beside the fireplace, which was again black and cold, I could see the fair light of the lamp on the desk, the bright whiteness of paper brimming over the open drawer and one sheet of foolscap lying alone on the blue carpet, half in shade, cut diagonally by the limit of the light. For a moment I seemed to see a transparent Sebastian at his desk; or rather I thought of that passage about the wrong Roquebrune: perhaps he preferred doing his writing in bed?

After a while I went on with my business, examining and roughly classifying the contents of the drawers. There were many letters. These I set aside to be gone through later. Newspaper cuttings in a gaudy book, an impossible butterfly on its cover. No, none of them were reviews of his own books: Sebastian was much too vain to collect them; nor would his sense of humour allow him to paste them in patiently when they did come his way. Still, as I say, there was an album with cuttings, all of them referring (as I found out later when perusing them at leisure) to incongruous or dream-absurd incidents which had occurred in the most trivial places and conditions. Mixed metaphors too, I perceived, met with his approval, as he probably considered them to belong to the same faintly nightmare category. Between some legal documents I found a slip of paper on which he had begun to write a story—there was only one sentence, stopping short but it gave me the opportunity of observing the queer way Sebastian had—in the process of writing—of not striking out the words which he had replaced by others, so that, for instance, the phrase I encountered ran thus: "As he a heavy A heavy sleeper, Roger Rogerson, old Rogerson bought old Rogers bought, so afraid Being a heavy sleeper, old Rogers was so afraid of missing to-morrows. He was a heavy sleeper. He was mortally afraid of missing to-morrow's event glory early train glory so what he did was to buy and bring home in a to buy that evening and bring home not one but eight alarm clocks of different sizes and vigour of ticking nine eight eleven alarm clocks of different sizes ticking which alarm clocks nine alarm clocks as a cat has nine which he placed which made his bedroom look rather like a"

I was sorry it stopped here.

Foreign coins in a chocolate box: francs, marks, schillings, crowns,—and their small change. Several fountain pens. An Oriental amethyst, unset. A rubber band. A glass tube of tablets for headache, nervous breakdown, neuralgia, insomnia, bad dreams, toothache. The toothache sounded rather dubious. An old note-book (1926) filled with dead telephone numbers. Photographs.

I thought I should find lots of girls. You know the kind,—smiling in the sun, summer snapshots, continental tricks of shade, smiling in white on pavement, sand or snow,—but I was mistaken. The two dozen or so of photographs I shook out of a large envelope with the laconic Mr. H. written on top in Sebastian's hand, all featured one and the same person at different stages of his life: first a moonfaced urchin in a vulgarly cut sailor suit, next an ugly boy in a cricket-cap, then a pug-nosed youth and so on till one arrived at a series of full-grown Mr. H.—a rather repellent bulldog type of man, getting steadily fatter in a world of photographic backgrounds and real front gardens. I learnt who the man was supposed to be when I came across a newspaper clipping attached to one of the photographs:

"Author writing fictitious biography requires photos of gentleman, efficient appearance, plain, steady, teetotaller, bachelors preferred. Will pay for photos childhood, youth, manhood to appear in said work."

That was a book Sebastian never wrote, but possibly he was still contemplating doing so in the last year of his life, for the last photograph of Mr. H. standing happily near a brand-new car, bore the date "March 1935" and Sebastian had died but a year later.

Suddenly I felt tired and miserable. I wanted the face of his Russian correspondent. I wanted pictures of Sebastian himself. I wanted many things . . . Then, as I let my eyes roam around the room, I caught sight of a couple of framed photographs in the dim shadows above the bookshelves.

I got up and examined them. One was an enlarged snapshot of a Chinese stripped to the waist, in the act of being vigourously beheaded, the other was a banal photographic study of a curly child playing with a pup. The taste of their juxtaposition seemed to me questionable, but probably Sebastian had his own reasons for keeping and hanging them so.

I glanced too, at the books; they were numerous, untidy and miscellaneous. But one shelf was a little neater than the rest and here I noted the following sequence which for a moment seemed to form a vague musical phrase, oddly familiar: *Hamlet, La morte d'Arthur, The Bridge of San Luis Rey, Doctor Jekyll and Mr. Hyde, South Wind, The Lady with the Dog, Madame Bovary, The Invisible Man, Le Temps Retrouvé, Anglo-Persian Dictionary, The Author of Trixie, Alice in Wonderland, Ulysses, About Buying a Horse, King Lear* . . .

The melody gave a small gasp and faded. I returned to the desk and began sorting out the letters I had laid aside. They were mostly business letters, and I felt entitled to peruse them. Some bore no relation to Sebastian's profession, others did. The disorder was considerable and many allusions remained unintelligible to me. In a few cases he had kept copies of his own letters so that for instance I got in full a long zestful dialogue between him and his publisher in regard to a certain book. Then, there was a fussy soul in Rumania of all places, clamouring for an option . . . I learnt too of the sales in England and the Dominions . . . Nothing very brilliant—but in one case at least perfectly satisfactory. A few letters from friendly authors. One gentle writer, the author of a single famous book, rebuked Sebastian (April 4, 1928) for being "Conradish" and suggested his leaving out the "con" and cultivating the "radish" in future works—a singularly silly idea, I thought.

Lastly, at the very bottom of the bundle, I came to my mother's and my own letters, together with several from one of his undergraduate friends; and as I struggled a little with their pages (old letters resent being unfolded) I suddenly realised what my next hunting-ground ought to be.

5

SEBASTIAN KNIGHT'S college years were not particularly happy. To be sure he enjoyed many of the things he found at Cambridge,—he was in fact quite overcome at first to see and smell and feel the country for which he had always longed. A real hansom-cab took him from the station to Trinity College: the vehicle, it seemed, had been waiting there especially for him, desperately holding out against extinction till that moment, and then gladly dying out to join side whiskers and the Large Copper. The slush of streets gleaming wet in the misty darkness with its promised counterpoint—a cup of strong tea and a generous fire—formed a harmony which somehow he knew by heart. The pure chimes of tower-clocks, now hanging over the town, now overlapping and echoing afar, in some odd, deeply familiar way blended with the piping cries of the newspaper vendors. And as he entered the stately gloom of Great Court with gowned shadows passing in the mist and the porter's bowler hat bobbing in front of him, Sebastian felt that he somehow recognised every sensation, the wholesome reek of damp turf, the ancient sonority of stone slabs under heel, the blurred outlines of dark walls overhead—everything. That special feeling of elation probably endured for quite a long time, but there was something else intermingled with it, and later on predominant. Sebastian in spite of himself realised with perhaps a kind of helpless amazement (for he had expected more from England than she could do for him) that no matter how wisely and sweetly his new surroundings played up to his old dreams, he himself, or rather still the most precious part of himself, would remain as hopelessly alone as it had always been. The keynote of Sebastian's life was solitude and the kindlier fate tried to make him feel at home by counterfeiting admirably the things he thought he wanted, the more he was aware of his inability to fit into the picture,—into any kind of picture. When at last he thoroughly understood this and grimly started to cultivate self-consciousness as if it had been some rare talent or passion, only then did Sebastian derive satisfaction from its rich and monstrous growth, ceasing to worry about his awkward un-congeniality,—but that was much later.

Apparently, at first he was frantically afraid of not doing the right thing or, worse still, of doing it clumsily. Someone told him that the hard cornered part of the academical cap ought to be broken, or even removed altogether, leaving only the limp black cloth. No sooner had he done so, than he found out that he had lapsed into the worst "undergrad" vulgarity and that perfect taste consisted in ignoring the cap and gown one wore, thus granting them the faultless appearance of insignificant things which otherwise would have dared to matter. Again, whatever the weather, hats and umbrellas were tabooed, and Sebastian piously got wet and caught colds until a certain day when he came to know one D. W. Gorget, a delightful, flippant, lazy, easy-going fellow, famed for his row-diness, elegance and wit: and Gorget coolly went about in a town-hat plus umbrella. Fifteen years later, when I visited Cambridge and was told by Sebastian's best college friend (now a prominent scholar) of all these things, I remarked that everybody seemed to be carrying—— "Exactly," said he, "Gorget's umbrella has bred."

"And tell me," I asked, "what about games? Was Sebastian good at games?"

My informant smiled.

"I am afraid," he answered, "that except a little mild tennis on a rather soggy green court with a daisy or two on the worst patches, neither Sebastian nor I went in very much for that sort of thing. His racket, I remember, was a remarkably ex-pensive one, and his flannels very becoming—and generally he looked very tidy and nice and all that; but his service was a feminine pat and he rushed about a lot without hitting any-thing, and as I was not much better than he, our game mainly consisted in retrieving damp green balls or throwing them back to players on the adjacent courts—all this under a steady drizzle. Yes, he was definitely poor at games."

"Did that upset him?"

"It did in a way. In fact, his first term was quite poisoned by the thought of his inferiority in those matters. The first time he met Gorget,—that was in my rooms—poor Sebastian talked so much about tennis that at last Gorget asked whether the game was played with a stick. This rather soothed Sebastian as he supposed that Gorget, whom he liked from the start, was bad at games, too."

"And was he?"

"Oh, well, he was a Rugby Blue, but perhaps he did not much care for lawn-tennis. Anyway, Sebastian soon got over the game complex. And generally speaking—"

We sat there in that dimly lit oak-panelled room, our armchairs so low that it was quite easy to reach the tea things which stood humbly on the carpet, and Sebastian's spirit seemed to hover about us with the flicker of the fire reflected in the brass knobs of the hearth. My interlocutor had known him so intimately that I think he was right in suggesting that Sebastian's sense of inferiority was based on his trying to out-England England, and never succeeding, and going on trying, until finally he realised that it was not these outward things that betrayed him, not the mannerisms of fashionable slang, but the very fact of his striving to be and act like other people when he was blissfully condemned to the solitary confinement of his own self.

Still, he had done his best to be a standard undergraduate. Clad in a brown dressing-gown and old pumps, carrying soap-box and sponge-bag, he had strolled out on winter mornings on his way to the Baths round the corner. He had had breakfast in Hall, with the porridge as grey and dull as the sky above Great Court and the orange marmalade of exactly the same hue as the creeper on its walls. He had mounted his "push-bike," as my informant called it, and with his gown across his shoulder had pedalled to this or that lecture hall. He had lunched at the Pitt (which, I understood, was a kind of club, probably with horsey pictures on the walls and very old waiters asking their eternal riddle: thick or clear?). He had played fives (whatever that may be) or some other tame game, and then had had tea with two or three friends; the talk had hobbled along between crumpet and pipe, carefully avoiding anything that had not been said by others. There may have been another lecture or two before dinner, and then again Hall, a very fine place which I was duly shown. It was being swept at the moment, and the fat white calves of Henry the Eighth looked as if they might get tickled.

"And where did Sebastian sit?"

"Down there, against the wall."

"But how did one get there? The tables seem miles long."

"He used to step up on the outer bench and walk across the table. One trod on a plate now and then, but it was the usual method."

Then, after dinner, he would go back to his rooms, or perhaps make his way with some silent companion to the little cinema on the market place where a Wild West film would be shown, or Charlie Chaplin stiffly trotting away from the big wicked man and skidding on the street corner.

Then, after three or four terms of this sort of thing a curious change came over Sebastian. He stopped enjoying what he thought he ought to enjoy and serenely turned to what really concerned him. Outwardly, this change resulted in his dropping out of the rhythm of college life. He saw no one, except my informant, who remained perhaps the only man in his life with whom he had been perfectly frank and natural—it was a handsome friendship and I quite understood Sebastian, for that quiet scholar struck me as being the finest and gentlest soul imaginable. They were both interested in English literature, and Sebastian's friend was already then planning that first work of his, *The Laws of Literary Imagination*, which, two or three years later, won for him the Montgomery Prize.

"I must confess," said he as he stroked a soft blue cat with celadon eyes which had appeared from nowhere and now made itself comfortable in his lap, "I must confess that Sebastian rather pained me at that particular period of our friendship. Missing him in the lecture hall, I would go to his rooms and find him still in bed, curled up like a sleeping child, but gloomily smoking, with cigarette ash all over his crumpled pillow and inkstains on the sheet which hung loosely to the floor. He would only grunt in reply to my energetic greeting, not deigning even to change his position, so after hovering around and satisfying myself that he was not ill, I would go off to lunch, and then call upon him again only to find him lying on his other side and using a slipper for an ashtray. I would suggest getting him something to eat, for his cupboard was always empty, and presently, when I brought him a bunch of bananas, he would cheer up like a monkey and immediately start to annoy me with a series of obscurely immoral statements, related to Life, Death or God, which he specially relished making because he knew that they annoyed me—although I never believed that he really meant what he said.

"At last, about three or four in the afternoon, he would put on his dressing-gown and shuffle into the sitting-room where, in disgust, I would leave him, huddled up by the fire and scratching his head. And next day, as I sat working in my digs, I would suddenly hear a great stamping up the stairs, and Sebastian would bounce into the room, clean, fresh and excited, with the poem he had just finished."

All this, I trust, is very true to type, and one little detail strikes me as especially pathetic. It appears that Sebastian's English, though fluent and idiomatic, was decidedly that of a foreigner. His "r"s, when beginning a word, rolled and rasped, he made queer mistakes, saying, for instance, "I have seized a cold" or "that fellow is sympathetic"—merely meaning that he was a nice chap. He misplaced the accent in such words as "interesting" or "laboratory." He mispronounced names like "Socrates" or "Desdemona." Once corrected, he would never repeat the mistake, but the very fact of his not being quite sure about certain words distressed him enormously and he used to blush a bright pink when, owing to a chance verbal flaw, some utterance of his would not be quite understood by an obtuse listener. In those days, he wrote far better than he spoke, but still there was something vaguely un-English about his poems. None of them have reached me. True, his friend thought that perhaps one or two . . .

He put down the cat and rummaged awhile among some papers in a drawer, but he could not lay his hand on anything. "Perhaps, in some trunk at my sister's place," he said vaguely, "but I'm not even sure . . . Little things like that are the darlings of oblivion, and moreover I know Sebastian would have applauded their loss."

"By the way," I said, "the past you recall seems dismally wet meteorologically speaking,—as dismal, in fact, as to-day's weather (it was a bleak day in February). Tell me, was it never warm and sunny? Does not Sebastian himself refer somewhere to the 'pink candlesticks of great chestnut trees' along the bank of some beautiful little river?"

Yes, I was right, spring and summer did happen in Cambridge almost every year (that mysterious "almost" was singularly pleasing). Yes, Sebastian quite liked to loll in a punt on the Cam. But what he liked above all was to cycle in the dusk along a certain path skirting meadows. There, he would sit on a fence looking at the wispy salmon-pink clouds turning to a dull copper in the pale evening sky and think about things. What things? That cockney girl with her soft hair still in plaits whom he once followed across the common, and accosted and kissed, and never saw again? The form of a particular cloud? Some misty sunset beyond a black Russian firwood (oh, how much I would give for such a memory coming to him!)? The inner meaning of grassblade and star? the unknown language of silence? the terrific weight of a dew-drop? the heartbreaking beauty of a pebble among millions and millions of pebbles, all making sense, but what sense? The old, old question of Who are you? to one's own self grown strangely evasive in the gloaming, and to God's world around to which one has never been really introduced. Or, perhaps, we shall be nearer the truth in supposing that while Sebastian sat on that fence, his mind was a turmoil of words and fancies, uncomplete fancies and insufficient words, but already he knew that this and only this was the reality of his life, and that his destiny lay beyond that ghostly battlefield which he would cross in due time.

"Did I like his books? Oh, enormously. I didn't see much of him after he left Cambridge, and he never sent me any of his works. Authors, you know, are forgetful. But one day I got three of them at the library and read them in as many nights. I was always sure he would produce something fine, but I never expected it would be as fine as that. In his last year here—I don't know what's the matter with this cat, she does not seem to know milk all of a sudden."

In his last Cambridge year Sebastian worked a good deal; his subject—English literature—was a vast and complicated one; but this same period was marked by his sudden trips to London, generally without the authorities' leave. His tutor, the late Mr. Jefferson, had been, I learnt, a mighty dull old gentleman, but a fine linguist, who insisted upon considering Sebastian as a Russian. In other words, he drove Sebastian to the limit of exasperation by telling him all the Russian words he knew,—a nice bagful collected on a journey to Moscow years ago,—and asking him to teach him some more. One day, at last, Sebastian blurted out that there was some mistake—he had not been born in Russia really, but in Sofia. Upon which, the delighted old man at once started to speak Bulgarian. Sebastian lamely answered that it was not the special dialect he knew, and when challenged to furnish a sample, invented a new idiom on the spur of the moment, which greatly puzzled the old linguist until it dawned upon him that Sebastian—

"Well, I think you have drained me now," said my informant with a smile. "My reminiscences are getting shallower and sillier—and I hardly think it worth while to add that Sebastian got a first and that we had our picture taken in full glory—I shall try and find it some day and send it to you if you like. Must you really leave now? Would you not like to see the Backs? Come along and visit the crocuses, Sebastian used to call them 'the poet's mushrooms,' if you see what he meant."

But it was raining too hard. We stood for a minute or two under the porch, and then I said I thought I'd better be going.

"Oh, look here," called Sebastian's friend after me, as I was already picking my way among the puddles. "I quite forgot to tell you. The Master told me the other day that somebody wrote to him asking whether Sebastian Knight had really been a Trinity man. Now, what was the fellow's name? Oh, bother . . . My memory has shrunk in the washing. Well, we did give it a good rinsing, didn't we? Anyway, I gathered that somebody was collecting data for a book on Sebastian Knight. Funny, you don't seem to have—"

"Sebastian Knight?" said a sudden voice in the mist, "Who is speaking of Sebastian Knight?"

6

THE STRANGER who uttered these words now approached—Oh, how I sometimes yearn for the easy swing of a well-oiled novel! How comfortable it would have been had the voice belonged to some cheery old don with long downy ear-lobes and that puckering about the eyes which stands for wisdom and humour . . . A handy character, a welcome passer-by who had also known my hero, but from a different angle. "And now," he would say, "I am going to tell you the real story of Sebastian Knight's college years." And then and there he would have launched on that story. But alas, nothing of the kind really happened. That Voice in the Mist rang out in the dimmest passage of my mind. It was but the echo of some possible truth, a timely reminder: don't be too certain of learning the past from the lips of the present. Beware of the most honest broker. Remember that what you are told is really threefold: shaped by the teller, reshaped by the listener, concealed from both by the dead man of the tale. Who is speaking of Sebastian Knight? repeats that voice in my conscience. Who indeed? His best friend and his half-brother. A gentle scholar, remote from life, and an embarrassed traveller visiting a distant land. And where is the third party? Rotting peacefully in the cemetery of St. Damier. Laughingly alive in five volumes. Peering unseen over my shoulder as I write this (although I dare say he mistrusted too strongly the commonplace of eternity to believe even now in his own ghost).

Anyway, here was I with the booty that friendship could yield. To this I added a few casual facts occurring in Sebastian's very short letters belonging to that period and the chance references to University life found scattered amongst his books. I then returned to London where I had neatly planned my next move.

At our last meeting Sebastian had happened to mention a kind of secretary whom he had employed from time to time between 1930 and 1934. Like many authors in the past, and as very few in the present (or perhaps we are simply unaware of

those who fail to manage their affairs in a sound pushing manner), Sebastian was ridiculously helpless in business matters
and once having found an adviser (who incidentally might be
a shark or a blockhead—or both) he gave himself up to him
entirely with the greatest relief. Had I perchance inquired
whether he was perfectly certain that So-and-So now handling
his affairs was not a meddlesome old rogue, he would have
hurriedly changed the subject, so in dread was he that the
discovery of another's mischief might force his own laziness
into action. In a word he preferred the worst assistant to no
assistant at all, and would convince himself and others that he
was perfectly content with his choice. Having said all this I
should like to stress the fact as definitely as possible that none
of my words are—from a legal point of view—slanderous, and
that the name I am about to mention has *not* appeared in this
particular paragraph.

Now what I wanted from Mr. Goodman was not so much
an account of Sebastian's last years—that I did not yet need—
(for I intended to follow his life stage by stage without overtaking him), but merely to obtain a few suggestions as to what
people I ought to see who might know something of Sebastian's post-Cambridge period.

So on March first, 1936, I called on Mr. Goodman at his
office in Fleet Street. But before describing our interview I
must be allowed a short digression.

Amongst Sebastian's letters I found as already mentioned
some correspondence between him and his publisher dealing
with a certain novel. It appears that in Sebastian's first book
(1925), *The Prismatic Bezel*, one of the minor characters is an
extremely comic and cruel skit upon a certain living author
whom Sebastian found necessary to chastise. Naturally the
publisher knew it immediately and this fact made him so uncomfortable that he advised Sebastian to modify the whole
passage, a thing which Sebastian flatly refused to do, saying
finally that he would get the book printed elsewhere,—and
this he eventually did.

"You seem to wonder," he wrote in one letter, "what on
earth could make me, a budding author (as you say—but that
is a misapplied term, for your authentic budding author remains budding all his life; others, like me, spring into blossom

in one bound), you seem to wonder, let me repeat (which
does not mean I am apologising for that Proustian parenthe-
sis), why the hell I should take a nice porcelain blue contemporary (X. does remind one, doesn't he, of those cheap china
things which tempt one at fairs to an orgy of noisy destruction) and let him drop from the tower of my prose to the
gutter below. You tell me he is widely esteemed; that his sales
in Germany are almost as tremendous as his sales here; that
an old story of his has just been selected for *Modern Master-
pieces*; that together with Y. and Z. he is considered one of
the leading writers of the 'post-war' generation; and that, last
but not least, he is dangerous as a critic. You seem to hint
that we should all keep the dark secret of his success, which
is to travel second-class with a third-class ticket,—or if my
simile is not sufficiently clear,—to pamper the taste of the
worst category of the reading public—not those who revel in
detective yarns, bless their pure souls—but those who buy the
worst banalities because they have been shaken up in a modern way with a dash of Freud or 'stream of consciousness' or
whatnot,—and incidentally do not and never will understand
that the pretty cynics of to-day are Marie Corelli's nieces and
old Mrs. Grundy's nephews. Why should we keep that shameful secret? What is this masonic bond of triteness—or indeed
tritheism? Down with these shoddy gods! And then you go
and tell me that my 'literary career' will be hopelessly handicapped from the start by my attacking an influential and esteemed writer. But even if there were such a thing as a 'literary
career' and I were disqualified merely for riding my own
horse, still I would refuse to change one single word in what
I have written. For, believe me, no imminent punishment can
be violent enough to make me abandon the pursuit of my
pleasure, especially when this pleasure is the firm young
bosom of truth. There are in fact not many things in life comparable to the delight of satire, and when I imagine the hum-
bug's face as he reads (and read he shall) that particular
passage and knows as well as we do that it is the truth, then
delight reaches its sweetest climax. Let me add that if I have
faithfully rendered not only X.'s inner world (which is no
more than a tube-station during rush hours) but also his tricks

of speech and demeanour, I emphatically deny that he or any other reader may discern the least trace of vulgarity in the passage which causes you such alarm. So do not let this haunt you any longer. Remember too that I take all responsibility, moral and commercial, in case you really 'get into trouble' with my innocent little volume."

My point in quoting this letter (apart from its own value as showing Sebastian in that bright boyish mood which later remained as a rainbow across the stormy gloom of his darkest tales) is to settle a rather delicate question. In a minute or two Mr. Goodman will appear in flesh and blood. The reader already knows how thoroughly I disapprove of that gentleman's book. However, at the time of our first (and last) interview I knew nothing about his work (insofar as a rapid compilation may be called work). I approached Mr. Goodman with an open mind; it is no longer open now, and naturally this is bound to influence my description. At the same time I do not very well see how I can discuss my visit to him without alluding even as discreetly as in the case of Sebastian's college-friend, to Mr. Goodman's manner if not appearance. Shall I be able to stop at that? Will not Mr. Goodman's face suddenly pop out to the owner's rightful annoyance when he reads these lines? I have studied Sebastian's letter and arrived at the conclusion that what Sebastian Knight might permit himself in respect to Mr. X. is denied me in regard to Mr. Goodman. The frankness of Sebastian's genius cannot be mine, and I should only succeed in being rude there where he might have been brilliant. So that I am treading on very thin ice and must try to step warily as I enter Mr. Goodman's study.

"Pray be seated," he said, courteously waving me into a leather armchair near his desk. He was remarkably well-dressed though decidedly with a city flavour. A black mask covered his face. "What can I do for you?" He went on looking at me through the eyeholes and still holding my card.

I suddenly realised that my name conveyed nothing to him. Sebastian had made his mother's name his own very completely.

"I am," I answered, "Sebastian Knight's half-brother." There was a short silence.

"Let me see," said Mr. Goodman, "am I to understand, that you are referring to the late Sebastian Knight, the well-known author?"

"Exactly," said I.

Mr. Goodman with finger and thumb stroked his face . . . I mean the face under his mask . . . stroked it down, down, reflectively.

"I beg your pardon," he said, "but are you quite sure that there is not some mistake?"

"None whatever," I replied, and in as few words as possible I explained my relationship to Sebastian.

"Oh, is that so?" said Mr. Goodman, growing more and more pensive. "Really, really, it never entered my head. I was certainly quite aware that Knight was born and brought up in Russia. But I somehow missed the point about his name. Yes, now I see . . . Yes, it ought to be a Russian one . . . His mother . . ."

Mr. Goodman drummed the blotting-pad for a minute with his fine white fingers and then faintly sighed.

"Well, what's done is done," he remarked. "Too late now to add a . . . I mean," he hurriedly continued, "that I'm sorry not to have gone into the matter before. So you are his half-brother? Well, I am delighted to meet you."

"First of all," I said, "I should like to settle the business-question. Mr. Knight's papers, at least those that refer to his literary occupations, are not in very great order and I don't quite know exactly how things stand. I haven't yet seen his publishers, but I gather that at least one of them—the firm that brought out *The Funny Mountain*—no longer exists. Before going further into the matter I thought I'd better have a talk with you."

"Quite so," said Mr. Goodman. "As a matter of fact you may not be cognizant of my having interest in two Knight books, *The Funny Mountain* and *Lost Property*. Under the circumstances the best thing would be for me to give you some details which I can send you by letter to-morrow morning as well as a copy of my contract with Mr. Knight. Or should I call him Mr. . . ." and smiling under his mask Mr. Goodman tried to pronounce our simple Russian name.

"Then there is another matter," I continued. "I have

decided to write a book on his life and work, and I sorely need certain information. Could you perhaps . . ."

It seemed to me that Mr. Goodman stiffened. Then he coughed once or twice and even went as far as to select a black-currant lozenge from a small box on his distinguished-looking desk.

"My dear Sir," he said, suddenly veering together with his seat and whirling his eyeglass on his ribbon. "Let us be perfectly outspoken. I have certainly known poor Knight better than anyone else, but . . . look here, have you started writing that book?"

"No," I said.

"Then don't. You must excuse my being so very blunt. An old habit,—a bad habit, perhaps. You don't mind, do you? Well, what I mean is . . . how should I put it? . . . You see, Sebastian Knight was not what you might call a great writer . . . Oh, yes, I know,—a fine artist and all that,—but with no appeal to the general public. I don't wish to say that a book could not be written about him. It could. But then it ought to be written from a special point of view which would make the subject fascinating. Otherwise it is bound to fall flat, because, you see, I really don't think that Sebastian Knight's fame is strong enough to sustain anything like the work you are contemplating."

I was so taken aback by this outburst that I kept silent. And Mr. Goodman went on:

"I trust my bluntness does not offend you. Your half-brother and I were such good pals that you quite understand how I feel about it. Better not, my dear sir, better not. Leave it to some professional fellow, to one who knows the book-market—and he will tell you that anybody trying to complete an exhaustive study of Knight's life and work, as you put it, would be wasting his and the reader's time. Why, even So-and-So's book about the late . . . [a famous name was mentioned] with all those photographs and facsimiles did not sell."

I thanked Mr. Goodman for his advice and reached for my hat. I felt he had proved a failure and that I had followed a false scent. Somehow or other I did not care to ask him to enlarge upon those days when he and Sebastian had been "such pals." I wonder now what his answer would have been had I begged him to tell me the story of his secretaryship. After shaking hands with me most cordially, he returned the black mask which I pocketed, as I supposed it might come in usefully on some other occasion. He saw me to the nearest glass door and there we parted. As I was about to go down the stairs, a vigourous-looking girl whom I had noticed steadily typing in one of the rooms ran after me and stopped me (queer,—that Sebastian's Cambridge friend had also called me back).

"My name," she said, "is Helen Pratt. I have overheard as much of your conversation as I could stand and there is a little thing I want to ask you. Clare Bishop is a great friend of mine. There's something she wants to find out. Could I talk to you one of these days?"

I said yes, most certainly, and we fixed the time.

"I knew Mr. Knight quite well," she added, looking at me with bright round eyes.

"Oh, really," said I, not quite knowing what else to say.

"Yes," she went on, "he was an amazing personality, and I don't mind telling you that I loathed Goodman's book about him."

"What do you mean?" I asked. "What book?"

"Oh, the one he has just written. I was going over the proofs with him this last week. Well, I must be running. Thank you so much."

She darted away and very slowly I descended the steps. Mr. Goodman's large soft pinkish face was, and is, remarkably like a cow's udder.

7

MR. GOODMAN's book *The Tragedy of Sebastian Knight* has enjoyed a very good press. It has been lengthily reviewed in the leading dailies and weeklies. It has been called "impressive and convincing." The author has been credited with "deep insight" into an "essentially modern" character. Passages have been quoted to demonstrate his efficient handling of nutshells. One critic even went as far as to take his hat off to Mr. Goodman—who, let it be added, had used his own merely to talk through it. In a word, Mr. Goodman has been patted on the back when he ought to have been rapped on the knuckles.

I, for one, would have ignored that book altogether had it been just another bad book, doomed with the rest of its kind to oblivion by next spring. The Lethean Library, for all its incalculable volumes, is, I know, sadly incomplete without Mr. Goodman's effort. But bad as the book may be, it is something else besides. Owing to the quality of its subject, it is bound to become quite mechanically the satellite of another man's enduring fame. As long as Sebastian Knight's name is remembered, there always will be some learned inquirer conscientiously climbing up a ladder to where *The Tragedy of Sebastian Knight* keeps half awake between Godfrey Goodman's *Fall of Man* and Samuel Goodrich's *Recollections of a Lifetime*. Thus, if I continue to harp on the subject, I do so for Sebastian Knight's sake.

Mr. Goodman's method is as simple as his philosophy. His sole object is to show "poor Knight" as a product and victim of what he calls "our time"—though why some people are so keen to make others share in their chronometric concepts, has always been a mystery to me. "Postwar Unrest," "Postwar Generation" are to Mr. Goodman magic words opening every door. There is, however, a certain kind of "open sesame" which seems less a charm than a skeleton-key, and this, I am afraid, is Mr. Goodman's kind. But he is quite wrong in thinking that he found something once the lock had been forced. Not that I wish to suggest that Mr. Goodman *thinks*. He could not if he tried. His book concerns itself only with such ideas as have been shown (commercially) to attract mediocre minds.

For Mr. Goodman, young Sebastian Knight "freshly emerged from the carved chrysalid of Cambridge" is a youth of acute sensibility in a cruel cold world. In this world, "outside realities intrude so roughly upon one's most intimate dreams" that a young man's soul is forced into a state of siege before it is finally shattered. "The War," says Mr. Goodman without so much as a blush, "had changed the face of the universe." And with much gusto he goes on to describe those special aspects of postwar life which met a young man at "the troubled dawn of his career": a feeling of some great deception; weariness of the soul and feverish physical excitement (such as the "vapid lewdness of the fox-trot"); a sense of futility—and its result: gross liberty. Cruelty, too; the reek of blood still in the air; glaring picture-palaces; dim couples in dark Hyde Park; the glories of standardisation; the cult of machinery; the degradation of Beauty, Love, Honour, Art . . . and so on. It is really a wonder that Mr. Goodman himself who, as far as I know, was Sebastian's coeval, managed to live through those terrific years.

But what Mr. Goodman could stand, his Sebastian Knight apparently could not. We are given a picture of Sebastian restlessly pacing the rooms of his London flat in 1923, after a short trip to the Continent, which Continent "shocked him indescribably by the vulgar glamour of its gambling-hells." Yes, "pacing up and down . . . clutching at his temples . . . in a passion of discontent . . . angry with the world . . . alone . . . eager to do something, but weak, weak . . ." The dots are not Mr. Goodman's tremolos, but denote sentences I have kindly left out. "No," Mr. Goodman goes on, "this was not the world for an artist to live in. It was all very well to flaunt a brave countenance, to make a great display of that cynicism which so irritates one in Knight's earlier work and so pains one in his last two volumes . . . it was all very well to appear contemptuous and ultrasophisticated, but the thorn was there, the sharp, poisonous thorn." I don't know why, but the presence of this (perfectly mythical) thorn seems to give Mr. Goodman a grim satisfaction.

It would be unfair of me if I let it seem that this first chapter of *The Tragedy of Sebastian Knight* consists exclusively of a thick flow of philosophical treacle. Word-pictures and anecdotes which form the body of the book (that is, when Mr. Goodman arrives at the stage of Sebastian's life when he met him personally) appear here too, as rockcakes dotting the syrup. Mr. Goodman was no Boswell; still, no doubt, he kept a note-book where he jotted down certain remarks of his employer—and apparently some of these related to his employer's past. In other words, we must imagine that Sebastian in between work would say: Do you know, my dear Goodman, this reminds me of a day in my life, some years ago, when . . . Here would come the story. Half a dozen of these seem to Mr. Goodman sufficient to fill out what is to him a blank— Sebastian's youth in England.

The first of these stories (which Mr. Goodman considers to be extremely typical of "postwar undergraduate life") depicts Sebastian showing a girl-friend from London the sights of Cambridge. "And this is the Dean's window," he said; then smashing the pane with a stone, he added: "And this is the Dean." Needless to say that Sebastian has been pulling Mr. Goodman's leg: the story is as old as the University itself.

Let us look at the second one. During a short vacation trip to Germany (1921? 1922?) Sebastian, one night, being annoyed by the caterwauls in the street, started to pelt the offenders with miscellaneous objects including an egg. Presently, a policeman knocked at his door, bringing back all these objects minus the egg.

This is from an old (or, as Mr. Goodman would say, "prewar") Jerome K. Jerome book. Leg-pulling again.

Third story: Sebastian speaking of his very first novel (unpublished and destroyed) explained that it was about a fat young student who travels home to find his mother married to his uncle; this uncle, an ear-specialist, had murdered the student's father.

Mr. Goodman misses the joke.

Fourth: Sebastian in the summer of 1922 had overworked himself and, suffering from hallucinations, used to see a kind of optical ghost,—a black-robed monk moving swiftly towards him from the sky.

This is a little harder: a short story by Chekhov.

Fifth:

But I think we had better stop, or else Mr. Goodman might be in danger of becoming a centipede. Let us have him remain quadrupedal. I am sorry for him, but it cannot be helped. And if only he had not padded and commented these "curious incidents and fancies" so ponderously, with such a rich crop of deductions! Churlish, capricious, mad Sebastian, struggling in a naughty world of Juggernauts, and aeronauts, and naughts, and what-nots . . . Well, well, there may be something in all that.

I want to be scientifically precise. I should hate being balked of the tiniest particle of truth only because at a certain point of my search I was blindly enraged by a trashy concoction . . . Who is speaking of Sebastian Knight? His former secretary. Were they ever friends? No,—as we shall see later. Is there anything real or possible in the contrast between a frail eager Sebastian and a wicked tired world? Not a thing. Was there perhaps some other kind of chasm, breach, fissure? There was.

It is enough to turn to the first thirty pages or so of *Lost Property* to see how blandly Mr. Goodman (who incidentally never quotes anything that may clash with the main idea of his fallacious work) misunderstands Sebastian's inner attitude in regard to the outer world. Time for Sebastian was never 1914 or 1920 or 1936—it was always year 1. Newspaper headlines, political theories, fashionable ideas meant to him no more than the loquacious printed notice (in three languages, with mistakes in at least two) on the wrapper of some soap or toothpaste. The lather might be thick and the notice convincing—but that was an end of it. He could perfectly well understand sensitive and intelligent thinkers not being able to sleep because of an earthquake in China; but, being what he was, he could not understand why these same people did not feel exactly the same spasm of rebellious grief when thinking of some similar calamity that had happened as many years ago as there were miles to China. Time and space were to him measures of the same eternity, so that the very idea of his reacting in any special "modern" way to what Mr. Goodman calls "the atmosphere of postwar Europe" is utterly preposterous. He was intermittently happy and uncomfortable in the

world into which he came, just as a traveller may be exhila-
rated by visions of his voyage and be almost simultaneously
sea-sick. Whatever age Sebastian might have been born in, he
would have been equally amused and unhappy, joyful and apprehensive, as a child at a pantomime now and then thinking
of to-morrow's dentist. And the reason of his discomfort was
not that he was moral in an immoral age, or immoral in a
moral one, neither was it the cramped feeling of his youth not
blowing naturally enough in a world which was too rapid a
succession of funerals and fireworks; it was simply his becoming aware that the rhythm of his inner being was so much
richer than that of other souls. Even then, just at the close of
his Cambridge period, and perhaps earlier too, he knew that
his slightest thought or sensation had always at least one more
dimension than those of his neighbours. He might have
boasted of this had there been anything lurid in his nature.
As there was not, it only remained for him to feel the awkwardness of being a crystal among glass, a sphere among
circles (but all this was nothing when compared to what he
experienced as he finally settled down to his literary task).

"I was," writes Sebastian in *Lost Property*, "so shy that I
always managed somehow to commit the fault I was most
anxious to avoid. In my disastrous attempt to match the colour of my surroundings I could only be compared to a colour-
blind chameleon. My shyness would have been easier to
bear—for me and for others—had it been of the normal
clammy-and-pimply kind: many a young fellow passes through
this stage and nobody really minds. But with me it assumed
a morbid secret form which had nothing to do with the throes
of puberty. Among the most hackneyed inventions of the torture house there is one consisting of denying the prisoner
sleep. Most people live through the day with this or that part
of their mind in a happy state of somnolence: a hungry man
eating a steak is interested in his food and not, say, in the
memory of a dream about angels wearing top-hats which he
happened to see seven years ago; but in my case all the shutters and lids and doors of the mind would be open at once at
all times of the day. Most brains have their Sundays, mine was
even refused a half-holiday. This state of constant wakefulness
was extremely painful not only in itself, but in its direct results.

Every ordinary act which, as a matter of course, I had to perform, took on such a complicated appearance, provoked such a multitude of associative ideas in my mind, and these associations were so tricky and obscure, so utterly useless for practical application, that I would either shirk the business at hand or else make a mess of it out of sheer nervousness. When one morning I went to see the editor of a review who, I thought, might print some of my Cambridge poems, a particular stammer he had, blending with a certain combination of angles in the pattern of roofs and chimneys, all slightly distorted owing to a flaw in the glass of the window-pane,—this and a queer musty smell in the room (of roses rotting in the waste-paper basket?) sent my thoughts on such long and intricate errands that, instead of saying what I had meant to say, I suddenly started telling this man whom I was seeing for the first time, about the literary plans of a mutual friend, who, I remembered too late, had asked me to keep them secret . . .

". . . Knowing, as I did, the dangerous vagrancies of my consciousness I was afraid of meeting people, of hurting their feelings or making myself ridiculous in their eyes. But this same quality or defect which tormented me so, when confronted with what is called the practical side of life (though, between you and me, bookkeeping or bookselling looks singularly unreal in the starlight), became an instrument of exquisite pleasure whenever I yielded to my loneliness. I was deeply in love with the country which was my home (as far as my nature could afford the notion of home); I had my Kipling moods and my Rupert Brooke moods, and my Housman moods. The blind man's dog near Harrods or a pavement-artist's coloured chalks; brown leaves in a New Forest ride or a tin bath hanging outside on the black brick wall of a slum; a picture in Punch or a purple passage in Hamlet, all went to form a definite harmony, where I, too, had the shadow of a place. My memory of the London of my youth is the memory of endless vague wanderings, of a sun-dazzled window suddenly piercing the blue morning mist or of beautiful black wires with suspended raindrops running along them. I seem to pass with intangible steps across ghostly lawns and through dancing-halls full of the whine of Hawaiian music and down dear drab little streets with pretty names, until I come to a certain warm hollow where something very like the selfest of my own self sits huddled up in the darkness."

It is a pity Mr. Goodman had not the leisure to peruse this passage, though it is doubtful whether he would have grasped its inner meaning.

He was kind enough to send me a copy of his work. In the letter accompanying it he explained in heavily bantering tones, with what was epistolarily meant to be a good-natured wink, that if he had not mentioned the book in the course of our interview, it was because he wanted it to be a splendid surprise. His tone, his guffaws, his pompous wit—all this suggested an old gruff friend of the family turning up with a precious gift for the youngest. But Mr. Goodman is not a very good actor. Not for a moment did he really think that I would be delighted either with the book he wrote or with the mere fact that he had gone out of his way to advertise the name of a member of my family. He knew all along that his book was rubbish, and he knew that neither its binding, nor its jacket, nor the blurb on the jacket, nor indeed any of the reviews and notices in the press would deceive me. Why he had considered it wiser to keep me in the dark is not quite evident. Perhaps he thought I might wickedly sit down and dash off my own volume, just in time to have it collide with his.

But he not only sent me his book. He also produced the account he had promised me. This is not the place to discuss these matters. I have handed them over to my solicitor who has already acquainted me with his conclusions. Here I may only say that Sebastian's candour in practical affairs was taken advantage of in the coarsest fashion. Mr. Goodman has never been a regular literary agent. He has only betted on books. He does not rightfully belong to that intelligent, honest and hardworking profession. We will leave it at that; but I have not yet done with *The Tragedy of Sebastian Knight* or rather—*The Farce of Mr. Goodman.*

8

TWO YEARS had elapsed after my mother's death before I saw Sebastian again. One picture postcard was all I had had from him during that time, except the cheques he insisted on sending me. On a dull gray afternoon in November or December, 1924, as I was walking up the Champs Elysées towards the Etoile I suddenly caught sight of Sebastian through the glass front of a popular café. I remember my first impulse was to continue on my way, so pained was I by the sudden revelation that having arrived in Paris he had not communicated with me. Then on second thought I entered. I saw the back of Sebastian's glossy dark head and the downcast bespectacled face of the girl sitting opposite him. She was reading a letter which, as I approached, she handed back to him with a faint smile and took off her horn-rimmed glasses.

"Isn't it rich?" asked Sebastian, and at the same moment I laid my hand on his thin shoulder.

"Oh, hullo, V.," he said looking up. "This is my brother, Miss Bishop. Sit down and make yourself comfortable." She was pretty in a quiet sort of way with a pale faintly freckled complexion, slightly hollowed cheeks, blue-gray near-sighted eyes, a thin mouth. She wore a gray tailor-made with a blue scarf and a small three-cornered hat. I believe her hair was bobbed.

"I was just going to ring you up," said Sebastian, not very truthfully I am afraid. "You see I am only here for the day and going back to London to-morrow. What will you have?"

They were drinking coffee. Clare Bishop, her lashes beating, rummaged in her bag, found her handkerchief, and dabbed first one pink nostril and then the other. "Cold getting worse," she said and clicked her bag.

"Oh, splendidly," said Sebastian, in reply to an obvious question. "As a matter of fact I have just finished writing a novel, and the publisher I've chosen seems to like it judging by his encouraging letter. He even seems to approve of the title *Cock Robin Hits Back* though Clare doesn't."

"I think it sounds silly," said Clare, "and besides a bird can't hit."

"It alludes to a well-known nursery-rhyme," said Sebastian, for my benefit.

"A silly allusion," said Clare; "your first title was much better."

"I don't know . . . The prism . . . The prismatic edge . . ." murmured Sebastian, "that's not quite what I want . . . Pity Cock Robin is so unpopular. . . ."

"A title," said Clare, "must convey the colour of the book,—not its subject."

It was the first time and also the last that I ever heard Sebastian discuss literary matters in my presence. Rarely, too, had I seen him in such a lighthearted mood. He appeared well-groomed and fit. His finely-shaped white face with that slight shading on the cheeks—he was one of those unfortunate men who have to shave twice a day when dining out—did not show a trace of that dull unhealthy tinge it so often had. His rather large slightly pointed ears were aflame as they were when he was pleasurably excited. I, for my part, was tongue-tied and stiff. Somehow, I felt that I had barged in.

"Shall we go to a cinema or something," asked Sebastian diving into his waistcoat pocket, with two fingers.

"Just as you like," said Clare.

"Gah-song," said Sebastian. I had noticed before that he tried to pronounce French as a real healthy Britisher would.

For some time we searched under the table and under the plush seats for one of Clare's gloves. She used a nice cool perfume. At last I retrieved it, a gray suede glove with a white lining and a fringed gauntlet. She put them on leisurely as we pushed through the revolving door. Rather tall, very straight-backed, good ankles, flat-heeled shoes.

"Look here," I said, "I don't think I can go with you to the pictures. I'm dreadfully sorry, but I have got some things to attend to. Perhaps . . . But when exactly are you leaving?"

"Oh, to-night," replied Sebastian, "but I'll soon be over again . . . Stupid of me not to have let you know earlier. At any rate we can walk with you a little way . . ."

"Do you know Paris well?" I asked of Clare. . . .

"My parcel," she said stopping short.

"Oh, all right, I'll fetch it," said Sebastian and went back to the café.

We two proceeded very slowly up the wide side-walk. I lamely repeated my question.

"Yes, fairly," she said. "I've got friends here—I'm staying with them until Christmas."

"Sebastian looks remarkably well," I said.

"Yes, I suppose he does," said Clare looking over her shoulder and then blinking at me. "When I first met him he looked a doomed man."

"When was that," I probably asked, for now I remember her answer: "This spring in London at a dreadful party, but then he always looks doomed at parties."

"Here are your bongs-bongs," said Sebastian's voice behind us. I told them I was going to the Etoile underground station and we skirted the place from the left. As we were about to cross the Avenue Kleber, Clare nearly got knocked down by a bicycle.

"You little fool," said Sebastian, gripping her by the elbow.

"Far too many pigeons," she said, as we reached the curb.

"Yes, and they smell," added Sebastian.

"What kind of smell? My nose is stuffed up," she asked sniffing and peering at the dense crowd of fat birds strutting about our feet.

"Iris and rubber," said Sebastian.

The groan of a motor-lorry in the act of avoiding a furniture-van sent the birds wheeling across the sky. They settled among the pearl-gray and black frieze of the Arc de Triomphe and when some of them fluttered off again it seemed as if bits of the carved entablature were turned into flaky life. A few years later I found that picture, "that stone melting into wing," in Sebastian's third book.

We crossed more avenues and then came to the white banisters of the underground station. Here we parted, quite cheerfully . . . I remember Sebastian's receding raincoat and Clare's blue-gray figure. She took his arm and altered her step to fall in with his swinging stride.

Now, I learnt from Miss Pratt a number of things which made me wish to learn a good deal more. Her object in applying to me was to find out whether any of Clare Bishop's letters to Sebastian had remained among his things. She stressed the point that it was not Clare Bishop's commission; that in fact Clare Bishop knew nothing of our interview. She had been married now for three or four years and was much too proud to speak of the past. Miss Pratt had seen her a week or so after Sebastian's death had got into the papers, but although the two women were very old friends (that is, knew more about each other than each of them thought the other knew) Clare did not dwell upon the event.

"I hope he was not too unhappy," she said quietly and then added, "I wonder if he kept my letters?"

The way she said this, the narrowing of her eyes, the quick sigh she gave before changing the subject, convinced her friend that it would be a great relief for her to know the letters had been destroyed. I asked Miss Pratt whether I could get in touch with Clare; whether Clare might be coaxed into talking to me about Sebastian. Miss Pratt answered that knowing Clare she would not even dare to transmit my request. "Hopeless," was what she said. For a moment I was basely tempted to hint that I had the letters in my keeping and would hand them over to Clare provided she granted me a personal interview, so passionate was my longing to meet her, just to see and to watch the shadow of the name I would mention flit across her face. But no,—I could not blackmail Sebastian's past. That was out of the question.

"The letters are burnt," I said. I then continued to plead, repeating again and again that surely there could be no harm in trying; could she not convince Clare, when telling her of our talk, that my visit would be very short, very innocent?

"What is it exactly you want to know?" asked Miss Pratt, "because, you see, I can tell you lots myself."

She spoke for a long time about Clare and Sebastian. She did it very well, although, like most women, she was inclined to be somewhat didactic in retrospection.

"Do you mean to say," I interrupted her at a certain point of her story, "that nobody ever found out what that other woman's name was?"

"No," said Miss Pratt.

"But how shall I find her," I cried.

"You never will."

"When do you say it began?" I interrupted again, as she referred to his illness.

"Well," she said, "I'm not quite sure. What I witnessed wasn't his first attack. We were coming out of some restaurant. It was very cold and he could not find a taxi. He got nervous and angry. He started to run towards one that had drawn up a little way off. Then he stopped and said he was not feeling well. I remember he took a pill or something out of a little box and crushed it in his white silk scarf, sort of pressing it to his face as he did so. That must have been in twenty-seven or twenty-eight."

I asked several more questions. She answered them all in the same conscientious fashion and went on with her dismal tale.

When she had gone, I wrote it all down—but it was dead, dead. I simply had to see Clare! One glance, one word, the mere sound of her voice would be sufficient (and necessary, absolutely necessary) to animate the past. Why it was thus I did not understand, just as I have never understood why on a certain unforgettable day some weeks earlier I had been so sure that if I could find a dying man alive and conscious I would learn something which no human being had yet learnt.

Then one Monday morning I made a call.

The maid showed me into a small sitting-room. Clare was at home, this at least I learnt from that ruddy and rather raw young female. (Sebastian mentions somewhere that English novelists never depart from a certain fixed tone when describing housemaids.) On the other hand I knew from Miss Pratt that Mr. Bishop was busy in the City on week-days; queer—her having married a man with the same name, no relation either, just pure coincidence. Would she not see me? Fairly well off, I should say, but not very . . . Probably an L-shaped drawing room on the first floor and over that a couple of bedrooms. The whole street consisted of just such close-pressed narrow houses. She was long in making up her mind . . . Should I have risked telephoning first? Had Miss Pratt already told her about the letters? Suddenly I heard soft footfalls coming down the stairs and a huge man in a black dressing-gown with purple facings came bouncing into the room.

"I apologise for my attire," he said, "but I am suffering

from a severe cold. My name is Bishop and I gather you want to see my wife."

Had he caught that cold, I thought in a curious flash of fancy, from the pink-nosed husky-voiced Clare I had seen twelve years ago?

"Why, yes," I said, "if she hasn't forgotten me. We met once in Paris."

"Oh, she remembered your name all right," said Mr. Bishop, looking at me squarely, "but I am sorry to say she can't see you."

"May I call later?" I asked.

There was a slight silence, and then Mr. Bishop asked.

"Am I right in presuming that your visit is connected in some way with your brother's death?" There he stood before me, hands thrust into his dressing-gown pockets, looking at me, his fair hair brushed back with an angry brush—a good fellow, a decent fellow, and I hope he will not mind my saying so here. Quite recently, I may add, in very sad circumstances, letters have been exchanged between us, which have quite done away with any ill-feeling that might have crept into our first conversation.

"Would that prevent her seeing me?" I asked in my turn. It was a foolish phrase, I admit.

"You are not going to see her in any case," said Mr. Bishop. "Sorry," he added, relenting a little, as he felt I was safely drifting out. "I am sure that in other circumstances . . . but you see my wife is not overkeen to recall past friendships, and you will forgive me if I say quite frankly I do not think you should have come."

I walked back feeling I had bungled it badly. I pictured to myself what I would have said to Clare had I found her alone. Somehow I managed to convince myself now that had she been alone, she would have seen me: so an unforeseen obstacle belittles those one had imagined. I would have said: "Let us not talk of Sebastian. Let us talk of Paris. Do you know it well? Do you remember those pigeons? Tell me what have you been reading lately . . . And what about films? Do you still lose your gloves, parcels?" Or else I might have resorted to a bolder method, a direct attack. "Yes, I know how you must feel about it, but please, please, talk to me about him.

For the sake of his portrait. For the sake of little things which will wander away and perish if you refuse to let me have them for my book about him." Oh, I was sure she would never have refused.

And two days later with this last intention firm in my mind, I made still another attempt. This time I was resolved to be much more circumspect. It was a fine morning, quite early yet, and I was sure she would not stay indoors. I would unobtrusively take up my position at the corner of her street, wait for her husband's departure to the City, wait for her to come out and then accost her. But things did not work out quite as I had expected.

I had still some little way to go when suddenly Clare Bishop appeared. She had just crossed from my side of the street to the opposite pavement. I knew her at once although I had seen her only for a short half-hour years before. I knew her although her face was now pinched and her body strangely full. She walked slowly and heavily, and as I crossed towards her I realised that she was in an advanced stage of pregnancy. Owing to the impetuous strain in my nature, which has often led me astray, I found myself walking towards her with a smile of welcome, but in those few instants I was already overwhelmed by the perfectly clear consciousness that I might neither talk to her nor greet her in any manner. It had nothing to do with Sebastian or my book, or my words with Mr. Bishop, it was solely on account of her stately concentration. I knew I was forbidden even to make myself known to her, but as I say my impetus had carried me across the street and in such a way that I nearly bumped into her upon reaching the pavement. She side-stepped heavily and lifted her nearsighted eyes. No, thank God, she did not recognise me. There was something heartrending in the solemn expression of her pale saw-dusty face. We had both stopped short. With ridiculous presence of mind I brought out of my pocket the first thing my hand met with, and I said: "I beg your pardon, but have you dropped this?"

"No," she said, with an impersonal smile. She held it for a moment close to her eyes, "no," she repeated, and giving it back to me went on her way. I stood with a key in my hand, as if I had just picked it up off the pavement. It was the latch-key of Sebastian's flat, and with a queer pang I now realised that she had touched it with her innocent blind fingers. . . .

9

THEIR RELATIONSHIP lasted six years. During that period Sebastian produced his two first novels: *The Prismatic Bezel* and *Success*. It took him some seven months to compose the first (April–October, 1924) and twenty-two months to compose the second (July, 1925–April, 1927). Between autumn, 1927, and summer, 1929, he wrote the three stories which later (1932) were re-published together under the title *The Funny Mountain*. In other words, Clare intimately witnessed the first three fifths of his entire production (I skip the juvenilia—the Cambridge poems for instance—which he himself destroyed); and as in the intervals between the above-mentioned books Sebastian kept twisting and laying aside and re-twisting this or that imaginative scheme it may be safely assumed that during those six years he was continuously occupied. And Clare loved his occupation.

She entered his life without knocking, as one might step into the wrong room because of its vague resemblance to one's own. She stayed there forgetting the way out and quietly getting used to the strange creatures she found there and petted despite their amazing shapes. She had no special intention of being happy or of making Sebastian happy, nor had she the slightest misgivings as to what might come next; it was merely a matter of naturally accepting life with Sebastian because life without him was less imaginable than a tellurian's camping-tent on a mountain in the moon. Most probably, if she had borne him a child they would have slipped into marriage since that would have been the simplest way for all three; but that not being the case it did not enter their heads to submit to those white and wholesome formalities which very possibly both would have enjoyed had they given them necessary thought. There was nothing of your advanced prejudice-be-damned stuff about Sebastian. Well did he know that to flaunt one's contempt for a moral code was but smuggled smugness and prejudice turned inside out. He usually chose the easiest ethical path (just as he chose the thorniest aesthetic one) merely because it happened to be the shortest cut to his chosen object; he was far too lazy in everyday life (just as he was far too hardworking in his artistic life) to be bothered by problems set and solved by others.

Clare was twenty-two when she met Sebastian. She did not remember her father; her mother was dead too, and her step-father had married again, so that the faint notion of home which that couple presented to her might be compared to the old sophism of changed handle and changed blade, though of course she could hardly expect to find and join the original parts—this side of Eternity at least. She lived alone in London, rather vaguely attending an Art-school and taking a course in Eastern languages, of all things. People liked her because she was quietly attractive with her charming dim face and soft husky voice, somehow remaining in one's memory as if she were subtly endowed with the gift of being remembered: she came out well in one's mind, she was mnemogenic. Even her rather large and knuckly hands had a singular charm, and she was a good light silent dancer. But best of all she was one of those rare, very rare women who do not take the world for granted and who see everyday things not merely as familiar mirrors of their own feminity. She had imagination—the mus-cle of the soul—and her imagination was of a particularly strong, almost masculine quality. She possessed, too, that real sense of beauty which has far less to do with Art than with the constant readiness to discern the halo round a frying-pan or the likeness between a weeping-willow and a Skye terrier. And finally she was blest with a keen sense of humour. No wonder she fitted into his life so well.

Already during the first season of their acquaintance they saw a great deal of each other; in the autumn she went to Paris and he visited her there more than once, I suspect. By then his first book was ready. She had learnt to type and the summer evenings of 1924 had been to her as many pages slipped into the slit and rolled out again alive with black and violet words. I should like to imagine her tapping the glisten-ing keys to the sound of a warm shower rustling in the dark elms beyond the open window, with Sebastian's slow and se-rious voice (he did not merely dictate, said Miss Pratt,—he officiated) coming and going across the room. He used to spend most of the day writing, but so labourious was his progress that there would hardly be more than a couple of fresh pages for her to type in the evening and even these had to be done over again, for Sebastian used to indulge in an orgy of corrections; and sometimes he would do what I daresay no author ever did—recopy the typed sheet in his own slanting un-English hand and then dictate it anew. His struggle with words was unusually painful and this for two reasons. One was the common one with writers of his type: the bridging of the abyss lying between expression and thought; the maddening feeling that the right words, the only words are awaiting you on the opposite bank in the misty distance, and the shudderings of the still unclothed thought clamouring for them on this side of the abyss. He had no use for ready-made phrases because the things he wanted to say were of an exceptional build and he knew moreover that no real idea can be said to exist without the words made to measure. So that (to use a closer simile) the thought which only seemed naked was but pleading for the clothes it wore to become visible, while the words lurking afar were not empty shells as they seemed, but were only waiting for the thought they already concealed to set them aflame and in motion. At times he felt like a child given a farrago of wires and ordered to produce the wonder of light. And he did produce it; and sometimes he would not be conscious at all of the way he succeeded in doing so, and at other times he would be worrying the wires for hours in what seemed the most rational way—and achieve nothing. And Clare, who had not composed a single line of imaginative prose or poetry in her life, understood so well (and that was her private miracle) every detail of Sebastian's struggle, that the words she typed were to her not so much the conveyors of their natural sense, but the curves and gaps and zigzags showing Sebastian's groping along a certain ideal line of expression.

This, however, was not all. I know, I know as definitely as I know we had the same father, I know Sebastian's Russian was better and more natural to him than his English. I quite believe that by not speaking Russian for five years he may have forced himself into thinking he had forgotten it. But a language is a live physical thing which cannot be so easily dismissed. It should moreover be remembered that five years before his first book—that is, at the time he left Russia,—his English was as thin as mine. I have improved mine artificially years later (by dint of hard study abroad); he tried to let his thrive naturally in its own surroundings. It did thrive wonderfully but still I maintain that had he started to write in Russian, those particular linguistic throes would have been spared him. Let me add that I have in my possession a letter written by him not long before his death. And that short letter is couched in a Russian purer and richer than his English ever was, no matter what beauty of expression he attained in his books.

I know too that as Clare took down the words he disentangled from his manuscript she sometimes would stop tapping and say with a little frown, slightly lifting the outer edge of the imprisoned sheet and re-reading the line: "No, my dear. You can't say it so in English." He would stare at her for an instant or two and then resume his prowl, reluctantly pondering on her observation, while she sat with her hands softly folded in her lap quietly waiting. "There is no other way of expressing it," he would mutter at last. "And if for instance," she would say—and then an exact suggestion would follow.

"Oh, well, if you like," he would reply.

"I'm not insisting, my dear, just as you wish, if you think bad grammar won't hurt . . ."

"Oh, go on," he would cry, "you are perfectly right, go on . . ."

By November, 1924, *The Prismatic Bezel* was completed. It was published in the following March and fell completely flat. As far as I can find out by looking up newspapers of that period, it was alluded to only once. Five lines and a half in a Sunday paper, between other lines referring to other books. "*The Prismatic Bezel* is apparently a first novel and as such ought not to be judged as severely as (So-and-So's book mentioned previously). Its fun seemed to me obscure and its obscurities funny, but possibly there exists a kind of fiction the niceties of which will always elude me. However, for the benefit of readers who like that sort of stuff I may add that Mr. Knight is as good at splitting hairs as he is at splitting infinitives."

That spring was probably the happiest period of Sebastian's

existence. He had been delivered of one book and was already feeling the throbs of the next one. He was in excellent health. He had a delightful companion. He suffered from none of those petty worries which formerly used to assail him at times with the perseverance of a swarm of ants spreading over a hacienda. Clare posted letters for him, and checked laundry returns, and saw that he was well supplied with shaving blades, tobacco and salted almonds for which he had a special weakness. He enjoyed dining out with her and then going to a play. The play almost invariably made him writhe and groan afterwards, but he derived a morbid pleasure from dissecting platitudes. An expression of greed, of wicked eagerness, would make his nostrils expand while his back teeth ground in a paroxysm of disgust, as he pounced upon some poor triviality. Miss Pratt remembered one particular occasion when her father, who had at one time had some financial interest in the cinema industry, invited Sebastian and Clare to the private view of a very gorgeous and expensive film. The leading actor was a remarkably handsome young man wearing a luxurious turban and the plot was powerfully dramatic. At the highest point of tension, Sebastian, to Mr. Pratt's extreme surprise and annoyance, began to shake with laughter, with Clare bubbling too but plucking at his sleeve in a helpless effort to make him stop. They must have had a glorious time together, those two. And it is hard to believe that the warmth, the tenderness, the beauty of it has not been gathered, and is not treasured somewhere, somehow, by some immortal witness of mortal life. They must have been seen wandering in Kew Gardens, or Richmond Park (personally I have never been there but the names attract me), or eating ham and eggs at some pretty inn in their summer rambles in the country, or reading on the vast divan in Sebastian's study with the fire cheerfully burning and an English Christmas already filling the air with faintly spicy smells on a background of lavender and leather. And Sebastian must have been overheard telling her of the extraordinary things he would try to express in his next book *Success*.

One day in the summer of 1926, as he was feeling parched and fuzzled after battling with a particularly rebellious chapter, he thought he might take a month's holiday abroad. Clare having some business in London said she would join him a week or two later. When she eventually arrived at the German seaside resort which Sebastian had decided upon, she was un-expectedly informed at the hotel that he had left for an un-known destination but would be back in a couple of days. This puzzled Clare, although, as she afterwards told Miss Pratt, she did not feel unduly anxious or distressed. We may picture her, a thin tall figure in a blue mackintosh (the weather was overcast and unfriendly) strolling rather aimlessly on the promenade, the sandy beach, empty except for a few undis-mayed children, the three-coloured flags flapping mournfully in a dying breeze, and a steely gray sea breaking here and there into crests of foam. Farther down the coast there was a beech-wood, deep and dark with no undergrowth except bindwood patching the undulating brown soil; and a strange brown still-ness stood waiting among the straight smooth tree-trunks: she thought she might find at any moment a red-capped German gnome peeping bright-eyed at her from among the dead leaves of a hollow. She unpacked her bathing things and passed a pleasant though somewhat listless day lying on the soft white sand. Next morning was rainy again and she stayed in her room until lunch time, reading Donne, who for ever after remained to her associated with the pale gray light of that damp and hazy day and the whine of a child wanting to play in the corridor. And presently Sebastian arrived. He was certainly glad to see her but there was something not quite natural in his demeanour. He seemed nervous and troubled, and averted his face whenever she tried to meet his look. He said he had come across a man he had known ages ago, in Russia, and they had gone in the man's car to—he named a place on the coast some miles away. "But what *is* the matter, my dear?" she asked peering into his sulky face.

"Oh, nothing, nothing," he cried peevishly, "I can't sit and do nothing, I want my work," he added and looked away.

"I wonder if you are telling me the truth," she said.

He shrugged his shoulders and slid the edge of his palm along the groove of the hat he was holding.

"Come along," he said. "Let's have lunch and then go back to London."

But there was no convenient train before evening. As the weather had cleared they went out for a stroll. Sebastian tried once or twice to be as bright with her as he usually was, but it somehow fizzled out and they were both silent. They reached the beech-wood. There was the same mysterious and dull suspense about it, and he said, though she had not told him she had been there before: "What a funny quiet place. Eerie, isn't it? One half-expects to see a brownie among those dead leaves and convolvulus."

"Look here, Sebastian," she suddenly exclaimed, putting her hands on his shoulders. "I want to know what's the matter. Perhaps you've stopped loving me. Is it that?"

"Oh my darling, what nonsense," said he with perfect sincerity. "But . . . if you must know . . . you see . . . I'm not good at deceiving, and well, I'd rather you knew. The fact is I felt a confounded pain in my chest and arm, so I thought I'd better dash to Berlin and see a doctor. He packed me off to bed there . . . Serious? . . . No, I hope not. We discussed coronary arteries and blood supply and sinuses of Salva and he generally seemed to be a very knowing old beggar. I'll see another man in London and get a second opinion, though I feel fit as a fiddle to-day . . ."

I suppose Sebastian already knew from what exact heart-disease he was suffering. His mother had died of the same complaint, a rather rare variety of angina pectoris, called by some doctors "Lehmann's disease." It appears, however, that after the first attack he had at least a year's respite, though now and then he did experience a queer twinge as of inner itch in his left arm.

He sat down to his task again and worked steadily through the autumn, spring and winter. The composing of *Success* turned out to be even more arduous than that of his first novel and took him much longer, although both books were about the same length. By a stroke of luck I have a direct picture of the day *Success* was finished. This I owe to someone I met later—and indeed many of the impressions I have offered in this chapter have been formed by corroborating the statements of Miss Pratt with those of another friend of Sebastian's, though the spark which had kindled it all belongs in some mysterious manner to that glimpse I had of Clare Bishop walking heavily down a London street.

The door opens. Sebastian Knight is disclosed lying spread-eagled on the floor of his study. Clare is making a neat bundle of the typed sheets on the desk. The person who entered stops short.

"No, Leslie," says Sebastian from the floor, "I'm not dead. I have finished building a world, and this is my Sabbath rest."

10

"THE PRISMATIC BEZEL" was appreciated at its true worth only when Sebastian's first real success caused it to be presented anew by another firm (Bronson), but even then it did not sell as well as *Success*, or *Lost Property*. For a first novel it shows remarkable force of artistic will and literary self-control. As often was the way with Sebastian Knight he used parody as a kind of springboard for leaping into the highest region of serious emotion. J. L. Coleman has called it "a clown developing wings, an angel mimicking a tumbler pigeon," and the metaphor seems to me very apt. Based cunningly on a parody of certain tricks of the literary trade, *The Prismatic Bezel* soars skyward. With something akin to fanatical hate Sebastian Knight was ever hunting out the things which had once been fresh and bright but which were now worn to a thread, dead things among living ones; dead things shamming life, painted and repainted, continuing to be accepted by lazy minds serenely unaware of the fraud. The decayed idea might be in itself quite innocent and it may be argued that there is not much sin in continually exploiting this or that thoroughly worn subject or style if it still pleases and amuses. But for Sebastian Knight, the merest trifle, as, say, the adopted method of a detective story, became a bloated and malodorous corpse. He did not mind in the least "penny dreadfuls" because he wasn't concerned with ordinary morals; what annoyed him invariably was the second rate, not the third or N-th rate, because here, at the readable stage, the shamming began, and this was, in an *artistic* sense, immoral. But *The Prismatic Bezel* is not only a rollicking parody of the setting of a detective tale; it is also a wicked imitation of many other things: as for instance a certain literary habit which Sebastian Knight, with his uncanny perception of secret decay, noticed in the modern novel, namely the fashionable trick of grouping a medley of people in a limited space (a hotel, an island, a street). Then also different kinds of styles are satirized in the course of the book as well as the problem of blending direct speech with narration and description which an elegant

pen solves by finding as many variations of "he said" as may
be found in the dictionary between "acceded" and "yelped."
But all this obscure fun is, I repeat, only the author's springboard.

Twelve persons are staying at a boarding-house; the house
is very carefully depicted but in order to stress the "island"
note, the rest of the town is casually shown as a secondary
cross between natural mist and a primary cross between stage-
properties and a real-estate agent's nightmare. As the author
points out (indirectly) this method is somewhat allied to the
cinema practice of showing the leading lady in her impossible
dormitory years as glamorously different from a crowd of
plain and fairly realistic schoolmates. One of the lodgers, a
certain G. Abeson, art-dealer, is found murdered in his room.
The local police-officer, who is described solely in terms of
boots, rings up a London detective, asking him to come at
once. Owing to a combination of mishaps (his car runs over
an old woman and then he takes the wrong train) he is very
long in arriving. In the meantime the inhabitants of the
boarding house plus a chance passer-by, old Nosebag, who
happened to be in the lobby when the crime was discovered,
are thoroughly examined. All of them except the last named,
a mild old gentleman with a white beard yellowish about the
mouth, and a harmless passion for collecting snuffboxes, are
more or less open to suspicion; and one of them, a fishy art-
student, seems particularly so: half a dozen blood-stained
handkerchiefs are found under his bed. Incidentally, it may be
noted that in order to simplify and "concentrate" things not
a single servant or hotel employee is specifically mentioned
and nobody bothers about their non-existence. Then, with a
quick sliding motion, something in the story begins to shift
(the detective, it must be remembered, is still on the way and
G. Abeson's stiff corpse lying on the carpet). It gradually tran-
spires that all the lodgers are in various ways connected with
one another. The old lady in No. 3 turns out to be the mother
of the violinist in No. 11. The novelist occupying the front
bedroom is really the husband of the young lady in the third
floor back. The fishy art-student is no less than this lady's
brother. The solemn moon-faced person who is so very polite
to everyone, happens to be butler to the crusty old colonel

who, it appears, is the violinist's father. The gradual melting process continues through the art-student's being engaged to the fat little woman in No. 5, and she is the old lady's daughter by a previous marriage. And when the amateur lawn tennis champion in No. 6 turns out to be the violinist's brother and the novelist their uncle and the old lady in No. 3 the crusty old colonel's wife, then the numbers on the doors are quietly wiped out and the boarding-house motif is painlessly and smoothly replaced by that of a country-house, with all its natural implications. And here the tale takes on a strange beauty. The idea of time, which was made to look comic (detective losing his way . . . stranded somewhere in the night) now seems to curl up and fall asleep. Now the lives of the characters shine forth with a real and human significance and G. Abeson's sealed door is but that of a forgotten lumber-room. A new plot, a new drama utterly unconnected with the opening of the story, which is thus thrust back into the region of dreams, seems to struggle for existence and break into light. But at the very moment when the reader feels quite safe in an atmosphere of pleasurable reality and the grace and glory of the author's prose seems to indicate some lofty and rich intention, there is a grotesque knocking at the door and the detective enters. We are again wallowing in a morass of parody. The detective, a shifty fellow, drops his h's, and this is meant to look as if it were meant to look quaint; for it is not a parody of the Sherlock Holmes vogue but a parody of the modern reaction from it. The lodgers are examined afresh. New clues are guessed at. Mild old Nosebag potters about, very absent-minded and harmless. He had just dropped in to see if they had a spare room, he explains. The old gag of making the most innocent-looking person turn out to be the master-villain seems to be on the point of being exploited. The sleuth suddenly gets interested in snuff-boxes. "'Ullo," he says, "'ow about Hart?" Suddenly a policeman lumbers in, very red in the face and reports that the corpse has gone. The detective: "What dy'a mean by gorn?" The policeman: "Gone Sir, the room is empty." There was a moment of ridiculous suspense. "I think," said old Nosebag quietly, "that I can explain." Slowly and very carefully he removes his beard, his gray wig, his dark spectacles, and the face of G. Abeson is disclosed. "You see," says Mr. Abeson with a self-deprecating smile, "one dislikes being murdered."

I have tried my best to show the workings of the book, at least some of its workings. Its charm, humour and pathos can only be appreciated by direct reading. But for enlightenment of those who felt baffled by its habit of metamorphosis, or merely disgusted at finding something incompatible with the idea of a "nice book" in the discovery of a book's being an utterly new one, I should like to point out that *The Prismatic Bezel* can be thoroughly enjoyed once it is understood that the heroes of the book are what can be loosely called "methods of composition." It is as if a painter said: look, here I'm going to show you not the painting of a landscape, but the painting of different ways of painting a certain landscape, and I trust their harmonious fusion will disclose the landscape as I intend you to see it. In the first book Sebastian brought this experiment to a logical and satisfactory conclusion. By putting to the *ad absurdum* test this or that literary manner and then dismissing them one after the other, he deduced his own manner and fully exploited it in his next book *Success*. Here he seems to have passed from one plane to another rising a step higher, for, if his first novel is based on methods of literary composition,—the second one deals mainly with the methods of human fate. With scientific precision in the classification, examination and rejection of an immense amount of data (the accumulation of which is rendered possible by the fundamental assumption that an author is able to discover anything he may want to know about his characters, such capacity being limited only by the manner and purpose of his selection in so far as it ought to be not a haphazard jumble of worthless details but a definite and methodical quest), Sebastian Knight devotes the three hundred pages of *Success* to one of the most complicated researches that has ever been attempted by a writer. We are informed that a certain commercial traveller Percival Q. at a certain stage of his life and in certain circumstances meets the girl, a conjuror's assistant, with whom he will be happy ever after. The meeting is or seems accidental: both happen to use the same car belonging to an amiable stranger on a day the buses went on strike. This is the formula: quite uninteresting if viewed as an actual happening, but becoming a source of remarkable mental enjoyment and excitement, when examined from a special angle. The author's task is to find out how this formula has been arrived at; and all the magic and force of his art are summoned in order to discover the exact way in which two lines of life were made to come into contact,—the whole book indeed being but a glorious gamble on causalities or, if you prefer, the probing of the aetiological secret of aleatory occurrences. The odds seem unlimited. Several obvious lines of inquiry are followed with varying success. Working backwards the author finds out why the strike was fixed to take place that particular day and a certain politician's life-long predilection for the number nine is found to be at the root of the business. This leads us nowhere and the trail is abandoned (not without having given us the opportunity of witnessing a heated party debate). Another false scent is the stranger's car. We try to find out who he was and what caused him to pass at a given moment along a given street; but when we do learn that he had passed there on his way to his office every week day at the same time for the last ten years of his life, we are left none the wiser. Thus we are forced to assume that the outward circumstances of the meeting are not samples of fate's activity in regard to two subjects but a given entity, a fixed point, of no causal import; and so, with a clear conscience we turn to the problem of why Q. and the girl Anne of all people were made to come and stand side by side for a minute on the curb at that particular spot. So the girl's line of fate is traced back for a time, then the man's, notes are compared, and then again both lives are followed up in turn.

We learn a number of curious things. The two lines which have finally tapered to the point of meeting are really not the straight lines of a triangle which diverge steadily towards an unknown base, but wavy lines, now running wide apart, now almost touching. In other words there have been at least two occasions in these two peoples' lives when unknowingly to one another they all but met. In each case fate seemed to have prepared such a meeting with the utmost care; touching up now this possibility now that one; screening exits and repainting signposts; narrowing in its creeping grasp the bag of the net where the butterflies were flapping; timing the least detail and leaving nothing to chance. The disclosure of these secret preparations is a fascinating one and the author seems argus-eyed as he takes into account all the colours of place and cir-cumstance. But, every time, a minute mistake (the shadow of a flaw, the stopped hole of an unwatched possibility, a caprice of free will) spoils the necessitarian's pleasure and the two lives are diverging again with increased rapidity. Thus, Percival Q. is prevented, by a bee stinging him on the lip, at the last minute, from coming to the party, to which fate with endless difficulty had managed to bring Anne; thus, by a trick of tem-per she fails to get the carefully prepared job in the lost prop-erty office where Q.'s brother is employed. But fate is much too persevering to be put off by failure. And when finally success is achieved it is reached by such delicate machinations that not the merest click is audible when at last the two are brought together.

I shall not go into further details of this clever and delight-ful novel. It is the best-known of Sebastian Knight's works, although his three later books surpass it in many ways. As in my demonstration of *The Prismatic Bezel*, my sole object is to show the workings, perhaps detrimentally to the impression of beauty left by the book itself, apart from its artifices. It contains, let me add, a passage so strangely connected with Sebastian's inner life at the time of the completing of the last chapters, that it deserves being quoted in contrast to a series of observations referring rather to the meanders of the au-thor's brain than to the emotional side of his art.

"William [Anne's first queer effeminate fiancé, who after-wards jilted her] saw her home as usual and cuddled her a little in the darkness of the doorway. All of a sudden, she felt that his face was wet. He covered it with his hand and groped for his handkerchief. 'Raining in Paradise,' he said . . . 'the onion of happiness . . . poor Willy is willy nilly a willow.' He kissed the corner of her mouth and then blew his nose with a faint moist squizzle. 'Grown-up men don't cry,' said Anne. 'But I'm not a grown-up,' he replied with a whimper. 'That moon is childish, and that wet pavement is childish, and Love is a honey-suckling babe . . .' 'Please stop,' she said. 'You know I hate when you go on talking like that. It's so silly, so . . .' 'So Willy,' he sighed. He kissed her again and they stood like some soft dark statue with two dim heads. A policeman passed leading the night on a leash and then paused to let it sniff at a pillar-box. 'I'm as happy as you,' she said, 'but I don't want to cry in the least or to talk nonsense.' 'But can't you see,' he whispered, 'can't you see that happiness at its very best is but the zany of its own mortality?' 'Good-night,' said Anne. 'To-morrow at eight,' he cried as she slipped away. He patted the door gently and presently was strolling down the street. She is warm and she is pretty, he mused, and I love her, and it's all no good, no good, because we are dying. I cannot bear that backward glide into the past. That last kiss is already dead and *The Woman in White* [a film they had been to see that night] is stone-dead, and the policeman who passed is dead too, and even the door is as dead as its nail. And that last thought is already a dead thing by now. Coates (the doctor) is right when he says that my heart is too small for my size. And sighs. He wandered on talking to himself, his shadow now pulling a long nose, now dropping a curtsey, as it slipped back round a lamp-post. When he reached his dismal lodgings he was a long time climbing the dark stairs. Before going to bed he knocked at the conjuror's door and found the old man standing in his underwear and inspecting a pair of black trousers. 'Well?' said William . . . 'They don't kinda like my accent,' he replied, 'but I guess I'm going to get that turn all the same.' William sat down on the bed and said: 'You ought to dye your hair.' 'I'm more bald than gray,' said the conjuror. 'I sometimes wonder,' said William, 'where the things we shed are—because they must go *somewhere*, you know,—lost hair, fingernails . . .' 'Been drinking again,' suggested the conjuror without much curiosity. He folded his trousers with care and told William to quit the bed, so that he might put them under the mattress. William sat down on a chair and the conjuror went on with his business; the hairs bristled on his calves, his lips were pursed, his soft hands moved tenderly. 'I am merely happy,' said William. 'You don't look it,' said the solemn old man. 'May I buy you a rabbit?' asked William. 'I'll hire one when necessary,' the conjuror re-plied drawing out the 'necessary' as if it were an endless rib-bon. 'A ridiculous profession,' said William, 'a pick-pocket gone mad, a matter of patter. The pennies in a beggar's cap and the omelette in your top hat. Absurdly the same.' 'We are used to insult,' said the conjuror. He calmly put out the light and William groped his way out. The books on the bed in his room seemed reluctant to move. As he undressed he imagined the forbidden bliss of a sunlit laundry: blue water and scarlet wrists. Might he beg Anne to wash his shirt? Had he really annoyed her again? Did she really believe they would be married some day? The pale little freckles on the glistening skin under her innocent eyes. The right front-tooth that protruded a little. Her soft warm neck. He felt again the pressure of tears. Would she go the way of May, Judy, Juliette, Augusta and all the rest of his love-embers? He heard the dancing-girl in the next room locking the door, washing, bumping down a jug, wistfully clearing her throat. Something dropped with a tinkle. The conjuror began to snore."

II

I AM fast approaching the crucial point of Sebastian's sentimental life and as I consider the work already done in the pale light of the task still before me I feel singularly ill at ease. Have I given as fair an idea of Sebastian's life up to now as I had hoped, and as I now hope to do, in regard to its final period? The dreary tussle with a foreign idiom and a complete lack of literary experience do not predispose one to feeling overconfident. But badly as I may have blundered over my task in the course of the preceding chapters I am determined to persevere and in this I am sustained by the secret knowledge that in some unobtrusive way Sebastian's shade is trying to be helpful.

I have received less abstract help too. P. G. Sheldon, the poet, who saw a great deal of Clare and Sebastian between 1927 and 1930 was kindly willing to tell me anything he might know, when I called upon him very soon after my strange half-meeting with Clare. And it is he again who a couple of months later (when I had already begun upon this book) informed me of poor Clare's fate. She had seemed to be such a normal and healthy young woman, how was it that she bled to death next to an empty cradle? He told me of her delight when *Success* lived up to its title. For it *was* a success this time. Why it is so, why this excellent book should flop and that other, as excellent, receive its due, will always remain something of a mystery. As had been the case, too, with his first novel, Sebastian had not moved a finger, not pulled the least string in order to have *Success* brightly heralded and warmly acclaimed. When a press-cutting agency began to pepper him with samples of praise, he refused either to subscribe to the clippings or thank the kindly critics. To express his gratitude to a man who by saying what he thought of a book was merely doing his duty, seemed to Sebastian improper and even insulting as implying a tepidly human side to the frosty serenity of dispassionate judgement. Moreover, once having begun he would have been forced to go on thanking and thanking for every following line lest the man should be hurt by a sudden lapse; and finally, such a damp dizzy warmth would develop that, in spite of this or that critic's well-known honesty, the grateful author might never be quite, quite certain that here or there personal sympathy had not tiptoed in.

Fame in our day is too common to be confused with the enduring glow around a deserving book. But whatever it was, Clare meant to enjoy it. She wanted to see people who wanted to see Sebastian, who emphatically did not want to see them. She wanted to hear strangers talk about *Success* but Sebastian said he was no longer interested in that particular book. She wanted Sebastian to join a literary club and mix with other authors. And once or twice Sebastian got into a starched shirt and got out of it again without having uttered one single word at the dinner arranged in his honour. He was not feeling too well. He slept badly. He had dreadful fits of temper—and this was a thing new to Clare. One afternoon as he was working at *The Funny Mountain* in his study and trying to keep to a steep slippery track among the dark crags of neuralgia, Clare entered and in her gentlest voice inquired whether he would not mind seeing a visitor.

"No," he said, baring his teeth at the word he had just written.

"But you asked him to come at five and . . ."

"Now you've done it . . ." cried Sebastian, and dashed his fountain-pen at the shocked white wall. "Can't you let me work in peace," he shouted in such a crescendo that P. G. Sheldon who had been playing chess with Clare in the next room got up and closed the door leading to the hall, where a meek little man was waiting.

Now and then, a wild frolicsome mood came over him. One afternoon with Clare and a couple of friends, he devised a beautiful practical joke to be played on a person they were going to meet after dinner. Sheldon curiously enough had forgotten what it was exactly, that scheme. Sebastian laughed and turned on his heel knocking his fists together as he did when genuinely amused. They were all about to start and very eager and all that, and Clare had 'phoned for a taxi and her new silver shoes glittered and she had found her bag, when suddenly Sebastian seemed to lose all interest in the proceedings. He looked bored and yawned almost without opening his mouth in a very annoying manner and presently said he would take the dog out and then go to bed. In those days he had a little black bull-terrier; eventually it fell ill and had to be destroyed.

The Funny Mountain was completed, then *Albinos in Black* and then his third and last short story, *The Back of the Moon.* You remember that delightful character in it—the meek little man waiting for a train who helped three miserable travellers in three different ways? This Mr. Siller is perhaps the most alive of Sebastian's creatures and is incidentally the final representative of the "research theme," which I have discussed in conjunction with *The Prismatic Bezel* and *Success.* It is as though a certain idea steadily growing through two books has now burst into real physical existence, and so Mr. Siller makes his bow, with every detail of habit and manner, palpable and unique—: the bushy eyebrows and the modest mustache, the soft collar and the Adam's apple "moving like the bulging shape of an arrased eavesdropper," the brown eyes, the wine-red veins on the big strong nose, "whose form made one wonder whether he had not lost his hump somewhere"; the little black tie and the old umbrella ("a duck in deep mourning"); the dark thickets in the nostrils; the beautiful surprise of shiny perfection when he removes his hat. But the better Sebastian's work was the worse he felt—especially in the intervals. Sheldon thinks that the world of the last book he was to write several years later (*The Doubtful Asphodel*) was already casting its shadow on all things surrounding him and that his novels and stories were but bright masks, sly tempters under the pretense of artistic adventure leading him unerringly towards a certain imminent goal. He was presumably as fond of Clare as he had always been, but the acute sense of mortality which had begun to obsess him, made his relations with her appear more brittle than they perhaps were. As for Clare, she had quite inadvertently in her well-meaning innocence dallied at some pleasant sunlit corner of Sebastian's life, where Sebastian himself had not paused; and now she was left behind and did not quite know whether to try and catch up with him or attempt to call him back. She was kept cheerfully busy, what with looking after Sebastian's literary affairs and keeping his life tidy in general, and although she surely felt that something was awry, that it was dangerous to lose touch with his imaginative existence, she probably comforted herself by presuming it to be a passing restlessness, and that "it would all settle down by-and-by." Naturally, I cannot touch upon the intimate side of their relationship, firstly, because it would be ridiculous to discuss what no one can definitely assert, and secondly because the very sound of the word "sex" with its hissing vulgarity and the "ks, ks" catcall at the end, seems so inane to me that I cannot help doubting whether there *is* any real idea behind the word. Indeed, I believe that granting "sex" a special situation when tackling a human problem, or worse still, letting the "sexual idea," if such a thing exists, pervade and "explain" all the rest is a grave error of reasoning. "The breaking of a wave cannot explain the whole sea, from its moon to its serpent; but a pool in the cup of a rock and the diamond-rippled road to Cathay are both water." (*The Back of the Moon.*)

"Physical love is but another way of saying the same thing and not a special sexophone note, which once heard is echoed in every other region of the soul" (*Lost Property*, page 82). "All things belong to the same order of things, for such is the oneness of human perception, the oneness of individuality, the oneness of matter, whatever matter may be. The only real number is one, the rest are mere repetition" (*ibid*, page 83). Had I even known from some reliable source that Clare was not quite up to the standards of Sebastian's love-making I would still never dream of selecting this dissatisfaction as the reason for his general feverishness and nervousness. But being dissatisfied with things in general, he might have been dissatisfied with the colour of his romance too. And mind you, I use the word dissatisfaction very loosely, for Sebastian's mood at that period of his life was something far more complicated than mere Weltschmerz or the blues. It can only be grasped through the medium of his last book *The Doubtful Asphodel.* That book was as yet but a distant haze. Presently it would become the outline of a shore. In 1929, a famous heart-specialist, Dr. Oates, advised Sebastian to spend a month at Blauberg, in Alsace, where a certain treatment had proved beneficial in several similar cases. It seems to have been tacitly agreed that he would go alone. Before he left, Miss Pratt,

Sheldon, Clare and Sebastian had tea together at his flat and he was cheerful and talkative, and teased Clare for having dropped her own crumpled handkerchief among the things she had been packing for him in his fussy presence. Then he made a dart at Sheldon's cuff (he never wore a wristwatch himself), peeped at the time and suddenly began to rush, although there was almost an hour to spare. Clare did not suggest seeing him to the train—she knew he disliked that. He kissed her on the temple and Sheldon helped him carry out his bag (have I already mentioned that, apart from a vague charwoman and the waiter who brought him his meals from a neighbouring restaurant, Sebastian did not employ servants?). When he had gone, the three of them sat in silence for a while.

All at once Clare put down the teapot and said: "I think that handkerchief had wanted to go with him, I've a great mind to take that hint."

"Don't be silly," said Mr. Sheldon.

"Why not?" she asked.

"If you mean that you want to catch the same train," began Miss Pratt . . .

"Why not," Clare repeated. "I have forty minutes in which to do it. I'll dash to my place, pack a thing or two, bolt into a taxi . . ."

And she did it. What happened at Victoria is not known, but an hour or so later she rang up Sheldon who had gone home, and told him with a rather pathetic little laugh that Sebastian had not even wanted her to stay on the platform until his train left. I have a very definite vision somehow of her arriving there, with her bag, her lips ready to part in a humorous smile, her dim eyes peering through the windows of the train, looking for him, then finding him, or perhaps he saw her first . . . "Hullo, here I am," she must have said brightly, a little too brightly perhaps . . .

He wrote to her, a few days later, to tell her that the place was very pleasant and that he felt remarkably well. Then there was a silence, and only when Clare had sent an anxious telegram did a card arrive with the information that he was curtailing his stay at Blauberg and would spend a week in Paris before coming home.

Towards the end of that week he rang me up and we dined together at a Russian restaurant. I had not seen him since 1924 and this was 1929. He looked worn and ill, and owing to his pallor seemed unshaven although he had just been to the barber. There was a boil at the back of his neck patched up with pink plaster.

After he had asked me a few questions about myself, we both found it a strain to carry on the conversation. I asked him what had become of the nice girl with whom I had seen him last time. "What girl?" he asked. "Oh, Clare. Yes, she's all right. We're sort of married."

"You look a bit seedy," I said.

"And I don't give a damn if I do. Will you have 'pelmenies' now?"

"Fancy your still remembering what they taste like," I said.

"Why shouldn't I?" he said drily.

We ate in silence for some minutes. Then we had coffee.

"What did you say the place was called? Blauberg?"

"Yes, Blauberg."

"Was it nice there?"

"It depends on what you call nice," he said and his jaw-muscles moved as he scrunched a yawn. "Sorry," he said, "I hope I get some sleep in the train."

He suddenly fumbled at my wrist.

"Half-past eight," I replied.

"I've got to telephone," he muttered and strode across the restaurant with his napkin in his hand. Five minutes later he was back with the napkin half-stuffed into his coat-pocket. I pulled it out.

"Look here," he said, "I'm dreadfully sorry, I must be going. I forgot I had an appointment."

"It has always distressed me," writes Sebastian Knight in *Lost Property*, "that people in restaurants never notice the animated mysteries, who bring them their food and check their overcoats and push doors open for them. I once reminded a businessman with whom I had lunched a few weeks before, that the woman who had handed us our hats had had cotton wool in her ears. He looked puzzled and said he hadn't been aware of there having been any woman at all. . . . A person who fails to notice a taxi-driver's hare-lip because he is in a hurry to get somewhere, is to me a monomaniac. I have often felt as if I were sitting among blind men and madmen, when I thought that I was the only one in the crowd to wonder about the chocolate-girl's slight, very slight limp."

As we left the restaurant and were making our way towards the taxi-rank, a bleary-eyed old man wetted his thumb and offered Sebastian or me or both, one of the printed advertisements he was distributing. Neither of us took it, both looked straight ahead, sullen dreamers ignoring the offer. "Well, good-bye," I said to Sebastian, as he beckoned to a cab.

"Come and see me one day in London," he said and glanced over his shoulder, "Wait a minute," he added, "this won't do. I have cut a beggar . . ." He left me and presently returned, a small sheet of paper in his hand. He read it carefully before throwing it away.

"Want a lift?" he asked.

I felt he was madly anxious to get rid of me.

"No, thanks," I said. I did not catch the address he gave to the chauffeur, but I recall his telling him to go fast.

When he returned to London . . . No, the thread of the narrative breaks off and I must ask others to tie up the threads again.

Did Clare notice at once that something had happened? Did she suspect at once what that something was? Shall we try to guess what she asked Sebastian, and what he answered, and what she said then? I think we will not . . . Sheldon saw them soon after Sebastian's return and found that Sebastian looked queer. But he had looked queer before, too . . .

"Presently it began to worry me," said Mr. Sheldon. He met Clare alone and asked her whether she thought Sebastian was all right. "Sebastian?" said Clare with a slow dreadful smile, "Sebastian has gone mad. Quite mad," she repeated, widely opening her pale eyes.

"He has stopped talking to me," she added in a small voice.

Then Sheldon saw Sebastian and asked him what was amiss.

"Is it any of your business?" inquired Sebastian with a kind of wretched coolness.

"I like Clare," said Sheldon, "and I want to know why she walks about like a lost soul." (She would come to Sebastian every day and sit in odd corners where she never used to sit. She brought sweets sometimes or a tie for Sebastian. The sweets remained uneaten and the tie hung lifelessly on the back of a chair. She seemed to pass through Sebastian like a ghost. Then she would fade away as silently as she had come.)

"Well," said Sheldon, "out with it, man. What have you done to her?"

S HELDON learnt nothing from him whatsoever. What he did learn was from Clare herself; and this amounted to very little. After his return to London Sebastian had been getting letters in Russian from a woman he had met at Blauberg. She had been living at the same hotel as he. Nothing else was known.

Six weeks later (in September, 1929) Sebastian left England again and was absent until January of the following year. Nobody knew where he had been. Sheldon suggested it might have been Italy "because lovers usually go there." He did not cling to his suggestion.

Whether Sebastian had some final explanation with Clare, or whether he left a letter for her when he departed, is not clear. She wandered away as quietly as she had come. She changed her lodgings: they were too close to Sebastian's flat. On a certain gloomy November day Miss Pratt met her in the fog on her way home from a life-insurance office where she had found work. After that, the two girls saw each other fairly often, but Sebastian's name was seldom mentioned. Five years later, Clare married.

Lost Property which Sebastian had begun at that time appears as a kind of halt in his literary journey of discovery: a summing up, a counting of the things and souls lost on the way, a setting of bearings; the clinking sound of unsaddled horses browsing in the dark; the glow of a campfire; stars overhead. There is in it a short chapter dealing with an aeroplane crash (the pilot and all the passengers but one were killed); the survivor, an elderly Englishman, was discovered by a farmer some way from the place of the accident, sitting on a stone. He sat huddled up—the picture of misery and pain. "Are you badly hurt?" asked the farmer. "No," answered the Englishman, "toothache. I've had it all the way." Half a dozen letters were found scattered in a field: remnants of the air-mail bag. Two of these were business letters of great importance; a third was addressed to a woman, but began: "Dear Mr. Mortimer, in reply to yours of the 6th inst . . ." and dealt with the placing of an order; a fourth was a birthday greeting; a fifth was the letter of a spy with its steely secret hidden in a haystack of idle prattle; and the last was an envelope directed to a firm of traders with the wrong letter inside, a love letter. "This will smart, my poor love. Our picnic is finished; the dark road is bumpy and the smallest child in the car is about to be sick. A cheap fool would tell you: you must be brave. But then, anything I might tell you in the way of support or consolation is sure to be milk-puddingy,—you know what I mean. You always knew what I meant. Life with you was lovely—and when I say lovely, I mean doves and lilies, and velvet, and that soft pink 'v' in the middle and the way your tongue curved up to the long, lingering 'l.' Our life together was alliterative, and when I think of all the little things which will die, now that we cannot share them, I feel as if we were dead too. And perhaps we are. You see, the greater our happiness was, the hazier its edges grew, as if its outlines were melting, and now it has dissolved altogether. I have not stopped loving you; but something is dead in me, and I cannot see you in the mist . . . This is all poetry. I am lying to you. Lily-livered. There can be nothing more cowardly than a poet beating about the bush. I think you have guessed how things stand: the damned formula of 'another woman.' I am desperately unhappy with her—here is one thing which is true. And I think there is nothing much more to be said about that side of the business.

"I cannot help feeling there is something essentially wrong about love. Friends may quarrel or drift apart, close relations too, but there is not this pang, this pathos, this fatality which clings to love. Friendship never has that doomed look. Why, what is the matter? I have not stopped loving you, but because I cannot go on kissing your dim dear face, we must part, we must part. Why is it so? What is this mysterious exclusiveness? One may have a thousand friends, but only one love-mate. Harems have nothing to do with this matter: I am speaking of dance, not gymnastics. Or can one imagine a tremendous Turk loving every one of his four hundred wives as I love you? For if I say 'two' I have started to count and there is no end to it. There is only one real number: One. And love, apparently, is the best exponent of this singularity.

"Good-bye, my poor love. I shall never forget you and never replace you. It would be absurd of me to try and persuade you that you were the pure love, and that this other passion is but a comedy of the flesh. All is flesh and all is purity. But one thing is certain: I have been happy with you and now I am miserable with another. And so life will go on. I shall joke with the chaps at the office and enjoy my dinners (until I get dyspepsia), and read novels, and write verse, and keep an eye on the stocks—and generally behave as I have always behaved. But that does not mean that I shall be happy without you . . . Every small thing which will remind me of you—the look of disapproval about the furniture in the rooms where you have patted cushions and spoken to the poker, every small thing which we have descried together—will always seem to me one half of a shell, one half of a penny, with the other half kept by you. Good-bye. Go away, go away. Don't write. Marry Charlie or any other good man with a pipe in his teeth. Forget me now, but remember me afterwards, when the bitter part is forgotten. This blot is not due to a tear. My fountain-pen has broken down and I am using a filthy pen in this filthy hotel room. The heat is terrific and I have not been able to clinch the business I was supposed to bring 'to a satisfactory close,' as that ass Mortimer says. I think you have got a book or two of mine—but that is not really important. *Please*, don't write. L."

If we abstract from this fictitious letter everything that is personal to its supposed author, I believe that there is much in it that may have been felt by Sebastian, or even written by him, to Clare. He had a queer habit of endowing even his most grotesque characters with this or that idea, or impression, or desire which he himself might have toyed with. His hero's letter may possibly have been a kind of code in which he expressed a few truths about his relations with Clare. But I fail to name any other author who made use of his art in such a baffling manner—baffling to me who might desire to see the real man behind the author. The light of personal truth is hard to perceive in the shimmer of an imaginary nature, but what is still harder to understand is the amazing fact that a man writing of things which he really felt at the time of writing, could have had the power to create simultaneously—and out of the very things which distressed his mind—a fictitious and faintly absurd character.

Sebastian returned to London in the beginning of 1930 and took to his bed after a very bad heart attack. Somehow or other he managed to go on with the writing of *Lost Property*: his easiest book, I think. Now, it ought to be understood in connection with what follows that Clare had been solely responsible for the managing of his literary affairs. After her departure, these soon became wildly entangled. In many cases Sebastian had not the vaguest idea how things stood and what his exact relations with this or that publisher were. He was so muddled, so utterly incompetent, so hopelessly incapable of remembering a single name or address, or the place where he put things, that now he got into the most absurd predicaments. Curiously enough, Clare's girlish forgetfulness had been replaced by a perfect clarity and steadiness of purpose when handling Sebastian's affairs; but now it all went amuck. He had never learnt to use a typewriter and was much too nervous to begin now. *The Funny Mountain* was published simultaneously in two American magazines, and Sebastian was at a loss to remember how he had managed to sell it to two different people. Then there was a complicated affair with a man who wanted to make a film of *Success* and who had paid Sebastian in advance (without his noticing it, so absent-mindedly did he read letters) for a shortened and "intensified" version, which Sebastian never even dreamt of making. *The Prismatic Bezel* was in the market again, but Sebastian hardly knew of it. Invitations were not even answered. Telephone numbers proved delusions, and the harassing search for the envelope where he had scrawled this or that number exhausted him more than the writing of a chapter. And then—his mind was elsewhere, following in the tracks of an absent mistress, waiting for her call,—and presently the call would come, or he himself could stand the suspense no longer, and there he would be as Roy Carswell had once seen him: a gaunt man in a great coat and bedroom slippers getting into a Pullman car.

It was in the beginning of this period that Mr. Goodman made his appearance. Little by little, Sebastian handed over to him all his literary affairs, and felt greatly relieved to meet so

efficient a secretary. "I usually found him," writes Mr. Goodman, "lying in bed like a sulky leopard" (which somehow
reminds one of the nightcapped wolf in "Little Red Riding
Hood") . . . "Never in my life had I seen," he goes on in
another passage, "such a dejected-looking being . . . I am
told that the French author M. Proust, whom Knight consciously or subconsciously copied, also had a great inclination
towards a certain listless 'interesting' pose . . ." And further:
"Knight was very thin, with a pale countenance and sensitive
hands, which he liked to display with feminine coquetry. He
confessed to me once that he liked to pour half a bottle of
French perfume into his morning bath, but with all that he
looked singularly badly got up . . . Knight was extraordinarily
vain, like most modernist authors. Once or twice I caught him
pasting cuttings, most certainly reviews concerning his books,
into a beautiful and expensive album which he kept locked up
in his desk, feeling perhaps a little ashamed to let my critical
eye consider the fruit of his human weakness . . . He often
went abroad, twice a year, I daresay, presumably to Gay Paree
. . . But he was very mysterious about it and made a great
show of Byronic languor. I cannot help feeling that trips to
the Continent formed part of his artistic program . . . he was
the perfect 'poseur.' "

But where Mr. Goodman waxes really eloquent is when he
starts to discourse upon deeper matters. His idea is to show
and explain the "fatal split between Knight the artist and the
great booming world about him"—(a circular fissure, obviously). "Knight's uncongeniality was his undoing," exclaims
Goodman and clicks out three dots. "Aloofness is a cardinal
sin in an age when a perplexed humanity eagerly turns to its
writers and thinkers, and demands of them attention to, if not
the cure of, its woes and wounds . . . The 'ivory tower' cannot be suffered unless it is transformed into a lighthouse or a
broadcasting station . . . In such an age . . . brimming with
burning problems when . . . economic depression . . .
dumped . . . cheated . . . the man in the street . . . the
growth of totalitarian . . . unemployment . . . the next
super-great war . . . new aspects of family life . . . sex . . .
structure of the universe." Mr. Goodman's interests are wide,
as we see. "Now, Knight," he goes on, "absolutely refused to

take any interest whatsoever in contemporary questions . . .
When asked to join in this or that movement, to take part in
some momentous meeting, or merely to append his signature,
among more famous names, to some manifest of undying
truth or denunciation of great iniquity . . . he flatly refused
in spite of all my admonishments and even pleadings . . .
True, in his last (and most obscure) book, he does survey the
world . . . but the angle he chooses and the aspects he notes
are totally different from what a serious reader naturally expects from a serious author . . . It is as though a conscientious inquirer into the life and machinery of some great
enterprise were shown, with elaborate circumlocution, a dead
bee on a window sill . . . Whenever I called his attention to
this or that just published book which had fascinated me because it was of general and vital interest, he childishly replied
that it was 'claptrap,' or made some other completely irrelevant remark . . . He confused solitude with altitude and the
Latin for sun. He failed to realise that it was merely a dark
corner . . . However, as he was hypersensitive (I remember
how he used to wince when I pulled my fingers to make the
joints crack,—a bad habit I have when meditating), he could
not help feeling that something was wrong . . . that he was
steadily cutting himself away from Life . . . and that the
switch would not function in his solarium. The misery which
had begun as an earnest young man's reaction to the rude
world into which his temperamental youth had been thrust,
and which later continued to be displayed as a fashionable
mask in the days of his success as a writer, now took on a new
and hideous reality. The board adorning his breast read no
more 'I am the lone artist'; invisible fingers had changed it
into 'I am blind.' "

It would be an insult to the reader's acumen were I to
comment on Mr. Goodman's glibness. If Sebastian was blind,
his secretary, in any case, plunged lustily into the part of a
barking and pulling leader. Roy Carswell, who in 1933 was
painting Sebastian's portrait, told me he remembered roaring
with laughter at Sebastian's accounts of his relations with Mr.
Goodman. Very possibly he would never have been energetic
enough to get rid of that pompous person had the latter not
become a shade too enterprising. In 1934 Sebastian wrote to

Roy Carswell from Cannes telling him that he had found out by chance (he seldom reread his own books) that Goodman had changed an epithet in the Swan edition of *The Funny Mountain*. "I have given him the sack," he added. Mr. Goodman modestly refrains from mentioning this minor detail. After exhausting his stock of impressions, and concluding that the real cause of Sebastian's death was the final realisation of having been "a human failure, and therefore an artistic one too," he cheerfully mentions that his work as secretary came to an end owing to his entering another branch of business. I shall not refer any more to Goodman's book. It is abolished.

But as I look at the portrait Roy Carswell painted I seem to see a slight twinkle in Sebastian's eyes, for all the sadness of their expression. The painter has wonderfully rendered the moist dark greenish-grey of their iris, with a still darker rim and a suggestion of gold dust constellating round the pupil. The lids are heavy and perhaps a little inflamed, and a vein or two seems to have burst on the glossy eye-ball. These eyes and the face itself are painted in such a manner as to convey the impression that they are mirrored Narcissus-like in clear water—with a very slight ripple on the hollow cheek, owing to the presence of a water-spider which has just stopped and is floating backward. A withered leaf has settled on the reflected brow, which is creased as that of a man peering intently. The crumpled dark hair over it is partly suffused by another ripple, but one strand on the temple has caught a glint of humid sunshine. There is a deep furrow between the straight eyebrows, and another down from the nose to the tightly shut dusky lips. There is nothing much more than this head. A dark opalescent shade clouds the neck, as if the upper part of the body were receding. The general back-ground is a mysterious blueness with a delicate trellis of twigs in one corner. Thus Sebastian peers into a pool at himself.

"I wanted to hint at a woman somewhere behind him or over him,—the shadow of a hand, perhaps . . . something . . . But then I was afraid of story-telling instead of painting."

"Well, nobody seems to know anything about her. Not even Sheldon."

"She smashed his life, that sums her up, doesn't it?"

"No, I want to know more. I want to know all. Otherwise

he will remain as incomplete as your picture. Oh, it is very good, the likeness is excellent, and I love that floating spider immensely. Especially its club-footed shadow at the bottom. But the face is only a chance reflection. Any man can look into water."

"But don't you think that he did it particularly well?"

"Yes, I can see your point. But all the same I must find that woman. She is the missing link in his evolution, and I must obtain her—it's a scientific necessity."

"I'll bet you this picture that you won't find her," said Roy Carswell.

13

THE FIRST THING was to learn her identity. How should I start upon my quest? What data did I possess? In June, 1929, Sebastian had dwelt at the Beaumont Hotel at Blauberg, and there he had met her. She was Russian. No other clue was available.

I have Sebastian's aversion for postal phenomena. It seems easier to me to travel a thousand miles than to write the shortest letter, then find an envelope, find the right address, buy the right stamp, post the letter (and rack my brain trying to remember whether I have signed it). Moreover, in the delicate affair I was about to tackle, correspondence was out of the question. In March, 1936, after a month's stay in England, I consulted a tourist office and set out for Blauberg.

So here he has passed, I reflected, as I looked at wet fields with long trails of white mist where upright poplar trees dimly floated. A small red-tiled town crouched at the foot of a soft grey mountain. I left my bag in the cloakroom of a forlorn little station where invisible cattle lowed sadly in some shunted truck, and went up a gentle slope towards a cluster of hotels and sanitariums beyond a damp-smelling park. There were very few people about, it was not "the height of the season," and I suddenly realised with a pang that I might find the hotel shut.

But it was not; thus far, luck was with me.

The house seemed fairly pleasant with its well kept garden and budding chestnut trees. It looked as if it could not hold more than some fifty people—and this braced me: I wanted my choice restricted. The hotel manager was a grey-haired man with a trimmed beard and velvet black eyes. I proceeded very carefully.

First I said that my late brother, Sebastian Knight, a celebrated English author, had greatly liked his stay and that I was thinking of staying at the hotel myself in the summer. Perhaps I ought to have taken a room, sliding in, ingratiating myself, so to speak, and postponing my special request until a more favourable moment; but somehow I thought that the matter might be settled on the spot. He said yes, he remembered the Englishman who had stayed in 1929 and had wanted a bath every morning.

"He did not make friends readily, did he?" I asked with sham casualness. "He was always alone?"

"Oh, I think he was here with his father," said the hotel manager vaguely.

We wrestled for some time disentangling the three or four Englishmen who had happened to have stayed at Hotel Beaumont during the last ten years. I saw that he did not remember Sebastian any too clearly.

"Let me be frank," I said off-handedly, "I am trying to find the address of a lady, my brother's friend, who had stayed here at the same time as he."

The hotel manager lifted his eyebrows slightly, and I had the uneasy feeling that I had committed some blunder.

"Why?" he said. ("Ought I to bribe him?" I thought quickly.)

"Well," I said, "I'm ready to pay you for the trouble of finding the information I want."

"What information?" he asked. (He was a stupid and suspicious old party—may he never read these lines.)

"I was wondering," I went on patiently, "whether you would be so very, very kind as to help me to find the address of a lady who stayed here at the same time as Mr. Knight, that is in June, 1929?"

"What lady?" he asked in the elenctic tones of Lewis Carroll's caterpillar.

"I'm not sure of her name," I said nervously.

"Then how do you expect me to find her?" he said with a shrug.

"She was Russian," I said. "Perhaps you remember a Russian lady,—a *young* lady,—and well . . . good-looking?"

"Nous avons eu beaucoup de jolies dames," he replied getting more and more distant. "How should I remember?"

"Well," said I, "the simplest way would be to have a look at your books and sort out the Russian names for June, 1929."

"There are sure to be several," he said. "How will you pick out the one you need, if you do not know it?"

"Give me the names and addresses," I said desperately, "and leave the rest to me."

He sighed deeply and shook his head.

"No," he said.

"Do you mean to say you don't keep books?" I asked trying to speak quietly.

"Oh, I keep them all right," he said. "My business requires great order in these matters. Oh, yes, I have got the names all right . . ."

He wandered away to the back of the room and produced a large black volume.

"Here," he said. "First week of July, 1935 . . . Professor Ott with wife, Colonel Samain . . ."

"Look here," I said, "I'm not interested in July, 1935. What I want . . ." He shut his book and carried it away.

"I only wanted to show you," he said with his back turned to me,—"to show you [a lock clicked] that I keep my books in good order."

He came back to his desk and folded a letter that was lying on the blotting-pad.

"Summer, 1929," I pleaded. "Why don't you want to show me the pages I want?"

"Well," he said, "the thing is not done. Firstly, because I don't want a person who is a complete stranger to me to bother people who were and will be my clients. Secondly, because I cannot understand why you should be so eager to find a woman whom you do not want to name. And thirdly—I do not want to get into any kind of trouble. I have enough troubles as it is. In the hotel round the corner a Swiss couple committed suicide in 1929," he added rather irrelevantly.

"Is that your last word?" I asked.

He nodded and looked at his watch. I turned on my heel and slammed the door after me,—at least, I tried to slam it,—it was one of those confounded pneumatic doors which resist.

Slowly, I went back to the station. The park. Perhaps Sebastian recalled that particular stone bench under that cedar tree at the time he was dying. The outline of that mountain yonder may have been the paraph of a certain unforgettable evening. The whole place seemed to me a huge refuse heap

where I knew a dark jewel had been lost. My failure was
absurd, horrible, excruciating. The leaden sluggishness of
dream-endeavour. Hopeless gropings among dissolving
things. Why was the past so rebellious?

"And what shall I do now?" The stream of the biography
on which I longed so to start, was, at one of its last bends,
enshrouded in pale mist; like the valley I was contemplating.
Could I leave it thus and write the book all the same? A book
with a blind spot. An unfinished picture,—uncoloured limbs
of the martyr with the arrows in his side.

I had the feeling that I was lost, that I had nowhere to go.
I had pondered long enough the means to find Sebastian's
last love to know that there was practically no other way of
finding her name. Her name! I felt I should recognise it at
once if I got at those greasy black folios. Ought I to give it
up and turn to the collection of a few other minor details
concerning Sebastian which I still needed and which I knew
where to obtain?

It was in this bewildered state of mind that I got into the
slow local train which was to take me back to Strasburg.
Then I would go on to Switzerland perhaps . . . But no, I
could not get over the tingling pain of my failure; though I
tried hard enough to bury myself in an English paper I had
with me: I was in training, so to speak, reading only English
in view of the work I was about to begin . . . But could one
begin something so incomplete in one's mind?

I was alone in my compartment (as one usually is in a second-class carriage on that sort of train), but then, at the next
station, a little man with bushy eyebrows got in, greeted me
continentally, in thick guttural French, and sat down opposite.
The train ran on, right into the sunset. All of a sudden, I
noticed that the passenger opposite was beaming at me.

"Marrvellous weather," he said and took off his bowler hat
disclosing a pink bald head. "You are English?" he asked nodding and smiling.

"Well, yes, for the moment," I answered.

"I see, saw, you read English djornal," he said pointing
with his finger,—then hurriedly taking off his fawn glove and
pointing again (perhaps he had been told that it was rude to
point with a gloved index). I murmured something and

looked away: I do not like chatting in a train, and at the moment I was particularly disinclined to do so. He followed my gaze. The low sun had set aflame the numerous windows of a large building which turned slowly, demonstrating one huge chimney, then another, as the train clattered by.

"Dat," said the little man, "is 'Flambaum and Roth,' great fabric, factory. Paper."

There was a little pause. Then he scratched his big shiny nose and leaned towards me.

"I have been," he said, "London, Manchester, Sheffield, Newcastle." He looked at the thumb which had been left uncounted.

"Yes," he said. "De toy-business. Before de war. And I was playing a little football," he added, perhaps because he noticed that I glanced at a rough field with two goals dejectedly standing at the ends,—one of the two had lost its crossbar.

He winked; his small moustache bristled.

"Once, you know," he said and was convulsed with silent laughter, "once, you know, I fling, flung de ball from 'out' direct into goal."

"Oh," I said wearily, "and did you score?"

"De wind scored. Dat was a robinsonnada!"

"A what?"

"A robinsonnada—a marrvellous trick. Yes . . . Are you voyaging farr?" he inquired in a coaxing super-polite voice.

"Well," I said, "this train does not go farther than Strasburg, does it?"

"No; I mean, meant in generahl. You are a traveller?"

I said yes.

"In what?" he asked, cocking his head.

"Oh, in the past I suppose," I replied.

He nodded as if he had understood. Then, leaning again towards me, he touched me on the knee and said: "Now I sell ledder—you know—ledder balls, for odders to play. Old! No force! Also hound-muzzles and fings like dat."

Again he tapped my knee lightly. "But earlier," he said, "last year, four last years, I was in de police—no, no, not once, not quite . . . Plain-clotheses. Understand me?"

I looked at him with sudden interest.

"Let me see," I said, "this gives me an idea . . ."

"Yes," he said, "if you want help, good ledder, *cigarette-etuis*, straps, advice, boxing-gloves . . ."

"Fifth and perhaps first," I said.

He took his bowler which lay on the seat near him, put it on carefully (his Adam's apple rolling up and down), and then, with a shiny smile, briskly took it off to me.

"My name is Silbermann," he said, and stretched out his hand. I shook it and named myself too.

"But dat is not English," he cried slapping his knee. "Dat is Russian! *Gavrit parussky?* I know also some odder words . . . Wait! Yes! Cookolkah—de little doll."

He was silent for a minute. I rolled in my head the idea he had given me. Should I try to consult a private detective agency? Would this little man be of any use himself?

"Rebah!" he cried. "Der's anodder. Fish, so? and . . . Yes. *Braht, millee braht*—dear brodder."

"I was thinking," I said, "that perhaps, if I told you of the bad fix I am in . . ."

"But dat is all," he said with a sigh. "I speak (again the fingers were counted) Lithuanian, German, English, French (and again the thumb remained). Forgotten Russian. Once! Quite!"

"Could you perhaps . . ." I began.

"Anyfing," he said. "Ledder-belts, purses, notice-books, suggestions."

"Suggestions," I said. "You see, I am trying to trace a person . . . a Russian lady whom I never have met, and whose name I do not know. All I know is that she lived for a certain stretch of time at a certain hotel at Blauberg."

"Ah, good place," said Mr. Silbermann, "very good"—and he screwed down the ends of his lips in grave approbation. "Good water, walks, caseeno. What you want me to do?"

"Well," I said, "I should first like to know what *can* be done in such cases."

"Better leave her alone," said Mr. Silbermann, promptly.

Then he thrust his head forward and his bushy eyebrows moved.

"Forget her," he said. "Fling her out of your head. It is dangerous and ewsyless." He flicked something off my trouser knee, nodded and sat back again.

"Never mind that," I said. "The question is how, not why."

"Every how has its why," said Mr. Silbermann. "You find, found her build, her picture, and now want to find herself yourself? Dat is not love. Ppah! Surface!"

"Oh, no," I cried, "it is not like that. I haven't the vaguest idea what she is like. But, you see, my dead brother loved her, and I want to hear her talk about him. It's really quite simple."

"Sad!" said Mr. Silbermann and shook his head.

"I want to write a book about him," I continued, "and every detail of his life interests me."

"What was he ill?" Mr. Silbermann asked huskily.

"Heart," I replied.

"Harrt,—dat's bad. Too many warnings, too many . . . general . . . general . . ."

"Dress rehearsals of death. That's right."

"Yes. And how old?"

"Thirty-six. He wrote books, under his mother's name. Knight. Sebastian Knight."

"Write it here," said Mr. Silbermann handing me an extraordinarily nice new note-book enclosing a delightful silver pencil. With a trk-trk-trk sound, he neatly removed the page, put it into his pocket and handed me the book again.

"You like it, no?" he said with an anxious smile. "Permit me a little present."

"Really," I said, "that's very kind . . ."

"Nofing, nofing," he said, waving his hand. "Now, what you want?"

"I want," I replied, "to get a complete list of all the people who have stayed in the Hotel Beaumont during June, 1929. I also want some particulars of who they are, the women at least. I want their addresses. I want to be sure that under a foreign name a Russian woman is not hidden. Then I shall choose the most probable one or ones and . . ."

"And try to reach dem," said Mr. Silbermann nodding. "Well! Very well! I had, have all the hotel-gentlemans here [he showed his palm], and it will be simple. Your address, please."

He produced another note-book, this time a very worn one, with some of the bescribbled pages falling off like autumn-leaves. I added that I should not move from Strasburg until he called.

"Friday," he said. "Six, punctly."

Then the extraordinary little man sank back in his seat, folded his arms and closed his eyes, as if clinched business had somehow put a full stop to our conversation. A fly inspected his bald brow, but he did not move. He dozed until Strasburg. There we parted.

"Look here," I said as we shook hands. "You must tell me your fee . . . I mean, I'm ready to pay you whatever you think suitable . . . And perhaps you would like something in advance . . ."

"You will send me your book," he said lifting a stumpy finger. "And pay for possible depences," he added under his breath. "Cerrtainly!"

14

So this was the way I got a list of some forty-two names among which Sebastian's (S. Knight, 36 Oak Park Gdns., London S.W.) seemed strangely lovely and lost. I was rather struck (pleasantly) by the fact that all the addresses were there too, affixed to the names: Silbermann hurriedly explained that people often die in Blauberg. Out of forty-one unknown persons as many as thirty-seven "did not come to question" as the little man put it. True, three of these (unmarried women) bore Russian names, but two of them were German and one Alsatian: they had often stayed at the hotel. There was also a somewhat baffling girl, Vera Rasine; Silbermann however knew for certain that she was French; that, in fact, she was a dancer and the mistress of a Strasburg banker. There was also an aged Polish couple whom we let pass without a qualm. All the rest of this "out-of-the-question" group, that is thirty-one persons, consisted of twenty adult males; of these only eight were married or at least had brought their wives (Emma, Hildegard, Pauline and so on), all of whom Silbermann swore were elderly, respectable and eminently non-Russian.

Thus we were left with four names:

Mademoiselle Lidya Bohemsky with an address in Paris. She had spent nine days in the hotel at the beginning of Sebastian's stay and the manager did not remember anything about her.

Madame de Rechnoy. She had left the hotel for Paris on the eve of Sebastian's departure for the same city. The manager remembered that she was a smart young woman and very generous with her tips. The "de" denoted, I knew, a certain type of Russian who likes to accent gentility, though really the use of the French *particule* before a Russian name is not only absurd but illegal. She might have been an adventuress; she might have been the wife of a snob.

Helene Grinstein. The name was Jewish but in spite of the "stein" it was not German-Jewish. That "i" in "grin" displacing the natural "u" pointed to its having grown in Russia.

She had arrived but a week before Sebastian left and had stayed three days longer. The manager said she was a pretty woman. She had been to his hotel once before and lived in Berlin.

Helene von Graun. That was a real German name. But the manager was positive that several times during her stay she had sung songs in Russian. She had a splendid contralto, he said, and was ravishing. She had remained a month in all, leaving for Paris five days before Sebastian.

I meticulously noted all these particulars and the four addresses. Any of these four might prove to be the one I wanted. I warmly thanked Mr. Silbermann as he sat there before me with his hat on his joined knees. He sighed and looked down at the toes of his small black boots adorned by old mousegrey spats.

"I have made dis," he said, "because you are to me sympathetic. But . . . [he looked at me with mild appeal in his bright brown eyes] but please, I fink it is ewsyless. You can't see de odder side of de moon. Please donnt search de woman. What is past is past. She donnt remember your brodder."

"I shall jolly well remind her," I said grimly.

"As you desire," he muttered squaring his shoulders and buttoning up his coat. He got up. "Good djorney," he said without his usual smile.

"Oh, wait a bit, Mr. Silbermann, we've got to settle something. What do I owe you?"

"Yes, dat is correct," he said seating himself again. "Moment." He unscrewed his fountain pen, jotted down a few figures, looked at them tapping his teeth with the holder: "Yes, sixty-eight francs."

"Well, that's not much," I said, "won't you perhaps . . ."

"Wait," he cried, "dat is false. I have forgotten . . . do you guard dat notice-book dat I give, gave you?"

"Why, yes," I said, "in fact, I've begun using it. You see . . . I thought . . ."

"Den it is not sixty-eight," he said, rapidly revising his addition. "It is . . . It is only eighteen, because de book costs fifty. Eighteen francs in all. Travelling depences . . ."

"But," I said, rather flabbergasted at his arithmetic . . .

"No, dat's now right," said Mr. Silbermann.

I found a twenty franc coin though I would have gladly given him a hundred times as much, if he had only let me.

"So," he said, "I owe you now . . . Yes, dat's right, Eighteen and two make twenty." He knitted his brows. "Yes, twenty. Dat's yours." He put my coin on the table and was gone.

I wonder how I shall send him this work when it is finished: the funny little man has not given me his address, my head was too full of other things to think of asking him for it. But if he ever does come across *The Real Life of Sebastian Knight* I should like him to know how grateful I am for his help. And for the note-book. It is well filled by now, and I shall have a new set of pages clipped in when these are completed.

After Mr. Silbermann had gone I studied at length the four addresses he had so magically obtained for me, and I decided to begin with the Berlin one. If that proved a disappointment I should be able to grapple with a trio of possibilities in Paris without undertaking another long journey, a journey all the more enervating because then I should know for sure I was playing my very last card. If on the contrary, my first try was lucky, then . . . But no matter . . . Fate amply rewarded me for my decision.

Large wet snowflakes were drifting aslant the Passauer Strasse in West-Berlin as I approached an ugly old house, its face half-hidden in a mask of scaffolding. I tapped on the glass of the porter's lodge, a muslin curtain was roughly drawn aside, a small window was knocked open and a blowsy old woman gruffly informed me that Frau Helene Grinstein did live in the house. I felt a queer little shiver of elation and went up the stairs. "Grinstein," said a brass plate on the door.

A silent boy in a black tie with a pale swollen face let me in and without so much as asking my name, turned and walked down the passage. There was a crowd of coats on the rack in the tiny hall. A bunch of snow-wet chrysanthemums lay on the table between two solemn top hats. As no one seemed to come, I knocked at one of the doors, then pushed it open and then shut it again. I had caught a glimpse of a dark-haired little girl, lying fast asleep on a divan, under a moleskin coat. I stood for a minute in the middle of the hall.

I wiped my face which was still wet from snow. I blew my nose. Then I ventured down the passage. A door was ajar and I caught the sound of low voices, speaking in Russian. There were many people in the two large rooms joined by a kind of arch. One or two faces turned towards me vaguely as I strolled in, but otherwise my entry did not arouse the slightest interest. There were glasses with half-finished tea on the table, and a plateful of crumbs. One man in a corner was reading a newspaper. A woman in a grey shawl was sitting at the table with her cheek propped on her hand and a tear-drop on her wrist. Two or three other persons were sitting quite still on the divan. A little girl rather like the one I had seen sleeping was stroking an old dog curled up on a chair. Somebody began to laugh or gasp or something in the adjacent room, where there were more people sitting or wandering about. The boy who had met me in the hall passed carrying a glass of water and I asked him in Russian whether I might speak to Mrs. Helene Grinstein.

"Aunt Elena," he said to the back of a dark slim woman who was bending over an old man hunched up in an armchair. She came up to me and invited me to walk into a small parlour on the other side of the passage. She was very young and graceful with a small powdered face and long soft eyes which appeared to be pulled up towards the temples. She wore a black jumper and her hands were as delicate as her neck.

"*Kahk eto oojahsno* . . . isn't it dreadful?" she whispered.

I replied rather foolishly that I was afraid I had called at the wrong moment.

"Oh," she said, "I thought" . . . She looked at me. "Sit down," she said, "I thought I saw your face just now at the funeral . . . No? Well, you see, my brother-in-law has died and . . . No, no, sit down. It has been an awful day."

"I don't want to disturb you," I said, "I'd better go . . . I only wanted to talk to you about a relation of mine . . . whom I think you knew . . . at Blauberg . . . but it does not matter . . ."

"Blauberg? I have been there twice," she said and her face twitched as the telephone began ringing somewhere.

"His name was Sebastian Knight," I said looking at her unpainted tender trembling lips.

"No, I have never heard that name," she said, "no."

"He was half-English," I said, "he wrote books."

She shook her head and then turned to the door which had been opened by the sullen boy, her nephew.

"Sonya is coming up in half-an-hour," he said. She nodded and he withdrew.

"In fact I did not know any one at the hotel," she continued. I bowed and apologised again.

"But what is *your* name," she asked peering at me with her dim soft eyes which somehow reminded me of Clare. "I think you mentioned it, but to-day my brain seems to be in a daze . . . Ach," she said when I had told her. "But that sounds familiar. Wasn't there a man of that name killed in a duel in St. Petersburg? Oh, your father? I see. Wait a minute. Somebody . . . just the other day . . . somebody had been recalling the case. How funny . . . It always happens like that, in heaps. Yes . . . the Rosanovs . . . They knew your family and all that . . ."

"My brother had a school-fellow called Rosanov," I said.

"You'll find them in the telephone book," she went on rapidly, "you see, I don't know them very well, and I am quite incapable just now of looking up anything."

She was called away and I wandered alone toward the hall. There I found an elderly gentleman pensively sitting on my overcoat and smoking a cigar. At first he could not quite make out what I wanted but then was effusively apologetic.

Somehow I felt sorry it had not been Helene Grinstein. Although of course she never *could* have been the woman who had made Sebastian so miserable. Girls of her type do not smash a man's life—they build it. There she had been steadily managing a house that was bursting with grief and had found it possible to attend to the fantastic affairs of a completely superfluous stranger. And not only had she listened to me, she had given me a tip which I then and there followed, and though the people I saw had nothing to do with Blauberg and the unknown woman, I collected one of the most precious pages of Sebastian's life. A more systematic mind than mine would have placed them in the beginning of this book, but my quest had developed its own magic and logic and though I sometimes cannot help believing that it had gradually grown into a dream, that quest, using the pattern of reality for the weaving of its own fancies, I am forced to recognise that I was being led right, and that in striving to render Sebastian's life I must now follow the same rhythmical interlacements.

There seems to have been a law of some strange harmony in the placing of a meeting relating to Sebastian's first adolescent romance in such close proximity to the echoes of his last dark love. Two modes of his life question each other and the answer is his life itself, and that is the nearest one ever can approach a human truth. He was sixteen and so was she. The lights go out, the curtain rises and a Russian summer landscape is disclosed: the bend of a river half in the shade because of the dark fir trees growing on one steep clay bank and almost reaching out with their deep black reflections to the other side which is low and sunny and sweet, with marsh-flowers and silver-tufted grass. Sebastian, his close-cropped head hatless, his loose silk blouse now clinging to his shoulder-blades, now to his chest according to whether he bends or leans back, is lustily rowing in a boat painted a shiny green. A girl is sitting at the helm, but we shall let her remain achromatic: a mere outline, a white shape not filled in with colour by the artist. Dark blue dragonflies in a slow skipping flight pass hither and thither and alight on the flat waterlily leaves. Names, dates and even faces have been hewn in the red clay of the steeper bank and swifts dart in and out of holes therein. Sebastian's teeth glisten. Then, as he pauses and looks back, the boat with a silky swish slides into the rushes.

"You're a very poor cox," he says.

The picture changes: another bend of that river. A path leads to the water edge, stops, hesitates and turns to loop around a rude bench. It is not quite evening yet, but the air is golden and midges are performing a primitive native dance in a sunbeam between the aspen leaves which are quite quite still at last, forgetful of Judas.

Sebastian is sitting upon the bench and reading aloud some English verse from a black copybook. Then he stops suddenly: a little to the left a naiad's head with auburn hair is seen just above the water, receding slowly, the long tresses floating behind. Then the nude bather emerges on the opposite bank, blowing his nose with the aid of his thumb; it is the long-haired village priest. Sebastian goes on reading to the girl beside him. The painter has not yet filled in the white space except for a thin sunburnt arm streaked from wrist to elbow along its outer side with glistening down.

As in Byron's dream, again the picture changes. It is night. The sky is alive with stars. Years later Sebastian wrote that gazing at the stars gave him a sick and squeamish feeling, as for instance when you look at the bowels of a ripped-up beast. But at the time, this thought of Sebastian's had not yet been expressed. It is very dark. Nothing can be discerned of what is possibly an alley in the park. Sombre mass on sombre mass and somewhere an owl hooting. An abyss of blackness where all of a sudden a small greenish circle moves up: the luminous dial of a watch (Sebastian disapproved of watches in his riper years).

"Must you go?" asks his voice.

A last change: a V-shaped flight of migrating cranes; their tender moan melting in a turquoise-blue sky high above a tawny birch-grove. Sebastian, still not alone, is seated on the white-and-cinder-grey trunk of a felled tree. His bicycle rests, its spokes a-glitter among the bracken. A Camberwell Beauty skims past and settles on the kerf, fanning its velvety wings. Back to town to-morrow, school beginning on Monday.

"Is this the end? Why do you say that we shall not see each other this winter?" he asks for the second or third time. No answer. "Is it true that you think you've fallen in love with that student chap?—*vetovo studenta?*" The seated girl's shape remains blank except for the arm and a thin brown hand toying with a bicycle pump. With the end of the holder it slowly writes on the soft earth the word "yes," in English, to make it gentler.

The curtain is rung down. Yes, that is all. It is very little but it is heartbreaking. Never more may he ask of the boy who sits daily at the next school desk, "And how is your sister?" Nor must he ever question old Miss Forbes, who still drops in now and then, about the little girl to whom she had also given lessons. And how shall he tread again the same paths next summer, and watch the sunset and cycle down to the river? (But next summer was mainly devoted to the futurist poet Pan.)

By a chance conjuncture of circumstances it was Natasha Rosanov's brother that drove me to the Charlottenburg station to catch the Paris express. I said how curious it had been to have talked to his sister, now the plump mother of two boys, about a distant summer in the dreamland of Russia. He answered that he was perfectly content with his job in Berlin. I tried, as I had vainly tried before, to make him talk of Sebastian's school life. "My memory is appallingly bad," he replied, "and anyway I am too busy to be sentimental about such ordinary things."

"Oh, but surely, surely," I said, "you can recall some little outstanding fact, anything would be welcome . . ." He laughed. "Well," he said, "haven't you just spent hours talking to my sister? She adores the past, doesn't she? She says, you are going to put her in a book as she was in those days, she is quite looking forward to it, in fact."

"Please, try and remember something," I insisted stubbornly.

"I am telling you that I do not remember, you queer person. It's useless, quite useless. There is nothing to relate except ordinary rot about cribbing and cramming and nicknaming teachers. We had quite a good time, I suppose . . . But you know, your brother . . . how shall I put it? . . . your brother was not very popular at school . . ."

As THE READER may have noticed, I have tried to put into this book as little of my own self as possible. I have tried not to allude (though a hint now and then might have made the background of my research somewhat clearer) to the circumstances of my own life. So at this point of my story I shall not dwell upon certain business difficulties I experienced on my arrival in Paris, where I had a more or less permanent home; they were in no way related to my quest, and if I mention them in passing, it is only to stress the fact that I was so engrossed in the attempt to discover Sebastian's last love that I cheerfully dismissed any personal troubles which my taking such a long holiday might entail.

I was not sorry that I had started off with the Berlin clue. It had at least led me to obtain an unexpected glimpse of another chapter of Sebastian's past. And now one name was erased, and I had three more chances before me. The Paris telephone directory yielded the information that "Graun (von), Helene" and "Rechnoy, Paul" (the "de," I noticed, was absent) corresponded to the addresses I possessed. The prospect of meeting a husband was unpleasant but unavoidable. The third lady, Lydia Bohemsky, was ignored by both directories, that is the telephone book and that other Bottin masterpiece, where addresses are arranged according to streets. Anyway, the address I had might help me to get at her. I knew my Paris well, so that I saw at once the most time-saving sequence in which to dispose my calls if I wanted to have done with them in one day. Let it be added, in case the reader be surprised at the rough-and-ready style of my activity, that I dislike telephoning as much as I do writing letters.

The door at which I rang was opened by a lean, tall, shock-headed man in his shirtsleeves and with a brass stud at his collarless throat. He held a chessman—a black knight—in his hand. I greeted him in Russian.

"Come in, come in," he said cheerfully, as if he had been expecting me.

"My name is so-and-so," I said.

"And mine," he cried, "is Pahl Pahlich Rechnoy,"—and he guffawed heartily as if it were a good joke. "If you please," he said, pointing with the chessman to an open door.

I was ushered into a modest room, with a sewing machine standing in one corner and a faint smell of ribbon-and-linen in the air. A heavily built man was sitting sideways at a table on which an oilcloth chessboard was spread, with pieces too large for the squares. He looked at them askance while the empty cigarette-holder in the corner of his mouth looked the other way. A pretty little boy of four or five was kneeling on the floor, surrounded by tiny motor cars. Pahl Pahlich chucked the black knight onto the table and its head came off. Black carefully screwed it on again.

"Sit down," said Pahl Pahlich. "This is my cousin," he added. Black bowed. I sat down on the third (and last) chair. The child came up to me and silently showed me a new red-and-blue pencil.

"I could take your rook now if I wished," said Black darkly, "but I have a much better move."

He lifted his queen and delicately crammed it into a cluster of yellowish pawns—one of which was represented by a thimble.

Pahl Pahlich made a lightning swoop and took the queen with his bishop. Then he roared with laughter.

"And now," said Black calmly, when White had stopped roaring, "now you are in the soup. Check, my dove."

While they were arguing over the position, with White trying to take his move back, I looked round the room. I noted the portrait of what had been in the past an Imperial Family. And the moustache of a famous general, moscowed a few years ago. I noted, too, the bulging springs of the bug-brown couch, which served, I felt, as a triple bed—for husband and wife and child. For a minute, the object of my coming seemed to me madly absurd. Somehow, too, I remembered Chichikov's round of weird visits in Gogol's "Dead Souls." The little boy was drawing a motor car for me.

"I am at your service," said Pahl Pahlich (he had lost, I saw, and Black was putting the pieces back into an old cardboard box—all except the thimble). I said what I had carefully prepared beforehand: namely that I wanted to see his wife, because she had been friends with some . . . well, German friends of mine. (I was afraid of mentioning Sebastian's name too soon.)

"You'll have to wait a bit then," said Pahl Pahlich. "She is busy in town, you see. I think, she'll be back in a moment."

I made up my mind to wait, although I felt that to-day I should hardly manage to see his wife alone. I hoped however that a little deft questioning might at once settle whether she had known Sebastian; then, bye-and-bye, I could make her talk.

"In the meantime," said Pahl Pahlich, "we shall clap down a little brandy—*cognachkoo*."

The child, finding that I had been sufficiently interested in his pictures, wandered off to his uncle, who at once took him on his knee and proceeded to draw with incredible rapidity and very beautifully a racing car.

"You are an artist," I said—to say something.

Pahl Pahlich, who was rinsing glasses in the tiny kitchen, laughed and shouted over his shoulder: "Oh, he's an all round genius. He can play the violin standing upon his head, and he can multiply one telephone number by another in three seconds, and he can write his name upside down in his ordinary hand."

"And he can drive a taxi," said the child, dangling its thin, dirty little legs.

"No, I shan't drink with you," said Uncle Black, as Pahl Pahlich put the glasses on the table. "I think, I shall take the boy out for a walk. Where are his things?"

The boy's coat was found, and Black led him away. Pahl Pahlich poured out the brandy and said: "You must excuse me for these glasses. I was rich in Russia and I got rich again in Belgium ten years ago, but then I went broke. Here's to yours."

"Does your wife sew?" I asked, so as to set the ball rolling.

"Oh, yes, she has taken up dressmaking," he said with a happy laugh. "And I'm a type-setter, but I have just lost my job. She's sure to be back in a moment. I did not know she had German friends," he added.

"I think," I said, "they met her in Germany, or was it

Alsace?" He had been refilling his glass eagerly, but suddenly he stopped and looked at me agape.

"I'm afraid, there's some mistake," he exclaimed. "It must have been my first wife. Varvara Mitrofanna has never been out of Paris—except Russia, of course,—she came here from Sebastopol via Marseilles." He drained his glass and began to laugh.

"That's a good one," he said eyeing me curiously. "Have I met you before? Do you know my first one personally?"

I shook my head.

"Then you're lucky," he cried. "Damned lucky. And your German friends have sent you upon a wild goose-chase because you'll never find her."

"Why?" I asked getting more and more interested.

"Because soon after we separated, and that was years ago, I lost sight of her absolutely. Somebody saw her in Rome, and somebody saw her in Sweden,—but I'm not sure even of that. She may be here, and she may be in hell. *I* don't care."

"And you could not suggest any way of finding her?"

"None," he said

"Mutual acquaintances?"

"They were *her* acquaintances, not mine," he answered with a shudder.

"You haven't got a photo of her or something?"

"Look here," he said, "what are you driving at? Are the police after her? Because, you know, I shouldn't be surprised if she turned out to be an international spy. Mata Hari! That's her type. Oh, absolutely. And then . . . Well, she's not a girl you can easily forget once she's got into your system. She sucked me dry, and in more ways than one. Money and soul, for instance. I would have killed her . . . if it had not been for Anatole."

"And who's that?" I asked.

"Anatole? Oh, that's the executioner. The man with the guillotine here. So you're not of the police, after all. No? Well, it's your own business, I suppose. But, really, she drove me mad. I met her, you know, in Ostende, that must have been, let me see, in 1927,—she was twenty then, no, not even twenty. I knew she was another fellow's mistress and all that, but I did not care. Her idea of life was drinking cocktails, and

eating a large supper at four o'clock in the morning, and dancing the shimmy or whatever it was called, and inspecting
brothels because that was fashionable among Parisian snobs,
and buying expensive clothes, and raising hell in hotels when
she thought the maid had stolen her small change which she
afterwards found in the bathroom . . . Oh, and all the rest of
it,—you may find her in any cheap novel, she's a type,
a type. And she loved inventing some rare illness and going to
some famous kurort, and . . ."

"Wait a bit." I said. "That interests me. In June, 1929, she
was alone in Blauberg."

"Exactly, but that was at the very end of our marriage. We
were living in Paris then, and soon after we separated, and I
worked for a year at a factory in Lyon. I was broke, you see."

"Do you mean to say she met some man in Blauberg?"

"No, that I don't know. You see, I don't think she really
went very far in deceiving me, not really, you know, not the
whole hog,—at least I tried to think so, because there were
always lots of men around her, and she didn't mind being
kissed by them, I suppose, but I should have gone mad, had
I let myself brood over the matter. Once, I remember . . ."

"Pardon me," I interrupted again, "but are you quite sure
you never heard of an English friend of hers?"

"English? I thought you said German. No, I don't know.
There was a young American at Ste. Maxime in 1928, I believe,
who almost swooned every time Ninka danced with him,—
and, well, there may have been Englishmen at Ostende and
elsewhere, but really I never bothered about the nationality
of her admirers."

"So you are quite, quite sure that you don't know about
Blauberg and . . . well, about what happened afterwards?"

"No," he said. "I don't think that she was interested in
anybody there. You see, she had one of her illness-phases at
the time—and she used to eat only lemon-ice and cucumbers,
and talk of death and the Nirvana or something—she had a
weakness for Lhassa—you know what I mean . . ."

"What exactly was her name?" I asked.

"Well, when I met her her name was Nina Toorovetz—but
whether—— No, I think, you won't find her. As a matter of
fact, I often catch myself thinking that she has never existed.

I told Varvara Mitrofanna about her, and she said it was merely a bad dream after seeing a bad cinema film. Oh, you are not going yet, are you? She'll be back in a minute . . ." He looked at me and laughed (I think he had had a little too much of that brandy).

"Oh, I forget," he said. "It is not my present wife that you want to find. And by the way," he added, "my papers are in perfect order. I can show you my *carte de travail*. And if you do find her, I should like to see her before she goes to prison. Or perhaps better not."

"Well, thank you for our conversation," I said, as we were, rather too enthusiastically, shaking hands—first in the room, then in the passage, then in the doorway.

"*I* thank you," Pahl Pahlich cried. "You see, I quite like talking about her and I am sorry I did not keep any of her photographs."

I stood for a moment reflecting. Had I pumped him enough . . . Well, I could always see him once more . . . Might there not be a chance photo in one of those illustrated papers with cars, furs, dogs, Riviera fashions? I asked about that.

"Perhaps," he answered, "perhaps. She got a prize once at a fancy-dress ball, but I don't quite remember where it happened. All towns seemed restaurants and dancing-halls to me."

He shook his head laughing boisterously, and slammed the door. Uncle Black and the child were slowly coming up the stairs as I went down.

"Once upon a time," Uncle Black was saying, "there was a racing motorist who had a little squirrel; and one day . . ."

16

M Y FIRST IMPRESSION was that I had got what I wanted,—that at least I knew *who* Sebastian's mistress had been; but presently I cooled down. Could it have been she, that wind-bag's first wife? I wondered as a taxi took me to my next address. Was it really worth while following that plausible, too plausible trail? Was not the image Pahl Pahlich had conjured up a trifle too obvious? The whimsical wanton that ruins a foolish man's life. But was Sebastian foolish? I called to mind his acute distaste for the obvious bad and the obvious good; for ready-made forms of pleasure and hack-neyed forms of distress. A girl of that type would have got on his nerves immediately. For what could her conversation have been, if indeed she *had* managed to get acquainted with that quiet, unsociable, absent-minded Englishman at the Beau-mont hotel? Surely, after the very first airing of her notions, he would have avoided her. He used to say, I know, that fast girls had slow minds and that there could be nothing duller than a pretty woman who likes fun; even more: that if you looked well at the prettiest girl while she was exuding the cream of the commonplace, you were sure to find some mi-nute blemish in her beauty, corresponding to her habits of thought. He would not mind perhaps having a bite at the apple of sin because, apart from solecisms, he was indifferent to the idea of sin; but he did mind apple-jelly, potted and patented. He might have forgiven a woman for being a flirt, but he would never have stood a sham mystery. He might have been amused by a hussy getting drunk on beer, but he could not have tolerated a *grande cocotte* hinting at a craving for bhang. The more I thought of it, the less possible it seemed . . . At any rate, I ought not to bother about that girl until I had examined the two other possibilities.

So it was with an eager step that I entered the very imposing house (in a very fashionable part of the town) at which my taxi had stopped. The maid said Madame was not in but, on seeing my disappointment, asked me to wait a moment and then returned with the suggestion that if I liked, I could talk to Madame von Graun's friend, Madame Lecerf. She turned out to be a small, slight, pale faced young woman with smooth black hair. I thought I had never seen a skin so evenly pale; her black dress was high at the neck, and she used a long black cigarette holder.

"So you would like to see my friend?" she said, and there was, I thought, a delightful old-world suavity in her crystal clear French.

I introduced myself.

"Yes," she said, "I saw your card. You are Russian, aren't you?"

"I have come," I explained, "on a very delicate errand. But first tell me, am I right in assuming that Madame Graun is a compatriot of mine?"

"Mais oui, elle est tout ce qu'il y a de plus russe," she answered in her soft tinkling voice. "Her husband was German, but he spoke Russian, too."

"Ah," I said, "that past tense is most welcome."

"You may be quite frank with me," said Madame Lecerf. "I rather like delicate errands."

"I am related," I went on, "to the English author, Sebastian Knight, who died two months ago; and I am attempting to work out his biography. He had a close friend whom he met at Blauberg where he stayed in 1929. I am trying to trace her. This is about all."

"Quelle drôle d'histoire!" she exclaimed. "What a curious story. And what do you want her to tell you?"

"Oh, anything she pleases . . . But am I to understand . . . Do you mean that Madame Graun is the person in question?"

"Very possibly," she said, "though I don't think I ever heard her mentioning that particular name . . . What did you say it was?"

"Sebastian Knight."

"No. But still it's quite possible. She always picks up friends at the places where she stays. *Il va sans dire,*" She added, "that you ought to speak to her personally. Oh, I'm sure you'll find her charming. But what a strange story," she repeated looking at me with a smile. "Why must you write a book about him, and how is it you don't know the woman's name?"

"Sebastian Knight was rather secretive," I explained. "And that lady's letters which he kept . . . Well, you see—he wished them destroyed after his death."

"That's right," she said cheerfully, "I quite understand him. By all means, burn love-letters. The past makes noble fuel. Would you like a cup of tea?"

"No," I said. "What I would like is to know when I can see Madame Graun."

"Soon," said Madame Lecerf. "She is not in Paris for the moment, but I think you might call again to-morrow. Yes, that'll be all right, I suppose. She may even return to-night."

"Might I ask you," I said, "to tell me more about her?"

"Well, that's easy," said Madame Lecerf. "She is quite a good singer, tzigan songs, you know, that kind. She is extraordinarily beautiful. *Elle fait des passions.* I like her awfully and I have a room at this flat whenever I stay in Paris. Here is her picture, by the way."

Slowly and noiselessly she moved across the thick-carpeted drawing room, and took a large framed photograph which was standing on the piano. I stared for a moment at an exquisite face half turned away from me. The soft curve of the cheek and the upward dart of the ghostly eyebrow were very Russian, I thought. There was a gleam on the lower eyelid, and a gleam on the full dark lips. The expression seemed to me a strange mixture of dreaminess and cunning.

"Yes," I said, "yes . . ."

"Why, is it she?" asked Madame Lecerf inquisitively.

"It might be," I replied, "and I am much looking forward to meeting her."

"I'll try to find out myself," said Madame Lecerf with a charming air of conspiracy. "Because, you see, I think writing a book about people you know is so much more honest than making a hash of them and then presenting it as your own invention!"

I thanked her and made my adieux as the French have it. Her hand was remarkably small, and as I inadvertently pressed it too hard, she winced, for there was a big sharp ring on the middle finger. It hurt me too a little.

"To-morrow at the same time," she said and laughed gently. A nice quiet, quietly moving person.

I had learnt really nothing as yet, but I felt I was proceeding successfully. Now it remained to set my mind at ease in regard to Lydia Bohemsky. When I called at the address I had, I was told by the concierge that the lady had moved some months ago. He said he thought she lived at a small hotel across the street. There I was told that she had gone three weeks ago and was living at the other end of the town. I asked my informant whether he thought she was Russian. He said she was. "A handsome dark woman?" I suggested, using an old Sherlock Holmes stratagem. "Exactly," he replied rather putting me off (the right answer would have been: Oh, no, she is an ugly blond). Half an hour later, I entered a gloomy-looking house not far from the Santé prison. My ring was answered by a fat elderly woman with waved bright orange hair, purplish jowls and some dark fluff over her painted lip.

"May I speak to Mademoiselle Lydia Bohemsky?" I said.

"C'est moi," she replied with a terrific Russian accent.

"Then I'll bring the things," I muttered and hurriedly left the house. I sometimes think that she may be still standing in the doorway.

When next day I called again at Madame von Graun's flat, the maid showed me into another room—a kind of boudoir doing its best to look charming. I had already noticed on the day before the intense warmth in the flat—and as the weather outside was, though decidedly damp, yet hardly what you would call chilly, this orgy of central heating seemed rather exaggerated. I was kept waiting a long time. There were several oldish French novels on the console; most of them by literary prize-winners, and a well thumbed copy of Dr. Axel Munthe's *San Michele*. A bunch of carnations stood in a self-conscious vase. There were a few other fragile knick-knacks about—probably quite nice and expensive, but I always have shared Sebastian's almost pathological dislike for anything made of glass or china. Last but not least, there was a sham piece of polished furniture, containing, I felt, that horror of horrors: a radio set. Still, all things considered, Helene von Graun seemed to be a person of "taste and culture."

At last, the door opened and the lady I had seen on the previous day sidled in,—I say sidled because she was turning her head back and down, talking to what turned out to be a frog-faced, wheezing, black bull-dog, which seemed reluctant to waddle in.

"Remember my sapphire," she said giving me her little cold hand. She sat down on the blue sofa and pulled up the heavy bull-dog. *"Viens, mon vieux,"* she panted, *"viens.* He is pining away without Helene," she said when the beast was made comfortable among the cushions. "It's a shame, you know, I thought she would be back this morning, but she rang up from Dijon and said she would not arrive till Saturday (to-day was Tuesday). I'm dreadfully sorry. I did not know where to reach you. Are you very disappointed?"—and she looked at me with her chin on her clasped hands and her sharp elbows in close-fitting velvet propped on her knees.

"Well," I said, "if you tell me something more about Madame Graun, perhaps I may be consoled."

I don't know why, but the atmosphere of the place drove me somehow to affected speech and manner.

"And what is more," she said, lifting a sharp-nailed finger, *"j'ai une petite surprise pour vous.* But first we'll have tea." I saw that I could not avoid the farce of tea this time; indeed, the maid had already wheeled in a movable table with glittering tea things.

"Put it here, Jeanne," said Madame Lecerf. "Yes, that will do."

"Now you must tell me as explicitly as possible," said Madame Lecerf, *"tout ce que vous croyez raisonnable de demander à une tasse de thé.* I suspect you would like some cream in it, if you have lived in England. You *look* English, you know."

"I prefer looking Russian," I said.

"I'm afraid I don't know any Russians, except Helene, of course. These biscuits, I think, are rather amusing."

"And what is your surprise?" I asked.

She had a funny manner of looking at you intently—not into your eyes though, but at the lower part of your face, as if you had got a crumb or something that ought to be wiped off. She was very lightly made up for a French woman, and I thought her transparent skin and dark hair quite attractive.

"Ah!" she said. "I asked her something when she telephoned, and—" she stopped and seemed to enjoy my impatience.

"And she replied," I said, "that she had never heard the name."

"No," said Madame Lecerf, "she just laughed, but I know that laugh of hers."

I got up, I think, and walked up and down the room.

"Well," I said at length, "it is not exactly a laughing matter, is it? Doesn't she know that Sebastian Knight is dead?"

Madame Lecerf closed her dark velvety eyes in a silent "yes" and then looked again at my chin.

"Have you seen her lately,—I mean did you see her in January when the news of his death was in the papers? Wasn't she sorry?"

"Look here, my dear friend, you are strangely naïve," said Madame Lecerf. "There are many kinds of love and many kinds of sorrow. Let us assume that Helene is the person you are seeking. But why ought we to assume that she loved him enough to be upset by his dying? Or perhaps she did love him, but held special views about death which excluded hysterics? What do we know of such matters? It's her personal affair. She'll tell you, I suppose, but until then it's hardly fair to insult her."

"I did not insult her," I cried. "I am sorry if I sounded unfair. But do talk about her. How long have you known her?"

"Oh, I haven't seen much of her these last years until this one—she travels a lot, you know—but we used to go to the same school—here in Paris. Her father was a Russian painter, I believe. She was still very young when she married that fool."

"What fool?" I queried.

"Well, her husband, of course. Most husbands are fools, but that one was *hors concours*. It didn't last long, happily. Have one of mine." She handed me her lighter too. The bulldog growled in its sleep. She moved and curled up on the sofa, making room for me. "You don't seem to know much about women, do you?" she asked, stroking her own heel.

"I'm only interested in one," I answered.

"And how old are you?" she went on. "Twenty-eight? Have I guessed? No? Oh, well, then you're older than me. But no matter. What was I telling you? . . . I know a few things about her,—what she told me herself and what I have picked up. The only man she really loved was a married man and that was before her marriage, and she was a mere slip of a girl then, mind you—and he got tired of her or something. She had a few affairs after that, but it didn't much matter really. *Un coeur de femme ne ressuscite jamais.* Then there was one story which she told me in full—it was rather a sad one."

She laughed. Her teeth were a little too large for her small pale mouth.

"You look as if my friend were your own sweetheart," she said teasingly. "By the way, I wanted to ask you how did you come to this address—I mean, what led you to look up Helene?"

I told her about the four addresses I had obtained in Blauberg. I mentioned the names.

"That's superb," she cried, "that's what I call energy! *Voyez vous ça!* And you went to Berlin? She was a Jewess? Adorable! And you have found the others too?"

"I saw one," I said, "and that was enough."

"Which?" she asked with a spasm of uncontrollable mirth. "Which? The Rechnoy woman?"

"No," I said. "Her husband has married again, and she has vanished."

"You are charming, charming," said Madame Lecerf, wiping her eyes and rippling with new laughter. "I can see you crashing in and being confronted by an innocent couple. Oh, I never heard anything so funny. Did his wife throw you downstairs, or what?"

"Let us drop the matter," I said rather curtly. I had had enough of that girl's merriment. She had, I am afraid, that French sense of humour in connection with connubial matters, which at another moment might have appealed to me too; but just now I felt that the flippantly indecent view she took of my inquiry was somehow slighting Sebastian's memory. As this feeling deepened, I found myself thinking all of a sudden that perhaps the whole thing was indecent and that my clumsy efforts to hunt down a ghost had swamped any idea that I might ever form of Sebastian's last love. Or would Sebastian have been tickled at the grotesque side of the quest I had undertaken for his sake? Would the biographee have found that special "Knightian twist" about it which would have fully compensated the blundering biographer?

"Please, forgive me," she said, putting her ice-cold hand on mine and looking at me from under her brows. "You must not be so touchy, you know."

She got up quickly and went to the mahogany affair in the corner. I looked at her thin girlish back as she bent down,— and I guessed what she was about to do.

"No, not that, for God's sake!" I cried.

"No?" she said. "I thought a little music might soothe you. And generally create the right atmosphere for our talk. No? Well, just as you like."

The bull-dog shook himself and lay down again.

"That's right," she said in a coaxing-and-pouting voice.

"You were about to tell me," I reminded her.

"Yes," she said sitting down again at my side and pulling at the hem of her skirt, as she curled one leg under her. "Yes. You see, I don't know who the man was, but I gathered he was a difficult sort of man. She says she liked his looks and his hands and his manner of talking, and she thought it would be rather good fun to have him make love to her—because, you see, he looked so very intellectual, and it is always entertaining to see that kind of refined, distant,—brainy fellow suddenly go on all fours and wag his tail. What's the matter now, *cher Monsieur*?"

"What on earth are you talking about?" I cried. "When . . . When and where did it happen, that affair?"

"*Ah non merci, je ne suis pas le calendrier de mon amie. Vous ne voudriez pas!* I didn't bother about asking her dates and names, and if she told me them herself, I have forgotten. Now, please, don't ask me any more questions: I am telling you what *I* know, and not what *you'd* like to know. I don't think he was a relation of yours, because he was so unlike you—of course, as far as I can judge by what she told me and by what I have seen of you. You are a nice eager boy—and he, well, he was anything but nice—he got positively wicked when he found out that he was falling in love with Helene. Oh no, *he* did not turn into a sentimental pup, as she had expected. He told her bitterly that she was cheap and vain, and then he kissed her to make sure that she was not a porcelain figure. Well, she wasn't. And presently he found out that he could not live without her, and presently she found out that she had had quite enough of hearing him talk of his dreams, and the dreams in his dreams, and the dreams in the dreams of his dreams. Mind you, I do not condemn either. Perhaps both were right and perhaps neither,—but, you see, my friend was not quite the ordinary woman he thought she was—oh, she was something quite different, and she knew a bit more about life and death and people than he thought he knew. He was the kind of man, you know, who thinks all modern books are trashy, and all modern young people fools, merely because he is much too preoccupied with his own sensations and ideas to understand those of others. She says, you can't imagine his tastes and his whims, and the way he spoke of religion,—it must have been appalling, I suppose. And my friend, you know, is, or rather was, very gay, *très vive*, and all that, but she felt she was getting old and sour whenever he arrived. Because he never stayed long with her, you know,— he would come *à l'improviste* and plump down on a pouf with his hands on the knob of his cane, without taking off his gloves—and stare gloomily. She got friendly with another man soon, who worshipped her and was oh, much, much more attentive and kind and thoughtful than the man you wrongly suppose to have been your brother (don't scowl, please), but she did not much care for either and she says it was a scream to see the way they were polite to each other when they met. She liked travelling, but whenever she found some really nice place, where she could forget her troubles and everything, there he would blot out the landscape again, and sit down on the terrace at her table, and say that she was vain and cheap, and that he could not live without her. Or else, he would make a long speech in front of her friends—you know, *des jeunes gens qui aiment à rigoler*—some long and obscure speech about the form of an ashtray or the colour of time,— and there he would be left on that chair all alone, smiling foolishly to himself, or counting his own pulse. I'm sorry if he really turns out to be your relative because I don't think that she has retained a particularly pleasant souvenir of those days. He became quite a pest at last, she says, and she didn't even let him touch her anymore, because he would have a fit or something when he got excited. One day, at last, when she knew he was going to arrive by the night train, she asked a young man who would do anything to please her, to meet him and tell him that she did not want to see him ever again, and that if he attempted to see her, he would be regarded by her friends as a troublesome stranger and dealt with accordingly. It was not very nice of her, I think, but she supposed it would be better for him in the long run. And it worked. He did not even send her any more of his usual entreating letters, which she never read, anyway. No, no, really, I don't think it can be the man in question,—if I tell you all this it is merely because I want to give you a portrait of Helene—and not of her lovers. She was so full of life, so ready to be sweet to everybody, so brimming with that *vitalité joyeuse qui est, d'ailleurs, tout-à-fait conforme à une philosophie innée, à un sens quasi-religieux des phénomènes de la vie.* And what did it amount to? The men she liked proved dismal disappointments, all women with a very few exceptions were nothing but cats, and she spent the best part of her life in trying to be happy in a world which did its best to break her. Well, you'll meet her and see for yourself whether the world has succeeded."

We were silent for quite a long time. Alas, I had no more doubts, though the picture of Sebastian was atrocious,—but then, too, I had got it secondhand.

"Yes," I said, "I shall see her at all costs. And this for two reasons. Firstly, because I want to ask her a certain question,—one question only. And secondly . . ."

"Yes?" said Madame Lecerf sipping her cold tea. "Secondly?"

"Secondly, I am at a loss to imagine how such a woman could attract my brother; so I want to see her with my own eyes."

"Do you mean to say," asked Madame Lecerf, "that you think she is a dreadful, dangerous woman? *Une femme fatale?* Because, you know, that's not so. She's good as good bread."

"Oh, no," I said. "Not dreadful, not dangerous. Clever, if you like, and all that. But . . . No, I must see for myself."

"He who will live will see," said Madame Lecerf. "Now, look here, I've got a suggestion. I am going away to-morrow.

I am afraid that if you drop in here on Saturday, Helene may be in such a rush—she is always rushing, you know,—that she'll put you off till next day, forgetting that next day she is coming for a week to my place in the country: so you'll miss her again. In other words, I think that the best thing would be for you to come down to my place, too. Because then you are quite, quite sure to meet her. So, what I suggest is that you come Sunday morning—and stay as long as you choose. We've got four spare bedrooms, and I think you'll be comfortable. And then, you know, if I talk to her first a little, she'll be just in the right mood for a talk with you. *Eh bien, êtes-vous d'accord?*"

17

V ERY CURIOUS, I mused: there seemed to be a slight
family likeness between Nina Rechnoy and Helene von
Graun,—or at least between the two pictures which the
husband of one and the friend of the other had painted for
me. Between the two there was not much to choose, Nina
was shallow and glamourous, Helene cunning and hard; both
were flighty; neither was much to my taste,—nor should I
have thought to Sebastian's. I wondered if the two women
had known each other at Blauberg: they would have gone
rather well together,—theoretically; in reality they would
probably have hissed and spat at each other. On the other
hand, I could now drop the Rechnoy clue altogether—and
that was a great relief. What that French girl had told me
about her friend's lover could hardly have been a coincidence.
Whatever the feelings I experienced at learning the way Sebastian had been treated, I could not help being satisfied that
my enquiry was nearing its end and that I was spared the
impossible task of unearthing Pahl Pahlich's first wife, who for
all I knew might be in jail or in Los Angeles.

I knew I was being given my last chance, and as I was anxious to make sure I would get at Helene von Graun, I made
a tremendous effort and sent her a letter to her Paris address,
so that she might find it on her arrival. It was quite short: I
merely informed her that I was her friend's guest at Lescaux
and had accepted this invitation with the sole object of meeting her; I added that there was an important piece of literary
business which I wished to discuss with her. This last sentence
was not very honest, but I thought it sounded enticing. I had
not quite understood whether her friend had told her anything about my desire to see her when she telephoned from
Dijon. I was desperately afraid that on Sunday Madame Lecerf
might blandly inform me that Helene had left for Nice instead. After posting that letter I felt that at any rate I had
done all in my power to fix our rendezvous.

I started at nine in the morning, so as to reach Lescaux
around noon as arranged. I was already boarding the train

when I realised with a shock that on my way I would pass St. Damier where Sebastian had died and was buried. Here I had travelled one unforgettable night. But now I failed to recognize anything: when the train stopped for a minute at the little St. Damier platform, its inscription alone told me that I had been there. The place looked so simple and staid and definite compared to the distorted dream impression which lingered in my memory. Or was it distorted now?

I felt strangely relieved when the train moved on: no more was I treading the ghostly tracks I had followed two months before. The weather was fair and every time the train stopped I seemed to hear the light uneven breathing of spring, still barely visible but unquestionably present: "cold-limbed ballet-girls waiting in the wings," as Sebastian put it once.

Madame Lecerf's house was large and ramshackle. A score of unhealthy old trees represented the park. There were fields on one side and a hill with a factory on the other. Everything about the place had a queer look of weariness, and shabbiness, and dustiness; when later I learned that it had only been built some thirty-odd years ago I felt still more surprised by its decrepitude. As I approached the main entrance I met a man hastily scrunching down the gravel walk; he stopped and shook hands with me:

"Enchanté de vous connaître," he said, summing me up with a melancholy glance, "my wife is expecting you. *Je suis navré* . . . but I am obliged to go to Paris this Sunday."

He was a middle-aged rather common-looking Frenchman with tired eyes and an automatic smile. We shook hands once more.

"*Mon ami,* you'll miss that train," came Madame Lecerf's crystal voice from the veranda, and he trotted off obediently.

To-day she wore a beige dress, her lips were brightly made up but she had not dreamt of meddling with her diaphanous complexion. The sun gave a blueish sheen to her hair and I found myself thinking that she was after all quite a pretty young woman. We wandered through two or three rooms which looked as if the idea of a drawing-room had been vaguely divided between them. I had the impression that we were quite alone in that unpleasant rambling house. She picked up a shawl lying on a green silk settee and drew it about her.

"Isn't it cold," she said. "That's one thing I hate in life, cold. Feel my hands. They are always like that except in summer. Lunch will be ready in a minute. Sit down."

"When exactly is she coming?" I asked.

"Ecoutez," said Madame Lecerf, "can't you forget her for a minute and talk to me about other things? *Ce n'est pas très poli, vous savez.* Tell me something about yourself. Where do you live, and what do you do?"

"Will she be here in the afternoon?"

"Yes, yes, you obstinate man, *Monsieur l'entêté.* She's sure to come. Don't be so impatient. You know, women don't much care for men with an *idée fixe.* How did you like my husband?"

I said that he must be much older than she.

"He is quite kind but a dreadful bore," she went on, laughing. "I sent him away on purpose. We've been married for only a year, but it feels like a diamond wedding already. And I just hate this house. Don't you?"

I said it seemed rather old-fashioned.

"Oh, that's not the right term. It looked brand new when I first saw it. But it has faded and crumbled away since. I once told a doctor that all flowers except pinks and daffodils withered if I touched them,—isn't it bizarre?"

"And what did he say?"

"He said he wasn't a botanist. There used to be a Persian princess like me. She blighted the Palace Gardens."

An elderly and rather sullen maid looked in and nodded to her mistress.

"Come along," said Madame Lecerf. "*Vous devez mourir de faim,* judging by your face."

We collided in the doorway because she suddenly turned back as I was following her. She clutched my shoulder and her hair brushed my cheek. "You clumsy young man," she said, "I have forgotten my pills."

She found them and we went over the house in search of the dining-room. We found it at last. It was a dismal place with a bay-window which had seemed to change its mind at

the last moment and had made a half-hearted attempt to re-
vert to an ordinary state. Two people drifted in silently,
through different doors. One was an old lady who, I gathered,
was a cousin of Monsieur Lecerf. Her conversation was strictly
limited to polite purrs when passing eatables. The other was
a rather handsome man in plus-fours with a solemn face and
a queer grey streak in his fair sparse hair. He never uttered a
single word during the whole lunch. Madame Lecerf's manner of introducing consisted of a hurried gesture which did
not bother about names. I noticed that she ignored his presence at table,—that indeed he seemed to sit apart. The lunch
was well-cooked but haphazard. The wine, however, was quite
good.

After we had clattered through the first course the blond
gentleman lit a cigarette and wandered away. He came back
in a minute with an ashtray. Madame Lecerf who had been
engaged with her food now looked at me and said:

"So you have travelled a good deal, lately? I have never
been to England you know,—somehow it never happened. It
seems to be a dull place. *On doit s'y ennuyer follement, n'est-
ce-pas?* And then the fogs . . . And no music, no art of any
sort . . . This is a special way of preparing rabbit, I think you
will like it."

"By the way," I said, "I forgot to tell you, I've written a
letter to your friend warning her I would be down here and
. . . sort of reminding her to come."

Madame Lecerf put down knife and fork. She looked surprised and annoyed. "You haven't!" she exclaimed.

"But it can't do any harm, can it, or do you think—"

We finished the rabbit in silence. Chocolate cream followed.
The blond gentleman carefully folded his napkin, inserted it
into a ring, got up, bowed slightly to our hostess and withdrew.

"We shall take our coffee in the green room," said Madame
Lecerf to the maid.

"I am furious with you," she said as we settled down. "I
think you have spoiled it all."

"Why, what have I done?" I asked.

She looked away. Her small hard bosom heaved (Sebastian
once wrote that it happened only in books but here was proof

that he was mistaken). The blue vein on her pale girlish neck seemed to throb (but of that I am not so sure). Her lashes fluttered. Yes, she was decidedly a pretty woman. Did she come from the Midi, I wondered. From Arles perhaps. But no, her accent was Parisian.

"Were you born in Paris?" I asked.

"Thank you," she said without looking, "that's the first question you've asked about me. But that does not atone for your blunder. It was the silliest thing you could have done. Perhaps, if I tried . . . Excuse me, I'll be back in a minute."

I sat back and smoked. Dust was swarming in a slanting sunbeam; volutes of tobacco-smoke joined it and rotated softly, insinuatingly, as if they might form a live picture at any moment. Let me repeat here that I am loth to trouble these pages with any kind of matter relating personally to me; but I think it may amuse the reader (and who knows, Sebastian's ghost too) if I say that for a moment I thought of making love to that woman. It was really very odd,—at the same time she got rather on my nerves,—I mean the things she said. I was losing my grip somehow. I shook myself mentally as she returned.

"Now you've done it," she said. "Helene is not at home."

"Tant mieux," I replied, "she's probably on her way here, and really you ought to understand how terribly impatient I am to see her."

"But why on earth did you have to write to her!" Madame Lecerf cried. "You don't even know her. And I had promised you she would be here to-day. What more could you wish? And if you didn't believe me, if you wanted to control me— *alors vous êtes ridicule, cher Monsieur.*"

"Oh, look here," I said quite sincerely, "that never entered my head. I only thought, well . . . butter can't spoil the porridge, as we Russians say."

"I think I don't much care for butter . . . or Russians," she said. What could I do? I glanced at her hand lying near mine. It was trembling slightly, her frock was flimsy—and a queer little shiver not exactly of cold passed down my spine. Ought I to kiss that hand? Could I manage to achieve courteousness without feeling rather a fool?

She sighed and stood up.

"Well, there's nothing to be done about it. I'm afraid you have put her off and if she does come—well, no matter. We shall see. Would you like to go over our domain? I think it is warmer outside than in this miserable house—*que dans cette triste demeure*."

The "domain" consisted of the garden and grove I had already noticed. It was all very still. The black branches, here and there studded with green, seemed to be listening to their own inner life. Something dreary and dull hung over the place. Earth had been dug out and heaped against a brick wall by a mysterious gardener who had gone and forgotten his rusty spade. For some odd reason I recalled a murder that had happened lately, a murderer who had buried his victim in just such a garden as this.

Madame Lecerf was silent; then she said: "You must have been very fond of your half-brother, if you make such a fuss about his past. How did he die? Suicide?"

"Oh, no," I said, "he suffered from heart-disease."

"I thought you said he had shot himself. That would have been so much more romantic. I'll be disappointed in your book if it all ends in bed. There are roses here in summer,— here, on that mud,—but catch me spending the summer here ever again."

"I shall certainly never think of falsifying his life in any way," I said.

"Oh, all right. I knew a man who published the letters of his dead wife and distributed them among his friends. Why do you suppose the biography of your brother will interest people?"

"Haven't you ever read"—I began, when suddenly a smart-looking though rather mud-bespattered car stopped at the gate.

"Oh, bother," said Madame Lecerf.

"Perhaps it's she," I exclaimed.

A woman had scrambled out of the car right into a puddle.

"Yes, it's she all right," said Madame Lecerf. "Now you stay where you are, please."

She ran down the path, waving her hand, and upon reaching the newcomer, kissed her and led her to the left where they both disappeared behind a clump of bushes. I espied them again a moment later when they had skirted the garden and were going up the steps. They vanished into the house. I had really seen nothing of Helene von Graun except her unfastened fur coat and bright-coloured scarf.

I found a stone bench and sat down. I was excited and rather pleased with myself for having captured my prey at last. Somebody's cane was lying on the bench and I poked the rich brown earth. I had succeeded! This very night after talking to her I would return to Paris, and . . . A thought strange to the rest, a changeling, a trembling oaf, slipped in, mingling with the crowd . . . Would I return to-night? How was it, that breathless phrase in that second-rate Maupassant story: "I have forgotten a book." But I was forgetting mine too.

"So that's where you are," said Madame Lecerf's voice. "I thought perhaps you had gone home."

"Well, is everything all right?"

"Far from it," she answered calmly. "I have no idea what you wrote, but she thought it referred to a film affair she's trying to arrange. She says you've entrapped her. Now you'll do what I tell you. You won't speak to her to-day or to-morrow or the day after. But you'll stay here and be very nice to her. And she has promised to tell me everything, and afterwards perhaps you may talk to her. Is that a bargain?"

"It's really awfully good of you to take all this trouble," I said.

She sat down on the bench beside me, and as the bench was very short and I am rather—well—on the sturdy side— her shoulder touched mine. I moistened my lips with my tongue and scrawled lines on the ground with the stick I was holding.

"What are you trying to draw?" she asked and then cleared her throat.

"My thought-waves," I answered foolishly.

"Once upon a time," she said softly, "I kissed a man just because he could write his name upside down."

The stick dropped from my hand. I stared at Madame Lecerf. I stared at her smooth white brow, I saw her violet dark eyelids, which she had lowered, possibly mistaking my stare,— saw a tiny pale birth-mark on the pale cheek, the delicate wings of her nose, the pucker of her upper lip, as she bent her dark head, the dull whiteness of her throat, the laquered rose-red nails of her thin fingers. She lifted her face, her queer velvety eyes with that iris placed slightly higher than usual, looked at my lips.

I got up.

"What's the matter," she said, "what are you thinking about?"

I shook my head. But she was right. I was thinking of something now—something that had to be solved, at once.

"Why, are we going in?" she asked as we moved up the path.

I nodded.

"But she won't be down before another minute, you know. Tell me why you are sulking?"

I think I stopped and stared at her again, this time at her slim little figure in that buff, close fitting frock.

I moved on, brooding heavily, and the sun-dappled path seemed to frown back at me.

"*Vous n'êtes guère aimable,*" said Madame Lecerf.

There was a table and several chairs on the terrace. The silent blond person whom I had seen at lunch was sitting there examining the works of his watch. As I sat down I clumsily jolted his elbow and he let drop a tiny screw.

"*Boga radi,*" he said (don't mention it) as I apologised.

(Oh, he was Russian, was he? Good, that would help me.)

The lady stood with her back to us, humming gently, her foot tapping the stone flags.

It was then that I turned to my silent compatriot who was ogling his broken watch.

"*Ah-oo-neigh na-sheiky pah-ook,*" I said softly.

The lady's hand flew up to the nape of her neck, she turned on her heel.

"Shto?" (what?) asked my slow-minded compatriot, glancing at me. Then he looked at the lady, grinned uncomfortably and fumbled with his watch.

"*J'ai quelque chose dans le cou* . . . There's something on my neck, I feel it," said Madame Lecerf.

"As a matter of fact," I said, "I have just been telling this Russian gentleman that I thought there was a spider on your neck. But I was mistaken, it was a trick of light."

"Shall we put on the gramophone?" she asked brightly.

"I'm awfully sorry," I said, "but I think I must be going home. You'll excuse me won't you?"

"Mais vous êtes fou," she cried, "you are mad, don't you want to see my friend?"

"Another time perhaps," I said soothingly, "another time."

"Tell me," she said following me into the garden, "what *is* the matter?"

"It was very clever of you," I said, in our liberal grand Russian language, "it was very clever of you to make me believe you were talking about your friend when all the time you were talking about yourself. This little hoax would have gone on for quite a long time if fate had not pushed your elbow, and now you've spilled the curds and whey. Because I happen to have met your former husband's cousin, the one who could write upside down. So I made a little test. And when you subconsciously caught the Russian sentence I muttered aside. . . ." No, I did not say a word of all this. I just bowed myself out of the garden. She will be sent a copy of this book and will understand.

18

THAT QUESTION which I had wished to ask Nina remained unuttered. I had wished to ask her whether she ever realised that the wan-faced man, whose presence she had found so tedious, was one of the most remarkable writers of his time. What was the use of asking! Books mean nothing to a woman of her kind; her own life seems to her to contain the thrills of a hundred novels. Had she been condemned to spend a whole day shut up in a library, she would have been found dead about noon. I am quite sure that Sebastian never alluded to his work in her presence: it would have been like discussing sundials with a bat. So let us leave that bat to quiver and wheel in the deepening dusk: the clumsy mimic of a swallow.

In those last and saddest years of his life Sebastian wrote *The Doubtful Asphodel*, which is unquestionably his masterpiece. Where and how did he write it? In the reading-room of the British Museum (far from Mr. Goodman's vigilant eye). At a humble table deep in the corner of a Parisian "bistro" (not of the kind that his mistress might patronise). In a deck-chair under an orange parasol somewhere in Cannes or Juan, when she and her gang had deserted him for a spree elsewhere. In the waiting-room of an anonymous station, between two heart-attacks. In a hotel, to the clatter of plates being washed in the yard. In many other places which I can but vaguely conjecture. The theme of the book is simple: a man is dying: you feel him sinking throughout the book; his thought and his memories pervade the whole with greater or lesser distinction (like the swell and fall of uneven breathing), now rolling up this image, now that, letting it ride in the wind, or even tossing it out on the shore, where it seems to move and live for a minute on its own and presently is drawn back again by grey seas where it sinks or is strangely transfigured. A man is dying, and he is the hero of the tale; but whereas the lives of other people in the book seem perfectly realistic (or at least realistic in a Knightian sense), the reader is kept ignorant as to who the dying man is, and where his deathbed stands or floats, or whether it is a bed at all. The man is the book; the book itself is heaving and dying, and drawing up a ghostly knee. One thought-image, then another breaks upon the shore of consciousness, and we follow the thing or the being that has been evoked: stray remnants of a wrecked life; sluggish fancies which crawl and then unfurl eyed wings. They are, these lives, but commentaries to the main subject. We follow the gentle old chess player Schwarz, who sits down on a chair in a room in a house, to teach an orphan boy the moves of the knight; we meet the fat Bohemian woman with that grey streak showing in the fast colour of her cheaply dyed hair; we listen to a pale wretch noisily denouncing the policy of oppression to an attentive plainclothes man in an ill-famed public-house. The lovely tall primadonna steps in her haste into a puddle, and her silver shoes are ruined. An old man sobs and is soothed by a soft-lipped girl in mourning. Professor Nussbaum, a Swiss scientist, shoots his young mistress and himself dead in a hotel-room at half past three in the morning. They come and go, these and other people, opening and shutting doors, living as long as the way they follow is lit, and are engulfed in turn by the waves of the dominant theme: a man is dying. He seems to move an arm or turn his head on what might be a pillow, and as he moves, this or that life we have just been watching, fades or changes. At moments, his personality grows conscious of itself, and then we feel that we are passing down some main artery of the book. "Now, when it was too late, and Life's shops were closed, he regretted not having bought a certain book he had always wanted; never having gone through an earthquake, a fire, a train-accident; never having seen Tatsienlu in Tibet, or heard blue magpies chattering in Chinese willows; not having spoken to that errant schoolgirl with shameless eyes, met one day in a lonely glade; not having laughed at the poor little joke of a shy ugly woman, when no one had laughed in the room; having missed trains, allusions and opportunities; not having handed the penny he had in his pocket to that old street-violinist playing to himself tremulously on a certain bleak day in a certain forgotten town."

Sebastian Knight had always liked juggling with themes, making them clash or blending them cunningly, making *them* express that hidden meaning, which could only be expressed in a succession of waves, as the music of a Chinese buoy can be made to sound only by undulation. In *The Doubtful Asphodel*, his method has attained perfection. It is not the parts that matter, it is their combinations.

There seems to be a method, too, in the author's way of expressing the physical process of dying: the steps leading into darkness; action being taken in turns by the brain, the flesh, the lungs. First the brain follows up a certain hierarchy of ideas—ideas about death: sham-clever thoughts scribbled in the margin of a borrowed book (the episode of the philosopher): "Attraction of death: physical growth considered upside down as the lengthening of a suspended drop; at last falling into nothing." Thoughts, poetical, religious: ". . . the swamp of rank materialism and the golden paradises of those whom Dean Park calls the optimystics . . ." "But the dying man knew that these were not real ideas; that only one half of the notion of death can be said really to exist: *this* side of the question—the wrench, the parting, the quay of life gently moving away aflutter with handkerchiefs: ah! he was already on the other side, if he could see the beach receding; no, not quite—if he was still thinking." (Thus, one who has come to see a friend away, may stay on deck too late, but still not become a traveller.)

Then, little by little, the demons of physical sickness smother with mountains of pain all kinds of thought, philosophy, surmise, memories, hope, regret. We stumble and crawl through hideous landscapes, nor do we mind where we go—because it is all anguish and nothing but anguish. The method is now reversed. Instead of those thought-images which radiated fainter and fainter, as we followed them down blind alleys, it is now the slow assault of horrible uncouth visions drawing upon us and hemming us in: the story of a tortured child; an exile's account of life in the cruel country whence he fled; a meek lunatic with a black eye; a farmer kicking his dog—lustily, wickedly. Then the pain fades too. "Now he was left so exhausted that he failed to be interested in death." Thus "sweaty men snore in a crowded third-class carriage; thus a schoolboy falls asleep over his unfinished sum." "I am tired, tired . . . a tyre rolling and rolling by itself, now wobbling, now slowing down, now . . ."

This is the moment when a wave of light suddenly floods the book: ". . . as if somebody had flung open the door and people in the room have started up, blinking, feverishly picking up parcels." We feel that we are on the brink of some absolute truth, dazzling in its splendour and at the same time almost homely in its perfect simplicity. By an incredible feat of suggestive wording, the author makes us believe that he knows the truth about death and that he is going to tell it. In a moment or two, at the end of this sentence, in the middle of the next, or perhaps a little further still, we shall learn something that will change all our concepts, as if we discovered that by moving our arms in some simple, but never yet attempted manner, we could fly. "The hardest knot is but a meandering string; tough to the finger nails, but really a matter of lazy and graceful loopings. The eye undoes it, while clumsy fingers bleed. He (the dying man) was that knot, and he would be untied at once, if he could manage to see and follow the thread. And not only himself, everything would be unravelled,—everything that he might imagine in our childish terms of space and time, both being riddles invented by man *as* riddles, and thus coming back at us: the boomerangs of nonsense . . . Now he had caught something real, which had nothing to do with any of the thoughts or feelings, or experiences he might have had in the kindergarten of life . . ."

The answer to all questions of life and death, "the absolute solution" was written all over the world he had known: it was like a traveller realising that the wild country he surveys is not an accidental assembly of natural phenomena, but the page in a book where these mountains and forests, and fields, and rivers are disposed in such a way as to form a coherent sentence; the vowel of a lake fusing with the consonant of a sibilant slope; the windings of a road writing its message in a round hand, as clear as that of one's father; trees conversing in dumb-show, making sense to one who has learnt the gestures of their language . . . Thus the traveller spells the landscape and its sense is disclosed, and likewise, the intricate pattern of human life turns out to be monogrammatic, now quite clear to the inner eye disentangling the interwoven letters. And the word, the meaning which appears is astounding in its simplicity: the greatest surprise being perhaps that in the course of one's earthly existence, with one's brain encompassed by an iron ring, by the close-fitting dream of one's own personality—one had not made by chance that simple mental jerk, which would have set free imprisoned thought and granted it the great understanding. Now the puzzle was solved. "And as the meaning of all things shone through their shapes, many ideas and events which had seemed of the utmost importance dwindled not to insignificance, for nothing could be insignificant now, but to the same size which other ideas and events, once denied any importance, now attained." Thus, such shining giants of our brain as science, art or religion fell out of the familiar scheme of their classification, and joining hands, were mixed and joyfully levelled. Thus, a cherry stone and its tiny shadow which lay on the painted wood of a tired bench, or a bit of torn paper, or any other such trifle out of millions and millions of trifles grew to a wonderful size. Re-modelled and re-combined, the world yielded its sense to the soul as naturally as both breathed.

And now we shall know what exactly it is; the word will be uttered—and you, and I, and everyone in the world will slap himself on the forehead: What fools we have been! At this last bend of his book the author seems to pause for a minute, as if he were pondering whether it were wise to let the truth out. He seems to lift his head and to leave the dying man, whose thoughts he was following, and to turn away and to think: Shall we follow him to the end? Shall we whisper the word which will shatter the snug silence of our brains? We shall. We have gone too far as it is, and the word is being already formed, and will come out. And we turn and bend again over a hazy bed, over a grey, floating form,—lower and lower . . . But that minute of doubt was fatal: the man is dead.

The man is dead and we do not know. The asphodel on the other shore is as doubtful as ever. We hold a dead book in our hands. Or are we mistaken? I sometimes feel when I turn the pages of Sebastian's masterpiece that the "absolute solution" is there, somewhere, concealed in some passage I have read too hastily, or that it is intertwined with other words whose familiar guise deceived me. I don't know any other book that gives one this special sensation, and perhaps this was the author's special intention.

I recall vividly the day when I saw *The Doubtful Asphodel* announced in an English paper. I had come across a copy of that paper in the lobby of a hotel in Paris, where I was waiting for a man whom my firm wanted wheedled into settling a certain deal. I am not good at wheedling, and generally the business seemed to me less promising than it seemed to my employers. And as I sat there alone in the lugubriously comfortable hall, and read the publisher's advertisement and Sebastian's handsome black name in block letters, I envied his lot more acutely than I had ever envied it before. I did not know where he was at the time, I had not seen him for at least six years, nor did I know of his being so ill and so miserable. On the contrary, that announcement of his book seemed to me a token of happiness—and I imagined him standing in a warm cheerful room at some club, with his hands in his pockets, his ears glowing, his eyes moist and bright, a smile fluttering on his lips,—and all the other people in the room standing round him, holding glasses of port, and laughing at his jokes. It was a silly picture, but it kept shining in its trembling pattern of white shirtfronts and black dinner jackets and mellow-coloured wine, and clear-cut faces, as one of those coloured photographs you see on the back of magazines. I decided to get that book as soon as it was published, I always used to get his books at once, but somehow I was particularly impatient to get this one. Presently the person I was waiting for came down. He was an Englishman, and fairly well-read. As we talked for a few moments about ordinary things before broaching the business in hand, I pointed casually to the advertisement in the paper and asked whether he had read any of Sebastian Knight's books. He said he had read one or two—*The Prismatic Something* and *Lost Property.* I asked him whether he had liked them. He said he had in a way, but the author seemed to him a terrible snob, intellectually, at least. Asked to explain, he added that Knight seemed to him to be constantly playing some game of his own invention, without telling his partners its rules. He said he preferred books that made one think, and Knight's books didn't,—they left you puzzled and cross. Then he talked of another living author, whom he thought so much better than Knight. I took advantage of a pause to enter on our business conversation. It did not prove as successful as my firm had expected.

The Doubtful Asphodel obtained many reviews, and most of them were long and quite flattering. But here and there the hint kept recurring that the author was a tired author, which seemed another way of saying that he was just an old bore. I even caught a faint suggestion of commiseration, as if *they* knew certain sad dreary things about the author which were not really in the book, but which permeated their attitude towards it. One critic even went as far as to say that he read it "with mingled feelings, because it was a rather unpleasant experience for the reader, to sit beside a deathbed and never be quite sure whether the author was the doctor or the patient." Nearly all the reviews gave to understand that the book was a little too long, and that many passages were obscure and obscurely aggravating. All praised Sebastian Knight's "sincerity"—whatever that was. I wondered what Sebastian thought of those reviews.

I lent my copy to a friend who kept it several weeks without reading it, and then lost it in a train. I got another and never lent it to anybody. Yes, I think that of all his books this is my favourite one. I don't know whether it makes one "think," and I don't much care if it does not. I like it for its own sake. I like its manners. And sometimes I tell myself that it would not be inordinately hard to translate it into Russian.

19

I HAVE MANAGED to reconstruct more or less the last year of Sebastian's life: 1935. He died in the very beginning of 1936, and as I look at this figure I cannot help thinking that there is an occult resemblance between a man and the date of his death. Sebastian Knight d. 1936 . . . This date to me seems the reflection of that name in a pool of rippling water. There is something about the curves of the last three numerals that recalls the sinuous outlines of Sebastian's personality . . . I am trying, as I have often tried in the course of this book, to express an idea that might have appealed to him . . . If here and there I have not captured at least the shadow of his thought, or if now and then unconscious cerebration has not led me to take the right turn in his private labyrinth, then my book is a clumsy failure.

The appearance of *The Doubtful Asphodel* in the spring of 1935 coincided with Sebastian's last attempt to see Nina. When he was told by one of her sleek-haired young ruffians that she wished to be rid of him for ever, he returned to London and stayed there for a couple of months, making a pitiful effort to deceive solitude by appearing in public as much as he could. A thin, mournful and silent figure, he would be seen in this place or that, wearing a scarf round his neck even in the warmest dining-room, exasperating hostesses by his absent-mindedness and his gentle refusal to be drawn out, wandering away in the middle of a party, or being discovered in the nursery, engrossed in a jigsaw-puzzle. One day, near Charing Cross, Helen Pratt saw Clare into a bookshop, and a few seconds later, as she was continuing her way, she ran into Sebastian. He coloured slightly as he shook hands with Miss Pratt, and then accompanied her to the underground station. She was thankful he had not appeared a minute earlier, and still more thankful when he did not trouble to allude to the past. He told her instead an elaborate story about a couple of men who had attempted to swindle him at a game of poker the night before.

"Glad to have met you," he said as they parted. "I think I shall get it here."

"Get what?" asked Miss Pratt.

"I was on my way to [he named the bookshop], but I see I can get what I want at this stall."

He went to concerts and plays, and drank hot milk in the middle of the night at coffee stalls with taxi drivers. He is said to have been three times to see the same film—a perfectly insipid one called *The Enchanted Garden*. A couple of months after his death, and a few days after I had learnt who Madame Lecerf really was, I discovered that film in a French cinema where I sat through the performance, with the sole intent of learning why it had attracted him so. Somewhere in the middle the story shifted to the Riviera, and there was a glimpse of bathers basking in the sun. Was Nina among them? Was it her naked shoulder? I thought that one girl who glanced back at the camera looked rather like her, but sun-oil and sun tan, and an eye-shade are much too good at disguising a passing face. He was very ill for a week in August, but he refused to take to his bed, as Doctor Oates prescribed. In September, he went to see some people in the country: he was but very slightly acquainted with them; and they had invited him out of mere politeness, because he happened to have said he had seen the picture of their house in the *Prattler*. For a whole week he wandered about a coldish house where all the other guests knew one another intimately, and then one morning he walked ten miles to the station and quietly travelled back to town, leaving dinner jacket and sponge-bag behind. In the beginning of November, he had lunch with Sheldon at Sheldon's club and was so taciturn that his friend wondered why he had come at all. Then comes a blank. Apparently he went abroad, but I hardly believe that he had any definite plan about trying to meet Nina again, though perhaps some faint hope of that kind was at the source of his restlessness.

I had spent most of the winter of 1935 in Marseilles, attending to some of my firm's business. In the middle of January, 1936, I got a letter from Sebastian. Strangely enough, it was written in Russian.

"I am, as you see, in Paris, and presumably shall be stuck [*zasstrianoo*] here for some time. If you can come, come; if you can't, I shall not be offended; but it might be perhaps better if you came. I am fed up [*osskomina*] with a number of tortuous things and especially with the patterns of my shed snake-skins [*vypolziny*] so that now I find a poetic solace in the obvious and the ordinary which for some reason or other I had overlooked in the course of my life. I should like for example to ask you what you have been doing during all these years, and to tell you about myself: I hope you have done better than I. Lately I have been seeing a good deal of old Dr. Starov, who treated *maman* [so Sebastian called my mother]. I met him by chance one night in the street, when I was taking a forced rest on the running-board of somebody's parked car. He seemed to think that I had been vegetating in Paris since *maman's* death, and I have agreed to his version of my emigré existence, because [*eeboh*] any explanation seemed to me far too complicated. Some day you may come upon certain papers; you will burn them at once; true, they have heard voices in [one or two indecipherable words: *Dot chetu?*], but now they must suffer the stake. I kept them, and gave them night-lodgings [*notchleg*], because it is safer to let such things sleep, lest, when killed, they haunt us as ghosts. One night, when I felt particularly mortal, I signed their death-warrant, and by it you will know them. I had been staying at the same hotel as usual, but now I have moved to a kind of sanatorium out of town, note the address. This letter was begun almost a week ago, and up to the word 'life' it had been destined [*prednaznachalos*] to quite a different person. Then somehow or other it turned towards you, as a shy guest in a strange house will talk at unusual length to the near relative with whom he came to the party. So forgive me if I bore you [*dokoochayou*], but somehow I don't much like those bare branches and twigs which I see from my window."

This letter upset me, of course, but it did not make me as anxious as I should have been, had I known that since 1926 Sebastian had been suffering from an incurable disease, growing steadily worse during the last five years. I must shamefully confess that my natural alarm was somewhat subdued by the thought that Sebastian was very high-strung and nervous and had always been inclined to undue pessimism when his health was impaired. I had, I repeat, not the smallest inkling of his heart-trouble, and so I managed to convince myself that he was suffering from overwork. Still, he was ill and begging me to come in a tone that was novel to me. He had never seemed to need my presence, but now he was positively pleading for it. It moved me, and it puzzled me, and I would certainly have jumped into the very first train had I known the whole truth. I got the letter on Thursday and at once resolved to go to Paris on Saturday, so as to journey back on Sunday night, for I felt that my firm would not expect me to take a holiday at the critical stage of the business I was supposed to be looking after in Marseilles. I decided that instead of writing and explaining I would send him a telegram Saturday morning, when I should know whether, perhaps, I could take the earlier train.

And that night I dreamt a singularly unpleasant dream. I dreamt I was sitting in a large dim room which my dream had hastily furnished with odds and ends collected in different houses I vaguely knew, but with gaps or strange substitutions, as for instance that shelf which was at the same time a dusty road. I had a hazy feeling that the room was in a farmhouse or a country-inn—a general impression of wooden walls and planking. We were expecting Sebastian—he was due to come back from some long journey. I was sitting on a crate or something, and my mother was also in the room, and there were two more persons drinking tea at the table round which we were seated—a man from my office and his wife, both of whom Sebastian had never known, and who had been placed there by the dream-manager—just because anybody would do to fill the stage.

Our wait was uneasy, laden with obscure forebodings, and I felt that they knew more than I, but I dreaded to inquire why my mother worried so much about a muddy bicycle which refused to be crammed into the wardrobe: its doors kept opening. There was the picture of a steamer on the wall, and the waves on the picture moved like a procession of caterpillars, and the steamer rocked and this annoyed me—until I remembered that the hanging of such a picture was an old and commonplace custom, when awaiting a traveller's return. He might arrive at any moment, and the wooden floor near the door had been sprinkled with sand, so that he might not slip. My mother wandered away with the muddy spurs and stirrups she could not hide, and the vague couple was quietly abolished, for I was alone in the room, when a door opened in a gallery upstairs, and Sebastian appeared, slowly descending a rickety flight of stairs which came straight down into the room. His hair was tousled and he was coatless: he had, I understood, just been taking a nap after his journey. As he came down, pausing a little on every step, with always the same foot ready to continue and with his arm resting on the wooden hand-rail, my mother came back again and helped him to get up when he stumbled and slithered down on his back. He laughed as he came up to me, but I felt that he was ashamed of something. His face was pale and unshaven, but it looked fairly cheerful. My mother, with a silver cup in her hand, sat down on what proved to be a stretcher, for she was presently carried away by two men who slept on Saturdays in the house, as Sebastian told me with a smile. Suddenly I noticed that he wore a black glove on his left hand, and that the fingers of that hand did not move, and that he never used it—I was afraid horribly, squeamishly, to the point of nausea, that he might inadvertently touch me with it, for I understood now that it was a sham thing attached to the wrist,—that he had been operated upon, or had had some dreadful accident. I understood too why his appearance and the whole atmosphere of his arrival seemed so uncanny, but though he perhaps noticed my shudder, he went on with his tea. My mother came back for a moment to fetch the thimble she had forgotten and quickly went away, for the men were in a hurry. Sebastian asked me whether the manicurist had already come, as he was anxious to get ready for the banquet. I tried to dismiss the subject, because the idea of his maimed hand was insufferable, but presently I saw the whole room in terms of jagged fingernails, and a girl I had known (but she had strangely faded now) arrived with her manicure case and sat down on a stool in front of Sebastian. He asked me not to look, but I could not help looking. I saw him undoing his black glove and slowly pulling it off; and as it came off, it spilt its only contents—a number of tiny hands, like the front paws of a mouse, mauve-pink and soft,—lots of them,—and they dropped to the floor, and the girl in black went on her knees.

I bent down to see what she was doing under the table and I saw that she was picking up the little hands and putting them into a dish,—I looked up and Sebastian had vanished, and when I bent down again, the girl had vanished too. I felt I could not stay in that room for a moment longer. But as I turned and groped for the latch I heard Sebastian's voice behind me; it seemed to come from the darkest and remotest corner of what was now an enormous barn with grain trickling out of a punctured bag at my feet. I could not see him and was so eager to escape that the throbbing of my impatience seemed to drown the words he said. I knew he was calling me and saying something very important—and promising to tell me something more important still, if only I came to the corner where he sat or lay, trapped by the heavy sacks that had fallen across his legs. I moved, and then his voice came in one last loud insistent appeal, and a phrase which made no sense when I brought it out of my dream, then, in the dream itself, rang out laden with such absolute moment, with such an unfailing intent to solve for me a monstrous riddle, that I would have run to Sebastian after all, had I not been half out of my dream already.

I know that the common pebble you find in your fist after having thrust your arm shoulder deep into water, where a jewel seemed to gleam on pale sand, is really the coveted gem though it looks like a pebble as it dries in the sun of everyday. Therefore I felt that the nonsensical sentence which sang in my head as I awoke was really the garbled translation of a striking disclosure; and as I lay on my back listening to the familiar sounds in the street and to the inane musical hash of the wireless brightening somebody's early breakfast in the room above my head, the prickly cold of some dreadful apprehension produced an almost physical shudder in me and I decided to send a wire telling Sebastian I was coming that very day. Owing to some idiotic piece of commonsense (which otherwise was never my forte), I thought I'd better find out at the Marseilles branch of my office whether my presence might be spared. I discovered that not only it might not, but that it was doubtful whether I could absent myself at all for the weekend. That Friday I came home very late after a harassing day. There was a telegram waiting for me since noon,—but so strange is the sovereignty of daily platitudes over the delicate revelations of a dream that I had quite forgotten its earnest whisper, and was simply expecting some business news as I burst the telegram open.

"Sevastian's state hopeless come immediately Starov." It was worded in French; the "v" in Sebastian's name was a transcription of its Russian spelling; for some reason unknown, I went to the bathroom and stood there for a moment in front of the looking-glass. Then I snatched my hat and ran downstairs. The time was a quarter to twelve when I reached the station, and there was a train at 0.02, arriving at Paris about half past two p.m. on the following day.

Then I discovered that I had not enough cash about me to afford a second-class ticket, and for a minute I debated with myself the question whether generally it would not be better to go back for some more and fly to Paris as soon as I could get a plane. But the train's near presence proved too tempting. I took the cheapest opportunity, as I usually do in life. And no sooner had the train moved than I realised with a shock that I had left Sebastian's letter in my desk and did not remember the address he had given.

20

THE CROWDED COMPARTMENT was dark, stuffy and full of legs. Rain drops trickled down the panes: they did not trickle straight but in a jerky, dubious, zig-zag course, pausing every now and then. The violet-blue night-lamp was reflected in the black glass. The train rocked and groaned as it rushed through the night. What on earth was the name of that sanitorium? It began with an "M." It began with an "M." It began with an . . . the wheels got mixed up in their repetitive rush and then found their rhythm again. Of course, I would obtain the address from Doctor Starov. Ring him up from the station as soon as I arrived. Somebody's heavily-booted dream tried to get in between my shins and then was slowly withdrawn. What had Sebastian meant by "the usual hotel?" I could not recall any special place in Paris where he had stayed. Yes, Starov would know where he was. Mar . . . Man . . . Mat . . . Would I get there in time? My neighbor's hip pushed at mine, as he switched from one kind of snore to another, sadder one. Would I arrive in time to find him alive . . . arrive . . . alive . . . arrive . . . He had something to tell me, something of boundless importance. The dark, rocking compartment, chock-full of sprawling dummies, seemed to me a section of the dream I had had. What would he tell me before he died? The rain spat and tinkled against the glass and a ghost-like snowflake settled in one corner and melted away. Somebody in front of me slowly came to life; rustled paper and munched in the dark, and then lit a cigarette, and its round glow stared at me like a Cyclopean eye. I must, I must get there in time. Why had I not dashed to the aerodrome as soon as I got that letter? I would have been with Sebastian by now! What was the illness he was dying of? Cancer? Angina pectoris—like his mother? As it happens with many people who do not trouble about religion in the ordinary trend of life, I hastily invented a soft, warm, tear-misty God, and whispered an informal prayer. Let me get there in time, let him hold out till I come, let him tell me his secret. Now it was all snow: the glass had grown a grey beard. The man who had munched and smoked was asleep again. Could I try and stretch out my legs, and put my feet up on something? I groped with my burning toes, but the night was all bone and flesh. I yearned in vain for a wooden something under my ankles and calves. Mar . . . Matamar . . . Mar . . . How far was that place from Paris? Doctor Starov. Alexander Alexandrovich Starov. The train clattered over the points, repeating those x's. Some unknown station. As the train stopped voices came from the next compartment, somebody was telling an endless tale. There was also the shifting sound of doors being moved aside, and some mournful traveller drew our door open too, and saw it was hopeless. Hopeless. *Etat désespéré.* I must get there in time. How long that train stopped at stations! My righthand neighbour sighed and tried to wipe the window-pane, but it remained misty with a faint yellowish light glimmering through. The train moved on again. My spine ached, my bones were leaden. I tried to shut my eyes and to doze, but my eyelids were lined with floating designs— and a tiny bundle of light, rather like an infusoria, swam across, starting again from the same corner. I seemed to recognise in it the shape of the station lamp which had passed by long ago. Then colours appeared, and a pink face with a large gazelle eye slowly turned towards me—and then a basket of flowers, and then Sebastian's unshaven chin. I could not stand that optical paintbox any longer, and with endless, cautious manoeuvering, resembling the steps of some ballet dancer filmed in slow motion, I got out into the corridor. It was brightly lit and cold. For a time I smoked and then staggered towards the end of the carriage, and swayed for a moment over a filthy roaring hole in the train's bottom, and staggered back, and smoked another cigarette. Never in my life had I wanted a thing as fiercely as I wanted to find Sebastian alive,— to bend over him and catch the words he would say. His last book, my recent dream, the mysteriousness of his letter—all made me firmly believe that some extraordinary revelation would come from his lips. If I found them still moving. If I were not too late. There was a map on the panel between the windows, but it had nothing to do with the course of my journey. My face was darkly reflected in the window-pane. *Il est dangereux . . . E pericoloso . . .* a soldier with red eyes

brushed past me and for some seconds a horrible tingle remained in my hand, because it had touched his sleeve. I craved
for a wash. I longed to wash the coarse world away and appear
in a cold aura of purity before Sebastian. He had done with
mortality now and I could not offend his nostrils with its reek.
Oh, I would find him alive. Starov would not have worded
his telegram that way, had he been sure that I would be late.
The telegram had come at noon. The telegram, my God, had
come at noon! Sixteen hours had already passed, and when
might I reach Mar . . . Mat . . . Ram . . . Rat . . . No, not
"R"—it began with an "M." For a moment I saw the dim
shape of the name, but it faded before I could grasp it. And
there might be another setback: money. I should dash from
the station to my office and get some at once. The office was
quite near. The bank was farther. Did anybody of my numerous friends live near the station? No, they all lived in Passy or
around the Porte St. Cloud,—the two Russian quarters of
Paris. I squashed my third cigarette and looked for a less
crowded compartment. There was, thank God, no luggage to
keep me in the one I had left. But the carriage was crammed
and I was much too sick in mind to go down the train. I am
not even sure whether the compartment into which I groped,
was another or the old one: it was just as full of knees and
feet and elbows—though perhaps the air was a little less
cheesy. Why had I never visited Sebastian in London? He had
invited me once or twice. Why had I kept away from him so
stubbornly, when he was the man I admired most of all men?
Those bloody asses who sneered at his genius . . . There was,
in particular, one old fool whose skinny neck I longed to
wring—ferociously. Ah, that bulky monster rolling on my left
was a woman; eau-de-Cologne and sweat struggling for ascendancy, the former losing. Not a single soul in that carriage
knew who Sebastian Knight was. That chapter out of *Lost
Property* so poorly translated in *Cadran*. Or was it *La Vie
Littéraire*? Or was I too late, too late—was Sebastian dead
already, while I sat on this accursed bench with a derisive bit
of thin leather padding which could not deceive my aching
buttocks? Faster, please faster! Why do you think it worth
stopping at this station? and why stop so long? Move, move
on. So—that's better.

Very gradually the darkness faded to a greyish dimness, and a snow-covered world became faintly perceptible through the window. I felt dreadfully cold in my thin raincoat. The faces of my travelling companions became visible as if layers of webs and dust were slowly brushed away. The woman next to me had a thermos flask of coffee and she handled it with a kind of maternal love. I felt sticky all over and excruciatingly unshaven. I think that if my bristly cheek had come into contact with satin, I should have fainted. There was a flesh-coloured cloud among the drab ones, and a dull pink flushed the patches of thawing snow in the tragic loneliness of barren fields. A road drew out and glided for a minute along the train, and just before it turned away a man on a bicycle wobbled among snow and slush and puddles. Where was he going? Who was he? Nobody will ever know.

I think I must have dozed for an hour or so—or at least I managed to keep my inner vision dark. My companions were talking and eating when I opened my eyes and I suddenly felt so sick that I scrambled out and sat on a strapontin for the rest of the journey, my mind as blank as the wretched morning. The train, I learnt, was very late, owing to the night blizzard or something, so it was only at a quarter to four in the afternoon that we reached Paris. My teeth chattered as I walked down the platform and for an instant I had a foolish impulse to spend the two or three francs jingling in my pocket on some strong liquor. But I went to the telephone instead. I thumbed the soft greasy book, looking for Dr. Starov's number and trying not to think that presently I should know whether Sebastian was still alive. Starkaus, cuirs, peaux; Starley, jongleur, humoriste; Starov . . . ah, there it was: Jasmin 61-93. I performed some dreadful manipulations and forgot the number in the middle, and struggled again with the book, and re-dialled, and listened for a while to an ominous buzzing. I sat for a minute quite still: somebody threw the door open and with an angry muttering retreated. Again the dial turned and clicked back, five, six, seven times, and again there was that nasal drone: donne, donne, donne . . . Why was I so unlucky? "Have you finished?" asked the same person—a cross old man with a bull-dog face. My nerves were on edge and I quarreled with that nasty old fellow. Fortunately a neighbouring booth was free by now; he slammed himself in. I went on trying. At last I succeeded. A woman's voice replied that the doctor was out, but could be reached at half past five,—she gave me the number. When I got to my office I could not help noticing that my arrival provoked a certain surprise. I showed the telegram I had got to my chief and he was less sympathetic than one might have reasonably expected. He asked me some awkward questions about the business in Marseilles. Finally I got the money I wanted and paid the taxi which I had left at the door. It was twenty minutes to five by then so that I had almost an hour before me.

I went to have a shave and then ate a hurried breakfast. At twenty past five I rang up the number I had been given, and was told that the doctor had gone home and would be back in a quarter of an hour. I was too impatient to wait and dialled his home number. The female voice I already knew answered that he had just left. I leant against the wall (the booth was in a café this time) and knocked at it with my pencil. Would I never get to Sebastian? Who were those idle idiots who wrote on the wall "Death to the Jews" or *"Vive le front populaire,"* or left obscene drawings? Some anonymous artist had begun blacking squares—a chess board, *ein Schachbrett, un damier* . . . There was a flash in my brain and the word settled on my tongue: St. Damier! I rushed out and hailed a passing taxicab. Would he take me to St. Damier, wherever the place was? He leisurely unfolded a map and studied it for some time. Then he replied that it would take two hours at least to get there—seeing the condition of the road. I asked him whether he thought I had better go by train. He did not know.

"Well, try and go fast," I said, and knocked my hat off as I plunged into the car.

We were a long time getting out of Paris. Every kind of known obstacle was put in our way, and I think I have never hated anything so much as I did a certain policeman's arm at one of the cross-roads. At last we wriggled out of the traffic jam into a long dark avenue. But still we did not go fast enough. I pushed the glass open and implored the chauffeur to increase his speed. He answered that the road was far too slippery—as it was we badly skidded once or twice. After an hour's drive he stopped and asked his way of a policeman on a bicycle. They both pored at length over the policeman's map, and then the chauffeur drew his own out, and they compared both. We had taken a wrong turning somewhere and now had to go back for at least a couple of miles. I tapped again on the pane: the taxi was positively crawling. He shook his head without as much as turning round. I looked at my watch, it was nearing seven o'clock. We stopped at a filling-station and the driver had a confidential talk with the garage man. I could not guess where we were, but as the road now ran along a vast expanse of fields, I hoped that we were getting nearer my goal. Rain swept and swished against the window-panes and when I pleaded once more with the driver for a little acceleration, he lost his temper and was volubly rude. I felt helpless and numb as I sank back in my seat. Lighted windows blurredly passed by. Would I ever get to Sebastian? Would I find him alive if I did ever reach St. Damier? Once or twice we were overtaken by other cars and I drew my driver's attention to their speed. He did not answer, but suddenly stopped and with a violent gesture unfolded his ridiculous map. I inquired whether he had lost his way again. He kept silent but the expression of his fat neck was vicious. We drove on. I noticed with satisfaction that he was going much faster now. We passed under a railway bridge and drew up at a station. As I was wondering whether it was St. Damier at last, the driver got out of his seat and wrenched open the door. "Well," I asked, "what's the matter now?"

"You shall go by train after all," said the driver, "I'm not willing to smash my car for your sake. This is the St. Damier line, and you're lucky to have been brought here."

I was even luckier than he thought for there was a train in a few minutes. The station-guard swore I would be at St. Damier by nine. That last phase of my journey was the darkest. I was alone in the carriage and a queer torpor had seized me: in spite of my impatience, I was terribly afraid lest I might fall asleep and miss the station. The train stopped often and it was every time a sickening task to find and decipher the station's name. At one stage I experienced the hideous feeling that I had just been jerked awake after dozing heavily for an unknown length of time—and when I looked at my watch it was a quarter past nine. Had I missed it? I was half-inclined to use the alarm signal, but then I felt the train was slowing down, and as I leant out of the window, I espied a lighted sign floating past and stopping: St. Damier.

A quarter of an hour's stumble through dark lanes and what seemed by its sough to be a pine-wood, brought me to the St. Damier hospital. I heard a shuffling and wheezing behind the door and a fat old man clad in a thick grey sweater instead of a coat and in worn felt slippers let me in. I entered a kind of office dimly lit by a weak bare electric lamp, which seemed coated with dust on one side. The man looked at me blinking, his bloated face glistening with the slime of sleep, and for some odd reason I spoke at first in a whisper.

"I have come," I said, "to see Monsieur Sebastian Knight, K, n, i, g, h, t. Knight. Night."

He grunted and sat down heavily at a writing-desk under the hanging lamp.

"Too late for visitors," he mumbled as if talking to himself.

"I got a wire," I said, "my brother is very ill,"—and as I spoke I felt I was trying to imply that there was not the shade of a doubt of Sebastian still being alive.

"What was the name?" he asked with a sigh.

"Knight," I said. "It begins with a 'K'. It is an English name."

"Foreign names ought to be always replaced by numbers," muttered the man, "it would simplify matters. There was a patient who died last night, and he had a name . . ."

I was struck by the horrible thought that he might be referring to Sebastian . . . Was I too late after all?

"Do you mean to say . . ." I began, but he shook his head and turned the pages of a ledger on his desk.

"No," he growled, "the English Monsieur is not dead. K, K, K . . ."

"K, n, i, g . . ." I began once again.

"C'est bon, c'est bon," he interrupted. "K, n, K, g . . . n . . . I'm not an idiot, you know. Number thirty-six."

He rang the bell and sank back in his armchair with a yawn. I paced up and down the room in a tremor of uncontrollable impatience. At last a nurse entered and the night-porter pointed at me.

"Number thirty-six," he said to the nurse.

I followed her down a white passage and up a short flight of stairs. "How is he?" I could not help asking.

"I don't know," she said and led me to a second nurse who was sitting at the end of another white passage, the exact copy of the first, and reading a book at a little table.

"A visitor for number thirty-six," said my guide and slipped away.

"But the English Monsieur is asleep," said the nurse, a round-faced young woman, with a very small and very shiny nose.

"Is he better?" I asked. "You see, I'm his brother, and I got a telegram . . ."

"I think he's a little better," said the nurse with a smile, which was to me the loveliest smile I could have ever imagined.

"He had a very, very bad heart attack yesterday morning. Now he is asleep."

"Look here," I said, handing her a ten or twenty franc coin. "I'll come to-morrow again, but I'd like to go into his room and wait for a minute there."

"Oh, but you shouldn't wake him," she said smiling again.

"I shan't wake him. I shall just sit near him and stay only a minute."

"Well, I don't know," she said. "You might, of course, peep in here, but you must be very careful."

She led me to the door, Number thirty-six, and we entered a tiny room or closet with a couch; she pushed slightly an inner door which was standing ajar and I peered for a moment into a dark room. At first I could only hear my heart thumping, but then I discerned a quick soft breathing. I strained my eyes; there was a screen or something half round the bed, and anyway it would have been too dark to distinguish Sebastian.

"There," whispered the nurse. "I shall leave the door open an inch and you may sit here, on this couch, for a minute."

She lit a small blue-shaded lamp and left me alone. I had a stupid impulse to draw my cigarette-case out of my pocket. My hands still shook, but I felt happy. He was alive. He was peacefully asleep. So it was his heart—was it?—that had let him down . . . The same as his mother. He was better, there was hope. I would get all the heart specialists in the world to have him saved. His presence in the next room, the faint sound of breathing, gave me a sense of security, of peace, of wonderful relaxation. And as I sat there and listened, and clasped my hands, I thought of all the years that had passed, of our short, rare meetings and I knew that now, as soon as he could listen to me, I should tell him that whether he liked it or not I would never be far from him any more. The strange dream I had had, the belief in some momentous truth he would impart to me before dying—now seemed vague, abstract, as if it had been drowned in some warm flow of simpler, more human emotion, in the wave of love I felt for the man who was sleeping beyond that half-opened door. How had we managed to drift apart? Why had I always been so silly and sullen, and shy during our short interviews in Paris? I would go away presently and spend the night in the hotel, or perhaps they could give me a room at the hospital—just until I could see him? For a moment it seemed to me that the faint rhythm of the sleeper's breath had been suspended, that he had awaked and made a light champing sound, before sinking again into sleep: now the rhythm continued, so low that I could hardly distinguish it from my own breath, as I sat and listened. Oh, I would tell him thousands of things—I would talk to him about *The Prismatic Bezel* and *Success*, and *The Funny Mountain*, and *Albinos in Black*, and *The Back of the Moon*, and *Lost Property*, and *The Doubtful Asphodel*,—all these books that I knew as well as if I had written them myself. And he would talk, too. How little I knew of his life! But now I was learning something every instant. That door standing slightly ajar was the best link imaginable. That gentle breathing was telling me more of Sebastian than I had ever known before. If I could have smoked, my happiness would have been perfect. A spring clanked in the couch as I shifted my position slightly, and I was afraid that it might have disturbed his sleep. But no: the soft sound was there, following a thin trail which seemed to skirt time itself, now dipping into a hollow, now appearing again,—steadily travelling across a landscape formed of the symbols of silence—darkness, and curtains, and a glow of blue light at my elbow.

Presently I got up and tiptoed out into the corridor.

"I hope," the nurse said, "you did not disturb him? It is good that he sleeps."

"Tell me," I asked, "when does Doctor Starov come?"

"Doctor who?" she said. "Oh, the Russian doctor. *Non, c'est le docteur Guinet qui le soigne.* You'll find him here to-morrow morning."

"You see," I said, "I'd like to spend the night somewhere here. Do you think that perhaps . . ."

"You could see Doctor Guinet even now," continued the nurse in her quiet pleasant voice. "He lives next door. So you are the brother, are you? And to-morrow his mother is com-ing from England, n'est-ce pas?"

"Oh, no," I said, "his mother died years ago. And tell me, how is he during the day, does he talk? does he suffer?"

She frowned and looked at me queerly.

"But . . ." she said. "I don't understand . . . What is your name, please?"

"Right," I said. "I haven't explained. We are half-brothers, really. My name is [I mentioned my name]."

"Oh-la-la!" she exclaimed getting very red in the face. "Mon Dieu! The Russian gentleman died yesterday, and you've been visiting Monsieur Kegan . . ."

So I did not see Sebastian after all, or at least I did not see him alive. But those few minutes I spent listening to what I thought was his breathing changed my life as completely as it would have been changed, had Sebastian spoken to me before dying. Whatever his secret was, I have learnt one secret too, and namely: that the soul is but a manner of being—not a constant state—that any soul may be yours, if you find and follow its undulations. The hereafter may be the full ability of consciously living in any chosen soul, in any number of souls, all of them unconscious of their interchangeable burden. Thus—I am Sebastian Knight. I feel as if I were impersonating him on a lighted stage, with the people he knew coming and going—the dim figures of the few friends he had, the scholar, and the poet, and the painter,—smoothly and noiselessly pay-ing their graceful tribute; and here is Goodman, the flat-footed buffoon, with his dicky hanging out of his waistcoat; and there—the pale radiance of Clare's inclined head, as she is led away weeping by a friendly maiden. They move round Sebastian—round me who am acting Sebastian,—and the old conjuror waits in the wings with his hidden rabbit; and Nina sits on a table in the brightest corner of the stage, with a wineglass of fuchsined water, under a painted palm. And then the masquerade draws to a close. The bald little prompter shuts his book, as the light fades gently. The end, the end. They all go back to their everyday life (and Clare goes back to her grave)—but the hero remains, for, try as I may, I cannot get out of my part: Sebastian's mask clings to my face, the likeness will not be washed off. I am Sebastian, or Sebastian is I, or perhaps we both are someone whom neither of us knows.

THE END

BEND SINISTER

To Véra

Introduction

BEND SINISTER was the first novel I wrote in America, and that was half a dozen years after she and I had adopted each other. The greater part of the book was composed in the middle 'Forties, at a particularly cloudless and vigorous period of life. My health was excellent. My daily consumption of cigarettes had reached the four-package mark. I slept at least four or five hours, the rest of the night walking pencil in hand about the dingy little flat in Craigie Circle, Cambridge, Massachusetts, where I lodged under an old lady with feet of stone and above a young woman with hypersensitive hearing. Every day including Sundays, I would spend up to 10 hours studying the structure of certain butterflies in the laboratorial paradise of the Harvard Museum of Comparative Zoology; but three times a week I stayed there only till noon and then tore myself away from microscope and camera lucida to travel to Wellesley (by tram and bus, or subway and railway), where I taught college girls Russian grammar and literature.

The book was finished on a warm rainy night, more or less as described at the end of Chapter Eighteen. A kind friend, Edmund Wilson, read the typescript and recommended the book to Allen Tate, who had Holt publish it in 1947. I was deeply immersed in other labors but nonetheless managed to discern the dull thud it made. Praises, as far as I can recall, rang out only in two weeklies—TIME and *The New Yorker*, I think.

The term "bend sinister" means a heraldic bar or band drawn from the left side (and popularly, but incorrectly, supposed to denote bastardy). This choice of title was an attempt to suggest an outline broken by refraction, a distortion in the mirror of being, a wrong turn taken by life, a sinistral and sinister world. The title's drawback is that a solemn reader looking for "general ideas" or "human interest" (which is much the same thing) in a novel may be led to look for them in this one.

There exist few things more tedious than a discussion of

general ideas inflicted by author or reader upon a work of
fiction. The purpose of this foreword is not to show that *Bend
Sinister* belongs or does not belong to "serious literature"
(which is a euphemism for the hollow profundity and the ever-
welcome commonplace). I have never been interested in what
is called the literature of social comment (in journalistic and
commercial parlance: "great books"). I am not "sincere," I
am not "provocative," I am not "satirical." I am neither a
didacticist nor an allegorizer. Politics and economics, atomic
bombs, primitive and abstract art forms, the entire Orient,
symptoms of "thaw" in Soviet Russia, the Future of Mankind,
and so on, leave me supremely indifferent. As in the case of
my *Invitation to a Beheading*—with which this book has obvious affinities—automatic comparisons between *Bend Sinister*
and Kafka's creations or Orwell's clichés would go merely to
prove that the automaton could not have read either the great
German writer or the mediocre English one.

Similarly, the influence of my epoch on my present book is
as negligible as the influence of my books, or at least of this
book, on my epoch. There can be distinguished, no doubt,
certain reflections in the glass directly caused by the idiotic
and despicable regimes that we all know and that have
brushed against me in the course of my life: worlds of tyranny
and torture, of Fascists and Bolshevists, of Philistine thinkers
and jack-booted baboons. No doubt, too, without those in-
famous models before me I could not have interlarded this
fantasy with bits of Lenin's speeches, and a chunk of the
Soviet constitution, and gobs of Nazist pseudo-efficiency.

While the system of holding people in hostage is as old as
the oldest war, a fresher note is introduced when a tyrannic
state is at war with its own subjects and may hold any citizen
in hostage with no law to restrain it. An even more recent
improvement is the subtle use of what I shall term "the lever
of love"—the diabolical method (applied so successfully by
the Soviets) of tying a rebel to his wretched country by his
own twisted heartstrings. It is noteworthy, however, that in
Bend Sinister Paduk's still young police state—where a certain
dull-wittedness is a national trait of the people (augmenting
thereby the possibilities of muddling and bungling so typical,
thank God, of all tyrannies)—lags behind actual regimes in

successfully working this lever of love, for which at first it rather haphazardly gropes, losing time on the needless persecution of Krug's friends, and only by chance realizing (in Chapter Fifteen) that by grabbing his little child one would force him to do whatever one wished.

The story in *Bend Sinister* is not really about life and death in a grotesque police state. My characters are not "types," not carriers of this or that "idea." Paduk, the abject dictator and Krug's former schoolmate (regularly tormented by the boys, regularly caressed by the school janitor); Doctor Alexander, the government's agent; the ineffable Hustav; icy Crystalsen and hapless Kolokololiteishchikov; the three Bachofen sisters; the farcical policeman Mac; the brutal and imbecile soldiers— all of them are only absurd mirages, illusions oppressive to Krug during his brief spell of being, but harmlessly fading away when I dismiss the cast.

The main theme of *Bend Sinister*, then, is the beating of Krug's loving heart, the torture an intense tenderness is subjected to—and it is for the sake of the pages about David and his father that the book was written and should be read. Two other themes accompany the main one: the theme of dim-brained brutality which thwarts its own purpose by destroying the right child and keeping the wrong one; and the theme of Krug's blessed madness when he suddenly perceives the simple reality of things and knows but cannot express in the words of his world that he and his son and his wife and everybody else are merely my whims and megrims.

Is there any judgment on my part carried out, any sentence pronounced, any satisfaction given to the moral sense? If imbeciles and brutes can punish other brutes and imbeciles, and if crime still retains an objective meaning in the meaningless world of Paduk (all of which is doubtful), we may affirm that crime *is* punished at the end of the book when the uniformed waxworks are really hurt, and the dummies are at last in quite dreadful pain, and pretty Mariette gently bleeds, staked and torn by the lust of 40 soldiers.

The plot starts to breed in the bright broth of a rain puddle. The puddle is observed by Krug from a window of the hospital where his wife is dying. The oblong pool, shaped like a cell that is about to divide, reappears subthematically throughout the novel, as an ink blot in Chapter Four, an ink-stain in Chapter Five, spilled milk in Chapter Eleven, the in-fusoria-like image of ciliated thought in Chapter Twelve, the footprint of a phosphorescent islander in Chapter Eighteen, and the imprint a soul leaves in the intimate texture of space in the closing paragraph. The puddle thus kindled and rekin-dled in Krug's mind remains linked up with the image of his wife not only because he had contemplated the inset sunset from her death-bedside, but also because this little puddle vaguely evokes in him my link with him: a rent in his world leading to another world of tenderness, brightness and beauty.

And a companion image even more eloquently speaking of Olga is the vision of her divesting herself of herself, of her jewels, of the necklace and tiara of earthly life, in front of a brilliant mirror. It is this picture that appears six times in the course of a dream, among the liquid, dream-refracted mem-ories of Krug's boyhood (Chapter Five).

Paronomasia is a kind of verbal plague, a contagious sick-ness in the world of words; no wonder they are monstrously and ineptly distorted in Padukgrad, where everybody is merely an anagram of everybody else. The book teems with stylistic distortions, such as puns crossed with anagrams (in Chapter Two, the Russian circumference, *krug*, turns into a Teutonic cucumber, *gurk*, with an additional allusion to Krug's revers-ing his journey across the bridge); suggestive neologisms (the *amorandola*—a local guitar); parodies of narrative clichés ("who had overheard the last words" and "who seemed to be the leader of the group," Chapter Two); spoonerisms ("si-lence" and "science" playing leapfrog in Chapter Seventeen); and of course the hybridization of tongues.

The language of the country, as spoken in Padukgrad and Omigod, as well as in the Kur valley, the Sakra mountains and the region of Lake Malheur, is a mongrel blend of Slavic and Germanic with a strong strain of ancient Kuranian running through it (and especially prominent in ejaculations of woe); but colloquial Russian and German are also used by represen-tatives of all groups, from the vulgar Ekwilist soldier to the discriminating intellectual. Ember, for instance, in Chapter Seven, gives his friend a sample of the three first lines of Ham-let's soliloquy (Act III, Scene I) translated into the vernacular (with a pseudo-scholarly interpretation of the first phrase taken to refer to the contemplated killing of Claudius, i.e., "is the murder to be or not to be?"). He follows this up with a Russian version of part of the Queen's speech in Act IV, Scene VII (also not without a built-in scholium) and a splendid Russian rendering of the prose passage in Act III, Scene II, beginning, "Would not this, Sir, and a forest of feathers. . . ." Problems of translation, fluid transitions from one tongue to another, semantic transparencies yielding layers of receding or welling sense are as characteristic of Sinisterbad as are the monetary problems of more habitual tyrannies.

In this crazy-mirror of terror and art a pseudo-quotation made up of obscure Shakespeareanisms (Chapter Three) somehow produces, despite its lack of literal meaning, the blurred diminutive image of the acrobatic performance that so gloriously supplies the bravura ending for the next chapter. A chance selection of iambic incidents culled from the prose of *Moby Dick* appears in the guise of "a famous American poem" (Chapter Twelve). If the "admiral" and his "fleet" in a trite official speech (Chapter Four) are at first mis-heard by the widower as "animal" and its "feet," this is because the chance reference, coming just before, to a man losing his wife dims and distorts the next sentence. When in Chapter Three Ember recalls four best-selling novels, the alert commuter cannot fail to notice that the titles of three of them form, roughly, the lavatorial injunction not to Flush the Toilet when the Train Passes through Towns and Villages, while the fourth alludes to Werfel's trashy *Song of Bernadette*, half altar bread and half bonbon. Similarly, at the beginning of Chapter Six, where some other popular romances of the day are mentioned, a slight shift in the spectrum of meaning replaces the title *Gone with the Wind* (filched from Dowson's *Cynara*) with that of *Flung Roses* (filched from the same poem), and a fusion between two cheap novels (by Remarque and Sholokhov) produces the neat *All Quiet on the Don*.

Stéphane Mallarmé has left three or four immortal bagatelles, and among these is *L'Après-Midi d'un Faune* (first drafted in 1865). Krug is haunted by a passage from this voluptuous eclogue where the faun accuses the nymph of disengaging herself from his embrace *"sans pitié du sanglot dont j'étais encore ivre"* ("spurning the spasm with which I still was drunk"). Fractured parts of this line re-echo through the book, cropping up for instance in the *malarma ne donje* of Dr. Azureus' wail of rue (Chapter Four) and in the *donje te zankoriv* of apologetic Krug when he interrupts the kiss of the university student and his little Carmen (foreshadowing Mariette) in the same chapter. Death, too, is a ruthless interruption; the widower's heavy sensuality seeks a pathetic outlet in Mariette, but as he avidly clasps the haunches of the chance nymph he is about to enjoy, a deafening din at the door breaks the throbbing rhythm forever.

It may be asked if it is really worth an author's while to devise and distribute these delicate markers whose very nature requires that they be not too conspicuous. Who will bother to notice that Pankrat Tzikutin, the shabby old pogromystic (Chapter Thirteen) is Socrates Hemlocker; that "the child is bold" in the allusion to immigration (Chapter Eighteen) is a stock phrase used to test a would-be American citizen's reading ability; that Linda did not steal the porcelain owlet after all (beginning of Chapter Ten); that the urchins in the yard (Chapter Seven) have been drawn by Saul Steinberg; that the "other rivermaid's father" (Chapter Seven) is James Joyce who wrote *Winnipeg Lake* (ibid.); and that the last word of the book is *not* a misprint (as assumed in the past by at least one proofreader)? Most people will not even mind having missed all this; well-wishers will bring their own symbols and mobiles, and portable radios, to my little party; ironists will point out the fatal fatuity of my explications in this foreword and advise me to have footnotes next time (footnotes always seem comic to a certain type of mind). In the long run, however, it is only the author's private satisfaction that counts. I reread my books rarely, and then only for the utilitarian purpose of controlling a translation or checking a new edition; but when I do go through them again, what pleases me most is the wayside murmur of this or that hidden theme.

Thus, in the second paragraph of Chapter Five comes the first intimation that "someone is in the know"—a mysterious intruder who takes advantage of Krug's dream to convey his own peculiar code message. The intruder is not the Viennese Quack (all my books should be stamped Freudians, Keep

Out), but an anthropomorphic deity impersonated by me. In the last chapter of the book this deity experiences a pang of pity for his creature and hastens to take over. Krug, in a sudden moonburst of madness, understands that he is in good hands: nothing on earth really matters, there is nothing to fear, and death is but a question of style, a mere literary device, a musical resolution. And as Olga's rosy soul, emblemized already in an earlier chapter (Nine), bombinates in the damp dark at the bright window of my room, comfortably Krug returns unto the bosom of his maker.

September 9, 1963   —VLADIMIR NABOKOV
Montreux

I

A N OBLONG PUDDLE inset in the coarse asphalt; like a fancy footprint filled to the brim with quicksilver; like a spatulate hole through which you can see the nether sky. Surrounded, I note, by a diffuse tentacled black dampness where some dull dun dead leaves have stuck. Drowned, I should say, before the puddle had shrunk to its present size.

It lies in shadow but contains a sample of the brightness beyond, where there are trees and two houses. Look closer. Yes, it reflects a portion of pale blue sky—mild infantile shade of blue—taste of milk in my mouth because I had a mug of that color thirty-five years ago. It also reflects a brief tangle of bare twigs and the brown sinus of a stouter limb cut off by its rim and a transverse bright cream-colored band. You have dropped something, this is yours, creamy house in the sunshine beyond.

When the November wind has its recurrent icy spasm, a rudimentary vortex of ripples creases the brightness of the puddle. Two leaves, two triskelions, like two shuddering three-legged bathers coming at a run for a swim, are borne by their impetus right into the middle where with a sudden slowdown they float quite flat. Twenty minutes past four. View from a hospital window.

November trees, poplars, I imagine, two of them growing straight out of the asphalt: all of them in the cold bright sun, bright richly furrowed bark and an intricate sweep of numberless burnished bare twigs, old gold—because getting more of the falsely mellow sun in the higher air. Their immobility is in contrast with the spasmodic ruffling of the inset reflection—for the visible emotion of a tree is the mass of its leaves, and there remain hardly more than thirty-seven or so here and there on one side of the tree. They just flicker a little, of a neutral tint, but burnished by the sun to the same ikontint as the intricate trillions of twigs. Swooning blue of the sky crossed by pale motionless superimposed cloud wisps.

The operation has not been successful and my wife will die.

Beyond a low fence, in the sun, in the bright starkness, a slaty house front has for frame two cream-colored lateral pilasters and a broad blank unthinking cornice: the frosting of a shop-worn cake. Windows look black by day. Thirteen of them; white lattice, green shutters. All very clear, but the day will not last. Something has moved in the blackness of one window: an ageless housewife—ope as my dentist in my milk-tooth days used to say, a Dr. Wollison—opens the window, shakes out something and you may now close.

The other house (to the right, beyond a jutting garage) is quite golden now. The many-limbed poplars cast their alembic ascending shadow bands upon it, in between their own burnished black-shaded spreading and curving limbs. But it all fades, it fades, she used to sit in a field, painting a sunset that would never stay, and a peasant child, very small and quiet and bashful in spite of its mousy persistence would stand at her elbow, and look at the easel, at the paints, at her wet aquarelle brush poised like the tongue of a snake—but the sunset had gone, leaving only a clutter of the purplish remnants of the day, piled up anyhow—ruins, junk.

The dappled surface of that other house is crossed by an outer stairway, and the dormer window to which this leads is now as bright as the puddle was—for the latter has now changed to a dull liquid white traversed by dead black, so that it looks like an achromatic copy of the painting previously seen.

I shall probably never forget the dull green of the narrow lawn in front of the first house (to which the dappled one stands sideways). A lawn both disheveled and baldish, with a middle parting of asphalt, and all studded with pale dun leaves. The colors go. There is a last glow in the window to which the stairs of the day still lead. But it is all up, and if the lights were turned on inside they would kill what remains of the outside day. The cloud wisps are flushed with flesh pink, and the trillions of twigs are becoming extremely distinct; and now there is no more color below: the houses, the lawn, the fence, the vistas in between, everything has been toned down to a kind of auburn gray. Oh, the glass of the puddle is bright mauve.

They have turned on the lights in the house I am in, and the view in the window has died. It is all inky black with a pale blue inky sky—"runs blue, writes black" as that ink bottle said, but it did not, nor does the sky, but the trees do with their trillions of twigs.

KRUG HALTED in the doorway and looked down at her upturned face. The movement (pulsation, radiation) of its features (crumpled ripples) was due to her speaking, and he realized that this movement had been going on for some time. Possibly all the way down the hospital stairs. With her faded blue eyes and long wrinkled upper lip she resembled someone he had known for years but could not recall—funny. A side line of indifferent cognition led him to place her as the head nurse. The continuation of her voice came into being as if a needle had found its groove. Its groove in the disc of his mind. Of his mind that had started to revolve as he halted in the doorway and looked down at her upturned face. The movement of its features was now audible.

She pronounced the word that meant "fighting" with a northwestern accent: "*fakhtung*" instead of "*fahtung*." The person (male?) whom she resembled peered out of the mist and was gone before he could identify her—or him.

"They are still fighting," she said. ". . . dark and dangerous. The town is dark, the streets are dangerous. Really, you had better spend the night here. . . . In a hospital bed" (*gospitalisha kruvka*—again that marshland accent and he felt like a heavy crow—*kruv*—flapping against the sunset). "Please! Or you could wait at least for Dr. Krug who has a car."

"No relative of mine," he said. "Pure coincidence."

"I know," she said, "but still you ought not to not to not to not to"—(the world went on revolving although it had expended its sense).

"I have," he said, "a pass." And, opening his wallet, he went so far as to unfold the paper in question with trembling fingers. He had thick (let me see) clumsy (there) fingers which always trembled slightly. The inside of his cheeks was methodically sucked in and smacked ever so slightly when he was in the act of unfolding something. Krug—for it was he—showed her the blurred paper. He was a huge tired man with a stoop.

"But it might not help," she whined, "a stray bullet might hit you."

(You see the good woman thought that bullets were still *flukhtung* about in the night, meteoric remnants of the firing that had long ceased.)

"I am not interested in politics," he said. "And I have only the river to cross. A friend of mine will come to fix things tomorrow morning."

He patted her on the elbow and went on his way.

He yielded, with what pleasure there was in the act, to the soft warm pressure of tears. The sense of relief did not last, for as soon as he let them flow they became atrociously hot and abundant so as to interfere with his eyesight and respiration. He walked through a spasmodic fog down the cobbled Omigod Lane towards the embankment. Tried clearing his throat but it merely led to another gasping sob. He was sorry now he had yielded to that temptation for he could not stop yielding and the throbbing man in him was soaked. As usual he discriminated between the throbbing one and the one that looked on: looked on with concern, with sympathy, with a sigh, or with bland surprise. This was the last stronghold of the dualism he abhorred. The square root of I is I. Footnotes, forget-me-nots. The stranger quietly watching the torrents of local grief from an abstract bank. A familiar figure, albeit anonymous and aloof. He saw me crying when I was ten and led me to a looking glass in an unused room (with an empty parrot cage in the corner) so that I might study my dissolving face. He has listened to me with raised eyebrows when I said things which I had no business to say. In every mask I tried on, there were slits for his eyes. Even at the very moment when I was rocked by the convulsion men value most. My savior. My witness. And now Krug reached for his handkerchief which was a dim white blob somewhere in the depths of his private night. Having at last crept out of a labyrinth of pockets, he mopped and wiped the dark sky and amorphous houses; then he saw he was nearing the bridge.

On other nights it used to be a line of lights with a certain lilt, a metrical incandescence with every foot rescanned and prolonged by reflections in the black snaky water. This night there was only a diffused glow where a Neptune of granite loomed upon his square rock which rock continued as a parapet which parapet was lost in the mist. As Krug, trudging steadily, approached, two Ekwilist soldiers barred his way. More were lurking around, and when a lantern moved, knightwise, to check him, he noticed a little man dressed as a *meshchaniner* [petty bourgeois] standing with folded arms and smiling a sickly smile. The two soldiers (both, oddly enough, had pock-marked faces) were asking, Krug understood, for his (Krug's) papers. While he was fumbling for the pass they bade him hurry and mentioned a brief love affair they had had, or would have, or invited him to have with his mother.

"I doubt," said Krug as he went through his pockets, "whether these fancies which have bred maggotlike from ancient taboos could be really transformed into acts—and this for various reasons. Here it is" (it almost wandered away while I was talking to the orphan—I mean, the nurse).

They grabbed it as if it had been a hundred krun note. While they were subjecting the pass to an intense examination, he blew his nose and slowly put back his handkerchief into the left-hand pocket of his overcoat; but on second thought transferred it to his right-hand trouser pocket.

"What's this?" asked the fatter of the two, marking a word with the nail of the thumb he was pressing against the paper. Krug, holding his reading spectacles to his eyes, peered over the man's hand. "University," he said. "Place where things are taught—nothing very important."

"No, this," said the soldier.

"Oh, 'philosophy.' *You* know. When you try to imagine a *mirok* [small pink potato] without the least reference to any you have eaten or will eat." He gestured vaguely with his glasses and then slipped them into their lecture-hall nook (vest pocket).

"What is your business? Why are you loafing near the bridge?" asked the fat soldier while his companion tried to decipher the permit in his turn.

"Everything can be explained," said Krug. "For the last ten

days or so I have been going to the Prinzin Hospital every morning. A private matter. Yesterday my friends got me this document because they foresaw that the bridge would be guarded after dark. My home is on the south side. I am returning much later than usual."

"Patient or doctor?" asked the thinner soldier.

"Let me read you what this little paper is meant to convey," said Krug, stretching out a helpful hand.

"Read on while I hold it," said the thin one, holding it upside down.

"Inversion," said Krug, "does not trouble me, but I need my glasses." He went through the familiar nightmare of over-coat—coat—trouser pockets, and found an empty spectacle case. He was about to resume his search.

"Hands up," said the fatter soldier with hysterical suddenness.

Krug obeyed, holding the case heavenward.

The left part of the moon was so strongly shaded as to be almost invisible in the pool of clear but dark ether across which it seemed to be swiftly floating, an illusion due to the moonward movement of some small chinchilla clouds; its right part, however, a somewhat porous but thoroughly talc-powdered edge or cheek, was vividly illumined by the artificial-looking blaze of an invisible sun. The whole effect was remarkable.

The soldiers searched him. They found an empty flask which quite recently had contained a pint of brandy. Although a burly man, Krug was ticklish and he uttered little grunts and squirmed slightly as they rudely investigated his ribs. Something jumped and dropped with a grasshopper's click. They had located the glasses.

"All right," said the fat soldier. "Pick them up, you old fool."

Krug stooped, groped, side-stepped—and there was a horrible scrunch under the toe of his heavy shoe.

"Dear, dear, this is a singular position," he said. "For now there is not much to choose between my physical illiteracy and your mental one."

"We are going to arrest you," said the fat soldier. "It will put an end to your clowning, you old drunkard. And when we get fed up with guarding you, we'll chuck you into the water and shoot at you while you drown."

Another soldier came up idly juggling with a flashlight and again Krug had a glimpse of a pale-faced little man standing apart and smiling.

"I want some fun too," the third soldier said.

"Well, well," said Krug. "Fancy seeing you here. How is your cousin, the gardener?"

The newcomer, an ugly, ruddy-cheeked country lad, looked at Krug blankly and then pointed to the fat soldier.

"It is his cousin, not mine."

"Yes, of course," said Krug quickly. "Exactly what I meant. How is he, that gentle gardener? Has he recovered the use of his left leg?"

"We have not seen each other for some time," answered the fat soldier moodily. "He lives in Bervok."

"A fine fellow," said Krug. "We were all so sorry when he fell into that gravel pit. Tell him, since he exists, that Professor Krug often recalls the talks we had over a jug of cider. Anyone can create the future but only a wise man can create the past. Grand apples in Bervok."

"This is his permit," said the fat moody one to the rustic ruddy one, who took the paper gingerly and at once handed it back.

"You had better call that *ved'min syn* [son of a witch] there," he said.

It was then that the little man was brought forward. He seemed to labor under the impression that Krug was some sort of superior in relation to the soldiers for he started to complain in a thin almost feminine voice, saying that he and his brother owned a grocery store on the other side and that both had venerated the Ruler since the blessed seventeenth of that month. The rebels were crushed, thank God, and he wished to join his brother so that a Victorious People might obtain the delicate foods he and his deaf brother sold.

"Cut it out," said the fat soldier, "and read this."

The pale grocer complied. Professor Krug had been given full liberty by the Committee of Public Welfare to circulate after dusk. To cross from the south town to the north one. And back. The reader desired to know why he could not

accompany the professor across the bridge. He was briskly
kicked back into the darkness. Krug proceeded to cross the
black river.

This interlude had turned the torrent away: it was now running unseen behind a wall of darkness. He remembered
other imbeciles he and she had studied, a study conducted
with a kind of gloating enthusiastic disgust. Men who got
drunk on beer in sloppy bars, the process of thought satisfactorily replaced by swine-toned radio music. Murderers.
The respect a business magnate evokes in his home town.
Literary critics praising the books of their friends or parti-
sans. Flaubertian *farceurs*. Fraternities, mystic orders. People
who are amused by trained animals. The members of reading clubs. All those who *are* because they do *not* think, thus
refuting Cartesianism. The thrifty peasant. The booming
politician. Her relatives—her dreadful humorless family.
Suddenly, with the vividness of a praedormital image or of a
bright-robed lady on stained glass, she drifted across his ret-
ina, in profile, carrying something—a book, a baby, or just
letting the cherry paint on her fingernails dry—and the wall
dissolved, the torrent was loosed again. Krug stopped, trying to control himself, with the palm of his ungloved hand
resting on the parapet as in former days frock-coated men of
parts used to be photographed in imitation of portraits by
old masters—hand on book, on chair back, on globe—but as
soon as the camera had clicked everything started to move, to
gush, and he walked on—jerkily, because of the sobs shaking
his ungloved soul. The lights of the thither side were nearing in a shudder of concentric prickly iridescent circles,
dwindling again to a blurred glow when you blinked, and
extravagantly expanding immediately afterwards. He was a big
heavy man. He felt an intimate connection with the black lacquered water lapping and heaving under the stone arches of
the bridge.

Presently he stopped again. Let us touch this and look at
this. In the faint light (of the moon? of his tears? of the few
lamps the dying fathers of the city had lit from a mechanical
sense of duty?) his hand found a certain pattern of roughness:
a furrow in the stone of the parapet and a knob and a hole
with some moisture inside—all of it highly magnified as the

thirty thousand pits in the crust of the plastic moon are on the large glossy print which the proud selenographer shows his young wife. On this particular night, just after they had tried to turn over to me her purse, her comb, her cigarette holder, I found and touched this—a selected combination, details of the bas-relief. I had never touched this particular knob before and shall never find it again. This moment of conscious contact holds a drop of solace. The emergency brake of time. Whatever the present moment is, I have stopped it. Too late. In the course of our, let me see, twelve, twelve and three months, years of life together, I ought to have immobilized by this simple method millions of moments; paying perhaps terrific fines, but stopping the train. Say, why did you do it? the popeyed conductor might ask. Because I liked the view. Because I wanted to stop those speeding trees and the path twisting between them. By stepping on its receding tail. What happened to her would perhaps not have happened, had I been in the habit of stopping this or that bit of our common life, prophylactically, prophetically, letting this or that moment rest and breathe in peace. Taming time. Giving her pulse respite. Pampering life, life—our patient.

Krug—for it was still he—walked on, with the impression of the rough pattern still tingling and clinging to the ball of his thumb. This end of the bridge was brighter. The soldiers who bade him halt looked livelier, better shaven, wore neater uniforms. There were also more of them, and more nocturnal travelers had been held up: two old men with their bicycles and what might be termed a gentleman (velvet collar of overcoat set up, hands thrust into pockets) and his girl, a bedraggled bird of paradise.

Pietro—or at least the soldier resembled Pietro, the head waiter at the University Club—Pietro the soldier examined Krug's pass and said in cultured accents:

"I fail to understand, Professor, what enabled you to effect the crossing of the bridge. You had no right whatever to do so since this pass has not been signed by my colleagues of the north side guard. I am afraid you must go back and have it done by them according to emergency regulations. Otherwise I cannot let you enter the south side of the city. *Je regrette* but a law is a law."

"Quite true," said Krug. "Unfortunately they are unable to read, let alone write."

"This does not concern us," said bland grave handsome Pietro—and his companions nodded in grave judicious assent. "No, I cannot let you pass, unless, I repeat, your identity and innocence are guaranteed by the signature of the opposite sentry."

"But cannot we turn the bridge the other way round, so to speak?" said Krug patiently. "I mean—give it a full turn. You sign the permits of those who cross from the south side to the north one, don't you? Well, let us reverse the process. Sign this valuable paper and suffer me to go to my bed in Peregolm Lane."

Pietro shook his head: "I do not follow you, Professor. We have exterminated the enemy—aye, we have crushed him under our heels. But one or two hydra heads are still alive, and we cannot take any chances. In a week or so, Professor, I can assure you the city will go back to normal conditions. Isn't that a promise, lads?" Pietro added, turning to the other soldiers who assented eagerly, their honest intelligent faces lit up by that civic ardor which transfigures even the plainest man.

"I appeal to your imagination," said Krug. "Imagine I was going the other way. In fact, I *was* going the other way this morning, when the bridge was not guarded. To place sentries only at nightfall is a very conventional notion—but let it pass. Let me pass too."

"Not unless this paper is signed," said Pietro and turned away.

"Aren't you lowering to a considerable extent the standards by which the function, if any, of the human brain is judged?" rumbled Krug.

"Hush, hush," said another soldier, putting his finger to his cleaved lip and then quickly pointing at Pietro's broad back. "Hush. Pietro is perfectly right. Go."

"Yes, go," said Pietro who had overheard the last words. "And when you come again with your pass signed and everything in order—think of the inner satisfaction you will feel when we countersign it. And for us, too, it will be a pleasure. The night is still young, and anyway, we should not shirk a certain amount of physical exertion if we want to be worthy of our Ruler. Go, Professor."

Pietro looked at the two bearded old men patiently gripping their bicycle handles, their knuckles white in the lamplight, their lost dog eyes watching him intently. "You may go, too," said the generous fellow.

With an alacrity that was in odd contrast with their advanced age and spindle legs, the bearded ones jumped upon their mounts and pedaled off, wobbling in their eagerness to get away and exchanging rapid guttural remarks. What were they discussing? The pedigree of their bicycles? The price of some special make? The condition of the race track? Were their cries exclamations of encouragement? Friendly taunts? Did they banter the ball of a joke seen years before in the *Simplizissimus* or the *Strekoza*? One always desires to find out what people who ride by are saying to each other.

Krug walked as fast as he could. Clouds had masked our siliceous satellite. Somewhere near the middle of the bridge he overtook the grizzled cyclists. Both were inspecting the anal ruby of one of the bicycles. The other lay on its side like a stricken horse with half-raised sad head. He walked fast and held his pass in his fist. What would happen if I threw it into the Kur? Doomed to walk back and forth on a bridge which has ceased to be one since neither bank is really attainable. Not a bridge but an hourglass which somebody keeps reversing, with me, the fluent fine sand, inside. Or the grass stalk you pick with an ant running up it, and you turn the stalk upside down the moment he gets to the tip, which becomes the pit, and the poor little fool repeats his performance. The old men overtook him in their turn, clattering lickety-split through the mist, gallantly galloping, goading their old black horses with blood-red spurs.

" 'Tis I again," said Krug as his slovenly friends clustered around him. "You forgot to sign my pass. Here it is. Let us get it over with promptly. Scrawl a cross, or a telephone booth curlicue, or a gammadion, or something. I dare not hope that you have one of those stamping affairs at hand."

While still speaking, he realized that they did not recognize him at all. They looked at his pass. They shrugged their shoulders as if ridding themselves of the burden of knowledge. They even scratched their heads, a quaint method used in that country because supposed to prompt a richer flow of blood to the cells of thought.

"Do you *live* on the bridge?" asked the fat soldier.

"No," said Krug. "Do try to understand. *C'est simple comme bonjour*, as Pietro would say. They sent me back because they had no evidence that you let me pass. From a formal point of view I am not on the bridge at all."

"He may have climbed up from a barge," said a dubious voice.

"No, no," said Krug. "I not bargee-bargee. You still do not understand. I am going to put it as simply as possible. They of the solar side saw heliocentrically what you tellurians saw geocentrically, and unless these two aspects are somehow combined, I, the visualized object, must keep shuttling in the universal night."

"It is the man who knows Gurk's cousin," cried one of the soldiers in a burst of recognition.

"Ah, excellent," said Krug much relieved. "I was forgetting the gentle gardener. So one point is settled. Now, come on, do something."

The pale grocer stepped forward and said:

"I have a suggestion to make. I sign his, he signs mine, and we both cross."

Somebody was about to cuff him, but the fat soldier, *who seemed to be the leader of the group*, intervened and remarked that it was a sensible idea.

"Lend me your back," said the grocer to Krug; and hastily unscrewing his fountain pen, he proceeded to press the paper against Krug's left shoulder blade. "What name shall I put, brothers?" he asked of the soldiers.

They shuffled and nudged each other, none of them willing to disclose a cherished incognito.

"Put Gurk," said the bravest at last, pointing to the fat soldier.

"Shall I?" asked the grocer, turning nimbly to Gurk.

They got his consent after a little coaxing. Having dealt with Krug's pass, the grocer in his turn stood before Krug.

Leapfrog, or the admiral in his cocked hat resting the telescope on the young sailor's shoulder (the gray horizon going
seesaw, a white gull veering, but no land in sight).

"I hope," said Krug, "that I will be able to do it as nicely
as I would if I had my glasses."

On the dotted line it will not be. Your pen is hard. Your
back is soft. Cucumber. Blot it with a branding iron.

Both papers were passed around and bashfully approved of.

Krug and the grocer started walking across the bridge; at
least Krug walked: his little companion expressed his delirious
joy by running in circles around Krug, he ran in widening
circles and imitated a railway engine: chug-chug, his elbows
pressed to his ribs, his feet moving almost together, taking
small firm staccato steps with knees slightly bent. Parody of a
child—*my* child.

"*Stoy, chort* [stop, curse you]," cried Krug, for the first time
that night using his real voice.

The grocer ended his gyrations by a spiral that brought him
back into Krug's orbit whereupon he fell in with the latter's
stride and walked beside him, chatting airily.

"I must apologize," he said, "for my demeanor. But I am
sure you feel the same as I do. This has been quite an ordeal.
I thought they would never let me go—and those allusions
to strangling and drowning were a bit tactless. Nice boys, I
admit, hearts of gold, but uncivilized—their only defect really.
Otherwise, I agree with you, they are grand. While I was
standing——"

This is the fourth lamppost, and one tenth of the bridge.
Few of them are alight.

". . . My brother who is practically stone deaf has a store
on Theod—sorry, Emrald Avenue. In fact we are partners, but
I have a little business of my own which keeps me away most
of the time. In view of the present events he needs my help,
as we all do. You might think——"

Lamppost number ten.

". . . but I look at it this way. Of course our Ruler is a
great man, a genius, a one-man-in-a-century-man. The kind
of boss people like you and me have been always wanting. But
he is bitter. He is bitter because for the last ten years our so-
called liberal government has kept hounding him, torturing

him, clapping him into jail for every word he said. I shall always remember—and shall pass it on to our grandsons—what he said that time they arrested him at the big meeting in the Godeon: I, he said, am born to lead as naturally as a bird flies. I think it is the greatest thought ever expressed in human language, and the most poetical one. Name me the writer who has said anything approaching it? I shall go even further and say——"

This is number fifteen. Or sixteen?

". . . if we look at it from another angle. We are quiet people, we want a quiet life, we want our business to go on smoothly. We want the quiet pleasures of life. For instance, everybody knows that the best moment of the day is when one comes back from work, unbuttons one's vest, turns on some light music, and sits in one's favorite armchair, enjoying the jokes in the evening paper or discussing one's neighbors with the little woman. That is what we mean by true culture, true human civilization, the things for the sake of which so much blood and ink have been shed in ancient Rome or Egypt. But nowadays you continuously hear silly people say that for the likes of you and me that kind of life has gone. Do not believe them—it has not. And not only has it not gone——"

Are there more than forty? This must be at least half of the bridge.

". . . shall I tell you what has really been going on all those years? Well, firstly, we were made to pay impossible taxes; secondly, all those Parliament members and Ministers of State whom we never saw or heard, kept drinking more and more champagne and sleeping with fatter and fatter whores. That is what they call liberty! And what happened in the meantime? Somewhere deep in the woods, in a log cabin, the Ruler was writing his manifestoes, like a tracked beast. The things they did to his followers! Jesus! I have heard dreadful stories from my brother-in-law who has belonged to the party since his youth. He is certainly the brainiest man I have ever met. So you see——"

No, less than half.

". . . you are a professor I understand. Well, Professor, from now on a great future lies before you. We must now

educate the ignorant, the moody, the wicked—but educate
them in a new way. Just think of all the trash we used to be
taught. . . . Think of the millions of unnecessary books accumulating in libraries. The books they print! You know—
you will never believe me—but I have been told by a reliable
person that in one bookshop there actually is a book of at
least a hundred pages which is wholly devoted to the anatomy
of bedbugs. Or things in foreign languages which nobody can
read. And all the money spent on nonsense. All those huge
museums—just one long hoax. Make you gape at a stone that
somebody picked up in his backyard. Less books and more
commonsense—that's my motto. People are made to live together, to do business with one another, to talk, to sing songs
together, to meet in clubs and stores, and at street corners—
and in churches and stadiums on Sundays—and not sit alone,
thinking dangerous thoughts. My wife had a lodger——"

The man with the velvet collar and his girl passed by quickly
with a pit-a-pat of fugitive footfalls, not looking back.

". . . change it all. You will teach young people to count,
to spell, to tie a parcel, to be tidy and polite, to take a bath
every Saturday, to speak to prospective buyers—oh, thousands
of necessary things, all the things that make sense to all people
alike. I wish I was a teacher myself. Because I maintain that
every man, no matter how humble, the last gaberloon, the
last——"

If all were alight I should not have got so confused.

". . . for which I paid a ridiculous fine. And now? Now it
is the State that will help me along with my business. It will
be there to control my earnings—and what does that mean?
It means that my brother-in-law who belongs to the party and
now sits in a big office, if you please, at a big glass-topped
writing desk, will help me in every possible way to get my
accounts straight: I shall make much more than I ever did
because from now on we all belong to one happy community.
It is all in the family now—one huge family, all linked up, all
snug and no questions asked. Because every man has some
kind of relative in the party. My sister says how sorry she is
that our old father is no more, he who was so afraid of bloodshed. Greatly exaggerated. What I say is the sooner we shoot

the smart fellows who raise hell because a few dirty anti-Ekwilists at last got what was coming to them——"

This is the end of the bridge. And lo—there is no one to greet us.

Krug was perfectly right. The south side guards had deserted their post and only the shadow of Neptune's twin brother, a compact shadow that looked like a sentinel but was not one, remained as a reminder of those that had gone. True, some paces ahead, on the embankment, three or four, possibly uniformed, men, smoking two or three glowing cigarettes, relaxed on a bench while a seven-stringed amorandola was being discreetly, romantically thumbed in the dark, but they did not challenge Krug and his delightful companion, nor indeed pay any attention to them as the two passed.

3

H E ENTERED the elevator which greeted him with the small sound he knew, half stamp, half shiver, and its features lit up. He pressed the third button. The brittle, thin-walled, old-fashioned little room blinked but did not move. He pressed again. Again the blink, the uneasy stillness, the inscrutable stare of a thing that does not work and knows it will not. He walked out. And at once, with an optical snap, the lift closed its bright brown eyes. He went up the neglected but dignified stairs.

Krug, a hunchback for the nonce, inserted his latchkey and slowly reverting to normal stature stepped into the hollow, humming, rumbling, rolling, roaring silence of his flat. Alone, a mezzotint of the Da Vinci miracle—thirteen persons at such a narrow table (crockery lent by the Dominican monks) stayed aloof. The lightning struck her stubby tortoise-shell-handled umbrella as it leant away from his own gamp, which was spared. He took off the one glove he had on, disposed of his overcoat and hung up his wide-brimmed black felt hat. His wide-brimmed black hat, no longer feeling at home, fell off the peg and was left lying there.

He walked down the long passage on the walls of which black oil paintings, the overflow from his study, showed nothing but cracks in the blindly reflected light. A rubber ball the size of a large orange was asleep on the floor.

He entered the dining room. A plate of cold tongue garnished with cucumber slices and the painted cheek of a cheese were quietly expecting him.

The woman had a remarkable ear. She slipped out of her room next to the nursery and joined Krug. Her name was Claudina and for the last week or so she had been the sole servant in Krug's household: the male cook had left, disapproving of what he had neatly described as its "subversive atmosphere."

"Thank goodness," she said, "you have come safely home. Would you like some hot tea?"

He shook his head, turning his back to her, groping in the

vicinity of the sideboard as if he were looking for something.

"How is madame tonight?" she asked.

Not answering, in the same slow blundering fashion, he made for the Turkish sitting room which nobody used and, traversing it, reached another bend of the passage. There he opened a closet, lifted the lid of an empty trunk, looked inside and then came back.

Claudina was standing quite still in the middle of the dining room where he had left her. She had been in the family for several years and, as conventionally happens in such cases, was pleasantly plump, middle-aged, and sensitive. There she stood staring at him with dark liquid eyes, her mouth slightly opened showing a gold spotted tooth, her coral earrings staring too and one hand pressed to her formless gray-worsted bosom.

"I want you to do something for me," said Krug. "Tomorrow I am taking the child to the country for a few days and while I am away will you please collect all her dresses and put them into the empty black trunk. Also her personal affairs, the umbrella and such things. Put it all, please, into the closet and lock it up. Anything you find. The trunk may be too small——"

He wandered out of the room without looking at her, was about to inspect another closet but thought better of it, turned on his heel and then automatically switched into tiptoe gear as he approached the nursery. There at the white door he stopped and the thumping of his heart was suddenly interrupted by his little son's special bedroom voice, detached and courteous, employed by David with graceful precision to notify his parents (when they returned, say, from a dinner in town) that he was still awake and ready to receive anybody who would like to wish him a second good night.

This was bound to happen. Only a quarter past ten. I thought the night was almost over. Krug closed his eyes for a moment, then went in.

He distinguished a rapid dim tumbling movement of bedclothes; the switch of a bed lamp clicked and the boy sat up, shielding his eyes. At that age (eight) children cannot be said to smile in any settled way. The smile is not localized; it is diffused throughout the whole frame—if the child is happy of course. This child was still a happy child. Krug said the conventional thing about time and sleep. No sooner had he said it than a fierce rush of rough tears started from the bottom of his chest, made for his throat, was stopped by inferior forces, remained in wait, maneuvering in black depths, getting ready for another leap. *Pourvu qu'il ne pose pas la question atroce.* I pray thee, local deity.

"Have they been shooting at you?" David asked.

"What nonsense," he said. "Nobody shoots at night."

"But they have. I heard the pops. Look, here's a new way of wearing pajamas."

He stood up nimbly, spreading his arms, balancing on small powdery-white, blue-veined feet that seemed to cling monkeywise to the disarranged linen on the dimpled creaking mattress. Blue pants, pale-green vest (the woman must be color-blind).

"I dropped the right ones into my bath," he explained cheerfully.

Possibilities of buoyancy exerted a sudden attraction, and with the collaboration of popping sounds he jumped, once, twice, three times, higher, higher—then from a dizzy suspension fell down on his knees, rolled over, stood up again on the tossed bed, tottering, swaying.

"Lie down, lie down," said Krug, "it is getting very late. I must go now. Come, lie down. Quick."

(He may not ask.)

He fell this time on his bottom and, fumbling with incurved toes got them under the blanket, between blanket and sheet, laughed, got them right this time, and Krug rapidly tucked him in.

"There has been no story tonight," said David, lying quite flat, his own long upper lashes sweeping up, his elbows thrown back and resting like wings on both sides of his head on the pillow.

"I shall tell you a double one tomorrow."

As he bent over the child, Krug was held at arm's length for a moment, both looking into each other's faces: the child hurriedly trying hard to think up something to ask in order to gain time, the father frantically praying that one particular question would not be asked. How tender the skin looked in its bedtime glory, with a touch of the palest violet above the eyes and with that golden bloom on the forehead, below the thick ruffled fringe of golden brown hair. The perfection of nonhuman creatures—birds, young dogs, moths asleep, colts—and these little mammals. A combination of three tiny brown spots, birthmarks on the faintly flushed cheek near the nose recalled some combination he had seen, touched, taken in recently—what was it? The parapet.

He quickly kissed them, turned off the light and went out. Thank God, it has not been asked—he thought as he closed the door. But, as he gently released the handle, there it came, high-pitched, brightly remembered.

"Soon," he replied. "As soon as the doctor tells her she can. Sleep. I beg you."

At least a merciful door was between him and me.

In the dining room, on a chair near the sideboard, Claudina sat crying lustily into a paper napkin. Krug settled down to his meal, dispatched it in haste, briskly handling the unnecessary pepper and salt, clearing his throat, moving plates, dropping a fork and catching it on his instep, while she sobbed intermittently.

"Please, go to your room," he said at last. "The child is not asleep. Call me at seven tomorrow. Mr. Ember will probably attend to the arrangements tomorrow. I shall leave with the child as early as possible."

"But it's so sudden," she moaned. "You said yesterday—Oh, it ought not to have happened like this!"

"And I shall wring your neck," added Krug, "if you breathe one blessed word to the child."

He pushed away his plate, went to his study, locked the door.

Ember might be out. The telephone might not work. But from the feel of the receiver as he took it up he knew the faithful instrument was alive. I could never remember Ember's number. Here is the back of the telephone book on which we used to jot down names and figures, our hands mixed, slanting and curving in opposite directions. Her concavity fitting my convexity exactly. Extraordinary—I am able to make out the shadow of eyelashes on a child's cheek but fail to decipher my own handwriting. He found his spare glasses and then the

familiar number with the 6 in the middle resembling Ember's Persian nose, and Ember put down his pen, removed the
long amber cigarette-holder from his thickly pursed lips and
listened.

"I was in the middle of this letter when Krug rang up and
told me a terrible thing. Poor Olga is no more. She died today
following an operation of the kidney. I had gone to see her
at the hospital last Tuesday and she was as sweet as ever and
admired so much the really lovely orchids I had brought her;
there was no real danger in sight—or if there was, the doctors
did not tell him. I have registered the shock but cannot ana-
lyze yet the impact of the news. I shall probably not be able
to sleep for several nights. My own tribulations, all those petty
theatrical intrigues I have just described, will, I am afraid,
seem as trivial to you as they now seem to me.

"At first I was struck by the unpardonable thought that he
was delivering himself of a monstrous joke like the time he
read backwards from end to beginning that lecture on space
to find out whether his students would react in any manner.
They did not, nor do I for the moment. You will see him
probably before you receive this muddled epistle: he is going
tomorrow to the Lakes with his poor little boy. It is a wise
decision. The future is not too clear but I suppose the University will resume its functions before long, though of course
nobody knows what sudden changes may occur. Of late there
have been some appalling rumors; the only newspaper I read
has not come for at least a fortnight. He asked me to take
care of the cremation tomorrow, and I wonder what people
will think when he does not turn up; but of course his attitude
towards death prevents his going to the ceremony though it
will be as brief and formal as I can possibly make it—if only
Olga's family does not intrude. Poor dear fellow—she was a
brilliant helper to him in his brilliant career. In normal times,
I suppose, I would be supplying her picture to American
newspapermen."

Ember put down his pen again and sat lost in thought. He
too had participated in that brilliant career. An obscure
scholar, a translator of Shakespeare in whose green, damp
country he had spent his studious youth—he innocently
shambled into the limelight when a publisher asked him to

apply the reverse process to the *Komparatiwn Stuhdar en Sophistat tuen Pekrekh* or, as the title of the American edition had it, a little more snappily, *The Philosophy of Sin* (banned in four states and a best seller in the rest). What a strange trick of chance—this masterpiece of esoteric thought endearing itself at once to the middle-class reader and competing for first honors during one season with that robust satire *Straight Flush*, and then, next year, with Elisabeth Ducharme's romance of Dixieland, *When the Train Passes*, and for twenty-nine days (leap year) with the book club selection *Through Towns and Villages*, and for two consecutive years with that remarkable cross between a certain kind of wafer and a lollipop, Louis Sontag's *Annunciata*, which started so well in the Caves of St. Barthelemy and ended in the funnies.

In the beginning, Krug, although professing to be amused, was greatly annoyed by the whole business, while Ember felt abashed and apologetic and covertly wondered whether perhaps his particular brand of rich synthetic English had contained some outlandish ingredient, some dreadful additional spice that might account for the unexpected excitement; but with a greater perspicacity than the two puzzled scholars showed, Olga prepared herself to enjoy thoroughly, for years to come, the success of a work whose very special points she knew better than its ephemeral reviewers could know. She it was who made the horrified Ember persuade Krug to go on that American lecture tour, as if she foresaw that its plangent reverberations would win him at home the esteem which his work in its native garb had neither wrung from academic stolidity nor induced in the comatose mass of amorphous readerdom. Not that the trip itself had been displeasing. Far from it. Although Krug, being as usual chary of squandering in idle conversation such experiences as might undergo unpredictable metamorphoses later on (if left to pupate quietly in the alluvium of the mind), had spoken little of his tour, Olga had managed to recompose it in full and to relay it gleefully to Ember who had vaguely expected a flow of sarcastic disgust. "Disgust?" cried Olga. "Why, he has known enough of that here. Disgust, indeed! Elation, delight, a quickening of the imagination, a disinfection of the mind, *togliwn ochnat divodiv* [the daily surprise of awakening]!"

"Landscapes as yet unpolluted with conventional poetry, and life, that self-conscious stranger, being slapped on the back and told to relax." He had written this upon his return, and Olga, with devilish relish, had pasted into a shagreen album indigenous allusions to the most original thinker of our times. Ember evoked her ample being, her thirty-seven resplendent years, the bright hair, the full lips, the heavy chin which went so well with the cooing undertones of her voice—something ventriloquial about her, a continuous soliloquy following in willowed shade the meanderings of her actual speech. He saw Krug, the ponderous dandruffed maestro, sitting there with a satisfied and sly smile on his big swarthy face (recalling that of Beethoven in the general correlation of its rugged features)—yes, lolling in that old rose armchair while Olga buoyantly took charge of the conversation—and how vividly one remembered the way she had of letting a sentence bounce and ripple over the three quick bites she took at the raisin cake she held, and the brisk triple splash of her plump hand over the sudden stretch of her lap as she brushed the crumbs away and went on with her story. Almost extravagantly healthy, a regular *radabarbára* [full-blown handsome woman]: those wide radiant eyes, that flaming cheek to which she would press the cool back of her hand, that shining white forehead with a whiter scar—the consequence of an automobile accident in the gloomy Lagodan mountains of legendary fame. Ember could not see how one might dispose of the recollection of such a life, the insurrection of such a widowhood. With her small feet and large hips, with her girlish speech and her matronly bosom, with her bright wits and the torrents of tears she shed that night, while dripping with blood herself, over the crippled crying doe that had rushed into the blinding lights of the car, with all this and with many other things that Ember knew he could not know, she would lie now, a pinch of blue dust in her cold columbarium.

He had liked her enormously, and he loved Krug with the same passion that a big sleek long-flewed hound feels for the high-booted hunter who reeks of the marsh as he leans towards the red fire. Krug could take aim at a flock of the most popular and sublime human thoughts and bring down a wild goose any time. But he could not kill death.

Ember hesitated, then dialed fluently. The line was engaged. That sequence of small bar-shaped hoots was like the long vertical row of superimposed I's in an index by first lines to a verse anthology. I am a lake. I am a tongue. I am a spirit. I am fevered. I am not covetous. I am the Dark Cavalier. I am the torch. I arise. I ask. I blow. I bring. I cannot change. I cannot look. I climb the hill. I come. I dream. I envy. I found. I heard. I intended an Ode. I know. I love. I must not grieve, my love. I never. I pant. I remember. I saw thee once. I traveled. I wandered. I will. I will. I will. I will.

He thought of going out to mail his letter as bachelors are wont to do around eleven o'clock at night. He hoped a timely aspirin tablet had nipped his cold in the bud. The unfinished translation of his favorite lines in Shakespeare's greatest play—

> follow the perttaunt jauncing 'neath the rack
> with her pale skeins-mate.

crept up tentatively but it would not scan because in his native tongue "rack" was anapaestic. Like pulling a grand piano through a door. Take it to pieces. Or turn the corner into the next line. But the berth there was taken, the table was reserved, the line was engaged.

It was not now.

"I thought perhaps you might like me to come. We might play chess or something. I mean, tell me frankly——"

"I would," said Krug. "But I have had an unexpected call from—well, an unexpected call. They want me to come immediately. They call it an emergency session—I don't know—important, they say. All rubbish, of course, but as I can neither work nor sleep, I thought I might go."

"Had you any trouble in getting home tonight?"

"I am afraid I was drunk. I broke my glasses. They are sending——"

"Is it what you alluded to the other day?"

"No. Yes. No—I do not remember. *Ce sont mes collègues et le vieux et tout le trimbala.* They are sending a car for me in a few minutes."

"I see. Do you think——"

"You will be at the hospital as early as possible, won't you?—At nine, at eight, even earlier. . . ."

"Yes, of course."

"I told the maid—and perhaps you will look into the matter too when I am gone—I told her——"

Krug heaved horribly, could not finish—crushed down the receiver. His study was unusually cold. All of them so blind and sooty, and hung up so high above the bookshelves, that he could hardly make out the cracked complexion of an up-turned face under a rudimentary halo or the jigsaw indentures of a martyr's parchmentlike robe dissolving into grimy black-ness. A deal table in one corner supported loads of unbound volumes of the *Revue de Psychologie* bought secondhand, crabbed 1879 turning into plump 1880, their dead-leaf covers frayed or crumpled at the edges and almost cut through by the crisscross string eating its way into their dusty bulk. Re-sults of the pact never to dust, never to unmake the room. A comfortable hideous bronze stand lamp with a thick glass shade of lumpy garnet and amethyst portions set in asym-metrical interspaces between bronze veins had grown to a great height, like some enormous weed, from the old blue carpet beside the striped sofa where Krug will lie tonight. The spontaneous generation of unanswered letters, reprints, uni-versity bulletins, disemboweled envelopes, paper clips, pencils in various stages of development littered the desk. Gregoire, a huge stag beetle wrought of pig iron which had been used by his grandfather to pull off by the heel (hungrily gripped by these burnished mandibles) first one riding boot, then the other, peered, unloved, from under the leathern fringe of a leathern armchair. The only pure thing in the room was a copy of Chardin's "House of Cards," which she had once placed over the mantelpiece (to ozonize your dreadful lair, she had said)—the conspicuous cards, the flushed faces, the lovely brown background.

He walked down the passage again, listened to the rhyth-mic silence in the nursery—and Claudina again slipped out of the adjacent room. He told her he was going out and asked her to make his bed on the divan in the study. Then he picked up his hat from the floor and went downstairs to wait for the car.

It was cold outside and he regretted not having refilled his flask with that brandy which had helped him to live through the day. It was also very quiet—quieter than usual. The old-fashioned genteel house fronts across the cobbled lane had extinguished most of their lights. A man he knew, a former Member of Parliament, a mild bore who used to take out his two polite paletoted dachshunds at nightfall, had been removed a couple of days before from number fifty in a motor truck already crammed with other prisoners. Obviously the Toad had decided to make his revolution as conventional as possible. The car was late.

He had been told by University President Azureus that a Dr. Alexander, Assistant Lecturer in Biodynamics, whom Krug had never met, would come to fetch him. The man Alexander had been collecting people all evening and the President had been trying to get in touch with Krug since the early afternoon. A peppy, dynamic, efficient gentleman, Dr. Alexander—one of those people who in times of disaster emerge from dull obscurity to blossom forth suddenly with permits, passes, coupons, cars, connections, lists of addresses. The University bigwigs had crumpled up helplessly, and of course no such gathering would have been possible had not a perfect organizer been evolved from the periphery of their species by a happy mutation which almost suggested the discreet intermediation of a transcendental force. One could distinguish in the dubious light the emblem (bearing a remarkable resemblance to a crushed dislocated but still writhing spider) of the new government upon a red flaglet affixed to the bonnet, when the officially sanctioned car obtained by the magician in our midst drew up at the curb which it grazed with a purposeful tire.

Krug seated himself beside the driver, who was none other than Dr. Alexander himself, a pink-faced, very blond, very well-groomed man in his thirties, with a pheasant's feather in his nice green hat and a heavy opal ring on his fourth finger. His hands were very white and soft, and lay lightly on the steering wheel. Of the two (?) persons in the back Krug recognized Edmond Beuret, the Professor of French literature.

"Bonsoir, cher collègue," said Beuret. *"On m'a tiré du lit au grand désespoir de ma femme. Comment va la vôtre?"*

"A few days ago," said Krug, "I had the pleasure of reading your article on—" (he could not recall the name of that

French general, an honest if somewhat limited historical figure
who had been driven to suicide by slanderous politicians).

"Yes," said Beuret, "it did me good to write it. *'Les morts,
les pauvres morts ont de grandes douleurs.—Et quand Octobre
souffle'*——"

Dr. Alexander turned the wheel very gently and spoke without looking at Krug, then giving him a rapid glance, then
looking again straight ahead:

"I understand, Professor, that you are going to be our
savior tonight. The fate of our Alma Mater lies in good
hands."

Krug grunted noncommittally. He had not the vaguest—or
was it a veiled allusion to the fact that the Ruler, colloquially
known as the Toad, had been a schoolmate of his—but that
would have been too silly.

The car was stopped in the middle of Skotoma (ex Liberty,
ex Imperial) Place by three soldiers, two policemen, and the
raised hand of poor Theodor the Third who permanently
wanted a lift or to go to a smaller place, teacher; but they
were motioned by Dr. Alexander to look at the little red
and black flag—whereupon they saluted and retired into the
darkness.

The streets were deserted as usually happens in the gaps of
history, in the *terrains vagues* of time. Taken all in all the only
live creature encountered was a young man going home from
an ill-timed and apparently badly truncated fancy ball: he was
dressed up as a Russian mujik—embroidered shirt spreading
freely from under a tasseled sash, *culotte bouffante*, soft crimson boots, and wrist watch.

"On va lui torcher le derrière, à ce gaillard-là," remarked
Professor Beuret grimly. The other—anonymous—person in
the back seat, muttered something inaudible and replied to
himself in an affirmative but likewise inarticulate way.

"I cannot drive much faster," said Dr. Alexander steadily
looking ahead, "because the wrestle-cap of the lower slammer
is what they call muckling. If you will put your hand into my
right-hand pocket, Professor, you will find some cigarettes."

"I am a nonsmoker," said Krug. "And anyway I do not
believe there are any there."

They drove on for some time in silence.

"Why?" asked Dr. Alexander, gently treading, gently releasing.

"A passing thought," said Krug.

Discreetly the gentle driver allowed one hand to leave the wheel and grope, then the other. Then, after a moment, the right one again.

"I must have mislaid them," he said after another minute of silence. "And you, Professor, are not only a nonsmoker—and not only a man of genius, everybody knows that, but also (quick glance) an exceedingly lucky gambler."

"Eez eet zee verity," said Beuret, suddenly shifting to English, which he knew Krug understood, and speaking it like a Frenchman in an English book, "eez eet zee verity zat, as I have been informed by zee reliable sources, zee disposed *chef* of the state has been captured together with a couple of other blokes (when the author gets bored by the process—or forgets) somewhere in the hills—and shot? But no, I ziss cannot credit—eet eez too orrible" (when the author remembers again).

"Probably a slight exaggeration," observed Dr. Alexander in the vernacular. "Various kinds of ugly rumors are apt to spread nowadays, and although of course *domusta barbarn kapusta* [the ugliest wives are the truest], still I do not think that in this particular case," he trailed off with a pleasant laugh and there was another silence.

O my strange native town! Your narrow lanes where the Roman once passed dream in the night of other things than do the evanescent creatures that tread your stones. O you strange town! Your every stone holds as many old memories as there are motes of dust. Every one of your gray quiet stones has seen a witch's long hair catch fire, a pale astronomer mobbed, a beggar kicked in the groin by another beggar— and the King's horses struck sparks from you, and the dandies in brown and the poets in black repaired to the coffee houses while you dripped with slops to the merry echoes of gardyloo. Town of dreams, a changing dream, O you, stone changeling. The little shops all shuttered in the clean night, the gaunt walls, the niche shared by the homeless pigeon with a sculptured churchman, the rose window, the exuded gargoyle, the jester who slapped Christ—lifeless carvings and dim life

mingling their feathers. . . . Not for the wheels of oil-
maddened engines were your narrow and rough streets designed—and as the car stopped at last and bulky Beuret
crawled out in the wake of his beard, the anonymous muser
who had been sitting beside him was observed to split into
two, producing by sudden gemination Gleeman, the frail Professor of Medieval Poetry, and the equally diminutive Yanovsky, who taught Slavic scansion—two newborn homunculi
now drying on the paleolithic pavement.

"I shall lock the car and follow you presently," said Dr.
Alexander with a little cough.

An Italianate mendicant in picturesque rags who had over-
done it by having an especially dramatic hole in the one place
which normally would never have had any—the bottom of his
expectant hat—stood, shaking diligently with the ague in the
lamplight at the front door. Three consecutive coppers fell—
and are still falling. Four silent professors flocked up the rococo stairs.

But they did not have to ring or knock or anything for the
door on the topmost landing was flung open to greet them
by the prodigious Dr. Alexander who was there already, having zoomed perhaps, up some special backstairs, or by means
of those nonstop things as when I used to rise from the
twinned night of the Keeweenawatin and the horrors of the
Laurentian Revolution, through the ghoul-haunted Province
of Perm, through Early Recent, Slightly Recent, Not So Recent, Quite Recent, Most Recent—warm, warm!—up to *my*
room number on *my* hotel floor in a remote country, up, up,
in one of those express elevators manned by the delicate
hands—my own in a negative picture—of dark-skinned men
with sinking stomachs and rising hearts, never attaining Paradise, which is not a roof garden; and from the depths of the
stag-headed hall old President Azureus came at a quick pace,
his arms open, his faded blue eyes beaming in advance, his
long wrinkled upper lip quivering——

"Yes, of course—how stupid of me," thought Krug, the
circle in Krug, one Krug in another one.

4

OLD Azureus's manner of welcoming people was a silent rhapsody. Ecstatically beaming, slowly, tenderly, he would take your hand between his soft palms, hold it thus as if it were a long sought treasure or a sparrow all fluff and heart, in moist silence, peering at you the while with his beaming wrinkles rather than with his eyes, and then, very slowly, the silvery smile would start to dissolve, the tender old hands would gradually release their hold, a blank expression replace the fervent light of his pale fragile face, and he would leave you as if he had made a mistake, as if after all you were not the loved one—the loved one whom, the next moment, he would espy in another corner, and again the smile would dawn, again the hands would enfold the sparrow, again it would all dissolve.

A score of prominent representatives of the University, some of them Dr. Alexander's recent passengers, were standing or sitting in the spacious, more or less glittering drawing-room (not all the lamps were lit under the green cumuli and cherubs of its ceiling) and perhaps half a dozen more co-existed in the adjacent *mussikisha* [music room], for the old gentleman was a mediocre harpist *à ses heures* and liked to fix up trios, with himself as the hypotenuse, or have some very great musician do things to the piano, after which the very small and not overabundant sandwiches and some triangled *bouchées*, which, he fondly believed had a special charm of their own due to their shape, were passed around by two maids and his unmarried daughter, who smelt vaguely of eau de Cologne and distinctly of sweat. Tonight, in lieu of these dainties, there were tea and hard biscuits; and a tortoise-shell cat (stroked alternately by the Professor of Chemistry, and Hedron, the Mathematician) lay on the dark-shining Bechstein. At the dry-leaf touch of Gleeman's electric hand, the cat rose like boiling milk and proceeded to purr intensely; but the little medievalist was absent-minded and wandered away. Economics, Divinity, and Modern History stood talking near one of the heavily draped windows. A thin but virulent draught was perceptible in spite of the drapery. Dr. Alexander had sat down at a small table, had carefully removed to its north-western corner the articles upon it (a glass ashtray, a porcelain donkey with paniers for matches, a box made to mimic a book) and was going through a list of names, crossing out some of them by means of an incredibly sharp pencil. The President hovered over him in a mixed state of curiosity and concern. Now and then Dr. Alexander would stop to ponder, his unoccupied hand cautiously stroking the sleek fair hair at the back of his head.

"What about Rufel?" (Political Science) asked the President. "Could you not get him?"

"Not available," replied Dr. Alexander. "Apparently arrested. For his own safety, I am told."

"Let us hope so," said old Azureus thoughtfully. "Well, no matter. I suppose we may start."

Edmond Beuret, rolling his big brown eyes, was telling a phlegmatic fat person (Drama) of the bizarre sight he had witnessed.

"Oh, yes," said Drama. "Art students. I know all about it."

"Ils ont du toupet pourtant," said Beuret.

"Or merely obstinacy. When young people cling to tradition they do so with as much passion as the riper man shows when demolishing it. They broke into the *Klumba* [Pigeon Hole—a well-known theater] since all the dancing halls proved closed. Perseverance."

"I hear that the *Parlamint* and the *Zud* [Court of Justice] are still burning," said another Professor.

"You hear wrongly," said Drama, "because we are not talking of that, but of the sad case of history encroaching upon an annual ball. They found a provision of candles and danced on the stage," he went on, turning again to Beuret, who stood with his stomach protruding and both hands thrust deep into his trouser pockets. "Before an empty house. A picture which has a few nice shadows."

"I think we may start," said the President, coming up to them and then passing through Beuret like a moonbeam, to notify another group.

"Then it is admirable," said Beuret, as he suddenly saw the thing in a different light. "I do hope the *pauvres gosses* had some fun."

"The police," said Drama, "dispersed them about an hour ago. But I presume it was exciting while it lasted."

"I think we may start in a moment," said the President confidently, as he drifted past them again. His smile gone long ago, his shoes faintly creaking, he slipped in between Yanovksy and the Latinist and nodded yes to his daughter, who was showing him surreptitiously a bowl of apples through the door.

"I have heard from two sources (one was Beuret, the other Beuret's presumable informer)," said Yanovsky—and sank his voice so low that the Latinist had to bring down and lend him a white-fluffed ear.

"I have heard another version," the Latinist said, slowly unbending. "They were caught while attempting to cross the frontier. One of the Cabinet Ministers whose identity is not certain was executed on the spot, but (he subdued his voice as he named the former President of the State) . . . was brought back and imprisoned."

"No, no," said Yanovsky, "not Me Nisters. He all alone. Like King Lear."

"Yes, this will do nicely," said Dr. Azureus with sincere satisfaction to Dr. Alexander who had shifted some of the chairs and had brought in a few more, so that by magic the room had assumed the necessary poise.

The cat slid down from the piano and slowly walked out, on the way brushing for one mad instant against the pencil-striped trouser leg of Gleeman who was busy peeling a dark-red Bervok apple.

Orlik, the Zoologist, stood with his back to the company as he intently examined at various levels and from various angles the spines of books on the shelves beyond the piano, now and then pulling out one which showed no title—and hurriedly putting it back: they were all zwiebacks, all in German—German poetry. He was bored and had a huge noisy family at home.

"I disagree with you there—with both of you," the Professor of Modern History was saying. "My client never repeats herself. At least not when people are all agog to see the repetition coming. In fact, it is only unconsciously that Clio can repeat herself. Because her memory is too short. As with so many phenomena of time, recurrent combinations are perceptible as such only when they cannot affect us any more—when they are imprisoned so to speak in the past, which *is* the past just because it is disinfected. To try to map our tomorrows with the help of data supplied by our yesterdays means ignoring the basic element of the future which is its complete nonexistence. The giddy rush of the present into this vacuum is mistaken by us for a rational movement."

"Pure Krugism," murmured the Professor of Economics.

"To take an example"—continued the Historian without noticing the remark: "no doubt we can single out occasions in the past that parallel our own period, when the snowball of an idea has been rolled and rolled by the red hands of schoolboys and got bigger and bigger until it became a snowman in a crumpled top hat set askew and with a broom perfunctorily affixed to his armpit—and then suddenly the bogey eyes blinked, the snow turned to flesh, the broom became a weapon and a full-fledged tyrant beheaded the boys. Oh, yes, a parliament or a senate has been upset before, and it is not the first time that an obscure and unlovable but marvelously obstinate man has gnawed his way into the bowels of a country. But to those who watch these events and would like to ward them, the past offers no clues, no *modus vivendi*—for the simple reason that it had none itself when toppling over the brink of the present into the vacuum it eventually filled."

"If this be so," said the Professor of Divinity, "then we go back to the fatalism of inferior nations and disown the thousands of past occasions when the capacity to reason, and act accordingly, proved more beneficial than skepticism and submission would have been. Your academic distaste for applied history rather suggests its vulgar utility, my friend."

"Oh, I was not talking of submission or anything in that line. That is an ethical question for one's own conscience to solve. I was merely refuting your contention that history could predict what Paduk would say or do tomorrow. There can be no submission—because the very fact of our discussing these matters implies curiosity, and curiosity in its turn is insubordination in its purest form. Speaking of curiosity, can you explain the strange infatuation of our President for that pink-faced gentleman yonder—the kind gentleman who brought us here? What is his name, who is he?"

"One of Maler's assistants, I think; a laboratory worker or something like that," said Economics.

"And last term," said the Historian, "we saw a stuttering imbecile being mysteriously steered into the Chair of Paedology because he happened to play the indispensable contrabass. Anyhow the man must be a very Satan of persuasiveness considering that he has managed to get Krug to come here."

"Did he not use," asked the Professor of Divinity with a mild suggestion of slyness, "did he not use somewhere that simile of the snowball and the snowman's broom?"

"Who?" asked the Historian. "Who used it? That man?"

"No," said the Professor of Divinity. "The other. The one whom it was so hard to get. It is curious the way ideas he expressed ten years ago——"

They were interrupted by the President who stood in the middle of the room asking for attention and lightly clapping his hands.

The person whose name had just been mentioned, Professor Adam Krug, the philosopher, was seated somewhat apart from the rest, deep in a cretonned armchair, with his hairy hands on its arms. He was a big heavy man in his early forties, with untidy, dusty, or faintly grizzled locks and a roughly hewn face suggestive of the uncouth chess master or of the morose composer, but more intelligent. The strong compact dusky forehead had that peculiar hermetic aspect (a bank safe? a prison wall?) which the brows of thinkers possess. The brain consisted of water, various chemical compounds and a group of highly specialized fats. The pale steely eyes were half closed in their squarish orbits under the shaggy eyebrows which had protected them once from the poisonous droppings of extinct birds—Schneider's hypothesis. The ears were of goodly size with hair inside. Two deep folds of flesh diverged from the nose along the large cheeks. The morning had been shaveless. He wore a badly creased dark suit and a bow tie, always the same, hyssop violet with (pure white in the type, here Isabella) interneural macules and a crippled left hindwing. The not so recent collar was of the low open variety, i.e., with a comfortable triangular space for his namesake's apple. Thick-soled

shoes and old-fashioned black spats were the distinctive
characters of his feet. What else? Oh, yes—the absent-minded
beat of his forefinger against the arm of his chair.

Under this visible surface, a silk shirt enveloped his robust
torso and tired hips. It was tucked deep into his long under-
pants which in their turn were tucked into his socks: it was
rumored, he knew, that he wore none (hence the spats) but
that was not true; they were in fact nice expensive lavender
silk socks.

Under this was the warm white skin. Out of the dark an
ant trail, a narrow capillary caravan, went up the middle of his
abdomen to end at the brink of his navel; and a blacker and
denser growth was spread-eagled upon his chest.

Under this was a dead wife and a sleeping child.

The President bent his head over a rosewood bureau which
had been drawn by his assistant into a conspicuous position.
He put on his spectacles using one hand, shaking his silvery
head to get their bows into place, and proceeded to collect,
equate, tap-tap, the papers he had been counting. Dr. Alexander tiptoed into a far corner where he sat down on an introduced chair. The President put down his thick even batch
of typewritten sheets, removed his spectacles and, holding
them away from his right ear, began his preliminary speech.
Soon Krug became aware that he was a kind of focal center
in respect to the Argus-eyed room. He knew that except for
two people in the assembly, Hedron and, perhaps, Orlik, nobody really liked him. To each, or about each, of his colleagues he had said at one time or other, something . . .
something impossible to recall in this or that case and difficult
to define in general terms—some careless bright and harsh
trifle that had grazed a stretch of raw flesh. Unchallenged and
unsought, a plump pale pimply adolescent entered a dim classroom and looked at Adam who looked away.

"I have called you together, gentlemen, to inform you of
certain very grave circumstances, circumstances which it
would be foolish to ignore. As you know, our University has
been virtually closed since the end of last month. I have now
been given to understand that unless our intentions, our program and conduct are made clear to the Ruler, this organism, this old and beloved organism, will cease to function

altogether, and some other institution with some other staff
be established in its stead. In other words, the glorious edifice
which those bricklayers, Science and Administration, have
built stone by stone during centuries, will fall. . . . It will fall
because of our lack of initiative and tact. At the eleventh hour
a line of conduct has been planned which, I hope, may prevent
the disaster. Tomorrow it might have been too late.

"You all know how distasteful the spirit of compromise is
to me. But I do not think the gallant effort in which we shall
all join can be branded by that obnoxious term. Gentlemen!
When a man has lost a beloved wife, when an animal has lost
his feet in the aging ocean; when a great executive sees the
work of his life shattered to bits—he regrets. He regrets too
late. So let us not by our own fault place ourselves in the
position of the bereaved lover, of the admiral whose fleet is
lost in the raging waves, of the bankrupt administrator—let
us take our fate like a flaming torch into both hands.

"First of all, I shall read you a short memorandum—a kind
of manifesto if you wish—which is to be submitted to the
Government and duly published . . . and here comes the second point I wish to raise—a point which some of you have
already guessed. In our midst we have a man . . . a great man
let me add, who by a singular coincidence happened in by-
gone days to be the schoolmate of another great man, the
man who leads our State. Whatever political opinions we
hold—and during my long life I have shared most of them—
it cannot be denied that a government is a government and
as such cannot be expected to suffer a tactless demonstration
of unprovoked dissension or indifference. What seemed to us
a mere trifle, the mere snowball of a transient political creed
gathering no moss, has assumed enormous proportions, has
become a flaming banner while we were blissfully slumbering
in the security of our vast libraries and expensive laboratories.
Now we are awake. The awakening is rough, I admit, but
perhaps this is not solely the fault of the bugler. I trust that
the delicate task of wording this . . . this that has been prepared . . . this historical paper which we all will promptly
sign, has been accomplished with a deep sense of the enormous importance this task presents. I trust too that Adam
Krug will recall his happy schooldays and carry this document

in person to the Ruler, who, I know, will appreciate greatly
the visit of a beloved and world-famous former playmate, and
thus will lend a kinder ear to our sorry plight and good res-
olutions than he would if this miraculous coincidence had not
been granted us. Adam Krug, will you save us?''

Tears stood in the old man's eyes and his voice had trembled while uttering this dramatic appeal. A page of foolscap
skimmed off the table and gently settled on the green roses
of the carpet. Dr. Alexander noiselessly walked over to it and
restored it to the desk. Orlik, the old zoologist, opened a little
book lying next to him and discovered that it was an empty
box with a lone pink peppermint on the bottom.

"You are the victim of a sentimental delusion, my dear
Azureus," said Krug. "What I and the Toad hoard *en fait de
souvenirs d'enfance* is the habit I had of sitting upon his face."

There was a sudden crash of wood against wood. The
zoologist had looked up and at the same time put down
Buxum biblioformis with too much force. A hush followed.
Dr. Azureus slowly sat down and said in a changed voice:

"I do not quite follow you, Professor. I do not know who
the . . . whom the word or name you used refers to and—
what you mean by recalling that singular game—probably
some childish tussle . . . lawn tennis or something like that."

"Toad was his nickname," said Krug. "And it is doubtful
whether you would call it lawn tennis—or even leapfrog for
that matter. *He* did not. I was something of a bully, I am
afraid, and I used to trip him up and sit upon his face—a kind
of rest cure."

"Please, my dear Krug, please," said the President, wincing.
"This is in questionable taste. You were boys at school, and
boys will be boys, and I am sure you have many enjoyable
memories in common—discussing lessons or talking of your
grand plans for the future as boys will do——"

"I sat upon his face," said Krug stolidly, "every blessed day
for about five school years—which makes, I suppose, about a
thousand sittings."

Some looked at their feet, others at their hands, others
again got busy with cigarettes. The zoologist, after showing a
momentary interest in the proceedings, turned to a newfound

bookcase. Dr. Alexander negligently avoided the shifting eye of old Azureus, who apparently was seeking help in that unexpected quarter.

"The details of the ritual," continued Krug—but was interrupted by the ching-ching of a little cowbell, a Swiss trinket that the old man's desperate hand had found on the bureau.

"All this is quite irrelevant," cried the President. "I really must call you to order, my dear colleague. We have wandered away from the main——"

"But look here," said Krug. "Really, I have not said anything dreadful, have I? I do not suggest for instance that the present face of the Toad retains after twenty-five years the immortal imprint of my weight. In those days, although thinner than I am now——"

The President had slipped out of his chair and fairly ran towards Krug.

"I have remembered," he said with a catch in his voice, "something I wanted to tell you—most important—*sub rosa* —will you please come with me into the next room for a minute?"

"All right," said Krug, heaving out of his armchair.

The next room was the President's study. Its tall clock had stopped at a quarter past six. Krug calculated rapidly, and the blackness inside him sucked at his heart. Why am I here? Shall I go home? Shall I stay?

". . . My dear friend, you know well my esteem for you. But you are a dreamer, a thinker. You do not realize the circumstances. You say impossible, unmentionable things. Whatever we think of—of that person, we must keep it to ourselves. We are in deathly danger. You are jeopardizing the—everything. . . ."

Dr. Alexander, whose courtesy, assistance and *savoir-vivre* were really supreme, slipped in with an ash tray which he placed at Krug's elbow.

"In that case," said Krug, ignoring the redundant article, "I have to note with regret that the tact you mentioned was but its helpless shadow—namely an afterthought. You ought to have warned me, you know, that for reasons I still cannot fathom you intended to ask me to visit the——"

"Yes, to visit the Ruler," interpolated Azureus hurriedly. "I am sure that when you take cognizance of the manifesto, the reading of which has been so unexpectedly postponed——"

The clock began striking. For Dr. Alexander, who was an expert in such matters and a methodical man, had not been able to curb the tinkerer's instinct and was now standing on a chair and pawing the danglers and the naked face. His ear and dynamic profile were reflected in pink pastel by the opened glass door of the clock.

"I think I prefer going home," said Krug.

"Stay, I implore you. We shall now quickly read and sign that really historical document. And you must agree, you must be the messenger, you must be the dove——"

"Confound that clock," said Krug. "Can't you stop its striking, man? You seem to confuse the olive branch with the fig leaf," he went on, turning again to the President. "But this is neither here nor there, since for the life of me——"

"I only beg you to think it over, to avoid any rash decision. Those school recollections are delightful *per se*—little quarrels—a harmless nickname—but we must be serious now. Come, let us go back to our colleagues and do our duty."

Dr. Azureus, whose oratorical zest seemed to have waned, briefly informed his audience that the declaration which all had to read and sign, had been typed in the same number of copies as there would be signatures. He had been given to understand, he said, that this would lend a dash of individuality to every copy. What was the real object of this arrangement he did not explain, and, let us hope, did not know, but Krug thought he recognized in the apparent imbecility of the procedure the eerie ways of the Toad. The good doctors, Azureus and Alexander, distributed the sheets with the celerity that a conjuror and his assistant display when passing around for inspection articles which should not be examined too closely.

"You take one too," said the older doctor to the younger one.

"No, really," exclaimed Dr. Alexander, and everybody could see his handsome face express a rosy confusion. "Indeed, no. I would not dare. My humble signature must not hobnob with those of this august assembly. I am nothing."

"Here—this is yours," said Dr. Azureus with an odd burst of impatience.

The zoologist did not bother to read his, signed it with a borrowed pen, returned the pen over his shoulder and became engrossed again in the only inspectable stuff he had found so far—an old Baedeker with views of Egypt and ships of the desert in silhouette. Poor collecting ground on the whole—except perhaps for the orthopterist.

Dr. Alexander sat down at the rosewood desk, unbuttoned his jacket, shot out his cuffs, tuned the chair proximally, checked its position as a pianist does; then produced from his vest pocket a beautiful glittering instrument made of crystal and gold; looked at its nib; tested it on a bit of paper; and, holding his breath, slowly unfolded the convolutions of his name. Having completed the ornamentation of its complex tail, he raised his pen and surveyed the glamour he had wrought. Unfortunately at this precise moment, his golden wand (perhaps resentful of the concussions that its master's various exertions had been transmitting to it throughout the evening) shed a big black tear on the valuable typescript.

Really flushing this time, the V vein swelling on his forehead, Dr. Alexander applied the leech. When the corner of the blotting paper had drunk its fill without touching the bottom, the unfortunate doctor gingerly dabbed the remains. Adam Krug from a vantage point near by saw these pale blue remains: a fancy footprint or the spatulate outline of a puddle.

Gleeman reread the document twice, frowned twice, remembered the grant and the stained-glass window frontispiece and the special type he had chosen, and the footnote on page three hundred and six that would explode a rival theory concerning the exact age of a ruined wall, and affixed his dainty but strangely illegible signature.

Beuret who had been brusquely roused from a pleasant nap in a screened armchair, read, blew his nose, cursed the day he had changed his citizenship—then told himself that after all it was not his business to combat exotic politics, folded his handkerchief and seeing that others signed, signed.

Economics and History held a brief consultation during

which a skeptic but slightly strained smile appeared on the latter's face. They appended their signatures in unison and then noticed with dismay that while comparing notes they had somehow swapped copies, for each copy had the name and address of the potential undersigner typed out in the left-hand corner.

The rest sighed and signed, or did not sigh and signed, or signed—and sighed afterwards, or did neither the one nor the other, but then thought better of it and signed. Adam Krug too, he too, he too, unclipped his rusty wobbly fountain pen. The telephone rang in the adjacent study.

Dr. Azureus had personally handed the document to him and had hung around while Krug had leisurely put on his spectacles and had started to read, throwing his head back so as to rest it on the antimacassar and holding the sheets rather high in his slightly trembling thick fingers. They trembled more than usually because it was after midnight and he was unspeakably tired. Dr. Azureus stopped hovering and felt his old heart stumble as it went upstairs (metaphorically) with its guttering candle when Krug nearing the end of the manifesto (three pages and a half, sewn) pulled at the pen in his breast pocket. A sweet aura of intense relief made the candle rear its flame as old Azureus saw Krug spread the last page on the flat wooden arm of his cretonned armchair and unscrew the muzzle part of his pen, turning it into a cap.

With a quick flip-like delicately precise stroke quite out of keeping with his burly constitution, Krug inserted a comma in the fourth line. Then (*chmok*) he remuzzled, reclipped his pen (*chmok*) and handed the document to the distracted President.

"Sign it," said the President in a funny automatic voice.

"Legal documents excepted," answered Krug, "and not all of them at that, I never have signed, nor ever shall sign, anything not written by myself."

Old Azureus glanced around, his arms slowly rising. Somehow nobody was looking his way save Hedron, the mathematician, a gaunt man with a so-called "British" mustache and a pipe in his hand. Dr. Alexander was in the next room attending to the telephone. The cat was asleep in the stuffy room of the President's daughter who was dreaming of not being able to find a certain pot of apple jelly which she knew was a ship she had once seen in Bervok and a sailor was leaning and spitting overboard, watching his spit fall, fall, fall into the apple jelly of the heart-rending sea for her dream was shot with golden-yellow, as she had not put out the lamp, wishing to keep awake until her old father's guests had gone.

"Moreover," said Krug, "the metaphors are all mongrels whereas the sentence about being ready to add to the curriculum such matters as would prove necessary to promote political understanding and to do our utmost is miserable grammar which even my comma cannot save. I want to go home now."

"Prakhtata meta!" poor Dr. Azureus cried to the very quiet assembly. *"Prakhta tuen vadust, mohen kern! Profsar Krug malarma ne donje . . . Prakhtata!"*

Dr. Alexander, faintly resembling the fading sailor, reappeared and signaled, then called the President, who, still clutching the unsigned paper, sped wailing towards his faithful assistant.

"Come on, old boy, don't be a fool. Sign that darned thing," said Hedron, leaning over Krug and resting the fist with the pipe on Krug's shoulder. "What on earth does it matter? Affix your commercially valuable scrawl. Come on! Nobody can touch our circles—but we must have some place to draw them."

"Not in the mud, sir, not in the mud," said Krug, smiling his first smile of the evening.

"Oh, don't be a pompous pedant," said Hedron. "Why do you want to make me feel so uncomfortable? I signed it—and my gods did not stir."

Without looking, Krug put up his hand to touch lightly Hedron's tweed sleeve.

"It's all right," he said. "I don't care a damn for your morals so long as you draw your circles and show conjuring tricks to my boy."

For one dangerous moment he felt again the hot black surge of grief and the room almost melted . . . but Dr. Azureus was speeding back.

"My poor friend," said the President with great gusto. "You are a hero to have come. Why did not you tell me? I understand everything now! Of course, you could not have given the necessary attention—your decision and signature may be postponed—and I am sure we all are heartily ashamed of ourselves for having bothered you at such a moment."

"Go on speaking," said Krug. "Go on. Your words are conundrums to me but don't let that stop you."

With an awful feeling that a piece of utter misinformation had bedeviled him, Azureus stared, then stammered:

"I hope, I am not . . . I mean, I hope I am . . . I mean, haven't you . . . isn't there sorrow in your family?"

"If there is, it is no concern of yours," said Krug. "I want to go home," he added, blasting out suddenly in the terrible voice that would come like a thunderclap when he arrived at the climax of a lecture. "Will that man—what's his name— drive me back?"

From afar Dr. Alexander nodded to Dr. Azureus.

The mendicant had been relieved. Two soldiers sat huddled on the treadboard of the car, presumably guarding it. Krug, being eager to avoid a chat with Dr. Alexander, promptly got into the back. To his great annoyance, however, Dr. Alexander, instead of taking the wheel, joined him there. With one of the soldiers driving while the other protruded a comfortable elbow, the car screeched, cleared its throat and hummed through the dark streets.

"Perhaps you would like——" said Dr. Alexander, and, groping on the floor, attempted to draw up a rug so as to unite under it his and his bedfellow's legs. Krug grunted and kicked the thing off. Dr. Alexander tugged, fidgeted, tucked himself in all alone, and then relaxed, one hand languidly resting in the strap on his side of the car. An incidental street lamp found and mislaid his opal.

"I must confess I admired you, Professor. Of course you were the only real man among those poor dear fossils. I understand, you do not see much of your colleagues, do you? Oh, you must have felt rather out of place——"

"Wrong again," said Krug, breaking his vow to keep silent. "I esteem my colleagues as I do my own self. I esteem them for two things: because they are able to find perfect felicity in specialised knowledge and because they are not apt to commit physical murder."

Dr. Alexander mistook this for one of the obscure quips which, he had been told, Adam Krug liked to indulge in, and laughed cautiously.

Krug glanced at him through the running darkness and turned away for good.

"And you know," continued the young biodynamicist, "I have a curious feeling, Professor, that somehow or other the numerous sheep are prized less than the one lone wolf. I wonder what is going to happen next. I wonder, for instance, what would be your attitude if our whimsical government with apparent inconsistency ignored the sheep but offered the wolf the most munificent position imaginable. It is a passing thought of course and you may laugh at the paradox (the speaker briefly demonstrated the way it might be done) but this and other possibilities, perhaps of a quite opposite nature, somehow or other come to the mind. You know, when I was a student and lived in a garret, my landlady, the wife of the grocer below, used to insist that I should end by setting the house on fire, so many candles did I burn every night while poring over the pages of your admirable in every respect——"

"Shut up, will you?" said Krug, all of a sudden revealing a queer streak of vulgarity and even cruelty, for nothing in the innocent and well-meaning, if not very intelligent prattle of the young scientist (who quite obviously had been turned into a chatterbox by the shyness characteristic of overstrung and perhaps undernourished young folks, victims of capitalism, communism and masturbation, when they find themselves in the company of really big men, such as for instance someone whom they know to be a personal friend of the boss, or the head of the firm himself, or even the head's brother-in-law Gogolevitch, and so on) warranted the rudeness of the interjection; which interjection however had the effect of insuring complete silence for the rest of the trip.

Only when the somewhat roughly driven car swerved into Peregolm Lane, did the unresentful young man, who realized no doubt the bewildered state of mind of the widower, open his mouth again.

"Here we are," he said genially. "I hope you have your
sesamka [latchkey]. We must be dashing back, I'm afraid.
Good night! Happy dreams! *Proshchevantze!*" [jocose
"adieu"].

The car vanished while the square echo of its slammed door
was still suspended in mid-air like an empty picture frame of
ebony. But Krug was not alone: a thing that resembled a helmet had rolled down the steps of the porch and lay at his feet.

Close up, close up! In the farewell shadows of the porch,
his moon-white monstrously padded shoulder in pathetic dis-
harmony with his slender neck, a youth, dressed up as an
American Football Player, stood in one last deadlock with a
sketchy little Carmen,—and even the sum of their years was
at least ten less than the spectator's age. Her short black skirt
with its suggestion of jet and petal half veiled the quaint garb
of her lover's limbs. A spangled wrap drooped from her left
hand and the inner side of her limp arm shone through black
gauze. Her other arm circled up and around the boy's neck
and the tense fingers were thrust from behind into his dark
hair; yes, one distinguished everything—even the short clumsily lacquered fingernails, the rough schoolgirl knuckles. He,
the tackler, held Laocoön, and a brittle shoulder-blade, and a
small rhythmical hip, in his throbbing coils through which
glowing globules were traveling in secret, and her eyes were
closed.

"I am really sorry," said Krug, "but I have to pass. *Donje
te zankoriv* [do please excuse me]."

They separated and he caught a glimpse of her pale, dark-
eyed, not very pretty face with its glistening lips as she slipped
under his door-holding arm and after one backward glance
from the first landing ran upstairs trailing her wrap with all its
constellation—Cepheus and Cassiopeia in their eternal bliss,
and the dazzling tear of Capella, and Polaris the snowflake on
the grizzly fur of the Cub, and the swooning galaxies—those
mirrors of infinite space *qui m'effrayent, Blaise*, as they did
you, and where Olga is not, but where mythology stretches
strong circus nets, lest thought, in its ill-fitting tights, should
break its old neck instead of rebouncing with a hep and a
hop—hopping down again into this urine-soaked dust to take
that short run with the half pirouette in the middle and display

the extreme simplicity of heaven in the acrobat's amphiphor-
ical gesture, the candidly open hands that start a brief shower
of applause while he walks backwards and then, reverting to
virile manners, catches the little blue handkerchief, which his
muscular flying mate, after her own exertions, takes from her
heaving hot bosom—heaving more than her smile suggests—
and tosses to him, so that he may wipe the palms of his aching
weakening hands.

5

IT BRISTLED with farcical anachronism; it was suffused with a sense of gross maturity (as in Hamlet the churchyard scene); its somewhat meager setting was patched up with odds and ends from other (later) plays; but still the recurrent dream we all know (finding ourselves in the old classroom, with our homework not done because of our having unwittingly missed ten thousand days of school) was in Krug's case a fair rendering of the atmosphere of the original version. Naturally, the script of daytime memory is far more subtle in regard to factual details, since a good deal of cutting and trimming and conventional recombination has to be done by the dream producers (of whom there are usually several, mostly illiterate and middle-class and pressed by time); but a show is always a show, and the embarrassing return to one's former existence (with the off-stage passing of years translated in terms of forgetfulness, truancy, inefficiency) is somehow better enacted by a popular dream than by the scholarly precision of memory.

But is it really as crude as all that? Who is behind the timid producers? No doubt, this desk at which Krug finds himself sitting has been hastily borrowed from a different set and is more like the general equipment of the university auditorium than like the individual affair of Krug's boyhood, with its smelly (prunes, rust) inkhole and the penknife scars on its lid (which could bang) and that special inkstain in the shape of Lake Malheur. No doubt, too, there is something wrong about the position of the door, and some of Krug's students, vague supes (Danes today, Romans tomorrow), have been hurriedly rounded up to fill gaps left by those of his schoolmates who proved less mnemogenic than others. But among the producers or stagehands responsible for the setting there has been one . . . it is hard to express it . . . a nameless, mysterious genius who took advantage of the dream to convey his own peculiar code message which has nothing to do with school days or indeed with any aspect of Krug's physical existence, but which links him up somehow with an unfathomable mode of being, perhaps terrible, perhaps blissful, perhaps neither, a kind of transcendental madness which lurks behind the corner of consciousness and which cannot be defined more accurately than this, no matter how Krug strains his brain. O yes—the lighting is poor and one's field of vision is oddly narrowed as if the memory of closed eyelids persisted intrinsically within the sepia shading of the dream, and the orchestra of the senses is limited to a few native instruments, and Krug reasons in his dream worse than a drunken fool; but a closer inspection (made when the dream-self is dead for the ten thousandth time and the day-self inherits for the ten thousandth time those dusty trifles, those debts, those bundles of illegible letters) reveals the presence of someone in the know. Some intruder has been there, has tiptoed upstairs, has opened closets and very slightly disarranged the order of things. Then the shrunken, chalk-dusty, incredibly light and dry sponge imbibes water until it is as plump as a fruit; it makes glossy black arches all over the livid blackboard as it sweeps away the dead white symbols; and we start afresh now combining dim dreams with the scholarly precision of memory.

You entered a tunnel of sorts; it ran through the body of an irrelevant house and brought you into an inner court coated with old gray sand which turned to mud at the first spatter of rain. Here soccer was played in the windy pale interval between two series of lessons. The yawn of the tunnel and the door of the school, at the opposite ends of the yard, became football goals much in the same fashion as the commonplace organ of one species of animal is dramatically modified by a new function in another.

At times, a regular association football with its red liver tightly tucked in under its leather corset and the name of an English maker running across the almost palatable sections of its hard ringing rotundity, would be surreptitiously brought and cautiously dribbled about in a corner, but this was a forbidden object in the yard, bounded as it was by brittle windows.

Here is the ball, the ball, the smooth indiarubber ball, approved by the authorities, suddenly disclosed in a glass case like some museum exhibit: three balls, in fact, in three cases; for we are shown all its instars: first the new one, so clean as

to be almost white—the white of a shark's belly; then the dirty
gray adult with grains of gravel adhering to its weather-beaten
cheek; then a flabby and formless corpse. A bell tinkles. The
museum gets dark and empty again.

Pass the ball, Adamka! A shot wide of the mark or a deliberate punt seldom resulted in a crash of broken glass; but,
conversely, a puncture would usually follow the collision with
a certain vicious projection formed by an angle of the roofed
porch. The stricken ball's collapse would not be noticeable at
once. Then, at the next hard kick, its life-air would start to
ooze, and presently it would be flopping about like an old
galosh, before coming to rest, a miserable jellyfish of soiled
indiarubber, on the muddy ground where fiendishly disappointed boots would at last kick it to pieces. The end of the
ballona [festive gathering with dances]. She doffs her diamond
tiara before her mirror.

Krug played football [*vooter*], Paduk did not [*nekht*]. Krug,
a burly, fat-faced, curly-headed boy, sporting tweed knickerbockers with buttons below the knee (soccer shorts were taboo), pounded through the mud with more zest than skill.
Now he found himself running (by night, ugly? Yah, by night,
folks) down something that looked like a railway track
through a long damp tunnel (the dream stage management
having used the first set available for rendering "tunnel,"
without bothering to remove either the rails or the ruby lamps
that glowed at intervals along the rocky black sweating walls).
There was a heavy ball at his toes; he kept treading upon it
whenever he tried to kick it; finally it got stuck somehow or
other on a ledge of the rock wall, which, here and there, had
small inset show windows, neatly illumined and enlivened by
a quaint aquarian touch (corals, sea urchins, champagne bubbles). Within one of them she sat, taking off her dew-bright
rings and unclasping the diamond *collier de chien* that encircled her full white throat; yes, divesting herself of all earthly
jewels. He groped for the ball on the ledge and fished out a
slipper, a little red pail with the picture of a sailing boat upon
it and an eraser, all of which somehow summed up to the ball.
It was difficult to go on dribbling through the tangle of rickety scaffolding where he felt he was getting in the way of the
workmen who were fixing wires or something, and when he

reached the diner the ball had rolled under one of the tables; and there, half hidden by a fallen napkin, was the threshold of the goal, because the goal was a door.

If you opened that door you found a few *zaftpupen* ["softies"] mooning on the broad window seats behind the clothes racks, and Paduk would be there, too, eating something sweet and sticky given him by the janitor, a bemedaled veteran with a venerable beard and lewd eyes. When the bell rang, Paduk would wait for the bustle of flushed begrimed classbound boys to subside, whereupon he would quietly make his way up the stairs, his agglutinate palm caressing the banisters. Krug, whom the putting away of the ball had detained (there was a big box for playthings and fake jewelry under the stairs), overtook him and pinched his plump buttocks in passing.

Krug's father was a biologist of considerable repute. Paduk's father was a minor inventor, a vegetarian, a theosophist, a great expert in cheap Hindu lore; at one time he seems to have been in the printing business—printing mainly the works of cranks and frustrated politicians. Paduk's mother, a flaccid lymphatic woman from the Marshland, had died in childbirth, and soon after this the widower had married a young cripple for whom he had been devising a new type of braces (she survived him, braces and all, and is still limping about somewhere). The boy Paduk had a pasty face and a gray-blue cranium with bumps: his father shaved his head for him personally once a week—some kind of mystic ritual, no doubt.

It is not known how the nickname "toad" originated, for there was nothing in his face suggestive of that animal. It was an odd face with all its features in their proper position but somehow diffuse and abnormal as if the little fellow had undergone one of those facial operations when the skin is borrowed from some other part of the body. The impression was due perhaps to the motionless cast of his features: he never laughed and when he happened to sneeze he had a way of doing it with a minimum of contraction and no sound at all. His small dead-white nose and neat blue galatea made him resemble *en laid* the wax schoolboys in the shopwindows of tailors, but his hips were much plumper than those of mannikins, and he walked with a slight waddle and wore sandals which used to provoke a good deal of caustic comment. Once, when he was being badly mauled it was discovered that he had right against the skin a green undershirt, green as a billiard cloth and apparently made of the same texture. His hands were permanently clammy. He spoke in a curiously smooth nasal voice with a strong northwestern accent and had an irritating trick of calling his classmates by anagrams of their names—Adam Krug for instance was Gumakrad or Dramaguk; this he did not from any sense of humor, which he totally lacked, but because, as he carefully explained to new boys, one should constantly bear in mind that all men consist of the same twenty-five letters variously mixed.

Such traits would have been readily excused had he been a likable fellow, a good pal, a co-operative vulgarian or a pleasantly queer boy with most matter-of-fact muscles (Krug's case). Paduk, in spite of his oddities, was dull, commonplace and insufferably mean. Thinking of it later, one comes to the unexpected conclusion that he was a veritable hero in the domain of meanness, since every time he indulged in it he must have known that he was heading again towards that hell of physical pain which his revengeful classmates put him through every time. Curiously enough, we cannot recall any single definite example of his meanness, albeit vividly remembering what Paduk had to suffer in retaliation of his recondite crimes. There was for instance the case of the padograph.

He must have been fourteen or fifteen when his father invented this only contraption of his that was destined to have some commercial success. It was a portable affair looking like a typewriter made to reproduce with repellent perfection the hand of its owner. You supplied the inventor with numerous specimens of your penmanship, he would study the strokes and the linkage, and then turn out your individual padograph. The resulting script copied exactly the average "tone" of your handwriting while the minor variations of each character were taken care of by the several keys serving each letter. Punctuation marks were carefully diversified within the limits of this or that individual manner, and such details as spacing and what experts call "clines" were so rendered as to mask mechanical regularity. Although, of course, a close examination of the script never failed to reveal the presence of a mechanical medium, a good deal of more or less foolish deceit could be practiced. You could, for instance, have your padograph based on the handwriting of a correspondent and then play all kinds of pranks on him and his friends. Despite this inane undertow of clumsy forgery, the thing caught the fancy of the honest consumer: devices which in some curious new way imitate nature are attractive to simple minds. A really good padograph, reproducing a multitude of shades, was a very expensive article. Orders, however, poured in, and one purchaser after another enjoyed the luxury of seeing the essence of his incomplex personality distilled by the magic of an elaborate instrument. In the course of a year, three thousand padographs were sold, and of this number, more than one tenth were optimistically used for fraudulent purposes (both cheaters and cheated displaying remarkable stupidity in the process). Paduk senior had been just about to build a special factory for production on a grand scale when a Parliamentary decree put a ban on the manufacture and sale of padographs throughout the country. Philosophically speaking, the padograph subsisted as an Ekwilist symbol, as a proof of the fact that a mechanical device can reproduce personality, and that Quality is merely the distributional aspect of Quantity.

One of the first samples issued by the inventor was a birthday present for his son. Young Paduk applied it to the needs of homework. His handwriting was a thin arachnoid scrawl of the reverse type with strongly barred *t*'s standing out conspicuously among the other limp letters, and all this was perfectly mimicked. He had never got rid of infantile inkstains, so his father had thrown in additional keys for an hourglass-shaped blot and two round ones. These adornments, however, Paduk ignored, and quite rightly. His teachers only noticed that his work had become somewhat tidier and that such question marks as he happened to use were in darker and purpler ink than the rest of the characters: by one of those mishaps which are typical of a certain kind of inventor, his father had forgotten that sign.

Soon, however, the pleasures of secrecy waned and one morning Paduk brought his machine to school. The teacher of mathematics, a tall, blue-eyed Jew with a tawny beard, had to attend a funeral, and the resulting free hour was devoted to a demonstration of the padograph. It was a beautiful object and a shaft of spring sunlight promptly located it; snow was melting and dripping outside, jewels glittered in the mud, iridescent pigeons cooed on the wet window ledge, the roofs of the houses beyond the yard shone with a diamond shimmer; and Paduk's stumpy fingers (the edible part of each fingernail gone except for a dark linear limit embedded in a roll of yellowish flesh) drummed upon the bright keys. One must admit that the whole procedure showed considerable pluck on his part: he was surrounded by rough boys who disliked him intensely and there was nothing to prevent their pulling his magic instrument to pieces. But there he sat coolly transcribing some text and explaining in his high-pitched drawl the niceties of the demonstration. Schimpffer, a red-haired boy of Alsatian descent, with extremely efficient fingers, said: "Now let me try!" and Paduk made room for him and directed his—at first somewhat suspensive—taps. Krug tried next, and Paduk helped him, too, until he realized that his mechanized double under Krug's strong thumb was submissively setting down: I am an imbecile imbecile am I and I promise to pay ten fifteen twenty-five kruns—"Please, oh, please," said Paduk quickly, "somebody is coming, let us put it away." He clapped it into his desk, pocketed the key and hurried to the lavatory, as he always did when he got excited.

Krug conferred with Schimpffer and a simple plan of action was devised. After lessons they coaxed Paduk into giving them another look at the instrument. As soon as its case was unlocked, Krug removed Paduk and sat upon him, while Schimpffer laboriously typed out a short letter. This he slipped into the mailbox and Paduk was released.

On the following day the young wife of the rheumy and dithering teacher of history received a note (on lined paper with two holes punched out in the margin) pleading for a rendezvous. Instead of complaining to her husband, as was expected, this amiable woman, wearing a heavy blue veil, waylaid Paduk, told him he was a big naughty boy and with an eager jiggle of her rump (which in those days of tight waists looked like an inverted heart) suggested taking a *kuppe* [closed carriage] and driving to a certain unoccupied flat, where she might scold him in peace. Although since the preceding day Paduk had been on the lookout for something nasty to

happen, he was not prepared for anything of this particular
sort and actually followed her into the dowdy cab before recovering his wits. A few minutes later, in the traffic jam of
Parliament Square, he slithered out and ignominiously fled.
How all these *trivesta* [details of amorous doings] reached his
comrades, is difficult to conjecture; anyway, the incident became a school legend. For a few days Paduk kept away; nor
did Schimpffer appear for some time: by an amusing coincidence the latter's mother had been badly burned by a mysterious explosive that some practical joker had put into her
bag while she was out shopping. When Paduk turned up
again, he was his usual quiet self but he did not refer to his
padograph or bring it to school any more.

That same year, or perhaps the next, a new headmaster with
ideas resolved to develop what he termed "the politico-social
consciousness" of the older boys. He had quite a program—meetings, discussions, the formation of party groups—
oh, lots of things. The healthier boys avoided these gatherings
for the simple reason that, being held after classes or
during recess, they encroached upon one's freedom. Krug
made violent fun of the fools or trucklers who fell for this
civic nonsense. The headmaster, while stressing the purely voluntary nature of attendance, warned Krug (who was at the
top of his class) that his individualistic behavior constituted a
dreadful example. There was an etching representing the Sand
Bread Riot, 1849, above the headmaster's horsehair couch.
Krug did not dream of yielding and stoically ignored the mediocre marks which from that moment fell to his lot despite
his work's remaining on the same level. Again the headmaster
spoke to him. There was also a colored print depicting a lady
in cherry red, sitting before her mirror. The position was interesting: here was this headmaster, a liberal with robust lean-
ings towards the Left, an eloquent advocate of Uprightness and
Impartiality, ingeniously blackmailing the brightest boy in his
school and acting thus not because he wished him to join a
certain definite group (say, a Leftist one), but because the boy
would not join any group whatsoever. For it should be remarked in all fairness to the headmaster that, far from enforc-
ing his own political predilections, he allowed his pupils to
adhere to any party they chose, even if this proved to be a

new combination unrelated to any of the factions represented in the then flourishing Parliament. Indeed so broad-minded was he that he positively *wanted* the richer boys to form strongly capitalistic clusters, or the sons of reactionary nobles to keep in tune with their caste and unite in *"Rutterheds."* All he asked for was that they follow their social and economic instincts, while the only thing he condemned was the complete absence of such instincts in an individual. He saw the world as a lurid interplay of class passions amid a landscape of conventional gauntness, with Wealth and Work emitting Wagnerian thunder in their predetermined parts; a refusal to act in the show appeared to him as a vicious insult to his dynamic myth as well as to the Trade Union to which the actors belonged. Under these circumstances he felt justified in pointing out to the teachers that if Adam Krug passed the final examinations with honors, his success would be dialectically unfair in regard to those of Krug's schoolmates who had less brains but were better citizens. The teachers entered so heartily into the spirit of the thing that it is a wonder how our young friend managed to pass at all.

That last term was also marked by the sudden rise of Paduk. Although he had seemed to be disliked by all, a kind of small court and bodyguard was there to greet him when he gently rose to the surface and gently founded the party of the Average Man. Every one of his followers had some little defect or "background of insecurity" as an educationist after a fruit cocktail might put it: one boy suffered from permanent boils, another was morbidly shy, a third had by accident beheaded his baby sister, a fourth stuttered so badly that you could go out and buy yourself a chocolate bar while he was wrestling with an initial *p* or *b*: he would never try to by-pass the obstacle by switching to a synonym, and when finally the explosion did occur, it convulsed his whole frame and sprayed his interlocutor with triumphant saliva. A fifth disciple was a more sophisticated stutterer, since the flaw in his speech took the form of an additional syllable coming *after* the critical word like a kind of halfhearted echo. Protection was provided by a truculent simian youth who at seventeen could not memorize the multiplication tables but was able to hold up a chair majestically occupied by yet another disciple, the fattest boy

in the school. Nobody had noticed how this rather incongruous little crowd had gathered around Paduk and nobody
could understand what exactly had given Paduk the leadership.

A couple of years before these events his father had become
acquainted with Fradrik Skotoma of pathetic fame. The old
iconoclast as he liked to be called, was at the time steadily
slipping into misty senility. With his moist bright red mouth
and fluffy white whiskers he had begun to look, if not respectable, at least harmless, and his shrunken body had assumed
such a gossamery aspect that the matrons of his dingy neighborhood, as they watched him shuffle along in the fluorescent
halo of his dotage, felt almost like crooning over him and
would buy him cherries and hot raisin cakes and the loud
socks he affected. People who had been stirred in their youth
by his writings had long forgotten that passionate flow of in-
sidious pamphlets and mistook the shortness of their own
memory for the curtailment of his objective existence, so that
they would frown a quick frown of incredulity if told that
Skotoma, the *enfant terrible* of the sixties, was still alive. Skotoma himself, at eight-five, was inclined to consider his tumultuous past as a preliminary stage far inferior to his present
philosophical period, for, not unnaturally, he saw his decline
as a ripening and an apotheosis, and was quite sure that the
rambling treatise he had Paduk senior print would be recognized as an immortal achievement.

He expressed his new-found conception of mankind with
the solemnity befitting a tremendous discovery. At every given
level of world-time there was, he said, a certain computable
amount of human consciousness distributed throughout the
population of the world. This distribution was uneven, and
herein lay the root of all our woes. Human beings, he said,
were so many vessels containing unequal portions of this essentially uniform consciousness. It was however quite possible, he maintained, to regulate the capacity of the human
vessels. If, for instance, a given amount of water were contained in a given number of heterogeneous bottles—wine bottles, flagons and vials of varying shape and size, and all the
crystal and gold scent bottles that were reflected in her mirror,
the distribution of the liquid would be uneven and unjust, but

could be made even and just either by grading the contents
or by eliminating the fancy vessels and adopting a standard
size. He introduced the idea of balance as a basis for universal
bliss and called his theory "Ekwilism." This he claimed was
quite new. True, socialism had advocated uniformity on an
economic plane, and religion had grimly promised the same
in spiritual terms as an inevitable status beyond the grave. But
the economist had not seen that no leveling of wealth could
be successfully accomplished, nor indeed was of any real moment, so long as there existed some individuals with more
brains or guts than others; and similarly the priest had failed
to perceive the futility of his metaphysical promise in relation
to those favored ones (men of bizarre genius, big game
hunters, chess players, prodigiously robust and versatile lovers,
the radiant woman taking her necklace off after the ball) for
whom this world was a paradise in itself and who would be
always one point up no matter what happened to everyone in
the melting pot of eternity. And even, said Skotoma, if the
last became the first and vice versa, imagine the patronizing
smile of the *ci-devant* William Shakespeare on seeing a former
scribbler of hopelessly bad plays blossom anew as the Poet
Laureate of heaven.

It is important to note that while suggesting a remolding
of human individuals in conformity with a well-balanced pattern, the author prudently omitted to define both the practical
method to be pursued and the kind of person or persons responsible for planning and directing the process. He contented himself with repeating throughout his book that the
difference between the proudest intellect and the humblest
stupidity depended entirely upon the degree of "world consciousness" condensed in this or that individual. He seemed
to think that its redistribution and regulation would automatically follow as soon as his readers perceived the truth of
his main assertion. It is also to be observed that the good
Utopian had the whole misty blue world in view, not only his
own morbidly self-conscious country. He died soon after his
treatise appeared and so was spared the discomfort of seeing
his vague and benevolent Ekwilism transformed (while retaining its name) into a violent and virulent political doctrine, a
doctrine that proposed to enforce spiritual uniformity upon

his native land through the medium of the most standardized section of the inhabitants, namely the Army, under the supervision of a bloated and dangerously divine State.

When young Paduk instituted the Party of the Average Man as based on Skotoma's book, the metamorphosis of Ekwilism had only just started and the frustrated boys who conducted those dismal meetings in a malodorous classroom were still groping for the means to make the contents of the human vessel conform to an average scale. That year a corrupt politician had been assassinated by a college student called Emrald (not Amrald, as his name is usually misspelled abroad), who at the trial came out quite irrelevantly with a poem of his own composition, a piece of jagged neurotic rhetorism extolling Skotoma because he

> . . . taught us to worship the Common Man,
> and showed us that no tree
> can exist without a forest,
> no musician without an orchestra,
> no wave without an ocean,
> and no life without death.

Poor Skotoma, of course, had done nothing of the kind, but this poem was now sung to the tune of *"Ustra mara, donjet domra"* (a popular ditty lauding the intoxicating properties of gooseberry wine) by Paduk and his friends and later became an Ekwilist classic. In those days a blatantly bourgeois paper happened to be publishing a cartoon sequence depicting the home life of Mr. and Mrs. Etermon (Everyman). With conventional humor and sympathy bordering upon the obscene, Mr. Etermon and the little woman were followed from parlor to kitchen and from garden to garret through all the mentionable stages of their daily existence, which, despite the presence of cozy armchairs and all sorts of electric thingumbobs and one thing-in-itself (a car), did not differ essentially from the life of a Neanderthal couple. Mr. Etermon taking a z-nap on the divan or stealing into the kitchen to sniff with erotic avidity the sizzling stew, represented quite unconsciously a living refutation of individual immortality, since his whole habitus was a dead-end with nothing in it capable or worthy of transcending the mortal condition. Neither, however, could one imagine Etermon actually dying, not only because the

rules of gentle humor forbade his being shown on his deathbed, but also because not a single detail of the setting (not
even his playing poker with life-insurance salesmen) suggested
the fact of absolutely inevitable death; so that in one sense
Etermon, while personifying a refutation of immortality, was
immortal himself, and in another sense he could not hope to
enjoy any kind of afterlife simply because he was denied the
elementary comfort of a death chamber in his otherwise well
planned home. Within the limits of this airtight existence, the
young couple were as happy as any young couple ought to
be: a visit to the movies, a raise in one's salary, a yum-yum
something for dinner—life was positively crammed with these
and similar delights, whereas the worst that might befall one,
was hitting a traditional thumb with a traditional hammer or
mistaking the date of the boss's birthday. Poster pictures of
Etermon showed him smoking the brand that millions smoke,
and millions could not be wrong, and every Etermon was supposed to imagine every other Etermon, up to the President
of the State, who had just replaced dull, stolid Theodore the
Last, returning at the close of the office day to the (rich) cu-
linary and (meager) connubial felicities of the Etermon home.
Skotoma, quite apart from the senile divagations of his
Ekwilism (and even they implied some kind of drastic
change, some kind of dissatisfaction with given conditions) had
viewed what he called "the petty bourgeois" with the wrath
of orthodox anarchism and would have been appalled, just as
Emrald the terrorist would have been, to know that a group
of youths was worshiping Ekwilism in the guise of a cartoon-
engendered Mr. Etermon. Skotoma, however, had been the
victim of a common delusion: his "petty bourgeois" existed
only as a printed label on an empty filing box (the iconoclast,
like most of his kind, relied entirely upon generalizations and
was quite incapable of noting, say, the wallpaper in a chance
room or talking intelligently to a child). Actually, with a little
perspicacity, one might learn many curious things about Eter-
mons, things that made them so different from one another
that Etermon, except as a cartoonist's transient character,
could not be said to exist. All of a sudden transfigured, his
eyes narrowly glowing, Mr. Etermon (whom we have just seen
mildly pottering about the house) locks himself up in the

bathroom with his prize—a prize we prefer not to name; another Etermon, straight from his shabby office, slips into the silence of a great library to gloat over certain old maps of which he will not speak at home; a third Etermon with a fourth Etermon's wife anxiously discusses the future of a child she has managed to bear him in secret during the time her husband (now back in his armchair at home) was fighting in a remote jungle land where, in his turn, he has seen moths the size of a spread fan, and trees at night pulsating rhythmically with countless fireflies. No, the average vessels are not as simple as they appear: it is a conjuror's set and nobody, not even the enchanter himself, really knows what and how much they hold.

Skotoma had dwelt in his day upon the economic aspect of Etermon; Paduk deliberately copied the Etermon cartoon in its sartorial sense. He wore the tall collar of celluloid, the famous shirt-sleeve bands and the expensive footgear—for the only brilliance Mr. Etermon permitted himself was related to parts as far as possible removed from the anatomic center of his being: glossy shoes, glossy hair. With his father's reluctant consent, the top of Paduk's pale-blue cranium was allowed to grow just enough hair to resemble Etermon's beautifully groomed pate and Etermon's washable cuffs with starlike links were affixed to Paduk's weak wrists. Although in later years this mimetic adaptation was no longer consciously pursued (while on the other hand the Etermon strip was eventually discontinued, and afterwards seemed quite atypical when looked up at a different period of fashion) Paduk never got over this stiff superficial neatness; he was known to endorse the views of a doctor, belonging to the Ekwilist party, who affirmed that if a man kept his clothes scrupulously clean, he might, and should, limit his weekday ablutions to washing nothing but his face, ears, and hands. Throughout all his later adventures, in all places, under all circumstances, in the blurry back rooms of suburban cafés, in the miserable offices where this or that obstinate newspaper of his was concocted, in barracks, in public halls, in the forests and hills where he hid with a bunch of barefooted red-eyed soldiers, and in the palace where, through an incredible whim of local history, he found himself vested with more power than any national ruler had

ever enjoyed, Paduk still retained something of the late Mr.
Etermon, a sort of cartoon angularity, a cracked and soiled
cellophane wrapper effect, through which, nevertheless, one
could discern a brand-new thumbscrew, a bit of rope, a rusty
knife and a specimen of the most sensitive of human organs
wrenched out together with its blood-clotted roots.

In the classroom where the final examination was being
held, young Paduk, his sleek hair resembling a wig too small
for his shaven head, sat between Brun the Ape and a lacquered
dummy representing an absentee. Adam Krug, wearing a
brown dressing gown, sat directly behind. Somebody on his
left asked him to pass a book to the family of his right-hand
neighbor, and this he did. The book, he noticed, was in
reality a rosewood box shaped and painted to look like a volume of verse and Krug understood that it contained some
secret commentaries that would assist an unprepared student's
panic-stricken mind. Krug regretted that he had not opened
the box or book while it passed through his hands. The theme
to be tackled was an afternoon with Mallarmé, an uncle of his
mother, but the only part he could remember seemed to be
"le sanglot dont j'étais encore ivre."

Everybody around was scribbling with zest and a very black
fly which Schimpffer had especially prepared for the occasion
by dipping it into India ink was walking on the shaven part
of Paduk's studiously bent head. It left a blot near his pink
ear and a black colon on his shiny white collar. A couple of
teachers—her brother-in-law and the teacher of mathematics—were busily arranging a curtained something which
would be a demonstration of the next theme to be discussed.
They reminded one of stagehands or morticians but Krug
could not see well because of the Toad's head. Paduk and all
the rest wrote on steadily, but Krug's failure was complete, a
baffling and hideous disaster, for he had been busy becoming an elderly man instead of learning the simple but now
unobtainable passages which they, mere boys, had memorized. Smugly, noiselessly, Paduk left his seat to take his paper
to the examiner, tripped over the foot that Schimpffer shot
out and through the gap which he left Krug clearly perceived
the outlines of the next theme. It was not quite ready for
demonstration but the curtains were still drawn. Krug found

a scrap of clean paper and got ready to write his impressions. The two teachers pulled the curtains apart. Olga was revealed sitting before her mirror and taking off her jewels after the ball. Still clad in cherry-red velvet, her strong gleaming elbows thrown back and lifted like wings, she had begun to unclasp at the back of her neck her dazzling dog collar. He knew it would come off together with her vertebrae—that in fact it was the crystal of her vertebrae—and he experienced an agonizing sense of impropriety at the thought that everybody in the room would observe and take down in writing her inevitable, pitiful, innocent disintegration. There was a flash, a click: with both hands she removed her beautiful head and, not looking at it, carefully, carefully, dear, smiling a dim smile of amused recollection (who could have guessed at the dance that the real jewels were pawned?), she placed the beautiful imitation upon the marble ledge of her toilet table. Then he knew that all the rest would come off too, the rings together with the fingers, the bronze slippers with the toes, the breasts with the lace that cupped them . . . his pity and shame reached their climax, and at the ultimate gesture of the tall cold stripteaser, prowling pumalike up and down the stage, with a horrible qualm Krug awoke.

6

"WE MET YESTERDAY," said the room. "I am the spare bedroom in the Maximovs' *dacha* [country house, cottage]. These are windmills on the wallpaper." "That's right," replied Krug. Somewhere in the thin-walled, pine-fragrant house a stove was comfortably crackling and David was speaking in his tinkling voice—probably answering Anna Petrovna, probably having breakfast with her in the next room.

Theoretically there is no absolute proof that one's awakening in the morning (the finding oneself again in the saddle of one's personality) is not really a quite unprecedented event, a perfectly original birth. One day Ember and he had happened to discuss the possibility of their having invented *in toto* the works of William Shakespeare, spending millions and millions on the hoax, smothering with hush money countless publishers, librarians, the Stratford-on-Avon people, since in order to be responsible for all references to the poet during three centuries of civilization, these references had to be assumed to be spurious interpolations injected by the inventors into actual works which they had re-edited; there still was a snag here, a bothersome flaw, but perhaps it might be eliminated, too, just as a cooked chess problem can be cured by the addition of a passive pawn.

The same might be true of one's personal existence as perceived in retrospect upon waking up: the retrospective effect itself is a fairly simple illusion, not unlike the pictorial values of depth and remoteness produced by a paintbrush on a flat surface; but it takes something better than a paintbrush to create the sense of compact reality backed by a plausible past, of logical continuity, of picking up the thread of life at the exact point where it was dropped. The subtlety of the trick is nothing short of marvelous, considering the immense number of details to be taken into account, arranged in such a way as to suggest the action of memory. Krug at once knew that his wife had died; that he had beaten a hasty retreat to the country with his little son, and that the view framed in the

casement (wet leafless trees, brown earth, white sky, a hill with
a farmhouse in the distance) was not only a sample picture of
that particular region but was also there to tell him that David
had pulled the shade up and had left the room without awakening him; whereupon, with almost obsequious apropos, a
couch at the other end of the room displayed by means of
mute gestures—see this and this—all that was necessary to
convince one that a child had slept there.

On the morning after her death her relatives had arrived.
The night before Ember had informed them of her death.
Note how smoothly the retrospective machinery works: everything fits into everything else. They (to switch into a lower
past-gear) arrived, they invaded Krug's flat. David was
finishing his velvetina. They came in full force: her sister Viola,
Viola's revolting husband, a half brother of sorts and his wife,
two remote female cousins scarcely visible in the mist and a
vague old man whom Krug had never met before. Augment
the vanity of the illusive depth. Viola had always disliked her
sister; they had seldom seen each other during the last twelve
years. She wore a heavily blotched little veil: it came down to
the bridge of her freckled nose, no further than that, and
behind its black violets one could distinguish a brightness
which was both voluptuous and hard. Her blond-bearded
husband gently supported her, although actually the solicitude
with which the pompous rogue surrounded her sharp elbow
only hampered her swift masterful movements. She soon
shook him away. When last seen, he was staring in dignified
silence through the window at two black limousines waiting
at the curb. A gentleman in black with powdered blue jowls,
the representative of the incinerating firm, came to say that it
was high time to start. Meanwhile Krug had escaped with
David by the back door.

Carrying a suitcase, still wet from Claudina's tears, he led
the child to the nearest trolley stop, and, in company with a
band of sleepy soldiers who were going on to their barracks,
arrived at the railway station. Before he was allowed to board
the train for the Lakes, governmental agents examined his papers and the balls of David's eyes. The Lakes hotel turned out
to be closed, and after they had wandered around for a while,

a jovial postman in his yellow automobile took them (and Ember's letter) to the Maximovs. This completes the reconstruction.

The common bathroom in a friendly house is its only inhospitable section, especially when the water runs at first tepid, then stone cold. A long silvery hair was imbedded in a cake of cheap almond soap. Toilet paper had been difficult to get lately and was replaced by bits of newspaper impaled on a hook. At the bottom of the bowl a safety razor blade envelope with Dr. S. Freud's face and signature floated. If I stay for a week, he thought, this alien wood will be gradually tamed and purified by repeated contacts with my wary flesh. He rinsed the bath gingerly. The rubber tube of the spraying affair came off the tap with a plop. Two clean towels hung on a rope together with some black stockings that had been or would be washed. A bottle of mineral oil, half full, and a gray cardboard cylinder which had been the kernel of a toilet paper roll, stood side by side on a shelf. The shelf also held two popular novels (*Flung Roses* and *All Quiet on the Don*). David's toothbrush gave him a smile of recognition. He dropped his shaving soap on the floor and there was a silvery hair sticking to it when he picked it up.

In the dining room Maximov was alone. The portly old gentleman slipped a marker into his book, stood up with a genial jerk and vigorously shook hands with Krug, as if a night's sleep had been a long and hazardous journey. "How did you rest [*Kak pochivali*]?" he asked, and then, with a worried frown, tested the temperature of the coffee-pot under its coxcomb cozy. His shiny pink face was clean-shaven like that of an actor (old-fashioned simile); a tasseled skullcap protected his perfectly bald head; he wore a warm jacket with toggles. "I recommend this," he said, pointing with his fifth finger. "I find it is the only cheese of its kind that does not clog the bowels."

He was one of those persons whom one loves not because of some lustrous streak of talent (this retired businessman possessed none), but because every moment spent with them fits exactly the gauge of one's life. There are friendships like circuses, waterfalls, libraries; there are others comparable to old dressing gowns. You found nothing especially attractive about

Maximov's mind if you took it apart: his ideas were conservative, his tastes undistinguished: but somehow or other these dull components formed a wonderfully comfortable and harmonious whole. No subtlety of thought tainted his honesty, he was as reliable as iron and oak, and when Krug mentioned once that the word "loyalty" phonetically and visually reminded him of a golden fork lying in the sun on a smooth spread of pale yellow silk, Maximov replied somewhat stiffly that to *him* loyalty was limited to its dictionary denotation. Commonsense with him was saved from smug vulgarity by a delicate emotional undercurrent, and the somewhat bare and birdless symmetry of his branching principles was ever so slightly disturbed by a moist wind blowing from regions which he naïvely thought did not exist. The misfortunes of others worried him more than did his own troubles, and had he been an old sea captain, he would have dutifully gone down with his ship rather than plump apologetically into the last lifeboat. At the present moment he was bracing himself to give a piece of his mind to Krug, and was playing for time by talking politics.

"The milkman," he said, "told me this morning that posters have been put up all over the village inviting the population to celebrate spontaneously the restoration of complete order. A plan of conduct is suggested. We are supposed to collect in our usual holiday haunts, in cafés, in clubs and in the halls of our corporations and sing communal songs in praise of the Government. Directors of civic *ballonas* have been elected for every district. One wonders of course what people who cannot sing and who do not belong to any corporation are expected to do."

"I dreamed of him," said Krug. "Apparently this is the only way that my old schoolmate can hope to associate with me nowadays."

"I understand you were not particularly fond of each other at school?"

"Well, that needs analyzing. I certainly loathed him, but the question is—was it mutual? I remember one queer incident. The lights went out suddenly—short circuit or something."

"Does happen sometimes. Try that jam. Your son thought highly of it."

"I was in the classroom reading," continued Krug. "Goodness knows why it was in the evening. The Toad had slipped in and was fumbling in his desk—he kept candy there. It was then that the lights went out. I leaned back, waiting in perfect darkness. Suddenly I felt something wet and soft on the back of my hand. The Kiss of the Toad. He managed to bolt before I could catch him."

"Pretty sentimental, I should say," remarked Maximov.

"And loathsome," added Krug.

He buttered a bun and proceeded to recount the details of the meeting at the President's house. Maximov sat down too, pondered for a moment, then pounced across the table at a basket with *knakerbrod*, bumped it down near Krug's plate and said:

"I want to tell you something. When you hear it, you may be cross and call me a meddler, but I shall risk incurring your displeasure because the matter is really much too serious and I do not mind whether you growl or not. *Ia, sobstvenno, uzhe vchera khotel* [I should have broached the subject yesterday] but Anna thought you were too tired. It would be rash to postpone this talk any longer."

"Go ahead," said Krug, taking a bite and bending forward as the jam was about to drip.

"I perfectly understand your refusal to deal with those people. I should have acted likewise, I guess. They will make another attempt at getting you to sign things and you will refuse again. This point is settled."

"Most definitely," said Krug.

"Good. Now, since this point is settled, it follows that something else is settled too. Namely, your position under the new regime. It takes on a peculiar aspect, and what I wish to point out is that you do not seem to realize the danger of this aspect. In other words, as soon as the Ekwilists lose hope of obtaining your co-operation they will arrest you."

"Non-Sense," said Krug.

"Precisely. Let us call this hypothetical occurrence an utterly nonsensical thing. But the utterly nonsensical is a natural and logical part of Paduk's rule. You have to take this into consideration, my friend, you have to prepare some kind of defense, no matter how unlikely the danger may seem."

"*Yer un dah* [stuff and nonsense]," said Krug. "He will go on licking my hand in the dark. I am invulnerable. Invulnerable—the rumbling sea wave [*volna*] rolling the rabble of pebbles as it recedes. Nothing can happen to Krug the Rock. The two or three fat nations (the one that is blue on the map and the one that is fallow) from which my Toad craves recognition, loans, and whatever else a bullet-riddled country may want to obtain from a sleek neighbor—these nations will simply ignore him and his government, if he . . . molests me. Is that the right kind of growl?"

"It is not. Your conception of practical politics is romantic and childish, and altogether false. We can imagine him forgiving you the ideas you expressed in your former works. We can also imagine him suffering an outstanding mind to exist in the midst of a nation which by his own law must be as plain as its plainest citizen. But in order to imagine these things we are forced to postulate an attempt on his part to put you to some special use. If nothing comes of it—then he will not bother about public opinion abroad, and on the other hand no state will bother about you if it finds some profit in dealing with this country."

"Foreign academies will protest. They will offer fabulous sums, my weight in *Ra*, to buy my liberty."

"You may jest as much as you please, but still I want to know—look here, Adam, what do you expect to do? I mean, you surely cannot believe you will be permitted to lecture or publish your works, or keep in touch with foreign scholars and publishers, or do you?"

"I do not. *Je resterai coi.*"

"My French is limited," said Maximov dryly.

"I shall," said Krug (beginning to feel very bored), "lie *doggo*. In due time what intelligence I have left will be dovetailed into some leisurely book. Frankly I do not give a damn for this or any other university. Is David out of doors?"

"But, my dear fellow, they will not let you sit still! This is the crux of the matter. I or any other plain citizen can and must sit still, but you cannot. You are one of the very few celebrities our country has produced in modern times, and——"

"Who are the other stars of this mysterious constellation?"

queried Krug, crossing his legs and inserting a comfortable hand between thigh and knee.

"All right: the only one. And for this reason they will want you to be as active as possible. They will do all they can to make you boost their way of thinking. The style, the *begonia* [brilliancy], will be yours, of course. Paduk will be satisfied with merely arranging the program."

"And I shall remain deaf and dumb. Really, my dear fellow, this is all journalism on your part. I want to be left alone."

"Alone is the wrong word!" cried Maximov, flushing. "You are not alone! You have a child."

"Come, come," said Krug, "let us please——"

"We shall not. I warned you that I would ignore your irritation."

"Well, what do you want me to do?" asked Krug with a sigh and helped himself to another cup of lukewarm coffee.

"Leave the country at once."

The stove crackled gently, and a square clock with two cornflowers painted on its white wooden face and no glass rapped out the seconds in pica type. The window attempted a smile. A faint infusion of sunshine spread over the distant hill and brought out with a kind of pointless distinction the little farm and its three pine trees on the opposite slope which seemed to move forward and then to retreat again as the wan sun swooned.

"I do not see the necessity of leaving right now," said Krug. "If they pester me too persistently I probably shall—but for the present the only move I care to make is to rook my king the long side."

Maximov got up and then sat down in another chair.

"I see it is going to be quite difficult to make you realize your position. Please, Adam, use your wits: neither today, nor tomorrow, nor at any time will Paduk allow you to go abroad. But today you can escape, as Berenz and Marbel and others have escaped; tomorrow it will be impossible, the frontiers are being stitched up more and more closely, there will not be a single interstice left by the time you make up your mind."

"Well, why then don't you escape yourself?" grunted Krug.

"My position is somewhat different," answered Maximov

quietly. "And what is more, you know it. Anna and I are too old—and besides I am the perfect type of the average man and present no danger whatever to the Government. You are as healthy as a bull, and everything about you is criminal."

"Even if I thought it wise to leave the country I should not have the faintest idea how to manage the business."

"Go to Turok—he knows, he will put you in touch with the necessary people. It will cost you a good deal of money but you can afford it. I too do not know how it is done, but I know it can and has been done. Think of the peace in a civilized country, of the possibilities to work, of the schooling available for your child. Under your present circumstances——"

He checked himself. After an exceedingly awkward supper the night before he had told himself he would not refer again to the subject which this strange widower seemed so stoically to avoid.

"No," said Krug. "No. I am not up to it [*ne do tovo*] for the moment. It is kind of you to worry about me [*obo mne*] the way you do, but really [*pravo*] you exaggerate the danger. I shall keep your suggestion in mind, of course [*koneshno*]. Let us not talk of it any more [*bol'she*]. What is David doing?"

"Well, you know what I think at least [*po kraïneï mere*]," said Maximov, picking up the historical novel he had been reading when Krug came in. "But we are not through with you yet. I shall have Anna talk to you, too, whether you like it or not. She may fare better. I believe David is with her in the kitchen garden. We lunch at one."

The night had been stormy, heaving and gasping with brutal torrents of rain; and in the starkness of the cold quiet morning the sodden brown asters were in disorder and drops of quicksilver blotched the pungent-smelling purple cabbage leaves, between the coarse veins of which grubs had made ugly holes. David was dreamily sitting in a wheelbarrow and the little old lady was trying to push it along on the muddy clay of the path. "*Ne mogoo!* [I cannot]," she exclaimed with a laugh and brushed a strand of thin silvery hair away from her temple. David tumbled out of the wheelbarrow. Krug, not looking at her, said he wondered whether it was not too chilly for the boy to go about without his coat, and Anna Petrovna replied that the white sweater he had on was sufficiently thick and comfy. Olga somehow had never much liked Anna Petrovna and her sweet saintliness.

"I want to take him for a good long walk," said Krug. "You must have had quite enough of him. Lunch at one, is that right?"

What he said, what words he used, did not matter; he kept avoiding her brave kind eyes to which he felt he could not live up, and listened to his own voice stringing trivial sounds in the silence of a shriveled world.

She stood watching them as father and son went hand in hand towards the road. Very still, fumbling keys and a thimble in the strained pockets of her black jumper.

Broken clusters of mountain ash corals lay here and there on the chocolate-brown road. The berries were puckered and soiled, but even if they had been juicy and clean you certainly could not eat them. Jam is a different matter. No. I said: no. To *taste* is the same as to eat. Some of the maples in the silent damp wood through which the road wandered retained their painted leaves but the birches were quite naked. David slipped and with great presence of mind prolonged the slide so as to have the pleasure of sitting down on the sticky earth. Get up, get up. But he kept sitting there for another moment looking up with sham stupefaction and laughing eyes. His hair was moist and hot. Get up. Surely, this is a dream, thought Krug, this silence, the deep ridicule of late autumn, miles away from home. Why are we here of all places? A sickly sun again attempted to enliven the white sky: for a second or two a couple of wavering shadows, K ghost and D ghost, marching on shadowy stilts, copied the human gait and then faded out. An empty bottle. If you like, he said, you can pick up that Skotomic bottle and throw it hard at the trunk of a tree. It will explode with a beautiful bang. But it fell intact into the rusty waves of the bracken, and he had to wade in after it himself, because the place was much too damp for the wrong pair of shoes David was wearing. Try again. It refused to break. All right, I shall do it myself. There was a post with a sign: Hunting Prohibited. Against this he hurled the green vodka bottle violently. He was a big heavy man. David backed. The bottle burst like a star.

Presently they emerged into open country. Who was that idly sitting on a fence? He wore long boots and a peaked cap but did not look like a peasant. He smiled and said: "Good morning, Professor." "Good morning to you," answered Krug without stopping. Possibly one of the people who supplied the Maximovs with game and berries.

The *dachas* on the right-hand side of the road were mostly deserted. Here and there, however, some remnants of vacational life still persisted. In front of one of the porches a black trunk with brass knobs, a couple of bundles, and a helpless looking bicycle with swathed pedals stood, sat, and lay, awaiting some means of transportation, and a child in town clothes was rocking for the last time in a doleful swing between the boles of two pine trees that had seen better days. A little further, two elderly women with tear-stained faces were engaged in burying a mercifully killed dog together with the old croquet ball that bore the signs of its gay young teeth. In yet another garden a white-bearded waltwhitmanesque man wearing a jaeger suit was seated before an easel, and although the time was a quarter to eleven of a nondescript morning, a cindery red-barred sunset sprawled on his canvas, and he was painting in the trees and various other details which, on the day before, advancing dusk had prevented him from completing. On a bench in a pine grove on the left a straight-backed girl was rapidly speaking (retaliation . . . bombs . . . cowards . . . oh, Phokus, if I were a man . . .) with nervous gestures of perplexity and dismay to a blue-capped student who sat with bent head and poked at scraps of paper, bus tickets, pine needles, the eye of a doll or a fish, the soft soil, with the point of the slim, tightly buttoned umbrella belonging to his pale companion. But otherwise the once cheerful resort was forlorn, the shutters were closed, a battered perambulator lay upside down in a ditch and the telegraph poles, those armless laggards, hummed in mournful unison with the blood that throbbed in one's head.

The road dipped slightly and then the village appeared, with a misty wilderness on one side and Lake Malheur on the other. The posters the milkman had mentioned gave a delightful touch of civilization and civic maturity to the humble hamlet squatting under its low mossy roofs. Several scrawny peasant women and their drum-bellied children, had collected in front of the village hall, which was being prettily decorated for the coming festivities; and from the windows of the post office on the left and from the windows of the police station on the right uniformed clerks followed the progress of the good work with eager intelligent eyes full of pleasant anticipation. All of a sudden, with a sound akin to the cry of a newborn infant, a radio loud-speaker which had just been installed burst into life, then abruptly collapsed.

"There are some toys there," remarked David, pointing across the road towards a small but eclectic store which carried everything from groceries to Russian felt boots.

"All right," said Krug; "let us see what there is."

But as the impatient child started to cross alone, a big black automobile emerged at full speed from the direction of the district highway, and Krug, plunging forward, jerked David back as the car thundered by, leaving the mangled body of a hen in its tingling wake.

"You hurt me," said David.

Krug felt weak in the knees and bade David make haste so that he would not notice the dead bird.

"How many times——" said Krug.

A small replica of the murderous vehicle (the vibration of which still haunted Krug's solar plexus, although by that time it had probably reached or even passed the spot where the neighborly loafer had been perched on his fence) was immediately detected by David among the cheap dolls and the tins of preserves. Though somewhat dusty and scratched, it had the kind of detachable tires he approved of and was especially acceptable because it had been found in an out-of-the-way place. Krug asked the red-cheeked young grocer for a pocket flask of brandy (the Maximovs were teetotalers). As he was paying for it and for the little car which David was delicately rolling backwards and forwards upon the counter, the Toad's nasal tones, prodigiously magnified, burst forth from outside. The grocer stood to attention, fixing in civic fervor the flags decorating the village hall, which, together with a strip of white sky, could be seen through the doorway.

". . . and to those who trust me as they trust themselves," roared the loud-speaker, as it ended a sentence.

The clatter of applause that followed was presumably interrupted by the gesture of the orator's hand.

"From now on," continued the tremendously swollen Tyrannosaurus, "the way to total joy lies open. You will attain it, brothers, by dint of ardent intercourse with one another, by being like happy boys in a whispering dormitory, by adjusting ideas and emotions to those of a harmonious majority; you will attain it, citizens, by weeding out all such arrogant notions as the community does not and should not share; you will attain it, adolescents, by letting your person dissolve in the virile oneness of the State; then, and only then, will the goal be reached. Your groping individualities will become interchangeable and, instead of crouching in the prison cell of an illegal ego, the naked soul will be in contact with that of every other man in this land; nay, more: each of you will be able to make his abode in the elastic inner self of any other citizen, and to flutter from one to another, until you know not whether you are Peter or John, so closely locked will you be in the embrace of the State, so gladly will you be krum karum——"

The speech disintegrated in a succession of cackles. There was a kind of stunned silence: evidently the village radio was not yet in perfect working order.

"One could almost butter one's bread with the modulations of that admirable voice," remarked Krug.

What followed was most unexpected: the grocer gave him a wink.

"Good gracious," said Krug, "a gleam in the gloom!"

But the wink contained a specific injunction. Krug turned. An Ekwilist soldier was standing right behind him.

All he wanted however was a pound of sunflower seeds. Krug and David inspected a cardboard house which stood on the floor in a corner. David sank down on his little haunches to peep inside through the windows. But these were simply painted upon the wall. He slowly drew himself up, still looking at the house and automatically slipping his hand into Krug's.

They left the shop and in order to overcome the monotony of the return journey decided to skirt the lake and then to follow a path that meandered through meadows and would bring them back to the Maximovs' cottage after going round the wood.

Was the fool trying to save me? From what? From whom? Excuse me, I am invulnerable. Not much more foolish in fact than suggesting I grow a beard and cross the frontier.

There were a number of things to be settled before giving thought to political matters—if indeed that drivel could be called a political matter. If, moreover, in a fortnight or so some impatient admirer did not murder Paduk. Misunderstanding, so to speak, the drift of the spiritual cannibalism advocated by the poor fellow. One wondered also (at least somebody might wonder—the question was of little interest) what the peasants made of that eloquence. Maybe it vaguely reminded them of church. First of all I shall have to get him a good nurse—a picture-book nurse, kind and wise and scrupulously clean. Then I must do something about you, my love. We have imagined that a white hospital train with a white Diesel engine has taken you through many a tunnel to a mountainous country by the sea. You are getting well there. But you cannot write because your fingers are so very weak. Moonbeams cannot hold even a white pencil. The picture is pretty, but how long can it stay on the screen? We expect the next slide, but the magic-lantern man has none left. Shall we let the theme of a long separation expand till it breaks into tears? Shall we say (daintily handling the disinfected white symbols) that the train is Death and the nursing home Paradise? Or shall we leave the picture to fade by itself, to mingle with other fading impressions? But we want to write letters to you even if you cannot answer. Shall we suffer the slow wobbly scrawl (we can manage our name and two or three words of greeting) to work its conscientious and unnecessary way across a post card which will never be mailed? Are not these problems so hard to solve because my own mind is not made up yet in regard to your death? My intelligence does not accept the transformation of physical discontinuity into the permanent continuity of a nonphysical element escaping the obvious law, nor can it accept the inanity of accumulating incalculable treasures of thought and sensation, and thought-behind-thought and sensation-behind-sensation, to lose them all at once and forever in a fit of black nausea followed by infinite nothingness. Unquote.

"See if you can climb on top of that stone. I don't think you can."

David trotted across a dead meadow towards a boulder shaped like a sheep (left behind by some careless glacier). The brandy was bad but would serve. He suddenly recalled a summer day when he had walked through these very fields in the company of a tall black-haired girl with thick lips and downy arms whom he had courted just before he met Olga.

"Yes, I *am* looking. Splendid. Now try to get down."

But David could not. Krug walked up to the boulder and tenderly removed him. This little body. They sat for a while on a lamb-boulder near by and contemplated an endless freight train puffing beyond the fields towards the station near the lake. A crow ponderously flapped by, the slow swish-swish of its wings making the rotting grassland and the colorless sky seem even sadder than they actually were.

"You will lose it that way. Better let me put it into my pocket."

Presently they started moving again, and David was curious to know how far they had to walk yet. Only a little way. They followed the edge of the forest and then turned into a very muddy road which led them to what was for the moment home.

A cart was standing in front of the cottage. The old white horse looked at them across its shoulder. On the threshold of the porch two people were sitting side by side: the farmer who lived on the hill and his wife who did the housework for the Maximovs.

"They are gone," said the farmer.

"I hope they did not go out to meet us on the road because we came by another way. Go in, David, and wash your hands."

"No," said the farmer. "They are quite gone. They have been taken away in a police car."

At this point his wife became very voluble. She had just come down from the hill when she saw the soldiers leading the aged couple away. She had been afraid to come near. Her wages had not been paid since October. She would take, she said, all the jars of jam in the house.

Krug went in. The table was laid for four. David wanted to have his toy which, he hoped, his father had not lost. A piece of raw meat was lying on the kitchen table.

Krug sat down. The farmer had also come in and was stroking his grizzled chin.

"Could you drive us to the station?" asked Krug after a while.

"I might get into trouble," said the farmer.

"Oh, come, I offer you more than the police will ever pay you for whatever you do for them."

"You are not the police and so cannot bribe me," replied the honest and meticulous old farmer.

"You mean you refuse?"

The farmer was silent.

"Well," said Krug, getting to his feet, "I am afraid, I shall have to insist. The child is tired, I do not intend to carry him and the bag."

"How much was it again?" asked the farmer.

Krug put on his glasses and opened his wallet.

"You will stop at the police station on the way," he added.

The toothbrushes and the pajamas were quickly packed. David accepted the sudden departure with perfect equanimity but suggested eating something first. The kind woman got him some biscuits and an apple. A fine rain had set in. David's hat could not be found and Krug gave him his own broad-brimmed black one, but David kept taking it off because it covered his ears and he wanted to hear the sloshing hoofs, the creaking wheels.

As they were passing the spot where two hours before a man with a heavy mustache and twinkling eyes had been sitting on a rustic fence, Krug noticed that now, instead of the man, there were but a couple of *rudobrustki* or *ruddocks* [a small bird allied to the robin] and that a square of cardboard had been nailed to the fence. It bore a rough inscription in ink (already somewhat affected by the drizzle):

Bon Voyage!

To this Krug drew the attention of the driver; who, without

turning his head, remarked that there were many inexplicable things happening *nowadays* (a euphemism for "new regime") and that it was better not to study current phenomena too closely. David tugged at his father's sleeve and wanted to know what it was all about. Krug explained that they were discussing the strange ways of people who arranged picnics in dreary November.

"I had better drive you straight on, folks, or you might miss the one forty," said the farmer tentatively, but Krug made him pull up at the brick house where the local police had their headquarters. Krug got out and entered an office room where a bewhiskered old man, his uniform unbuttoned at the neck, was sipping tea from a blue saucer and blowing upon it between sips. He said he knew nothing about the business. It was, he said, the City Guard, and not his department, which had made the arrest. He could only presume that they had been taken to some prison in town as political offenders. He suggested that Krug stop playing the busybody and thank his stars for not having been in the house when the arrest took place. Krug said that, on the contrary, he intended doing everything in his power to find out why two aged and respectable persons who had lived quietly in the country for a number of years and had no connection whatever with—— The police officer, interrupting him, said that the best a professor could do (if Krug *was* a professor) would be to keep his mouth shut and leave the village. Again the saucer was lifted to the bearded lips. Two young members of the force hovered around and stared at Krug.

He stood there for a moment looking at the wall, at a poster calling attention to the plight of aged policemen, at a calendar (monstrously *in copula* with a barometer); pondered a bribe; decided that they really knew nothing here; and with a shrug of his heavy shoulders walked out.

David was not in the cart.

The farmer turned his head, looked at the empty seat and said the child had probably followed Krug into the police station. Krug went back. The chief eyed him with irritation and suspicion and said that he had seen the cart from the window and that there had been no child in it from the very start. Krug tried to open another door in the corridor but it was locked. "Stop that," growled the man losing his temper, "or else we'll arrest you for making a nuisance of yourself."

"I want my little boy," said Krug (another Krug, horribly handicapped by a spasm in the throat and a pounding heart).

"Hold your horses," said one of the younger policemen. "This is not a kindergarten, there are no children here."

Krug (now a man in black with an ivory face) pushed him aside and went out again. He cleared his throat and bellowed for David. Two villagers in medieval *kappen* who stood near the cart gazed at him and then at each other, and then one of them turned and glanced in a given direction. "Have you——?" asked Krug. But they did not reply and looked once more at each other.

I must not lose my head, thought Adam the Ninth—for by now there were quite a number of these serial Krugs: turning this way and that like the baffled buffeted seeker in a game of blindman's buff; battering with imaginary fists a cardboard police station to pulp; running through nightmare tunnels; half-hiding together with Olga behind a tree to watch David warily tiptoe around another, his whole body ready for a little shiver of glee; searching an intricate dungeon where, somewhere, a shrieking child was being tortured by experienced hands; hugging the boots of a uniformed brute; strangling the brute amid a chaos of overturned furniture; finding a small skeleton in a dark cellar.

At this point it may be mentioned that David wore on the fourth finger of his left hand a child's enameled ring.

He was about to attack the police once more, but then noticed that a narrow lane fringed with shriveled nettles ran along the side of the brick police house (the two peasants had been glancing in that direction for quite a while), and turned into it, stumbling painfully over a log as he did so.

"Take care, don't break your pins, you'll need 'em," said the farmer with an amiable laugh.

In the lane, a barefooted scrofulous boy in a pink red-patched shirt was whipping a top and David stood looking on with his hands behind his back.

"This is intolerable," cried Krug. "You ought never, never to wander away like that. Shut up! Yes. I *will* hold you. Get in. Get in."

One of the peasants tapped his temple slightly with a judicious air, and his crony nodded. In an open window a young policeman aimed a half-eaten apple at Krug's back but was restrained by a staider comrade.

The cart moved on. Krug groped for his handkerchief, did not find it, wiped his face with the palm of his still shaking hand.

The well-named lake was a featureless expanse of gray water, and as the cart turned onto the highway that ran along the shore to the station, a cold breeze lifted with invisible finger and thumb the thin silvery mane of the old mare.

"Will my mummy be back when we come?" asked David.

A FLUTED GLASS with a blue-veined violet and a jug of hot punch stand on Ember's bedtable. The buff wall directly above his bed (he has a bad cold) bears a sequence of three engravings.

Number one represents a sixteenth-century gentleman in the act of handing a book to a humble fellow who holds a spear and a bay-crowned hat in his left hand. Note the sinistral detail (Why? Ah, "that is the question," as Monsieur Homais once remarked, quoting *le journal d'hier*, a question which is answered in a wooden voice by the Portrait on the title page of the First Folio). Note also the legend: "Ink, a Drug." Somebody's idle pencil (Ember highly treasures this scholium) has numbered the letters so as to spell *Grudinka* which means "bacon" in several Slavic languages.

Number two shows the rustic (now clad in the clothes of the gentleman) removing from the head of the gentleman (now writing at a desk) a kind of shapska. Scribbled underneath in the same hand: "*Ham-let*, or *Homelette au Lard*."

Finally, number three has a road, a traveler on foot (wearing the stolen shapska) and a road sign "To High Wycombe."

His name is protean. He begets doubles at every corner. His penmanship is unconsciously faked by lawyers who happen to write a similar hand. On the wet morning of November 27, 1582, he is Shaxpere and she is a Wately of Temple Grafton. A couple of days later he is Shagspere and she is a Hathway of Stratford-on-Avon. Who is he? William X, cunningly composed of two left arms and a mask. Who else? The person who said (not for the first time) that the glory of God is to hide a thing, and the glory of man is to find it. However, the fact that the Warwickshire fellow wrote the plays is most satisfactorily proved on the strength of an applejohn and a pale primrose.

There are two themes here: the Shakespearian one rendered in the present tense, with Ember presiding in his ruelle; and another theme altogether, a complex mixture of past, present, and future, with Olga's monstrous absence causing dreadful embarrassment. This was, this is, their first meeting since she died. Krug will not speak of her, will not even inquire about her ashes; and Ember, who feels the shame of death too, does not know what to say. Had he been able to move about freely, he might have embraced his fat friend in silence (a miserable defeat in the case of philosophers and poets accustomed to believe that words are superior to deeds), but this is not feasible when one of the two lies in bed. Krug, semi-intentionally, keeps out of reach. He is a difficult person. Describe the bedroom. Allude to Ember's bright brown eyes. Hot punch and a touch of fever. His strong shining blue-veined nose and the bracelet on his hairy wrist. Say something. Ask about David. Relate the horror of those rehearsals.

"David is also laid up with a cold [*ist auk beterkeltet*] but that is not why we had to come back [*zueruk*]. What [*shto bish*] were you saying about those rehearsals [*repetitia*]?"

Ember gratefully adopts the subject selected. He might have asked: "Why then?" He will learn the reason a little later. Vaguely he perceives emotional dangers in that dim region. So he prefers to talk shop. Last chance of describing the bedroom.

Too late. Ember gushes. He exaggerates his own gushing manner. In a dehydrated and condensed form Ember's new impressions as Literary Adviser to the State Theater may be rendered thus:

"The two best Hamlets we had, indeed the only respectable ones, have both left the country in disguise and are now said to be fiercely intriguing in Paris after having almost murdered each other en route. None of the youngsters we have interviewed are any good, though one or two have at least the full habit of body required for the part. For reasons I shall presently make clear Osric and Fortinbras have acquired a tremendous ascendancy over the rest of the cast. The Queen is with child. Laertes is constitutionally unable to learn the elements of fencing. I have lost all interest in the staging of the thing as I am helpless to change the grotesque course it has taken. My sole poor object now is to have the players adopt my own translation instead of the abominable one to which they are used. On the other hand this work of love commenced long ago is not yet quite finished and the fact of having to speed it up for what is a rather incidental purpose (to say the least) causes me intense irritation, which, however, is nothing to the horror of hearing the actors lapse with a kind of atavistic relief into the gibberish of the traditional version (Kronberg's) whenever Wern, who is weak and prefers ideas to words, allows them to behind my back."

Ember goes on to explain why the new Government found it worth while to suffer the production of a muddled Elizabethan play. He explains the idea on which the production is based. Wern, who humbly submitted the project, took his conception of the play from the late Professor Hamm's extraordinary work "The Real Plot of *Hamlet*."

" 'Iron and ice' (wrote the Professor)—'this is the physical amalgamation suggested by the personality of the strangely rigid and ponderous Ghost. Of this union Fortinbras (Ironside) will be presently born. According to the immemorial rules of the stage what is boded must be embodied: the eruption must come at all cost. In *Hamlet* the exposition grimly promises the audience a play founded upon young Fortinbras' attempt to recover the lands lost by his father to King Hamlet. This is the conflict, this is the plot. To surreptitiously shift the stress from this healthy, vigorous and clear-cut Nordic theme to the chameleonic moods of an impotent Dane would be, on the modern stage, an insult to determinism and commonsense.

" 'Whatever Shakespeare's or Kyd's intentions were, there can be no doubt that the keynote, the impelling power of the action, is the corruption of civil and military life in Denmark. Imagine the morale of an army where a soldier, who must fear neither thunder nor silence, says that he is "sick at heart"! Consciously or unconsciously, the author of *Hamlet* has created the tragedy of the masses and thus has founded the sovereignty of society over the individual. This, however, does not mean that there is no tangible hero in the play. But he is not Hamlet. The real hero is of course Fortinbras, a blooming young knight, beautiful and sound to the core. With God's sanction, this fine Nordic youth assumes the control of miserable Denmark which had been so criminally misruled by degenerate King Hamlet and Judeo-Latin Claudius.

" 'As with all decadent democracies, everybody in the

Denmark of the play suffers from a plethora of words. If the state is to be saved, if the nation desires to be worthy of a new robust government, then everything must be changed; popular commonsense must spit out the caviar of moonshine and poetry, and the simple word, *verbum sine ornatu*, intelligible to man and beast alike, and accompanied by fit action, must be restored to power. Young Fortinbras possesses an ancient claim and hereditary rights to the throne of Denmark. Some dark deed of violence or injustice, some base trick on the part of degenerate feudalism, some masonic maneuver engendered by the Shylocks of high finance, has dispossessed his family of their just claims, and the shadow of this crime keeps hanging in the dark background until, with the closing scene, the idea of mass justice impresses upon the whole play its seal of historical significance.

" 'Three thousand crowns and a week or so of available time would not have been sufficient to conquer Poland (at least in those days); but they proved amply sufficient for another purpose. Wine-besotted Claudius is completely deceived by young Fortinbras' suggestion, that he, Fortinbras, pass through the dominion of Claudius on his (singularly roundabout) way to Poland with an army levied for quite a different purpose. No, the bestial Polacks need not tremble: *that* conquest will not take place; it is not *their* bogs and forests that our hero covets. Instead of proceeding to the port, Fortinbras, that soldier of genius, will be lying in waiting and the "go softly on" (which he whispers to his troops after sending a captain to greet Claudius) can only mean one thing: go softly into hiding while the enemy (the Danish King) thinks you have embarked for Poland.

" 'The real plot of the play will be readily grasped if the following is realized: the Ghost on the battlements of Elsinore is not the ghost of King Hamlet. It is that of Fortinbras the Elder whom King Hamlet has slain. The ghost of the victim posing as the ghost of the murderer—what a wonderful bit of farseeing strategy, how deeply it excites our intense admiration! The glib and probably quite untrue account of old Hamlet's death which this admirable imposter gives is intended solely to create *innerliche Unruhe* in the state and to soften the morale of the Danes. The poison poured into the sleeper's

ear is a symbol of the subtle injection of lethal rumors, a
symbol which the groundlings of Shakespeare's day could
hardly have missed. Thus, old Fortinbras, disguised as his enemy's ghost, prepares the peril of his enemy's son and the triumph of his own offspring. No, the "judgments" were not
so accidental, the "slaughters" not so casual as they seemed
to Horatio the Recorder, and there is a note of deep satisfaction (which the audience cannot help sharing) in the young
hero's guttural exclamation—Ha-ha, this quarry cries on
havoc (meaning: the foxes have devoured one another)—as
he surveys the rich heap of dead bodies, all that is left of the
rotten state of Denmark. We can easily imagine him adding
in an outburst of rough filial gratitude: Yah, the old mole has
done a good job!

" 'But to return to Osric. Garrulous Hamlet has just been
speaking to the skull of a jester; now it is the skull of jesting
death that speaks to Hamlet. Note the remarkable juxtaposition: the skull—the shell; "Runs away with a shell on his
head." Osric and Yorick almost rime, except that the yolk
of one has become the bone (os) of the other. Mixing as he
does the language of the shop and the ship, this middleman,
wearing the garb of a fantastic courtier, is in the act of selling
death, the very death that Hamlet has just escaped at sea. The
winged doublet and the aureate innuendoes mask a deep purpose, a bold and cunning mind. Who is this master of cere-
monies? He is young Fortinbras' most brilliant spy.' Well, this
gives you a fair sample of what I have to endure."

Krug cannot help smiling at little Ember's complaints. He
remarks that somehow or other the whole business reminds
him of Paduk's mannerisms. I mean these intricate convolutions of sheer stupidity. To stress the artist's detachment from
life, Ember says he does not know and does not care to know
(a telltale dismissal) who this Paduk or Padock—*bref, la per-
sonne en question*—is. By way of explanation Krug tells Ember
about his visit to the Lakes and how it all ended. Naturally
Ember is aghast. He vividly visualizes Krug and the child wandering through the rooms of the deserted cottage whose two
clocks (one in the dining room, the other in the kitchen)
are probably still going, alone, intact, pathetically sticking
to man's notion of time after man has gone. He wonders

whether Maximov had time to receive the well-written letter he sent him about Olga's death and Krug's helpless condition. What shall I say? The priest mistook a blear-eyed old man belonging to Viola's party for the widower and while making his oration, and while the beautiful big body was burning behind a thick wall, kept addressing himself to that person (who nodded back). Not even an uncle, not even her mother's lover.

Ember turns his face to the wall and bursts into tears. In order to bring things back to a less emotional level Krug tells him about a curious character with whom he once traveled in the States, a man who was fanatically eager to make a film out of *Hamlet.*

"We'd begin, he had said, with
Ghostly apes swathed in sheets
haunting the shuddering Roman streets.
And the mobled moon . . .

Then: the ramparts and towers of Elsinore, its dragons and florid ironwork, the moon making fish scales of its shingle tiles, the integument of a mermaid multiplied by the gable roof, which shimmers in an abstract sky, and the green star of a glowworm on the platform before the dark castle. Hamlet's first soliloquy is delivered in an unweeded garden that has gone to seed. Burdock and thistle are the main invaders. A toad breathes and blinks on the late king's favorite garden seat. Somewhere the cannon booms as the new king drinks. By dream law and screen law the cannon is gently transformed into the obliquity of a rotten tree trunk in the garden. The trunk points cannonwise at the sky where for one instant the deliberate loops of canescent smoke form the floating word 'self-slaughter.'

"Hamlet at Wittenberg, always late, missing G. Bruno's lectures, never using a watch, relying on Horatio's timepiece which is slow, saying he will be on the battlements between eleven and twelve and turning up after midnight.

"The moonlight following on tiptoe the Ghost in complete steel, a gleam now settling on a rounded pauldron, now stealing along the taces.

"We shall also see Hamlet dragging the dead Ratman from under the arras and along the floor and up the winding stairs, to stow him away in an obscure passage, with some weird light effects anon, when the torch-bearing Switzers are sent to find the body. Another thrill will be provided by Hamlet's sea-gowned figure, unhampered by the heavy seas, heedless of the spray, clambering over bales and barrels of Danish butter and creeping into the cabin where Rosenstern and Guildenkranz, those gentle interchangeable twins 'who came to heal and went away to die,' are snoring in their common bunk. As the sagebrush country and leopard-spotted hills sped past the window of the men's lounge, more and more pictorial possibilities were evolved. We might be shown, he said (he was a hawk-faced shabby man whose academic career had been suddenly brought to a close by an awkwardly timed love affair), R. following young L. through the Quartier Latin, Polonius in his youth acting Caesar at the University Playhouse, the skull in Hamlet's gloved hands developing the features of a live jester (with the censor's permission); perhaps even lusty old King Hamlet smiting with a poleax the Polacks skidding and sprawling on the ice. Then he produced a flask from his hip pocket and said: 'take a shot.' He added he had thought she was eighteen at least, judging by her bust, but, in fact, she was hardly fifteen, the little bitch. And then there was Ophelia's death. To the sounds of Liszt's *Les Funérailles* she would be shown wrestling—or, as another rivermaid's father would have said, 'wrustling'—with the willow. A lass, a salix. He recommended here a side shot of the glassy water. To feature a phloating leaph. Then back again to her little white hand, holding a wreath, trying to reach, trying to wreathe a phallacious sliver. Now comes the difficulty of dealing in a dramatic way with what had been in prevocal days the *pièce de résistance* of comic shorts—the getting-unexpectedly-wet stunt. The hawk-man in the toilet lounge pointed out (between cigar and cuspidor) that the difficulty might be neatly countered by showing only her shadow, her falling shadow, falling and glancing across the edge of the turfy bank amid a shower of shadowy flowers. See? Then: a garland afloat. That puritanical leather (on which they sat) was the very last remnant of a phylogenetic link between the modern highly differentiated Pullman idea and a bench in the primitive stagecoach: from oats to oil. Then—and only then—we see her, he said, on her back in the brook (which table-forks further on to form eventually the Rhine, the Dnepr and the Cottonwood Canyon or Nova Avon) in a dim ectoplastic cloud of soaked, bulging bombast-quilted garments and dreamily droning hey non nonny nonny or any other old laud. This is transformed into a tinkling of bells, and now we are shown a liberal shepherd on marshy ground where *Orchis mascula* grows: period rags, sun-margined beard, five sheep and one cute lamb. An important point, this lamb, despite the brevity—one heartthrob —of the bucolic theme. Song moves to Queen's shepherd, lamb moves to brook.''

Krug's anecdote has the desired effect. Ember stops sniffling. He listens. Presently he smiles. Finally, he enters into the spirit of the game. Yes, she was found by a shepherd. In fact her name can be derived from that of an amorous shepherd in Arcadia. Or quite possibly it is an anagram of Alpheios, with the "S" lost in the damp grass—Alpheus the rivergod, who pursued a long-legged nymph until Artemis changed her into a stream, which of course suited his liquidity to a tee (*cp.* Winnipeg Lake, ripple 585, Vico Press edition). Or again we can base it on the Greek rendering of an old Danske serpent name. Lithe, lithping, thin-lipped Ophelia, Amleth's wet dream, a mermaid of Lethe, a rare water serpent, *Russalka letheana* of science (to match your long purples). While he was busy with German servant maids, she at home, in an embayed window, with the icy spring wind rattling the pane, innocently flirted with Osric. Her skin was so tender that if you merely looked at it a rosy spot would appear. The uncommon cold of a Botticellian angel tinged her nostrils with pink and suffused her upperlip—you know, when the rims of the lips merge with the skin. She proved to be a kitchen wench too—but in the kitchen of a vegetarian. Ophelia, serviceableness. Died in passive service. The fair Ophelia. A first Folio with some neat corrections and a few bad mistakes. "My dear fellow" (we might have Hamlet say to Horatio), "she was as hard as nails in spite of her physical softness. And slippery: a posy made of eels. She was one of those thin-blooded pale-eyed lovely slim slimy ophidian maidens that are both hotly hysterical and hopelessly frigid. Quietly, with a kind of devilish daintiness she minced her dangerous course the way her

father's ambition pointed. Even mad, she went on teasing her
secret with the dead man's finger. Which kept pointing at me.
Oh, of course I loved her like forty thousand brothers, as thick
as thieves (terracotta jars, a cypress, a fingernail moon) but we
all were Lamord's pupils, if you know what I mean." He
might add that he had caught a cold in the head during the
dumb show. Undine's pink gill, iced watermelon, *l'aurore gre-
lottant en robe rose et verte.* Her sleazy lap.

Speaking of the word-droppings on a German scholar's decrepit hat, Krug suggests tampering with Hamlet's name too.
Take "Telemachos," he says, which means "fighting from
afar"—which again was Hamlet's idea of warfare. Prune it,
remove the unnecessary letters, all of them secondary additions, and you get the ancient "Telmah." Now read it backwards. Thus does a fanciful pen elope with a lewd idea and
Hamlet in reverse gear becomes the son of Ulysses slaying his
mother's lovers. *Worte, worte, worte.* Warts, warts, warts. My
favorite commentator is Tschischwitz, a madhouse of con-
sonants—or a *soupir de petit chien.*

Ember, however, has not quite finished with the girl. After
hurriedly noting that Elsinore is an anagram of Roseline,
which has possibilities, he returns to Ophelia. He likes her, he
says. Quite apart from Hamlet's notions about her, the girl
had charm, a kind of heartbreaking charm: those quick gray-
blue eyes, the sudden laugh, the small even teeth, the pause
to see whether you were not making fun of her. Her knees
and calves, though quite shapely, were a little too sturdy in
comparison with her thin arms and light bosom. The palms
of her hands were like a damp Sunday and she wore a cross
round her neck where a tiny raisin of flesh, a coagulated but
still transparent bubble of dove's blood, seemed always in danger of being sliced off by that thin golden chain. Then, too,
there was her morning breath, it smelled of narcissi before
breakfast and of curdled milk after. She had something the
matter with her liver. The lobes of her ears were naked,
though they had been minutely pierced for small corals—not
pearls. The combination of all these details, her sharp elbows,
very fair hair, tight glossy cheekbones and the ghost of a blond
fluff (most delicately bristly to the eye) at the corners of her
mouth, remind him (says Ember remembering his childhood)

of a certain anemic Esthonian housemaid, whose pathetically parted poor little breasts palely dangled in her blouse when she went low, very low, to pull on for him his striped socks.

Here Ember suddenly raises his voice to a petulant scream of distress. He says that instead of this authentic Ophelia the impossible Gloria Bellhouse, hopelessly plump, with a mouth like the ace of hearts, has been selected for the part. He is especially incensed at the greenhouse carnations and lilies that the management gives her to play with in the "mad" scene. She and the producer, like Goethe, imagine Ophelia in the guise of a canned peach: "her whole being floats in sweet ripe passion," says Johann Wolfgang, Ger. poet, nov., dram. & phil. Oh, horrible.

"Or her father . . . We all know him and love him, don't we? and it would be so simple to have him right: Polonius-Pantolonius, a pottering dotard in a padded robe, shuffling about in carpet slippers and following the sagging spectacles at the end of his nose, as he waddles from room to room, vaguely androgynous, combining the pa and the ma, a hermaphrodite with the comfortable pelvis of a eunuch—instead of which they have a stiff tall man who played Metternich in *The World Waltzes* and insists on remaining a wise and wily statesman for the rest of his days. Oh, most horrible."

But there is worse to come. Ember asks his friend to hand him a certain book—no, the red one. Sorry, the *other* red one.

"As you have noticed, perhaps, the Messenger mentions a certain Claudio as having given him letters which Claudio 'received . . . of him that brought them [from the ship]'; there is no reference to this person anywhere else in the play. Now let us open the great Hamm's second book. What does he do? Here we are. He takes this Claudio and—well, just listen.

"That he was the King's fool is evident from the fact that in the German original (*Bestrafter Brudermord*) it is the clown Phantasmo who brings the news. It is amazing that nobody as yet has troubled to follow up this prototypical clue. No less obvious is the fact that in his quibbling mood Hamlet would of course make a special point of having the sailors deliver his message to the *King's fool*, since he, Hamlet, has *fooled* the *King*. Finally, when we recall that in those days a court jester would often assume the name of his master, with only a slight change in the ending, the picture becomes complete. We have thus the interesting figure of this Italian or Italianate jester haunting the gloomy halls of a Northern castle, a man in his forties, but as alert as he was in his youth, twenty years ago, when he replaced Yorick. Whereas Polonius had been the 'father' of good news, Claudio is the 'uncle' of bad news. His character is more subtle than that of the wise and good old man. He is afraid to confront the King directly with a message with which his nimble fingers and prying eye have already acquainted themselves. He knows that he cannot very well come to the King and tell him 'your beer is sour' with a quibble on 'beer,' meaning 'your beard is soar'd' (to soar—to pull, to twitch off). So, with superb cunning he invents a stratagem which speaks more for his intelligence than for his moral courage. What is this stratagem? It is far deeper than anything 'poor Yorick' could ever have devised. While the sailors hurry away to such abodes of pleasure as a long-yearned-for port can provide, Claudio, the dark-eyed schemer, neatly refolds the dangerous letter and casually hands it to *another messenger*, the 'Messenger' of the play, who innocently takes it to the King."

But enough of this, let us hear Ember's rendering of some famous lines:

> *Ubit' il' ne ubit'? Vot est' oprosen.*
> *Vto bude edler: v rasume tzerpieren*
> *Ogneprashchi i strely zlovo roka—*

(or as a Frenchman might have it:)

> *L'égorgerai-je ou non? Voici le vrai problème.*
> *Est-il plus noble en soi de supporter quand même*
> *Et les dards et le feu d'un accablant destin—*

Yes, I am still jesting. We now come to the real thing.

> *Tam nad ruch'om rostiot naklonno iva,*
> *V vode iavliaia list'ev sedinu;*
> *Guirliandy fantasticheskie sviv*
> *Iz etikh list'ev—s primes'u romashek,*
> *Krapivy, lutikov—*

(Over yon brook there grows aslant a willow
Showing in the water the hoariness of its leaves;
Having tressed fantastic garlands
Of these leaves, with a sprinkling of daisies,
Nettles, crowflowers—)

You see I have to choose my commentators.
    Or this difficult passage:

Ne dumaete-li vy, sudar', shto vot eto (the song about
the wounded deer), *da les per'ev na shliape, da dve kamchatye rozy na proreznykh bashmakakh, mogli by, kol' for-
tuna zadala by mne turku, zasluzhit' mne uchast'e v
teatralnoi arteli; a, sudar'?*

Or the beginning of my favorite scene:
As he sits listening to Ember's translation, Krug cannot help
marveling at the strangeness of the day. He imagines himself
at some point in the future recalling this particular moment.
He, Krug, was sitting beside Ember's bed. Ember, with knees
raised under the counterpane, was reading bits of blank verse
from scraps of paper. Krug had recently lost his wife. A new
political order had stunned the city. Two people he was fond
of had been spirited away and perhaps executed. But the room
was warm and quiet and Ember was deep in *Hamlet*. And
Krug marveled at the strangeness of the day. He listened to
the rich-toned voice (Ember's father had been a Persian mer-
chant) and tried to simplify the terms of his reaction. Nature
had once produced an Englishman whose domed head had
been a hive of words; a man who had only to breathe on any
particle of his stupendous vocabulary to have that particle live
and expand and throw out tremulous tentacles until it became
a complex image with a pulsing brain and correlated limbs.
Three centuries later, another man, in another country, was
trying to render these rhythms and metaphors in a different
tongue. This process entailed a prodigious amount of labor,
for the necessity of which no real reason could be given. It
was as if someone, having seen a certain oak tree (further
called Individual T) growing in a certain land and casting its
own unique shadow on the green and brown ground, had
proceeded to erect in his garden a prodigiously intricate piece

of machinery which in itself was as unlike that or any other tree as the translator's inspiration and language were unlike those of the original author, but which, by means of ingenious combinations of parts, light effects, breeze-engendering engines, would, when completed, cast a shadow exactly similar to that of Individual T—the same outline, changing in the same manner, with the same double and single spots of suns rippling in the same position, at the same hour of the day. From a practical point of view, such a waste of time and material (those headaches, those midnight triumphs that turn out to be disasters in the sober light of morning!) was almost criminally absurd, since the greatest masterpiece of imitation presupposed a voluntary limitation of thought, in submission to another man's genius. Could this suicidal limitation and submission be compensated by the miracle of adaptive tactics, by the thousand devices of shadography, by the keen pleasure that the weaver of words and their witness experienced at every new wile in the warp, or was it, taken all in all, but an exaggerated and spiritualized replica of Paduk's writing machine?

"Do you like it, do you accept it?" asked Ember anxiously.

"I think it is wonderful," said Krug, frowning. He got up and paced the room. "Some lines need oiling," he continued, "and I do not like the color of dawn's coat—I see 'russet' in a less leathery, less proletarian way, but you may be right. The whole thing is really quite wonderful."

He went to the window as he spoke, unconsciously peering into the yard, a deep well of light and shade (for, curiously enough, it was some time in the afternoon, and not in the middle of the night).

"I am so pleased," said Ember. "Of course, there are lots of little things to be changed. I think, I shall stick to '*laderod kappe.*'"

"Some of his puns——" said Krug. "Hullo, that's queer."

He had become aware of the yard. Two organ-grinders were standing there, a few paces from each other, neither of them playing—in fact, both looked depressed and self-conscious. Several heavy-chinned urchins with zigzag profiles (one little chap holding a toy cart by a string) gaped at them quietly.

"Never in my life," said Krug, "have I seen *two* organ-grinders in the same back yard at the same time."

"Nor have I," admitted Ember. "I shall now proceed to show you——"

"I wonder what has happened?" said Krug. "They look most uncomfortable, and they do not, or cannot, play."

"Perhaps one of them butted into the other's beat," suggested Ember, sorting out a fresh set of papers.

"Perhaps," said Krug.

"And perhaps each is afraid that the other will plunge into some competitive music as soon as one of them starts to play."

"Perhaps," said Krug. "All the same—it is a very singular picture. An organ-grinder is the very emblem of oneness. But here we have an absurd duality. They do not play but they do glance upwards."

"I shall now proceed," said Ember, "to read you——"

"I know of only one other profession," said Krug, "that has that upward movement of the eyeballs. And that is our clergy."

"Well, Adam, sit down and listen. Or am I boring you?"

"Oh, nonsense," said Krug, going back to his chair. "I was only trying to think what exactly was wrong. The children seem also perplexed by their silence. There is something familiar about the whole thing, something I cannot quite disentangle—a certain line of thought. . . ."

"The chief difficulty that assails the translator of the following passage," said Ember, licking his fat lips after a draught of punch and readjusting his back to his large pillow, "the chief difficulty——"

The remote sound of the doorbell interrupted him.

"Are you expecting someone?" asked Krug.

"Nobody in particular. Maybe some of those actor fellows have come to see whether I am dead. They will be disappointed."

The footfalls of the valet passed down the corridor. Then returned.

"Gentleman and lady to see you, sir," he said.

"Curse them," said Ember. "Could you, Adam . . . ?"

"Yes of course," said Krug. "Shall I tell them you are asleep?"

"And unshaven," said Ember. "And anxious to go on with my reading."

A handsome lady in a dove-gray tailor-made suit and a gentleman with a glossy red tulip in the buttonhole of his cutaway coat stood side by side in the hall.

"We——" began the gentleman, fumbling in his left trouser pocket and accompanying this gesture with a kind of wriggle as if he had a touch of cramp or were uncomfortably clothed.

"Mr. Ember is in bed with a cold," said Krug. "And he asked me——"

The gentleman bowed: "I understand perfectly, but this (his free hand proffered a card) will tell you my name and standing. I have my orders as you can see. Prompt submission to them tore me away from my very private duties as host. I too was giving a party. And no doubt Mr. Ember, if that is his name, will act as promptly as I did. This is my secretary— in fact, something more than a secretary."

"Oh, come, Hustav," said the lady, nudging him. "Surely, Professor Krug is not interested in our relations."

"Our relations?" said Hustav, looking at her with an expression of fond facetiousness on his aristocratic face. "Say that again. It sounded lovely."

She lowered her thick eyelashes and pouted.

"I did not mean what you mean, you bad boy. The Professor will think *Gott weiss was.*"

"It sounded," pursued Hustav tenderly, "like the rhythmic springs of a certain blue couch in a certain guest room."

"All right. It is sure not to happen again if you go on being so nasty."

"Now she is cross with us," sighed Hustav, turning to Krug. "Beware of women, as Shakespeare says! Well, I have to perform my sad duty. Lead me to the patient, Professor."

"One moment," said Krug. "If you are not actors, if this is not some fatuous hoax——"

"Oh, I know what you are going to say"—purred Hustav; "this element of gracious living strikes you as queer, does it not? One is accustomed to consider such things in terms of sordid brutality and gloom, rifle butts, rough soldiers, muddy boots—*und so weiter*. But headquarters knew that Mr. Ember was an artist, a poet, a sensitive soul, and it was thought that something a little dainty and uncommon in the way of arrests, an atmosphere of high life, flowers, the perfume of feminine beauty, might sweeten the ordeal. Please, notice that I am wearing civilian clothes. Whimsical perhaps, I grant you, but then—imagine his feelings if my uncouth assistants (the thumb of his free hand pointed in the direction of the stairs) crashed in and started to rip up the furniture."

"Show the Professor that big ugly thing you carry about in your pocket, Hustav."

"Say that again?"

"I mean your pistol of course," said the lady stiffly.

"I see," said Hustav. "I misunderstood you. But we shall go into that later. You need not mind her, Professor, she is apt to exaggerate. There is really nothing special about this weapon. A humdrum official article, No. 184682, of which you can see dozens any time."

"I think I have had enough of this," said Krug. "I do not believe in pistols and—well, no matter. You can put it back. All I want to know is: do you intend to take him away right now?"

"Yep," said Hustav.

"I shall find some way to complain about these monstrous intrusions," rumbled Krug. "It cannot go on like this. They were a perfectly harmless old couple, both in rather indifferent health. You shall certainly regret it."

"It has just occurred to me," remarked Hustav to his fair companion, as they moved through the flat in Krug's wake, "that the Colonel had one schnapps too many when we left him, so that I doubt whether your little sister will be quite the same by the time we get back."

"I thought that story he told about the two sailors and the *barbok* [a kind of pie with a hole in the middle for melted butter] most entertaining," said the lady. "You must tell it to Mr. Ember; he is a writer and might put it into his next book."

"Well, for that matter, your own pretty mouth——" began Hustav—but they had reached the bedroom door and the lady modestly remained behind while Hustav, again thrusting a fumbling hand into his trouser pocket, jerkily went in after Krug.

The valet was in the act of removing a *mida* [small table with incrustations] from the bedside. Ember was inspecting his uvula in a hand mirror.

"This idiot here has come to arrest you," said Krug in English.

Hustav, who had been quietly beaming at Ember from the threshold, suddenly frowned and glanced at Krug suspiciously.

"But surely this is a mistake," said Ember. "Why should anyone want to arrest me?"

"*Heraus, Mensch, marsch,*" said Hustav to the valet and, when the latter had left the room:

"We are not in a classroom, Professor," he said, turning to Krug, "so please use language that everybody can understand. Some other time I may ask you to teach me Danish or Dutch; at this moment, however, I am engaged in the performance of duties which are perhaps as repellent to me and to Miss Bachofen as they are to you. Therefore I must call your attention to the fact that, although I am not averse to a little mild bantering——"

"Wait a minute, wait a minute," cried Ember. "I know what it is. It is because I did not open my windows when those very loud speakers were on yesterday. But I can explain. . . . My doctor will certify I was ill. Adam, it is all right, there is no need to worry."

The sound of an idle finger touching the keys of a cold piano came from the drawing room, as Ember's valet returned with some clothes over his arm. The man's face was the color of veal and he avoided looking at Hustav. To his master's exclamation of surprise he replied that the lady in the drawing room had told him to get Ember dressed or be shot.

"But this is ridiculous!" cried Ember. "I cannot just jump into my clothes. I must have a bath first, I must shave."

"There is a barber at the nice quiet place you are going to," remarked the kindly Hustav. "Come, get up, you really must not be so disobedient."

(How if I answer "no"?)

"I refuse to dress while you are all staring at me," said Ember.

"We are not looking," said Hustav.

Krug left the room and walked past the piano towards the study. Miss Bachofen rose up from the piano stool and nimbly overtook him.

"*Ich will etwas sagen* [I want to say something]," she said and dropped her light hand upon his sleeve. "Just now, when we were talking, I had the impression you thought Hustav and I were rather absurd young people. But that is only a way he has, you know, always making *witze* [jokes] and teasing me, and really I am not the sort of girl you may think I am."

"These odds and ends," said Krug, touching a shelf near which he was passing, "have no special value, but he treasures them, and if you have slipped a little porcelain owl—which I do not see—into your bag——"

"Professor, we are not thieves," she said very quietly, and he must have had a heart of stone who would not have felt ashamed of his evil thought as she stood there, a narrow-hipped blonde with a pair of symmetrical breasts moistly heaving among the frills of her white silk blouse.

He reached the telephone and dialed Hedron's number. Hedron was not at home. He talked to Hedron's sister. Then he discovered that he had been sitting on Hustav's hat. The girl came towards him again and opened her white bag to show him she had not purloined anything of real or sentimental value.

"And you may search me, too," she said defiantly, unbuttoning her jacket. "Provided you do not tickle me," added the doubly innocent, perspiring German girl.

He went back to the bedroom. Near the window Hustav was turning the pages of an encyclopedia in search of exciting words beginning with M and V. Ember stood half-dressed, a yellow tie in his hand.

"*Et voilà . . . et me voici. . . .*" he said with an infantile little whine in his voice. "*Un pauvre bonhomme qu'on traine en prison.* Oh, I don't want to go *at all*! Adam, isn't there anything that can be done? Think up something, please! *Je suis souffrant, je suis en détresse.* I shall confess I had been preparing a *coup d'état* if they start torturing me."

The valet whose name was or had been Ivan, his teeth

chattering, his eyes half-closed, helped his poor master into his coat.

"May I come in now?" queried Miss Bachofen with a kind of musical coyness. And slowly she sauntered in, rolling her hips.

"Open your eyes wide, Mr. Ember," exclaimed Hustav. "I want you to admire the lady who has consented to grace your home."

"You are incorrigible," murmured Miss Bachofen with a slanting smile.

"Sit down, dear. On the bed. Sit down, Mr. Ember. Sit down, Professor. A moment of silence. Poetry and philosophy must brood, while beauty and strength— Your apartment is nicely heated, Mr. Ember. Now, if I were *quite, quite* sure that you two would not try to get shot by the men outside, I might ask you to leave the room, while Miss Bachofen and I remain here for a brisk business conference. I need it badly."

"No, *Liebling*, no," said Miss Bachofen. "Let us get moving. I am sick of this place. We'll do it at home, honey."

"I think it is a beautiful place," muttered Hustav reproachfully.

"*Il est saoul*," said Ember.

"In fact, these mirrors and rugs suggest certain tremendous Oriental sensations which I cannot resist."

"*Il est complètement saoul,*" said Ember and began to weep.

Pretty Miss Bachofen took her boy friend firmly by the arm and after some coaxing he was made to convey Ember to the black police car waiting for them. When they had gone, Ivan became hysterical, produced an old bicycle from the attic, carried it downstairs and rode away. Krug locked the apartment and slowly went home.

8

THE TOWN was curiously bright in the late sunlight: this was one of the Painted Days peculiar to the region. They came in a row after the first frost, and happy the foreign tourist who visited Padukgrad at such a time. The mud left by the recent rains made one's mouth water, so rich did it look. The house fronts on one side of the street were bathed in an amber light which brought out every, oh, every, detail; some displayed mosaic designs; the principal city bank, for instance, had seraphs amid a yuccalike flora. On the fresh blue paint of the boulevard benches children had made with their fingers the words: Glory to Paduk—a sure way of enjoying the properties of the sticky substance without getting one's ears twisted by the policeman, whose strained smile indicated the quandary in which he found himself. A ruby-red toy balloon hung in the cloudless sky. Grimy chimney sweeps and flour-powdered baker boys were fraternizing in open cafés, where they drowned their ancient feud in cider and grenadine. A man's rubber overshoe and a bloodstained cuff lay in the middle of the sidewalk and passers-by gave them a wide berth without, however, slowing down or looking at those two articles or indeed revealing their awareness of them in any way beyond stepping off the curb into the mud and then stepping back onto the sidewalk. The window of a cheap toyshop had been starred by a bullet, and, as Krug approached, a soldier came out carrying a clean paper bag into which he proceeded to cram the overshoe and the cuff. You remove the obstacle and the ants resume a straight course. Ember never wore detachable cuffs, nor would he have dared jump out of a moving vehicle and run, and gasp, and run and duck as that unfortunate person had done. This is becoming a nuisance. I must awake. The victims of my nightmares are increasing in numbers too fast, thought Krug as he walked, ponderous, black-overcoated, black-hatted, the overcoat flappily unbuttoned, the wide-brimmed felt hat in his hand.

Weakness of habit. A former official, a very *ancien régime* old party, had avoided arrest, or worse, by slipping out from his genteel plush-and-dust apartment, Peregolm Lane 4, and transferring his quarters to the dead elevator in the house where Krug dwelt. In spite of the "Not Working" sign on the door, that strange automaton Adam Krug would invariably try to get in and would be met by the frightened face and white goatee of the harassed refugee. Fright, however, would at once be replaced by a worldly display of hospitality. The old fellow had managed to transform his narrow abode into quite a comfortable little den. He was neatly dressed and carefully shaven and with pardonable pride would show you such fixtures as, for example, an alcohol lamp and a trousers press. He was a Baron.

Krug boorishly refused the cup of coffee he was offered and tramped up to his own flat. Hedron was waiting for him in David's room. He had been told of Krug's telephone call; had come over at once. David did not want them to leave the nursery and threatened to get out of bed if they did. Claudina brought the boy his supper but he refused to eat. From the study to which Krug and Hedron retired, they could indistinctly hear him arguing with the woman.

They discussed what could be done: planning a certain course of action; well knowing that neither this course nor any other would avail. Both wanted to know why people of no political importance had been seized: though, to be sure, they might have guessed the answer, the simple answer that was to be given them half an hour later.

"Incidentally, we are having another meeting on the twelfth," remarked Hedron. "I am afraid you are going to be the guest of honor again."

"Not I," said Krug. "I shall not be there."

Hedron carefully scooped out the black contents of his pipe into the bronze ash tray at his elbow.

"I must be getting back," he said with a sigh. "Those Chinese delegates are coming to dinner."

He was referring to a group of foreign physicists and mathematicians who had been invited to take part in a congress that had been called off at the last moment. Some of the least important members had not been notified of this cancellation and had come all the way for nothing.

At the door, just before leaving, he looked at the hat in his hand and said:

"I hope she did not suffer . . . I——"

Krug shook his head and hurriedly opened the door.

The staircase presented a remarkable spectacle. Hustav, now in full uniform, with a look of utter dejection on his swollen face, was sitting on the steps. Four soldiers in various postures formed a martial bas-relief along the wall. Hedron was immediately surrounded and shown the order for his arrest. One of the men pushed Krug out of the way. There was a vague sort of scuffle, in the course of which Hustav lost his footing and bumpily fell down the steps, dragging Hedron after him. Krug tried to follow the soldiers downstairs but was made to desist. The clatter subsided. One imagined the Baron cowering in the darkness of his unconventional hiding place and still not daring to believe that he remained uncaptured.

9

HOLDING your cupped hands together, dear, and progressing with the cautious and tremulous steps of tremendous age (although hardly fifteen) you crossed the porch; stopped; gently worked open the glass door by means of your elbow; made your way past the caparisoned grand piano, traversed the sequence of cool carnation-scented rooms, found your aunt in the *chambre violette*———

I think I want to have the whole scene repeated. Yes, from the beginning. As you came up the stone steps of the porch, your eyes never left your cupped hands, the pink chink between the two thumbs. Oh, what were you carrying? Come on now. You wore a striped (dingy white and pale-blue) sleeveless jersey, a dark-blue girl-scout skirt, untidy orphan-black stockings and a pair of old chlorophyl-stained tennis shoes. Between the pillars of the porch geometrical sunlight touched your reddish brown bobbed hair, your plump neck and the vaccination mark on your sunburned arm. You moved slowly through a cool and sonorous drawing room, then entered a room where the carpet and armchairs and curtains were purple and blue. From various mirrors your cupped hands and lowered head came towards you and your movements were mimicked behind your back. Your aunt, a lay figure, was writing a letter.

"Look," you said.

Very slowly, rosewise, you opened your hands. There, clinging with all its six fluffy feet to the ball of your thumb, the tip of its mouse-gray body slightly excurved, its short, red, blue-ocellated inferior wings oddly protruding forward from beneath the sloping superior ones which were long and marbled and deeply notched———

I think I shall have you go through your act a third time, but in reverse—carrying that hawk moth back into the orchard where you found it.

As you went the way you had come (now with the palm of your hand open), the sun that had been lying in state on the parquetry of the drawing room and on the flat tiger (spread-eagled and bright-eyed beside the piano), leaped at you, climbed the dingy soft rungs of your jersey and struck you right in the face so that all could see (crowding, tier upon tier, in the sky, jostling one another, pointing, feasting their eyes on the young *radabarbára*) its high color and fiery freckles, and the hot cheeks as red as the hind wings basally, for the moth was still clinging to your hand and you were still looking at it as you progressed towards the garden, where you gently transferred it to the lush grass at the foot of an apple tree far from the beady eyes of your little sister.

Where was I at the time? An eighteen-year-old student sitting with a book (*Les Pensées*, I imagine) on a station bench miles away, not knowing you, not known to you. Presently I shut the book and took what was called an omnibus train to the country place where young Hedron was spending the summer. This was a cluster of rentable cottages on a hillside overlooking the river, the opposite bank of which revealed in terms of fir trees and alder bushes the heavily timbered acres of your aunt's estate.

We shall now have somebody else arrive from nowhere—*à pas de loup*, a tall boy with a little black mustache and other signs of hot uncomfortable puberty. Not I, not Hedron. That summer we did nothing but play chess. The boy was your cousin, and while my comrade and I, across the river, pored over Tarrash's collection of annotated games, he would drive you to tears during meals by some intricate and maddening piece of teasing and then, under the pretense of reconciliation, would steal after you into some attic where you were hiding your frantic sobbing, and there would kiss your wet eyes, and hot neck and tumbled hair and try to get at your armpits and garters for you were a remarkably big ripe girl for your age; but he, in spite of his fine looks and hungry hard limbs, died of consumption a year later.

And still later, when you were twenty and I twenty-three, we met at a Christmas party and discovered that we had been neighbors that summer, five years before—five years lost! And at the precise moment when in awed surprise (awed by the bungling of destiny) you put your hand to your mouth and looked at me with very round eyes and muttered: "But that's where *I* lived!"—I recalled in a flash a green lane near an orchard and a sturdy young girl carefully carrying a lost fluffy nestling, but whether it had been really you no amount of probing and poking could either confirm or disprove.

Fragment from a letter addressed to a dead woman in heaven by her husband in his cups.

H E GOT RID of her furs, of all her photographs, of her huge English sponge and supply of lavender soap, of her umbrella, of her napkin ring, of the little porcelain owl she had bought for Ember and never given him—but she refused to be forgotten. When (some fifteen years before) both his parents had been killed in a railway accident, he had managed to alleviate the pain and the panic by writing Chapter III (Chapter IV in later editions) of his *"Mirokonzepsia"* wherein he looked straight into the eyesockets of death and called him a dog and an abomination. With one strong shrug of his burly shoulders he shook off the burden of sanctity enveloping the monster, and as with a thump and a great explosion of dust the thick old mats and carpets and things fell, he had experienced a kind of hideous relief. But could he do it again?

Her dresses and stockings and hats and shoes mercifully disappeared together with Claudina when the latter, soon after Hedron's arrest, was bullied by police agents into leaving. The agencies he called, in an attempt to find a trained nurse to replace her, could not help him; but a couple of days after Claudina had gone, the bell rang and there, on the landing, was a very young girl with a suitcase offering her services. "I answer," she amusingly said, "to the name of Mariette"; she had been employed as maid and model in the household of the well-known artist who had lived in apartment 30 right above Krug; but now he was obliged to depart with his wife and two other painters for a much less comfortable prison camp in a remote province. Mariette brought down a second suitcase and quietly moved into the room near the nursery. She had good references from the Department of Public Health, graceful legs and a pale, delicately shaped, not particularly pretty but attractively childish face with parched-looking lips, always parted, and strange lusterless dark eyes; the pupil almost merged in tint with the iris, which was placed somewhat higher than is usual and was obliquely shaded by sooty lashes. No paint or powder touched her singularly bloodless, evenly translucid cheeks. She wore her hair long. Krug had a confused feeling that he had seen her before, probably on the stairs. Cinderella, the little slattern, moving and dusting in a dream, always ivory pale and unspeakably tired after last night's ball. On the whole, there was something rather irritating about her, and her wavy brown hair had a strong chestnutty smell; but David liked her, so she might do after all.

II

O N HIS BIRTHDAY, Krug was informed by telephone that the Head of the State desired to grant him an interview, and hardly had the fuming philosopher laid down the receiver than the door flew open and—very much like one of those stage valets that march in stiffly half a second before their fictitious master (insulted and perhaps beaten up by them between acts) claps his hands—a dapper, heel-clicking aide-de-camp saluted from the threshold. By the time that the palace motor car, a huge black limousine, which made one think of first-class funerals in alabaster cities, arrived at its destination, Krug's annoyance had given way to a kind of grim curiosity. Though otherwise fully dressed, he was wearing bedroom slippers, and the two gigantic janitors (whom Paduk had inherited together with the abject caryatids supporting the balconies) stared at his absent-minded feet as he shuffled up the marble steps. From then on a multitude of uninformed rascals kept silently seething around him, causing him to follow this or that course by means of a bodiless elastic pressure rather than by definite gestures or words. He was steered into a waiting room where, instead of the usual magazines, one was offered various games of skill (such as for instance glass gadgets within which little bright hopelessly mobile balls had to be coaxed into the orbits of eyeless clowns). Presently two masked men came in and searched him thoroughly. Then one of them retired behind the screen while the other produced a small vial marked H_2SO_4, which he proceeded to conceal under Krug's left armpit. Having had Krug assume a "natural position," he called his companion, who approached with an eager smile and immediately found the object: upon which he was accused of having peeped through the *kwazinka* [a slit between the folding parts of a screen]. A rapidly mounting squabble was stopped by the arrival of the *zemberl* [chamberlain]. This prim old personage noticed at once that Krug was inadequately shod; there followed a feverish search through the oppressive vastness of the palace. A small collection of footgear began accumulating around Krug—a number of seedy-looking pumps, a girl's tiny slipper trimmed with moth-eaten squirrel fur, some bloodstained arctics, brown shoes, black shoes and even a pair of half boots with screwed on skates. Only the last fitted Krug and some more time elapsed before adequate hands and instruments were found to deprive the soles of their rusty but gracefully curved supplements.

Then the *zemberl* ushered Krug into the presence of the *ministr dvortza*, a von Embit, of German extraction. Embit at once pronounced himself a humble admirer of Krug's genius. His mind had been formed by *"Mirokonzepsia,"* he said. Moreover, a cousin of his had been a student of Professor Krug's—the famous physician—was he any relation? He wasn't. The *ministr* kept up this social patter for a few minutes (he had a queer way of emitting a quick little snort before saying something) and then took Krug by the arm and they walked down a long passage with doors on one side and a stretch of pale-green and spinach-green tapestry on the other, displaying what seemed to be an endless hunt through a sub-tropical forest. The visitor was made to inspect various rooms, i.e., his guide would softly open a door and in a reverent whisper direct his attention to this or that interesting item. The first room to be shown contained a contour map of the State, made of bronze with towns and villages represented by precious and semiprecious stones of various colors. In the next, a young typist was poring over the contents of some documents, and so absorbed was she in deciphering them, and so noiselessly had the *ministr* entered, that she emitted a wild shriek when he snorted behind her back. Then a classroom was visited: a score of brown-skinned Armenian and Sicilian lads were diligently writing at rosewood desks while their *eunig*, a fat old man with dyed hair and bloodshot eyes, sat in front of them painting his fingernails and yawning with closed mouth. Of special interest was a perfectly empty room, in which some extinct furniture had left squares of honey-yellow color on the brown floor: von Embit lingered there and bade Krug linger, and mutely pointed at a vacuum cleaner, and lingered on, eyes moving this way and that as if flitting over the sacred treasures of an ancient chapel.

But something even more curious than that was kept *pour la bonne bouche. Notamment, une grande pièce bien claire* with chairs and tables of a clean-cut laboratory type and what looked like an especially large and elaborate radio set. From this machine came a steady thumping sound not unlike that of an African drum, and three doctors in white were engaged in checking the number of beats per minute. In their turn, two violent-looking members of Paduk's bodyguard controlled the doctors by keeping count separately. A pretty nurse was reading *Flung Roses* in a corner, and Paduk's private physician, an enormous baby-faced man in a dusty-looking frockcoat, was fast asleep behind a projection screen. Thump-ah, thump-ah, thump-ah, went the machine, and every now and then there was an additional systole, causing a slight break in the rhythm.

The owner of the heart to the amplified beatings of which the experts were listening, was in his study some fifty feet away. His guardian soldiers, all leather and cartridges, carefully examined Krug's and von Embit's papers. The latter gentleman had forgotten to provide himself with a photostat of his birth certificate and so could not pass, much to his good-natured discomfiture. Krug went in alone.

Paduk, clothed from carbuncle to bunion in field gray, stood with his hands behind his back and his back to the reader. He stood, thus oriented and clothed, before a bleak French window. Ragged clouds rode the white sky and the windowpane rattled slightly. The room, alas, had been formerly a ballroom. A good deal of stucco ornamentation enlivened the walls. The few chairs that floated about in the mirrory wilderness were gilt. So was the radiator. One corner of the room was cut off by a great writing desk.

"Here I am," said Krug.

Paduk wheeled around and without looking at his visitor marched to the desk. There he sank in a leathern armchair. Krug, whose left shoe had begun to hurt, sought a seat and not finding one in the vicinity of the table, looked back at the gilt chairs. His host, however, saw to that: there was a click, and a replica of Paduk's *klubzessel* [armchair] Jack-in-the-boxed from a trap near the desk.

Physically the Toad had hardly changed except that every particle of his visible organism had been expanded and roughened. On the top of his bumpy, bluish, shaven head a patch of hair was neatly brushed and parted. His blotched complexion was worse than ever, and one wondered what tremendous will power a man must possess to refrain from squeezing out the blackheads that clogged the coarse pores on and near the wings of his fattish nose. His upper lip was disfigured by a scar. A bit of porous plaster adhered to the side of his chin, and a still larger bit, with a soiled corner turned back and a pad of cotton awry, could be seen in the fold of his neck just above the stiff collar of his semimilitary coat. In a word, he was a little too repulsive to be credible, and so let us ring the bell (held by a bronze eagle) and have him beautified by a mortician. Now the skin is thoroughly cleansed and has assumed a smooth marchpane color. A glossy wig with auburn and blond tresses artistically intermixed covers his head. Pink paint has dealt with the unseemly scar. Indeed, it would be an admirable face, were we able to close his eyes for him. But no matter what pressure we exert upon the lids, they snap open again. I never noticed his eyes, or else his eyes have changed.

They were those of a fish in a neglected aquarium, muddy meaningless eyes, and moreover the poor man was in a state of morbid embarrassment at being in the same room with big heavy Adam Krug.

"You wanted to see me. What is your trouble? What is your truth? People always want to see me and talk of their troubles and truths. I am tired, the world is tired, we are both tired. The trouble of the world is mine. I tell them to tell me their troubles. What do you want?"

This little speech was delivered in a slow flat toneless mumble. And having delivered it Paduk bent his head and stared at his hands. What remained of his fingernails looked like thin strings sunk deep in the yellowish flesh.

"Well," said Krug, "if you put it like this, *dragotzennyĭ* [my precious], I think I want a drink."

The telephone emitted a discreet tinkle. Paduk attended to it. His cheek twitched as he listened. Then he handed the receiver to Krug who comfortably clasped it and said "Yes."

"Professor," said the telephone, "this is merely a suggestion. The chief of the State is not generally addressed as '*dragotzennyĭ*.'"

"I see," said Krug, stretching out one leg. "By the way, will you please send up some brandy? Wait a bit——"

He looked interrogatively at Paduk who had made a somewhat ecclesiastical and Gallic gesture of lassitude and disgust, raising both hands and letting them sink again.

"One brandy and a glass of milk," said Krug and hung up.

"More than twenty-five years, Mugakrad," said Paduk after a silence. "You have remained what you were, but the world spins on. Gumakrad, poor little Gumradka."

"And then," said Krug, "the two proceeded to speak of old times, to remember the names of teachers and their idiosyncrasies—curiously the same throughout the ages, and what can be funnier than a habitual oddity? Come, *dragotzennyĭ*, come, sir, I know all that, and really we have more important things to discuss than snowballs and ink blots."

"You might regret it," said Paduk.

Krug drummed for a while on his side of the desk. Then he fingered a long paper knife of ivory.

The telephone rang again. Paduk listened.

"You are not supposed to touch knives here," he said to Krug as, with a sigh, he replaced the receiver. "Why did you want to see me?"

"*I* did not. You did."

"Well—why did I? Do you know that, mad Adam?"

"Because," said Krug, "I am the only person who can stand on the other end of the seesaw and make your end rise."

Knuckles briskly rapped on the door and the *zemberl* marched in with a tinkling tray. He deftly served the two friends and presented a letter to Krug. Krug took a sip and read the note. "Professor," it said, "this is still not the right manner. You should bear in mind that notwithstanding the narrow and fragile bridge of school memories uniting the two sides, these are separated in depth by an abyss of power and dignity which even a great philosopher (and that is what *you* are—yes, sir!) cannot hope to measure. You must not indulge in this atrocious familiarity. One has to warn you again. One beseeches you. Hoping that the shoes are not too uncomfortable, one remains a well-wisher."

"And that's that," said Krug.

Paduk moistened his lips in the pasteurized milk and spoke in a huskier voice.

"Now let me tell you. They come and say to me: Why is this good and intelligent man idle? Why is he not in the service of the State? And I answer: I don't know. And they are puzzled also."

"Who are they?" asked Krug dryly.

"Friends, friends of the law, friends of the lawmaker. And the village fraternities. And the city clubs. And the great lodges. Why is it so, why is he not with us? I only echo their query."

"The hell you do," said Krug.

The door opened slightly and a fat gray parrot with a note in its beak walked in. It waddled towards the desk on clumsy hoary legs and its claws made the kind of sound that unmanicured dogs make on varnished floors. Paduk jumped out of his chair, walked rapidly towards the old bird and kicked it like a football out of the room. Then he shut the door with a bang. The telephone was ringing its heart out on the desk. He disconnected the current and clapped the whole thing into a drawer.

"And now the answer," he said.

"Which you owe me," said Krug. "First of all I wish to know why you had those four friends of mine arrested. Was it to make a vacuum around me? To leave me shivering in a void?"

"The State is your only true friend."

"I see."

Gray light from long windows. The dreary wail of a tugboat.

"A nice picture we make—you as a kind of *Erlkönig* and myself as the male baby clinging to the matter-of-fact rider and peering into the magic mists. Pah!"

"All we want of you is that little part where the handle is."

"There is none," cried Krug and hit his side of the table with his fist.

"I beseech you to be careful. The walls are full of camouflaged holes, each one with a rifle which is trained upon you. Please, do not gesticulate. They are jumpy today. It's the weather. This gray menstratum."

"If," said Krug, "you cannot leave me and my friends in peace, then let them and me go abroad. It would save you a world of trouble."

"What is it exactly you have against my government?"

"I am not in the least interested in your government. What I resent is your attempt to make me interested in it. Leave me alone."

" 'Alone' is the vilest word in the language. Nobody is alone. When a cell in an organism says 'leave me alone,' the result is cancer."

"In what prison or prisons are they kept?"

"I beg your pardon?"

"Where is Ember, for instance?"

"You want to know too much. These are dull technical matters of no real interest to your type of mind. And now——"

No, it did not go on quite like that. In the first place Paduk was silent during most of the interview. What he did say amounted to a few curt platitudes. To be sure, he did do some drumming on the desk (they all drum) and Krug retaliated with some of his own drumming but otherwise neither showed nervousness. Photographed from above, they would have come out in Chinese perspective, doll-like, a little limp but possibly with a hard wooden core under their plausible clothes—one slumped at his desk in a shaft of gray light, the other seated sideways to the desk, legs crossed, the toe of the upper foot moving up and down,—and the secret spectator (some anthropomorphic deity, for example) surely would be amused by the shape of human heads seen from above. Paduk curtly asked Krug whether his (Krug's) apartment were warm enough (nobody, of course, could have expected a revolution *without* a shortage of coal), and Krug said yes, it was. And did he have any trouble in getting milk and radishes? Well, yes, a little. He made a note of Krug's answer on a calendar slip. He had learned with sorrow of Krug's bereavement. Was Professor Martin Krug a relative of his? Were there any relatives on his late wife's side? Krug supplied him with the necessary data. Paduk leaned back in his chair and tapped his nose with the rubber end of his six-faceted pencil. As his thoughts took a different course, he changed the position of the pencil: he now held it by the end, horizontally, rolling it slightly between the finger and thumb of either hand, seemingly interested in the disappearance and reappearance of Eberhard Faber No. 2⅜. It is not a difficult part but still the actor must be careful not to overdo what Graaf somewhere calls "villainous deliberation." Krug in the meantime sipped his brandy and tenderly nursed the glass. Suddenly Paduk plunged towards his desk; a drawer shot out, a beribboned typescript was produced. This he handed to Krug.

"I must put on my spectacles," said Krug.

He held them before his face and looked through them at a distant window. The left glass showed a dim spiral nebula in the middle not unlike the imprint of a ghostly thumb. While he breathed upon it and rubbed it away with his handkerchief, Paduk explained matters. Krug was to be nominated college president in place of Azureus. His salary would be three times that of his predecessor which had been five thousand kruns. Moreover, he would be provided with a motorcar, a bicycle, and a padograph. At the public opening of the University he would kindly deliver a speech. His works would be republished in new editions, revised in the light of political events. There might be bonuses, sabbatical years, lottery tickets, a cow—lots of things.

"And this, I presume, is the speech," said Krug cozily. Paduk remarked that in order to save Krug the trouble of composing it, the speech had been prepared by an expert.

"We hope you will like it as well as we do."

"So this," repeated Krug, "is the speech."

"Yes," said Paduk. "Now take your time. Read it carefully. Oh, by the way, there was one word to be changed. I wonder if that has been done. Will you please——"

He stretched his hand to take the typescript from Krug, and in doing so knocked down the tumbler of milk with his elbow. What was left of the milk made a kidney-shaped white puddle on the desk.

"Yes," said Paduk, handing the typescript back, "it has been changed."

He busied himself with removing various things from the desk (a bronze eagle, a pencil, a picture post card of Gainsborough's "Blue Boy," and a framed reproduction of Aldobrandini's "Wedding," of the half-naked wreathed, adorable

minion whom the groom is obliged to renounce for the sake
of a lumpy, muffled-up bride), and then messily dabbed at the
milk with a piece of blotting paper. Krug read *sotto voce*:

" 'Ladies and gentlemen! Citizens, soldiers, wives and
mothers! Brothers and sisters! The revolution has brought to
the fore problems [*zadachi*] of unusual difficulty, of colossal
importance, of world-wide scope [*mirovovo mashtaba*]. Our
leader has resorted to most resolute revolutionary measures
calculated to arouse the unbounded heroism of the oppressed
and exploited masses. In the shortest [*kratchaishiĭ*] time [*srok*]
the State has created central organs for providing the country
with all the most important products which are to be distributed at fixed prices in a playful manner. Sorry—*planful* manner. Wives, soldiers and mothers! The hydra of the reaction
may still raise its head . . . !'

"This won't do, the creature has more heads than one, has
it not?"

"Make a note of it," said Paduk through his teeth. "Make
a note in the margin and for goodness' sake go on."

" 'As our old proverb has it, "the ugliest wives are the
truest," but surely this cannot apply to the "ugly rumors"
which our enemies are spreading. It is rumored for instance
that the cream of our intelligentsia is opposed to the present
regime.'

"Wouldn't 'whipped cream' be fitter? I mean, pursuing the
metaphor——"

"Make a note, make a note, these details do not matter."

" 'Untrue! A mere phrase, an untruth. Those who rage,
storm, fulminate, gnash their teeth, pour a ceaseless stream
[*potok*] of abusive words upon us do not accuse us of anything
directly, they only "insinuate." This insinuation is stupid. Far
from opposing the regime, we professors, writers, philosophers, and so forth, support it with all possible learning and
enthusiasm.

" 'No, gentlemen; no, traitors, your most "categorical"
words, declarations and notes will not diminish these facts.
You may gloss over the fact that our foremost professors and
thinkers support the regime, but you cannot dismiss the fact
that they do support it. We are happy and proud to march
with the masses. Blind matter regains the use of its eyes and

knocks off the rosy spectacles which used to adorn the long
nose of so-called Thought. Whatever I have thought and written in the past, one thing is clear to me now: no matter to
whom they belong, two pairs of eyes looking at a boot see
the same boot since it is identically reflected in both; and further, that the larynx is the seat of thought so that the working
of the mind is a kind of gargling.'

"Well, well, this last sentence seems to be a garbled passage
from one of my works. A passage turned inside out by somebody who did not understand the gist of my remarks. I was
criticizing that old——"

"Please, go on. Please."

" 'In other words, the new Education, the new University
which I am happy and proud to direct will inaugurate the era
of Dynamic Living. In result, a great and beautiful simplifi-
cation will replace the evil refinements of a degenerate past.
We shall teach and learn, first of all, that the dream of Plato
has come true in the hands of the Head of our State. . . .'

"This is sheer drivel. I refuse to go on. Take it away."

He pushed the typescript towards Paduk, who sat with
closed eyes.

"Do not make any hasty decisions, mad Adam. Go home.
Think it over. Nay, do not speak. They cannot hold their fire
much longer. Prithee, go."

Which, of course, terminated the interview. Thus? Or perhaps in some other way? Did Krug really glance at the prepared speech? And if he did, was it really as silly as all that?
He did; it was. The seedy tyrant or the president of the State,
or the dictator, or whoever he was—the man Paduk in a word,
the Toad in another—did hand my favorite character a mysterious batch of neatly typed pages. The actor playing the re-
cipient should be taught not to look at his hand while he takes
the papers *very slowly* (keeping those lateral lower-jaw muscles
in movement, please) but to stare straight at the giver: in
short, look at the giver first, *then* lower your eyes to the gift.
But both were clumsy and cross men, and the experts in the
cardiarium exchanged solemn nods at a certain point (when
the milk was upset), and they, too, were not acting. Tentatively scheduled to take place in three months' time, the opening of the new University was to be a most ceremonious and

widely publicized affair, with a host of reporters from foreign countries, ignorant overpaid correspondents, with noiseless little typewriters in their laps, and photographers with souls as cheap as dried figs. And the one great thinker in the country would appear in scarlet robes (click) beside the chief and symbol of the State (click, click, click, click, click, click) and proclaim in a thundering voice that the State was bigger and wiser than any mortal could be.

12

THINKING of that farcical interview, he wondered how long it would be till the next attempt. He still believed that so long as he kept lying low nothing harmful could happen. Oddly enough, at the end of the month his usual check arrived although for the time being the University had ceased to exist, at least on the outside. Behind the scenes there was an endless sequence of sessions, a turmoil of administrative activity, a regrouping of forces, but he declined either to attend these meetings or to receive the various delegations and special messengers that Azureus and Alexander kept sending to his house. He argued that, when the Council of Elders had exhausted its power of seduction, he would be left alone since the Government, while not daring to arrest him and being reluctant to grant him the luxury of exile, would still keep hoping with forlorn obstinacy that finally he might relent. The drab color the future took matched well the gray world of his widowhood, and had there been no friends to worry about and no child to hold against his cheek and heart, he might have devoted the twilight to some quiet research: for example he had always wished to know more about the Aurignacian Age and those portraits of singular beings (perhaps Neanderthal half-men—direct ancestors of Paduk and his likes—used by Aurignacians as slaves) that a Spanish nobleman and his little daughter had discovered in the painted cave of Altamira. Or he might take up some dim problem of Victorian telepathy (the cases reported by clergymen, nervous ladies, retired colonels who had seen service in India) such as the remarkable dream a Mrs. Storie had of her brother's death. And in our turn we shall follow the brother as he walks along the railway line on a very dark night: having gone sixteen miles, he felt a little tired (as who would not); he sat down to take off his boots and dozed off to the chirp of the crickets, and then a train lumbered by. Seventy-six sheep trucks (in a curious "count-sheep-sleep" parody) passed without touching him, but then some projection came in contact with the back of his head killing him instantly. And we might also probe the

"illusions hypnagogiques" (only illusion?) of dear Miss Bidder
who once had a nightmare from which a most distinct demon
survived after she woke so that she sat up to inspect its hand
which was clutching the bedrail but it faded into the ornaments over the mantelpiece. Silly, but I can't help it, he
thought as he got out of his armchair and crossed the room
to rearrange the leering folds of his brown dressing gown
which, as it sprawled across the divan, showed at one end a
very distinct medieval face.

He looked up various odds and ends he had stored at odd
moments for an essay which he had never written and would
never write because by now he had forgotten its leading idea,
its secret combination. There was for instance the papyrus a
person called Rhind bought from some Arabs (who said they
had found it among the ruins of small buildings near Rames-
seum); it began with the promise to disclose "all the secrets,
all the mysteries" but (like Miss Bidder's demon) turned out
to be merely a schoolbook with blank spaces which some unknown Egyptian farmer in the seventeenth century B.C. had
used for his clumsy calculations. A newspaper clipping mentioned that the State Entomologist had retired to become Adviser on Shade Trees, and one wondered whether this was not
some dainty oriental euphemism for death. On the next slip
of paper he had transcribed passages from a famous American
poem:

> A curious sight—these bashful bears,
> These timid warrior whalemen
> . . . . .
> And now the time of tide has come;
> The ship casts off her cables
> . . . . .
> It is not shown on any map;
> True places never are
> . . . . .
> This lovely light, it lights not me;
> All loveliness is anguish—

and, of course, that bit about the delicious death of an Ohio
honey hunter (for my humor's sake I shall preserve the style
in which I once narrated it at Thula to a lounging circle of
my Russian friends).

Truganini, the last Tasmanian, died in 1877, but the last Kruganini could not remember how this was linked up with the fact that the edible Galilean fishes in the first century A.D. would be principally chromids and barbels although in Raphael's representation of the miraculous draught we find among nondescript piscine forms of the young painter's fancy two specimens which obviously belong to the skate family, never found in fresh water. Speaking of Roman *venationes* (shows with wild beasts) of the same epoch, we note that the stage, on which ridiculously picturesque rocks (the later ornaments of "romantic" landscapes) and an indifferent forest were represented, was made to rise out of the crypts below the urine-soaked arena with Orpheus on it among real lions and bears with gilded claws; but this Orpheus was acted by a criminal and the scene ended with a bear killing him, while Titus or Nero, or Paduk, looked on with that complete pleasure which "art" shot through with "human interest" is said to produce.

The nearest star is Alpha Centauri. The Sun is about 93 millions of miles away. Our solar system emerged from a spiral nebula. De Sitter, a man of leisure, has estimated the circumference of the "finite though boundless" universe at about one hundred million light-years and its mass at about a quintillion quadrillions of grams. We can easily imagine people in 3000 A.D. sneering at our naïve nonsense and replacing it by some nonsense of their own.

"Civil war is destroying Rome which none could ruin, not even the wild beast Germany with its blue-eyed youth." How I envy Cruquius who had actually seen the Blandinian MSS of Horace (destroyed in 1556 when the Benedictine abbey of St. Peter at Blankenbergh near Ghent was sacked by the mob). Oh, what was it like, traveling along the Appian Way in that large four-wheeled coach for long journeys known as the *rhēda*? Same Painted Ladies fanning their wings on the same thistleheads.

Lives that I envy: longevity, peaceful times, peaceful country, quiet fame, quiet satisfaction: Ivar Aasen, Norwegian philologist, 1813–1896, who invented a language. Down here we have too much of *homo civis* and too little of *sapiens*.

Dr. Livingstone mentions that on one occasion, after

talking with a Bushman for some time about the Deity, he found that the savage thought he was speaking of Sakomi, a local chief. The ant lives in a universe of shaped odors, of chemical configurations.

Old Zoroastrian motif of the rising sun, origin of Persian ogee design. The blood-and-gold horrors of Mexican sacrifices as told by Catholic priests or the eighteen thousand Formosan boys under nine whose little hearts were burned out upon an altar at the command of the spurious prophet Psalmanazar—the whole thing being a European forgery of the pale-green eighteenth century.

He tossed the notes back into the drawer of his desk. They were dead and unusable. Leaning his elbow on the desk and swaying slightly in his armchair, he slowly scratched his scalp through his coarse hair (as coarse as that of Balzac, he had a note of that too somewhere). A dismal feeling grew upon him: he was empty, he would never write another book, he was too old to bend and rebuild the world which had crashed when she died.

He yawned and wondered what individual vertebrate had yawned first and whether one might suppose that this dull spasm was the first sign of exhaustion on the part of the whole subdivision in its evolutionary aspect. Perhaps, if I had a new fountain pen instead of this wreck, or a fresh bouquet of, say, twenty beautifully sharpened pencils in a slim vase, and a ream of ivory smooth paper instead of these, let me see, thirteen, fourteen more or less frumpled sheets (with a two-eyed dolichocephalic profile drawn by David upon the top one) I might start writing the unknown thing I want to write; unknown, except for a vague shoe-shaped outline, the infusorial quiver of which I feel in my restless bones, a feeling of *shchekotiki* (as we used to say in our childhood) half-tingle, half-tickle, when you are trying to remember something or understand something or find something, and probably your bladder is full, and your nerves are on edge, but the combination is on the whole not unpleasant (if not protracted) and produces a minor orgasm or *"petit éternuement intérieur"* when at last you find the picture-puzzle piece which exactly fits the gap.

As he completed his yawn, he reflected that his body was

much too big and healthy for him: had he been all shriveled
up and flaccid and pestered by petty diseases, he might have
been more at peace with himself. Baron Munchausen's horse-
decorpitation story. But the individual atom is free: it pulsates
as it wants, in low or high gear; it decides itself when to absorb
and when to radiate energy. There is something to be said for
the method employed by male characters in old novels: it is
indeed soothing to press one's brow to the deliciously cold
windowpane. So he stood, poor percipient. The morning was
gray with patches of thawing snow.

David would have to be fetched from the kindergarten in
a few minutes (if his watch was right). The slow languid
sounds and half-hearted thumps coming from the next room
meant that Mariette was engaged in expressing her vague notions of order. He heard the sloppy tread of her old bed slippers trimmed with dirty fur. She had an irritating way of
performing her household duties with nothing on to conceal
her miserably young body save a dim nightgown, the frayed
hem of which hardly reached to her knees. *Femineum lucet
per bombycina corpus.* Lovely ankles: she had won a prize for
dancing, she said. A lie, I guess, like most of her utterances;
though, on second thoughts, she did have in her room a Spanish fan and a pair of castanets. For no special reason (or was
he looking for something? No) he had been led to peep into
her room in passing while she was out with David. It smelt
strongly of her hair and of *Sanglot* (a cheap musky perfume);
flimsy soiled odds and ends lay on the floor and the bedtable
was occupied by a brownish-pink rose in a glass and a large
X-ray picture of her lungs and vertebrae. She had proved such
an execrable cook that he was forced to have at least one
square meal a day brought for all three from a good restaurant
round the corner, while relying on eggs and gruels and various
preserves to provide breakfasts and suppers.

Having glanced at his watch again (and even listened to it)
he decided to take his restlessness out for a walk. He found
Cinderella in David's bedroom: she had interrupted her
labors to pick up one of David's animal books and was now
engrossed in it, half-sitting, half-lying athwart the bed, with
one leg stretched far out, the bare ankle resting on the back
of a chair, the slipper off, the toes moving.

"I shall fetch David myself," he said, averting his eyes from the brownish-pink shadows she showed.

"What?" (The queer child did not trouble to change her attitude—merely stopped twitching her toes and lifted her lusterless eyes.)

He repeated the sentence.

"Oh, all right," she said, her eyes back on the book.

"And do, please, dress," Krug added before leaving the room.

Ought to get somebody else, he thought, as he walked down the street; somebody totally different, an elderly person, completely clothed. It was, he had understood, merely a matter of habit, the result of having constantly posed naked for the black-bearded artist in apartment 30. In fact, during summer, none of them, she said, wore anything at all indoors—neither he, nor she, nor the artist's wife (who, according to sundry oils exhibited before the revolution had a grand body with numerous navels, some frowning, others looking surprised).

The kindergarten was a bright little institution run by one of his former students, a woman called Clara Zerkalsky and her brother Miron. The main enjoyment of the eight little children in their care was provided by an intricate set of padded tunnels, just high enough to let one crawl through on all fours, but there were also brilliantly painted cardboard bricks, and mechanical trains and picture books and a live shaggy dog called Basso. The place had been found by Olga the year before and David was getting a little too big for it though he still loved to crawl through the tunnels. In order to avoid exchanging salutations with the other parents, Krug stopped at the gate beyond which was the little garden (now mostly consisting of puddles) with benches for visitors. David was the first to run out of the gaily colored wooden house.

"Why didn't Mariette come?"

"Instead of me? Put on your cap."

"You and she could have come together."

"Didn't you have any rubbers?"

"Uh-uh."

"Then give me your hand. And if you walk into a puddle but once. . . ."

"And if I do it by chance [*nechaianno*]?"

"I shall see to that. Come, *raduga moia* [my rainbow], give me your hand and let us be moving."

"Billy brought a bone today. Gee whizz—some bone. I want to bring one, too."

"Is it the dark Billy or the little fellow with the glasses?"

"The glasses. He said my mother was dead. Look, look, a woman chimney sweep."

(These had recently appeared owing to some obscure shift or rift or sift or drift in the economics of the State—and much to the delight of the children.) Krug was silent. David went on talking.

"*That* was your fault, not mine. My left shoe is full of water. Daddy!"

"Yes."

"My left shoe is full of water."

"Yes. I'm sorry. Let's walk a little faster. What did you answer?"

"When?"

"When Billy said that stupid thing about your mother."

"Nothing. What should I have said?"

"But you knew it *was* a stupid remark?"

"I guess so."

"Because even *if* she were dead she would not be dead for you or me."

"Yes, but she isn't, is she?"

"Not in our sense. A bone is nothing to you or me but it means a lot to Basso."

"Daddy, he *growled* over it. He just lay there and growled with his paw on it. Miss Zee said we must not touch him or talk to him while he had it."

"Raduga moia"!

They were now in Peregolm Lane. A bearded man whom Krug knew to be a spy and who always appeared punctually at noon was at his post before Krug's home. Sometimes he hawked apples, once he had come disguised as a postman. On very cold days he would try standing in the window of a tailor, mimicking a dummy, and Krug had amused himself by outstaring the poor chap. Today he was inspecting the house fronts and jotting down something on a pad.

"Counting the raindrops, inspector?"

The man looked away; moved; and in moving stubbed his toe against the curb. Krug smiled.

"Yesterday," said David, "as we were going by, that man winked at Mariette."

Krug smiled again.

"You know what, Daddy? I think she talks to him on the telephone. She talks on the telephone every time you go out."

Krug laughed. That queer little girl, he imagined, enjoyed the love-making of quite a number of swains. She had two afternoons off, probably full of fauns and footballers and matadors. Is this getting to be an obsession? Who is she—a servant? an adopted child? Or what? Nothing. I know perfectly well, thought Krug, as he stopped laughing, that she merely goes to the pictures with a stumpy girl friend—so she says—and I have no reason to disbelieve her; and if I really did think she was what she certainly is, I should have fired her instantly: because of the germs she might bring into the nursery. Just as Olga would have done.

Sometime during the last month the elevator had been removed bodily. Men had come, sealed the door of the unfortunate Baron's tiny house and carried it into a van, intact. The bird inside was too terrified to flutter. Or had he been a spy, too?

"It's all right. Don't ring. I have the key."

"Mariette!" shouted David.

"I suppose she is out shopping," said Krug and made his way to the bathroom.

She was standing in the tub, sinuously soaping her back or at least such parts of her narrow, variously dimpled, glistening back which she could reach by throwing her arm across her shoulder. Her hair was up, with a kerchief or something twisted around it. The mirror reflected a brown armpit and a poppling pale nipple. "Ready in a sec," she sang out.

Krug slammed the door with a great show of disgust. He stalked to the nursery and helped David to change his shoes. She was still in the bathroom when the man from the Angliskiĭ Club brought a meat pie, a rice pudding, and her adolescent buttocks. When the waiter had gone, she emerged, shaking her hair, and ran into her room where she slipped into a black frock and a minute later ran out again and started to lay the table. By the time dinner was over, the newspaper had come and the afternoon mail. What news could there be?

T HE GOVERNMENT had taken to sending him a good deal of printed matter advertising its achievements and aims. Together with the telephone bill and his dentist's Christmas greeting he would find in his mailbox some mimeographed circular running thus:

Dear Citizen, according to Article 521 of our Constitution the following four freedoms are to be enjoyed by the nation: 1. freedom of speech, 2. freedom of the press, 3. freedom of meetings, and 4. freedom of processions. These freedoms are guaranteed by placing at the disposal of the people efficient printing machines, adequate supplies of paper, well-aerated halls and broad streets. What should one understand by the first two freedoms? For a citizen of our State a newspaper is a collective organizer whose business is to prepare its readers for the accomplishment of various assignments allotted to them. Whereas in other countries newspapers are purely business ventures, firms that sell their printed wares to the public (and therefore do their best to attract the public by means of lurid headlines and naughty stories), the main object of *our* press is to supply such information as would give every citizen a clear perception of the knotty problems presented by civic and international affairs; consequently, they guide the activities and the emotions of their readers in the necessary direction.

In other countries we observe an enormous number of competing organs. Each newspaper tugs its own way and this baffling diversity of tendencies produces complete confusion in the mind of the man in the street; in our truly democratic country a homogeneous press is responsible before the nation for the correctness of the political education which it provides. The articles in our newspapers are not the outcome of this or that individual fancy but a mature carefully prepared message to the reader who, in turn, receives it with the same seriousness and intentness of thought.

Another important feature of our press is the voluntary collaboration of local correspondents—letters, suggestions, discussions, criticism, and so on. Thus we observe that our citizens have free access to the papers, a state of affairs which is unknown anywhere else. True, in other countries there is a lot of talk about "freedom" but in reality a lack of funds does not allow one the use of the printed word. A millionnaire and a working man clearly do not enjoy equal opportunities.

Our press is the public property of our nation. Therefore it is not run on a commercial basis. Even the advertisements in a capitalistic newspaper can influence its political trend; this of course would be quite impossible here.

Our newspapers are published by governmental and public organizations and are absolutely independent of individuals, private and commercial interests. Independence, in its turn, is synonymous with freedom. This is obvious.

Our newspapers are completely and absolutely independent of all such influences as do not coincide with the interests of the People to whom they belong and whom they serve to the exclusion of all other masters. Thus our country enjoys the use of free speech not in theory but in real practice. Obvious again.

The constitutions of other countries also mention various "freedoms." In reality, however, these "freedoms" are extremely restricted. A shortage of paper limits the freedom of the press; unheated halls do not encourage free gatherings; and under the pretext of regulating traffic the police break up demonstrations and processions.

Generally the newspapers of other countries are in the service of capitalists who either have their own organs or acquire columns in other papers. Recently, for instance, a journalist called Ballplayer was sold by one businessman to another for several thousand dollars.

On the other hand, when half a million American textile workers went on strike, the papers wrote about kings and queens, movies and theaters. The most popular photograph which appeared in *all* capitalist newspapers of that period was a picture of two rare butterflies glittering *vsemi tzvetami radugi* [with all the hues of the rainbow]. But not a word about the strike of the textile workers!

As our Leader has said: "The workers know that 'freedom of speech' in the so-called 'democratic' countries is an empty sound." In our own country there cannot be any contradiction between reality and the rights granted to the citizens by Paduk's Constitution for we have sufficient supplies of paper, plenty of good printing presses, spacious and warm public halls, and splendid avenues and parks.

We welcome queries and suggestions. Photographs and detailed booklets mailed free on application.

(I will keep it, thought Krug, I shall have it treated by some special process which will make it endure far into the future to the eternal delight of free humorists. O yes, I will keep it.)

As for news, there was practically none in the *Ekwilist* or the *Evening Bell* or any of the other government-controlled dailies. The editorials, however, were superb:

We believe that the only true Art is the Art of Discipline. All other arts in our Perfect City are but submissive variations of the supreme Trumpet-call. We love the corporate body we belong to better than ourselves and still better do we love the Ruler who symbolizes that body in terms of our times. We are for perfect Cooperation blending and balancing the three orders of the State: the productive, the executive, and the contemplative one. We are for an absolute community of interests among fellow citizens. We are for the virile harmony between lover and beloved.

(As Krug read this he experienced a faint "Lacedaemonian" sensation: whips and rods; music; and strange nocturnal terrors. He knew slightly the author of the article—a shabby old man who under the pen name of "Pankrat Tzikutin" had edited a pogromystic magazine years ago.)

Another serious article—it was curious how austere newspapers had become.

"A person who has never belonged to a Masonic Lodge or

to a fraternity, club, union, or the like, is an abnormal and dangerous person. Of course, some organizations used to be pretty bad and are forbidden today, but nevertheless it is better for a man to have belonged to a politically incorrect organization than not to have belonged to any organization at all. As a model that every citizen ought to sincerely admire and follow we should like to mention a neighbor of ours who confesses that nothing in the world, not even the most thrilling detective story, not even his young wife's plump charms, not even the daydreams every young man has of becoming an executive some day, can vie with the weekly pleasure of foregathering with his likes and singing community songs in an atmosphere of good cheer and, let us add, good business."

Lately the elections to the Council of Elders were taking up a good deal of space. A list of candidates, thirty in number, drawn by a special commission under Paduk's management, was circulated throughout the country; of these the voters had to select eleven. The same commission nominated *"backer-grupps,"* that is, certain clusters of names received the support of special agents, called *"megaphonshchiki"* [megaphone-armed "backers"] that boosted the civic virtues of their candidates at street corners, thus creating the illusion of a hectic election fight. The whole business was extremely confused and it did not matter in the least who won, who lost, but nevertheless the newspapers worked themselves into a state of mad agitation, giving every day, and then every hour, by means of special editions, the results of the struggle in this or that district. An interesting feature was that at the most exciting moments teams of agricultural or industrial workers, like insects driven to copulation by some unusual atmospheric condition, would suddenly issue challenges to other such teams declaring their desire to arrange "production matches" in honor of the elections. Therefore the net result of these "elections" was not any particular change in the composition of the Council, but a tremendously enthusiastic albeit somewhat exhausting "zoom-curve" in the manufacture of reaping machines, cream caramels (in bright wrappers with pictures of naked girls soaping their shoulder blades), *kolbendeckelschrauben* [piston-follower-bolts], *nietwippen* [lever-dollies], *blechtafel* [sheet iron], *krakhmalchiki* [starched collars for men and boys], *glocken-metall* [bronzo da campane], *geschützbronze* [bronzo da cannoni], *blasebalgen* [vozdukhoduvnye mekha] and other useful gadgets.

Detailed accounts of various meetings of factory people or collective kitchen gardeners, snappy articles devoted to the problems of bookkeeping, denunciations, news of the activities of innumerable professional unions and the clipped accents of poems printed *en escalier* (incidentally tripling the per line honorarium) dedicated to Paduk, completely replaced the comfortable murders, marriages, and boxing matches of happier and more flippant times. It was as if one side of the globe had been struck with paralysis while the other smiled an incredulous—and slightly foolish—smile.

14

H E HAD never indulged in the search for the True Substance, the One, the Absolute, the Diamond suspended from the Christmas Tree of the Cosmos. He had always felt the faint ridicule of a finite mind peering at the iridescence of the invisible through the prison bars of integers. And even if the Thing could be caught, why should he, or anybody else for that matter, wish the phenomenon to lose its curls, its mask, its mirror, and become the bald noumenon?

On the other hand, if (as some of the wiser neo-mathematicians thought) the physical world could be said to consist of measure groups (tangles of stresses, sunset swarms of electric midgets) moving like *mouches volantes* on a shadowy background that lay outside the scope of physics, then, surely, the meek restriction of one's interest to measuring the measurable smacked of the most humiliating futility. Take yourself away, you, with your ruler and scales! For without your rules, in an unscheduled event other than the paper chase of science, barefooted Matter *does* overtake Light.

We shall imagine then a prism or prison where rainbows are but octaves of ethereal vibrations and where cosmogonists with transparent heads keep walking into each other and passing through each other's vibrating voids while, all around, various frames of reference pulsate with FitzGerald contractions. Then we give a good shake to the telescopoid kaleidoscope (for what is your cosmos but an instrument containing small bits of colored glass which, by an arrangement of mirrors, appear in a variety of symmetrical forms when rotated—mark: when rotated) and throw the damned thing away.

How many of us have begun building anew—or thought they were building anew! Then they surveyed their construction. And lo: Heraclitus the Weeping Willow was shimmering by the door and Parmenides the Smoke was coming out of the chimney and Pythagoras (already inside) was drawing the shadows of the window frames on the bright polished floor where the flies played (I settle and you buzz by; then I buzz up and you settle; then jerk-jerk-jerk; then we both buzz up).

Long summer days. Olga playing the piano. Music, order.

The trouble with Krug, thought Krug, was that for long summer years and with enormous success he had delicately taken apart the systems of others and had acquired thereby a reputation for an impish sense of humor and delightful common sense whereas in fact he was a big sad hog of a man and the "common sense" affair had turned out to be the gradual digging of a pit to accommodate pure smiling madness.

He was constantly being called one of the most eminent philosophers of his time but he knew that nobody could really define what special features his philosophy had, or what "eminent" meant or what "his time" exactly was, or who were the other worthies. When writers in foreign countries were called his disciples he never could find in their writings anything remotely akin to the style or temper of thought which, without his sanction, critics had assigned to him, so that he finally began regarding himself (robust rude Krug) as an illusion or rather as a shareholder in an illusion which was highly appreciated by a great number of cultured people (with a generous sprinkling of semicultured ones). It was much the same thing as is liable to happen in novels when the author and his yes-characters assert that the hero is a "great artist" or a "great poet" without, however, bringing any proofs (reproductions of his paintings, samples of his poetry); indeed, taking care *not* to bring such proofs since any sample would be sure to fall short of the reader's expectations and fancy. Krug, while wondering who had puffed him up, who had projected him onto the screen of fame, could not help feeling that in some odd way he did deserve it, that he really was bigger and brighter than most of the men around him; but he also knew that what people saw in him, without realizing it perhaps, was not an admirable expansion of positive matter but a kind of inaudible frozen explosion (as if the reel had been stopped at the point where the bomb bursts) with some debris gracefully poised in mid-air.

When this type of mind, so good at "creative destruction," says to itself as any poor misled philosopher (oh, that cramped uncomfortable "I," that chess-Mephisto concealed in the *cogito*!) might say: "Now I have cleared the ground, now I will build, and the gods of ancient philosophy shall not intrude"—the result generally is a cold little heap of truisms fished out of the artificial lake into which they had been especially put for the purpose. What Krug hoped to fish out was something belonging not only to an undescribed species or genus or family or order, but something representing a brand-new class.

Now let us have this quite clear. What is more important to solve: the "outer" problem (space, time, matter, the unknown without) or the "inner" one (life, thought, love, the unknown within) or again their point of contact (death)? For we agree, do we not, that problems *as* problems do exist even if the world be something made of nothing within nothing made of something. Or is "outer" and "inner" an illusion too, so that a great mountain may be said to stand a thousand dreams high and hope and terror can be as easily charted as the capes and bays they helped to name?

Answer! Oh, that exquisite sight: a wary logician picking his way among the thorn bushes and pitfalls of thought, marking a tree or a cliff (this I have passed, this Nile is settled), looking back ("in other words") and cautiously testing some quaggy ground (now let us proceed——); having his carload of tourists stop at the base of a metaphor or Simple Example (let us suppose that an elevator——); pressing on, surmounting all difficulties and finally arriving in triumph at the very first tree he had marked!

And then, thought Krug, on top of everything, I am a slave of images. We speak of one thing being like some other thing when what we are really craving to do is to describe something that is like nothing on earth. Certain mind pictures have become so adulterated by the concept of "time" that we have come to believe in the actual existence of a permanently moving bright fissure (the point of perception) between our retrospective eternity which we cannot recall and the prospective one which we cannot know. We are not really able to measure time because no gold second is kept in a case in Paris but, quite frankly, do you not imagine a length of several hours more exactly than a length of several miles?

And now, ladies and gentlemen, we come to the problem

of death. It may be said with as fair an amount of truth as is practically available that to seek perfect knowledge is the attempt of a point in space and time to identify itself with every other point; death is either the instantaneous gaining of perfect knowledge (similar say to the instantaneous disintegration of stone and ivy composing the circular dungeon where formerly the prisoner had to content himself with only two small apertures optically fusing into one; whilst now, with the disappearance of all walls, he can survey the entire circular landscape), or absolute nothingness, *nichto.*

And this, snorted Krug, is what you call a brand-new class of thinking! Have some more fish.

Who could have believed that his powerful brain would become so disorganized? In the old days whenever he took up a book, the underscored passages, his lightning notes in the margin used to come together almost automatically, and a new essay, a new chapter was ready—but now he was almost incapable of lifting the heavy pencil from the dusty thick carpet where it had fallen from his limp hand.

O N THE FOURTH, he searched through some old papers and found a reprint of a Henry Doyle Lecture which he had delivered before the Philosophical Society of Washington. He reread a passage he had polemically quoted in regard to the idea of substance: "When a body is sweet and white all over, the notions of whiteness and sweetness are repeated in various places and intermixed. . . ." [*Da mi basia mille.*]

On the fifth, he went on foot to the Ministry of Justice and demanded an interview in connection with the arrest of his friends but it gradually transpired that the place had been turned into a hotel and that the man whom he had taken for a high official was merely the headwaiter.

On the eighth, as he was showing David how to touch a pellet of bread with the tips of two crossed fingers so as to produce a kind of mirror effect in terms of contact (the feel of a second pellet), Mariette laid her bare forearm and elbow upon his shoulder and watched with interest, fidgeting all the time, tickling his temple with her brown hair and scratching her thigh with a knitting needle.

On the tenth, a student called Phokus attempted to see him but was not admitted, partly because he never allowed any scholastic matters to bother him outside his (for the moment nonexistent) office, but mainly because there were reasons to think that this Phokus might be a Government spy.

On the night of the twelfth, he dreamt that he was surreptitiously enjoying Mariette while she sat, wincing a little, in his lap during the rehearsal of a play in which she was supposed to be his daughter.

On the night of the thirteenth, he was drunk.

On the fifteenth, an unknown voice on the telephone informed him that Blanche Hedron, his friend's sister, had been smuggled abroad and was now safe in Budafok, a place situated apparently somewhere in Central Europe.

On the seventeenth, he received a curious letter:

"Rich Sir, an agent of mine abroad has been informed by two of your friends, Messrs. Berenz and Marbel, that you are seeking to purchase a reproduction of Turok's masterpiece 'Escape.' If you care to visit my shop ('Brikabrak,' Dimmerlamp Street 14) around five in the afternoon Monday, Tuesday or Friday, I shall be glad to discuss the possibility of your——" a large blot eclipsed the end of the sentence. The letter was signed "Peter Quist, Antiques."

After a prolonged study of a map of the city, he discovered the street in its northwestern corner. He laid down his magnifying glass and removed his spectacles. Making those little sticky sounds he was wont to make at such times, he put his spectacles on again, and took up the glass and tried to discover whether any of the bus routes (marked in red) would bring him there. Yes, it could be done. In a casual flash, for no reason at all, he recollected a way Olga had of lifting her left eyebrow when she looked at herself in the mirror.

Do all people have that? A face, a phrase, a landscape, an air bubble from the past suddenly floating up as if released by the head warden's child from a cell in the brain while the mind is at work on some totally different matter? Something of the sort also occurs just before falling asleep when what you think you are thinking is not at all what you think. Or two parallel passenger trains of thought, one overtaking the other.

Outside, the roughish edges of the air had a touch of spring about them although the year had only begun.

An amusing new law demanded that everyone boarding a motor bus not only show his or her passport, but also give the conductor a signed and numbered photograph. The process of checking whether the likeness, signature and number corresponded to those of the passport was a lengthy one. It had been further decreed that in case a passenger did not have the exact fare ($17\frac{1}{3}$ cents per mile), whatever surplus he paid would be refunded to him at a remote postoffice, provided he took his place in the queue there not more than thirty-three hours after leaving the bus. The writing and stamping of receipts by a harassed conductor resulted in some more delay; and since, in accordance with the same decree, the bus stopped only at those points at which not fewer than three passengers wished to alight, a good deal of confusion was added to the delay. In spite of these measures buses were singularly crowded these days.

Nevertheless, Krug managed to reach his destination: together with two youths whom he had bribed (ten kruns each) for helping to make up the necessary trio, he landed precisely where he had decided to land. His two companions (who frankly confessed that they were making a living of it) immediately boarded a moving trolley car (where the regulations were still more complicated).

It had grown dark while he had been traveling and the crooked little street lived up to its name. He felt excited, insecure, apprehensive. He saw the possibility of escaping from Padukgrad into a foreign country as a kind of return into his own past because his own country had been a free country in the past. Granted that space and time were one, escape and return became interchangeable. The peculiar character of the past (bliss unvalued at the time, her fiery hair, her voice reading of small humanized animals to her child) looked as if it could be replaced or at least mimicked by the character of a country where his child could be brought up in security, liberty, peace (a long long beach dotted with bodies, a sunny honey and her satin Latin—advertisement of some American stuff somewhere seen, somehow remembered). My God, he thought, *que j'ai été veule*, this ought to have been done months ago, the poor dear man was right. The street seemed to be full of bookshops and dim little pubs. Here we are. Pictures of birds and flowers, old books, a polka-dotted china cat. He went in.

The owner of the shop, Peter Quist, was a middle-aged man with a brown face, a flat nose, a clipped black mustache and wavy black hair. He was simply but neatly attired in a blue-and-white striped washable summer suit. As Krug entered he was saying good-by to an old lady who had an old-fashioned feathery gray boa round her neck. She glanced at Krug keenly before lowering her *voilette* and swept out.

"Know who that was?" asked Quist.

Krug shook his head.

"Ever met the late President's widow?"

"Yes," said Krug, "I have."

"And what about his sister—ever met her?"

"I do not think so."

"Well, that was his sister," said Quist negligently. Krug

blew his nose and while wiping it cast a look at the contents of the shop: mainly books. A heap of *Librairie Hachette* volumes (Molière and the like), vile paper, disintegrating covers, were rotting in a corner. A beautiful plate from some early nineteenth-century insect book showed an ocellated hawk moth and its shagreen caterpillar which clung to a twig and arched its neck. A large discolored photograph (1894) representing a dozen or so bewhiskered men in tights with artificial limbs (some had as many as two arms and one leg) and a brightly colored picture of a Mississippi flatboat graced one of the panels.

"Well," said Quist, "I am certainly glad to meet you."

Shake hands.

"It was Turok who gave me your address," said the genial antiquarian as he and Krug settled down in two armchairs in the depth of the shop. "Before we come to any arrangement I want to tell you quite frankly: all my life I have been smuggling—dope, diamonds, old masters. . . . And now—people. I do it solely to meet the expenses of my private urges and orgies, but I do it well."

"Yes," said Krug, "yes, I see. I tried to locate Turok some time ago but he was away on business."

"Well, he got your eloquent letter just before he was arrested."

"Yes," said Krug, "yes. So he has been arrested. That I did not know."

"I am in touch with the whole group," explained Quist with a slight bow.

"Tell me," said Krug, "have you any news of my friends—the Maximovs, Ember, Hedron?"

"None, though I can easily imagine how distasteful they must find the prison regime. Allow me to embrace you, Professor."

He leaned forward and gave Krug an old-fashioned kiss on the left shoulder. Tears came to Krug's eyes. Quist coughed self-consciously and continued:

"However, let us not forget that I am a hard businessman and therefore above these . . . unnecessary emotions. True, I want to save you, but I also want money for it. You would have to pay me two thousand kruns."

"It is not much," said Krug.

"Anyway," said Quist dryly, "it is sufficient to pay the brave men who take my shivering clients across the border."

He got up, fetched a box of Turkish cigarettes, offered one to Krug (who refused), lit up, carefully arranged the burning match in a pink and violet sea shell for ashtray so that it would go on burning. Its end squirmed, blackened.

"You will excuse me," he said, "for having yielded to a movement of affection and exaltation. See this scar?"

He showed the back of his hand.

"This," he said, "I received in a duel, in Hungary, four years ago. We used cavalry sabers. In spite of my several wounds, I managed to kill my opponent. He was a great man, a brilliant brain, a gentle heart, but he had had the misfortune of jokingly referring to my young sister as '*cette petite Phryné qui se croit Ophélie.*' You see, the romantic little thing had attempted to drown herself in his swimming pool."

He smoked in silence.

"And there is no way to get them out of there?" asked Krug.

"Out of where? Oh, I see. No. My organization is of a different type. We call it *fruntgenz* [frontier geese] in our professional jargon, not *turmbrokhen* [prison breakers]. So you are willing to pay me what I ask? *Bene.* Would you still be willing if I asked as much money as you have in the world?"

"Certainly," said Krug. "Any of the foreign universities would repay me."

Quist laughed and became rather coyly engaged in fishing a bit of cotton out of a little bottle containing some tablets.

"You know what?" he said with a simper. "If I were an *agent provocateur*, which of course I am not, I would make at this point the following mental observation: Madamka (supposing this to be your nickname in the spying department) is eager to leave the country, no matter what it would cost him."

"And by golly you would be right," said Krug.

"You will also have to make a special present to me," continued Quist. "Namely, your library, your manuscripts, every scrap of writing. You would have to be as naked as an earthworm when you left this country."

"Splendid," said Krug. "I shall save the contents of my waste basket for you."

"Well," said Quist, "if so, then, this is about all."

"When could you arrange it?" asked Krug.

"Arrange what?"

"My flight."

"Oh, that. Well— Are you in a hurry?"

"Yes. In a tremendous hurry. I want to get my child out of here."

"Child?"

"Yes, a boy of eight."

"Yes. Of course, you have a child."

There was a curious pause. A dull red slowly suffused Quist's face. He looked down. With soft claws he plucked at his mouth and cheeks. What fools they had been! Now promotion was his.

"My clients," said Quist, "have to do about twenty miles on foot, through blueberry woods and cranberry bogs. The rest of the time they lie at the bottom of trucks, and every jolt tells. The food is scant and crude. The satisfaction of natural needs has to be denied one's self for ten hours at a stretch or more. Your physique is good, you will stand it. Of course, taking your child with you is quite out of the question."

"Oh, I think he would be as quiet as a mouse," said Krug. "And I could carry him as long as I can carry myself."

"One day," murmured Quist, "you were not able to carry him a couple of miles to the railway station."

"I beg your pardon?"

"I said: some day you will not be able to carry him as far as it is from here to the station. That, however, is not the essential point. Do you visualize the dangers?"

"Vaguely. But I could never leave my child behind."

There was another pause. Quist twisted a bit of cotton round the head of a match and probed the inner recesses of his left ear. He inspected with satisfaction the gold he obtained.

"Well," he said, "I shall see what can be done. We must keep in touch of course."

"Could we not fix an appointment?" suggested Krug, rising from his chair and looking for his hat. "I mean you might want some money in advance. Yes, I can see it. It is under the table. Thanks."

"You are welcome," said Quist. "What about some day next week? Would Tuesday do? Around five in the afternoon?"

"That would be perfect."

"Would you care to meet me on Neptune Bridge? Say, near the twentieth lamppost?"

"Gladly."

"At your service. I confess our little talk has clarified the whole situation to a most marvelous degree. It is a pity you cannot stay longer."

"I shudder," said Krug, "to think of the long journey home. It will take me hours to get back."

"Oh, but I can show you a shorter way," said Quist. "Wait a minute. A very short and pleasant cut."

He went to the foot of a winding staircase and looking up called:

"Mac!"

There was no answer. He waited, with his face now turned upwards, now half turned to Krug—not really looking at Krug; blinking, listening.

"Mac!"

Again there was no reply, and after a while Quist decided to go upstairs and fetch what he wanted himself.

Krug examined some poor things on a shelf: an old rusty bicycle bell, a brown tennis racket, an ivory penholder with a tiny peephole of crystal. He peeped, closing one eye; he saw a cinnabar sunset and a black bridge. *Gruss aus Padukbad.*

Quist came down the steps humming and skipping, with a bundle of keys in his hand. Of these he selected the brightest and unlocked a secret door under the stairs. Silently he pointed down a long passage. There were obsolete posters and elbowed water pipes on its dimly lit walls.

"Why, thank you very much," said Krug.

But Quist had already closed the door after him. Krug walked down the passage, his overcoat unbuttoned, his hands thrust into his trouser pockets. His shadow accompanied him like a Negro porter carrying too many bags.

Presently he came to another door consisting of rough boards roughly knocked together. He pushed it and stepped into his own back yard. Next morning he went down to inspect this exit from an ingressive angle. But now it was cunningly camouflaged, merging partly with some planks that were propped against the wall of the yard and partly with the door of a proletarian privy. On some bricks nearby the mournful detective assigned to his house and an organ-grinder of sorts sat playing *chemin de fer*; a soiled nine of spades lay on the ashstrewn ground at their feet, and, with a pang of impatient desire, he visualized a railway platform and glanced at a playing card and bits of orange peel enlivening the coal dust between the rails under a Pullman car which was still waiting for him in a blend of summer and smoke but a minute later would be gliding out of the station, away, away, into the fair mist of the incredible Carolinas. And following it along the darkling swamps, and hanging faithfully in the evening aether, and slipping through the telegraph wires, as chaste as a wove-paper watermark, as smoothly moving as the transparent tangle of cells that floats athwart an overworked eye, the lemon-pale double of the lamp that shone above the passenger would mysteriously travel across the turquoise landscape in the window.

"T HREE CHAIRS placed one behind the other. Same idea.
"The what?"

"The cowcatcher."

A Chinese checker board resting against the legs of the first chair represented the cowcatcher. The last chair was the observation car.

"I see. And now the engine driver must go to bed."

"Hurry up, daddy. Get on. The train is moving!"

"Look here, my darling——"

"Oh, *please*. Sit down just for a minute."

"No, my darling—I told you."

"But it's just one minute. Oh, daddy! Mariette does not want to, you don't want to. Nobody wants to travel with me on my supertrain."

"Not now. It is really time to——"

To be going to bed, to be going to school,—bedtime, dinnertime, tubtime, never just "time"; time to get up, time to go out, time to go home, time to put out all the lights, time to die.

And what agony, thought Krug the thinker, to love so madly a little creature, formed in some mysterious fashion (even more mysterious to us than it had been to the very first thinkers in their pale olive groves) by the fusion of two mysteries, or rather two sets of a trillion of mysteries each; formed by a fusion which is, at the same time, a matter of choice and a matter of chance and a matter of pure enchantment; thus formed and then permitted to accumulate trillions of its own mysteries; the whole suffused with consciousness, which is the only real thing in the world and the greatest mystery of all.

He saw David a year or two older, sitting on a vividly labeled trunk at the customs house on the pier.

He saw him riding a bicycle in between brilliant forsythia shrubs and thin naked birch trees down a path with a "no bicycles" sign. He saw him on the edge of a swimming pool, lying on his stomach, in wet black shorts, one shoulder blade sharply raised, one hand stretched shaking out iridescent water that clogged a toy destroyer. He saw him in one of those fabulous corner stores that have face creams on one side and ice creams on the other, perched there at the bar and craning towards the syrup pumps. He saw him throwing a ball with a special flip of the wrist, unknown in the old country. He saw him as a youth crossing a technicolored campus. He saw him wearing the curious garb (jockeylike except for the shoes and stockings) used by players in the American ball game. He saw him learning to fly. He saw him, aged two, sitting on his chamber pot, jerking, crooning, moving by jerks on his scraping chamber pot right across the nursery floor. He saw him as a man of forty.

On the eve of the day fixed by Quist he found himself on the bridge: he was out reconnoitering, since it had occurred to him that as a meeting place it might be unsafe because of the soldiers; but the soldiers had gone long ago, the bridge was deserted, Quist could come whenever he liked. Krug had only one glove, and he had forgotten his glasses, so could not reread the careful note Quist had given him with all the passwords and addresses and a sketch map and the key to the code of Krug's whole life. It mattered little however. The sky immediately overhead was quilted with a livid and billowy expanse of thick cloud; very large, grayish, semitransparent, irregularly shaped snowflakes slowly and vertically descended; and when they touched the dark water of the Kur, they floated upon it instead of melting at once, and this was strange. Further on, beyond the edge of the cloud, a sudden nakedness of heaven and river smiled at the bridge-bound observer, and a mother-of-pearl radiance touched up the curves of the remote mountains, from which the river, and the smiling sadness, and the first evening lights in the windows of riverside buildings were variously derived. Watching the snowflakes upon the dark and beautiful water, Krug argued that either the flakes were real, and the water was not real water, or else the latter was real, whereas the flakes were made of some special insoluble stuff. In order to settle the question, he let his mateless glove fall from the bridge; but nothing abnormal happened: the glove simply pierced the corrugated surface of the water with its extended index, dived and was gone.

On the south bank (from which he had come) he could see, further upstream, Paduk's pink palace and the bronze dome of the Cathedral, and the leafless trees of a public garden. On the other side of the river there were rows of old tenement houses beyond which (unseen but throbbingly present) stood the hospital where she had died. As he brooded thus, sitting sideways on a stone bench and looking at the river, a tugboat dragging a barge appeared in the distance and at the same time one of the last snowflakes (the cloud overhead seemed to be dissolving in the now generously flushed sky) grazed his underlip: it was a regular soft wet flake, he reflected, but perhaps those that had been descending upon the water itself had been different ones. The tug steadily approached. As it was about to plunge under the bridge, the great black funnel, doubly encircled with crimson, was pulled back, back and down by two men clutching at its rope and grinning with sheer exertion; one of them was a Chinese as were most of the river people and washermen of the town. On the barge behind half a dozen brightly colored shirts were drying and some potted geraniums could be seen aft, and a very fat Olga in the yellow blouse he disliked, arms akimbo, looked up at Krug as the barge in its turn was smoothly engulfed by the arch of the bridge.

He awoke (asprawl in his leather armchair) and immediately understood that something extraordinary had happened. It had nothing to do with the dream or the quite unprovoked and rather ridiculous physical discomfort he felt (a local congestion) or anything that he recalled in connection with the appearance of his room (untidy and dusty in an untidy and dusty light) or the time of the day (a quarter past eight P.M.; he had fallen asleep after an early supper). What had happened was that again he knew he could write.

He went to the bathroom, took a cold shower, like the good little boy scout he was, and tingling with mental eagerness and feeling comfortable and clean in pajamas and dressing gown, let his fountain pen suck in its fill, but then remembered that it was David's tucking-in hour, and decided to get it over with, so as not to be interrupted by nursery calls. In the passage three chairs still stood one behind the other. David was lying in bed and with rapid back and forth movements of his lead pencil was evenly shading a portion of a sheet of paper placed on the fibroid fine-grained cover of a big book. This produced a not unpleasant sound, both shuffling and silky with a kind of rising buzzing vibration underlying the scrabble. The punctate texture of the cover gradually appeared as a gray grating on the paper and then, with magical precision and quite independent of the (accidentally oblique) direction of the pencil strokes, the impressed word ATLAS came out in tall narrow white letters. One wondered if by shading one's life in like fashion——

The pencil cracked. David tried to straighten the loose tip in its pine socket and use the pencil in such a way as to have the longer projection of the wood act as a prop, but the lead broke off for good.

"And anyway," said Krug, who was impatient to get back to his own writing, "it is time to put out the lights."

"First the travel story," said David.

For several nights already Krug had been evolving a serial which dealt with the adventures awaiting David on his way to a distant country (we had stopped at the point where we crouched at the bottom of a sleigh, holding our breaths, very very quiet under sheepskin blankets and empty potato sacks).

"No, not tonight," said Krug. "It is much too late and I am busy."

"It is *not* too late," cried David sitting up suddenly, with blazing eyes, and striking the atlas with his fist.

Krug removed the book and bent over David to kiss him good night. David abruptly turned away to the wall.

"Just as you like," said Krug, "but you'd better say good night [*pokoĭnoĭ nochi*] because I'm not going to come again."

David drew the bedclothes over his head, sulking. With a little cough Krug unbent and put out the lamp.

"I am not going to sleep," said David in a muffled voice.

"That's up to you," said Krug, trying to imitate Olga's smooth pedagogic tones.

A pause in the dark.

"*Pokoĭnoĭ nochi, dushka* [*animula*]," said Krug from the threshold. Silence. He told himself with a certain degree of irritation that he would have to come back in ten minutes and go through the whole act in detail. This was, as often happened, only the first rough draft of the good night ritual. But then, of course, sleep might settle the matter. He closed the door and as he turned the bend of the passage bumped into Mariette. "Look where you are going, child," he said sharply, and hit his knee against one of the chairs left by David.

In this preliminary report on infinite consciousness a certain scumbling of the essential outline is unavoidable. We have to discuss sight without being able to see. The knowledge we may acquire in the course of such a discussion will necessarily stand in the same relation to the truth as the black peacock spot produced intraoptically by pressure on the palpebra does in regard to a garden path brindled with genuine sunlight.

Ah yes, the glair of the matter instead of its yolk, the reader will say with a sigh; *connu, mon vieux!* The same old sapless sophistry, the same old dust-coated alembics—and thought speeds along like a witch on her besom! But you are wrong, you captious fool.

Ignore my invective (a question of impetus) and consider the following point: can we work ourself into a state of abject panic by trying to imagine the infinite number of years, the infinite folds of dark velvet (stuff their dryness into your mouth), in a word the infinite past, which extends on the minus side of the day of our birth? We cannot. Why? For the simple reason that we have already gone through eternity, have already nonexisted once and have discovered that this *néant* holds no terrors whatever. What we are now trying (unsuccessfully) to do is to fill the abyss we have safely crossed with terrors borrowed from the abyss in front, which abyss is borrowed itself from the infinite past. Thus we live in a stocking which is in the process of being turned inside out, without our ever knowing for sure to what phase of the process our moment of consciousness corresponds.

Once launched he went on writing with a somewhat pathetic (if viewed from the side) gusto. He *was* wounded, something *had* cracked but, for the time being, a rush of second-rate inspiration and somewhat precious imagery kept him going nicely. After an hour or so of this sort of thing he stopped and reread the four and a half pages he had written.

The way was now clear. Incidentally in one compact sentence
he had referred to several religions (not forgetting "that wonderful Jewish sect whose dream of the gentle young rabbi
dying on the Roman *crux* had spread over all Northern
lands"), and had dismissed them together with ghosts and
kobolds. The pale starry heaven of untrammeled philosophy
lay before him, but he thought he would like a drink. With
his bared fountain pen still in his hand he trudged to the
dining room. She again.

"Is he asleep?" he asked in a kind of atonic grunt without
turning his head, while bending for the brandy in the lower
part of the sideboard.

"Should be," she replied.

He uncorked the bottle and poured some of its contents
into a green glass goblet.

"Thank you," she said.

He could not help glancing at her. She sat at the table
mending a stocking. Her bare neck and legs looked uncommonly pale in contrast to her black frock and black slippers.

She glanced up from her work, her head cocked, soft wrinkles on her forehead.

"Well?" she said.

"No liquor for you," he answered. "Root beer if you like.
I think there is some in the icebox."

"You nasty man," she said, lowering her untidy eyelashes
and crossing her legs anew. "You horrible man. I feel pretty
tonight."

"Pretty what?" he asked slamming the door of the sideboard.

"Just pretty. Pretty all over."

"Good night," he said. "Don't sit up too late."

"May I sit in your room while you are writing?"

"Certainly not."

He turned to go but she called him back:

"Your pen's on the sideboard."

Moaning, he came back with his goblet and took the pen.

"When I'm alone," she said, "I sit and do like this, like a
cricket. Listen, please."

"Listen to what?"

"Don't you hear?"

She sat with parted lips, slightly moving her tightly crossed thighs, producing a tiny sound, soft, labiate, with an alternate crepitation as if she were rubbing the palms of her hands which, however, lay idle.

"Chirruping like a poor cricket," she said.

"I happen to be partly deaf," remarked Krug and trudged back to his room.

He reflected he ought to have gone to see whether David was asleep. Oh, he should be, because otherwise he would have heard his father's footsteps and called. Krug did not care to pass again by the open door of the dining room and so told himself that David was at least half asleep and likely to be disturbed by an intrusion, however well-meant. It is not quite clear why he indulged in all this ascetic self-restraint business when he might have ridden himself so deliciously of his quite natural tension and discomfort with the assistance of that keen *puella* (for whose lively little abdomen younger Romans than he would have paid the Syrian slavers twenty thousand dinarii or more). Perhaps he was held back by certain subtle supermatrimonial scruples or by the dismal sadness of the whole thing. Unfortunately his urge to write had suddenly petered out and he did not know what to do with himself. He was not sleepy having slept after dinner. The brandy only added to the nuisance. He was a big heavy man of the hairy sort with a somewhat Beethovenlike face. He had lost his wife in November. He had taught philosophy. He was exceedingly virile. His name was Adam Krug.

He reread what he had written, crossed out the witch on her besom and started to pace the room with his hands in the pockets of his robe. Gregoire peered from under the armchair. The radiator purled. The street was silent behind thick dark-blue curtains. Little by little his thoughts resumed their mysterious course. The nutcracker cracking one hollow second after another, came to a full meaty one again. An indistinct sound like the echo of some remote ovation met the appearance of a new eidolon.

A fingernail scraped, tapped.

"What is it? What do you want?"

No answer. Smooth silence. Then an audible dimple. Then silence again.

He opened the door. She was standing there in her night-gown. A slow blink concealed and revealed again the queer stare of her dark opaque eyes. She had a pillow under her arm and an alarm clock in her hand. She sighed deeply.

"Please, let me come in," she said, the somewhat lemurian features of her small white face puckering up entreatingly. "I am terrified, I simply can't be alone. I feel something dreadful is about to happen. May I sleep here? Please!"

She crossed the room on tiptoe and with infinite care put the round-faced clock down on the night table. Penetrating her flimsy pink garment, the light of the lamp brought out her body in peachblow silhouette.

"Is it O.K.?" she whispered. "I shall make myself very small."

Krug turned away, and as he was standing near a bookcase, pressed down and released again a torn edge of calf's leather on the back of an old Latin poet. *Brevis lux. Da mi basia mille.* He pounded in slow motion the book with his fist.

When he looked at her again she had crammed the pillow under her nightgown in front and was shaking with mute laughter. She patted her false pregnancy. But Krug did not laugh.

Knitting her brow and letting the pillow and some peach petals drop to the floor between her ankles,

"Don't you like me at *all?*" she said [*inquit*].

If, he thought, my heart could be heard, as Paduk's heart is, then its thunderous thumping would awaken the dead. But let the dead sleep.

Going on with her act, she flung herself on the bedded sofa and lay there prone, her rich brown hair and the edge of a flushed ear in the full blaze of the lamp. Her pale young legs invited an old man's groping hand.

He sat down near her; morosely, with clenched teeth, he accepted the banal invitation, but no sooner had he touched her, than she got up and, lifting and twisting her thin white chestnutty-smelling bare arms, yawned.

"I guess I'll go back now," she said.

Krug said nothing, Krug sat there, sullen and heavy, burst-ing with vine-ripe desire, poor thing.

She sighed, put her knee against the bedding and, baring

her shoulder, investigated the marks that some playmate's teeth had left near a small, very dark birthmark on the diaphanous skin.

"Do you want me to go?" she asked.

He shook his head.

"Shall we make love if I stay?"

His hands compressed her frail hips as if he were taking her down from a tree.

"You know too little or much too much," he said. "If too little, then run along, lock yourself up, never come near me, because this is going to be a bestial explosion, and you might get badly hurt. I warn you. I am nearly three times your age and a great big sad hog of a man. And I don't love you."

She looked down at the agony of his senses. Tittered.

"Oh, you don't?"

Mea puella, puella mea. My hot, vulgar, heavenly, delicate little *puella.* This is the translucent amphora which I slowly set down by the handles. This is the pink moth clinging——

A deafening din (the door bell, loud knocking) interrupted these anthological preambulations.

"Oh, please, please," she muttered wriggling up to him, "let's go on, we have just enough time to do it before they break the door, please."

He pushed her away violently and snatched up his dressing gown from the floor.

"It's your last cha-ance," she sang out with that special rising note which produces as it were a faint interrogatory ripple, the liquid reflection of a question mark.

Catching up and hastily interlacing the ends of the brown cord of his somewhat monastic robe, he swung down the passage followed by Mariette and, a hunchback again, unlocked the impatient door.

Young woman with pistol in gloved hand; two raw youths of S.B. (Schoolboy Brigade): repulsive patches of unshaven skin and pustules, plaid wool shirts, worn loose and flapping.

"Hi, Linda," said Mariette.

"Hi, Mariechen," said the woman. She had an Ekwilist soldier's greatcoat carelessly hanging from her shoulders and a crumpled military cap was rakishly poised on her neatly waved honey-colored hair. Krug recognized her at once.

"My fiancé is waiting outside in a car," she explained to Mariette after giving her a smiling kiss. "The Professor can go as he is. He will get some nice sterilized regulation togs at the place we are taking him to."

"Is it my turn at last?" asked Krug.

"How are you, Mariechen? We shall go to a party after we drop the Professor. Is that O.K.?"

"That's fine," said Mariette, and then asked, lowering her voice: "Can I play with the nice boys?"

"Come, come, honey, you deserve better. Fact is, I have a big surprise for you. You, kids, get busy. The nursery is down there."

"No, you don't," said Krug blocking the way.

"Let them pass, Professor, they are doing their duty. And they will not steal a pin."

"Step aside, Doc, we are doing our duty."

There was a businesslike knuckle-rap on the half-closed hall door, and when Linda, who stood with her back to it and against whose spine it gently butted, flung it wide open, a tall, broad-shouldered man in a smart semipolice uniform walked in with a heavyweight wrestler's rotund step. He had bushy black eyebrows, a square heavy jaw and the whitest of white teeth.

"Mac," said Linda, "this here is my little sister. Escaped from a boarding school on fire. Mariette, this is my fiancé's best friend. I hope you two will like each other."

"I sure hope we do," said hefty Mac in a deep mellow voice. Dental display, extended palm the size of a steak for five.

"I sure am glad to meet a friend of Hustav," said Mariette demurely.

Mac and Linda exchanged a twinkling smile.

"I'm afraid, we have not made this too clear, honey. The fiancé in question is not Hustav. Definitely not Hustav. Poor Hustav is by now an abstraction."

("You shall not pass," rumbled Krug, holding the two youths at bay.)

"What happened?" asked Mariette.

"Well, they had to wring his neck. He was a *schlapp* [a failure], you see."

"A *schlapp* who during his short life made many a fine arrest," remarked Mac with the generosity and broadmindedness so characteristic of him.

"This here belonged to him," said Linda in confidential tones, showing the pistol to her sister.

"The flashlight too?"

"No, that's Mac's."

"My!" said Mariette reverently touching the huge leathery thing.

One of the youths, propelled by Krug, collided with the umbrella stand.

"Now, now, will you please stop this unseemly scuffle," said Mac pulling Krug back (poor Krug executed a cakewalk). The two youths at once made for the nursery.

"They will frighten him," muttered and gasped Krug trying to free himself from Mac's hold. "Let me go at once. Mariette, do me a favor": he frantically signalled to her to run, to run to the nursery and see that my child, my child, my child——

Mariette looked at her sister and giggled. With wonderful professional precision and *savoir-faire*, Mac suddenly dealt Krug a cutting backhand blow with the edge of his pig-iron paw: the blow caught Krug neatly on the inside of the right arm and instantly paralyzed it. Mac proceeded to treat Krug's left arm in like fashion. Krug, bent double holding his dead arms in his dead arms, sank down on one of the three chairs that stood (by now askew and meaningless) in the passage.

"Mac's awfully good at this sort of thing," remarked Linda.

"Yes, isn't he?" said Mariette.

The sisters had not seen each other for some time and kept smiling and blinking sweetly and touching each other with limp girlish gestures.

"That's a nice brooch," said the younger.

"Three fifty," said Linda, a fold adding itself to her chin.

"Shall I go and put on my black lace panties and the Spanish dress?" asked Mariette.

"Oh, I think you look just cute in this rumpled nighty. Doesn't she, Mac?"

"Sure," said Mac.

"And you won't catch cold because there is a mink coat in the car."

Owing to the door of the nursery suddenly opening (before slamming again) David's voice was heard for a moment: oddly enough, the child, instead of whimpering and crying for help, seemed to be trying to reason with his impossible visitors. Perhaps he had not been asleep after all. The sound of that dutiful and bland little voice was worse than the most anguished moaning.

Krug moved his fingers—the numbness was gradually passing away. As calmly as possible. As calmly as possible, he again appealed to Mariette.

"Does anybody know what he wants of me?" asked Mariette.

"Look," said Mac to Adam, "either you do what you're told or you don't. And if you don't, it's going to hurt like hell, see? Get up!"

"All right," said Krug. "I will get up. What next?"

"*Marsh vniz* [Go downstairs]!"

And then David began to scream. Linda made a tchk-tchk sound ("now those dumb kids have done it") and Mac looked at her for directions. Krug lurched towards the nursery. Simultaneously David in pale blue, the little mite, ran out but was immediately caught. "I want my daddy," he cried off stage. Humming, Mariette in the bathroom with the door open was making up her lips. Krug managed to reach his child. One of the hoodlums had pinned David to the bed. The other was trying to catch David's rapidly kicking feet.

"Leave him alone, *merzavtzy!*" [a term of monstrous abuse] cried Krug.

"They want him to be quiet, that's all," said Mac, who again had taken control of the situation.

"David, my love," said Krug, "it's all right, they won't hurt you."

The child, still held by the grinning youths, caught Krug by a fold of his dressing gown.

This little hand must be unclenched.

"It's all right, leave it to me, gentlemen. Don't touch him. My darling——"

Mac, who had had enough of it, briskly kicked Krug in the shins and bundled him out.

They have torn my little one in two.

"Look here, you brute," he said, half on his knees, clinging to the wardrobe in the passage (Mac was holding him by the front of his dressing gown and pulling), "I cannot leave my child to be tortured. Let him come with me wherever you are taking me."

A toilet was flushed. The two sisters joined the men and looked on with bored amusement.

"My dear man," said Linda, "we quite understand that it is your child, or at least your late wife's child, and not a little owl of porcelain or something, but our duty is to take you away and the rest does not concern us."

"Please, let us be moving," pleaded Mariette, "it's getting frightfully late."

"Allow me to telephone to Schamm," (one of the members of the Council of Elders) said Krug. "Just that. One telephone call."

"Oh, *do* let us go," repeated Mariette.

"The question is," said Mac, "will you go quietly, under your own power, or shall I have to maim you and then roll you down the steps as we do with logs in Lagodan?"

"Yes," said Krug suddenly making up his mind. "Yes. Logs. Yes. Let us go. Let us get there quickly. After all, the solution is simple!"

"Put out the lights, Mariette," said Linda, "or we shall be accused of stealing this man's electricity."

"I shall be back in ten minutes," shouted Krug in the direction of the nursery, using the full force of his lungs.

"Aw, for Christ's sake," muttered Mac pushing him towards the door.

"Mac," said Linda, "I'm afraid she might catch cold on the stairs. I think, you'd better carry her down. Look, why doesn't he go first, then me, then you. Come on, pick her up."

"I don't weigh much, you know," said Mariette, raising her elbows towards Mac. Blushing furiously, the young policeman cupped a perspiring paw under the girl's grateful thighs, put another around her ribs and lightly lifted her heavenwards. One of her slippers fell off.

"It's O.K.," she said quickly, "I can put my foot into your pocket. There. Lin will carry my slipper."

"Say, you sure don't weigh much," said Mac.

"Now hold me tight," she said. "Hold me tight. And give me that flashlight, it's hurting me."

The little procession made its way downstairs. The place was still and dark. Krug walked in front, with a circle of light playing upon his bent bare head and brown dressing gown—looking for all the world like a participant in some mysterious religious ceremony painted by a master of chiaroscuro, or copied from such a painting, or recopied from that or some other copy. Linda followed, her pistol pointing at his back, her prettily arched feet daintily negotiating the steps. Then came Mac carrying Mariette. Exaggerated parts of the banisters and sometimes the shadow of Linda's hair and cap slipped across Krug's back and along the ghostly wall, as the electric torch, fingered by sly Mariette, moved spasmodically. Her very thin wrist had a funny little bony knob on the outside. Now let us figure it out, let us look at it squarely. They have found the handle. On the night of the twenty-first Adam Krug was arrested. This was unexpected since he had not thought they would find the handle. In fact, he had hardly known there was any handle at all. Let us proceed logically. They will not harm the child. On the contrary, it is their most valued asset. Let us not imagine things, let us stick to pure reason.

"Oh, Mac, this is divine . . . I wish there were a billion steps!"

He may go to sleep. Let us pray he does. Olga once said that a billion was a million with a bad cold. Shin hurts. Anything, anything, anything, anything, anything. Your boots, *dragotzennyǐ*, have a taste of candied plums. And look, my lips bleed from your spurs.

"I can't see a thing," said Linda. "Quit fooling with that flashlight, Mariechen."

"Hold it straight, kiddo," grumbled Mac, breathing somewhat heavily, his great raw paw steadily melting; despite the lightness of his auburn burden; because of her burning rose.

Keep telling yourself that whatever they do they will not harm him. Their horrible stink and bitten nails—the smell and dirt of high-school boys. They may start breaking his playthings. Toss to each other, toss and catch, handy-dandy, one of his pet marbles, the opal one, unique, sacred, which even I dared not touch. He in the middle, trying to stop them, trying to catch it, trying to save it from them. Or, for instance, twisting his arm, or some filthy adolescent joke, or— no, this is all wrong, hold on, I must not imagine things. They will let him sleep. They will merely ransack the flat and have a good meal in the kitchen. And as soon as I reach Schamm or the Toad himself and say what I shall say——

A blustering wind took charge of our four friends as they came out of the house. An elegant car was waiting for them. At the wheel sat Linda's fiancé, a handsome blond man with white eyelashes and——

"Oh, but we do know each other. Yes, indeed. As a matter of fact, I have had the honor of being the Professor's chauffeur once before. And so this is the little sister. Glad to meet you, Mariechen."

"Get in, you fat numbskull," said Mac—and Krug heavily settled down next to the driver.

"Here's your slipper and here's your fur," said Linda, as she handed the promised coat to Mac who took it and started to help Mariette into it.

"No—just round my shoulders," said the debutante.

She shook her smooth brown hair; then, with a special disengaging gesture (the back of her hand rapidly passing along the nape of her delicate neck), she lightly swished it up so that it would not catch under the collar of the coat.

"There is room for three," she sang out sweetly in her best golden-oriole manner from the depths of the car, and sidling up to her sister, patted the free space on the outer side.

But Mac unfolded one of the front seats so as to be right behind his prisoner; resting both elbows on the partition and chewing the mint-flavored cud, he told Krug to behave.

"All aboard?" queried Dr. Alexander.

At this moment the nursery window (last one on the left, fourth floor) flew open and one of the youths leant out, bawling something in a questioning tone. Because of the gusty wind, nothing could be made out of the jumble of words that came forth.

"What?" cried Linda, her nose impatiently puckered.

"Uglowowgloowoo?" called the youth from the window.

"Okay," said Mac to no one in particular. "Okay," he grumbled. "We hear you."

"Okay!" cried Linda upwards, making a megaphone of her hands.

The second youth loomed in violent motion within the trapezoid of light. He was cuffing David who had climbed upon a table in a futile attempt to reach the window. The bright-haired pale-blue little figure disappeared. Krug, bellowing and plunging, was half out of the car, with Mac hanging on to him, tackling him round the waist. The car was moving. The struggle was useless. A procession of small colored animals raced along an oblique strip of wallpaper. Krug sank back in his seat.

"I wonder what he was asking," remarked Linda. "Are you quite sure it's all right, Mac? I mean——"

"Well, they have their instructions, haven't they?"

"I guess so."

"All six of you," said Krug gasping, "all six will be tortured and shot if my child gets hurt."

"Now, now, these are ugly words," said Mac, and none too gently rapped him with the loose joints of four fingers behind the ear.

It was Dr. Alexander who relieved the somewhat strained situation (for there is no doubt that for a moment everybody felt something had gone wrong):

"Well," he said with a sophisticated semismile, "ugly rumors and plain facts are not always as true as ugly brides and plain wives invariably are."

Mac spluttered with laughter—right into Krug's neck.

"I must say, your new steady has a regular sense of humor," whispered Mariette to her sister.

"He is a college man," said big-eyed Linda nodding in awe and protruding her lower lip. "He knows simply everything. It gives me the creeps. You should see him with a fuse or a monkey wrench."

The two girls settled down to some cozy chatting as girls in back seats are prone to do.

"Tell me some more about Hustav," asked Mariette. "How was he strangled?"

"Well, it was like this. They came by the back door while I was making breakfast and said they had instructions to get rid of him. I said aha but I don't want any mess on the floor and I don't want any shooting. He had bolted into a clothes closet. You could hear him shivering there and clothes falling down upon him and hangers jingling at every shiver. It was just too gruesome. I said, I don't want to see you guys doing it and I don't want to spend all day cleaning up. So they took him to the bathroom and started to work on him there. Of course, my morning was ruined. I had to be at my dentist's at ten, and there they were in the bathroom making simply hideous noises—especially Hustav. They must have been at it for at least twenty minutes. He had an Adam's apple as hard as a heel, they said—and of course I was late."

"As usual," commented Dr. Alexander.

The girls laughed. Mac turned to the younger of the two and stopped chewing to ask:

"Sure you not cold, Cin?"

His baritone voice was loaded with love. The teenager blushed and furtively pressed his hand. She said she was warm, oh, very warm. Feel for yourself. She blushed because he had employed a secret diminutive which none knew, which he had somehow divined. Intuition is the sesame of love.

"All right, all right, caramel eyes," said the shy young giant disengaging his hand. "Remember, I'm on duty."

And Krug felt again the man's drugstore breath.

17

THE CAR came to a stop at the north gate of the prison. Dr. Alexander, mellowly manipulating the plump rubber of the horn (white hand, white lover, pyriform breast of black concubine), honked.

A slow iron yawn was induced and the car crawled into yard No. 1. There a swarm of guards, some wearing gas masks (which in profile bore a striking resemblance to greatly magnified ant heads), clambered upon the footboards and other accessible parts of the car; two or three even grunted their way up to the roof. Numerous hands, several of which were heavily gloved, tugged at torpid recurved Krug (still in the larval stage) and pulled him out. Guards A and B took charge of him; the rest zigzagged away, darting this way and that, in search of new victims. With a smile and a semisalute Dr. Alexander said to guard A: "I'll be seeing you," then backed and proceeded to energetically unravel the wheel. Unraveled, the car turned, jerked forward: Dr. Alexander repeated his semisalute, while Mac, after wagging a great big forefinger at Krug, squeezed his haunches into the place Mariette had made for him next to herself. Presently the car was heard uttering festive honks as it sped away, down to a private musk-scented apartment. O joyous, red-hot, impatient youth!

Krug was led through several yards to the main building. In yards No. 3 and 4 outlines of condemned men for target practice had been chalked on a brick wall. An old Russian legend says that the first thing a *rastrelianyĭ* [person executed by the firing squad] sees on entering the "other world" (no interruption please, this is premature, take your hands away), is not a gathering of ordinary "shades" or "spirits" or repulsive dear repulsive unutterably dear unutterably repulsive dear ones in antiquated clothes, as you might think, but a kind of silent slow ballet, a welcoming group of these chalked outlines moving wavily like transparent Infusoria; but away with those bleak superstitions.

They entered the building and Krug found himself in a curiously empty room. It was perfectly round, with a well-scrubbed cement floor. So suddenly did his guards disappear that, had he been a character in fiction, he might well have wondered whether the strange doings and so on had not been some evil vision, and so forth. He had a throbbing headache: one of those headaches that seem to transcend on one side the limits of one's head, like the colors in cheap comics, and do not quite fill the head space on the other; and the dull throbs were saying: one, one, one, never reaching two, never. Of the four doors at the cardinal points of the circular room, only one, one, one was unlocked. Krug pushed it open.

"Yes?" said a pale-faced man, still looking down at the see-saw blotter with which he was dabbing whatever he had just written.

"I demand immediate action," said Krug.

The official looked at him with tired watery eyes.

"My name is Konkordiǐ Filadelfovich Kolokololiteǐshchi-kov," he said, "but they call me Kol. Take a seat."

"I——" began Krug anew.

Kol, shaking his head, hurriedly selected the necessary forms:

"Wait a minute. First of all we must have all the answers. Your name is——?"

"Adam Krug. Will you please have my child brought here at once, at once——"

"A little patience," said Kol dipping his pen. "I admit the procedure is tiresome but the sooner we get it over with the better. All right. K,r,u,g. Age?"

"Will this nonsense be necessary if I tell you straightaway that I have changed my mind?"

"It is necessary under all circumstances. Sex—male. Eyebrows—shaggy. Father's name——"

"Same as mine, curse you."

"Now, don't curse me. I am as tired as you are. Religion?"

"None."

" 'None' is no answer. The law requires every male to declare his religious affiliation. Catholic? Vitalist? Protestant?"

"There is no answer."

"My dear sir, you have been baptized at least?"

"I do not know what you are talking about."

"Well, this is most— Look here, I must put down *something*."

"How many questions more? Have you got to fill all this?" (pointing with a madly trembling finger at the page).

"I am afraid so."

"In that case I refuse to continue. Here I am with a declaration of the utmost importance to make—and you take up my time with nonsense."

"Nonsense is a harsh word."

"Look here, I will sign anything if my son——"

"One child?"

"One. A boy of eight."

"A tender age. Pretty hard upon you, sir, I admit. I mean— I am a father myself and all that. However I can assure you that your boy is perfectly safe."

"He is not!" cried Krug. "You delegated two ruffians——"

"I did not delegate anybody. You are in the presence of an underpaid *chinovnik*. As a matter of fact, I deplore everything that has happened in Russian literature."

"Anyway, whoever is responsible must choose: either I remain silent for ever, or else I speak, sign, swear—anything the Government wants. But I will do all this, and more, only if my child is brought here, to this room, at once."

Kol pondered. The whole thing was very irregular.

"The whole thing is very irregular," he said at length, "but I guess you are right. You see, the general procedure is something like this: first the questionnaire must be filled, then you go to your cell. There you have a heart-to-heart talk with a fellow prisoner who really is one of our agents. Then, around two in the morning, you are roused from a fitful sleep and I start to question you again. It was thought by competent people that you would break down between six forty and seven fifteen. Our meteorologist predicted a particularly cheerless dawn. Dr. Alexander, a colleague of yours, agreed to translate into everyday language your cryptic utterances, for no one could have predicted this bluntness, this . . . I suppose, I may also add that a child's voice would have been relayed to you emitting moans of artificial pain. I had been rehearsing it with my own little children—

they will be bitterly disappointed. Do you really mean to say that you are ready to pledge allegiance to the State and all that, if——"

"You had better hurry. The nightmare may get out of control."

"Why, of course, I shall have things fixed immediately. Your attitude is most satisfactory. Our great prison has made a man of you. It is a real treat. I shall be congratulated for having broken you so quickly. Excuse me."

He got up (a small slender State employee with a large pale head and black serrated jaws), plucked aside the folds of a velvet *portière*, and then the captive remained alone with his dull "one-one-one." A filing cabinet concealed the entrance Krug had used some minutes before. What looked like a curtained window turned out to be a curtained mirror. He rearranged the collar of his dressing gown.

Four years elapsed. Then disjointed parts of a century. Odds and ends of torn time. Say, twenty-two years in all. The oak tree before the old church had lost all its birds; alone, gnarled Krug had not changed.

Preceded by a slight hunching or bunching or both of the curtain and then by his own visible hand, Konkordiĭ Filadelfovich returned. He looked pleased.

"Your boy will be brought here in a jiffy," he said brightly. "Everybody is very much relieved. Been in the care of a trained nurse. She says, the kid behaved pretty badly. A problem child, I suppose? By the way, I am asked to ask you: would you like to write your own speech and submit it in advance or will you use the material prepared?"

"The material. I am terribly thirsty."

"We shall have some refreshments presently. Now, there is another question. Here are a few papers to be signed. We could start right now."

"Not before I see my child."

"You are going to be a very busy man, *sudar'* [sir], I warn you. There is sure to be a journalist or two hanging around already. Oh, the worries we have gone through! We thought, the University would never open again. I suppose, tomorrow there will be student demonstrations, processions, public thanksgiving. Do you know d'Abrikossov, the film producer?

Well, he said he had known all along you would suddenly
realize the greatness of the State and all that. He said it was
like *la grâce* in religion. A revelation. He said it was very difficult to explain things to anybody who had not experienced
this sudden dazzling shock of truth. Personally, I am very
happy to have had the privilege of witnessing your beautiful
conversion. Still sulking? Come, let us erase those wrinkles.
Hark! Music!"

He had apparently pressed a button or turned a knob for
some trumpety-strumpety sounds issued from somewhere,
and the good fellow added in a reverent whisper:

"Music in your honor."

The band was drowned, however, by a shrill telephone peal.
Capital news, evidently, for Kol replaced the receiver with a
triumphant flourish and motioned Krug towards the curtained
door. After you.

He was a man of the world; Krug was not and pressed
forward like a boorish boar.

Unnumbered scene (belonging to one of the last acts,
anyway): the spacious waiting room of a fashionable prison.
Cute little model of guillotine (with stiff top-hatted doll in
attendance) under glass bell on mantelpiece. Oil pictures
dealing darkly with various religious subjects. A collection of
magazines on a low table (the *Geographical Magazine*, *Stolitza i Usad'ba*, *Die Woche*, *The Tatler*, *L'Illustration*). One
or two bookcases with the usual books (*Little Women*, volume III of the *History of Nottingham* and so on). A bunch
of keys on a chair (mislaid there by one of the wardens). A
table with refreshments: a plate of herring sandwiches and a
pail of water surrounded with several mugs coming from
various German kurorts. (Krug's mug had a view of Bad
Kissingen.)

A door at the back swung open; several press photographers
and reporters formed a living gallery for the passage of two
burly men leading in a thin frightened boy of twelve or thirteen. His head was newly bandaged (nobody was to blame,
they said, he had slipped on a highly polished floor and hit
his forehead against a model of Stevenson's engine in the
Children's Museum). He wore a schoolboy's black uniform,
with belt. His elbow flew up to shield his face as one of the

men made a sudden gesture meant to curb the eagerness of the press people.

"This is not my child," said Krug.

"Your dad is always joking, always joking," said Kol to the boy kindly.

"I want my own child. This is somebody else's child."

"What's that?" asked Kol sharply. "Not your child? Nonsense, man. Use your eyes."

One of the burly men (a policeman in plain clothes) produced a document which he handed to Kol. The document said clearly: Arvid Krug, son of Professor Martin Krug, former Vice-President of the Academy of Medicine.

"The bandage perhaps changes him a little," said Kol hastily, a note of desperation creeping into his patter. "And then, of course, little boys grow so fast——"

The guards were knocking down the apparatus of the photographers and pushing the reporters out of the room. "Hold the boy," said a brutal voice.

The newcomer, a person called Crystalsen (red face, blue eyes, tall starched collar) who was, as it soon transpired, Second Secretary of the Council of Elders, came up close to Kol and asked poor Kol while holding him by the knot of his necktie whether Kol did not think he was sort of responsible for this idiotic misunderstanding. Kol was still hoping against hope——

"Are you *quite* sure," he kept asking Krug, "are you quite sure this little fellow is not your son? Philosophers are absent-minded, you know. The light in this room is not very grand——"

Krug closed his eyes and said through clenched teeth:

"I want my own child."

Kol turned to Crystalsen, spread out his hands and produced a helpless, hopeless, bursting sound with his lips (ppwt). Meanwhile, the unwanted boy was led away.

"We apologize," said Kol to Krug. "Such mistakes are bound to occur when there are so many arrests."

"Or not enough," interrupted Crystalsen crisply.

"He means," said Kol to Krug, "that those who made this mistake will be dearly punished."

Crystalsen, *même jeu*:

"Or pay for it severely."

"Exactly. Of course, matters will be straightened out without delay. There are four hundred telephones in this building. Your little lost child will be found at once. I understand now why my wife had that terrible dream last night. Ah, Crystalsen, *was ver a trum* [what a dream]!"

The two officials, the smaller one talking volubly and pawing at his tie, the other maintaining a grim silence, his Polar Sea eyes looking straight ahead, left the room.

Krug waited again.

At 11:24 P.M. a policeman (now in uniform) stole in, looking for Crystalsen. He wanted to know what was to be done with the wrong boy. He spoke in a hoarse whisper. When told by Krug that they had gone that way, he repointed to the door delicately, interrogatively, then tiptoed across the room, his Adam's apple moving diffidently. Was centuries long in closing, quite noiselessly, the door.

At 11:43, the same man, but now wild-eyed and disheveled, was led back through the waiting room by two Special Guards, to be shot later as a minor scapegoat, together with the other "burly man" (*vide* unnumbered scene) and poor Konkordiĭ.

At 12 punctually Krug was still waiting.

Little by little, however, various sounds, coming from the neighboring offices, increased in volume and agitation. Several times clerks crossed the room at a breathless run and once a telephone operator (a Miss Lovedale) who had been disgracefully manhandled, was carried to the prison hospital on a stretcher by two kind-hearted stone-faced colleagues.

At 1:08 A.M. rumors of Krug's arrest reached the little group of anti-Ekwilist conspirators of which the student Phokus was leader.

At 2:17, a bearded man who said he was an electro-technician came to inspect the heat radiator, but was told by a suspicious warden that no electricity was involved in their heating system and would he please come another day.

The windows had turned a ghostly blue when Crystalsen at last reappeared. He was glad to inform Krug that the child had been located. "You will be reunited in a few minutes," he said, adding that a new torture room completely modernized was right at the moment being prepared to receive those who had blundered. He wanted to know whether he had been correctly informed regarding Adam Krug's sudden conversion. Krug answered—yes, he was ready to broadcast to some of the richer foreign states his firm conviction that Ekwilism was all right, if, and only if, his child were returned to him safe and sound. Crystalsen led him to a police car, and on the way started to explain things.

It was quite clear that something had gone dreadfully wrong; the child had been taken to a kind of—well, Institute for Abnormal Children—instead of the best State Rest House, as had been arranged. You are hurting my wrist, sir. Unfortunately, the director of the Institute had understood, as who would not, that the child delivered to him was one of the so-called "Orphans," now and then used to serve as a "release-instrument" for the benefit of the most interesting inmates with a so-called "criminal" record (rape, murder, wanton destruction of State property, etc.). The theory—and we are not here to discuss its worth, and you shall pay for my cuff if you tear it—was that if once a week the really difficult patients could enjoy the possibility of venting in full their repressed yearnings (the exaggerated urge to hurt, destroy, etc.) upon some little human creature of no value to the community, then, by degrees, the evil in them would be allowed to escape, would be, so to say, "effundated," and eventually they would become good citizens. The experiment might be criticized, of course, but that was not the point (Crystalsen carefully wiped the blood from his mouth and offered his none too clean handkerchief to Krug—to wipe Krug's knuckles; Krug refused; they entered the car; several soldiers joined them). Well, the enclosure where the "release games" took place was so situated that the director from his window and the other doctors and research workers, male and female (Doktor Amalia von Wytwyl, for instance, one of the most fascinating personalities you have ever met, an aristocrat, you would enjoy meeting her under happier circumstances, sure you would) from other *gemütlich* points of vantage, could watch the proceedings and take notes. A nurse led the "orphan" down the marble steps. The enclosure was a beautiful expanse of turf, and the whole place, especially in summer, looked extremely attractive, reminding one of some of those open-air theaters that were so dear to the Greeks. The "orphan" or "little person" was left alone and allowed to roam all over the enclosure. One of the photographs showed him lying disconsolately on his stomach and uprooting a bit of turf with listless fingers (the nurse reappeared on the garden steps and clapped her hands to make him stop. He stopped). After a while the patients or "inmates" (eight all told) were let into the enclosure. At first, they kept at a distance, eyeing the "little person." It was interesting to observe how the "gang" spirit gradually asserted itself. They had been rough lawless unorganized individuals, but now something was binding them, the community spirit (positive) was conquering the individual whims (negative); for the first time in their lives they were *organized*; Doktor von Wytwyl used to say that this was a wonderful moment: one felt that, as she quaintly put it, "something was really happening," or in technical language: the "ego," he goes "ouf" (out) and the pure "egg" (common extract of egoes) "remains." And then the fun began. One of the patients (a "representative" or "potential leader"), a heavy handsome boy of seventeen went up to the "little person" and sat down beside him on the turf and said "open your mouth." The "little person" did what he was told and with unerring precision the youth spat a pebble into the child's open mouth. (This was a wee bit against the rules, because generally speaking, all missiles, instruments, arms and so forth were forbidden.) Sometimes the "squeezing game" started at once after the "spitting game" but in other cases the development from harmless pinching and poking or mild sexual investigations to limb tearing, bone breaking, deoculation, etc. took a considerable time. Deaths were of course unavoidable, but quite often the "little person" was afterwards patched up and gamely made to return to the fray. Next Sunday, dear, you will play with the big boys again. A patched up "little person" provided an especially satisfactory "release."

Now we take all this, press it into a small ball, and fit it into the center of Krug's brain where it gently expands.

The drive was a long one. Somewhere, in a rough mountain region four or five thousand feet above sea level they stopped: the soldiers wanted their *frishtik* [early luncheon] and were not loath to make a quiet picnic of it in that wild and pictur-esque place. The car stood inert, very slightly leaning on one side among dark rocks and patches of dead white snow. They took out their bread and cucumbers and regimental thermos bottles and moodily munched as they sat hunched up on the footboard or on the withered tousled coarse grass beside the highway. The Royal Gorge, one of nature's wonders, cut by sand-laden waters of the turbulent Sakra river through eons of time, offered scenes of splendor and glory. We try very hard at Bridal Veil Ranch to understand and appreciate the attitude of mind in which many of our guests arrive from their city homes and businesses, and this is the reason we endeavor to have our guests do just exactly as they wish in the way of fun, exercise, and rest.

Krug was allowed to get out of the car for a minute. Crys-talsen, who had no eye for beauty, remained inside eating an apple and skimming through a long private letter he had re-ceived the day before and had not had the time to peruse (even these men of steel have their domestic troubles). Krug stood with his back to the soldiers in front of a rock. This went on for such a long time that at last one of the soldiers remarked with a laugh:

"*Podi galonishcha dva vysvistal za-noch* [I fancy he must have drunk a couple of gallons during the night]."

Here she had her accident. Krug came back and slowly, painfully penetrated into the car where he joined Crystalsen who was still reading.

"Good morning," mumbled the latter withdrawing his foot. Presently he lifted his head, hastily crammed the letter into his pocket and called out to the soldiers.

Highway 76 brought them down into another part of the plain and very soon they saw the smoking chimneys of the little factory town in the neighborhood of which the famous experimental station was situated. Its director was a Dr. Ham-mecke: short, sturdy, with a bushy yellowish-white mustache, protruding eyes and stumpy legs. He, his assistants and the nurses were in a state of excitement bordering on ordinary panic. Crystalsen said he did not know yet whether they were to be destroyed or not; he expected, he said, to get destruc-tions (a froonerism for "instructions") by telephone (he looked at his watch) soon. They all were horribly obsequious, toadying to Krug, offering him a shower bath, the assistance of a pretty *masseuse*, a mouth organ requisitioned from an inmate, a glass of beer, brandy, breakfast, the morning paper, a shave, a game of cards, a suit of clothes, anything. They were obviously playing for time. Finally Krug was ushered into a projection hall. He was told that he would be led to his child in a minute (the child was still asleep, they said), and in the meantime would not he like to see a movie picture taken but a few hours ago? It showed, they said, how healthy and happy the child was.

He sat down. He accepted the flask of brandy which one of the shivering smiling nurses was thrusting into his face (so scared was she that she first attempted to feed him as she would an infant). Dr. Hammecke, his false teeth rattling in his head like dice, gave the order to start the performance. A young Chinese brought David's fur-trimmed little overcoat (yes, I recognize it, it is his) and turned it this way and that (newly cleaned, no more holes, see) with the flickering gestures of a conjuror to show there was no deceit: the child had been really found. Finally, with a twittering cry he turned out of one of the pockets a little toy car (yes, we bought it together) and a child's silver ring with most of the enamel gone (yes). Then he bowed and retired. Crystalsen, who sat next to Krug in the first row, looked gloomy and suspicious; his arms were crossed. "A trick, a damned trick," he kept muttering.

The lights went out and a square shimmer of light jumped onto the screen. But the whirr of the machine was again broken off (the engineer being affected by the general nervousness). In the dark Dr. Hammecke leant towards Krug and spoke in a thick stream of apprehensiveness and halitosis.

"We are happy to have you with us. We hope you will enjoy the picture. In the interest of silence. Put in a good word. We did our best."

The whirring noise was resumed, an inscription appeared upside down, again the engine stopped.

A nurse giggled.

"Science, please!" said the doctor.

Crystalsen who had had enough of it quickly left his place;

the unfortunate Hammecke tried to restrain him, but was shaken off by the gruff official.

A trembling legend appeared on the screen: Test 656. This melted into a subtle subtitle: "A Night Lawn Party." Armed nurses were shown unlocking doors. Blinking, the inmates trooped out. "Frau Doktor von Wytwyl, Leader of the Experiment (No Whistling, Please!)" said the next inscription. In spite of the dreadful predicament he was in, even Dr. Hammecke could not restrain an appreciative ha-ha. The woman Wytwyl, a statuesque blonde, holding a whip in one hand and a chronometer in the other, swept haughtily across the screen. "Watch Those Curves": a curving line on a blackboard was shown and a pointer in a rubber-gloved hand pointed out the climactic points and other points of interest in the yarovization of the ego.

"The Patients Are Grouped at the Rosebush Entrance of the Enclosure. They Are Searched for Concealed Weapons." One of the doctors drew out of the sleeve of the fattest boy a lumberman's saw. "Bad Luck, Fatso!" A collection of labeled implements was shown on a tray: the aforeseen saw, a piece of lead pipe, a mouth organ, a bit of rope, one of those penknives with twenty-four blades and things, a peashooter, a six-shooter, awls, augers, gramophone needles, an old-fashioned battle-ax. "Lying in Wait." They lay in wait. "The Little Person Appears."

Down the floodlit marble steps leading into the garden he came. A nurse in white accompanied him, then stopped and bade him descend alone. David had his warmest overcoat on, but his legs were bare and he wore his bedroom slippers. The whole thing lasted a moment: he turned his face up to the nurse, his eyelashes beat, his hair caught a gleam of lambent light; then he looked around, met Krug's eyes, showed no sign of recognition and uncertainly went down the few steps that remained. His face became larger, dimmer, and vanished as it met mine. The nurse remained on the steps, a faint not untender smile playing on her dark lips. "What a Treat," said the legend, "For a Little Person to be Out Walking in the Middle of the Night," and then "Uh-Uh. Who's that?"

Loudly Dr. Hammecke coughed and the whirr of the machine stopped. The light went on again.

I want to wake up. Where is he? I shall die if I do not wake up.

He declined the refreshments, refused to sign the distinguished visitors' book, walked through the people barring his way as if they were cobwebs. Dr. Hammecke, rolling his eyes, panting, pressing his hand to his diseased heart, motioned the head nurse to lead Krug to the infirmary.

There is little to add. In the passage Crystalsen with a big cigar in his mouth was engaged in jotting down the whole story in a little book which he pressed to the yellow wall on the level of his forehead. He jerked his thumb towards door A-1. Krug entered. Frau Doktor von Wytwyl née Bachofen (the third, eldest, sister) was gently, almost dreamily, shaking a thermometer as she looked down at the bed near which she stood in the far corner of the room. Then she turned to Krug and advanced towards him.

"Brace yourself," she said quietly. "There has been an accident. We have done our best——"

Krug pushed her aside with such force that she crashed into a white weighing machine and broke the thermometer she was holding.

"Oops," she said.

The murdered child had a crimson and gold turban around its head; its face was skilfully painted and powdered: a mauve blanket, exquisitely smooth, came up to its chin. What looked like a fluffy piebald toy dog was prettily placed at the foot of the bed. Before rushing out of the ward, Krug knocked this thing off the blanket, whereupon the creature, coming to life, gave a snarl of pain and its jaws snapped, narrowly missing his hand.

Krug was caught by a friendly soldier.

"*Yablochko, kuda-zh ty tak kotishsa* [little apple, whither are you rolling]?" asked the soldier and added:

"*A po zhabram, milaĭ, khochesh* [want me to hit you, friend]?"

Tut pocherk zhizni stanovitsa kraĭne nerazborchivym [here the long hand of life becomes extremely illegible]. *Ochevidtzy, sredi kotorykh byl i evo vnutrenniĭ sogliadataĭ* [witnesses among whom was his own something or other ("inner spy"? "private detective"? The sense is not at all clear)] *potom go-*

vorili [afterwards said] *shto evo prishlos' sviazat'* [that he had to be tied]. *Mezhdu tem* [among the themes? (Perhaps: among the subjects of his dreamlike state)] *Kristalsen, nevozmutimo dymia sigaroĭ* [Crystalsen calmly smoking his cigar], *sobral ves' shtat v aktovom zale* [called a meeting of the whole staff in the assembly hall] and informed them [*i soobshchil im*] that he had just received a telephone message according to which they would all be court-martialed for doing to death the only son of Professor Krug, celebrated philosopher, President of the University, Vice-President of the Academy of Medicine. Weak-hearted Hammecke slid from his chair and went on sliding, tobogganing down sinuous slopes, and after a smooth swoon-run finally came to rest like a derelict sleigh on the virgin snows of anonymous death. The woman Wytwyl, without losing her poise, swallowed a pill of poison. After trying and burying the rest of the staff and setting fire to the building where the buzzing patients were locked up, the soldiers carried Krug to the car.

They drove back to the capital across the wild mountains. Beyond Lagodan Pass the valleys were already brimming with dusk. Night took over among the great fir trees near the famous Falls. Olga was at the wheel, Krug, a nondriver, sat beside her, his gloved hands folded in his lap; behind sat Ember and an American professor of philosophy, a gaunt hollow-cheeked, white-haired man who had come all the way from his remote country to discuss with Krug the illusion of substance. Gorged with landscapes and rich local food (wrongly accented *piróshki*, wrongly spelled *schtschi* and an unpronounceable meat course followed by a hot crisscross-crusted cherry pie) the gentle scholar had fallen asleep. Ember was trying to recall the American name for a similar kind of fir tree in the Rocky Mountains. Two things happened together: Ember said "Douglas" and a dazzled doe plunged into the blaze of our lights.

18

"THIS OUGHT never to have happened. We are terribly sorry. Your child will be given the most scrumptious burial a white man's child could dream up; but still we quite understand, that for those who remain this is——" (two words indistinct). "We are more than sorry. Indeed, it can be safely asserted that never in the history of this great country has a group, a government, or a ruler been as sorry as we are today."

(Krug had been brought to a spacious room resplendent with megapod murals, in the Ministry of Justice. A picture of the building itself as it had been planned but not actually built yet—in consequence of fires Justice and Education shared the Hotel Astoria—showed a white skyscraper mounting like an albino cathedral into a morpho-blue sky. The voice belonging to one of the Elders who were holding an extraordinary session in the Palace two blocks away poured forth from a handsome walnut cabinet. Crystalsen and several clerks were whispering together in another part of the hall.)

"We feel, however," continued the walnut voice, "that nothing has changed in the relationship, the bond, the agreement which you, Adam Krug, so solemnly defined just before the personal tragedy occurred. Individual lives are insecure; but we guarantee the immortality of the State. Citizens die so that the city may live. We cannot believe that any personal bereavement can come between you and our Ruler. On the other hand, there is practically no limit to the amends we are ready to make. In the first place our foremost Funeral Home has agreed to deliver a bronze casket with garnet and turquoise incrustations. Therein your little Arvid will lie clasping his favorite toy, a box of tin soldiers, which at this very moment several experts at the Ministry of War are minutely checking in regard to the correctness of uniforms and weapons. In the second place, the six main culprits will be executed by an inexperienced headsman in your presence. This is a sensational offer."

(Krug had been shown these persons in their death cells a

347

few minutes before. The two dark pimply youths attended by
a Catholic priest were putting on a brave show, due mainly to
lack of imagination. Mariette sat with closed eyes, in a rigid
faint, bleeding gently. Of the other three the less said the
better.)

"You will certainly appreciate," said the walnut and fudge
voice, "the effort we make to atone for the worst blunder that
could have been committed under the circumstances. We are
ready to condone many things, including murder, but there
is one crime that can never, never be forgiven; and that is
carelessness in the performance of one's official duty. We also
feel that, having made the handsome amends just stated, we
are through with the whole miserable business and do not
have to refer to it any more. You will be pleased to hear that
we are ready to discuss with you the various details of your
new appointment."

Crystalsen came over to where Krug sat (still in his dressing
gown, his bristly cheek propped on his abrased knuckles) and
spread out several documents on the lion-clawed table whose
edge supported Krug's elbow. With his red and blue pencil
the blue-eyed, red-faced official made little crosses here and
there on the papers, showing Krug where to sign.

In silence, Krug took the papers and slowly crushed and
tore them with his big hairy hands. One of the clerks, a thin
nervous young man who knew how much thought and labor
the printing of the documents (on precious edelweiss paper!)
had demanded, clutched at his brow and uttered a shriek of
pure pain. Krug, without leaving his seat, caught the young
man by his coat and with the same ponderous crushing slow
gestures began to strangle his victim, but was made to desist.

Crystalsen, who alone had retained a most perfect calm,
notified the microphone in the following terms:

"The sounds you have just heard, gentlemen, are the
sounds made by Adam Krug in tearing the papers he had
promised to sign last night. He has also attempted to choke
one of my assistants."

Silence ensued. Crystalsen sat down and began cleaning his
nails with a steel shoe-buttoner contained, together with
twenty-three other instruments, in a fat pocketknife which he
had filched somewhere during the day. The clerks on their

hands and knees were collecting and smoothing out what remained of the documents.

Apparently there took place a consultation among the Elders. Then the voice said:

"We are ready to go even further. We offer to let you, Adam Krug, slaughter the culprits yourself. This is a very special offer and not likely to be renewed."

"Well?" asked Crystalsen without looking up.

"Go and——" (three words indistinct) said Krug.

There was another pause. ("The man is crazy . . . utterly crazy," whispered one effeminate clerk to another. "To turn down such an offer! Incredible! Never heard of such a thing." "Me neither." "Wonder where the boss got that knife.")

The Elders reached a certain decision but before making it known the more conscientious among them thought they would like to have the disc run again. They heard Krug's silence as he surveyed the prisoners. They heard one of the youths' wrist watch and a sad little gurgle inside the supperless priest. They heard a drop of blood fall upon the floor. They heard forty satisfied soldiers in the neighboring guardhouse compare carnal notes. They heard Krug being led to the radio room. They heard the voice of one of them saying how sorry they all were and how ready to make amends: a beautiful tomb for the victim of carelessness, a terrible doom for the careless. They heard Crystalsen sorting out papers and Krug tearing them. They heard the cry of the impressionable young clerk, the sounds of a struggle, then Crystalsen's crisp tones. They heard Crystalsen's firm fingernails getting at one twenty-fourth of the tight penknife. They heard themselves voicing their generous offer and Krug's vulgar reply. They heard Crystalsen closing the knife with a click and the clerks whispering. They heard themselves hearing all this.

The walnut cabinet moistened its lips:

"Let him be led to his bed," it said.

No sooner said than done. He was given a roomy cell in the prison; so roomy and pleasant, in fact, that the director had used it more than once to lodge some poor relatives of his wife when they came to town. On a second straw mattress right on the floor a man lay with his face to the wall, every inch of his body shivering. A huge curly brown wig sprawled all over his head. His clothes were those of an old-fashioned vagabond. His must have been a dark crime indeed. As soon as the door was closed and Krug had heavily sunk onto his own patch of straw and sackcloth, the tremor of his fellow prisoner ceased to be visible but at once became audible as a reedy quaking ably disguised voice:

"Do not seek to find who I am. My face will be turned to the wall. To the wall my face will be turned. Turned to the wall for ever and ever my face will be. Madman, you. Proud and black is your soul as the damp macadam at night. Woe! Woe! Question thy crime. 'Twill show the depth of thy guilt. Dark are the clouds, denser they grow. The Hunter comes riding his terrible steed. Ho-yo-to-ho! Ho-yo-to-ho!"

(Shall I tell him to stop? thought Krug. What's the use? Hell is full of these mummers.)

"Ho-yo-to-ho! Now listen, friend. Listen, Gurdamak. We are going to make you a last offer. Four friends you had, four staunch friends and true. Deep in a dungeon they languish and moan. Listen, Drug, listen Kamerad, I am ready to give them and some twenty other *liberalishki* their freedom, if you agree to what you had practically agreed to yesterday. Such a small thing! The lives of twenty-four men are in your hands. If you say 'no,' they will be destroyed, if it is 'aye,' they live. Think, what marvelous power! You sign your name and twenty-two men and two women flock out into the sunlight. It is your last chance. Madamka, say yes!"

"Go to hell, you filthy Toad," said Krug wearily.

The man uttered a cry of rage, and snatching a bronze cowbell from under his mattress shook it furiously. Masked guards with Japanese lanterns and lances invaded the cell and reverently helped him to his feet. Covering his face with the hideous locks of his red-brown wig he passed by Krug's elbow. His jack boots smelled of dung and glistened with innumerable teardrops. The darkness swept back into place. One could hear the prison governor's creaking spine and his voice telling the Toad what a dandy actor he was, what a swell performance, what a treat. The echoing steps retreated. Silence. Now, at last, you may think.

But swoon or slumber, he lost consciousness before he could properly grapple with his grief. All he felt was a slow sinking, a concentration of darkness and tenderness, a gradual growth of sweet warmth. His head and Olga's head, cheek to cheek, two heads held together by a pair of small experimenting hands which stretched up from a dim bed, were (or was—for the two heads formed one) going down, down, down towards a third point, towards a silently laughing face. There was a soft chuckle just as his and her lips reached the child's cool brow and hot cheek, but the descent did not stop there and Krug continued to sink into the heart-rending softness, into the black dazzling depths of a belated but—never mind—eternal caress.

In the middle of the night something in a dream shook him out of his sleep into what was really a prison cell with bars of light (and a separate pale gleam like the footprint of some phosphorescent islander) breaking the darkness. At first, as sometimes happens, his surroundings did not match any form of reality. Although of humble origin (a vigilant arc light outside, a livid corner of the prison yard, an oblique ray coming through some chink or bullet hole in the bolted and padlocked shutters) the luminous pattern he saw assumed a strange, perhaps fatal significance, the key to which was half-hidden by a flap of dark consciousness on the glimmering floor of a half-remembered nightmare. It would seem that some promise had been broken, some design thwarted, some opportunity missed—or so grossly exploited as to leave an afterglow of sin and shame. The pattern of light was somehow the result of a kind of stealthy, abstractly vindictive, groping, tampering movement that had been going on in a dream, or behind a dream, in a tangle of immemorial and by now formless and aimless machinations. Imagine a sign that warns you of an explosion in such cryptic or childish language that you wonder whether everything—the sign, the frozen explosion under the window sill and your quivering soul—has not been reproduced artificially, there and then, by special arrangement with the mind behind the mirror.

It was at that moment, just after Krug had fallen through the bottom of a confused dream and sat up on the straw with a gasp—and just before his reality, his remembered hideous misfortune could pounce upon him—it was then that I felt a pang of pity for Adam and slid towards him along an inclined beam of pale light—causing instantaneous madness, but at least saving him from the senseless agony of his logical fate.

With a smile of infinite relief on his tear-stained face, Krug lay back on the straw. In the limpid darkness he lay, amazed and happy, and listened to the usual nocturnal sounds peculiar to great prisons: the occasional akh-kha-kha-akha yawn of a guard, the laborious mumble of sleepless elderly prisoners studying their English grammar books (My aunt has a visa. Uncle Saul wants to see Uncle Samuel. The child is bold.), the heartbeats of younger men noiselessly digging an underground passage to freedom and recapture, the pattering sound made by the excrementa of bats, the cautious crackling of a page which had been viciously crumpled and thrown into the wastebasket and was making a pitiful effort to uncrumple itself and live just a little longer.

When at dawn four elegant officers (three counts and a Georgian prince) came to take him to a crucial meeting with friends, he refused to move and lay smiling at them and playfully trying to chuck them under their chins by means of his bare toes. He could not be made to put on any clothes and after a hurried consultation the four young guardsmen, swearing in old-fashioned French, carried him as he was, i.e., dressed only in (white) pajamas, to the very same car that had once been so smoothly driven by the late Dr. Alexander.

He was given a program of the confrontation ceremony and led through a kind of tunnel into a central yard.

As he contemplated the shape of the yard, the jutting roof of yonder porch, the gaping arch of the tunnellike entrance through which he had come, it dawned upon him with a kind of frivolous precision difficult to express, that this was the yard of his school; but the building itself had been altered, its windows had grown in length and through them one could see a flock of hired waiters from the Astoria laying a table for a fairy tale feast.

He stood in his white pajamas, bareheaded, barefooted, blinking, looking this way and that. He saw a number of unexpected people: near the dingy wall separating the yard from the workshop of a surly old neighbor who never threw back one's ball, there stood a stiff and silent little group of guards and bemedaled officials, and among them stood Paduk, one heel scraping the wall, his arms folded. In another, dimmer part of the yard several shabbily clothed men and two women "represented the hostages," as the program given to Krug said. His sister-in-law sat in a swing, her feet trying to catch the ground, and her blond-bearded husband was in the act of plucking at one of the ropes when she snarled at him for causing the swing to wobble, and slithered off with an ungraceful movement, and waved to Krug. Somewhat apart stood Hedron and Ember and Rufel and a man he could not quite place, and Maximov, and Maximov's wife. Everybody wanted to talk to the smiling philosopher (for it was not known that his son had died and that he himself was insane) but the soldiers had their orders and allowed the petitioners to approach only in pairs.

One of the Elders, a person called Schamm, bent his plumed head towards Paduk and half-pointing with a nervously diffident finger, taking back, as it were, every jerky poke he made with it and using some other finger to repeat the gesture, explained the goings on in a low voice. Paduk nodded and stared at nothing, and nodded again.

Professor Rufel, a high-strung, angular, extremely hirsute little man with hollow cheeks and yellow teeth came up to Krug together with——

"Goodness, Schimpffer!" exclaimed Krug. "Fancy meeting you here after all these years—let me see——"

"A quarter of a century," said Schimpffer in a deep voice.

"Well, well, this certainly is like old times," Krug went on with a laugh. "And what with the Toad there——"

A gust of wind overturned an empty sonorous ash can; a small vortex of dust raced across the yard.

"I have been elected as spokesman," said Rufel. "You know the situation. I shall not dwell upon details because time is short. We want you to know that we do not wish our plight to influence you in any way. We want to live very much, very much indeed, but we shall not bear you any grudge whatsoever——" He cleared his throat. Ember, still far away, was bobbing and straining, like Punch, trying to get a glimpse of Krug over the shoulders and heads.

"No grudge, none at all," Rufel continued rapidly. "In fact, we shall quite understand if you decline to yield—*Vy*

*ponimaete o chom rech? Daĭte zhe mne znak, shto vy poni-
maete*—[Do you understand what it is all about? Make me a
sign that you understand]."

"It's all right, go on," said Krug. "I was just trying to
remember. You were arrested—let me see—just before the cat
left the room. I suppose——" (Krug waved to Ember whose
big nose and red ears kept appearing here and there between
soldiers and shoulders). "Yes, I think I remember now."

"We have asked Professor Rufel to be our spokesman," said
Schimpffer.

"Yes, I see. A wonderful orator. I have heard you, Rufel, in
your prime, on a lofty platform, among flowers and flags. Why
is it that bright colors——"

"My friend," said Rufel, "time is short. Please, let me continue. We are no heroes. Death is hideous. There are two
women among us sharing our fate. Our miserable flesh would
throb with exquisite joy, if you consented to save our lives by
selling your soul. But we do not ask you to sell your soul. We
merely——"

Krug, interrupting him with a gesture, made a dreadful
grimace. The crowd waited in breathless suspense. Krug rent
the silence with a tremendous sneeze.

"You silly people," he said, wiping his nose with his hand,
"what on earth are you afraid of? What does it all matter?
Ridiculous! Same as those infantile pleasures—Olga and the
boy taking part in some silly theatricals, she getting drowned,
he losing his life or something in a railway accident. What on
earth does it matter?"

"Well, if it does not matter," said Rufel, breathing hard,
"then, damn it, tell them you are ready to do your best, and
stick to it, and we shall not be shot."

"You see, it's a horrible situation," said Schimpffer who
had been a brave banal red-haired boy, but now had a pale
puffy face with freckles showing through his sparse hair. "We
have been told that unless you accepted the Government's
terms this is our last day. I have a big factory of sport articles
in Ast-Lagoda. I was arrested in the middle of the night and
clapped into prison. I am a law-abiding citizen and do not
understand in the least why anybody should turn down a governmental offer, but I know that you are an exceptional

person and may have exceptional reasons, and believe me
I should hate to make you do anything dishonorable or
foolish."

"Krug, do you hear what we are saying?" asked Rufel
abruptly and as Krug continued to look at them with a benevolent and somewhat loose-lipped smile, they realized with
a shock that they were addressing a madman.

"*Khoroshen'koe polozhen'itze* [a pretty business]," remarked
Rufel to dumbfounded Schimpffer.

A colored photograph taken a moment or two later showed
the following: on the right (facing the exit) near the gray
wall, Paduk was seated with thighs parted, in a chair which
had just been fetched for him from the house. He wore
the green and brown mottled uniform of one of his favorite
regiments. His face was a dead pink blob under a waterproof
cap (which his father had once invented). He sported bottle-
shaped brown leggings. Schamm, a gorgeous person in a brass
breastplate and wide-brimmed white-feathered hat of black
velvet, was leaning toward him, saying something to the sulky
little dictator. Three other Elders stood near by, wrapped in
black cloaks, like cypresses or conspirators. Several handsome
young men in operatic uniforms, armed with brown and green
mottled automatic pistols, formed a protective semicircle
around this group. On the wall behind Paduk and just above
his head, an inscription in chalk, an obscene word scrawled
by some schoolboy, had been allowed to remain; this gross
negligence quite spoiled the right-hand part of the picture.
On the left, in the middle of the yard, hatless, his coarse dark
graying locks moving in the wind, clothed in ample white
pajamas with a silken girdle, and barefooted like a saint of old,
loomed Krug. Guards were pointing rifles at Rufel and
Schimpffer who were remonstrating with them. Olga's sister,
her face twitching, her eyes trying to look unconcerned, was
telling her inefficient husband to go a few steps forward and
occupy a more favorable position so that he and she might
get to Krug next. In the background, a nurse was giving Maximov an injection: the old man had collapsed, and his kneeling
wife was wrapping his feet in her black shawl (they both had
been cruelly treated in prison). Hedron, or rather an extremely gifted impersonator (for Hedron himself had com-

mitted suicide a few days before), was smoking a Dunhill pipe. Ember, shivering (the outline was blurred) despite the astrakhan coat he wore, had taken advantage of the altercation between the first pair and the guards and was almost at Krug's elbow. You can move again.

Rufel gesticulated. Ember caught Krug by the arm and Krug turned quickly to his friend.

"Wait a minute," said Krug. "Don't start complaining until I settle this misunderstanding. Because, you see, this *confrontation* is a complete misunderstanding. I had a dream last night, yes, a dream. . . . Oh, never mind, call it a dream or call it a haloed hallucination—one of those oblique beams across a hermit's cell—look at my bare feet—cold as marble, of course, but— Where was I? Listen, you are not as stupid as the others, are you? You know as well as I do that there is nothing to fear?"

"My dear Adam," said Ember, "let us not go into such details as fear. I am ready to die. . . . But there is one thing that I refuse to endure any longer, *c'est la tragédie des cabinets*, it is killing me. As you know, I have a most queasy stomach, and they lead me into an enseamed draught, an inferno of filth, once a day for a minute. *C'est atroce.* I prefer to be shot straightaway."

As Rufel and Schimpffer still kept struggling and telling the guards that they had not finished talking to Krug, one of the soldiers appealed to the Elders, and Schamm walked over and softly spoke.

"This will never do," he said in very careful accents (by sheer will power he had cured himself of an explosive stammer in his youth). "The program must be carried out without all this chatter and confusion. Let us have done with it. Tell them" (he turned to Krug) "that you have been elected Minister of Education and Justice and in this capacity are giving them back their lives."

"Your breastplate is fantastically beautiful," murmured Krug and with a rapid movement of all ten fingers drummed upon the convex metal.

"The days when we pup-played in this very yard are gone," said Schamm severely.

Krug reached for Schamm's headgear and deftly transferred it to his own locks.

It was a sissy sealskin bonnet. The boy, with a stutter of rage, tried to retrieve it. Adam Krug threw it to Pinkie Schimpffer who, in turn, threw it up a snow-fringed amassment of stacked birch logs where it stuck. Schamm ran back into the schoolhouse to complain. The Toad, homeward bound, stealthily walked along the low wall towards the exit. Adam Krug slung his book satchel across his shoulder and remarked to Schimpffer that it was funny—did Schimpffer also get sometimes that feeling of a "repeated sequence," as if all this had already happened before: fur cap, I threw it to you, you threw it up, logs, snow on logs, cap got stuck, the Toad came out . . . ? Being of a practical turn of mind, Schimpffer suggested they better give the Toad a good fright. The two boys watched him from behind the logs. The Toad stopped near the wall, apparently waiting for Mamsch. With a tremendous huzza, Krug led the attack.

"For God's sake, stop him," cried Rufel, "he has gone mad. We are not responsible for his actions. Stop him!"

In a burst of vigorous speed, Krug was running towards the wall, where Paduk, his features dissolving in the water of fear, had slipped from his chair and was trying to vanish. The yard seethed in wild commotion. Krug dodged the embrace of a guard. Then the left side of his head seemed to burst into flames (that first bullet took off part of his ear), but he stumbled on cheerfully:

"Come on, Schrimp, come on," he roared without looking back, "let us trim him, let us get at his guts, come on!"

He saw the Toad crouching at the foot of the wall, shaking, dissolving, speeding up his shrill incantations, protecting his dimming face with his transparent arm, and Krug ran towards him, and just a fraction of an instant before another and better bullet hit him, he shouted again: You, you—and the wall vanished, like a rapidly withdrawn slide, and I stretched myself and got up from among the chaos of written and rewritten pages, to investigate the sudden twang that something had made in striking the wire netting of my window.

As I had thought, a big moth was clinging with furry feet

to the netting, on the night's side; its marbled wings kept
vibrating, its eyes glowed like two miniature coals. I had just
time to make out its streamlined brownish-pink body and a
twinned spot of color; and then it let go and swung back
into the warm damp darkness.

Well, that was all. The various parts of my comparative paradise—the bedside lamp, the sleeping tablets, the glass of
milk—looked with perfect submission into my eyes. I knew
that the immortality I had conferred on the poor fellow was
a slippery sophism, a play upon words. But the very last lap
of his life had been happy and it had been proven to him that
death was but a question of style. Some tower clock which I
could never exactly locate, which, in fact, I never heard in the
daytime, struck twice, then hesitated and was left behind by
the smooth fast silence that continued to stream through the
veins of my aching temples; a question of rhythm.

Across the lane, two windows only were still alive. In one,
the shadow of an arm was combing invisible hair; or perhaps
it was a movement of branches; the other was crossed by the
slanting black trunk of a poplar. The shredded ray of a street-
lamp brought out a bright green section of wet boxhedge. I
could also distinguish the glint of a special puddle (the one
Krug had somehow perceived through the layer of his own
life), an oblong puddle invariably acquiring the same form
after every shower because of the constant spatulate shape of
a depression in the ground. Possibly, something of the kind
may be said to occur in regard to the imprint we leave in the
intimate texture of space. Twang. A good night for mothing.

SPEAK, MEMORY

An Autobiography Revisited

To Véra

Foreword

T̲HE PRESENT WORK is a systematically correlated assemblage of personal recollections ranging geographically from St. Petersburg to St. Nazaire, and covering thirty-seven years, from August 1903 to May 1940, with only a few sallies into later space-time. The essay that initiated the series corresponds to what is now Chapter Five. I wrote it in French, under the title of "Mademoiselle O," thirty years ago in Paris, where Jean Paulhan published it in the second issue of *Mesures*, 1936. A photograph (published recently in Gisèle Freund's *James Joyce in Paris*) commemorates this event, except that I am wrongly identified (in the *Mesures* group relaxing around a garden table of stone) as "Audiberti."

In America, whither I migrated on May 28, 1940, "Mademoiselle O" was translated by the late Hilda Ward into English, revised by me, and published by Edward Weeks in the January, 1943, issue of *The Atlantic Monthly* (which was also the first magazine to print my stories written in America). My association with *The New Yorker* had begun (through Edmund Wilson) with a short poem in April 1942, followed by other fugitive pieces; but my first prose composition appeared there only on January 3, 1948: this was "Portrait of My Uncle" (Chapter Three of the complete work), written in June 1947 at Columbine Lodge, Estes Park, Colo., where my wife, child, and I could not have stayed much longer had not Harold Ross hit it off so well with the ghost of my past. The same magazine also published Chapter Four ("My English Education," March 27, 1948), Chapter Six ("Butterflies," June 12, 1948), Chapter Seven ("Colette," July 31, 1948) and Chapter Nine ("My Russian Education," September 18, 1948), all written in Cambridge, Mass., at a time of great mental and physical stress, as well as Chapter Ten ("Curtain-Raiser," January 1, 1949), Chapter Two ("Portrait of My Mother," April 9, 1949), Chapter Twelve ("Tamara," December 10, 1949), Chapter Eight ("Lantern Slides," February 11, 1950; H. R.'s query: "Were the Nabokovs a *one*-nutcracker family?"), Chapter One ("Perfect

Past," April 15, 1950), and Chapter Fifteen ("Gardens and Parks," June 17, 1950), all written in Ithaca, N.Y.

Of the remaining three chapters, Chapters Eleven and Fourteen appeared in the *Partisan Review* ("First Poem," September, 1949, and "Exile," January–February, 1951), while Chapter Thirteen went to *Harper's Magazine* ("Lodgings in Trinity Lane," January, 1951).

The English version of "Mademoiselle O" has been republished in *Nine Stories* (New Directions, 1947), and *Nabokov's Dozen* (Doubleday, 1958; Heinemann, 1959; Popular Library, 1959; and Penguin Books, 1960); in the latter collection, I also included "First Love," which became the darling of anthologists.

Although I had been composing these chapters in the erratic sequence reflected by the dates of first publication given above, they had been neatly filling numbered gaps in my mind which followed the present order of chapters. That order had been established in 1936, at the placing of the cornerstone which already held in its hidden hollow various maps, timetables, a collection of matchboxes, a chip of ruby glass, and even—as I now realize—the view from my balcony of Geneva lake, of its ripples and glades of light, black-dotted today, at teatime, with coots and tufted ducks. I had no trouble therefore in assembling a volume which Harper & Bros. of New York brought out in 1951, under the title *Conclusive Evidence*; conclusive evidence of my having existed. Unfortunately, the phrase suggested a mystery story, and I planned to entitle the British edition *Speak, Mnemosyne* but was told that "little old ladies would not want to ask for a book whose title they could not pronounce." I also toyed with *The Anthemion* which is the name of a honeysuckle ornament, consisting of elaborate interlacements and expanding clusters, but nobody liked it; so we finally settled for *Speak, Memory* (Gollancz, 1951, and The Universal Library, N.Y., 1960). Its translations are: Russian, by the author (*Drugie Berega*, The Chekhov Publishing House, N.Y., 1954), French, by Yvonne Davet (*Autres Rivages*, Gallimard, 1961), Italian, by Bruno Oddera (*Parla, Ricordo*, Mondadori, 1962), Spanish, by Jaime Piñeiro Gonzáles (*¡Habla, memoria!*, 1963) and German, by Dieter E. Zimmer (Rowohlt, 1964). This exhausts the necessary amount of bibliographic information, which jittery critics who were annoyed by the note at the end of *Nabokov's Dozen* will be, I hope, hypnotized into accepting at the beginning of the present work.

While writing the first version in America I was handicapped by an almost complete lack of data in regard to family history, and, consequently, by the impossibility of checking my memory when I felt it might be at fault. My father's biography has been amplified now, and revised. Numerous other revisions and additions have been made, especially in the earlier chapters. Certain tight parentheses have been opened and allowed to spill their still active contents. Or else an object, which had been a mere dummy chosen at random and of no factual significance in the account of an important event, kept bothering me every time I reread that passage in the course of correcting the proofs of various editions, until finally I made a great effort, and the arbitrary spectacles (which Mnemosyne must have needed more than anybody else) were metamorphosed into a clearly recalled oystershell-shaped cigarette case, gleaming in the wet grass at the foot of an aspen on the Chemin du Pendu, where I found on that June day in 1907 a hawkmoth rarely met with so far west, and where a quarter of a century earlier, my father had netted a Peacock butterfly very scarce in our northern woodlands.

In the summer of 1953, at a ranch near Portal, Arizona, at a rented house in Ashland, Oregon, and at various motels in the West and Midwest, I managed, between butterfly-hunting and writing *Lolita* and *Pnin*, to translate *Speak, Memory*, with the help of my wife, into Russian. Because of the psychological difficulty of replaying a theme elaborated in my *Dar* (*The Gift*), I omitted one entire chapter (Eleven). On the other hand, I revised many passages and tried to do something about the amnesic defects of the original—blank spots, blurry areas, domains of dimness. I discovered that sometimes, by means of intense concentration, the neutral smudge might be forced to come into beautiful focus so that the sudden view could be identified, and the anonymous servant named. For the present, final, edition of *Speak, Memory* I have not only introduced basic changes and copious additions into the initial English text, but have availed myself of the corrections I made while turning it into Russian. This re-Englishing of a Russian re-version of what had been an English re-telling of Russian memories in the first place, proved to be a diabolical task, but some consolation was given me by the thought that such multiple metamorphosis, familiar to butterflies, had not been tried by any human before.

Among the anomalies of a memory, whose possessor and victim should never have tried to become an autobiographer, the worst is the inclination to equate in retrospect my age with that of the century. This has led to a series of remarkably consistent chronological blunders in the first version of this book. I was born in April 1899, and naturally, during the first third of, say, 1903, was roughly three years old; but in August of that year, the sharp "3" revealed to me (as described in "Perfect Past") should refer to the century's age, not to mine, which was "4" and as square and resilient as a rubber pillow. Similarly, in the early summer of 1906—the summer I began to collect butterflies—I was seven and not six as stated initially in the catastrophic second paragraph of Chapter 6. Mnemosyne, one must admit, has shown herself to be a very careless girl.

All dates are given in the New Style: we lagged twelve days behind the rest of the civilized world in the nineteenth century, and thirteen in the beginning of the twentieth. By the Old Style I was born on April 10, at daybreak, in the last year of the last century, and that was (if I could have been whisked across the border at once) April 22 in, say, Germany; but since all my birthdays were celebrated, with diminishing pomp, in the twentieth century, everybody, including myself, upon being shifted by revolution and expatriation from the Julian calendar to the Gregorian, used to add thirteen, instead of twelve days to the 10th of April. The error is serious. What is to be done? I find "April 23" under "birth date" in my most recent passport, which is also the birth date of Shakespeare, my nephew Vladimir Sikorski, Shirley Temple and Hazel Brown (who, moreover, shares my passport). This, then, is the problem. Calculatory ineptitude prevents me from trying to solve it.

When after twenty years of absence I sailed back to Europe, I renewed ties that had been undone even before I had left it. At these family reunions, *Speak, Memory* was judged. Details of date and circumstance were checked, and it was found that in many cases I had erred, or had not examined deeply enough an obscure but fathomable recollection. Certain matters were dismissed by my advisers as legends or rumors or, if genuine, were proven to be related to events or periods other than those to which frail memory had attached them. My cousin Sergey Sergeevich Nabokov gave me invaluable information on the history of our family. Both my sisters angrily remonstrated against my description of the journey to Biarritz (beginning of Chapter Seven) and by pelting me with specific details convinced me I had been wrong in leaving them behind ("with nurses and aunts"!). What I still have not been able to rework through want of specific documentation, I have now preferred to delete for the sake of over-all truth. On the other hand, a number of facts relating to ancestors and other personages have come to light and have been incorporated in this final version of *Speak, Memory.* I hope to write some day a "Speak on, Memory," covering the years 1940–60 spent in America: the evaporation of certain volatiles and the melting of certain metals are still going on in my coils and crucibles.

The reader will find in the present work scattered references to my novels, but on the whole I felt that the trouble of writing them had been enough and that they should remain in the first stomach. My recent introductions to the English translations of *Zashchita Luzhina*, 1930 (*The Defense*, Putnam, 1964), *Otchayanie*, 1936 (*Despair*, Putnam, 1966), *Priglashenie na kazn'*, 1938 (*Invitation to a Beheading*, Putnam, 1959), *Dar*, 1952, serialized 1937–38 (*The Gift*, Putnam, 1963) and *Soglyadatay*, 1938 (*The Eye*, Phaedra, 1965) give a sufficiently detailed, and racy, account of the creative part of my European past. For those who would like a fuller list of my publications, there is the detailed bibliography, worked out by Dieter E. Zimmer (*Vladimir Nabokov Bibliographie des Gesamtwerks*, Rowohlt, 1st ed. December, 1963; 2nd revised ed. May, 1964).

The two-mover described in the last chapter has been republished in *Chess Problems* by Lipton, Matthews & Rice (Faber, London 1963, p. 252). My most amusing invention, however, is a "White-retracts-move" problem which I dedicated to E. A. Znosko-Borovski, who published it, in the nineteen-thirties (1934?), in the émigré daily *Poslednie Novosti*, Paris. I do not recall the position lucidly enough to notate it here, but perhaps some lover of "fairy chess" (to which type of problem it belongs) will look it up some day in one of those blessed libraries where old newspapers are microfilmed, as all our memories should be. Reviewers read the first version more carelessly than they will this new edition: only one of them noticed my "vicious snap" at Freud in the first paragraph of Chapter Eight, section 2, and none discovered the name of a great cartoonist and a tribute to him in the last sentence of section 2, Chapter Eleven. It is most embarrassing for a writer to have to point out such things himself.

To avoid hurting the living or distressing the dead, certain proper names have been changed. These are set off by quotation marks in the index. Its main purpose is to list for my convenience some of the people and themes connected with my past years. Its presence will annoy the vulgar but may please the discerning, if only because

> Through the window of that index
>   Climbs a rose
> And sometimes a gentle wind *ex*
>   *Ponto* blows.

VLADIMIR NABOKOV
January 5, 1966
Montreux

Illustrations

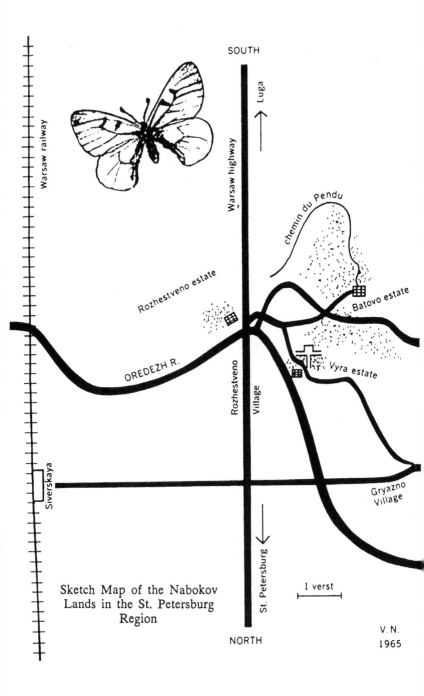

SOUTH

Luga

Warsaw railway

Warsaw highway

chemin du Pendu

Rozhestveno estate

Batovo estate

Vyra estate

OREDEZH R.

Rozhestveno

Village

Siverskaya

Gryazno Village

Sketch Map of the Nabokov
Lands in the St. Petersburg
Region

1 verst

St. Petersburg

NORTH

V. N.
1965

One

T HE CRADLE rocks above an abyss, and common sense tells us that our existence is but a brief crack of light between two eternities of darkness. Although the two are identical twins, man, as a rule, views the prenatal abyss with more calm than the one he is heading for (at some forty-five hundred heartbeats an hour). I know, however, of a young chronophobiac who experienced something like panic when looking for the first time at homemade movies that had been taken a few weeks before his birth. He saw a world that was practically unchanged—the same house, the same people—and then realized that he did not exist there at all and that nobody mourned his absence. He caught a glimpse of his mother waving from an upstairs window, and that unfamiliar gesture disturbed him, as if it were some mysterious farewell. But what particularly frightened him was the sight of a brand-new baby carriage standing there on the porch, with the smug, encroaching air of a coffin; even that was empty, as if, in the reverse course of events, his very bones had disintegrated.

Such fancies are not foreign to young lives. Or, to put it otherwise, first and last things often tend to have an adolescent note—unless, possibly, they are directed by some venerable and rigid religion. Nature expects a full-grown man to accept the two black voids, fore and aft, as stolidly as he accepts the extraordinary visions in between. Imagination, the supreme delight of the immortal and the immature, should be limited. In order to enjoy life, we should not enjoy it too much.

I rebel against this state of affairs. I feel the urge to take my rebellion outside and picket nature. Over and over again, my mind has made colossal efforts to distinguish the faintest of personal glimmers in the impersonal darkness on both sides of my life. That this darkness is caused merely by the walls of time separating me and my bruised fists from the free world of timelessness is a belief I gladly share with the most gaudily painted savage. I have journeyed back in thought—with thought hopelessly tapering off as I went—to remote regions where I groped for some secret outlet only to discover that the prison of time is spherical and without exits. Short of suicide, I have tried everything. I have doffed my identity in order to pass for a conventional spook and steal into realms that existed before I was conceived. I have mentally endured the degrading company of Victorian lady novelists and retired colonels who remembered having, in former lives, been slave messengers on a Roman road or sages under the willows of Lhasa. I have ransacked my oldest dreams for keys and clues— and let me say at once that I reject completely the vulgar, shabby, fundamentally medieval world of Freud, with its crankish quest for sexual symbols (something like searching for Baconian acrostics in Shakespeare's works) and its bitter little embryos spying, from their natural nooks, upon the love life of their parents.

Initially, I was unaware that time, so boundless at first blush, was a prison. In probing my childhood (which is the next best to probing one's eternity) I see the awakening of consciousness as a series of spaced flashes, with the intervals between them gradually diminishing until bright blocks of perception are formed, affording memory a slippery hold. I had learned numbers and speech more or less simultaneously at a very early date, but the inner knowledge that I was I and that my parents were my parents seems to have been established only later, when it was directly associated with my discovering their age in relation to mine. Judging by the strong sunlight that, when I think of that revelation, immediately invades my memory with lobed sun flecks through overlapping patterns of greenery, the occasion may have been my mother's birthday, in late summer, in the country, and I had asked questions and had assessed the answers I received. All this is as it should be according to the theory of recapitulation; the beginning of reflexive consciousness in the brain of our remotest ancestor must surely have coincided with the dawning of the sense of time.

Thus, when the newly disclosed, fresh and trim formula of my own age, four, was confronted with the parental formulas, thirty-three and twenty-seven, something happened to me. I was given a tremendously invigorating shock. As if subjected to a second baptism, on more divine lines than the Greek Catholic ducking undergone fifty months earlier by a howling, half-drowned half-Victor (my mother, through the half-closed door, behind which an old custom bade parents retreat, managed to correct the bungling archpresbyter, Father Konstantin Vetvenitski), I felt myself plunged abruptly into a radiant and mobile medium that was none other than the pure element of time. One shared it—just as excited bathers share shining seawater—with creatures that were not oneself but that were joined to one by time's common flow, an environment quite different from the spatial world, which not only man but apes and butterflies can perceive. At that instant, I became acutely aware that the twenty-seven-year-old being, in soft white and pink, holding my left hand, was my mother, and that the thirty-three-year-old being, in hard white and gold, holding my right hand, was my father. Between them, as they evenly progressed, I strutted, and trotted, and strutted again, from sun fleck to sun fleck, along the middle of a path, which I easily identify today with an alley of ornamental oaklings in the park of our country estate, Vyra, in the former Province of St. Petersburg, Russia. Indeed, from my present ridge of remote, isolated, almost uninhabited time, I see my diminutive self as celebrating, on that August day 1903, the birth of sentient life. If my left-hand-holder and my right-hand-holder had both been present before in my vague infant world, they had been so under the mask of a tender incognito; but now my father's attire, the resplendent uniform of the Horse Guards, with that smooth golden swell of cuirass burning upon his chest and back, came out like the sun, and for several years afterward I remained keenly interested in the age of my parents and kept myself informed about it, like a nervous passenger asking the time in order to check a new watch.

My father, let it be noted, had served his term of military training long before I was born, so I suppose he had that day put on the trappings of his old regiment as a festive joke. To a joke, then, I owe my first gleam of complete consciousness—which again has recapitulatory implications, since the first creatures on earth to become aware of time were also the first creatures to smile.

2

It was the primordial cave (and not what Freudian mystics might suppose) that lay behind the games I played when I was four. A big cretonne-covered divan, white with black trefoils, in one of the drawing rooms at Vyra rises in my mind, like some massive product of a geological upheaval before the beginning of history. History begins (with the promise of fair Greece) not far from one end of this divan, where a large potted hydrangea shrub, with pale blue blossoms and some greenish ones, half conceals, in a corner of the room, the pedestal of a marble bust of Diana. On the wall against which the divan stands, another phase of history is marked by a gray engraving in an ebony frame—one of those Napoleonic-battle pictures in which the episodic and the allegoric are the real adversaries and where one sees, all grouped together on the same plane of vision, a wounded drummer, a dead horse, trophies, one soldier about to bayonet another, and the invulnerable emperor posing with his generals amid the frozen fray.

With the help of some grown-up person, who would use first both hands and then a powerful leg, the divan would be moved several inches away from the wall, so as to form a narrow passage which I would be further helped to roof snugly with the divan's bolsters and close up at the ends with a couple of its cushions. I then had the fantastic pleasure of creeping through that pitch-dark tunnel, where I lingered a little to listen to the singing in my ears—that lonesome vibration so familiar to small boys in dusty hiding places—and then, in a burst of delicious panic, on rapidly thudding hands and knees I would reach the tunnel's far end, push its cushion away, and be welcomed by a mesh of sunshine on the parquet under the canework of a Viennese chair and two gamesome flies settling by turns. A dreamier and more delicate sensation was provided by another cave game, when upon awakening in the early morning I made a tent of my bedclothes and let my imagination play in a thousand dim ways with shadowy snowslides of linen and with the faint light that seemed to penetrate my penumbral covert from some immense distance, where I fancied that strange, pale animals roamed in a landscape of lakes.

The recollection of my crib, with its lateral nets of fluffy cotton cords, brings back, too, the pleasure of handling a certain beautiful, delightfully solid, garnet-dark crystal egg left over from some unremembered Easter; I used to chew a corner of the bedsheet until it was thoroughly soaked and then wrap the egg in it tightly, so as to admire and re-lick the warm, ruddy glitter of the snugly enveloped facets that came seeping through with a miraculous completeness of glow and color. But that was not yet the closest I got to feeding upon beauty.

How small the cosmos (a kangaroo's pouch would hold it), how paltry and puny in comparison to human consciousness, to a single individual recollection, and its expression in words! I may be inordinately fond of my earliest impressions, but then I have reason to be grateful to them. They led the way to a veritable Eden of visual and tactile sensations. One night, during a trip abroad, in the fall of 1903, I recall kneeling on my (flattish) pillow at the window of a sleeping car (probably on the long-extinct Mediterranean Train de Luxe, the one whose six cars had the lower part of their body painted in umber and the panels in cream) and seeing with an inexplicable pang, a handful of fabulous lights that beckoned to me from a distant hillside, and then slipped into a pocket of black velvet: diamonds that I later gave away to my characters to alleviate the burden of my wealth. I had probably managed to undo and push up the tight tooled blind at the head of my berth, and my heels were cold, but I still kept kneeling and peering. Nothing is sweeter or stranger than to ponder those first thrills. They belong to the harmonious world of a perfect childhood and, as such, possess a naturally plastic form in one's memory, which can be set down with hardly any effort; it is only starting with the recollections of one's adolescence that Mnemosyne begins to get choosy and crabbed. I would moreover submit that, in regard to the power of hoarding up impressions, Russian children of my generation passed through a period of genius, as if destiny were loyally trying what it could for them by giving them more than their share, in view of the cataclysm that was to remove completely the world they had known. Genius disappeared when everything had been stored, just as it does with those other, more specialized child prodigies—pretty, curly-headed youngsters waving batons or taming enormous pianos, who eventually turn into second-rate musicians with sad eyes and obscure ailments and something vaguely misshapen about their eunuchoid hindquarters. But even so, the individual mystery remains to tantalize the memoirist. Neither in environment nor in heredity can I find the exact instrument that fashioned me, the anonymous roller that pressed upon my life a certain intricate watermark whose unique design becomes visible when the lamp of art is made to shine through life's foolscap.

3

To fix correctly, in terms of time, some of my childhood recollections, I have to go by comets and eclipses, as historians do when they tackle the fragments of a saga. But in other cases there is no dearth of data. I see myself, for instance, clambering over wet black rocks at the seaside while Miss Norcott, a languid and melancholy governess, who thinks I am following her, strolls away along the curved beach with Sergey, my younger brother. I am wearing a toy bracelet. As I crawl over those rocks, I keep repeating, in a kind of zestful, copious, and deeply gratifying incantation, the English word "childhood," which sounds mysterious and new, and becomes stranger and stranger as it gets mixed up in my small, overstocked, hectic mind, with Robin Hood and Little Red Riding Hood, and the brown hoods of old hunchbacked fairies. There are dimples in the rocks, full of tepid seawater, and my magic muttering accompanies certain spells I am weaving over the tiny sapphire pools.

The place is of course Abbazia, on the Adriatic. The thing around my wrist, looking like a fancy napkin ring, made of semitranslucent, pale-green and pink, celluloidish stuff, is the fruit of a Christmas tree, which Onya, a pretty cousin, my coeval, gave me in St. Petersburg a few months before. I sentimentally treasured it until it developed dark streaks inside which I decided as in a dream were my hair cuttings which somehow had got into the shiny substance together with my tears during a dreadful visit to a hated hairdresser in nearby

Fiume. On the same day, at a waterside café, my father happened to notice, just as we were being served, two Japanese officers at a table near us, and we immediately left—not without my hastily snatching a whole *bombe* of lemon sherbet, which I carried away secreted in my aching mouth. The year was 1904. I was five. Russia was fighting Japan. With hearty relish, the English illustrated weekly Miss Norcott subscribed to reproduced war pictures by Japanese artists that showed how the Russian locomotives—made singularly toylike by the Japanese pictorial style—would drown if our Army tried to lay rails across the treacherous ice of Lake Baikal.

But let me see. I had an even earlier association with that war. One afternoon at the beginning of the same year, in our St. Petersburg house, I was led down from the nursery into my father's study to say how-do-you-do to a friend of the family, General Kuropatkin. His thickset, uniform-encased body creaking slightly, he spread out to amuse me a handful of matches, on the divan where he was sitting, placed ten of them end to end to make a horizontal line, and said, "This is the sea in calm weather." Then he tipped up each pair so as to turn the straight line into a zigzag—and that was "a stormy sea." He scrambled the matches and was about to do, I hoped, a better trick when we were interrupted. His aide-de-camp was shown in and said something to him. With a Russian, flustered grunt, Kuropatkin heavily rose from his seat, the loose matches jumping up on the divan as his weight left it. That day, he had been ordered to assume supreme command of the Russian Army in the Far East.

This incident had a special sequel fifteen years later, when at a certain point of my father's flight from Bolshevik-held St. Petersburg to southern Russia he was accosted while crossing a bridge, by an old man who looked like a gray-bearded peasant in his sheepskin coat. He asked my father for a light. The next moment each recognized the other. I hope old Kuropatkin, in his rustic disguise, managed to evade Soviet imprisonment, but that is not the point. What pleases me is the evolution of the match theme: those magic ones he had shown me had been trifled with and mislaid, and his armies had also vanished, and everything had fallen through, like my toy trains that, in the winter of 1904–05, in Wiesbaden, I tried to run over the frozen puddles in the grounds of the Hotel Oranien. The following of such thematic designs through one's life should be, I think, the true purpose of autobiography.

4

The close of Russia's disastrous campaign in the Far East was accompanied by furious internal disorders. Undaunted by them, my mother, with her three children, returned to St. Petersburg after almost a year of foreign resorts. This was in the beginning of 1905. State matters required the presence of my father in the capital; the Constitutionalist Democratic Party, of which he was one of the founders, was to win a majority of seats in the First Parliament the following year. During one of his short stays with us in the country that summer, he ascertained, with patriotic dismay, that my brother and I could read and write English but not Russian (except KAKAO and MAMA). It was decided that the village schoolmaster should come every afternoon to give us lessons and take us for walks.

With a sharp and merry blast from the whistle that was part of my first sailor suit, my childhood calls me back into that distant past to have me shake hands again with my delightful teacher. Vasiliy Martïnovich Zhernosekov had a fuzzy brown beard, a balding head, and china-blue eyes, one of which bore a fascinating excrescence on the upper lid. The first day he came he brought a boxful of tremendously appetizing blocks with a different letter painted on each side; these cubes he would manipulate as if they were infinitely precious things, which for that matter, they were (besides forming splendid tunnels for toy trains). He revered my father who had recently rebuilt and modernized the village school. In old-fashioned token of free thought, he sported a flowing black tie carelessly knotted in a bowlike arrangement. When addressing me, a small boy, he used the plural of the second person—not in the stiff way servants did, and not as my mother would do in moments of intense tenderness, when my temperature had gone up or I had lost a tiny train-passenger (as if the singular were too thin to bear the load of her love), but with the polite plainness of one man speaking to another whom he does not know well enough to use "thou." A fiery revolutionary, he would gesture vehemently on our country rambles and speak of humanity and freedom and the badness of warfare and the sad (but interesting, I thought) necessity of blowing up tyrants, and sometimes he would produce the then popular pacifist book *Doloy Oruzhie!* (a translation of Bertha von Suttner's *Die Waffen Nieder!*), and treat me, a child of six, to tedious quotations; I tried to refute them: at that tender and bellicose age I spoke up for bloodshed in angry defense of my world of toy pistols and Arthurian knights. Under Lenin's regime, when all non-Communist radicals were ruthlessly persecuted, Zhernosekov was sent to a hard-labor camp but managed to escape abroad, and died in Narva in 1939.

To him, in a way, I owe the ability to continue for another stretch along my private footpath which runs parallel to the road of that troubled decade. When, in July 1906, the Tsar unconstitutionally dissolved the Parliament, a number of its members, my father among them, held a rebellious session in Viborg and issued a manifesto that urged the people to resist the government. For this, more than a year and a half later they were imprisoned. My father spent a restful, if somewhat lonesome, three months in solitary confinement, with his books, his collapsible bathtub, and his copy of J. P. Muller's manual of home gymnastics. To the end of her days, my mother preserved the letters he managed to smuggle through to her—cheerful epistles written in pencil on toilet paper (these I have published in 1965, in the fourth issue of the Russian-language review *Vozdushnïe puti*, edited by Roman Grynberg in New York). We were in the country when he regained his liberty, and it was the village schoolmaster who directed the festivities and arranged the bunting (some of it frankly red) to greet my father on his way home from the railway station, under archivolts of fir needles and crowns of bluebottles, my father's favorite flower. We children had gone down to the village, and it is when I recall that particular day that I see with the utmost clarity the sun-spangled river; the bridge, the dazzling tin of a can left by a fisherman on its wooden railing; the linden-treed hill with its rosy-red church and marble mausoleum where my mother's dead reposed; the dusty road to the village; the strip of short, pastel-green grass,

with bald patches of sandy soil, between the road and the lilac
bushes behind which walleyed, mossy log cabins stood in a
rickety row; the stone building of the new schoolhouse near
the wooden old one; and, as we swiftly drove by, the little
black dog with very white teeth that dashed out from among
the cottages at a terrific pace but in absolute silence, saving
his voice for the brief outburst he would enjoy when his
muted spurt would at last bring him close to the speeding
carriage.

5

The old and the new, the liberal touch and the patriarchal
one, fatal poverty and fatalistic wealth got fantastically interwoven in that strange first decade of our century. Several times
during a summer it might happen that in the middle of luncheon, in the bright, many-windowed, walnut-paneled dining
room on the first floor of our Vyra manor, Aleksey, the butler,
with an unhappy expression on his face, would bend over and
inform my father in a low voice (especially low if we had company) that a group of villagers wanted to see the *barin* outside.
Briskly my father would remove his napkin from his lap and
ask my mother to excuse him. One of the windows at the west
end of the dining room gave upon a portion of the drive near
the main entrance. One could see the top of the honeysuckle
bushes opposite the porch. From that direction the courteous
buzz of a peasant welcome would reach us as the invisible
group greeted my invisible father. The ensuing parley, conducted in ordinary tones, would not be heard, as the windows
underneath which it took place were closed to keep out the
heat. It presumably had to do with a plea for his mediation
in some local feud, or with some special subsidy, or with the
permission to harvest some bit of our land or cut down a
coveted clump of our trees. If, as usually happened, the request was at once granted, there would be again that buzz,
and then, in token of gratitude, the good *barin* would be put
through the national ordeal of being rocked and tossed up
and securely caught by a score or so of strong arms.

In the dining room, my brother and I would be told to go
on with our food. My mother, a tidbit between finger and

thumb, would glance under the table to see if her nervous and gruff dachshund was there. *"Un jour ils vont le laisser tomber,"* would come from Mlle Golay, a primly pessimistic old lady who had been my mother's governess and still dwelt with us (on awful terms with our own governesses). From my place at table I would suddenly see through one of the west windows a marvelous case of levitation. There, for an instant, the figure of my father in his wind-rippled white summer suit would be displayed, gloriously sprawling in midair, his limbs in a curiously casual attitude, his handsome, imperturbable features turned to the sky. Thrice, to the mighty heave-ho of his invisible tossers, he would fly up in this fashion, and the second time he would go higher than the first and then there he would be, on his last and loftiest flight, reclining, as if for good, against the cobalt blue of the summer noon, like one of those paradisiac personages who comfortably soar, with such a wealth of folds in their garments, on the vaulted ceiling of a church while below, one by one, the wax tapers in mortal hands light up to make a swarm of minute flames in the mist of incense, and the priest chants of eternal repose, and funeral lilies conceal the face of whoever lies there, among the swimming lights, in the open coffin.

Two

As far back as I remember myself (with interest, with amusement, seldom with admiration or disgust), I have been subject to mild hallucinations. Some are aural, others are optical, and by none have I profited much. The fatidic accents that restrained Socrates or egged on Joaneta Darc have degenerated with me to the level of something one happens to hear between lifting and clapping down the receiver of a busy party-line telephone. Just before falling asleep, I often become aware of a kind of one-sided conversation going on in an adjacent section of my mind, quite independently from the actual trend of my thoughts. It is a neutral, detached, anonymous voice, which I catch saying words of no importance to me whatever—an English or a Russian sentence, not even addressed to me, and so trivial that I hardly dare give samples, lest the flatness I wish to convey be marred by a molehill of sense. This silly phenomenon seems to be the auditory counterpart of certain praedormitary visions, which I also know well. What I mean is not the bright mental image (as, for instance, the face of a beloved parent long dead) conjured up by a wing-stroke of the will; *that* is one of the bravest movements a human spirit can make. Nor am I alluding to the so-called *muscae volitantes*—shadows cast upon the retinal rods by motes in the vitreous humor, which are seen as transparent threads drifting across the visual field. Perhaps nearer to the hypnagogic mirages I am thinking of is the colored spot, the stab of an afterimage, with which the lamp one has just turned off wounds the palpebral night. However, a shock of this sort is not really a necessary starting point for the slow, steady development of the visions that pass before my closed eyes. They come and go, without the drowsy observer's participation, but are essentially different from dream pictures for he is still master of his senses. They are often grotesque. I am pestered by roguish profiles, by some coarse-featured and florid dwarf with a swelling nostril or ear. At times, however, my photisms take on a rather soothing *flou* quality, and then I see—projected, as it were, upon the inside of the eyelid—

gray figures walking between beehives, or small black parrots gradually vanishing among mountain snows, or a mauve remoteness melting beyond moving masts.

On top of all this I present a fine case of colored hearing. Perhaps "hearing" is not quite accurate, since the color sensation seems to be produced by the very act of my orally forming a given letter while I imagine its outline. The long *a* of the English alphabet (and it is this alphabet I have in mind farther on unless otherwise stated) has for me the tint of weathered wood, but a French *a* evokes polished ebony. This black group also includes hard *g* (vulcanized rubber) and *r* (a sooty rag being ripped). Oatmeal *n*, noodle-limp *l*, and the ivory-backed hand mirror of *o* take care of the whites. I am puzzled by my French *on* which I see as the brimming tension-surface of alcohol in a small glass. Passing on to the blue group, there is steely *x*, thundercloud *z*, and huckleberry *k*. Since a subtle interaction exists between sound and shape, I see *q* as browner than *k*, while *s* is not the light blue of *c*, but a curious mixture of azure and mother-of-pearl. Adjacent tints do not merge, and diphthongs do not have special colors of their own, unless represented by a single character in some other language (thus the fluffy-gray, three-stemmed Russian letter that stands for *sh*, a letter as old as the rushes of the Nile, influences its English representation).

I hasten to complete my list before I am interrupted. In the green group, there are alder-leaf *f*, the unripe apple of *p*, and pistachio *t*. Dull green, combined somehow with violet, is the best I can do for *w*. The yellows comprise various *e*'s and *i*'s, creamy *d*, bright-golden *y*, and *u*, whose alphabetical value I can express only by "brassy with an olive sheen." In the brown group, there are the rich rubbery tone of soft *g*, paler *j*, and the drab shoelace of *h*. Finally, among the reds, *b* has the tone called burnt sienna by painters, *m* is a fold of pink flannel, and today I have at last perfectly matched *v* with "Rose Quartz" in Maerz and Paul's *Dictionary of Color*. The word for rainbow, a primary, but decidedly muddy, rainbow, is in my private language the hardly pronounceable: *kzspygv*. The first author to discuss *audition colorée* was, as far as I know, an albino physician in 1812, in Erlangen.

The confessions of a synesthete must sound tedious and

pretentious to those who are protected from such leakings and drafts by more solid walls than mine are. To my mother, though, this all seemed quite normal. The matter came up, one day in my seventh year, as I was using a heap of old alphabet blocks to build a tower. I casually remarked to her that their colors were all wrong. We discovered then that some of her letters had the same tint as mine and that, besides, she was optically affected by musical notes. These evoked no chromatisms in me whatsoever. Music, I regret to say, affects me merely as an arbitrary succession of more or less irritating sounds. Under certain emotional circumstances I can stand the spasms of a rich violin, but the concert piano and all wind instruments bore me in small doses and flay me in larger ones. Despite the number of operas I was exposed to every winter (I must have attended *Ruslan* and *Pikovaya Dama* at least a dozen times in the course of half as many years), my weak responsiveness to music was completely overrun by the visual torment of not being able to read over Pimen's shoulder or of trying in vain to imagine the hawkmoths in the dim bloom of Juliet's garden.

My mother did everything to encourage the general sensitiveness I had to visual stimulation. How many were the aquarelles she painted for me; what a revelation it was when she showed me the lilac tree that grows out of mixed blue and red! Sometimes, in our St. Petersburg house, from a secret compartment in the wall of her dressing room (and my birth room), she would produce a mass of jewelry for my bedtime amusement. I was very small then, and those flashing tiaras and chokers and rings seemed to me hardly inferior in mystery and enchantment to the illumination in the city during imperial fêtes, when, in the padded stillness of a frosty night, giant monograms, crowns, and other armorial designs, made of colored electric bulbs—sapphire, emerald, ruby—glowed with a kind of charmed constraint above snow-lined cornices on housefronts along residential streets.

2

My numerous childhood illnesses brought my mother and me still closer together. As a little boy, I showed an abnormal aptitude for mathematics, which I completely lost in my singularly talentless youth. This gift played a horrible part in tussles with quinsy or scarlet fever, when I felt enormous spheres and huge numbers swell relentlessly in my aching brain. A foolish tutor had explained logarithms to me much too early, and I had read (in a British publication, the *Boy's Own Paper*, I believe) about a certain Hindu calculator who in exactly two seconds could find the seventeenth root of, say, 3529471145760275132301897342055866171392 (I am not sure I have got this right; anyway the root was 212). Such were the monsters that thrived on my delirium, and the only way to prevent them from crowding me out of myself was to kill them by extracting their hearts. But they were far too strong, and I would sit up and laboriously form garbled sentences as I tried to explain things to my mother. Beneath my delirium, she recognized sensations she had known herself, and her understanding would bring my expanding universe back to a Newtonian norm.

The future specialist in such dull literary lore as autoplagiarism will like to collate a protagonist's experience in my novel *The Gift* with the original event. One day, after a long illness, as I lay in bed still very weak, I found myself basking in an unusual euphoria of lightness and repose. I knew my mother had gone to buy me the daily present that made those convalescences so delightful. What it would be this time I could not guess, but through the crystal of my strangely translucent state I vividly visualized her driving away down Morskaya Street toward Nevski Avenue. I distinguished the light sleigh drawn by a chestnut courser. I heard his snorting breath, the rhythmic clacking of his scrotum, and the lumps of frozen earth and snow thudding against the front of the sleigh. Before my eyes and before those of my mother loomed the hind part of the coachman, in his heavily padded blue robe, and the leather-encased watch (twenty minutes past two) strapped to the back of his belt, from under which curved the pumpkin-like folds of his huge stuffed rump. I saw my mother's seal furs and, as the icy speed increased, the muff she raised to her face—that graceful, winter-ride gesture of a St. Petersburg lady. Two corners of the voluminous spread of bearskin that covered her up to the waist were attached by loops to the two side knobs of the low back of her seat. And behind her, holding on to these knobs, a footman in a cockaded hat stood on his narrow support above the rear extremities of the runners.

Still watching the sleigh, I saw it stop at Treumann's (writing implements, bronze baubles, playing cards). Presently, my mother came out of this shop followed by the footman. He carried her purchase, which looked to me like a pencil. I was astonished that she did not carry so small an object herself, and this disagreeable question of dimensions caused a faint renewal, fortunately very brief, of the "mind dilation effect" which I hoped had gone with the fever. As she was being tucked up again in the sleigh, I watched the vapor exhaled by all, horse included. I watched, too, the familiar pouting movement she made to distend the network of her close-fitting veil drawn too tight over her face, and as I write this, the touch of reticulated tenderness that my lips used to feel when I kissed her veiled cheek comes back to me—*flies* back to me with a shout of joy out of the snow-blue, blue-windowed (the curtains are not yet drawn) past.

A few minutes later, she entered my room. In her arms she held a big parcel. It had been, in my vision, greatly reduced in size—perhaps, because I subliminally corrected what logic warned me might still be the dreaded remnants of delirium's dilating world. Now the object proved to be a giant polygonal Faber pencil, four feet long and correspondingly thick. It had been hanging as a showpiece in the shop's window, and she presumed I had coveted it, as I coveted all things that were not quite purchasable. The shopman had been obliged to ring up an agent, a "Doctor" Libner (as if the transaction possessed indeed some pathological import). For an awful moment, I wondered whether the point was made of real graphite. It was. And some years later I satisfied myself, by drilling a hole in the side, that the lead went right through the whole length—a perfect case of art for art's sake on the part of Faber and Dr. Libner since the pencil was far too big for use and, indeed, was not meant to be used.

"Oh, yes," she would say as I mentioned this or that unusual sensation. "Yes, I know all that," and with a somewhat eerie ingenuousness she would discuss such things as double

This photograph, taken in 1955 by an obliging American tourist, shows the Nabokov house, of pink granite with frescoes and other Italianate ornaments, in St. Petersburg, now Leningrad, 47, Morskaya, now Hertzen Street. Aleksandr Ivanovich Hertzen (1812–1870) was a famous liberal (whom this commemoration by a police state would hardly have gratified) as well as the talented author of *Bïloe i Dumï* (translatable as "Bygones and Meditations"), one of my father's favorite books. My room was on the third floor, above the oriel. The lindens lining the street did not exist. Those green upstarts now hide the second-floor east-corner window of the room where I was born. After nationalization the house accommodated the Danish mission, and later, a school of architecture. The little sedan at the curb belongs presumably to the photographer.

sight, and little raps in the woodwork of tripod tables, and premonitions, and the feeling of the *déjà vu*. A streak of sectarianism ran through her direct ancestry. She went to church only at Lent and Easter. The schismatic mood revealed itself in her healthy distaste for the ritual of the Greek Catholic Church and for its priests. She found a deep appeal in the moral and poetical side of the Gospels, but felt no need in the support of any dogma. The appalling insecurity of an afterlife and its lack of privacy did not enter her thoughts. Her intense and pure religiousness took the form of her having equal faith in the existence of another world and in the impossibility of comprehending it in terms of earthly life. All one could do was to glimpse, amid the haze and the chimeras, something real ahead, just as persons endowed with an unusual persistence of diurnal cerebration are able to perceive in their deepest sleep, somewhere beyond the throes of an entangled and inept nightmare, the ordered reality of the waking hour.

3

To love with all one's soul and leave the rest to fate, was the simple rule she heeded. "*Vot zapomni* [now remember]," she would say in conspiratorial tones as she drew my attention to this or that loved thing in Vyra—a lark ascending the curds-and-whey sky of a dull spring day, heat lightning taking pictures of a distant line of trees in the night, the palette of maple leaves on brown sand, a small bird's cuneate footprints on new snow. As if feeling that in a few years the tangible part of her world would perish, she cultivated an extraordinary consciousness of the various time marks distributed throughout our country place. She cherished her own past with the same retrospective fervor that I now do her image and my past. Thus, in a way, I inherited an exquisite simulacrum—the beauty of intangible property, unreal estate—and this proved a splendid training for the endurance of later losses. Her special tags and imprints became as dear and as sacred to me as they were to her. There was the room which in the past had been reserved for her mother's pet hobby, a chemical laboratory; there was the linden tree marking the spot, by the side of the road that sloped up toward the village of Gryazno (accented on the

ultima), at the steepest bit where one preferred to take one's
"bike by the horns" (*bïka za roga*) as my father, a dedicated
cyclist, liked to say, and where he had proposed; and there
was, in the so-called "old" park, the obsolete tennis court,
now a region of moss, mole-heaps, and mushrooms, which
had been the scene of gay rallies in the eighties and nineties
(even her grim father would shed his coat and give the heaviest racket an appraisive shake) but which, by the time I was
ten, nature had effaced with the thoroughness of a felt eraser
wiping out a geometrical problem.

By then, an excellent modern court had been built at the
end of the "new" part of the park by skilled workmen imported from Poland for that purpose. The wire mesh of an
ample enclosure separated it from the flowery meadow that
framed its clay. After a damp night the surface acquired a
brownish gloss and the white lines would be repainted with
liquid chalk from a green pail by Dmitri, the smallest and
oldest of our gardeners, a meek, black-booted, red-shirted
dwarf slowly retreating, all hunched up, as his paintbrush went
down the line. A pea-tree hedge (the "yellow acacia" of
northern Russia), with a midway opening, corresponding to
the court's screen door, ran parallel to the enclosure and to a
path dubbed *tropinka Sfinksov* ("path of the Sphingids") because of the hawkmoths visiting at dusk the fluffy lilacs along
the border that faced the hedge and likewise broke in the
middle. This path formed the bar of a great T whose vertical
was the alley of slender oaks, my mother's coevals, that traversed (as already said) the new park through its entire length.
Looking down that avenue from the base of the T near the
drive one could make out quite distinctly the bright little gap
five hundred yards away—or fifty years away from where I am
now. Our current tutor or my father, when he stayed with us
in the country, invariably had my brother for partner in our
temperamental family doubles. "Play!" my mother would cry
in the old manner as she put her little foot forward and bent
her white-hatted head to ladle out an assiduous but feeble
serve. I got easily cross with her, and she, with the ballboys,
two barefooted peasant lads (Dmitri's pug-nosed grandson
and the twin brother of pretty Polenka, the head coachman's
daughter). The northern summer became tropical around har-

vest time. Scarlet Sergey would stick his racket between his knees and laboriously wipe his glasses. I see my butterfly net propped against the enclosure—just in case. Wallis Myers' book on lawn tennis lies open on a bench, and after every exchange my father (a first-rate player, with a cannonball service of the Frank Riseley type and a beautiful "lifting drive") pedantically inquires of my brother and me whether the "follow-through," that state of grace, has descended upon us. And sometimes a prodigious cloudburst would cause us to huddle under a shelter at the corner of the court while old Dmitri would be sent to fetch umbrellas and raincoats from the house. A quarter of an hour later he would reappear under a mountain of clothing in the vista of the long avenue which as he advanced would regain its leopard spots with the sun blazing anew and his huge burden unneeded.

She loved all games of skill and gambling. Under her expert hands, the thousand bits of a jigsaw puzzle gradually formed an English hunting scene; what had seemed to be the limb of a horse would turn out to belong to an elm and the hitherto unplaceable piece would snugly fill up a gap in the mottled background, affording one the delicate thrill of an abstract and yet tactile satisfaction. At one time, she was very fond of poker, which had reached St. Petersburg society via diplomatic circles, so that some of the combinations came with pretty French names—*brelan* for "three of a kind," *couleur* for "flush," and so on. The game in use was the regular "draw poker," with, occasionally, the additional tingle of jackpots and an omnivicarious joker. In town, she often played poker at the houses of friends until three in the morning, a society recreation in the last years before World War One; and later, in exile, she used to imagine (with the same wonder and dismay with which she recalled old Dmitri) the chauffeur Pirogov who still seemed to be waiting for her in the relentless frost of an unending night, although, in his case, rum-laced tea in a hospitable kitchen must have gone a long way to assuage those vigils.

One of her greatest pleasures in summer was the very Russian sport of *hodit' po gribï* (looking for mushrooms). Fried in butter and thickened with sour cream, her delicious finds appeared regularly on the dinner table. Not that the gustatory moment mattered much. Her main delight was in the quest, and this quest had its rules. Thus, no agarics were taken; all she picked were species belonging to the edible section of the genus *Boletus* (tawny *edulis*, brown *scaber*, red *aurantiacus*, and a few close allies), called "tube mushrooms" by some and coldly defined by mycologists as "terrestrial, fleshy, putrescent, centrally stipitate fungi." Their compact pilei—tight-fitting in infant plants, robust and appetizingly domed in ripe ones—have a smooth (not lamellate) under-surface and a neat, strong stem. In classical simplicity of form, boletes differ considerably from the "true mushroom," with its preposterous gills and effete stipal ring. It is, however, to the latter, to the lowly and ugly agarics, that nations with timorous taste buds limit their knowledge and appetite, so that to the Anglo-American lay mind the aristocratic boletes are, at best, reformed toadstools.

Rainy weather would bring out these beautiful plants in profusion under the firs, birches and aspens in our park, especially in its older part, east of the carriage road that divided the park in two. Its shady recesses would then harbor that special boletic reek which makes a Russian's nostrils dilate—a dark, dank, satisfying blend of damp moss, rich earth, rotting leaves. But one had to poke and peer for a goodish while among the wet underwood before something really nice, such as a family of bonneted baby *edulis* or the marbled variety of *scaber*, could be discovered and carefully teased out of the soil.

On overcast afternoons, all alone in the drizzle, my mother, carrying a basket (stained blue on the inside by somebody's whortleberries), would set out on a long collecting tour. Toward dinnertime, she could be seen emerging from the nebulous depths of a park alley, her small figure cloaked and hooded in greenish-brown wool, on which countless droplets of moisture made a kind of mist all around her. As she came nearer from under the dripping trees and caught sight of me, her face would show an odd, cheerless expression, which might have spelled poor luck, but which I knew was the tense, jealously contained beatitude of the successful hunter. Just before reaching me, with an abrupt, drooping movement of the arm and shoulder and a "Pouf!" of magnified exhaustion, she would let her basket sag, in order to stress its weight, its fabulous fullness.

Near a white garden bench, on a round garden table of iron, she would lay out her boletes in concentric circles to count and sort them. Old ones, with spongy, dingy flesh, would be eliminated, leaving the young and the crisp. For a moment, before they were bundled away by a servant to a place she knew nothing about, to a doom that did not interest her, she would stand there admiring them, in a glow of quiet contentment. As often happened at the end of a rainy day, the sun might cast a lurid gleam just before setting, and there, on the damp round table, her mushrooms would lie, very colorful, some bearing traces of extraneous vegetation—a grass blade sticking to a viscid fawn cap, or moss still clothing the bulbous base of a dark-stippled stem. And a tiny looper caterpillar would be there, too, measuring, like a child's finger and thumb, the rim of the table, and every now and then stretching upward to grope, in vain, for the shrub from which it had been dislodged.

4

Not only were the kitchen and the servants' hall never visited by my mother, but they stood as far removed from her consciousness as if they were the corresponding quarters in a hotel. My father had no inclination, either, to run the house. But he did order the meals. With a little sigh, he would open a kind of album laid by the butler on the dinner table after dessert and in his elegant, flowing hand write down the menu for the following day. He had a peculiar habit of letting his pencil or fountain pen vibrate just above the paper while he pondered the next ripple of words. My mother nodded a vague consent to his suggestions or made a wry face. Nominally, the housekeeping was in the hands of her former nurse, at that time a bleary, incredibly wrinkled old woman (born a slave around 1830) with the small face of a melancholy tortoise and big shuffling feet. She wore a nunnish brown dress and gave off a slight but unforgettable smell of coffee and decay. Her dreaded congratulation on our birthdays and namedays was the serfage kiss on the shoulder. Age had developed in her a pathological stinginess, especially in regard to sugar and preserves, so that by degrees, and with the sanction of my parents, other domestic arrangements, kept secret from her, had quietly come into force. Without knowing it (the knowledge would have broken her heart), she remained dangling as it were, from her own key ring, while my mother did her best to allay with soothing words the suspicions that now and then flitted across the old woman's weakening mind. Sole mistress of her moldy and remote little kingdom, which she thought was the real one (we would have starved had it been so), she was followed by the mocking glances of lackeys and maids as she steadily plodded through long corridors to store away half an apple or a couple of broken Petit-Beurre biscuits she had found on a plate.

Meanwhile, with a permanent staff of about fifty servants and no questions asked, our city household and country place were the scenes of a fantastic merry-go-round of theft. In this, according to nosy old aunts, whom nobody heeded but who proved to be right after all, the chief cook Nikolay Andreevich and the head gardener Egor, both staid-looking, bespectacled men with the hoary temples of trusty retainers, were the two masterminds. When confronted with stupendous and incomprehensible bills, or a sudden extinction of garden strawberries and hothouse peaches, my father, a jurist and a statesman, felt professionally vexed at not being able to cope with the economics of his own home; but every time a complicated case of larceny came to light, some legal doubt or scruple prevented him from doing anything about it. When common sense required the firing of a rascally servant, the man's little son would as likely as not fall desperately ill, and the resolution to get the best doctors in town for him would cancel all other considerations. So, with one thing and another, my father preferred to leave the whole housekeeping situation in a state of precarious equilibrium (not devoid of a certain quiet humor), with my mother deriving considerable comfort from the hope that her old nurse's illusory world would not be shattered.

My mother knew well how hurtful a broken illusion could be. The most trifling disappointment took on for her the dimensions of a major disaster. One Christmas Eve, in Vyra, not

long before her fourth baby was to be born, she happened to
be laid up with a slight ailment and made my brother and me
(aged, respectively, five and six) promise not to look into the
Christmas stockings that we would find hanging from our
bedposts on the following morning but to bring them over
to her room and investigate them there, so that she could
watch and enjoy our pleasure. Upon awakening, I held a furtive conference with my brother, after which, with eager
hands, each felt his delightfully crackling stocking, stuffed
with small presents; these we cautiously fished out one by one,
undid the ribbons, loosened the tissue paper, inspected everything by the weak light that came through a chink in the
shutters, wrapped up the little things again, and crammed
them back where they had been. I next recall our sitting on
our mother's bed, holding those lumpy stockings and doing
our best to give the performance she had wanted to see; but
we had so messed up the wrappings, so amateurish were our
renderings of enthusiastic surprise (I can see my brother casting his eyes upward and exclaiming, in imitation of our new
French governess, *"Ah, que c'est beau!"*), that, after observing
us for a moment, our audience burst into tears. A decade
passed. World War One started. A crowd of patriots and my
uncle Ruka stoned the German Embassy. *Peterburg* was sunk
to *Petrograd* against all rules of nomenclatorial priority. Beethoven turned out to be Dutch. The newsreels showed pho-
togenic explosions, the spasm of a cannon, Poincaré in his
leathern leggings, bleak puddles, the poor little Tsarevich in
Circassian uniform with dagger and cartridges, his tall sisters
so dowdily dressed, long railway trains crammed with troops.
My mother set up a private hospital for wounded soldiers. I
remember her, in the fashionable nurse's gray-and-white uniform she abhorred, denouncing with the same childish tears
the impenetrable meekness of those crippled peasants and the
ineffectiveness of part-time compassion. And, still later, when
in exile, reviewing the past, she would often accuse herself
(unjustly as I see it now) of having been less affected by the
misery of man than by the emotional load man dumps upon
innocent nature—old trees, old horses, old dogs.

Her particular fondness for brown dachshunds puzzled my
critical aunts. In the family albums illustrating her young

years, there was hardly a group that did not include one such animal—usually with some part of its flexible body blurred and always with the strange, paranoiac eyes dachshunds have in snapshots. A couple of obese old-timers, Box I and Loulou, still lolled in the sunshine on the porch when I was a child. Sometime in 1904 my father bought at a dog show in Munich a pup which grew into the bad-tempered but wonderfully handsome Trainy (as I named him because of his being as long and as brown as a sleeping car). One of the musical themes of my childhood is Trainy's hysterical tongue, on the trail of the hare he never got, in the depths of our Vyra park, whence he would return at dusk (after my anxious mother had stood whistling for a long time in the oak avenue) with the old corpse of a mole in his jaws and burs in his ears. Around 1915, his hind legs became paralyzed, and until he was chloroformed, he would dismally drag himself over long, glossy stretches of parquet floor like a *cul de jatte*. Then somebody gave us another pup, Box II, whose grandparents had been Dr. Anton Chekhov's Quina and Brom. This final dachshund followed us into exile, and as late as 1930, in a suburb of Prague (where my widowed mother spent her last years, on a small pension provided by the Czech government), he could be still seen going for reluctant walks with his mistress, waddling far behind in a huff, tremendously old and furious with his long Czech muzzle of wire—an émigré dog in a patched and ill-fitting coat.

During our last two Cambridge years, my brother and I used to spend vacations in Berlin, where our parents with the two girls and ten-year-old Kirill occupied one of those large, gloomy, eminently bourgeois apartments that I have let to so many émigré families in my novels and short stories. On the night of March 28, 1922, around ten o'clock, in the living room where as usual my mother was reclining on the red-plush corner couch, I happened to be reading to her Blok's verse on Italy—had just got to the end of the little poem about Florence, which Blok compares to the delicate, smoky bloom of an iris, and she was saying over her knitting, "Yes, yes, Florence does look like a *dïmnïy iris*, how true! I remember—" when the telephone rang.

After 1923, when she moved to Prague, and I lived in Germany and France, I was unable to visit her frequently; nor was I with her at her death, which occurred on the eve of World War Two. Whenever I did manage to go to Prague, there was always that initial pang one feels just before time, caught unawares, again dons its familiar mask. In the pitiable lodgings she shared with her dearest companion, Evgeniya Konstantinovna Hofeld (1884–1957), who had replaced, in 1914, Miss Greenwood (who, in her turn, had replaced Miss Lavington) as governess of my two sisters (Olga, born January 5, 1903, and Elena, born March 31, 1906), albums, in which, during the last years, she had copied out her favorite poems, from Maykov to Mayakovski, lay around her on odds and ends of decrepit, secondhand furniture. A cast of my father's hand and a watercolor picture of his grave in the Greek-Catholic cemetery of Tegel, now in East Berlin, shared a shelf with émigré writers' books, so prone to disintegration in their cheap paper covers. A soapbox covered with green cloth supported the dim little photographs in crumbling frames she liked to have near her couch. She did not really need them, for nothing had been lost. As a company of traveling players carry with them everywhere, while they still remember their lines, a windy heath, a misty castle, an enchanted island, so she had with her all that her soul had stored. With great clarity, I can see her sitting at a table and serenely considering the laid-out cards of a game of solitaire: she leans on her left elbow and presses to her cheek the free thumb of her left hand, in which, close to her mouth, she holds a cigarette, while her right hand stretches toward the next card. The double gleam on her fourth finger is two marriage rings—her own and my father's, which, being too large for her, is fastened to hers by a bit of black thread.

Whenever in my dreams I see the dead, they always appear silent, bothered, strangely depressed, quite unlike their dear, bright selves. I am aware of them, without any astonishment, in surroundings they never visited during their earthly existence, in the house of some friend of mine they never knew. They sit apart, frowning at the floor, as if death were a dark taint, a shameful family secret. It is certainly not then—not in dreams—but when one is wide awake, at moments of robust joy and achievement, on the highest terrace of consciousness, that mortality has a chance to peer beyond its own limits, from the mast, from the past and its castle tower. And although nothing much can be seen through the mist, there is somehow the blissful feeling that one is looking in the right direction.

Three

A N INEXPERIENCED HERALDIST resembles a medieval traveler who brings back from the East the faunal fantasies
influenced by the domestic bestiary he possessed all along
rather than by the results of direct zoological exploration.
Thus, in the first version of this chapter, when describing the
Nabokovs' coat of arms (carelessly glimpsed among some fa-
milial trivia many years before), I somehow managed to twist
it into the fireside wonder of two bears posing with a great
chessboard propped up between them. I have now looked it
up, that blazon, and am disappointed to find that it boils
down to a couple of lions—brownish and, perhaps, over-
shaggy beasts, but not really ursine—licking their chops, ram-
pant, regardant, arrogantly demonstrating the unfortunate
knight's shield, which is only one sixteenth of a checkerboard,
of alternate tinctures, azure & gules, with a botonée cross,
argent, in each rectangle. Above it one sees what remains of
the knight: his tough helmet and inedible gorget, as well as
one brave arm coming out of a foliate ornament, gules and
azure, and still brandishing a short sword. *Za hrabrost'*, "for
valour," says the scripture.

According to my father's first cousin Vladimir Viktorovich
Golubtsov, a lover of Russian antiquities, whom I consulted
in 1930, the founder of our family was Nabok Murza (*floruit*
1380), a Russianized Tatar prince in Muscovy. My own first
cousin, Sergey Sergeevich Nabokov, a learned genealogist, in-
forms me that in the fifteenth century our ancestors owned
land in the Moscow princedom. He refers me to a document
(published by Yushkov in *Acts of the XIII-XVII Centuries*,
Moscow, 1899) concerning a rural squabble which in the year
1494, under Ivan the Third, squire Kulyakin had with his
neighbors, Filat, Evdokim, and Vlas, sons of Luka Nabokov.
During the following centuries the Nabokovs were government officials and military men. My great-great-grandfather,
General Aleksandr Ivanovich Nabokov (1749–1807), was, in
the reign of Paul the First, chief of the Novgorod garrison
regiment called "Nabokov's Regiment" in official documents.

The youngest of his sons, my great-grandfather Nikolay Aleksandrovich Nabokov, was a young naval officer in 1817, when he participated, with the future admirals Baron von Wrangel and Count Litke, under the leadership of Captain (later Vice-Admiral) Vasiliy Mihaylovich Golovnin, in an expedition to map Nova Zembla (of all places) where "Nabokov's River" is named after my ancestor. The memory of the leader of the expedition is preserved in quite a number of place names, one of them being Golovnin's Lagoon, Seward Peninsula, W. Alaska, from where a butterfly, *Parnassius phoebus golovinus* (rating a big *sic*), has been described by Dr. Holland; but my great-grandfather has nothing to show except that very blue, almost indigo blue, even indignantly blue, little river winding between wet rocks; for he soon left the navy, *n'ayant pas le pied marin* (as says my cousin Sergey Sergeevich who informed me about him), and switched to the Moscow Guards. He married Anna Aleksandrovna Nazimov (sister of the Decembrist). I know nothing about his military career; whatever it was, he could not have competed with his brother, Ivan Aleksandrovich Nabokov (1787–1852), one of the heroes of the anti-Napoleon wars and, in his old age, commander of the Peter-and-Paul Fortress in St. Petersburg where (in 1849) one of his prisoners was the writer Dostoevski, author of *The Double*, etc., to whom the kind general lent books. Considerably more interesting, however, is the fact that he was married to Ekaterina Pushchin, sister of Ivan Pushchin, Pushkin's schoolmate and close friend. Careful, printers: two "chin" 's and one "kin."

The nephew of Ivan and the son of Nikolay was my paternal grandfather Dmitri Nabokov (1827–1904), Minister of Justice for eight years, under two Tsars. He married (September 24, 1859) Maria, the seventeen-year-old daughter of Baron Ferdinand Nicolaus Viktor von Korff (1805–1869), a German general in the Russian service.

In tenacious old families certain facial characteristics keep recurring as indicants and maker's marks. The Nabokov nose (e.g. my grandfather's) is of the Russian type with a soft round upturned tip and a gentle inslope in profile; the Korff nose (e.g. mine) is a handsome Germanic organ with a boldly boned bridge and a slightly tilted, distinctly grooved, fleshy end. The supercilious or surprised Nabokovs have rising eyebrows only proximally haired, thus fading toward the temples; the Korff eyebrow is more finely arched but likewise rather scanty. Otherwise the Nabokovs, as they recede through the picture gallery of time into the shadows, soon join the dim Rukavishnikovs of whom I knew only my mother and her brother Vasiliy, too small a sample for my present purpose. On the other hand, I see very clearly the women of the Korff line, beautiful, lily-and-rose girls, their high, flushed *pommettes*, pale blue eyes and that small beauty spot on one cheek, a patchlike mark, which my grandmother, my father, three or four of his siblings, some of my twenty-five cousins, my younger sister and my son Dmitri inherited in various stages of intensity as more or less distinct copies of the same print.

My German great-grandfather, Baron Ferdinand von Korff, who married Nina Aleksandrovna Shishkov (1819–1895), was born in Königsberg in 1805 and after a successful military career, died in 1869 in his wife's Volgan domain near Saratov. He was the grandson of Wilhelm Carl, Baron von Korff (1739–1799) and Eleonore Margarethe, Baroness von der Osten-Sacken (1731–1786), and the son of Nicolaus von Korff (d. 1812), a major in the Prussian army, and Antoinette Theodora Graun (d. 1859), who was the granddaughter of Carl Heinrich Graun, the composer.

Antoinette's mother, Elisabeth née Fischer (born 1760), was the daughter of Regina born Hartung (1732–1805), daughter of Johann Heinrich Hartung (1699–1765), head of a well-known publishing house in Königsberg. Elisabeth was a celebrated beauty. After divorcing her first husband, *Justizrat* Graun, the composer's son, in 1795, she married the minor poet Christian August von Stägemann, and was the "motherly friend," as my German source puts it, of a much better-known writer, Heinrich von Kleist (1777–1811), who, at thirty-three, had fallen passionately in love with her twelve-year-old daughter Hedwig Marie (later von Olfers). He is said to have called on the family, to say adieu before traveling to Wannsee—for the carrying out of an enthusiastic suicide pact with a sick lady—but was not admitted, it being laundry day in the Stägemann household. The number and diversity of contacts that my ancestors had with the world of letters are truly remarkable.

Carl Heinrich Graun, the great-grandfather of Ferdinand von Korff, *my* great-grandfather, was born in 1701, at Wahrenbrück, Saxony. His father, August Graun (born 1670), an exciseman (*"Königlicher Polnischer und Kurfürstlicher Sächsischer Akziseneinnehmer"*—the elector in question being his namesake, August II, King of Poland) came from a long line of parsons. His great-great-grandfather, Wolfgang Graun, was, in 1575, organist at Plauen (near Wahrenbrück), where a statue of his descendant, the composer, graces a public garden. Carl Heinrich Graun died at the age of fifty-eight, in 1759, in Berlin, where seventeen years earlier, the new opera house had opened with his *Caesar and Cleopatra*. He was one of the most eminent composers of his time, and even the greatest, according to local necrologists touched by his royal patron's grief. Graun is shown (posthumously) standing somewhat aloof, with folded arms, in Menzel's picture of Frederick the Great playing Graun's composition on the flute; reproductions of this kept following me through all the German lodgings I stayed in during my years of exile. I am told there is at the Sans-Souci Palace in Potsdam a contemporary painting representing Graun and his wife, Dorothea Rehkopp, sitting at the same clavecin. Musical encyclopedias often reproduce the portrait in the Berlin opera house where he looks very much like the composer Nikolay Dmitrievich Nabokov, my first cousin. An amusing little echo, to the tune of 250 dollars, from all those concerts under the painted ceilings of a guilded past, blandly reached me in heil-hitlering Berlin, in 1936, when the Graun family entail, basically a collection of pretty snuffboxes and other precious knickknacks, whose value after passing through many avatars in the Prussian state bank had dwindled to 43,000 reichsmarks (about 10,000 dollars), was distributed among the provident composer's descendants, the von Korff, von Wissmann and Nabokov clans (a fourth line, the Counts Asinari di San Marzano, had died out).

Two Baronesses von Korff have left their trace in the police records of Paris. One, born Anna-Christina Stegelman, daugh-

ter of a Swedish banker, was the widow of Baron Fromhold
Christian von Korff, colonel in the Russian army, a great-
granduncle of my grandmother. Anna-Christina was also the
cousin or the sweetheart, or both, of another soldier, the famous Count Axel von Fersen; and it was she who, in Paris,
in 1791, lent her passport and her brand-new custom-made
traveling coach (a sumptuous affair on high red wheels, upholstered in white Utrecht velvet, with dark green curtains and
all kinds of gadgets, then modern, such as a *vase de voyage*)
to the royal family for their escape to Varennes, the Queen
impersonating her, and the King, the tutor of the two children. The other police story involves a less dramatic masquerade.

With Carnival week nearing, in Paris, more than a century
ago, the Count de Morny invited to a fancy ball at his house
"une noble dame que la Russie a prêtée cet hiver à la France"
(as reported by Henrys in the *Gazette du Palais* section of the
Illustration, 1859, p. 251). This was Nina, Baroness von Korff,
whom I have already mentioned; the eldest of her five daughters, Maria (1842–1926), was to marry in September of the
same year, 1859, Dmitri Nikolaevich Nabokov (1827–1904), a
friend of the family who was also in Paris at the time. In view
of the ball, the lady ordered for Maria and Olga, flower-girl
costumes, at two hundred and twenty francs each. Their cost,
according to the glib *Illustration* reporter, represented six
hundred and forty-three days *"de nourriture, de loyer et
d'entretien du père Crépin* [food, rent and footwear]," which
sounds odd. When the costumes were ready, Mme de Korff
found them *"trop décolletés"* and refused to take them. The
dressmaker sent her *huissier* (warrant officer), upon which
there was a bad row, and my good great-grandmother (she
was beautiful, passionate and, I am sorry to say, far less austere
in her private morals than it would appear from her attitude
toward low necklines) sued the dressmaker for damages.

She contended that the *demoiselles de magasin* who brought
the dresses were *"des péronnelles* [saucy hussies]" who, in answer to her objecting that the dresses were cut too low for
gentlewomen to wear, *"se sont permis d'exposer des théories
égalitaires du plus mauvais goût* [dared to flaunt democratic
ideas in the worst of taste]"; she said that it had been too late

to have other fancy dresses made and that her daughters had not gone to the ball; she accused the *huissier* and his acolytes of sprawling on soft chairs while inviting the ladies to take hard ones; she also complained, furiously and bitterly, that the *huissier* had actually threatened to jail Monsieur Dmitri Nabokoff, "*Conseiller d'État, homme sage et plein de mesure* [a sedate, self-contained man]" only because the said gentleman had attempted to throw the *huissier* out of the window. It was not much of a case but the dressmaker lost it. She took back her dresses, refunded their cost and in addition paid a thousand francs to the plaintiff; on the other hand, the bill presented in 1791 to Christina by her carriage maker, a matter of five thousand nine hundred forty-four livres, had never been paid at all.

Dmitri Nabokov (the ending in *ff* was an old Continental fad), State Minister of Justice from 1878 to 1885, did what he could to protect, if not to strengthen, the liberal reforms of the sixties (trial by jury, for instance) against ferocious reactionary attacks. "He acted," says a biographer (Brockhaus' *Encyclopedia*, second Russian edition), "much like the captain of a ship in a storm who would throw overboard part of the cargo in order to save the rest." The epitaphical simile unwittingly echoes, I note, an epigraphical theme—my grandfather's earlier attempt to throw the law out of the window.

At his retirement, Alexander the Third offered him to choose between the title of count and a sum of money, presumably large—I do not know what exactly an earldom was worth in Russia, but contrary to the thrifty Tsar's hopes my grandfather (as also his uncle Ivan, who had been offered a similar choice by Nicholas the First) plumped for the more solid reward. (*"Encore un comte raté,"* dryly comments Sergey Sergeevich.) After that he lived mostly abroad. In the first years of this century his mind became clouded but he clung to the belief that as long as he remained in the Mediterranean region everything would be all right. Doctors took the opposite view and thought he might live longer in the climate of some mountain resort or in Northern Russia. There is an extraordinary story, which I have not been able to piece together adequately, of his escaping from his attendants some-

Dmitri Nikolaevich Nabokov, the author's grandfather (1827–1904), Minister of Justice (1878–1885).

The author's paternal grandmother, Baroness Maria von Korff (1842–1926) in the late eighteen-fifties.

where in Italy. There he wandered about, denouncing, with King Lear–like vehemence, his children to grinning strangers, until he was captured in a wild rocky place by some matter-of-fact *carabinieri*. During the winter of 1903, my mother, the only person whose presence, in his moments of madness, the old man could bear, was constantly at his side in Nice. My brother and I, aged three and four respectively, were also there with our English governess; I remember the windowpanes rattling in the bright breeze and the amazing pain caused by a drop of hot sealing wax on my finger. Using a candle flame (diluted to a deceptive pallor by the sunshine that invaded the stone slabs on which I was kneeling), I had been engaged in transforming dripping sticks of the stuff into gluey, marvelously smelling, scarlet and blue and bronze-colored blobs. The next moment I was bellowing on the floor, and my mother had hurried to the rescue, and somewhere nearby my grandfather in a wheelchair was thumping the resounding flags with his cane. She had a hard time with him. He used improper language. He kept mistaking the attendant who rolled him along the Promenade des Anglais for Count Loris-Melikov, a (long-deceased) colleague of his in the ministerial cabinet of the eighties. *"Qui est cette femme—chassez-la!"* he would cry to my mother as he pointed a shaky finger at the Queen of Belgium or Holland who had stopped to inquire about his health. Dimly I recall running up to his chair to show him a pretty pebble, which he slowly examined and then slowly put into his mouth. I wish I had had more curiosity when, in later years, my mother used to recollect those times.

He would lapse for ever-increasing periods into an unconscious state; during one such lapse he was transferred to his pied-à-terre on the Palace Quay in St. Petersburg. As he gradually regained consciousness, my mother camouflaged his bedroom into the one he had had in Nice. Some similar pieces of furniture were found and a number of articles rushed from Nice by a special messenger, and all the flowers his hazy senses had been accustomed to were obtained, in their proper variety and profusion, and a bit of house wall that could be just glimpsed from the window was painted a brilliant white, so every time he reverted to a state of comparative lucidity he found himself safe on the illusory Riviera artistically staged by my mother; and there, on March 28, 1904, exactly eighteen years, day for day, before my father, he peacefully died.

He left four sons and five daughters. The eldest was Dmitri, who inherited the Nabokov majorat in the then Tsardom of Poland; his first wife was Lidia Eduardovna Falz-Fein, his second, Marie Redlich; next, came Sergey, governor of Mitau, who married Daria Nikolaevna Tuchkov, the great-great-granddaughter of Field Marshal Kutuzov, Prince of Smolensk. Then came my father. The youngest was Konstantin, a confirmed bachelor. The sisters were: Natalia, wife of Ivan de Peterson, Russian consul at The Hague; Vera, wife of Ivan Pïhachev, sportsman and landowner; Nina, who divorced Baron Rausch von Traubenberg, military Governor of Warsaw, to marry Admiral Nikolay Kolomeytsev, hero of the Japanese war; Elizaveta, married to Henri, Prince Sayn-Wittgenstein-Berleburg, and after his death, to Roman Leikmann, former tutor of her sons; and Nadezhda, wife of Dmitri Vonlyarlyarski, whom she later divorced.

Uncle Konstantin was in the diplomatic service and, in the last stage of his career in London, conducted a bitter and unsuccessful struggle with Sablin as to which of them would head the Russian mission. His life was not particularly eventful, but he had had a couple of nice escapes from a fate less tame than the draft in a London hospital, which killed him in 1927. Once, in Moscow, on February 17, 1905, when an older friend, the Grand Duke Sergey, half a minute before the explosion, offered him a lift in his carriage, and my uncle said no, thanks, he'd rather walk, and away rolled the carriage to its fatal rendezvous with a terrorist's bomb; and the second time, seven years later, when he missed another appointment, this one with an iceberg, by chancing to return his *Titanic* ticket. We saw a good deal of him in London after we had escaped from Lenin's Russia. Our meeting at Victoria Station in 1919 is a vivid vignette in my mind: my father marching up to his prim brother with an unfolding bear hug; he, backing away and repeating: "*Mï v Anglii, mï v Anglii* [we are in England]." His charming little flat was full of souvenirs from India such as photographs of young British officers. He is the author of *The Ordeal of a Diplomat* (1921), easily obtainable in large public libraries, and of an English version of Pushkin's *Boris Godunov*; and he is portrayed, goatee and all (together with Count Witte, the two Japanese delegates and a benevolent Theodore Roosevelt), in a mural of the signing of the Portsmouth Treaty on the left side of the main entrance hall of the American Museum of Natural History—an eminently fit place to find my surname in golden Slavic characters, as I did the first time I passed there—with a fellow lepidopterist, who said "Sure, sure" in reply to my exclamation of recognition.

2

Diagrammatically, the three family estates on the Oredezh, fifty miles south of St. Petersburg, may be represented as three linked rings in a ten-mile chain running west-east across the Luga highway, with my mother's Vyra in the middle, her brother's Rozhestveno on the right, and my grandmother's Batovo on the left, the links being the bridges across the Oredezh (properly *Oredezh'*) which, in its winding, branching and looping course, bathed Vyra on either side.

Two other, much more distant, estates in the region were related to Batovo: my uncle Prince Wittgenstein's Druzhnoselie situated a few miles beyond the Siverski railway station, which was six miles northeast of our place; and my uncle Pïhachev's Mityushino, some fifty miles south on the way to Luga: I never once was there, but we fairly often drove the ten miles or so to the Wittgensteins and once (in August 1911) visited them at their other splendid estate, Kamenka, in the Province of Podolsk, S.W. Russia.

The estate of Batovo enters history in 1805 when it becomes the property of Anastasia Matveevna Rïleev, born Essen. Her son, Kondratiy Fyodorovich Rïleev (1795–1826), minor poet, journalist, and famous Decembrist, spent most of his summers in the region, addressed elegies to the Oredezh, and sang Prince Aleksey's castle, the jewel of its banks. Legend and logic, a rare but strong partnership, seem to indicate, as I have more fully explained in my notes to *Onegin*, that the Rïleev pistol duel with Pushkin, of which so little is known, took place in the Batovo park, between May 6 and 9 (Old Style),

1820. Pushkin, with two friends, Baron Anton Delvig and Pavel Yakovlev, who were accompanying him a little way on the first lap of his long journey from St. Petersburg to Ekaterinoslav, had quietly turned off the Luga highway, at Rozhestveno, crossed the bridge (hoof-thud changing to brief clatter), and followed the old rutty road westward to Batovo. There, in front of the manor house, Rïleev was eagerly awaiting them. He had just sent his wife, in her last month of pregnancy, to her estate near Voronezh, and was anxious to get the duel over—and, God willing, join her there. I can feel upon my skin and in my nostrils the delicious country roughness of the northern spring day which greeted Pushkin and his two seconds as they got out of their coach and penetrated into the linden avenue beyond the Batovo platbands, still virginally black. I see so plainly the three young men (the sum of their years equals my present age) following their host and two persons unknown, into the park. At that date small crumpled violets showed through the carpet of last year's dead leaves, and freshly emerged Orange-tips settled on the shivering dandelions. For one moment fate may have wavered between preventing a heroic rebel from heading for the gallows, and depriving Russia of *Eugene Onegin*; but then did neither.

A couple of decades after Rïleev's execution on the bastion of the Peter-and-Paul Fortress in 1826, Batovo was acquired from the state by my paternal grandmother's mother, Nina Aleksandrovna Shishkov, later Baroness von Korff, from whom my grandfather purchased it around 1855. Two tutor-and-governess-raised generations of Nabokovs knew a certain trail through the woods beyond Batovo as *"Le Chemin du Pendu,"* the favorite walk of The Hanged One, as Rïleev was referred to in society: callously but also euphemistically and wonderingly (gentlemen in those days were not often hanged) in preference to The Decembrist or The Insurgent. I can easily imagine young Rïleev in the green skeins of our woods, walking and reading a book, a form of romantic ambulation in the manner of his era, as easily as I can visualize the fearless lieutenant defying despotism on the bleak Senate Square with his comrades and puzzled troops; but the name of the long, "grown-up" *promenade* looked forward to by good children, remained throughout boyhood unconnected in our minds

with the fate of the unfortunate master of Batovo: my cousin
Sergey Nabokov, who was born at Batovo in *la Chambre du
Revenant*, imagined a conventional ghost, and I vaguely surmised with my tutor or governess that some mysterious
stranger had been found dangling from the aspen upon which
a rare hawkmoth bred. That Rïleev may have been simply the
"Hanged One" (*poveshenniy* or *visel'nik*) to the local peasants,
is not unnatural; but in the manorial families a bizarre taboo
prevented, apparently, parents from identifying the ghost, as
if a specific reference might introduce a note of nastiness into
the glamorous vagueness of the phrase designating a picturesque walk in a beloved country place. Still, I find it curious
to realize that even my father, who had so much information
about the Decembrists and so much more sympathy for them
than his relatives, never once, as far as I can recall, mentioned
Kondratiy Rïleev during our rambles and bicycle rides in the
environs. My cousin draws my attention to the fact that General Rïleev, the poet's son, was a close friend of Tsar Alexander
II and of my grandfather, D. N. Nabokov, and that *on ne
parle pas de corde dans la maison du pendu.*

From Batovo, the old rutty road (which we have followed
with Pushkin and now retrace) ran east for a couple of miles
to Rozhestveno. Just before the main bridge, one could either
turn north in open country toward our Vyra and its two parks
on each side of the road, or else continue east, down a steep
hill past an old cemetery choked with raspberry and racemosa
and cross the bridge toward my uncle's white-pillared house
aloof on its hill.

The estate Rozhestveno, with a large village of the same
name, extensive lands, and a manor house high above the Oredezh River, on the Luga (or Warsaw) highway, in the district
of Tsarskoe Selo (now Pushkin), about fifty miles south from
St. Petersburg (now Leningrad), had been known before the
eighteenth century as the Kurovitz domain, in the old Ko-
porsk district. Around 1715 it had been the property of Prince
Aleksey, the unfortunate son of that archbully, Peter the First.
Part of an *escalier dérobé* and something else I cannot recollect
were preserved in the new anatomy of the building. I have
touched that banister and have seen (or trod on?) the other,
forgotten, detail. From that palace, along that highway leading

to Poland and Austria, the prince had escaped only to be
lured back from as far south as Naples to the paternal torture
house by the Tsar's agent, Count Pyotr Andreevich Tolstoy,
one-time ambassador in Constantinople (where he had obtained for his master the little blackamoor whose great-grand-
son was to be Pushkin). Rozhestveno later belonged, I
believe, to a favorite of Alexander the First, and the manor
had been partly rebuilt when my maternal grandfather acquired the domain around 1880, for his eldest son Vladimir
who died at sixteen a few years later. His brother Vasiliy inherited it in 1901 and spent there ten summers out of the
fifteen that still remained to him. I particularly remember the
cool and sonorous quality of the place, the checkerboard flag-
stones of the hall, ten porcelain cats on a shelf, a sarcophagus
and an organ, the skylights and the upper galleries, the colored dusk of mysterious rooms, and carnations and crucifixes
everywhere.

3

In his youth Carl Heinrich Graun had a fine tenor voice;
one night, having to sing in an opera written by Schurmann,
chapel-master of Brunswick, he got so disgusted with some
airs in it that he replaced them by others of his own composition. Here I feel the shock of gleeful kinship; yet I prefer
two other ancestors of mine, the young explorer already mentioned and that great pathologist, my mother's maternal
grandfather, Nikolay Illarionovich Kozlov (1814–1889), first
president of the Russian Imperial Academy of Medicine and
author of such papers as "On the Development of the Idea
of Disease" or "On the Coarctation of the Jugular Foramen
in the Insane." At this convenient point, I may as well mention my own scientific papers, and especially my three favorite
ones, "Notes on Neotropical Plebejinae" (*Psyche*, Vol. 52,
Nos. 1–2 and 3–4, 1945), "A New Species of *Cyclargus* Nabokov" (*The Entomologist*, December 1948), and "The Nearctic Members of the Genus *Lycaeides* Hübner" (*Bulletin
Mus. Comp. Zool.*, Harvard Coll., 1949), after which year I
found it no longer physically possible to combine scientific

research with lectures, belles-lettres, and *Lolita* (for she was on her way—a painful birth, a difficult baby).

The Rukavishnikov blazon is more modest, but also less conventional than the Nabokov one. The escutcheon is a stylized version of a *domna* (primitive blast furnace), in allusion, no doubt, to the smelting of the Uralian ores that my adventurous ancestors discovered. I wish to note that these Rukavishnikovs—Siberian pioneers, gold prospectors and mining engineers—were *not* related, as some biographers have carelessly assumed, to the no less wealthy Moscow merchants of the same name. *My* Rukavishnikovs belonged (since the eighteenth century) to the landed gentry of Kazan Province. Their mines were situated at Alopaevsk near Nizhni-Tagilsk, Province of Perm, on the Siberian side of the Urals. My father had twice traveled there on the former Siberian Express, a beautiful train of the Nord-Express family, which I planned to take soon, though rather on an entomological than mineralogical trip, but the revolution interfered with that project.

My mother, Elena Ivanovna (August 29, 1876–May 2, 1939), was the daughter of Ivan Vasilievich Rukavishnikov (1841–1901), landowner, justice of the peace, and philanthropist, son of a millionaire industrialist, and Olga Nikolaevna (1845–1901), daughter of Dr. Kozlov. My mother's parents both died of cancer within the same year, he in March, she in June. Of her seven siblings, five died in infancy, and of her two older brothers, Vladimir died at sixteen at Davos, in the eighteen-eighties, and Vasiliy in Paris, in 1916. Ivan Rukavishnikov had a terrible temper and my mother feared him. In my childhood all I knew about him were his portraits (his beard, the magisterial chain around his neck) and such attributes of his main hobby as decoy ducks and elk heads. A pair of especially large bears he had shot stood upright with redoubtably raised front paws in the iron-barred vestibule of our country house. Every summer I gauged my height by the ability to reach their fascinating claws—first those of the lower forelimb, then those of the upper. Their bellies proved disappointingly hard, once your fingers (accustomed to palpate live dogs or toy animals) had sunk in their rough brown fur. Now and then they used to be taken out into a corner of the garden to be thoroughly

whacked and aired, and poor Mademoiselle, approaching from
the direction of the park, would utter a cry of alarm as she
caught sight of two savage beasts waiting for her in the mobile
shade of the trees. My father cared nothing for the shooting
of game, greatly differing in this respect from his brother Sergey, a passionate sportsman who since 1908 was Master of the
Hounds to His Majesty the Tsar.

One of my mother's happier girlhood recollections was
having traveled one summer with her aunt Praskovia to the
Crimea, where her paternal grandfather had an estate near
Feodosia. Her aunt and she went for a walk with him and
another old gentleman, the well-known seascape painter Ayvazovski. She remembered the painter saying (as he had said
no doubt many times) that in 1836, at an exhibition of pictures
in St. Petersburg, he had seen Pushkin, "an ugly little fellow
with a tall handsome wife." That was more than half a century
before, when Ayvazovski was an art student, and less than a
year before Pushkin's death. She also remembered the touch
nature added from its own palette—the white mark a bird left
on the painter's gray top hat. The aunt Praskovia, walking
beside her, was her mother's sister, who had married the celebrated syphilologist V. M. Tarnovski (1839–1906) and who
herself was a doctor, the author of works on psychiatry, an-
thropology and social welfare. One evening at Ayvazovski's
villa near Feodosia, Aunt Praskovia met at dinner the twenty-
eight-year-old Dr. Anton Chekhov whom she somehow offended in the course of a medical conversation. She was a very
learned, very kind, very elegant lady, and it is hard to imagine
how exactly she could have provoked the incredibly coarse
outburst Chekhov permits himself in a published letter of August 3, 1888, to his sister. Aunt Praskovia, or Aunt Pasha, as
we called her, often visited us at Vyra. She had an enchanting
way of greeting us, as she swept into the nursery with a sonorous *"Bonjour, les enfants!"* She died in 1910. My mother
was at her bedside, and Aunt Pasha's last words were: "That's
interesting. Now I understand. Everything is water, *vsyo—
voda.*"

My mother's brother Vasiliy was in the diplomatic service,
which he treated, however, far more lightly than my uncle
Konstantin did. For Vasiliy Ivanovich it was not a career, but

The author's maternal grandmother, Olga Nikolaevna Rukavishnikov, born Kozlov (1845–1901), St. Petersburg, around 1885.

a more or less plausible setting. French and Italian friends, being unable to pronounce his long Russian surname, had boiled it down to "Ruka" (with the accent on the last syllable), and this suited him far better than did his Christian name. Uncle Ruka appeared to me in my childhood to belong to a world of toys, gay picture books, and cherry trees laden with glossy black fruit: he had glass-housed a whole orchard in a corner of his country estate, which was separated from ours by the winding river. During the summer, almost every day at lunchtime his carriage might be seen crossing the bridge and then speeding toward our house along a hedge of young firs. When I was eight or nine, he would invariably take me upon his knee after lunch and (while two young footmen were clearing the table in the empty dining room) fondle me, with crooning sounds and fancy endearments, and I felt embarrassed for my uncle by the presence of the servants and relieved when my father called him from the veranda: *"Basile, on vous attend."* Once, when I went to meet him at the station (I must have been eleven or twelve then) and watched him descend from the long international sleeping car, he gave me one look and said: "How sallow and plain [*jaune et laid*] you have become, my poor boy." On my fifteenth nameday, he took me aside and in his brusque, precise and somewhat old-fashioned French informed me that he was making me his heir. "And now you may go," he added, *"l'audience est finie. Je n'ai plus rien à vous dire."*

I remember him as a slender, neat little man with a dusky complexion, gray-green eyes flecked with rust, a dark, bushy mustache, and a mobile Adam's apple bobbing conspicuously above the opal and gold snake ring that held the knot of his tie. He also wore opals on his fingers and in his cuff links. A gold chainlet encircled his frail hairy wrist, and there was usually a carnation in the buttonhole of his dove-gray, mouse-gray or silver-gray summer suit. It was only in summer that I used to see him. After a brief stay in Rozhestveno he would go back to France or Italy, to his château (called Perpigna) near Pau, to his villa (called Tamarindo) near Rome, or to his beloved Egypt, from which he would send me picture postcards (palm trees and their reflections, sunsets, pharaohs with their hands on their knees) crossed by his thick scrawl.

Then, in June again, when the fragrant *cheryomuha* (racemose old-world bird cherry or simply "racemosa" as I have baptized it in my work on "Onegin") was in foamy bloom, his private flag would be hoisted on his beautiful Rozhestveno house. He traveled with half-a-dozen enormous trunks, bribed the Nord-Express to make a special stop at our little country station, and with the promise of a marvelous present, on small, mincing feet in high-heeled white shoes would lead me mysteriously to the nearest tree and delicately pluck and proffer a leaf, saying, *"Pour mon neveu, la chose la plus belle au monde— une feuille verte."*

Or he would solemnly bring me from America the *Foxy Grandpa* series, and *Buster Brown*—a forgotten boy in a reddish suit: if one looked closely, one could see that the color was really a mass of dense red dots. Every episode ended in a tremendous spanking for Buster, which was administered by his wasp-waisted but powerful Ma, who used a slipper, a hairbrush, a brittle umbrella, anything—even the bludgeon of a helpful policeman—and drew puffs of dust from the seat of Buster's pants. Since I had never been spanked, those pictures conveyed to me the impression of strange exotic torture not different from, say, the burying of a popeyed wretch up to his chin in the torrid sand of a desert, as represented in the frontispiece of a Mayne Reid book.

4

Uncle Ruka seems to have led an idle and oddly chaotic life. His diplomatic career was of the vaguest kind. He prided himself, however, on being an expert in decoding ciphered messages in any of the five languages he knew. We subjected him to a test one day, and in a twinkle he turned the sequence "5.13 24.11 13.16 9.13.5 5.13 24.11" into the opening words of a famous monologue in Shakespeare.

Pink-coated, he rode to hounds in England or Italy; fur-coated, he attempted to motor from St. Petersburg to Pau; wearing an opera cloak, he almost lost his life in an airplane crash on a beach near Bayonne. (When I asked him how did the pilot of the smashed Voisin take it, Uncle Ruka thought for a moment and then replied with complete assurance: *"Il sanglotait assis sur un rocher."*) He sang barcaroles and modish lyrics (*"Ils se regardent tous deux, en se mangeant des yeux . . ." "Elle est morte en Février, pauvre Colinette! . . ." "Le soleil rayonnait encore, j'ai voulu revoir les grands bois . . ."* and dozens of others). He wrote music himself, of the sweet, rippling sort, and French verse, curiously scannable as English or Russian iambics, and marked by a princely disregard for the comforts of the mute *e*'s. He was extremely good at poker.

Because he stammered and had difficulty in pronouncing labials, he changed his coachman's name from Pyotr to Lev; and my father (who was always a little sharp with him) accused him of a slaveowner's mentality. Apart from this, his speech was a fastidious combination of French, English and Italian, all of which he spoke with vastly more ease than he did his native tongue. When he resorted to Russian, it was invariably to misuse or garble some extremely idiomatic or even folksy expression, as when he would say at table with a sudden sigh (for there was always something amiss—a spell of hay fever, the death of a peacock, a lost borzoi): *"Je suis triste et seul comme une bylinka v pole* [as lonesome as a 'grass blade in the field']."

He insisted that he had an incurable heart ailment and that, when the seizures came, he could obtain relief only by lying supine on the floor. Nobody took him seriously, and after he did die of angina pectoris, all alone, in Paris, at the end of 1916, aged forty-five, it was with a quite special pang that one recalled those after-dinner incidents in the drawing room—the unprepared footman entering with the Turkish coffee, my father glancing (with quizzical resignation) at my mother, then (with disapproval) at his brother-in-law spread-eagled in the footman's path, then (with curiosity) at the funny vibration going on among the coffee things on the tray in the seemingly composed servant's cotton-gloved hands.

From other, stranger torments that beset him in the course of his short life, he sought relief—if I understand these matters rightly—in religion, first in certain Russian sectarian outlets, and eventually in the Roman Catholic Church. His was the kind of colorful neurosis that should have been accompanied by genius but in his case was not, hence the search for a traveling shadow. In his youth he had been intensely disliked by his father, a country gentleman of the old school (bear hunting, a private theatre, a few fine Old Masters among a good deal of trash), whose uncontrollable temper was rumored to have been a threat to the boy's very life. My mother told me later of the tension in the Vyra household of her girlhood, of the atrocious scenes that took place in Ivan Vasilievich's study, a gloomy corner room giving on an old well with a rusty pumping wheel under five Lombardy poplars. Nobody used that room except me. I kept my books and spreading boards on its black shelves, and subsequently induced my mother to have some of its furniture transferred into my own sunny little study on the garden side, and therein staggered, one morning, its tremendous desk with nothing upon its waste of dark leather but a huge curved paper knife, a veritable scimitar of yellow ivory carved from a mammoth's tusk.

When Uncle Ruka died, at the end of 1916, he left me what would amount nowadays to a couple of million dollars and his country estate, with its white-pillared mansion on a green, escarped hill and its two thousand acres of wildwood and peat-bog. The house, I am told, still stood there in 1940, nationalized but aloof, a museum piece for any sightseeing traveler who might follow the St. Petersburg–Luga highway running below through the village Rozhestveno and across the branching river. Because of its floating islands of water lilies and algal brocade, the fair Oredezh had a festive air at that spot. Farther down its sinuous course, where the sand martins shot out of their holes in the steep red bank, it was deeply suffused with the reflections of great, romantic firs (the fringe of our Vyra); and still farther downstream, the endless tumultuous flow of a water mill gave the spectator (his elbows on the handrail) the sensation of receding endlessly, as if this were the stern of time itself.

5

The following passage is not for the general reader, but for the particular idiot who, because he lost a fortune in some crash, thinks he understands me.

My old (since 1917) quarrel with the Soviet dictatorship is wholly unrelated to any question of property. My contempt for the émigré who "hates the Reds" because they "stole" his money and land is complete. The nostalgia I have been cherishing all these years is a hypertrophied sense of lost childhood, not sorrow for lost banknotes.

And finally: I reserve for myself the right to yearn after an ecological niche:

> . . . Beneath the sky
> Of my America to sigh
> For *one* locality in Russia.

The general reader may now resume.

6

I was nearing eighteen, then was over eighteen; love affairs and verse-writing occupied most of my leisure; material questions left me indifferent, and, anyway, against the background of our prosperity no inheritance could seem very conspicuous; yet, upon looking back across the transparent abyss, I find queer and somewhat unpleasant to reflect that during the brief year that I was in the possession of that private wealth, I was too much absorbed by the usual delights of youth—youth that was rapidly losing its initial, non-usual fervor—either to derive any special pleasure from the legacy or to experience any annoyance when the Bolshevik Revolution abolished it overnight. This recollection gives me the sense of having been ungrateful to Uncle Ruka; of having joined in the general attitude of smiling condescension that even those who liked him usually took toward him. It is with the utmost repulsion that I force myself to recall the sarcastic comments that Monsieur Noyer, my Swiss tutor (otherwise a most kindly soul), used to make on my uncle's best composition, a *romance*, both the music and words of which he had written. One day, on the terrace of his Pau castle, with the amber vineyards below and the empurpled mountains in the distance, at a time when he was harassed by asthma, palpitations, shiverings, a Proustian excoriation of the senses, *se débattant*, as it were, under the impact of the autumn colors (described in his own words as the *"chapelle ardente de feuilles aux tons violents"*), of the distant voices from the valley, of a flight of doves striating the tender sky, he had composed that one-winged *ro-mance* (and the only person who memorized the music and all the words was my brother Sergey, whom he hardly ever noticed, who also stammered, and who is also now dead).

"L'air transparent fait monter de la plaine . . ." he would sing in his high tenor voice, seated at the white piano in our country house—and if I were at that moment hurrying through the adjacent groves on my way home for lunch (soon after seeing his jaunty straw hat and the black-velvet-clad bust of his handsome coachman in Assyrian profile, with scarlet-sleeved outstretched arms, skim rapidly along the rim of the hedge separating the park from the drive) the plaintive sounds

> *Un vol de tourterelles strie le ciel tendre,*
> *Les chrysanthèmes se parent pour la Toussaint*

reached me and my green butterfly net on the shady, tremulous trail, at the end of which was a vista of reddish sand and the corner of our freshly repainted house, the color of young fir cones, with the open drawing-room window whence the wounded music came.

7

The act of vividly recalling a patch of the past is something that I seem to have been performing with the utmost zest all my life, and I have reason to believe that this almost pathological keenness of the retrospective faculty is a hereditary trait. There was a certain spot in the forest, a footbridge across a brown brook, where my father would piously pause to recall the rare butterfly that, on the seventeenth of August, 1883, his German tutor had netted for him. The thirty-year-old scene would be gone through again. He and his brothers had stopped short in helpless excitement at the sight of the coveted insect poised on a log and moving up and down, as though in alert respiration, its four cherry-red wings with a pavonian eyespot on each. In tense silence, not daring to strike himself, he had handed his net to Herr Rogge, who was groping for it, his eyes fixed on the splendid fly. My cabinet inherited that specimen a quarter of a century later. One touching detail: its wings had "sprung" because it had been removed from the setting board too early, too eagerly.

In a villa which in the summer of 1904 we rented with my uncle Ivan de Peterson's family on the Adriatic (the name was either "Neptune" or "Apollo"—I can still identify its crenelated, cream-colored tower in old pictures of Abbazia), aged five, mooning in my cot after lunch, I used to turn over on my stomach and, carefully, lovingly, hopelessly, in an artistically detailed fashion difficult to reconcile with the ridiculously small number of seasons that had gone to form the inexplicably nostalgic image of "home" (that I had not seen since September 1903), I would draw with my forefinger on my pillow the carriage road sweeping up to our Vyra house, the stone steps on the right, the carved back of a bench on the left, the alley of oaklings beginning beyond the bushes of honeysuckle, and a newly shed horseshoe, a collector's item (much bigger and brighter than the rusty ones I used to find on the seashore), shining in the reddish dust of the drive. The recollection of that recollection is sixty years older than the latter, but far less unusual.

Once, in 1908 or 1909, Uncle Ruka became engrossed in some French children's books that he had come upon in our house; with an ecstatic moan, he found a passage he had loved in his childhood, beginning: *"Sophie n'était pas jolie . . ."* and many years later, my moan echoed his, when I rediscovered, in a chance nursery, those same "Bibliothèque Rose" volumes, with their stories about boys and girls who led in France an idealized version of the *vie de château* which my family led in Russia. The stories themselves (all those *Les Malheurs de Sophie, Les Petites Filles Modèles, Les Vacances*) are, as I see them now, an awful combination of preciosity and vulgarity; but in writing them the sentimental and smug Mme de Ségur, née Rostopchine, was Frenchifying the authentic surroundings of her Russian childhood which preceded mine by exactly one century. In my own case, when I come over Sophie's troubles again—her lack of eyebrows and love of thick cream—I not only go through the same agony and delight that my uncle did, but have to cope with an additional burden—the recollection I have of him, reliving his childhood with the help of those very books. I see again my schoolroom in Vyra, the blue roses of the wallpaper, the open window. Its reflection fills the oval mirror above the leathern couch where my uncle sits, gloating over a tattered book. A sense of security, of well-being, of summer warmth pervades my memory. That robust reality makes a ghost of the present. The mirror brims with brightness; a bumblebee has entered the room and bumps against the ceiling. Everything is as it should be, nothing will ever change, nobody will ever die.

Four

THE KIND of Russian family to which I belonged—a kind now extinct—had, among other virtues, a traditional leaning toward the comfortable products of Anglo-Saxon civilization. Pears' Soap, tar-black when dry, topaz-like when held to the light between wet fingers, took care of one's morning bath. Pleasant was the decreasing weight of the English collapsible tub when it was made to protrude a rubber underlip and disgorge its frothy contents into the slop pail. "We could not improve the cream, so we improved the tube," said the English toothpaste. At breakfast, Golden Syrup imported from London would entwist with its glowing coils the revolving spoon from which enough of it had slithered onto a piece of Russian bread and butter. All sorts of snug, mellow things came in a steady procession from the English Shop on Nevski Avenue: fruitcakes, smelling salts, playing cards, picture puzzles, striped blazers, talcum-white tennis balls.

I learned to read English before I could read Russian. My first English friends were four simple souls in my grammar—Ben, Dan, Sam and Ned. There used to be a great deal of fuss about their identities and whereabouts—"Who is Ben?" "He is Dan," "Sam is in bed," and so on. Although it all remained rather stiff and patchy (the compiler was handicapped by having to employ—for the initial lessons, at least—words of not more than three letters), my imagination somehow managed to obtain the necessary data. Wan-faced, big-limbed, silent nitwits, proud in the possession of certain tools ("Ben has an axe"), they now drift with a slow-motioned slouch across the remotest backdrop of memory; and, akin to the mad alphabet of an optician's chart, the grammar-book lettering looms again before me.

The schoolroom was drenched with sunlight. In a sweating glass jar, several spiny caterpillars were feeding on nettle leaves (and ejecting interesting, barrel-shaped pellets of olive-green frass). The oilcloth that covered the round table smelled of glue. Miss Clayton smelled of Miss Clayton. Fantastically, gloriously, the blood-colored alcohol of the outside thermometer had risen to 24° Réaumur (86° Fahrenheit) in the shade. Through the window one could see kerchiefed peasant girls weeding a garden path on their hands and knees or gently raking the sun-mottled sand. (The happy days when they would be cleaning streets and digging canals for the State were still beyond the horizon.) Golden orioles in the greenery emitted their four brilliant notes: dee-del-dee-O!

Ned lumbered past the window in a fair impersonation of the gardener's mate Ivan (who was to become in 1918 a member of the local Soviet). On later pages longer words appeared; and at the very end of the brown, inkstained volume, a real, sensible story unfolded its adult sentences ("One day Ted said to Ann: Let us—"), the little reader's ultimate triumph and reward. I was thrilled by the thought that some day I might attain such proficiency. The magic has endured, and whenever a grammar book comes my way, I instantly turn to the last page to enjoy a forbidden glimpse of the laborious student's future, of that promised land where, at last, words are meant to mean what they mean.

2

Summer *soomerki*—the lovely Russian word for dusk. Time: a dim point in the first decade of this unpopular century. Place: latitude 59° north from your equator, longitude 100° east from my writing hand. The day would take hours to fade, and everything—sky, tall flowers, still water—would be kept in a state of infinite vesperal suspense, deepened rather than resolved by the doleful moo of a cow in a distant meadow or by the still more moving cry that came from some bird beyond the lower course of the river, where the vast expanse of a misty-blue sphagnum bog, because of its mystery and remoteness, the Rukavishnikov children had baptized America.

In the drawing room of our country house, before going to bed, I would often be read to in English by my mother. As she came to a particularly dramatic passage, where the hero was about to encounter some strange, perhaps fatal danger, her voice would slow down, her words would be spaced portentously, and before turning the page she would place upon it her hand, with its familiar pigeon-blood ruby and diamond ring (within the limpid facets of which, had I been a better crystal-gazer, I might have seen a room, people, lights, trees in the rain—a whole period of émigré life for which that ring was to pay).

There were tales about knights whose terrific but wonderfully aseptic wounds were bathed by damsels in grottoes. From a windswept clifftop, a medieval maiden with flying hair and a youth in hose gazed at the round Isles of the Blessed. In "Misunderstood," the fate of Humphrey used to bring a more specialized lump to one's throat than anything in Dickens or Daudet (great devisers of lumps), while a shamelessly allegorical story, "Beyond the Blue Mountains," dealing with two pairs of little travelers—good Clover and Cowslip, bad Buttercup and Daisy—contained enough exciting details to make one forget its "message."

There were also those large, flat, glossy picture books. I particularly liked the blue-coated, red-trousered, coal-black Golliwogg, with underclothes buttons for eyes, and his meager harem of five wooden dolls. By the illegal method of cutting themselves frocks out of the American flag (Peg taking the motherly stripes, Sarah Jane the pretty stars) two of the dolls acquired a certain soft femininity, once their neutral articulations had been clothed. The Twins (Meg and Weg) and the Midget remained stark naked and, consequently, sexless.

We see them in the dead of night stealing out of doors to sling snowballs at one another until the chimes of a remote clock ("But Hark!" comments the rhymed text) send them back to their toybox in the nursery. A rude jack-in-the-box shoots out, frightening my lovely Sarah, and that picture I heartily disliked because it reminded me of children's parties at which this or that graceful little girl, who had bewitched me, happened to pinch her finger or hurt her knee, and would forthwith expand into a purple-faced goblin, all wrinkles and bawling mouth. Another time they went on a bicycle journey and were captured by cannibals; our unsuspecting travelers had been quenching their thirst at a palm-fringed pool when the tom-toms sounded. Over the shoulder of my past I admire again the crucial picture: the Golliwogg, still on his knees by the pool but no longer drinking; his hair stands on end and the normal black of his face has changed to a weird ashen hue.

There was also the motorcar book (Sarah Jane, always my favorite, sporting a long green veil), with the usual sequel—crutches and bandaged heads.

And, yes—the airship. Yards and yards of yellow silk went to make it, and an additional tiny balloon was provided for the sole use of the fortunate Midget. At the immense altitude to which the ship reached, the aeronauts huddled together for warmth while the lost little soloist, still the object of my intense envy notwithstanding his plight, drifted into an abyss of frost and stars—alone.

3

I next see my mother leading me bedward through the enormous hall, where a central flight of stairs swept up and up, with nothing but hothouse-like panes of glass between the upper landing and the light green evening sky. One would lag back and shuffle and slide a little on the smooth stone floor of the hall, causing the gentle hand at the small of one's back to propel one's reluctant frame by means of indulgent pushes. Upon reaching the stairway, my custom was to get to the steps by squirming under the handrail between the newel post and the first banister. With every new summer, the process of squeezing through became more difficult; nowadays, even my ghost would get stuck.

Another part of the ritual was to ascend with closed eyes. "Step, step, step," came my mother's voice as she led me up—and sure enough, the surface of the next tread would receive the blind child's confident foot; all one had to do was lift it a little higher than usual, so as to avoid stubbing one's toe against the riser. This slow, somewhat somnambulistic ascension in self-engendered darkness held obvious delights. The keenest of them was not knowing when the last step would come. At the top of the stairs, one's foot would be automatically lifted to the deceptive call of "Step," and then, with a momentary sense of exquisite panic, with a wild contraction of muscles, would sink into the phantasm of a step, padded, as it were, with the infinitely elastic stuff of its own nonexistence.

The author's father, Vladimir Dmitrievich Nabokov (1870–1922), as a school-boy around 1885 with his three brothers (from *left* to *right* Dmitri, Konstantin, and Sergey). My father was about to graduate from the Third Gymnasium and enter the university at an astonishingly early age. Uncle Konstantin, at eleven or twelve, was still being educated at home. Uncle Dmitri and Uncle Sergey were *pravoveds*, i.e. scholars of the fashionable Imperial School of Jurisprudence.

It is surprising what method there was in my bedtime daw-
dling. True, the whole going-up-the-stairs business now reveals certain transcendental values. Actually, however, I was
merely playing for time by extending every second to its utmost. This would still go on when my mother turned me over,
to be undressed, to Miss Clayton or Mademoiselle.

There were five bathrooms in our country house, and a
medley of venerable washstands (one of these I would seek
out in its dark nook whenever I had been crying, so as to feel
on my swollen face which I was ashamed to show, the healing
touch of its groping jet while I stepped on the rusty pedal).
Regular baths were taken in the evening. For morning ablutions, the round, rubber English tubs were used. Mine was
about four feet in diameter, with a knee-high rim. Upon the
lathered back of the squatting child, a jugful of water was
carefully poured by an aproned servant. Its temperature varied
with the hydrotherapeutic notions of successive mentors.
There was that bleak period of dawning puberty, when an icy
deluge was decreed by our current tutor, who happened to
be a medical student. On the other hand, the temperature of
one's evening bath remained pleasantly constant at 28° Réaumur (95° Fahrenheit) as measured by a large kindly thermometer whose wooden sheathing (with a bit of damp string
in the eye of the handle) allowed it to share in the buoyancy
of celluloid goldfishes and little swans.

The toilets were separate from the bathrooms, and the oldest among them was a rather sumptuous but gloomy affair
with some fine panelwork and a tasseled rope of red velvet,
which, when pulled, produced a beautifully modulated, discreetly muffled gurgle and gulp. From that corner of the
house, one could see Hesperus and hear the nightingales, and
it was there that, later, I used to compose my youthful verse,
dedicated to unembraced beauties, and morosely survey, in a
dimly illuminated mirror, the immediate erection of a strange
castle in an unknown Spain. As a small child, however, I was
assigned a more modest arrangement, rather casually situated
in a narrow recess between a wicker hamper and the door
leading to the nursery bathroom. This door I liked to keep
ajar; through it I drowsily looked at the shimmer of steam

above the mahogany bath, at the fantastic flotilla of swans and skiffs, at myself with a harp in one of the boats, at a furry moth pinging against the reflector of the kerosene lamp, at the stained-glass window beyond, at its two halberdiers consisting of colored rectangles. Bending from my warm seat, I liked to press the middle of my brow, its ophryon to be precise, against the smooth comfortable edge of the door and then roll my head a little, so that the door would move to and fro while its edge remained all the time in soothing contact with my forehead. A dreamy rhythm would permeate my being. The recent "Step, step, step," would be taken up by a dripping faucet. And, fruitfully combining rhythmic pattern with rhythmic sound, I would unravel the labyrinthian frets on the linoleum, and find faces where a crack or a shadow afforded a *point de repère* for the eye. I appeal to parents: never, never say, "Hurry up," to a child.

The final stage in the course of my vague navigation would come when I reached the island of my bed. From the veranda or drawing room, where life was going on without me, my mother would come up for the warm murmur of her goodnight kiss. Closed inside shutters, a lighted candle, Gentle Jesus, meek and mild, something-something little child, the child kneeling on the pillow that presently would engulf his humming head. English prayers and the little icon featuring a sun-tanned Greek Catholic saint formed an innocent association upon which I look back with pleasure; and above the icon, high up on the wall, where the shadow of something (of the bamboo screen between bed and door?) undulated in the warm candlelight, a framed aquarelle showed a dusky path winding through one of those eerily dense European beechwoods, where the only undergrowth is bindweed and the only sound one's thumping heart. In an English fairy tale my mother had once read to me, a small boy stepped out of his bed into a picture and rode his hobbyhorse along a painted path between silent trees. While I knelt on my pillow in a mist of drowsiness and talc-powdered well-being, half sitting on my calves and rapidly going through my prayer, I imagined the motion of climbing into the picture above my bed and plunging into that enchanted beechwood—which I did visit in due time.

4

A bewildering sequence of English nurses and governesses, some of them wringing their hands, others smiling at me enigmatically, come out to meet me as I re-enter my past.

There was dim Miss Rachel, whom I remember mainly in terms of Huntley and Palmer biscuits (the nice almond rocks at the top of the blue-papered tin box, the insipid cracknels at the bottom) which she unlawfully shared with me after my teeth had been brushed. There was Miss Clayton, who, when I slumped in my chair, would poke me in the middle vertebrae and then smilingly throw back her own shoulders to show what she wanted of me: she told me a nephew of hers at my age (four) used to breed caterpillars, but those she collected for me in an open jar with nettles all walked away one morning, and the gardener said they had hanged themselves. There was lovely, black-haired, aquamarine-eyed Miss Norcott, who lost a white kid glove at Nice or Beaulieu, where I vainly looked for it on the shingly beach among the colored pebbles and the glaucous lumps of sea-changed bottle glass. Lovely Miss Norcott was asked to leave at once, one night at Abbazia. She embraced me in the morning twilight of the nursery, pale-mackintoshed and weeping like a Babylonian willow, and that day I remained inconsolable, despite the hot chocolate that the Petersons' old Nanny had made especially for me and the special bread and butter, on the smooth surface of which my aunt Nata, adroitly capturing my attention, drew a daisy, then a cat, and then the little mermaid whom I had just been reading about with Miss Norcott and crying over, too, so I started to cry again. There was myopic little Miss Hunt, whose short stay with us in Wiesbaden came to an end the day my brother and I—aged four and five, respectively—managed to evade her nervous vigilance by boarding a steamer that took us quite a way down the Rhine before recapture. There was pink-nosed Miss Robinson. There was Miss Clayton again. There was one awful person who read to me Marie Corelli's *The Mighty Atom*. There were still others. At a certain point they faded out of my life. French and Russian took over; and what little time remained for the speaking of English was devoted to occasional sessions with two gentlemen, Mr. Burness and Mr.

Cummings, neither of whom dwelt with us. They are associated in my mind with winters in St. Petersburg, where we had a house on the Morskaya Street.

Mr. Burness was a large Scotsman with a florid face, light-blue eyes and lank, straw-colored hair. He spent his mornings teaching at a language school and then crammed into the afternoon more private lessons than the day could well hold. Traveling, as he did, from one part of the town to another and having to depend on the torpid trot of dejected *izvozchik* (cab) horses to get him to his pupils, he would be, with luck, only a quarter of an hour late for his two o'clock lesson (wherever that was), but would arrive after five for his four o'clock one. The tension of waiting for him and hoping that, for once, his superhuman doggedness might balk before the gray wall of some special snowstorm was the kind of feeling that one trusts never to meet with in mature life (but that I did experience again when circumstances forced me, in my turn, to give lessons and when, in my furnished rooms in Berlin, I awaited a certain stone-faced pupil, who would *always* turn up despite the obstacles I mentally piled in his way).

The very darkness that was gathering outside seemed a waste product of Mr. Burness' efforts to reach our house. Presently the valet would come to drop the blue voluminous blinds and draw the flowered window draperies. The tick-tock of the grandfather's clock in the schoolroom gradually assumed a dreary, nagging intonation. The tightness of my shorts in the groin and the rough touch of ribbed black stockings rubbing against the tender inside of my bent legs would mingle with the dull pressure of a humble need, the satisfaction of which I kept postponing. Nearly an hour would pass and there would be no sign of Mr. Burness. My brother would go to his room and play some practice piece on the piano and then plunge and replunge into some of the melodies that I loathed—the instruction to the artificial flowers in *Faust* (. . . *dites-lui qu'elle est belle* . . .) or Vladimir Lenski's wail (. . . *Koo-dah, koo-dah, koo-dah, vï udalilis'*). I would leave the upper floor, where we children dwelt, and slowly slide along the balustrade down to the second story, where my parents' rooms were situated. As often as not, they used to be out at that time, and in the gathering dusk the place acted upon my young senses in a curiously teleological way, as if this accumulation of familiar things in the dark were doing its utmost to form the definite and permanent image that repeated exposure did finally leave in my mind.

The sepia gloom of an arctic afternoon in midwinter invaded the rooms and was deepening to an oppressive black. A bronze angle, a surface of glass or polished mahogany here and there in the darkness, reflected the odds and ends of light from the street, where the globes of tall street lamps along its middle line were already diffusing their lunar glow. Gauzy shadows moved on the ceiling. In the stillness, the dry sound of a chrysanthemum petal falling upon the marble of a table made one's nerves twang.

My mother's boudoir had a convenient oriel for looking out on the Morskaya in the direction of the Maria Square. With lips pressed against the thin fabric that veiled the windowpane I would gradually taste the cold of the glass through the gauze. From that oriel, some years later, at the outbreak of the Revolution, I watched various engagements and saw my first dead man: he was being carried away on a stretcher, and from one dangling leg an ill-shod comrade kept trying to pull off the boot despite pushes and punches from the stretchermen—all this at a goodish trot. But in the days of Mr. Burness' lessons there was nothing to watch save the dark, muffled street and its receding line of loftily suspended lamps, around which the snowflakes passed and repassed with a graceful, almost deliberately slackened motion, as if to show how the trick was done and how simple it was. From another angle, one might see a more generous stream of snow in a brighter, violet-tinged nimbus of gaslight, and then the jutting enclosure where I stood would seem to drift slowly up and up, like a balloon. At last one of the phantom sleighs gliding along the street would come to a stop, and with gawky haste Mr. Burness in his fox-furred *shapka* would make for our door.

From the schoolroom, whither I had preceded him, I would hear his vigorous footsteps crashing nearer and nearer, and, no matter how cold the day was, his good, ruddy face would be sweating abundantly as he strode in. I remember the terrific energy with which he pressed on the spluttering pen as he wrote down, in the roundest of round hands, the tasks to be prepared for the next day. Usually at the end of the lesson a certain limerick was asked for and granted, the point of the performance being that the word "screamed" in it was to be involuntarily enacted by oneself every time Mr. Burness gave a formidable squeeze to the hand he held in his beefy paw as he recited the lines:

> There was a young lady from Russia
> Who (squeeze) whenever you'd crush her.
> She (squeeze) and she (squeeze) . . .

by which time the pain would have become so excruciating that we never got any farther.

5

The quiet, bearded gentleman with a stoop, old-fashioned Mr. Cummings, who taught me, in 1907 or 1908, to draw, had been my mother's drawing master also. He had come to Russia in the early nineties as foreign correspondent and illustrator for the London *Graphic*. Marital misfortunes were rumored to obscure his life. A melancholy sweetness of manner made up for the meagerness of his talent. He wore an ulster unless the weather was very mild, when he would switch to the kind of greenish-brown woolen cloak called a *loden*.

I was captivated by his use of the special eraser he kept in his waistcoat pocket, by the manner in which he held the page taut, and afterwards flicked off, with the back of his fingers, the "gutticles of the percha" (as he said). Silently, sadly, he illustrated for me the marble laws of perspective: long, straight strokes of his elegantly held, incredibly sharp pencil caused the lines of the room he created out of nothing (abstract walls, receding ceiling and floor) to come together in one remote hypothetical point with tantalizing and sterile accuracy. Tantalizing, because it made me think of railway tracks, symmetrically and trickily converging before the bloodshot eyes of my favorite mask, a grimy engine driver; sterile, because that room remained unfurnished and quite empty, being devoid even of the neutral statues one finds in the uninteresting first hall of a museum.

The rest of the picture gallery made up for its gaunt vestibule. Mr. Cummings was a master of the sunset. His little watercolors, purchased at different times for five or ten roubles apiece by members of our household, led a somewhat precarious existence, shifting, as they did, to more and more obscure nooks and finally getting completely eclipsed by some sleek porcelain beast or a newly framed photograph. After I had learned not only to draw cubes and cones but to shade properly with smooth, merging slants such parts of them as had to be made to turn away forever, the kind old gentleman contented himself with painting under my enchanted gaze his own wet little paradises, variations of one landscape: a summer evening with an orange sky, a pasture ending in the black fringe of a distant forest, and a luminous river, repeating the sky and winding away and away.

Later on, from around 1910 to 1912, the well-known "impressionist" (a term of the period) Yaremich took over; a humorless and formless person, he advocated a "bold" style, blotches of dull color, smears of sepia and olive-brown, by means of which I had to reproduce on huge sheets of gray paper, humanoid shapes that we modeled of plasticine and placed in "dramatic" positions against a backcloth of velvet with all kinds of folds and shadow effects. It was a depressing combination of at least three different arts, all approximative, and finally I rebelled.

He was replaced by the celebrated Dobuzhinski who liked to give me his lessons on the *piano nobile* of our house, in one of its pretty reception rooms downstairs, which he entered in a particularly noiseless way as if afraid to startle me from my verse-making stupor. He made me depict from memory, in the greatest possible detail, objects I had certainly seen thousands of times without visualizing them properly: a street lamp, a postbox, the tulip design on the stained glass of our own front door. He tried to teach me to find the geometrical coordinations between the slender twigs of a leafless boulevard tree, a system of visual give-and-takes, requiring a precision of linear expression, which I failed to achieve in my youth, but applied gratefully, in my adult instar, not only to the drawing of butterfly genitalia during my seven years at the Harvard Museum of Comparative Zoology, when immersing myself in

the bright wellhole of a microscope to record in India ink this
or that new structure; but also, perhaps, to certain camera-
lucida needs of literary composition. Emotionally, however, I
am still more indebted to the earlier color treats given me by
my mother and her former teacher. How readily Mr. Cummings would sit down on a stool, part behind with both hands
his—what? was he wearing a frock coat? I see only the gesture—and proceed to open the black tin paintbox. I loved the
nimble way he had of soaking his paintbrush in multiple color
to the accompaniment of a rapid clatter produced by the
enamel containers wherein the rich reds and yellows that the
brush dimpled were appetizingly cupped; and having thus collected its honey, it would cease to hover and poke, and, by
two or three sweeps of its lush tip, would drench the "Vat-
manski" paper with an even spread of orange sky, across
which, while that sky was still dampish, a long purple-black
cloud would be laid. "And that's all, dearie," he would say.
"That's all there is to it."

On one occasion, I had him draw an express train for me.
I watched his pencil ably evolve the cowcatcher and elaborate
headlights of a locomotive that looked as if it had been acquired secondhand for the Trans-Siberian line after it had
done duty at Promontory Point, Utah, in the sixties. Then
came five disappointingly plain carriages. When he had quite
finished them, he carefully shaded the ample smoke coming
from the huge funnel, cocked his head, and, after a moment
of pleased contemplation, handed me the drawing. I tried to
look pleased, too. He had forgotten the tender.

A quarter of a century later, I learned two things: that Burness, by then dead, had been well known in Edinburgh as a
scholarly translator of the Russian romantic poems that had
been the altar and frenzy of my boyhood; and that my humble
drawing master, whose age I used to synchronize with that of
granduncles and old family servants, had married a young Es-
tonian girl about the time I myself married. When I learned
these later developments, I experienced a queer shock; it was
as if life had impinged upon my creative rights by wriggling
on beyond the subjective limits so elegantly and economically
set by childhood memories that I thought I had signed and
sealed.

"And what about Yaremich?" I asked M. V. Dobuzhinski, one summer afternoon in the nineteen forties, as we strolled through a beech forest in Vermont. "Is he remembered?"

"Indeed, he is," replied Mstislav Valerianovich. "He was exceptionally gifted. I don't know what kind of teacher he was, but I do know that *you* were the most hopeless pupil I ever had."

Five

I HAVE often noticed that after I had bestowed on the characters of my novels some treasured item of my past, it would pine away in the artificial world where I had so abruptly placed it. Although it lingered on in my mind, its personal warmth, its retrospective appeal had gone and, presently, it became more closely identified with my novel than with my former self, where it had seemed to be so safe from the intrusion of the artist. Houses have crumbled in my memory as soundlessly as they did in the mute films of yore, and the portrait of my old French governess, whom I once lent to a boy in one of my books, is fading fast, now that it is engulfed in the description of a childhood entirely unrelated to my own. The man in me revolts against the fictionist, and here is my desperate attempt to save what is left of poor Mademoiselle.

A large woman, a very stout woman, Mademoiselle rolled into our existence in December 1905 when I was six and my brother five. There she is. I see so plainly her abundant dark hair, brushed up high and covertly graying; the three wrinkles on her austere forehead; her beetling brows; the steely eyes behind the black-rimmed pince-nez; that vestigial mustache; that blotchy complexion, which in moments of wrath develops an additional flush in the region of the third, and amplest, chin so regally spread over the frilled mountain of her blouse. And now she sits down, or rather she tackles the job of sitting down, the jelly of her jowl quaking, her prodigious posterior, with the three buttons on the side, lowering itself warily; then, at the last second, she surrenders her bulk to the wicker armchair, which, out of sheer fright, bursts into a salvo of crackling.

We had been abroad for about a year. After spending the summer of 1904 in Beaulieu and Abbazia, and several months in Wiesbaden, we left for Russia in the beginning of 1905. I fail to remember the month. One clue is that in Wiesbaden I had been taken to its Russian church—the first time I had been to church anywhere—and that might have been in the Lenten season (during the service I asked my mother what were the priest and deacon talking about; she whispered back in English that they were saying we should all love one another but I understood she meant that those two gorgeous personages in cone-shaped shining robes were telling each other they would always remain good friends). From Frankfurt we arrived in Berlin in a snowstorm, and next morning caught the Nord-Express, which thundered in from Paris. Twelve hours later it reached the Russian frontier. Against the background of winter, the ceremonial change of cars and engines acquired a strange new meaning. An exciting sense of *rodina*, "motherland," was for the first time organically mingled with the comfortably creaking snow, the deep footprints across it, the red gloss of the engine stack, the birch logs piled high, under their private layer of transportable snow, on the red tender. I was not quite six, but that year abroad, a year of difficult decisions and liberal hopes, had exposed a small Russian boy to grown-up conversations. He could not help being affected in some way of his own by a mother's nostalgia and a father's patriotism. In result, that particular return to Russia, my first *conscious* return, seems to me now, sixty years later, a rehearsal—not of the grand homecoming that will never take place, but of its constant dream in my long years of exile.

The summer of 1905 in Vyra had not yet evolved lepidoptera. The village schoolmaster took us for instructive walks ("What you hear is the sound of a scythe being sharpened"; "That field there will be given a rest next season"; "Oh, just a small bird—no special name"; "If that peasant is drunk, it is because he is poor"). Autumn carpeted the park with varicolored leaves, and Miss Robinson showed us the beautiful device—which the Ambassador's Boy, a familiar character in her small world, had enjoyed so much the preceding autumn—of choosing on the ground and arranging on a big sheet of paper such maple leaves as would form an almost complete spectrum (minus the blue—a big disappointment!), green shading into lemon, lemon into orange and so on through the reds to purples, purplish browns, reddish again and back through lemon to green (which was getting quite hard to find except as a part, a last brave edge). The first frosts hit the asters and still we did not move to town.

That winter of 1905–1906, when Mademoiselle arrived from Switzerland, was the only one of my childhood that I spent in the country. It was a year of strikes, riots and police-inspired massacres, and I suppose my father wished to keep his family away from the city, in our quiet country place, where his popularity with the peasants might mitigate, as he correctly surmised, the risks of unrest. It was also a particularly severe winter, producing as much snow as Mademoiselle might have expected to find in the hyperborean gloom of remote Muscovy. When she alighted at the little Siverski station, from which she still had to travel half-a-dozen miles by sleigh to Vyra, I was not there to greet her; but I do so now as I try to imagine what she saw and felt at that last stage of her fabulous and ill-timed journey. Her Russian vocabulary consisted, I know, of one short word, the same solitary word that years later she was to take back to Switzerland. This word, which in her pronunciation may be phonetically rendered as "giddy-eh" (actually it is *gde* with *e* as in "yet"), meant "Where?" And that was a good deal. Uttered by her like the raucous cry of some lost bird, it accumulated such interrogatory force that it sufficed for all her needs. "Giddy-eh? Giddy-eh?" she would wail, not only to find out her whereabouts but also to express supreme misery: the fact that she was a stranger, shipwrecked, penniless, ailing, in search of the blessed land where at last she would be understood.

I can visualize her, by proxy, as she stands in the middle of the station platform, where she has just alighted, and vainly my ghostly envoy offers her an arm that she cannot see. ("There I was, abandoned by all, *comme la Comtesse Karenine*," she later complained, eloquently, if not quite correctly.) The door of the waiting room opens with a shuddering whine peculiar to nights of intense frost; a cloud of hot air rushes out, almost as profuse as the steam from the panting engine; and now our coachman Zahar takes over—a burly man in sheepskin with the leather outside, his huge gloves protruding from his scarlet sash into which he has stuffed them. I hear the snow crunching under his felt boots while he busies him-

The author's father and mother, Elena Ivanovna Nabokov, born Rukavishnikov (1876–1939), in 1900, on the garden terrace at Vyra, their estate in the
Province of St. Petersburg. The birches and firs of the park behind my parents
belong to the same backdrop of past summers as the foliage of photograph
on p. 529.

self with the luggage, the jingling harness, and then his own nose, which he eases by means of a dexterous tweak-and-shake of finger and thumb as he trudges back around the sleigh. Slowly, with grim misgivings, *"Madmazelya,"* as her helper calls her, climbs in, clutching at him in mortal fear lest the sleigh move off before her vast form is securely encased. Finally, she settles down with a grunt and thrusts her fists into her skimpy plush muff. At the juicy smack of their driver's lips the two black horses, Zoyka and Zinka, strain their quarters, shift hooves, strain again; and then Mademoiselle gives a backward jerk of her torso as the heavy sleigh is wrenched out of its world of steel, fur, flesh, to enter a frictionless medium where it skims along a spectral road that it seems barely to touch.

For one moment, thanks to the sudden radiance of a lone lamp where the station square ends, a grossly exaggerated shadow, also holding a muff, races beside the sleigh, climbs a billow of snow, and is gone, leaving Mademoiselle to be swallowed up by what she will later allude to, with awe and gusto, as *"le steppe."* There, in the limitless gloom, the changeable twinkle of remote village lights seems to her to be the yellow eyes of wolves. She is cold, she is frozen stiff, frozen "to the center of her brain"—for she soars with the wildest hyperbole when not tagging after the most pedestrian dictum. Every now and then, she looks back to make sure that a second sleigh, bearing her trunk and hatbox, is following—always at the same distance, like those companionable phantoms of ships in polar waters which explorers have described. And let me not leave out the moon—for surely there must be a moon, the full, incredibly clear disc that goes so well with Russian lusty frosts. So there it comes, steering out of a flock of small dappled clouds, which it tinges with a vague iridescence; and, as it sails higher, it glazes the runner tracks left on the road, where every sparkling lump of snow is emphasized by a swollen shadow.

Very lovely, very lonesome. But what am I doing in this stereoscopic dreamland? How did I get here? Somehow, the two sleighs have slipped away, leaving behind a passportless spy standing on the blue-white road in his New England snowboots and stormcoat. The vibration in my ears is no longer their receding bells, but only my old blood singing. All is still, spellbound, enthralled by the moon, fancy's rear-vision mirror. The snow is real, though, and as I bend to it and scoop up a handful, sixty years crumble to glittering frost-dust between my fingers.

2

A large, alabaster-based kerosene lamp is steered into the gloaming. Gently it floats and comes down; the hand of memory, now in a footman's white glove, places it in the center of a round table. The flame is nicely adjusted, and a rosy, silk-flounced lamp shade, with inset glimpses of rococo winter sports, crowns the readjusted (cotton wool in Casimir's ear) light. Revealed: a warm, bright stylish ("Russian Empire") drawing room in a snow-muffled house—soon to be termed *le château*—built by my mother's grandfather, who, being afraid of fires, had the staircase fashioned of iron, so that when the house did get burned to the ground, sometime after the Soviet Revolution, those fine-wrought steps, with the sky shining through their openwork risers, remained standing, all alone but still leading up.

Some more about that drawing room, please. The gleaming white moldings of the furniture, the embroidered roses of its upholstery. The white piano. The oval mirror. Hanging on taut cords, its pure brow inclined, it strives to retain the falling furniture and a slope of bright floor that keep slipping from its embrace. The chandelier pendants. These emit a delicate tinkling (things are being moved in the upstairs room where Mademoiselle will dwell). Colored pencils. Their detailed spectrum advertised on the box but never completely represented by those inside. We are sitting at a round table, my brother and I and Miss Robinson, who now and then looks at her watch: roads must be dreadful with all that snow; and anyway many professional hardships lie in wait for the vague French person who will replace her.

Now the colored pencils in action. The green one, by a mere whirl of the wrist, could be made to produce a ruffled tree, or the eddy left by a submerged crocodile. The blue one drew a simple line across the page—and the horizon of all seas was there. A nondescript blunt one kept getting into one's way. The brown one was always broken, and so was the red, but sometimes, just after it had snapped, one could still make it serve by holding it so that the loose tip was propped, none too securely, by a jutting splinter. The little purple fellow, a special favorite of mine, had got worn down so short as to become scarcely manageable. The white one alone, that lanky albino among pencils, kept its original length, or at least did so until I discovered that, far from being a fraud leaving no mark on the page, it was the ideal implement since I could imagine whatever I wished while I scrawled.

Alas, these pencils, too, have been distributed among the characters in my books to keep fictitious children busy; they are not quite my own now. Somewhere, in the apartment house of a chapter, in the hired room of a paragraph, I have also placed that tilted mirror, and the lamp, and the chandelier drops. Few things are left, many have been squandered. Have I given away Box I (son and husband of Loulou, the housekeeper's pet), that old brown dachshund fast asleep on the sofa? No, I think he is still mine. His grizzled muzzle, with the wart at the puckered corner of the mouth, is tucked into the curve of his hock, and from time to time a deep sigh distends his ribs. He is so old and his sleep is so thickly padded with dreams (about chewable slippers and a few last smells) that he does not stir when faint bells jingle outside. Then a pneumatic door heaves and clangs in the vestibule. She has come after all; I had so hoped she would not.

3

Another dog, the sweet-tempered sire of a ferocious family, a Great Dane not allowed in the house, played a pleasant part in an adventure that took place on one of the following days, if not the very day after. It so happened that my brother and I were left completely in charge of the newcomer. As I reconstitute it now, my mother had probably gone, with her maid and young Trainy, to St. Petersburg (a distance of some fifty miles) where my father was deeply involved in the grave political events of that winter. She was pregnant and very nervous. Miss Robinson, instead of staying to break in

Mademoiselle, had gone too—back to that ambassador's family, about which we had heard from her as much as they would about us. In order to prove that this was no way of treating us, I immediately formed the project of repeating the exciting performance of a year before when we escaped from poor Miss Hunt in Wiesbaden. This time the countryside all around was a wilderness of snow, and it is hard to imagine what exactly could have been the goal of the journey I planned. We had just returned from our first afternoon walk with Mademoiselle and I was seething with frustration and hatred. With a little prompting, I had meek Sergey share some of my anger. To keep up with an unfamiliar tongue (all we knew in the way of French were a few household phrases), and on top of it to be crossed in all our fond habits, was more than one could bear. The *bonne promenade* she had promised us had turned out to be a tedious stroll near the house where the snow had been cleared and the icy ground sprinkled with sand. She had had us wear things we never used to wear, even on the frostiest day—horrible gaiters and hoods that hampered our every movement. She had restrained us when I induced Sergey to explore the creamy, smooth swellings of snow that had been flower beds in summer. She had not allowed us to walk under the organ-pipelike system of huge icicles that hung from the eaves and gloriously burned in the low sun. And she had rejected as *ignoble* one of my favorite pastimes (devised by Miss Robinson)—lying prone on a little plush sledge with a bit of rope tied to its front and a hand in a leathern mitten pulling me along a snow-covered path, under white trees, and Sergey, not lying but sitting on a second sledge, upholstered in red plush, attached to the rear of my blue one, and the heels of two felt boots, right in front of my face, walking quite fast with toes slightly turned in, now this, now that sole skidding on a raw patch of ice. (The hand and the feet belonged to Dmitri, our oldest and shortest gardener, and the path was the avenue of oaklings which seems to have been the main artery of my infancy.)

I explained to my brother a wicked plan and persuaded him to accept it. As soon as we came back from that walk, we left Mademoiselle puffing on the steps of the vestibule and dashed indoors, giving her the impression that we were about to conceal ourselves in some remote room. Actually, we trotted on till we reached the other side of the house, and then, through a veranda, emerged into the garden again. The above-mentioned Great Dane was in the act of fussily adjusting himself to a nearby snowdrift, but while deciding which hindleg to lift, he noticed us and at once joined us at a joyful gallop.

The three of us followed a fairly easy trail and after plodding through deeper snow, reached the road that led to the village. Meanwhile the sun had set. Dusk came with uncanny suddenness. My brother declared he was cold and tired, but I urged him on and finally made him ride the dog (the only member of the party to be still enjoying himself). We had gone more than two miles, and the moon was fantastically shiny, and my brother, in perfect silence, had begun to fall, every now and then, from his mount when Dmitri with a lantern overtook us and led us home. "Giddy-eh, giddy-eh?" Mademoiselle was frantically shouting from the porch. I brushed past her without a word. My brother burst into tears, and gave himself up. The Great Dane, whose name was Turka, returned to his interrupted affairs in connection with serviceable and informative snowdrifts around the house.

4

In our childhood we know a lot about hands since they live and hover at the level of our stature; Mademoiselle's were unpleasant because of the froggy gloss on their tight skin besprinkled with brown ecchymotic spots. Before her time no stranger had ever stroked my face. Mademoiselle, as soon as she came, had taken me completely aback by patting my cheek in sign of spontaneous affection. All her mannerisms come back to me when I think of her hands. Her trick of peeling rather than sharpening a pencil, the point held toward her stupendous and sterile bosom swathed in green wool. The way she had of inserting her little finger into her ear and vibrating it very rapidly. The ritual observed every time she gave me a fresh copybook. Always panting a little, her mouth slightly open and emitting in quick succession a series of asthmatic puffs, she would open the copybook to make a margin in it; that is, she would sharply imprint a vertical line with her

thumbnail, fold in the edge of the page, press, release, smooth
it out with the heel of her hand, after which the book would
be briskly twisted around and placed before me ready for use.
A new pen followed; she would moisten the glistening nib
with susurrous lips before dipping it into the baptismal ink
font. Then, delighting in every limb of every limpid letter (especially so because the preceding copybook had ended in utter
sloppiness), with exquisite care I would inscribe the word
Dictée while Mademoiselle hunted through her collection of
spelling tests for a good, hard passage.

5

Meanwhile the setting has changed. The berimed tree and
the high snowdrift with its xanthic hole have been removed
by a silent property man. The summer afternoon is alive with
steep clouds breasting the blue. Eyed shadows move on the
garden paths. Presently, lessons are over and Mademoiselle is
reading to us on the veranda where the mats and plaited chairs
develop a spicy, biscuity smell in the heat. On the white window ledges, on the long window seats covered with faded
calico, the sun breaks into geometrical gems after passing
through rhomboids and squares of stained glass. This is the
time when Mademoiselle is at her very best.

What a number of volumes she read through to us on that
veranda! Her slender voice sped on and on, never weakening,
without the slightest hitch or hesitation, an admirable reading
machine wholly independent of her sick bronchial tubes. We
got it all: *Les Malheurs de Sophie, Le Tour du Monde en Quatre
Vingts Jours, Le Petit Chose, Les Misérables, Le Comte de Monte
Cristo*, many others. There she sat, distilling her reading voice
from the still prison of her person. Apart from the lips, one
of her chins, the smallest but true one, was the only mobile
detail of her Buddha-like bulk. The black-rimmed pince-nez
reflected eternity. Occasionally a fly would settle on her stern
forehead and its three wrinkles would instantly leap up all together like three runners over three hurdles. But nothing
whatever changed in the expression of her face—the face I so
often tried to depict in my sketchbook, for its impassive and
simple symmetry offered a far greater temptation to my

stealthy pencil than the bowl of flowers or the decoy duck on the table before me, which I was supposedly drawing.

Presently my attention would wander still farther, and it was then, perhaps, that the rare purity of her rhythmic voice accomplished its true purpose. I looked at a tree and the stir of its leaves borrowed that rhythm. Egor was pottering among the peonies. A wagtail took a few steps, stopped as if it had remembered something—and then walked on, enacting its name. Coming from nowhere, a Comma butterfly settled on the threshold, basked in the sun with its angular fulvous wings spread, suddenly closed them just to show the tiny initial chalked on their dark underside, and as suddenly darted away. But the most constant source of enchantment during those readings came from the harlequin pattern of colored panes inset in a whitewashed framework on either side of the veranda. The garden when viewed through these magic glasses grew strangely still and aloof. If one looked through blue glass, the sand turned to cinders while inky trees swam in a tropical sky. The yellow created an amber world infused with an extra strong brew of sunshine. The red made the foliage drip ruby dark upon a pink footpath. The green soaked greenery in a greener green. And when, after such richness, one turned to a small square of normal, savorless glass, with its lone mosquito or lame daddy longlegs, it was like taking a draught of water when one is not thirsty, and one saw a matter-of-fact white bench under familiar trees. But of all the windows this is the pane through which in later years parched nostalgia longed to peer.

Mademoiselle never found out how potent had been the even flow of her voice. The subsequent claims she put forward were quite different. "Ah," she sighed, "*comme on s'aimait*— didn't we love each other! Those good old days in the *château*! The dead wax doll we once buried under the oak! [No— a wool-stuffed Golliwogg.] And that time you and Serge ran away and left me stumbling and howling in the depths of the forest! [Exaggerated.] *Ah, la fessée que je vous ai flanquée*— My, what a spanking I gave you! [She did try to slap me once but the attempt was never repeated.] *Votre tante, la Princesse*, whom you struck with your little fist because she had been rude to me! [Do not remember.] And the way you whispered

to me your childish troubles! [Never!] And the nook in my
room where you loved to snuggle because you felt so warm
and secure!"

Mademoiselle's room, both in the country and in town, was
a weird place to me—a kind of hothouse sheltering a thick-
leaved plant imbued with a heavy, enuretic odor. Although
next to ours, when we were small, it did not seem to belong
to our pleasant, well-aired home. In that sickening mist, reek-
ing, among other woolier effluvia, of the brown smell of oxi-
dized apple peel, the lamp burned low, and strange objects
glimmered upon the writing desk: a lacquered box with lic-
orice sticks, black segments of which she would hack off with
her penknife and put to melt under her tongue; a picture postcard of a lake and a castle with mother-of-pearl spangles for
windows; a bumpy ball of tightly rolled bits of silver paper
that came from all those chocolates she used to consume at
night; photographs of the nephew who had died, of his
mother who had signed her picture *Mater Dolorosa*, and of a
certain Monsieur de Marante who had been forced by his family to marry a rich widow.

Lording it over the rest was one in a fancy frame incrusted
with garnets; it showed, in three-quarter view, a slim young
brunette clad in a close-fitting dress, with brave eyes and
abundant hair. "A braid as thick as my arm and reaching down
to my ankles!" was Mademoiselle's melodramatic comment.
For this had been she—but in vain did my eyes probe her
familiar form to try and extract the graceful creature it had
engulfed. Such discoveries as my awed brother and I did make
merely increased the difficulties of that task; and the grown-
ups who during the day beheld a densely clothed Mademoiselle never saw what we children saw when, roused from her
sleep by one of us shrieking himself out of a bad dream, disheveled, candle in hand, a gleam of gilt lace on the blood-
red dressing gown that could not quite wrap her quaking
mass, the ghastly Jézabel of Racine's absurd play stomped
barefooted into our bedroom.

All my life I have been a poor go-to-sleeper. People in
trains, who lay their newspaper aside, fold their silly arms, and
immediately, with an offensive familiarity of demeanor, start
snoring, amaze me as much as the uninhibited chap who

cozily defecates in the presence of a chatty tubber, or partic-
ipates in huge demonstrations, or joins some union in order
to dissolve in it. Sleep is the most moronic fraternity in the
world, with the heaviest dues and the crudest rituals. It is a
mental torture I find debasing. The strain and drain of composition often force me, alas, to swallow a strong pill that gives
me an hour or two of frightful nightmares or even to accept
the comic relief of a midday snooze, the way a senile rake
might totter to the nearest euthanasium; but I simply cannot
get used to the nightly betrayal of reason, humanity, genius.
No matter how great my weariness, the wrench of parting
with consciousness is unspeakably repulsive to me. I loathe
Somnus, that black-masked headsman binding me to the
block; and if in the course of years, with the approach of a far
more thorough and still more risible disintegration, which
nowanights, I confess, detracts much from the routine terrors of
sleep, I have grown so accustomed to my bedtime ordeal as
almost to swagger while the familiar ax is coming out of its
great velvet-lined double-bass case, initially I had no such
comfort or defense: I had nothing—except one token light in
the potentially refulgent chandelier of Mademoiselle's bedroom, whose door, by our family doctor's decree (I salute
you, Dr. Sokolov!), remained slightly ajar. Its vertical line of
lambency (which a child's tears could transform into dazzling
rays of compassion) was something I could cling to, since in
absolute darkness my head would swim and my mind melt in
a travesty of the death struggle.

Saturday night used to be or ought to have been a pleasurable prospect, because that was the night Mademoiselle,
who belonged to the classical school of hygiene and regarded
our *toquades anglaises* as merely a source of colds, indulged
in the perilous luxury of a weekly bath, thus granting a longer
lease to my tenuous gleam. But then a subtler torment set in.

We have moved now to our town house, an Italianate construction of Finnish granite, built by my grandfather circa 1885,
with floral frescoes above the third (upper) story and a second-
floor oriel, in St. Petersburg (now Leningrad), 47, Morskaya
(now Hertzen Street). The children occupied the third floor.
In 1908, the year selected here, I still shared a nursery with
my brother. The bathroom assigned to Mademoiselle was at

the end of a Z-shaped corridor some twenty heartbeats' distance from my bed, and between dreading her premature return from the bathroom to her lighted bedroom next to our
nursery and envying my brother's regular little wheeze behind
the japanned screen separating us, I could never really put my
additional time to profit by deftly getting to sleep while a
chink in the dark still bespoke a speck of myself in nothingness. At length they would come, those inexorable steps, plodding along the passage and causing some fragile glass object,
which had been secretly sharing my vigil, to vibrate in dismay
on its shelf.

Now she has entered her room. A brisk interchange of light
values tells me that the candle on her bed table takes over the
job of the ceiling cluster of bulbs, which, having run up with
a couple of clicks two additional steps of natural, and then
supernatural, brightness, clicks off altogether. My line of light
is still there, but it has grown old and wan, and flickers whenever Mademoiselle makes her bed creak by moving. For I still
hear her. Now it is a silvery rustle spelling "Suchard"; now
the trk-trk-trk of a fruit knife cutting the pages of *La Revue
des Deux Mondes*. A period of decline has started: she is reading Bourget. Not one word of his will survive him. Doom is
nigh. I am in acute distress, desperately trying to coax sleep,
opening my eyes every few seconds to check the faded gleam,
and imagining paradise as a place where a sleepless neighbor
reads an endless book by the light of an eternal candle.

The inevitable happens: the pince-nez case shuts with a
snap, the review shuffles onto the marble of the bed table, and
gustily Mademoiselle's pursed lips blow; the first attempt fails,
a groggy flame squirms and ducks; then comes a second lunge,
and light collapses. In that pitchy blackness I lose my bearings,
my bed seems to be slowly drifting, panic makes me sit up
and stare; finally my dark-adapted eyes sift out, among entop-
tic floaters, certain more precious blurrings that roam in aimless amnesia until, half-remembering, they settle down as the
dim folds of window curtains behind which street lights are
remotely alive.

How utterly foreign to the troubles of the night were those
exciting St. Petersburg mornings when the fierce and tender,
damp and dazzling arctic spring bundled away broken ice

down the sea-bright Neva! It made the roofs shine. It painted the slush in the streets a rich purplish-blue shade which I have never seen anywhere since. On those glorious days *on allait se promener en équipage*—the old-world expression current in our set. I can easily refeel the exhilarating change from the thickly padded, knee-length *polushubok*, with the hot beaver collar, to the short navy-blue coat with its anchor-patterned brass buttons. In the open landau I am joined by the valley of a lap rug to the occupants of the more interesting back seat, majestic Mademoiselle, and triumphant, tear-bedabbled Sergey, with whom I have just had a row at home. I am kicking him slightly, now and then, under our common cover, until Mademoiselle sternly tells me to stop. We drift past the show windows of Fabergé whose mineral monstrosities, jeweled troykas poised on marble ostrich eggs, and the like, highly appreciated by the imperial family, were emblems of grotesque garishness to ours. Church bells are ringing, the first Brimstone flies up over the Palace Arch, in another month we shall return to the country; and as I look up I can see, strung on ropes from housefront to housefront high above the street, great, tensely smooth, semitransparent banners billowing, their three wide bands—pale red, pale blue, and merely pale—deprived by the sun and the flying cloud-shadows of any too blunt connection with a national holiday, but undoubtedly celebrating now, in the city of memory, the essence of that spring day, the swish of the mud, the beginning of mumps, the ruffled exotic bird with one bloodshot eye on Mademoiselle's hat.

6

She spent seven years with us, lessons getting rarer and rarer and her temper worse and worse. Still, she seemed like a rock of grim permanence when compared to the ebb and flow of English governesses and Russian tutors passing through our large household. She was on bad terms with all of them. In summer seldom less than fifteen people sat down for meals and when, on birthdays, this number rose to thirty or more, the question of place at table became a particularly burning one for Mademoiselle. Uncles and aunts and cousins would arrive on such days from neighboring estates, and the village doctor would come in his dogcart, and the village schoolmaster would be heard blowing his nose in the cool hall, where he passed from mirror to mirror with a greenish, damp, creaking bouquet of lilies of the valley or a sky-colored, brittle one of cornflowers in his fist.

If Mademoiselle found herself seated too far at the end of the huge table, and especially if she lost precedence to a certain poor relative who was almost as fat as she (*"Je suis une sylphide à côté d'elle,"* Mademoiselle would say with a shrug of contempt), then her sense of injury caused her lips to twitch in a would-be ironical smile—and when a naïve neighbor would smile back, she would rapidly shake her head, as if coming out of some very deep meditation, with the remark: *"Excusez-moi, je souriais à mes tristes pensées."*

And as though nature had not wished to spare her anything that makes one supersensitive, she was hard of hearing. Sometimes at table we boys would suddenly become aware of two big tears crawling down Mademoiselle's ample cheeks. "Don't mind me," she would say in a small voice, and she kept on eating till the unwiped tears blinded her; then, with a heartbroken hiccough she would rise and blunder out of the dining room. Little by little the truth would come out. The general talk had turned, say, on the subject of the warship my uncle commanded, and she had perceived in this a sly dig at her Switzerland that had no navy. Or else it was because she fancied that whenever French was spoken, the game consisted in deliberately preventing her from directing and adorning the conversation. Poor lady, she was always in such a nervous hurry to seize control of intelligible table talk before it bolted back into Russian that no wonder she bungled her cue.

"And your Parliament, sir, how is it getting along?" she would suddenly burst out brightly from her end of the table, challenging my father, who, after a harassing day, was not exactly eager to discuss troubles of the state with a singularly unreal person who neither knew nor cared anything about them. Thinking that someone had referred to music, "But Silence, too, may be beautiful," she would bubble. "Why, one evening, in a desolate valley of the Alps, I actually *heard* Silence." Sallies like these, especially when growing deafness led her to answer questions none had put, resulted in a painful hush, instead of touching off the rockets of a sprightly *causerie.*

And, really, her French was so lovely! Ought one to have minded the shallowness of her culture, the bitterness of her temper, the banality of her mind, when that pearly language of hers purled and scintillated, as innocent of sense as the alliterative sins of Racine's pious verse? My father's library, not her limited lore, taught me to appreciate authentic poetry; nevertheless, something of her tongue's limpidity and luster has had a singularly bracing effect upon me, like those sparkling salts that are used to purify the blood. This is why it makes me so sad to imagine now the anguish Mademoiselle must have felt at seeing how lost, how little valued was the nightingale voice which came from her elephantine body. She stayed with us long, much too long, obstinately hoping for some miracle that would transform her into a kind of Madame de Rambouillet holding a gilt-and-satin *salon* of poets, princes and statesmen under her brilliant spell.

She would have gone on hoping had it not been for one Lenski, a young Russian tutor, with mild myopic eyes and strong political opinions, who had been engaged to coach us in various subjects and participate in our sports. He had had several predecessors, none of whom Mademoiselle had liked, but he, as she put it, was *"le comble."* While venerating my father, Lenski could not quite stomach certain aspects of our household, such as footmen and French, which last he considered an aristocratic convention of no use in a liberal's home. On the other hand, Mademoiselle decided that if Lenski answered her point-blank questions only with short grunts (which he tried to Germanize for want of a better language), it was not because he could not understand French, but because he wished to insult her in front of everybody.

I can hear and see Mademoiselle requesting him in dulcet tones, but with an ominous quiver of her upper lip, to pass her the bread; and, likewise, I can hear and see Lenski Frenchlessly and unflinchingly going on with his soup; finally, with a slashing *"Pardon, monsieur,"* Mademoiselle would swoop right across his plate, snatch up the breadbasket, and recoil again with a *"Merci!"* so charged with irony that Lenski's downy ears would turn the hue of geraniums. "The brute! The cad! The Nihilist!" she would sob later in her room—which was no longer next to ours though still on the same floor.

If Lenski happened to come tripping downstairs while, with an asthmatic pause every ten steps or so, she was working her way up (for the little hydraulic elevator of our house in St. Petersburg would constantly, and rather insultingly, refuse to function), Mademoiselle maintained that he had viciously bumped into her, pushed her, knocked her down, and we already could see him trampling her prostrate body. More and more frequently she would leave the table, and the dessert she would have missed was diplomatically sent up in her wake. From her remote room she would write a sixteen-page letter to my mother, who, upon hurrying upstairs, would find her dramatically packing her trunk. And then, one day, she was allowed to go on with her packing.

7

She returned to Switzerland. World War One came, then the Revolution. In the early twenties, long after our correspondence had fizzled out, by a fluke move of life in exile I chanced to visit Lausanne with a college friend of mine, so I thought I might as well look up Mademoiselle, if she were still alive.

She was. Stouter than ever, quite gray and almost totally deaf, she welcomed me with a tumultuous outburst of affection. Instead of the Château de Chillon picture, there was now one of a garish troika. She spoke as warmly of her life in Russia as if it were her own lost homeland. Indeed, I found in the neighborhood quite a colony of such old Swiss governesses. Huddled together in a constant seething of competitive reminiscences, they formed a small island in an environment that had grown alien to them. Mademoiselle's bosom friend was now mummy-like Mlle Golay, my mother's former governess, still prim and pessimistic at eighty-five; she had remained in our family long after my mother had married, and her return to Switzerland had preceded only by a couple of years that of Mademoiselle, with whom she had not been on speaking terms when both had been living under our roof. One is always at home in one's past, which partly explains those pathetic ladies' posthumous love for a remote and, to be perfectly frank, rather appalling country, which they never had really known and in which none of them had been very content.

As no conversation was possible because of Mademoiselle's deafness, my friend and I decided to bring her next day the appliance which we gathered she could not afford. She adjusted the clumsy thing improperly at first, but no sooner had she done so than she turned to me with a dazzled look of moist wonder and bliss in her eyes. She swore she could hear every word, every murmur of mine. She could not for, having my doubts, I had not spoken. If I had, I would have told her to thank my friend, who had paid for the instrument. Was it, then, silence she heard, that Alpine Silence she had talked about in the past? In that past, she had been lying to herself; now she was lying to me.

Before leaving for Basle and Berlin, I happened to be walking along the lake in the cold, misty night. At one spot a lone light dimly diluted the darkness and transformed the mist into a visible drizzle. *"Il pleut toujours en Suisse"* was one of those casual comments which, formerly, had made Mademoiselle weep. Below, a wide ripple, almost a wave, and something vaguely white attracted my eye. As I came quite close to the lapping water, I saw what it was—an aged swan, a large, uncouth, dodo-like creature, making ridiculous efforts to hoist himself into a moored boat. He could not do it. The heavy, impotent flapping of his wings, their slippery sound against the rocking and plashing boat, the gluey glistening of the dark swell where it caught the light—all seemed for a moment laden with that strange significance which sometimes in dreams is attached to a finger pressed to mute lips and then pointed at something the dreamer has no time to distinguish before waking with a start. But although I soon forgot that dismal night, it was, oddly enough, that night, that compound image—shudder and swan and swell—which first came to my mind when a couple of years later I learned that Mademoiselle had died.

She had spent all her life in feeling miserable; this misery was her native element; its fluctuations, its varying depths, alone gave her the impression of moving and living. What bothers me is that a sense of misery, and nothing else, is not enough to make a permanent soul. My enormous and morose Mademoiselle is all right on earth but impossible in eternity. Have I really salvaged her from fiction? Just before the rhythm I hear falters and fades, I catch myself wondering whether, during the years I knew her, I had not kept utterly missing something in her that was far more she than her chins or her ways or even her French—something perhaps akin to that last glimpse of her, to the radiant deceit she had used in order to have me depart pleased with my own kindness, or to that swan whose agony was so much closer to artistic truth than a drooping dancer's pale arms; something, in short, that I could appreciate only after the things and beings that I had most loved in the security of my childhood had been turned to ashes or shot through the heart.

There is an appendix to Mademoiselle's story. When I first wrote it I did not know about certain amazing survivals. Thus, in 1960, my London cousin Peter de Peterson told me that their English nanny, who had seemed old to me in 1904 in Abbazia, was by now over ninety and in good health; neither was I aware that the governess of my father's two youngest sisters, Mlle Bouvier (later Mme Conrad), survived my father by almost half a century. She had entered their household in 1889 and stayed six years, being the last in a series of governesses. A pretty little keepsake drawn in 1895 by Ivan de Peterson, Peter's father, shows various events of life at Batovo vignetted over an inscription in my father's hand: *A celle qui a toujours su se faire aimer et qui ne saura jamais se faire oublier;* signatures have been appended by four young male Nabokovs and three of their sisters, Natalia, Elizaveta, and Nadezhda, as well as by Natalia's husband, their little son Mitik, two girl cousins, and Ivan Aleksandrovich Tihotski, the Russian tutor. Sixty-five years later, in Geneva, my sister Elena discovered Mme Conrad, now in her tenth decade. The ancient lady, skipping one generation, naïvely mistook Elena for our mother, then a girl of eighteen, who used to drive up with Mlle Golay from Vyra to Batovo, in those distant times whose long light finds so many ingenious ways to reach me.

Six

O N A SUMMER MORNING, in the legendary Russia of my boyhood, my first glance upon awakening was for the chink between the white inner shutters. If it disclosed a watery pallor, one had better not open them at all, and so be spared the sight of a sullen day sitting for its picture in a puddle. How resentfully one would deduce, from a line of dull light, the leaden sky, the sodden sand, the gruel-like mess of broken brown blossoms under the lilacs—and that flat, fallow leaf (the first casualty of the season) pasted upon a wet garden bench!

But if the chink was a long glint of dewy brilliancy, then I made haste to have the window yield its treasure. With one blow, the room would be cleft into light and shade. The foliage of birches moving in the sun had the translucent green tone of grapes, and in contrast to this there was the dark velvet of fir trees against a blue of extraordinary intensity, the like of which I rediscovered only many years later, in the montane zone of Colorado.

From the age of seven, everything I felt in connection with a rectangle of framed sunlight was dominated by a single passion. If my first glance of the morning was for the sun, my first thought was for the butterflies it would engender. The original event had been banal enough. On the honeysuckle, overhanging the carved back of a bench just opposite the main entrance, my guiding angel (whose wings, except for the absence of a Florentine limbus, resemble those of Fra Angelico's Gabriel) pointed out to me a rare visitor, a splendid, pale-yellow creature with black blotches, blue crenels, and a cinnabar eyespot above each chrome-rimmed black tail. As it probed the inclined flower from which it hung, its powdery body slightly bent, it kept restlessly jerking its great wings, and my desire for it was one of the most intense I have ever experienced. Agile Ustin, our town-house janitor, who for a comic reason (explained elsewhere) happened to be that summer in the country with us, somehow managed to catch it in my cap, after which it was transferred, cap and all, to a wardrobe, where domestic naphthalene was fondly expected by

Mademoiselle to kill it overnight. On the following morning, however, when she unlocked the wardrobe to take something out, my Swallowtail, with a mighty rustle, flew into her face, then made for the open window, and presently was but a golden fleck dipping and dodging and soaring eastward, over timber and tundra, to Vologda, Viatka and Perm, and beyond the gaunt Ural range to Yakutsk and Verkhne Kolymsk, and from Verkhne Kolymsk, where it lost a tail, to the fair Island of St. Lawrence, and across Alaska to Dawson, and southward along the Rocky Mountains—to be finally overtaken and captured, after a forty-year race, on an immigrant dandelion under an endemic aspen near Boulder. In a letter from Mr. Brune to Mr. Rawlins, June 14, 1735, in the Bodleian collection, he states that one Mr. Vernon followed a butterfly nine miles before he could catch him (*The Recreative Review or Eccentricities of Literature and Life*, Vol. 1, p. 144, London, 1821).

Soon after the wardrobe affair I found a spectacular moth, marooned in a corner of a vestibule window, and my mother dispatched it with ether. In later years, I used many killing agents, but the least contact with the initial stuff would always cause the porch of the past to light up and attract that blundering beauty. Once, as a grown man, I was under ether during appendectomy, and with the vividness of a decalcomania picture I saw my own self in a sailor suit mounting a freshly emerged Emperor moth under the guidance of a Chinese lady who I knew was my mother. It was all there, brilliantly reproduced in my dream, while my own vitals were being exposed: the soaking, ice-cold absorbent cotton pressed to the insect's lemurian head; the subsiding spasms of its body; the satisfying crackle produced by the pin penetrating the hard crust of its thorax; the careful insertion of the point of the pin in the cork-bottomed groove of the spreading board; the symmetrical adjustment of the thick, strong-veined wings under neatly affixed strips of semitransparent paper.

2

I must have been eight when, in a storeroom of our country house, among all kinds of dusty objects, I discovered some wonderful books acquired in the days when my mother's mother had been interested in natural science and had had a famous university professor of zoology (Shimkevich) give private lessons to her daughter. Some of these books were mere curios, such as the four huge brown folios of Albertus Seba's work (*Locupletissimi Rerum Naturalium Thesauri Accurata Descriptio . . .*), printed in Amsterdam around 1750. On their coarse-grained pages I found woodcuts of serpents and butterflies and embryos. The fetus of an Ethiopian female child hanging by the neck in a glass jar used to give me a nasty shock every time I came across it; nor did I much care for the stuffed hydra on plate CII, with its seven lion-toothed turtle-heads on seven serpentine necks and its strange, bloated body which bore buttonlike tubercules along the sides and ended in a knotted tail.

Other books I found in that attic, among herbariums full of alpine columbines, and blue palemoniums, and Jove's campions, and orange-red lilies, and other Davos flowers, came closer to my subject. I took in my arms and carried downstairs glorious loads of fantastically attractive volumes: Maria Sibylla Merian's (1647–1717) lovely plates of Surinam insects, and Esper's noble *Die Schmetterlinge* (Erlangen, 1777), and Boisduval's *Icones Historiques de Lépidoptères Nouveaux ou Peu Connus* (Paris, begun in 1832). Still more exciting were the products of the latter half of the century—Newman's *Natural History of British Butterflies and Moths*, Hofmann's *Die Gross-Schmetterlinge Europas*, the Grand Duke Nikolay Mihailovich's *Mémoires* on Asiatic lepidoptera (with incomparably beautiful figures painted by Kavrigin, Rybakov, Lang), Scudder's stupendous work on the *Butterflies of New England*.

Retrospectively, the summer of 1905, though quite vivid in many ways, is not animated yet by a single bit of quick flutter or colored fluff around or across the walks with the village schoolmaster: the Swallowtail of June, 1906, was still in the larval stage on a roadside umbellifer; but in the course of that month I became acquainted with a score or so of common things, and Mademoiselle was already referring to a certain forest road that culminated in a marshy meadow full of Small Pearl-bordered Fritillaries (thus called in my first unforgettable and unfadingly magical little manual, Richard South's *The*

Butterflies of the British Isles which had just come out at the time) as *le chemin des papillons bruns*. The following year I became aware that many of our butterflies and moths did not occur in England or Central Europe, and more complete atlases helped me to determine them. A severe illness (pneumonia, with fever up to 41° centigrade), in the beginning of 1907, mysteriously abolished the rather monstrous gift of numbers that had made of me a child prodigy during a few months (today I cannot multiply 13 by 17 without pencil and paper; I can add them up, though, in a trice, the teeth of the three fitting in neatly); but the butterflies survived. My mother accumulated a library and a museum around my bed, and the longing to describe a new species completely replaced that of discovering a new prime number. A trip to Biarritz, in August 1907, added new wonders (though not as lucid and numerous as they were to be in 1909). By 1908, I had gained absolute control over the European lepidoptera as known to Hofmann. By 1910, I had dreamed my way through the first volumes of Seitz's prodigious picture book *Die Gross-Schmetterlinge der Erde*, had purchased a number of rarities recently described, and was voraciously reading entomological periodicals, especially English and Russian ones. Great upheavals were taking place in the development of systematics. Since the middle of the century, Continental lepidopterology had been, on the whole, a simple and stable affair, smoothly run by the Germans. Its high priest, Dr. Staudinger, was also the head of the largest firm of insect dealers. Even now, half a century after his death, German lepidopterists have not quite managed to shake off the hypnotic spell occasioned by his authority. He was still alive when his school began to lose ground as a scientific force in the world. While he and his followers stuck to specific and generic names sanctioned by long usage and were content to classify butterflies by characters visible to the naked eye, English-speaking authors were introducing nomenclatorial changes as a result of a strict application of the law of priority and taxonomic changes based on the microscopic study of organs. The Germans did their best to ignore the new trends and continued to cherish the philately-like side of entomology. Their solicitude for the "average collector who should not be made to dissect" is comparable to the way

My brother Sergey and I, aged one and two, respectively (and looking like the same infant, wigless and wigged), in December 1901, in Biarritz. We had, I suppose, come there from Pau where we were living that winter. A shining wet roof—that is all I remember from that first trip to the South of France. It was followed by other trips, two to Biarritz (autumn 1907 and 1909) and two to the Riviera (late autumn 1903 and early summer 1904).

My father, aged thirty-five, with me aged seven, St. Petersburg, 1906.

nervous publishers of popular novels pamper the "average reader"—who should not be made to think.

There was another more general change, which coincided with my ardent adolescent interest in butterflies and moths. The Victorian and Staudingerian kind of species, hermetic and homogeneous, with sundry (alpine, polar, insular, etc.) "varieties" affixed to it from the outside, as it were, like incidental appendages, was replaced by a new, multiform and fluid kind of species, organically *consisting* of geographical races or subspecies. The evolutionary aspects of the case were thus brought out more clearly, by means of more flexible methods of classification, and further links between butterflies and the central problems of nature were provided by biological investigations.

The mysteries of mimicry had a special attraction for me. Its phenomena showed an artistic perfection usually associated with man-wrought things. Consider the imitation of oozing poison by bubblelike macules on a wing (complete with pseudo-refraction) or by glossy yellow knobs on a chrysalis ("Don't eat me—I have already been squashed, sampled and rejected"). Consider the tricks of an acrobatic caterpillar (of the Lobster Moth) which in infancy looks like bird's dung, but after molting develops scrabbly hymenopteroid appendages and baroque characteristics, allowing the extraordinary fellow to play two parts at once (like the actor in Oriental shows who *becomes* a pair of intertwisted wrestlers): that of a writhing larva and that of a big ant seemingly harrowing it. When a certain moth resembles a certain wasp in shape and color, it also walks and moves its antennae in a waspish, unmothlike manner. When a butterfly has to look like a leaf, not only are all the details of a leaf beautifully rendered but markings mimicking grub-bored holes are generously thrown in. "Natural selection," in the Darwinian sense, could not explain the miraculous coincidence of imitative aspect and imitative behavior, nor could one appeal to the theory of "the struggle for life" when a protective device was carried to a point of mimetic subtlety, exuberance, and luxury far in excess of a predator's power of appreciation. I discovered in nature the nonutilitarian delights that I sought in art. Both were a form of magic, both were a game of intricate enchantment and deception.

3

I have hunted butterflies in various climes and disguises: as a pretty boy in knickerbockers and sailor cap; as a lanky cosmopolitan expatriate in flannel bags and beret; as a fat hatless old man in shorts. Most of my cabinets have shared the fate of our Vyra house. Those in our town house and the small addendum I left in the Yalta Museum have been destroyed, no doubt, by carpet beetles and other pests. A collection of South European stuff that I started in exile vanished in Paris during World War Two. All my American captures from 1940 to 1960 (several thousands of specimens including great rarities and types) are in the Mus. of Comp. Zoology, the Am. Nat. Hist. Mus., and the Cornell Univ. Mus. of Entomology, where they are safer than they would be in Tomsk or Atomsk. Incredibly happy memories, quite comparable, in fact, to those of my Russian boyhood, are associated with my research work at the MCZ, Cambridge, Mass. (1941–1948). No less happy have been the many collecting trips taken almost every summer, during twenty years, through most of the states of my adopted country.

In Jackson Hole and in the Grand Canyon, on the mountain slopes above Telluride, Colo., and on a celebrated pine barren near Albany, N.Y., dwell, and will dwell, in generations more numerous than editions, the butterflies I have described as new. Several of my finds have been dealt with by other workers; some have been named after me. One of these, Nabokov's Pug (*Eupithecia nabokovi* McDunnough), which I boxed one night in 1943 on a picture window of James Laughlin's Alta Lodge in Utah, fits most philosophically into the thematic spiral that began in a wood on the Oredezh around 1910—or perhaps even earlier, on that Nova Zemblan river a century and a half ago.

Few things indeed have I known in the way of emotion or appetite, ambition or achievement, that could surpass in richness and strength the excitement of entomological exploration. From the very first it had a great many intertwinkling facets. One of them was the acute desire to be alone, since any companion, no matter how quiet, interfered with the concentrated enjoyment of my mania. Its gratification admitted of no compromise or exception. Already when I was ten, tutors and governesses knew that the morning was mine and cautiously kept away.

In this connection, I remember the visit of a schoolmate, a boy of whom I was very fond and with whom I had excellent fun. He arrived one summer night—in 1913, I think—from a town some twenty-five miles away. His father had recently perished in an accident, the family was ruined and the stout-hearted lad, not being able to afford the price of a railway ticket, had bicycled all those miles to spend a few days with me.

On the morning following his arrival, I did everything I could to get out of the house for my morning hike without his knowing where I had gone. Breakfastless, with hysterical haste, I gathered my net, pill boxes, killing jar, and escaped through the window. Once in the forest, I was safe; but still I walked on, my calves quaking, my eyes full of scalding tears, the whole of me twitching with shame and self-disgust, as I visualized my poor friend, with his long pale face and black tie, moping in the hot garden—patting the panting dogs for want of something better to do, and trying hard to justify my absence to himself.

Let me look at my demon objectively. With the exception of my parents, no one really understood my obsession, and it was many years before I met a fellow sufferer. One of the first things I learned was not to depend on others for the growth of my collection. One summer afternoon, in 1911, Mademoiselle came into my room, book in hand, started to say she wanted to show me how wittily Rousseau denounced zoology (in favor of botany), and by then was too far gone in the gravitational process of lowering her bulk into an armchair to be stopped by my howl of anguish: on that seat I had happened to leave a glass-lidded cabinet tray with long, lovely series of the Large White. Her first reaction was one of stung vanity: her weight, surely, could not be accused of damaging what in fact it had demolished; her second was to console me: *Allons donc, ce ne sont que des papillons de potager!*—which only made matters worse. A Sicilian pair recently purchased from Staudinger had been crushed and bruised. A huge Biarritz example was utterly mangled. Smashed, too, were some of my choicest local captures. Of these, an aberration resembling the Canarian race of the species might have been mended with a few drops of glue; but a precious gynandromorph, left side male, right side female, whose abdomen could not be traced and whose wings had come off, was lost forever: one might reattach the wings but one could not prove that all four belonged to that headless thorax on its bent pin. Next morning, with an air of great mystery, poor Mademoiselle set off for St. Petersburg and came back in the evening bringing me ("something better than your cabbage butterflies") a banal Urania moth mounted on plaster. "How you hugged me, how you danced with joy!" she exclaimed ten years later in the course of inventing a brand-new past.

Our country doctor, with whom I had left the pupae of a rare moth when I went on a journey abroad, wrote me that everything had hatched finely; but in reality a mouse had got at the precious pupae, and upon my return the deceitful old man produced some common Tortoiseshell butterflies, which, I presume, he had hurriedly caught in his garden and popped into the breeding cage as a plausible substitutes (so *he* thought). Better than he, was an enthusiastic kitchen boy who would sometimes borrow my equipment and come back two hours later in triumph with a bagful of seething invertebrate life and several additional items. Loosening the mouth of the net which he had tied up with a string, he would pour out his cornucopian spoil—a mass of grasshoppers, some sand, the two parts of a mushroom he had thriftily plucked on the way home, more grasshoppers, more sand, and one battered Small White.

In the works of major Russian poets I can discover only two lepidopteral images of genuinely sensuous quality: Bunin's impeccable evocation of what is certainly a Tortoiseshell:

> And there will fly into the room
> A colored butterfly in silk
> To flutter, rustle and pit-pat
> On the blue ceiling . . .

and Fet's "Butterfly" soliloquizing:

Whence have I come and whither am I hasting
Do not inquire;
Now on a graceful flower I have settled
And now respire.

In French poetry one is struck by Musset's well-known lines (in *Le Saule*):

Le phalène doré dans sa course légère
Traverse les prés embaumés

which is an absolutely exact description of the crepuscular flight of the male of the geometrid called in England the Orange moth; and there is Fargue's fascinatingly apt phrase (in *Les Quatres Journées*) about a garden which, at nightfall, *se glace de bleu comme l'aile du grand Sylvain* (the Poplar Admirable). And among the very few genuine lepidopterological images in English poetry, my favorite is Browning's

On our other side is the straight-up rock;
And a path is kept 'twixt the gorge and it
By boulder-stones where lichens mock
The marks on a moth, and small ferns fit
Their teeth to the polished block
                    ("By the Fire-side")

It is astounding how little the ordinary person notices butterflies. "None," calmly replied that sturdy Swiss hiker with Camus in his rucksack when purposely asked by me for the benefit of my incredulous companion if he had seen any butterflies while descending the trail where, a moment before, you and I had been delighting in swarms of them. It is also true that when I call up the image of a particular path remembered in minute detail but pertaining to a summer before that of 1906, preceding, that is, the date on my first locality label, and never revisited, I fail to make out one wing, one wingbeat, one azure flash, one moth-gemmed flower, as if an evil spell had been cast on the Adriatic coast making all its "leps" (as the slangier among us say) invisible. Exactly thus an entomologist may feel some day when plodding beside a jubilant, and already helmetless botanist amid the hideous flora of a parallel planet, with not a single insect in sight; and thus (in odd proof of the odd fact that whenever possible the scenery of our infancy is used by an economically minded producer as a ready-made setting for our adult dreams) the seaside hilltop of a certain recurrent nightmare of mine, whereinto I smuggle a collapsible net from my waking state, is gay with thyme and melilot, but incomprehensibly devoid of all the butterflies that should be there.

I also found out very soon that a "lepist" indulging in his quiet quest was apt to provoke strange reactions in other creatures. How often, when a picnic had been arranged, and I would be self-consciously trying to get my humble implements unnoticed into the tar-smelling charabanc (a tar preparation was used to keep flies away from the horses) or the tea-smelling Opel convertible (benzine forty years ago smelled that way), some cousin or aunt of mine would remark: "Must you *really* take that net with you? Can't you enjoy yourself like a normal boy? Don't you think you are spoiling everybody's pleasure?" Near a sign NACH BODENLAUBE, at Bad Kissingen, Bavaria, just as I was about to join for a long walk my father and majestic old Muromtsev (who, four years before, in 1906, had been President of the first Russian Parliament), the latter turned his marble head toward me, a vulnerable boy of eleven, and said with his famous solemnity: "Come with us by all means, but do not chase butterflies, child. It spoils the rhythm of the walk." On a path above the Black Sea, in the Crimea, among shrubs in waxy bloom, in March 1918, a bow-legged Bolshevik sentry attempted to arrest me for signaling (with my net, he said) to a British warship. In the summer of 1929, every time I walked through a village in the Eastern Pyrenees, and happened to look back, I would see in my wake the villagers frozen in the various attitudes my passage had caught them in, as if I were Sodom and they Lot's wife. A decade later, in the Maritime Alps, I once noticed the grass undulate in a serpentine way behind me because a fat rural policeman was wriggling after me on his belly to find out if I were not trapping songbirds. America has shown even more of this morbid interest in my retiary activities than other countries have—perhaps because I was in my forties when I came there to live, and the older the man, the queerer he looks with a butterfly net in his hand. Stern farmers have drawn my attention to NO FISHING signs; from cars passing me on the highway have come wild howls of derision; sleepy dogs, though unmindful of the worst bum, have perked up and come at me, snarling; tiny tots have pointed me out to their puzzled mamas; broad-minded vacationists have asked me whether I was catching bugs for bait; and one morning on a wasteland, lit by tall yuccas in bloom, near Santa Fe, a big black mare followed me for more than a mile.

4

When, having shaken off all pursuers, I took the rough, red road that ran from our Vyra house toward field and forest, the animation and luster of the day seemed like a tremor of sympathy around me.

Very fresh, very dark Arran Browns, which emerged only every second year (conveniently, retrospection has fallen here into line), flitted among the firs or revealed their red markings and checkered fringes as they sunned themselves on the roadside bracken. Hopping above the grass, a diminutive Ringlet called Hero dodged my net. Several moths, too, were flying—gaudy sun lovers that sail from flower to flower like painted flies, or male insomniacs in search of hidden females, such as that rust-colored Oak Eggar hurtling across the shrubbery. I noticed (one of the major mysteries of my childhood) a soft pale green wing caught in a spider's web (by then I knew what it was: part of a Large Emerald). The tremendous larva of the Goat Moth, ostentatiously segmented, flat-headed, flesh-colored and glossily flushed, a strange creature "as naked as a worm" to use a French comparison, crossed my path in frantic search for a place to pupate (the awful pressure of metamorphosis, the aura of a disgraceful fit in a public place). On the bark of that birch tree, the stout one near the park wicket, I had found last spring a dark aberration of Sievers' Carmelite (just another gray moth to the reader). In the ditch, under the bridgelet, a bright-yellow Silvius Skipper hobnobbed with a dragonfly (just a blue libellula to me). From a flower head two male Coppers rose to a tremendous height, fighting all the way up—and then, after a while, came the downward flash of one of them returning to his thistle. These were familiar insects, but at any moment something better might cause me to stop with a quick intake of breath. I remember one day when I warily brought my net closer and closer to an uncommon Hairstreak that had daintily settled on a sprig. I could clearly see the white W on its chocolate-brown underside. Its wings were closed and the inferior ones were rubbing against each other in a curious circular motion—possibly producing some small, blithe crepitation pitched too high for a human ear to catch. I had long wanted that particular species, and, when near enough, I struck. You have heard champion tennis players moan after muffing an easy shot. You may have seen the face of the world-famous grandmaster Wilhelm Edmundson when, during a simultaneous display in a Minsk café, he lost his rook, by an absurd oversight, to the local amateur and pediatrician, Dr. Schach, who eventually won. But that day nobody (except my older self) could see me shake out a piece of twig from an otherwise empty net and stare at a hole in the tarlatan.

5

Near the intersection of two carriage roads (one, well-kept, running north-south in between our "old" and "new" parks, and the other, muddy and rutty, leading, if you turned west, to Batovo) at a spot where aspens crowded on both sides of a dip, I would be sure to find in the third week of June great blue-black nymphalids striped with pure white, gliding and wheeling low above the rich clay which matched the tint of their undersides when they settled and closed their wings. Those were the dung-loving males of what the old Aurelians used to call the Poplar Admirable, or, more exactly, they belonged to its Bucovinan subspecies. As a boy of nine, not knowing that race, I noticed how much our North Russian specimens differed from the Central European form figured in Hofmann, and rashly wrote to Kuznetsov, one of the greatest Russian, or indeed world, lepidopterists of all time, naming my new subspecies *"Limenitis populi rossica."* A long month later he returned my description and aquarelle of "*rossica* Nabokov" with only two words scribbled on the back of my letter: "*bucovinensis* Hormuzaki." How I hated Hormuzaki! And how hurt I was when in one of Kuznetsov's later

A family group taken in our garden at Vyra by a St. Petersburg photographer in August 1908, between my father's recent return from prison and his departure on the following day, with my mother, for Stresa. The round thing on the tree trunk is an archery target. My mother has placed photophobic Trainy upon the iron table mentioned in connection with mushrooms in Chapter 2. My paternal grandmother is holding, in a decorative but precarious cluster, my two little sisters whom she never held in real life: Olga on her knee, Elena against her shoulder. The dark depth of the oldest part of our park provides the background. The lady in black is my mother's maternal aunt, Praskovia Nikolaevna Tarnovski, born Kozlov (1848–1910), who was to look after us and our mentors during our parents' trip to Italy. My brother Sergey is linked to her left elbow; her other hand supports me. I am perched on the bench arm, hating my collar and Stresa.

papers I found a gruff reference to "schoolboys who keep naming minute varieties of the Poplar Nymph!" Undaunted, however, by the *populi* flop, I "discovered" the following year a "new" moth. That summer I had been collecting assiduously on moonless nights, in a glade of the park, by spreading a bedsheet over the grass and its annoyed glowworms, and casting upon it the light of an acytelene lamp (which, six years later, was to shine on Tamara). Into that arena of radiance, moths would come drifting out of the solid blackness around me, and it was in that manner, upon that magic sheet, that I took a beautiful *Plusia* (now *Phytometra*) which, as I saw at once, differed from its closest ally by its mauve-and-maroon (instead of golden-brown) forewings, and narrower bractea mark and was not recognizably figured in any of my books. I sent its description and picture to Richard South, for publication in *The Entomologist.* He did not know it either, but with the utmost kindness checked it in the British Museum collection—and found it had been described long ago as *Plusia excelsa* by Kretschmar. I received the sad news, which was most sympathetically worded (". . . should be congratulated for obtaining . . . very rare Volgan thing . . . admirable figure . . .") with the utmost stoicism; but many years later, by a pretty fluke (I know I should not point out these plums to people), I got even with the first discoverer of *my* moth by giving his own name to a blind man in a novel.

Let me also evoke the hawkmoths, the jets of my boyhood! Colors would die a long death on June evenings. The lilac shrubs in full bloom before which I stood, net in hand, displayed clusters of a fluffy gray in the dusk—the ghost of purple. A moist young moon hung above the mist of a neighboring meadow. In many a garden have I stood thus in later years—in Athens, Antibes, Atlanta—but never have I waited with such a keen desire as before those darkening lilacs. And suddenly it would come, the low buzz passing from flower to flower, the vibrational halo around the streamlined body of an olive and pink Hummingbird moth poised in the air above the corolla into which it had dipped its long tongue. Its handsome black larva (resembling a diminutive cobra when it puffed out its ocellated front segments) could be found on dank willow herb two months later. Thus every hour and sea-

son had its delights. And, finally, on cold, or even frosty, autumn nights, one could sugar for moths by painting tree
trunks with a mixture of molasses, beer, and rum. Through
the gusty blackness, one's lantern would illumine the stickily
glistening furrows of the bark and two or three large moths
upon it imbibing the sweets, their nervous wings half open
butterfly fashion, the lower ones exhibiting their incredible
crimson silk from beneath the lichen-gray primaries. *"Cato-
cala adultera!"* I would triumphantly shriek in the direction
of the lighted windows of the house as I stumbled home to
show my captures to my father.

6

The "English" park that separated our house from the hayfields was an extensive and elaborate affair with labyrinthine
paths, Turgenevian benches, and imported oaks among the
endemic firs and birches. The struggle that had gone on since
my grandfather's time to keep the park from reverting to the
wild state always fell short of complete success. No gardener
could cope with the hillocks of frizzly black earth that the pink
hands of moles kept heaping on the tidy sand of the main
walk. Weeds and fungi, and ridgelike tree roots crossed and
recrossed the sun-flecked trails. Bears had been eliminated in
the eighties, but an occasional moose still visited the grounds.
On a picturesque boulder, a little mountain ash and a still
smaller aspen had climbed, holding hands, like two clumsy,
shy children. Other, more elusive trespassers—lost picnickers
or merry villagers—would drive our hoary gamekeeper Ivan
crazy by scrawling ribald words on the benches and gates. The
disintegrating process continues still, in a different sense, for
when, nowadays, I attempt to follow in memory the winding
paths from one given point to another, I notice with alarm
that there are many gaps, due to oblivion or ignorance, akin
to the terra-incognita blanks map makers of old used to call
"sleeping beauties."

Beyond the park, there were fields, with a continuous shimmer of butterfly wings over a shimmer of flowers—daisies,
bluebells, scabious, and others—which now rapidly pass by me
in a kind of colored haze like those lovely, lush meadows,

never to be explored, that one sees from the diner on a transcontinental journey. At the end of this grassy wonderland, the forest rose like a wall. There I roamed, scanning the tree trunks (the enchanted, the silent part of a tree) for certain tiny moths, called Pugs in England—delicate little creatures that cling in the daytime to speckled surfaces, with which their flat wings and turned-up abdomens blend. There, at the bottom of that sea of sunshot greenery, I slowly spun round the great boles. Nothing in the world would have seemed sweeter to me than to be able to add, by a stroke of luck, some remarkable new species to the long list of Pugs already named by others. And my pied imagination, ostensibly, and almost grotesquely, groveling to my desire (but all the time, in ghostly conspiracies behind the scenes, coolly planning the most distant events of my destiny), kept providing me with hallucinatory samples of small print: ". . . the only specimen so far known . . ." ". . . the only specimen known of *Eupithecia petropolitanata* was taken by a Russian schoolboy . . ." ". . . by a young Russian collector . . ." ". . . by myself in the Government of St. Petersburg, Tsarskoe Selo District, in 1910 . . . 1911 . . . 1912 . . . 1913 . . ." And then, thirty years later, that blessed black night in the Wasatch Range.

At first—when I was, say, eight or nine—I seldom roamed farther than the fields and woods between Vyra and Batovo. Later, when aiming at a particular spot half-a-dozen miles or more distant, I would use a bicycle to get there with my net strapped to the frame; but not many forest paths were passable on wheels; it was possible to ride there on horseback, of course, but, because of our ferocious Russian tabanids, one could not leave a horse haltered in a wood for any length of time: my spirited bay almost climbed up the tree it was tied to one day trying to elude them: big fellows with watered-silk eyes and tiger bodies, and gray little runts with an even more painful proboscis, but much more sluggish: to dispatch two or three of these dingy tipplers with one crush of the gloved hand as they glued themselves to the neck of my mount afforded me a wonderful empathic relief (which a dipterist might not appreciate). Anyway, on my butterfly hunts I always preferred hiking to any other form of locomotion (except, naturally, a flying seat gliding leisurely over the plant mats and

rocks of an unexplored mountain, or hovering just above the
flowery roof of a rain forest); for when you walk, especially in
a region you have studied well, there is an exquisite pleasure
in departing from one's itinerary to visit, here and there by
the wayside, this glade, that glen, this or that combination of
soil and flora—to drop in, as it were, on a familiar butterfly
in his particular habitat, in order to see if he has emerged, and
if so, how he is doing.

There came a July day—around 1910, I suppose—when I
felt the urge to explore the vast marshland beyond the Oredezh. After skirting the river for three or four miles, I found
a rickety footbridge. While crossing over, I could see the huts
of a hamlet on my left, apple trees, rows of tawny pine logs
lying on a green bank, and the bright patches made on the
turf by the scattered clothes of peasant girls, who, stark naked
in shallow water, romped and yelled, heeding me as little as
if I were the discarnate carrier of my present reminiscences.

On the other side of the river, a dense crowd of small,
bright blue male butterflies that had been tippling on the rich,
trampled mud and cow dung through which I trudged rose
all together into the spangled air and settled again as soon as
I had passed.

After making my way through some pine groves and alder
scrub I came to the bog. No sooner had my ear caught the
hum of diptera around me, the guttural cry of a snipe overhead, the gulping sound of the morass under my foot, than I
knew I would find here quite special arctic butterflies, whose
pictures, or, still better, nonillustrated descriptions I had wor-
shiped for several seasons. And the next moment I was among
them. Over the small shrubs of bog bilberry with fruit of a
dim, dreamy blue, over the brown eye of stagnant water, over
moss and mire, over the flower spikes of the fragrant bog
orchid (the *nochnaya fialka* of Russian poets), a dusky little
Fritillary bearing the name of a Norse goddess passed in low,
skimming flight. Pretty Cordigera, a gemlike moth, buzzed all
over its uliginose food plant. I pursued rose-margined Sul-
phurs, gray-marbled Satyrs. Unmindful of the mosquitoes that
furred my forearms, I stooped with a grunt of delight to snuff
out the life of some silver-studded lepidopteron throbbing in
the folds of my net. Through the smells of the bog, I caught

the subtle perfume of butterfly wings on my fingers, a perfume which varies with the species—vanilla, or lemon, or musk, or a musty, sweetish odor difficult to define. Still unsated, I pressed forward. At last I saw I had come to the end of the marsh. The rising ground beyond was a paradise of lupines, columbines, and pentstemons. Mariposa lilies bloomed under Ponderosa pines. In the distance, fleeting cloud shadows dappled the dull green of slopes above timber line, and the gray and white of Longs Peak.

I confess I do not believe in time. I like to fold my magic carpet, after use, in such a way as to superimpose one part of the pattern upon another. Let visitors trip. And the highest enjoyment of timelessness—in a landscape selected at random—is when I stand among rare butterflies and their food plants. This is ecstasy, and behind the ecstasy is something else, which is hard to explain. It is like a momentary vacuum into which rushes all that I love. A sense of oneness with sun and stone. A thrill of gratitude to whom it may concern—to the contrapuntal genius of human fate or to tender ghosts humoring a lucky mortal.

Seven

IN THE EARLY YEARS of this century, a travel agency on Nevski Avenue displayed a three-foot-long model of an oak-brown international sleeping car. In delicate verisimilitude it completely outranked the painted tin of my clockwork trains. Unfortunately it was not for sale. One could make out the blue upholstery inside, the embossed leather lining of the compartment walls, their polished panels, inset mirrors, tulip-shaped reading lamps, and other maddening details. Spacious windows alternated with narrower ones, single or geminate, and some of these were of frosted glass. In a few of the compartments, the beds had been made.

The then great and glamorous Nord-Express (it was never the same after World War One when its elegant brown became a nouveau-riche blue), consisting solely of such international cars and running but twice a week, connected St. Petersburg with Paris. I would have said: directly with Paris, had passengers not been obliged to change from one train to a superficially similar one at the Russo-German frontier (Verzhbolovo-Eydtkuhnen), where the ample and lazy Russian sixty-and-a-half-inch gauge was replaced by the fifty-six-and-a-half-inch standard of Europe and coal succeeded birch logs.

In the far end of my mind I can unravel, I think, at least five such journeys to Paris, with the Riviera or Biarritz as their ultimate destination. In 1909, the year I now single out, our party consisted of eleven people and one dachshund. Wearing gloves and a traveling cap, my father sat reading a book in the compartment he shared with our tutor. My brother and I were separated from them by a washroom. My mother and her maid Natasha occupied a compartment adjacent to ours. Next came my two small sisters, their English governess, Miss Lavington (later governess of the Tsar's children), and a Russian nurse. The odd one of our party, my father's valet, Osip (whom a decade later, the pedantic Bolsheviks were to shoot, because he appropriated our bicycles instead of turning them over to the nation), had a stranger for companion (Féaudi, a well-known French actor).

Historically and artistically, the year had started with a political cartoon in *Punch*: goddess England bending over goddess Italy, on whose head one of Messina's bricks has landed—probably, the worst picture *any* earthquake has ever inspired. In April of that year, Peary had reached the North Pole. In May, Shalyapin had sung in Paris. In June, bothered by rumors of new and better Zeppelins, the United States War Department had told reporters of plans for an aerial Navy. In July, Blériot had flown from Calais to Dover (with a little additional loop when he lost his bearings). It was late August now. The firs and marshes of Northwestern Russia sped by, and on the following day gave way to German pinewoods and heather.

At a collapsible table, my mother and I played a card game called *durachki*. Although it was still broad daylight, our cards, a glass and, on a different plane, the locks of a suitcase were reflected in the window. Through forest and field, and in sudden ravines, and among scuttling cottages, those discarnate gamblers kept steadily playing on for steadily sparkling stakes. It was a long, very long game: on this gray winter morning, in the looking glass of my bright hotel room, I see shining the same, the very same, locks of that now seventy-year-old valise, a highish, heavyish *nécessaire de voyage* of pigskin, with "H.N." elaborately interwoven in thick silver under a similar coronet, which had been bought in 1897 for my mother's wedding trip to Florence. In 1917 it transported from St. Petersburg to the Crimea and then to London a handful of jewels. Around 1930, it lost to a pawnbroker its expensive receptacles of crystal and silver leaving empty the cunningly contrived leathern holders on the inside of the lid. But that loss has been amply recouped during the thirty years it then traveled with me—from Prague to Paris, from St. Nazaire to New York and through the mirrors of more than two hundred motel rooms and rented houses, in forty-six states. The fact that of our Russian heritage the hardiest survivor proved to be a traveling bag is both logical and emblematic.

"*Ne budet-li, tï ved' ustal* [Haven't you had enough, aren't you tired]?" my mother would ask, and then would be lost in thought as she slowly shuffled the cards. The door of the compartment was open and I could see the corridor window, where the wires—six thin black wires—were doing their best to slant up, to ascend skywards, despite the lightning blows dealt them by one telegraph pole after another; but just as all six, in a triumphant swoop of pathetic elation, were about to reach the top of the window, a particularly vicious blow would bring them down, as low as they had ever been, and they would have to start all over again.

When, on such journeys as these, the train changed its pace to a dignified amble and all but grazed housefronts and shop signs, as we passed through some big German town, I used to feel a twofold excitement, which terminal stations could not provide. I saw a city, with its toylike trams, linden trees and brick walls, enter the compartment, hobnob with the mirrors, and fill to the brim the windows on the corridor side. This informal contact between train and city was one part of the thrill. The other was putting myself in the place of some passer-by who, I imagined, was moved as I would be moved myself to see the long, romantic, auburn cars, with their intervestibular connecting curtains as black as bat wings and their metal lettering copper-bright in the low sun, unhurriedly negotiate an iron bridge across an everyday thoroughfare and then turn, with all windows suddenly ablaze, around a last block of houses.

There were drawbacks to those optical amalgamations. The wide-windowed dining car, a vista of chaste bottles of mineral water, miter-folded napkins, and dummy chocolate bars (whose wrappers—Cailler, Kohler, and so forth—enclosed nothing but wood), would be perceived at first as a cool haven beyond a consecution of reeling blue corridors; but as the meal progressed toward its fatal last course, and more and more dreadfully one equilibrist with a full tray would back against our table to let another equilibrist pass with another full tray, I would keep catching the car in the act of being recklessly sheathed, lurching waiters and all, in the landscape, while the landscape itself went through a complex system of motion, the daytime moon stubbornly keeping abreast of one's plate, the distant meadows opening fanwise, the near trees sweeping up on invisible swings toward the track, a parallel rail line all at once committing suicide by anastomosis, a bank of nictitating grass rising, rising, rising, until the little witness of mixed velocities was made to disgorge his portion of *omelette aux confitures de fraises.*

It was at night, however, that the *Compagnie Internationale des Wagons-Lits et des Grands Express Européens* lived up to the magic of its name. From my bed under my brother's bunk (Was he asleep? Was he there at all?), in the semidarkness of our compartment, I watched things, and parts of things, and shadows, and sections of shadows cautiously moving about and getting nowhere. The woodwork gently creaked and crackled. Near the door that led to the toilet, a dim garment on a peg and, higher up, the tassel of the blue, bivalved nightlight swung rhythmically. It was hard to correlate those halting approaches, that hooded stealth, with the headlong rush of the outside night, which I knew *was* rushing by, sparkstreaked, illegible.

I would put myself to sleep by the simple act of identifying myself with the engine driver. A sense of drowsy well-being invaded my veins as soon as I had everything nicely arranged—the carefree passengers in their rooms enjoying the ride I was giving them, smoking, exchanging knowing smiles, nodding, dozing; the waiters and cooks and train guards (whom I had to place somewhere) carousing in the diner; and myself, goggled and begrimed, peering out of the engine cab at the tapering track, at the ruby or emerald point in the black distance. And then, in my sleep, I would see something totally different—a glass marble rolling under a grand piano or a toy engine lying on its side with its wheels still working gamely.

A change in the speed of the train sometimes interrupted the current of my sleep. Slow lights were stalking by; each, in passing, investigated the same chink, and then a luminous compass measured the shadows. Presently, the train stopped with a long-drawn Westinghousian sigh. Something (my brother's spectacles, as it proved next day) fell from above. It was marvelously exciting to move to the foot of one's bed, with part of the bedclothes following, in order to undo cautiously the catch of the window shade, which could be made to slide only halfway up, impeded as it was by the edge of the upper berth.

Like moons around Jupiter, pale moths revolved about a lone lamp. A dismembered newspaper stirred on a bench. Somewhere on the train one could hear muffled voices, somebody's comfortable cough. There was nothing particularly interesting in the portion of station platform before me, and still I could not tear myself away from it until it departed of its own accord.

Next morning, wet fields with misshapen willows along the radius of a ditch or a row of poplars afar, traversed by a horizontal band of milky-white mist, told one that the train was spinning through Belgium. It reached Paris at 4 P.M., and even if the stay was only an overnight one, I had always time to purchase something—say, a little brass *Tour Eiffel*, rather roughly coated with silver paint—before we boarded, at noon on the following day, the Sud-Express which, on its way to Madrid, dropped us around 10 P.M. at the La Négresse station of Biarritz, a few miles from the Spanish frontier.

2

Biarritz still retained its quiddity in those days. Dusty blackberry bushes and weedy *terrains à vendre* bordered the road that led to our villa. The Carlton was still being built. Some thirty-six years had to elapse before Brigadier General Samuel McCroskey would occupy the royal suite of the Hôtel du Palais, which stands on the site of a former palace, where in the sixties, that incredibly agile medium, Daniel Home, is said to have been caught stroking with his bare foot (in imitation of a ghost hand) the kind, trustful face of Empress Eugénie. On the promenade near the Casino, an elderly flower girl, with carbon eyebrows and a painted smile, nimbly slipped the plump torus of a carnation into the buttonhole of an intercepted stroller whose left jowl accentuated its royal fold as he glanced down sideways at the coy insertion of the flower.

The rich-hued Oak Eggars questing amid the brush were quite unlike ours (which did not breed on oak, anyway), and here the Speckled Woods haunted not woods, but hedges and had tawny, not pale-yellowish, spots. Cleopatra, a tropical-looking, lemon-and-orange Brimstone, languorously flopping about in gardens, had been a sensation in 1907 and was still a pleasure to net.

Along the back line of the *plage*, various seaside chairs and stools supported the parents of straw-hatted children who were playing in front on the sand. I could be seen on my knees trying to set a found comb aflame by means of a magnifying glass. Men sported white trousers that to the eye of today would look as if they had comically shrunk in the washing; ladies wore, that particular season, light coats with silk-faced lapels, hats with big crowns and wide brims, dense embroidered white veils, frill-fronted blouses, frills at their wrists, frills on their parasols. The breeze salted one's lips. At a tremendous pace a stray Clouded Yellow came dashing across the palpitating *plage*.

Additional movement and sound were provided by venders hawking *cacahuètes*, sugared violets, pistachio ice cream of a heavenly green, cachou pellets, and huge convex pieces of dry, gritty, waferlike stuff that came from a red barrel. With a distinctness that no later superpositions have dimmed, I see that waffleman stomp along through deep mealy sand, with the heavy cask on his bent back. When called, he would sling it off his shoulder by a twist of its strap, bang it down on the sand in a Tower of Pisa position, wipe his face with his sleeve, and proceed to manipulate a kind of arrow-and-dial arrangement with numbers on the lid of the cask. The arrow rasped and whirred around. Luck was supposed to fix the size of a sou's worth of wafer. The bigger the piece, the more I was sorry for him.

The process of bathing took place on another part of the beach. Professional bathers, burly Basques in black bathing suits, were there to help ladies and children enjoy the terrors of the surf. Such a *baigneur* would place the *client* with his back to the incoming wave and hold him by the hand as the rising, rotating mass of foamy, green water violently descended from behind, knocking one off one's feet with a mighty wallop. After a dozen of these tumbles, the *baigneur*, glistening like a seal, would lead his panting, shivering, moistly snuffling charge landward, to the flat foreshore, where an unforgettable old woman with gray hairs on her chin promptly

chose a bathing robe from several hanging on a clothesline.
In the security of a little cabin, one would be helped by yet
another attendant to peel off one's soggy, sand-heavy bathing
suit. It would plop onto the boards, and, still shivering, one
would step out of it and trample on its bluish, diffuse stripes.
The cabin smelled of pine. The attendant, a hunchback with
beaming wrinkles, brought a basin of steaming-hot water, in
which one immersed one's feet. From him I learned, and have
preserved ever since in a glass cell of my memory, that "butterfly" in the Basque language is *misericoletea*—or at least it
sounded so (among the seven words I have found in dictionaries the closest approach is *micheletea*).

3

On the browner and wetter part of the *plage*, that part
which at low tide yielded the best mud for castles, I found
myself digging, one day, side by side with a little French girl
called Colette.

She would be ten in November, I had been ten in April.
Attention was drawn to a jagged bit of violet mussel shell
upon which she had stepped with the bare sole of her narrow
long-toed foot. No, I was not English. Her greenish eyes
seemed flecked with the overflow of the freckles that covered
her sharp-featured face. She wore what might now be termed
a playsuit, consisting of a blue jersey with rolled-up sleeves
and blue knitted shorts. I had taken her at first for a boy and
then had been puzzled by the bracelet on her thin wrist and
the corkscrew brown curls dangling from under her sailor cap.

She spoke in birdlike bursts of rapid twitter, mixing governess English and Parisian French. Two years before, on the
same *plage*, I had been much attached to Zina, the lovely,
sun-tanned, bad-tempered little daughter of a Serbian natur-
opath—she had, I remember (absurdly, for she and I were
only eight at the time), a *grain de beauté* on her apricot skin
just below the heart, and there was a horrible collection of
chamber pots, full and half-full, and one with surface bubbles,
on the floor of the hall in her family's boardinghouse lodgings
which I visited early one morning to be given by her as she
was being dressed, a dead hummingbird moth found by the

cat. But when I met Colette, I knew at once that this was the real thing. Colette seemed to me so much stranger than all my other chance playmates at Biarritz! I somehow acquired the feeling that she was less happy than I, less loved. A bruise on her delicate, downy forearm gave rise to awful conjectures. "He pinches as bad as my mummy," she said, speaking of a crab. I evolved various schemes to save her from her parents, who were *"des bourgeois de Paris"* as I heard somebody tell my mother with a slight shrug. I interpreted the disdain in my own fashion, as I knew that those people had come all the way from Paris in their blue-and-yellow limousine (a fashionable adventure in those days) but had drably sent Colette with her dog and governess by an ordinary coach-train. The dog was a female fox terrier with bells on her collar and a most waggly behind. From sheer exuberance, she would lap up salt water out of Colette's toy pail. I remember the sail, the sunset and the lighthouse pictured on that pail, but I cannot recall the dog's name, and this bothers me.

During the two months of our stay at Biarritz, my passion for Colette all but surpassed my passion for Cleopatra. Since my parents were not keen to meet hers, I saw her only on the beach; but I thought of her constantly. If I noticed she had been crying, I felt a surge of helpless anguish that brought tears to my own eyes. I could not destroy the mosquitoes that had left their bites on her frail neck, but I could, and did, have a successful fistfight with a red-haired boy who had been rude to her. She used to give me warm handfuls of hard candy. One day, as we were bending together over a starfish, and Colette's ringlets were tickling my ear, she suddenly turned toward me and kissed me on the cheek. So great was my emotion that all I could think of saying was, "You little monkey."

I had a gold coin that I assumed would pay for our elopement. Where did I want to take her? Spain? America? The mountains above Pau? *"Là-bas, là-bas, dans la montagne,"* as I had heard Carmen sing at the opera. One strange night, I lay awake, listening to the recurrent thud of the ocean and planning our flight. The ocean seemed to rise and grope in the darkness and then heavily fall on its face.

Of our actual getaway, I have little to report. My memory retains a glimpse of her obediently putting on rope-soled canvas shoes, on the lee side of a flapping tent, while I stuffed a folding butterfly net into a brown-paper bag. The next glimpse is of our evading pursuit by entering a pitch-dark *ci-néma* near the Casino (which, of course, was absolutely out of bounds). There we sat, holding hands across the dog, which now and then gently jingled in Colette's lap, and were shown a jerky, drizzly, but highly exciting bullfight at San Sebastián. My final glimpse is of myself being led along the promenade by Linderovski. His long legs move with a kind of ominous briskness and I can see the muscles of his grimly set jaw working under the tight skin. My bespectacled brother, aged nine, whom he happens to hold with his other hand, keeps trotting out forward to peer at me with awed curiosity, like a little owl.

Among the trivial souvenirs acquired at Biarritz before leav-. ing, my favorite was not the small bull of black stone and not the sonorous seashell but something which now seems almost symbolic—a meerschaum penholder with a tiny peephole of crystal in its ornamental part. One held it quite close to one's eye, screwing up the other, and when one had got rid of the shimmer of one's own lashes, a miraculous photographic view of the bay and of the line of cliffs ending in a lighthouse could be seen inside.

And now a delightful thing happens. The process of re-creating that penholder and the microcosm in its eyelet stimulates my memory to a last effort. I try again to recall the name of Colette's dog—and, triumphantly, along those remote beaches, over the glossy evening sands of the past, where each footprint slowly fills up with sunset water, here it comes, here it comes, echoing and vibrating: Floss, Floss, Floss!

Colette was back in Paris by the time we stopped there for a day before continuing our homeward journey; and there, in a fawn park under a cold blue sky, I saw her (by arrangement between our mentors, I believe) for the last time. She carried a hoop and a short stick to drive it with, and everything about her was extremely proper and stylish in an autumnal, Parisian, *tenue-de-ville-pour-fillettes* way. She took from her governess and slipped into my brother's hand a farewell present, a box of sugar-coated almonds, meant, I knew, solely for me; and instantly she was off, tap-tapping her glinting hoop through light and shade, around and around a fountain choked with dead leaves, near which I stood. The leaves mingle in my memory with the leather of her shoes and gloves, and there was, I remember, some detail in her attire (perhaps a ribbon on her Scottish cap, or the pattern of her stockings) that reminded me then of the rainbow spiral in a glass marble. I still seem to be holding that wisp of iridescence, not knowing exactly where to fit it, while she runs with her hoop ever faster around me and finally dissolves among the slender shadows cast on the graveled path by the interlaced arches of its low looped fence.

Eight

I AM going to show a few slides, but first let me indicate the where and the when of the matter. My brother and I were born in St. Petersburg, the capital of Imperial Russia, he in the middle of March, 1900, and I eleven months earlier. The English and French governesses we had in our childhood were eventually assisted, and finally superseded, by Russian-speaking tutors, most of them graduate students at the capital's university. This tutorial era started about 1906 and lasted for almost a full decade, overlapping, from 1911 on, our high-school years. Each tutor, in turn, dwelt with us—at our St. Petersburg house during the winter, and the rest of the time either at our country estate, fifty miles from the city, or at the foreign resorts we often visited in the fall. Three years was the maximum it took me (I was better at such things than my brother) to wear out any one of those hardy young men.

In choosing our tutors, my father seems to have hit upon the ingenious idea of engaging each time a representative of another class or race, so as to expose us to all the winds that swept over the Russian Empire. I doubt that it was a completely deliberate scheme on his part, but in looking back I find the pattern curiously clear, and the images of those tutors appear within memory's luminous disc as so many magic-lantern projections.

The admirable and unforgettable village schoolmaster who in the summer of 1905 taught us Russian spelling used to come for only a few hours a day and thus does not really belong to the present series. He helps, however, to join its beginning and its end, since my final recollection of him refers to the Easter vacation in 1915, which my brother and I spent with my father and one Volgin—the last, and worst tutor—skiing in the snow-smothered country around our estate under an intense, almost violet sky. Our old friend invited us to his lodgings in the icicle-eaved school building for what he called a snack; actually it was a complex and lovingly planned meal. I can still see his beaming face and the beautifully simulated delight with which my father welcomed a dish (hare roasted in sour cream) that I knew he happened to detest. The room was overheated. My thawing ski boots were not as waterproof as they were supposed to be. My eyes, still smarting from the dazzling snows, kept trying to decipher, on the near wall, a so-called "typographical" portrait of Tolstoy. Like the tail of the mouse on a certain page in *Alice in Wonderland*, it was wholly composed of printed matter. A complete Tolstoy story ("Master and Man") had gone to make its author's bearded face, which, incidentally, our host's features somewhat resembled. We were just on the point of attacking the unfortunate hare, when the door flew open and Hristofor, a blue-nosed footman in a woman's woolen kerchief, ushered in sideways, with an idiotic smile, a huge luncheon basket packed with viands and wines that my tactless grandmother (who was wintering at Batovo) had thought necessary to send us, in case the schoolmaster's fare proved insufficient. Before our host had time to feel hurt, my father sent the untouched hamper back, with a brief note that probably puzzled the well-meaning old lady as most of his actions puzzled her. In a flowing silk gown and net mitts, a period piece rather than a live person, she spent most of her life on a couch, fanning herself with an ivory fan. A box of *boules de gomme*, or a glass of almond milk were always within her reach, as well as a hand mirror, for she used to repowder her face, with a large pink puff, every hour or so, the little mole on her cheekbone showing through all that flour, like a currant. Notwithstanding the languid aspects of her usual day, she remained an extraordinarily hardy woman and made a point of sleeping near a wide-open window all year round. One morning, after a nightlong blizzard, her maid found her lying under a layer of sparkling snow which had swept over her bed and her, without infringing upon the healthy glow of her sleep. If she loved anybody, it was only her youngest daughter, Nadezhda Vonlyarlyarski, for whose sake she suddenly sold Batovo in 1916, a deal which benefited no one at that dusking-tide of imperial history. She complained to all our relatives about the dark forces that had seduced her gifted son into scorning the kind of "brilliant" career in the Tsar's service his forefathers had pursued. What she found especially hard to understand was that my father, who, she knew, thoroughly appreciated all the pleasures of great wealth, could jeopardize its enjoyment by becoming a Liberal, thus helping to bring on a revolution that would, in the long run, as she correctly foresaw, leave him a pauper.

2

Our spelling master was a carpenter's son. In the magic-lantern sequence that follows, my first slide shows a young man we called Ordo, the enlightened son of a Greek Catholic deacon. On walks with my brother and me in the cool summer of 1907, he wore a Byronic black cloak with a silver S-shaped clasp. In the deep Batovo woods, at a spot near a brook where the ghost of a hanged man was said to appear, Ordo would give a rather profane and foolish performance for which my brother and I clamored every time we passed there. Bending his head and flapping his cloak in weird, vampiric fashion he would slowly cavort around a lugubrious aspen. One wet morning during that ritual he dropped his cigarette case and while helping to look for it, I discovered two freshly emerged specimens of the Amur hawkmoth, rare in our region—lovely, velvety, purplish-gray creatures—in tranquil copulation, cling-ing with chinchilla-coated legs to the grass at the foot of the tree. In the fall of that same year, Ordo accompanied us to Biarritz, and a few weeks later abruptly departed, leaving a present we had given him, a Gillette safety razor, on his pil-low, with a pinned note. It seldom happens that I do not quite know whether a recollection is my own or has come to me secondhand, but in this case I do waver, especially because, much later, my mother, in her reminiscent moods, used to refer with amusement to the flame she had unknowingly kin-dled. I seem to remember a door ajar into a drawing room, and there, in the middle of the floor, Ordo, our Ordo, crouch-ing on his knees and wringing his hands in front of my young, beautiful, and dumbfounded mother. The fact that I seem to see, out of the corner of my mind's eye, the undulations of a romantic cloak around Ordo's heaving shoulders suggests my having transferred something of the earlier forest dance to that blurred room in our Biarritz apartment (under the windows of which, in a roped-off section of the square, a huge custard-colored balloon was being inflated by Sigismond Lejoyeux, a local aeronaut).

Next came a Ukrainian, an exuberant mathematician with a dark mustache and a sparkling smile. He spent part of the winter of 1907–1908 with us. He, too, had his accomplishments, among which a vanishing-coin trick was particularly fetching. *A coin, placed on a sheet of paper, is covered with a tumbler and forthwith disappears.* Take an ordinary drinking glass. Paste neatly over its mouth a round piece of paper. The paper should be ruled (or otherwise patterned)—this will enhance the illusion. Place upon a similarly ruled sheet a small coin (a silver twenty-kopek piece will do). Briskly slip the tumbler over the coin, taking care to have both sets of rules or patterns tally. Coincidence of pattern is one of the wonders of nature. The wonders of nature were beginning to impress me at that early age. On one of his Sundays off, the poor conjuror collapsed in the street and was shoved by the police into a cold cell with a dozen drunks. Actually, he suffered from a heart condition, of which he died a few years later.

The next picture looks as if it had come on the screen upside down. It shows our third tutor standing on his head. He was a large, formidably athletic Lett, who walked on his hands, lifted enormous weights, juggled with dumbbells and in a trice could fill a large room with a garrison's worth of sweat reek. When he deemed it fit to punish me for some slight misdemeanor (I remember, for instance, letting a child's marble fall from an upper landing upon his attractive, hard-looking head as he walked downstairs), he would adopt the remarkable pedagogic measure of suggesting that he and I put on boxing gloves for a bit of sparring. He would then punch me in the face with stinging accuracy. Although I preferred this to the hand-cramping *pensums* Mademoiselle would think up, such as making me copy out two hundred times the proverb *Qui aime bien, châtie bien*, I did not miss the good man when he left after a stormy month's stay.

Then came a Pole. He was a handsome medical student, with liquid brown eyes and sleek hair, who looked rather like the French actor Max Linder, a popular movie comedian. Max lasted from 1908 to 1910 and won my admiration on a winter

day in St. Petersburg when a sudden commotion interrupted
our usual morning walk. Whip-brandishing Cossacks with
fierce, imbecile faces were urging their prancing and snorting
ponies against an excited crowd. Lots of caps and at least three
galoshes lay black on the snow. For a moment it seemed as if
one of the Cossacks was heading our way, and I saw Max half-
draw from an inside pocket a small automatic with which I
forthwith fell in love—but unfortunately the turmoil receded.
Once or twice he took us to see his brother, an emaciated
Roman Catholic priest of great distinction whose pale hands
absentmindedly hovered over our little Greek Catholic heads,
while Max and he discussed political or family matters in a
stream of sibilant Polish. I visualize my father on a summer
day in the country vying with Max in marksmanship—riddling
with pistol bullets a rusty NO HUNTING sign in our woods.
He was, this pleasant Max, a vigorous chap, and therefore I
used to be taken aback when he complained of migraine and
languidly refused to join me in kicking a football around or
going for a dip in the river. I know now that he was having
an affair that summer with a married woman whose property
lay a dozen miles away. At odd moments during the day, he
would sneak off to the kennels in order to feed and cajole our
chained watchdogs. They were set loose at II P.M. to rove
around the house, and he had to confront them in the dead
of night when he slipped out and made for the shrubbery
where a bicycle with all accessories—thumb bell, pump, tool
case of brown leather, and even trouser clips—had been secretly prepared for him by an ally, my father's Polish valet.
Holey dirt roads and humpy forest trails would take impatient
Max to the remote trysting place, which was a hunting
lodge—in the grand tradition of elegant adultery. The chill
mists of dawn and four Great Danes with short memories
would see him cycling back, and at 8 A.M. a new day would
begin. I wonder if it was not with a certain relief that, in the
autumn of that year (1909), Max left the scene of his nightly
exploits to accompany us on our second trip to Biarritz. Piously, penitently, he took a couple of days off to visit Lourdes
in the company of the pretty and fast Irish girl who was the
governess of Colette, my favorite playmate on the *plage*. Max
abandoned us the next year, for a job in the X-ray department

of a St. Petersburg hospital, and later on, between the two World Wars, became, I understand, something of a medical celebrity in Poland.

After the Catholic came the Protestant—a Lutheran of Jewish extraction. He will have to figure here under the name of Lenski. My brother and I went with him, late in 1910, to Germany, and after we came back in January of the following year, and began going to school in St. Petersburg, Lenski stayed on for about three years to help us with our homework. It was during his reign that Mademoiselle, who had been with us since the winter of 1905, finally gave up her struggle against intruding Muscovites and returned to Lausanne. Lenski had been born in poverty and liked to recall that between graduating from the *Gymnasium* of his native town, on the Black Sea, and being admitted to the University of St. Petersburg he had supported himself by ornamenting stones from the shingled shore with bright seascapes and selling them as paperweights. He had an oval pink face, short-lashed, curiously naked eyes behind a rimless pince-nez and a pale blue shaven head. We discovered at once three things about him: he was an excellent teacher; he lacked all sense of humor; and, in contrast to our previous tutors, he was someone we needed to defend. The security he felt as long as our parents were around might be shattered at any time in their absence by some sally on the part of our aunts. For them, my father's fierce writings against pogroms and other governmental practices were but the whims of a wayward nobleman, and I often overheard them discussing with horror Lenski's origins and my father's "insane experiments." After such an occasion, I would be dreadfully rude to them and then burst into hot tears in the seclusion of a water closet. Not that I particularly liked Lenski. There was something irritating about his dry voice, his excessive neatness, the way he had of constantly wiping his glasses with a special cloth or paring his nails with a special gadget, his pedantically correct speech and, perhaps most of all, his fantastic morning custom of marching (seemingly straight out of bed but already shod and trousered, with red braces hanging behind and a strange netlike vest enveloping his plump hairy torso) to the nearest faucet and limiting there his ablutions to a thorough sousing of his pink face, blue skull and fat neck, followed by some lusty Russian nose-blowing, after which he marched, with the same purposeful steps, but now dripping and purblind, back to his bedroom where he kept in a secret place three sacrosanct towels (incidentally he was so *brezgliv*, in the Russian untranslatable sense, that he would wash his hands after touching banknotes or banisters).

He complained to my mother that Sergey and I were little foreigners, freaks, fops, *snobï*, "pathologically indifferent," as he put it, to Goncharov, Grigorovich, Korolenko, Stanyukovich, Mamin-Sibiryak, and other stupefying bores (comparable to American "regional writers") whose works, according to him, "enthralled normal boys." To my obscure annoyance, he advised my parents to have their two boys—the three younger children were beyond his jurisdiction—lead a more democratic form of life, which meant, for example, switching, in Berlin, from the Adlon Hotel to a vast apartment in a gloomy pension in a lifeless lane and replacing pile-carpeted international express trains by the filthy floors and stale cigar smoke of swaying and pitching *Schnellzugs*. In foreign towns, as well as in St. Petersburg, he would freeze before shops to marvel at wares that left us completely indifferent. He was about to be married, had nothing but his salary, and was planning his future household with the utmost cunning and care. Now and then rash impulses interfered with his budget. Noticing one day a bedraggled hag who was gloating over a crimson-plumed hat on display at a milliner's, he bought it for her—and had quite a time getting rid of the woman. In his own acquisitions, he aimed at great circumspection. My brother and I patiently listened to his detailed daydreams as he analyzed every corner of the cozy yet frugal apartment he mentally prepared for his wife and himself. Sometimes his fancy would soar. Once it settled on an expensive ceiling lamp at Alexandre's, a St. Petersburg shop that featured rather painful bourgeois bric-a-brac. Not wishing the store to suspect what object he coveted, Lenski said he would take us to see it only if we swore to use self-control and not attract unnecessary attention by direct contemplation. With all kinds of precautions, he brought us under a dreadful bronze octopus and his only indication that this was the longed-for article was a

My mother at thirty-four, a pastel portrait (60 cm. × 40 cm.) by Leon Bakst, painted in 1910, in the music room of our St. Petersburg house. The reproduction printed here was made the same year, under his supervision. He had had tremendous trouble with the fluctuating outline of her lips, sometimes spending an entire sitting on one detail. The result is an extraordinary likeness and represents an interesting stage in his artistic development. My parents also possessed a number of watercolor sketches made for the Scheherazade ballet. Some twenty-five years later, in Paris, Alexandre Bénois told me that soon after the Soviet Revolution he had had all Bakst's works, as well as some of his own, such as the "Rainy Day in Brittany," transported from our house to the Alexander III (now State) Museum.

purring sigh. He used the same care—tiptoeing and whispering, in order not to wake the monster of fate (which, he
seemed to think, bore him a personal grudge)—when introducing us to his fiancée, a small, graceful young lady with
scared-gazelle eyes, and the scent of fresh violets clinging to
her black veil. We met her, I remember, near a pharmacy at
the corner of Potsdamerstrasse and Privatstrasse, a lane, full
of dead leaves, where our pension was, and he urged us to
keep his bride's presence in Berlin secret from our parents,
and a mechanical manikin in the pharmacy window was going
through the motions of shaving, and tramcars screeched by,
and it was beginning to snow.

3

We are now ready to tackle the main theme of this chapter.
Sometime during the following winter, Lenski conceived the
awful idea of showing, on alternate Sundays, Educational
Magic-Lantern Projections at our St. Petersburg home. By
their means he proposed to illustrate ("abundantly," as he
said with a smack of his thin lips) instructive readings before
a group that he fondly believed would consist of entranced
boys and girls sharing in a memorable experience. Besides
adding to our store of information, it might, he thought, help
make my brother and me into good little mixers. Using us as
a core, he accumulated around this sullen center several layers
of recruits—such coeval cousins of ours as happened to be at
hand, various youngsters we met every winter at more or less
tedious parties, some of our schoolmates (unusually quiet they
were—but, alas, registered every trifle), and the children of
the servants. Having been given a completely free hand by my
gentle and optimistic mother, he rented an elaborate apparatus and hired a dejected-looking university student to man it;
as I see it now, warmhearted Lenski was, among other things,
trying to help an impecunious comrade.

Never shall I forget that first reading. Lenski had selected
a narrative poem by Lermontov dealing with the adventures
of a young monk who left his Caucasian retreat to roam
among the mountains. As usual with Lermontov, the poem
combined pedestrian statements with marvelous melting fata

morgana effects. It was of goodly length, and its seven hundred and fifty rather monotonous lines were generously spread
by Lenski over a mere four slides (a fifth I had clumsily broken
just before the performance).

Fire-hazard considerations had led one to select for the
show an obsolete nursery in a corner of which stood a colum-
nar water heater, painted a bronzy brown, and a webfooted
bath, which, for the occasion, had been chastely sheeted. The
close-drawn window curtains prevented one from seeing the
yard below, the stacks of birch logs, and the yellow walls of
the gloomy annex containing the stables (part of which had
been converted into a two-car garage). Despite the ejection
of an ancient wardrobe and a couple of trunks, this depressing
back room, with the magic lantern installed at one end and
transverse rows of chairs, hassocks, and settees arranged for a
score of spectators (including Lenski's fiancée, and three or
four governesses, not counting our own Mademoiselle and
Miss Greenwood), looked jammed and felt stuffy. On my left,
one of my most fidgety girl cousins, a nebulous little blonde
of eleven or so with long, Alice-in-Wonderland hair and a
shell-pink complexion, sat so close to me that I felt the slender
bone of her hip move against mine every time she shifted in
her seat, fingering her locket, or passing the back of her hand
between her perfumed hair and the nape of her neck, or
knocking her knees together under the rustly silk of her yellow
slip, which shone through the lace of her frock. On my right,
I had the son of my father's Polish valet, an absolutely motionless boy in a sailor suit; he bore a striking resemblance to
the Tsarevich, and by a still more striking coincidence suffered
from the same tragic disease—hemophilia—so several times a
year a Court carriage would bring a famous physician to our
house and wait and wait in the slow, slanting snow, and if one
chose the largest of those grayish flakes and kept one's eye
upon it as it came down (past the oriel casement through
which one peered), one could discern its rather coarse, irregular shape and also its oscillation in flight, making one feel
dull and dizzy, dizzy and dull.

The lights went out. Lenski launched upon the opening
lines:

> The time—not many years ago;
> The place—a point where meet and flow
> In sisterly embrace the fair
> Aragva and Kurah; right there
> A monastery stood.

The monastery, with its two rivers, dutifully appeared and stayed on, in a lurid trance (if only one swift could have swept over it!), for about two hundred lines, when it was replaced by a Georgian maiden of sorts carrying a pitcher. When the operator withdrew a slide, the picture was whisked off the screen with a peculiar flick, magnification affecting not only the scene displayed, but also the speed of its removal. Otherwise, there was little magic. We were shown conventional peaks instead of Lermontov's romantic mountains, which

> Rose in the glory of the dawn
> Like smoking altars,

and while the young monk was telling a fellow recluse of his struggle with a leopard—

> O, I was awesome to behold!
> Myself a leopard, wild and bold,
> His flaming rage, his yells were mine

—a subdued caterwauling sounded behind me; it might have come from young Rzhevuski, with whom I used to attend dancing classes, or Alec Nitte who was to win some renown a year or two later for poltergeist phenomena, or one of my cousins. Gradually, as Lenski's reedy voice went on and on, I became aware that, with a few exceptions—such as, perhaps, Samuel Rosoff, a sensitive schoolmate of mine—the audience was secretly scoffing at the performance, and that afterward I would have to cope with various insulting remarks. I felt a quiver of acute pity for Lenski—for the meek folds at the back of his shaven head, for his pluck, for the nervous movements of his pointer, over which, in cold, kittenish paw-play, the colors would sometimes slip, when he brought it too close to the screen. Toward the end, the monotony of the proceedings became quite unbearable; the flustered operator could not find the fourth slide, having got it mixed up with the used ones, and while Lenski patiently waited in the dark, some of the spectators started to project the black shadows of their raised hands upon the frightened white screen, and presently, one ribald and agile boy (could it be I after all—the Hyde of my Jekyll?) managed to silhouette his foot, which, of course, started some boisterous competition. When at last the slide was found and flashed onto the screen, I was reminded of a journey, in my early childhood, through the long, dark St. Gothard Tunnel, which our train entered during a thunderstorm, but it was all over when we emerged, and then

> Blue, green and orange, wonderstruck
> With its own loveliness and luck,
> Across a crag a rainbow fell
> And captured there a poised gazelle.

I should add that during this and the following, still more crowded, still more awful Sunday afternoon sessions, I was haunted by the reverberations of certain family tales I had heard. In the early eighties, my maternal grandfather, Ivan Rukavishnikov, not finding for his sons any private school to his liking, had created an academy of his own by hiring a dozen of the finest professors available and assembling a score of boys for several terms of free education in the halls of his St. Petersburg house (No. 10, Admiralty Quay). The venture was not a success. Those friends of his whose sons he wanted to consort with his own were not always compliant, and of the boys he did get, many proved disappointing. I formed a singularly displeasing image of him, exploring schools for his obstinate purpose, his sad and strange eyes, so familiar to me from photographs, seeking out the best-looking boys among the best scholars. He is said to have actually paid needy parents in order to muster companions for his two sons. Little as our tutor's naïve lantern-slide shows had to do with Rukavishnikovian extravaganzas, my mental association of the two enterprises did not help me to put up with Lenski's making a fool and a bore of himself, so I was happy when, after three more performances ("The Bronze Horseman" by Pushkin; "Don Quixote"; and "Africa—the Land of Marvels"), my mother acceded to my frantic supplications and the whole business was dropped.

Now that I come to think of it, how tawdry and tumid they looked, those jellylike pictures, projected upon the damp linen screen (moisture was supposed to make them blossom more richly), but, on the other hand, what loveliness the glass slides as such revealed when simply held between finger and thumb and raised to the light—translucent miniatures, pocket wonderlands, neat little worlds of hushed luminous hues! In later years, I rediscovered the same precise and silent beauty at the radiant bottom of a microscope's magic shaft. In the glass of the slide, meant for projection, a landscape was reduced, and this fired one's fancy; under the microscope, an insect's organ was magnified for cool study. There is, it would seem, in the dimensional scale of the world a kind of delicate meeting place between imagination and knowledge, a point, arrived at by diminishing large things and enlarging small ones, that is intrinsically artistic.

4

Considering how versatile Lenski appeared to be, how thoroughly he could explain anything related to our school studies, his constant tribulations at the university came as something of a surprise. Their cause, it transpired eventually, was his complete lack of aptitude for the financial and political problems he so stubbornly tackled. I recall the jitters he was in when he had to take one of his most important final examinations. I was as worried as he and, just before the pending event, could not resist eavesdropping at the door of the room where my father, upon Lenski's urgent request, gave him a private rehearsal by testing his knowledge of Charles Gide's *Principles of Political Economy*. Thumbing the leaves of the book, my father might inquire, for instance: "What is the cause of value?" or: "What are the differences between the banknote and paper money?" and Lenski would eagerly clear his throat—and then remain perfectly silent, as if he had expired. After a while, he ceased to produce even that brisk little cough of his, and the intervals of silence were punctuated only by my father's drumming upon the table, except that once, in

a spurt of rapid and hopeful remonstration, the sufferer suddenly exclaimed: "This question is not in the book, sir!"—
but it was. Finally my father sighed, closed the textbook, gently but audibly, and remarked: "*Golubchik* [my dear fellow],
you cannot but fail—you simply don't know a thing." "I disagree with you there," retorted Lenski, not without dignity.
Sitting as stiffly as if he were stuffed, he was driven in our car
to the university, remained there till dusk, came back in a
sleigh, in a heap, in a snowstorm, and in silent despair went
up to his room.

Toward the end of his stay with us, he married and went
away on a honeymoon to the Caucasus, to Lermontov's
mountains, and then came back to us for another winter. During his absence, in the summer of 1913, a Swiss tutor, Monsieur Noyer, took over. He was a sturdily built man, with a
bristly mustache, and he read us Rostand's *Cyrano de Berge-
rac*, mouthing every line most lusciously and changing his
voice from flute to bassoon, according to the characters he
mimed. At tennis, when he was server, he would firmly stand
on the back line, with his thick legs, in wrinkled nankeens,
wide apart, and would abruptly bend them at the knees as he
gave the ball a tremendous but singularly inefficient whack.

When Lenski, in the spring of 1914, left us for good, we
had a young man from a Volgan province. He was a charming
fellow of gentle birth, a fair tennis player, an excellent horseman; on such accomplishments he was greatly relieved to rely,
since, at that late date, neither my brother nor I needed much
the educational help that an optimistic patron of his had
promised my parents the wretch could give us. In the course
of our very first colloquy he casually informed me that Dickens
had written *Uncle Tom's Cabin*, which led to a pounce bet on
my part, winning me his knuckle-duster. After that he was
careful not to refer to any literary character or subject in my
presence. He was very poor and a strange, dusty and etherish,
not altogether unpleasant smell came from his faded university
uniform. He had beautiful manners, a sweet temper, an unforgettable handwriting, all thorns and bristles (the like of
which I have seen only in the letters from madmen, that, alas,
I sometimes receive since the year of grace 1958), and an unlimited fund of obscene stories (which he fed me *sub rosa* in

a dreamy, velvety voice, without using one gross expression) about his pals and *poules*, and also about various relations of ours, one of whom, a fashionable lady, almost twice his age, he soon married only to get rid of her—during his subsequent career in Lenin's administration—by bundling her off to a labor camp, where she perished. The more I think of that man, the more I believe that he was completely insane.

I did not quite lose track of Lenski. On a loan from his father-in-law, he started, while still with us, some fantastic business that involved the buying up and exploiting of various inventions. It would be neither kind nor fair to say that he passed them off as his own; but he adopted them and talked about them with a warmth and tenderness which hinted at something like a natural fatherhood—an emotional attitude on his part with no facts in support and no fraud in view. One day, he proudly invited all of us to try out with our car a new type of pavement he was responsible for, composed of (so far as I can make out that strange gleam through the dimness of time) a weird weave of metallic strips. The outcome was a puncture. He was consoled, however, by the purchase of another hot thing: the blueprint of what he called an "electroplane," which looked like an old Blériot but had—and here I quote him again—a "voltaic" motor. It flew only in his dreams—and mine. During the war, he launched a miracle horse food in the form of *galette*-like flat cakes (he would nibble some himself and offer bites to friends), but most horses stuck to their oats. He trafficked in a number of other patents, all of them crazy, and was deep in debt when he inherited a small fortune through his father-in-law's death. This must have been in the beginning of 1918 because, I remember, he wrote to us (we were stranded in the Yalta region) offering us money and every kind of assistance. The inheritance he promptly invested in an amusement park on the East Crimean coast, and took no end of trouble to get a good orchestra and build a roller-skating rink of some special wood, and set up fountains and cascades illumed by red and green bulbs. In 1919, the Bolsheviks came and turned off the lights, and Lenski fled to France; the last I heard of him was in the twenties, when he was said to be earning a precarious living on the Riviera by painting pictures on seashells and stones. I do not know—and would rather not imagine—what happened to him during the Nazi invasion of France. Notwithstanding some of his oddities, he was, really, a very pure, very decent human being, whose private principles were as strict as his grammar and whose bracing *diktanti* I recall with joy: *kolokololiteyshchiki perekolotili vikarabkavshihsya vihuholey*, "the church-bell casters slaughtered the desmans that had scrambled out." Many years later, at the American Museum of Natural History in New York, I happened to quote that tongue twister to a zoologist who had asked me if Russian was as difficult as commonly supposed. We met again several months later and he said: "You know, I've been thinking a lot about those Muscovite muskrats: *why* were they said to have scrambled out? Had they been hibernating or hiding, or what?"

5

In thinking of my successive tutors, I am concerned less with the queer dissonances they introduced into my young life than with the essential stability and completeness of that life. I witness with pleasure the supreme achievement of memory, which is the masterly use it makes of innate harmonies when gathering to its fold the suspended and wandering tonalities of the past. I like to imagine, in consummation and resolution of those jangling chords, something as enduring, in retrospect, as the long table that on summer birthdays and namedays used to be laid for afternoon chocolate out of doors, in an alley of birches, limes and maples at its debouchment on the smooth-sanded space of the garden proper that separated the park and the house. I see the tablecloth and the faces of seated people sharing in the animation of light and shade beneath a moving, a fabulous foliage, exaggerated, no doubt, by the same faculty of impassioned commemoration, of ceaseless return, that makes me always approach that banquet table from the outside, from the depth of the park—not from the house—as if the mind, in order to go back thither, had to do so with the silent steps of a prodigal, faint with excitement. Through a tremulous prism, I distinguish the features of relatives and familiars, mute lips serenely moving in forgotten speech. I see the steam of the chocolate and the plates of blueberry tarts. I note the small helicopter of a revolving samara that gently descends upon the tablecloth, and, lying across the table, an adolescent girl's bare arm indolently extended as far as it will go, with its turquoise-veined underside turned up to the flaky sunlight, the palm open in lazy expectancy of something—perhaps the nutcracker. In the place where my current tutor sits, there is a changeful image, a succession of fade-ins and fade-outs; the pulsation of my thought mingles with that of the leaf shadows and turns Ordo into Max and Max into Lenski and Lenski into the schoolmaster, and the whole array of trembling transformations is repeated. And then, suddenly, just when the colors and outlines settle at last to their various duties—smiling, frivolous duties—some knob is touched and a torrent of sounds comes to life: voices speaking all together, a walnut cracked, the click of a nutcracker carelessly passed, thirty human hearts drowning mine with their regular beats; the sough and sigh of a thousand trees, the local concord of loud summer birds, and, beyond the river, behind the rhythmic trees, the confused and enthusiastic hullabaloo of bathing young villagers, like a background of wild applause.

Nine

I HAVE before me a large bedraggled scrapbook, bound in black cloth. It contains old documents, including diplomas, drafts, diaries, identity cards, penciled notes, and some printed matter, which had been in my mother's meticulous keeping in Prague until her death there, but then, between 1939 and 1961, went through various vicissitudes. With the aid of those papers and my own recollections, I have composed the following short biography of my father.

Vladimir Dmitrievich Nabokov, jurist, publicist and statesman, son of Dmitri Nikolaevich Nabokov, Minister of Justice, and Baroness Maria von Korff, was born on July 20, 1870, at Tsarskoe Selo near St. Petersburg, and was killed by an assassin's bullet on March 28, 1922, in Berlin. Till the age of thirteen he was educated at home by French and English governesses and by Russian and German tutors; from one of the latter he caught and passed on to me the *morbus et passio aureliani*. In the autumn of 1883, he started to attend the "Gymnasium" (corresponding to a combination of American "high school" and "junior college") on the then Gagarin Street (presumably renamed in the twenties by the shortsighted Soviets). His desire to excel was overwhelming. One winter night, being behind with a set task and preferring pneumonia to ridicule at the blackboard, he exposed himself to the polar frost, with the hope of a timely sickness, by sitting in nothing but his nightshirt at the open window (it gave on the Palace Square and its moon-polished pillar); on the morrow he still enjoyed perfect health, and, undeservedly, it was the dreaded teacher who happened to be laid up. At sixteen, in May 1887, he completed the Gymnasium course, with a gold medal, and studied law at the St. Petersburg University, graduating in January 1891. He continued his studies in Germany (mainly at Halle). Thirty years later, a fellow student of his, with whom he had gone for a bicycle trip in the Black Forest, sent my widowed mother the *Madame Bovary* volume which my father had had with him at the time and on the flyleaf of which he had written "The unsurpassed pearl of French literature"—a judgment that still holds.

On November 14 (a date scrupulously celebrated every subsequent year in our anniversary-conscious family), 1897, he married Elena Ivanovna Rukavishnikov, the twenty-one-year-old daughter of a country neighbor with whom he had six children (the first was a stillborn boy).

In 1895 he had been made Junior Gentleman of the Chamber. From 1896 to 1904 he lectured on criminal law at the Imperial School of Jurisprudence (*Pravovedenie*) in St. Petersburg. Gentlemen of the Chamber were supposed to ask permission of the "Court Minister" before performing a public act. This permission my father did not ask, naturally, when publishing in the review *Pravo* his celebrated article "The Blood Bath of Kishinev" in which he condemned the part played by the police in promoting the Kishinev pogrom of 1903. By imperial decree he was deprived of his court title in January 1905, after which he severed all connection with the Tsar's government and resolutely plunged into antidespotic politics, while continuing his juristic labors. From 1905 to 1915 he was president of the Russian section of the International Criminology Association and at conferences in Holland amused himself and amazed his audience by orally translating, when needed, Russian and English speeches into German and French and vice-versa. He was eloquently against capital punishment. Unswervingly he conformed to his principles in private and public matters. At an official banquet in 1904 he refused to drink the Tsar's health. He is said to have coolly advertised in the papers his court uniform for sale. From 1906 to 1917 he co-edited with I. V. Hessen and A. I. Kaminka one of the few liberal dailies in Russia, the *Rech* ("Speech") as well as the jurisprudential review *Pravo*. Politically he was a "Kadet," i.e. a member of the KD (*Konstitutsionno-demokraticheskaya partiya*), later renamed more aptly the party of the People's Freedom (*partiya Narodnoy Svobodi*). With his keen sense of humor he would have been tremendously tickled by the helpless though vicious hash Soviet lexicographers have made of his opinions and achievements in their rare biographical comments on him. In 1906 he was elected to the

First Russian Parliament (*Pervaya Duma*), a humane and heroic institution, predominantly liberal (but which ignorant foreign publicists, infected by Soviet propaganda, often confuse with the ancient "boyar dumas"!). There he made several splendid speeches with nationwide repercussions. When less than a year later the Tsar dissolved the Duma, a number of members, including my father (who, as a photograph taken at the Finland Station shows, carried his railway ticket tucked under the band of his hat), repaired to Vyborg for an illegal session. In May 1908, he began a prison term of three months in somewhat belated punishment for the revolutionary manifesto he and his group had issued at Vyborg. "Did V. get any 'Egerias' [Speckled Woods] this summer?" he asks in one of his secret notes from prison, which, through a bribed guard, and a faithful friend (Kaminka), were transmitted to my mother at Vyra. "Tell him that all I see in the prison yard are Brimstones and Cabbage Whites." After his release he was forbidden to participate in public elections, but (one of the paradoxes so common under the Tsars) could freely work in the bitterly liberal *Rech*, a task to which he devoted up to nine hours a day. In 1913, he was fined by the government the token sum of one hundred rubles (about as many dollars of the present time) for his reportage from Kiev, where after a stormy trial Beylis was found innocent of murdering a Christian boy for "ritual" purposes: justice and public opinion could still prevail occasionally in old Russia; they had only five years to go. He was mobilized soon after the beginning of World War One and sent to the front. Eventually he was attached to the General Staff in St. Petersburg. Military ethics prevented him from taking an active part in the first turmoil of the liberal revolution of March 1917. From the very start, History seems to have been anxious of depriving him of a full opportunity to reveal his great gifts of statesmanship in a Russian republic of the Western type. In 1917, during the initial stage of the Provisional Government—that is, while the Kadets still took part in it—he occupied in the Council of Ministers the responsible but inconspicuous position of Executive Secretary. In the winter of 1917–18, he was elected to the Constituent Assembly, only to be arrested by energetic Bolshevist sailors when it was disbanded. The November Revolution had already entered upon its gory course, its police was already active, but in those days the chaos of orders and counterorders sometimes took our side: my father followed a dim corridor, saw an open door at the end, walked out into a side street and made his way to the Crimea with a knapsack he had ordered his valet Osip to bring him to a secluded corner and a package of caviar sandwiches which good Nikolay Andreevich, our cook, had added of his own accord. From mid-1918 to the beginning of 1919, in an interval between two occupations by the Bolshevists, and in constant friction with trigger-happy elements in Denikin's army, he was Minister of Justice ("of minimal justice" as he used to say wryly) in one of the Regional Governments, the Crimean one. In 1919, he went into voluntary exile, living first in London, then in Berlin where, in collaboration with Hessen, he edited the liberal émigré daily *Rul'* ("Rudder") until his assassination in 1922 by a sinister ruffian whom, during World War Two, Hitler made administrator of émigré Russian affairs.

He wrote prolifically, mainly on political and criminological subjects. He knew *à fond* the prose and poetry of several countries, knew by heart hundreds of verses (his favorite Russian poets were Pushkin, Tyutchev, and Fet—he published a fine essay on the latter), was an authority on Dickens, and, besides Flaubert, prized highly Stendhal, Balzac and Zola, three detestable mediocrities from *my* point of view. He used to confess that the creation of a story or poem, *any* story or poem, was to him as incomprehensible a miracle as the construction of an electric machine. On the other hand, he had no trouble at all in writing on juristic and political matters. He had a correct, albeit rather monotonous style, which today, despite all those old-world metaphors of classical education and grandiloquent clichés of Russian journalism has—at least to my jaded ear—an attractive gray dignity of its own, in extraordinary contrast (as if belonging to some older and poorer relative) to his colorful, quaint, often poetical, and sometimes ribald, everyday utterances. The preserved drafts of some of his proclamations (beginning *"Grazhdane!"*, meaning *"Citoyens!"*) and editorials are penned in a copybook-slanted, beautifully sleek, unbelievably regular hand, almost free of corrections, a purity, a certainty, a mind-and-matter cofunction that I find amusing to compare to my own mousy hand and messy drafts, to the massacrous revisions and re-writings, and new revisions, of the very lines in which I am taking two hours now to describe a two-minute run of his flawless handwriting. His drafts were the fair copies of im-mediate thought. In this manner, he wrote, with phenomenal ease and rapidity (sitting uncomfortably at a child's desk in the classroom of a mournful palace) the text of the abdication of Grand Duke Mihail (next in line of succession after the Tsar had renounced his and his son's throne). No wonder he was also an admirable speaker, an "English style" cool orator, who eschewed the meat-chopping gesture and rhetorical bark of the demagogue, and here, too, the ridiculous cacologist I am, when not having a typed sheet before me, has inherited nothing.

Only recently have I read for the first time his important *Sbornik statey po ugolovnomu pravu* (a collection of articles on criminal law), published in 1904 in St. Petersburg, of which a very rare, possibly unique copy (formerly the property of a "Mihail Evgrafovich Hodunov," as stamped in violet ink on the flyleaf) was given me by a kind traveler, Andrew Field, who bought it in a secondhand bookshop, on his visit to Rus-sia in 1961. It is a volume of 316 pages containing nineteen papers. In one of these ("Carnal Crimes," written in 1902), my father discusses, rather prophetically in a certain odd sense, cases (in London) "of little girls *à l'âge le plus tendre* (*v nezh-neyshem vozraste*), i.e. from eight to twelve years, being sac-rificed to lechers (*slastolyubtsam*)." In the same essay he reveals a very liberal and "modern" approach to various ab-normal practices, incidentally coining a convenient Russian word for "homosexual": *ravnopoliy.*

It would be impossible to list the literally thousands of his articles in various periodicals, such as *Rech* or *Pravo.* In a later chapter I speak of his historically interesting book about a wartime semiofficial visit to England. Some of his memoirs pertaining to the years 1917–1919 have appeared in the *Arhiv russkoy revolyutsii,* published by Hessen in Berlin. On January 16, 1920, he delivered a lecture at King's College, London, on "Soviet Rule and Russia's Future," which was published a week later in the Supplement to *The New Commonwealth,*

No. 15 (neatly pasted in my mother's album). In the spring of the same year I learned by heart most of it when preparing to speak against Bolshevism at a Union debate in Cambridge; the (victorious) apologist was a man from *The Manchester Guardian*; I forget his name, but recall drying up utterly after reciting what I had memorized, and that was my first and last political speech. A couple of months before my father's death, the émigré review *Teatr i zhizn'* ("Theater and Life") started to serialize his boyhood recollections (he and I are overlapping now—too briefly). I find therein excellently described the terrible tantrums of his pedantic master of Latin at the Third Gymnasium, as well as my father's very early, and lifelong, passion for the opera: he must have heard practically every first-rate European singer between 1880 and 1922, and although unable to play anything (except very majestically the first chords of the "Ruslan" overture) remembered every note of his favorite operas. Along this vibrant string a melodious gene that missed me glides through my father from the sixteenth-century organist Wolfgang Graun to my son.

2

I was eleven years old when my father decided that the tutoring I had had, and was still having, at home might be profitably supplemented by my attending Tenishev School. This school, one of the most remarkable in St. Petersburg, was a comparatively young institution of a much more modern and liberal type than the ordinary Gymnasium, to which general category it belonged. Its course of study, consisting of sixteen "semesters" (eight Gymnasium classes), would be roughly equivalent in America to the last six years of school plus the first two years of college. Upon my admittance, in January 1911, I found myself in the third "semester," or in the beginning of the eighth grade according to the American system.

School was taught from the fifteenth of September to the twenty-fifth of May, with a couple of interruptions: a two-week intersemestral gap—to make place, as it were, for the huge Christmas tree that touched with its star the pale-green ceiling of our prettiest drawing room—and a one-week Easter vacation, during which painted eggs enlivened the breakfast table. Since snow and frost lasted from October well into April, no wonder the mean of my school memories is definitely hiemal.

When Ivan the first (who vanished one day) or Ivan the second (who was to see the time when I would send him forth on romantic errands) came to wake me around 8 A.M., the outside world was still cowled in brown hyperborean gloom. The electric light in the bedroom had a sullen, harsh, jaundiced tinge that made my eyes smart. Leaning my singing ear on my hand and propping my elbow on the pillow, I would force myself to prepare ten pages of unfinished homework. On my bed table, next to a stocky lamp with two bronze lion heads, stood a small unconventional clock: an upright container of crystal within which black-numbered, ivory-white, pagelike lamels flipped from right to left, each stopping for a minute the way commercial stills did on the old cinema screen. I gave myself ten minutes to tintype the text in my brain (nowadays it would take me two hours!) and, say, a dozen minutes to tub, dress (with Ivan's help), scutter downstairs, and swallow a cup of tepid cocoa from the surface of which I plucked off by the center a round of wrinkled brown skin. Mornings were botched, and such things as the lessons in boxing and fencing that a wonderful rubbery Frenchman, Monsieur Loustalot, used to give me had to be discontinued.

He still came, almost daily, however, to spar or fence with my father. I would dash, with my fur coat half on, through the green drawing room (where an odor of fir, hot wax and tangerines would linger long after Christmas had gone), toward the library, from which came a medley of stamping and scraping sounds. There, I would find my father, a big, robust man, looking still bigger in his white training suit, thrusting and parrying, while his agile instructor added brisk exclamations (*"Battez!" "Rompez!"*) to the click-clink of the foils.

Panting a little, my father would remove the convex fencing mask from his perspiring pink face to kiss me good morning. The place combined pleasantly the scholarly and the athletic, the leather of books and the leather of boxing gloves. Fat armchairs stood along the book-lined walls. An elaborate "punching ball" affair purchased in England—four steel posts supporting the board from which the pear-shaped striking bag hung—gleamed at the end of the spacious room. The purpose of this apparatus, especially in connection with the machine-gunlike ra-ta-ta of its bag, was questioned and the butler's explanation of it reluctantly accepted as true, by some heavily armed street fighters who came in through the window in 1917. When the Soviet Revolution made it imperative for us to leave St. Petersburg, that library disintegrated, but queer little remnants of it kept cropping up abroad. Some twelve years later, in Berlin, I picked up from a bookstall one such waif, bearing my father's *ex libris*. Very fittingly, it turned out to be *The War of the Worlds* by Wells. And after another decade had elapsed, I discovered one day in the New York Public Library, indexed under my father's name, a copy of the neat catalogue he had had privately printed when the phantom books listed therein still stood, ruddy and sleek, on his shelves.

3

He would replace his mask and go on with his stamping and lunging while I hurried back the way I had come. After the warmth in the entrance hall, where logs were crackling in the large fireplace, the outdoor air gave an icy shock to one's lungs. I would ascertain which of our two cars, the Benz or the Wolseley, was there to take me to school. The first, a gray landaulet, manned by Volkov, a gentle, pale-faced chauffeur, was the older one. Its lines had seemed positively dynamic in comparison with those of the insipid, noseless and noiseless, electric coupé that had preceded it; but, in its turn, it acquired an old-fashioned, top-heavy look, with a sadly shrunken bonnet, as soon as the comparatively long, black English limousine came to share its garage.

To get the newer car was to start the day zestfully. Pirogov, the second chauffeur, was a very short, pudgy fellow with a russet complexion that matched well the shade of the furs he wore over his corduroy suit and the orange-brown of his leggings. When some hitch in the traffic forced him to apply the brakes (which he did by suddenly distending himself in a peculiar springy manner), or when I bothered him by trying to communicate with him through the squeaky and not very ef-

ficient speaking tube, the back of his thick neck seen through
the glass partition would turn crimson. He frankly preferred
to drive the hardy convertible Opel that we used in the country during three or four seasons, and would do so at sixty miles
per hour (to realize how dashing that was in 1912, one should
take into account the present inflation of speed): indeed, the
very essence of summer freedom—schoolless untownishness—
remains connected in my mind with the motor's extravagant
roar that the opened muffler would release on the long, lone
highway. When in the second year of World War One Pirogov
was mobilized, he was replaced by dark, wild-eyed Tsiganov,
a former racing ace, who had participated in various contests
both in Russia and abroad and had had several ribs broken in
a bad smash in Belgium. Later, sometime in 1917, soon after
my father resigned from Kerenski's cabinet, Tsiganov decided—notwithstanding my father's energetic protests—to
save the powerful Wolseley car from possible confiscation by
dismantling it and distributing its parts over hiding places
known only to him. Still later, in the gloom of a tragic autumn, with the Bolshevists gaining the upper hand, one of
Kerenski's aides asked my father for a sturdy car the premier
might use if forced to leave in a hurry; but our debile old
Benz would not do and the Wolseley had embarrassingly vanished, and if I treasure the recollection of that request (recently denied by my eminent friend, but certainly made by his
aide-de-camp), it is only from a compositional viewpoint—
because of the amusing thematic echo of Christina von Korff's
part in the Varennes episode of 1791.

Although heavy snowfalls were much more usual in St. Petersburg than, say, around Boston, the several automobiles
that circulated among the numerous sleighs of the town before World War One somehow never seemed to get into the
kind of hideous trouble that modern cars get into on a good
New England white Christmas. Many strange forces had been
involved in the building of the city. One is led to suppose that
the arrangement of its snows—tidy drifts along the sidewalks
and a smooth solid spread on the octangular wood blocks of
the pavement—was arrived at by some unholy cooperation
between the geometry of the streets and the physics of the
snow clouds. Anyway, driving to school never took more than

a quarter of an hour. Our house was No. 47 in Morskaya Street. Then came Prince Oginski's (No. 45), then the Italian Embassy (No. 43), then the German Embassy (No. 41), and then the vast Maria Square, after which the house numbers continued to dwindle. There was a small public park on the north side of the square. In one of its linden trees an ear and a finger had been found one day—remnants of a terrorist whose hand had slipped while he was arranging a lethal parcel in his room on the other side of the square. Those same trees (a pattern of silver filigree in a mother-of-pearl mist out of which the bronze dome of St. Isaac's arose in the background) had also seen children shot down at random from the branches into which they had climbed in a vain attempt to escape the mounted gendarmes who were quelling the First Revolution (1905–06). Quite a few little stories like these were attached to squares and streets in St. Petersburg.

Upon reaching Nevski Avenue, one followed it for a long stretch, during which it was a pleasure to overtake with no effort some cloaked guardsman in his light sleigh drawn by a pair of black stallions snorting and speeding along under the bright blue netting that prevented lumps of hard snow from flying into the passenger's face. A street on the left side with a lovely name—Karavannaya (the Street of Caravans)—took one past an unforgettable toyshop. Next came the Cinizelli Circus (famous for its wrestling tournaments). Finally, after crossing an ice-bound canal one drove up to the gates of Tenishev School in Mohovaya Street (the Street of Mosses).

4

Belonging, as he did by choice, to the great classless intelligentsia of Russia, my father thought it right to have me attend a school that was distinguished by its democratic principles, its policy of nondiscrimination in matters of rank, race and creed, and its up-to-date educational methods. Apart from that, Tenishev School differed in nothing from any other school in time or space. As in all schools, the boys tolerated some teachers and loathed others, and, as in all schools, there was a constant interchange of obscene quips and erotic information. Being good at games, I would not have found the whole business too dismal if only my teachers had been less intent in trying to save my soul.

They accused me of not conforming to my surroundings; of "showing off" (mainly by peppering my Russian papers with English and French terms, which came naturally to me); of refusing to touch the filthy wet towels in the washroom; of fighting with my knuckles instead of using the slaplike swing with the underside of the fist adopted by Russian scrappers. The headmaster who knew little about games, though greatly approving of their consociative virtues, was suspicious of my always keeping goal in soccer "instead of running about with the other players." Another thing that provoked resentment was my driving to and from school in an automobile and not traveling by streetcar or horsecab as the other boys, good little democrats, did. With his face all screwed up in a grimace of disgust, one teacher suggested to me that the least I could do was to have the automobile stop two or three blocks away, so that my schoolmates might be spared the sight of a liveried chauffeur doffing his cap. It was as if the school were allowing me to carry about a dead rat by the tail with the understanding that I would not dangle it under people's noses.

The worst situation, however, arose from the fact that even then I was intensely averse to joining movements or associations of any kind. I enraged the kindest and most well-meaning among my teachers by declining to participate in extracurricular group work—debating societies with the solemn election of officers and the reading of reports on historical questions, and, in the higher grades, more ambitious gatherings for the discussion of current political events. The constant pressure upon me to belong to some group or other never broke my resistance but led to a state of tension that was hardly alleviated by everybody harping upon the example set by my father.

My father was, indeed, a very active man, but as often happens with the children of famous fathers, I viewed his activities through a prism of my own, which split into many enchanting colors the rather austere light my teachers glimpsed. In connection with his varied interests—criminological, legislative, political, editorial, philanthropic—he had to attend many committee meetings, and these were often held at our house.

That such a meeting was forthcoming might be always deduced from a peculiar sound in the far end of our large and resonant entrance hall. There, in a recess under the marble staircase, our *shveitsar* (doorman) would be busy sharpening pencils when I came home from school. For that purpose he used a bulky old-fashioned machine, with a whirring wheel, the handle of which he rapidly turned with one hand while holding with the other a pencil inserted into a lateral orifice. For years he had been the tritest type of "faithful retainer" imaginable, full of quaint wit and wisdom, with a dashing way of smoothing out, right and left, his mustache with two fingers, and a slight fried-fish smell always hanging about him: it originated in his mysterious basement quarters, where he had an obese wife and twins—a schoolboy of my age and a haunting, sloppy little aurora with a blue squint and coppery locks; but that pencil chore must have considerably embittered poor old Ustin—for I can readily sympathize with him, I who write my stuff only in very sharp pencil, keep bouquets of B 3's in vaselets around me, and rotate a hundred times a day the handle of the instrument (clamped to the table edge), which so speedily accumulates so much tawny-brown shag in its little drawer. It later turned out that he had long got into touch with the Tsar's secret police—tyros, of course, in comparison to Dzerzhinski's or Yagoda's men, but still fairly bothersome. As early as 1906, for instance, the police, suspecting my father of conducting clandestine meetings at Vyra, had engaged the services of Ustin who thereupon begged my father, under some pretext that I cannot recall, but with the deep purpose of spying on whatever went on, to take him to the country that summer as an extra footman (he had been pantry boy in the Rukavishnikov household); and it was he, omnipresent Ustin, who in the winter of 1917–18 heroically led representatives of the victorious Soviets up to my father's study on the second floor, and from there, through a music room and my mother's boudoir, to the southeast corner room where I was born, and to the niche in the wall, to the tiaras of colored fire, which formed an adequate recompense for the Swallowtail he had once caught for me.

Around eight in the evening, the hall would house an accumulation of greatcoats and overshoes. In a committee room, next to the library, at a long baize-covered table (where those beautifully pointed pencils had been laid out), my father and his colleagues would gather to discuss some phase of their opposition to the Tsar. Above the hubbub of voices, a tall clock in a dark corner would break into Westminster chimes; and beyond the committee room were mysterious depths—storerooms, a winding staircase, a pantry of sorts—where my cousin Yuri and I used to pause with drawn pistols on our way to Texas and where one night the police placed a fat, blear-eyed spy who went laboriously down on his knees before our librarian, Lyudmila Borisovna Grinberg, when discovered. But how on earth could I discuss all this with schoolteachers?

5

The reactionary press never ceased to attack my father's party, and I had got quite used to the more or less vulgar cartoons which appeared from time to time—my father and Milyukov handing over Saint Russia on a plate to World Jewry and that sort of thing. But one day, in the winter of 1911 I believe, the most powerful of the Rightist newspapers employed a shady journalist to concoct a scurrilous piece containing insinuations that my father could not let pass. Since the well-known rascality of the actual author of the article made him "non-duelable" (*neduelesposobniy*, as the Russian dueling code had it), my father called out the somewhat less disreputable editor of the paper in which the article had appeared.

A Russian duel was a much more serious affair than the conventional Parisian variety. It took the editor several days to make up his mind whether or not to accept the challenge. One the last of these days, a Monday, I went, as usual, to school. In consequence of my not reading the newspapers, I was absolutely ignorant of the whole thing. Sometime during the day I became aware that a magazine opened at a certain page was passing from hand to hand and causing titters. A well-timed swoop put me in possession of what proved to be the latest copy of a cheap weekly containing a lurid account of my father's challenge, with idiotic comments on the choice of weapons he had offered his foe. Sly digs were taken at his having reverted to a feudal custom that he had criticized in his own writings. There was also a good deal about the number of his servants and the number of his suits. I found out that he had chosen for second his brother-in-law, Admiral Kolomeytsev, a hero of the Japanese war. During the battle of Tsushima, this uncle of mine, then holding the rank of captain, had managed to bring his destroyer alongside the burning flagship and save the naval commander-in-chief.

After classes, I ascertained that the magazine belonged to one of my best friends. I charged him with betrayal and mockery. In the ensuing fight, he crashed backward into a desk, catching his foot in a joint and breaking his ankle. He was laid up for a month, but gallantly concealed from his family and from our teachers my share in the matter.

The pang of seeing him carried downstairs was lost in my general misery. For some reason or other, no car came to fetch me that day, and during the cold, dreary, incredibly slow drive home in a hired sleigh I had ample time to think matters over. Now I understood why, the day before, my mother had been so little with me and had not come down to dinner. I also understood what special coaching Thernant, a still finer *maître d'armes* than Loustalot, had of late been giving my father. What would his adversary choose, I kept asking myself—the blade or the bullet? Or had the choice already been made? Carefully, I took the beloved, the familiar, the richly alive image of my father at fencing and tried to transfer that image, minus the mask and the padding, to the dueling ground, in some barn or riding school. I visualized him and his adversary, both bare-chested, black-trousered, in furious battle, their energetic movements marked by that strange awkwardness which even the most elegant swordsmen cannot avoid in a real encounter. The picture was so repulsive, so vividly did I feel the ripeness and nakedness of a madly pulsating heart about to be pierced, that I found myself hoping for what seemed momentarily a more abstract weapon. But soon I was in even deeper distress.

As the sleigh crept along Nevski Avenue, where blurry lights swam in the gathering dusk, I thought of the heavy black Browning my father kept in the upper right-hand drawer of his desk. I knew that pistol as well as I knew all the other, more salient, things in his study; the *objets d'art* of crystal or veined stone, fashionable in those days; the glinting family photographs; the huge, mellowly illumined Perugino; the small, honey-bright Dutch oils; and, right over the desk, the rose-and-haze pastel portrait of my mother by Bakst: the artist had drawn her face in three-quarter view, wonderfully bringing out its delicate features—the upward sweep of the ash-colored hair (it had grayed when she was in her twenties), the pure curve of the forehead, the dove-blue eyes, the graceful line of the neck.

When I urged the old, rag-doll-like driver to go faster, he would merely lean to one side with a special half-circular movement of his arm, so as to make his horse believe he was about to produce the short whip he kept in the leg of his right felt boot; and that would be sufficient for the shaggy little hack to make as vague a show of speeding up as the driver had made of getting out his *knutishko*. In the almost hallucinatory state that our snow-muffled ride engendered, I refought all the famous duels a Russian boy knew so well. I saw Pushkin, mortally wounded at the first fire, grimly sit up to discharge his pistol at d'Anthès. I saw Lermontov smile as he faced Martïnov. I saw stout Sobinov in the part of Lenski crash down and send his weapon flying into the orchestra. No Russian writer of any repute had failed to describe *une rencontre*, a hostile meeting, always of course of the classical *duel à volonté* type (not the ludicrous back-to-back-march-face-about-bang-bang performance of movie and cartoon fame). Among several prominent families, there had been tragic deaths on the dueling ground in more or less recent years. Slowly my dreamy sleigh drove up Morskaya Street, and slowly dim silhouettes of duelists advanced upon each other and leveled their pistols and fired—at the crack of dawn, in damp glades of old country estates, on bleak military training grounds, or in the driving snow between two rows of fir trees.

And behind it all there was yet a very special emotional abyss that I was desperately trying to skirt, lest I burst into a tempest of tears, and this was the tender friendship underlying my respect for my father; the charm of our perfect accord; the Wimbledon matches we followed in the London papers; the chess problems we solved; the Pushkin iambics that rolled off his tongue so triumphantly whenever I mentioned some minor poet of the day. Our relationship was marked by that habitual exchange of homespun nonsense, comically garbled words, proposed imitations of supposed intonations, and all those private jokes which are the secret code of happy families. With all that he was extremely strict in matters of conduct and given to biting remarks when cross with a child or a servant, but his inherent humanity was too great to allow his rebuke to Osip for laying out the wrong shirt to be really offensive, just as a first-hand knowledge of a boy's pride tempered the harshness of reproval and resulted in sudden forgiveness. Thus I was more puzzled than pleased one day when upon learning that I had deliberately slashed my leg just above the knee with a razor (I still bear the scar) in order to avoid a recitation in class for which I was unprepared, he seemed unable to work up any real wrath; and his subsequent admission of a parallel transgression in his own boyhood rewarded me for not withholding the truth.

I remembered that summer afternoon (which already then seemed long ago although actually only four or five years had passed) when he had burst into my room, grabbed my net, shot down the veranda steps—and presently was strolling back holding between finger and thumb the rare and magnificent female of the Russian Poplar Admirable that he had seen basking on an aspen leaf from the balcony of his study. I remembered our long bicycle rides along the smooth Luga highway and the efficient way in which—mighty-calved, knickerbockered, tweed-coated, checker-capped—he would accomplish the mounting of his high-saddled "Dux," which his valet would bring up to the porch as if it were a palfrey. Surveying the state of its polish, my father would pull on his suede gloves and test under Osip's anxious eye whether the tires were sufficiently tight. Then he would grip the handlebars, place his left foot on a metallic peg jutting at the rear end of the frame, push off with his right foot on the other side of the hind wheel and after three or four such propelments (with the bicycle now set in motion), leisurely translate his right leg into pedal position, move up his left, and settle down on the saddle.

At last I was home, and immediately upon entering the vestibule I became aware of loud, cheerful voices. With the opportuneness of dream arrangements, my uncle the Admiral was coming downstairs. From the red-carpeted landing above, where an armless Greek woman of marble presided over a malachite bowl for visiting cards, my parents were still speaking to him, and as he came down the steps, he looked up with a laugh and slapped the balustrade with the gloves he had in his hand. I knew at once that there would be no duel, that the challenge had been met by an apology, that all was right. I brushed past my uncle and reached the landing. I saw my mother's serene everyday face, but I could not look at my father. And then it happened: my heart welled in me like that wave on which the *Buynïy* rose when her captain brought her alongside the burning *Suvorov*, and I had no handkerchief, and ten years were to pass before a certain night in 1922, at a public lecture in Berlin, when my father shielded the lecturer (his old friend Milyukov) from the bullets of two Russian Fascists and, while vigorously knocking down one of the assassins, was fatally shot by the other. But no shadow was cast by that future event upon the bright stairs of our St. Petersburg house; the large, cool hand resting on my head did not quaver, and several lines of play in a difficult chess composition were not blended yet on the board.

Ten

THE WILD WEST fiction of Captain Mayne Reid (1818–
1883), translated and simplified, was tremendously popular with Russian children at the beginning of this century, long
after his American fame had faded. Knowing English, I could
savor his *Headless Horseman* in the unabridged original. Two
friends swap clothes, hats, mounts, and the wrong man gets
murdered—this is the main whorl of its intricate plot. The
edition I had (possibly a British one) remains in the stacks of
my memory as a puffy book bound in red cloth, with a watery-
gray frontispiece, the gloss of which had been gauzed over
when the book was new by a leaf of tissue paper. I see this
leaf as it disintegrated—at first folded improperly, then torn
off—but the frontispiece itself, which no doubt depicted
Louise Pointdexter's unfortunate brother (and perhaps a coyote
or two, unless I am thinking of *The Death Shot*, another
Mayne Reid tale), has been so long exposed to the blaze of
my imagination that it is now completely bleached (but miraculously replaced by the *real* thing, as I noted when translating this chapter into Russian in the spring of 1953, and
namely, by the view from a ranch you and I rented that year:
a cactus-and-yucca waste whence came that morning the
plaintive call of a quail—Gambel's Quail, I believe—overwhelming me with a sense of undeserved attainments and
rewards).

We shall now meet my cousin Yuri, a thin, sallow-faced boy
with a round cropped head and luminous gray eyes. The son
of divorced parents, with no tutor to look after him, a town
boy with no country home, he was in many respects different
from me. He spent his winters in Warsaw, with his father,
Baron Evgeniy Rausch von Traubenberg, its military governor, and his summers at Batovo or Vyra, unless taken abroad
by his mother, my eccentric Aunt Nina, to dull Central European spas, where she went for long solitary walks leaving him
to the care of messenger boys and chambermaids. In the
country, Yuri got up late, and I did not see him before my
return to lunch, after four or five hours of butterfly hunting.

From his earliest boyhood, he was absolutely fearless, but was squeamish and wary of "natural history," could not make himself touch wriggly things, could not endure the amusing emprisoned tickle of a small frog groping about in one's fist like a person, or the discreet, pleasantly cool, rhythmically undulating caress of a caterpillar ascending one's bare shin. He collected little soldiers of painted lead—these meant nothing to me but he knew their uniforms as well as I did different butterflies. He did not play any ball games, was incapable of pitching a stone properly, and could not swim, but had never told me he could not, and one day, as we were trying to cross the river by walking over a jam of pine logs afloat near a sawmill, he nearly got drowned when a particularly slippery bole started to plop and revolve under his feet.

We had first become aware of each other around Christmas 1904 (I was five and a half, he seven), in Wiesbaden: I remember him coming out of a souvenir shop and running toward me with a breloque, an inch-long little pistol of silver, which he was anxious to show me—and suddenly sprawling on the sidewalk but not crying when he picked himself up, unmindful of a bleeding knee and still clutching his minuscule weapon. In the summer of 1909 or 1910, he enthusiastically initiated me into the dramatic possibilities of the Mayne Reid books. He had read them in Russian (being in everything save surname much more Russian than I) and, when looking for a playable plot, was prone to combine them with Fenimore Cooper and his own fiery inventions. I viewed our games with greater detachment and tried to keep to the script. The staging took place generally in the park of Batovo, where the trails were even more tortuous and trappy than those of Vyra. For our mutual manhunts we used spring pistols that ejected, with considerable force, pencil-long sticks (from the brass tips of which we had manfully twisted off the protective rubber suction cups). Later came airguns of various types, which shot wax pellets or small tufted darts, with nonlethal, but often quite painful consequences. In 1912, the impressive mother-of-pearl plated revolver he arrived with was calmly taken away and locked up by my tutor Lenski, but not before we had blown to pieces a shoebox lid (in prelude to the real thing, an ace), which we had been holding up by turns at a gentlemanly distance in a green avenue where a duel was rumored to have been fought many dim years ago. The following summer he was away in Switzerland with his mother—and soon after his death (in 1919), upon revisiting the same hotel and getting the same rooms they had occupied that July, she thrust her hand into the recesses of an armchair in quest of a fallen hairpin and brought up a tiny cuirassier, unhorsed but with bandy legs still compressing an invisible charger.

When he arrived for a week's visit in June 1914 (now sixteen and a half to my fifteen, and the interval was beginning to tell), the first thing he did, as soon as we found ourselves alone in the garden, was to take out casually an "ambered" cigarette from a smart silver case on the gilt inside of which he bade me observe the formula $3 \times 4 = 12$ engraved in memory of the three nights he had spent, at last, with Countess G. He was now in love with an old general's young wife in Helsingfors and a captain's daughter in Gatchina. I witnessed with a kind of despair every new revelation of his man-of-the-world style. "Where can I make some rather private calls?" he asked. So I led him past the five poplars and the old dry well (out of which we had been rope-hauled by three frightened gardeners only a couple of years before) to a passage in the servants' wing where the cooing of pigeons came from an inviting windowsill and where there hung on the sun-stamped wall the remotest and oldest of our country-house telephones, a bulky boxlike contraption which had to be clangorously cranked up to educe a small-voiced operator. Yuri was now even more relaxed and sociable than the mustanger of former years. Sitting on a deal table against the wall and dangling his long legs, he chatted with the servants (something I was not supposed to do, and did not know how to do)—with an aged footman with sideburns whom I had never seen grin before or with a kitchen flirt, of whose bare neck and bold eyes I became aware only then. After Yuri had concluded his third long-distance conversation (I noticed with a blend of relief and dismay how awful his French was), we walked down to the village grocery which otherwise I never dreamed of visiting, let alone buying there a pound of black-and-white sunflower seeds. Throughout our return stroll, among the late afternoon butterflies that were preparing to roost, we

munched and spat, he showing me how to perform it con-
veyer-wise: split the seed open between the right-side back
teeth, ease out the kernel with the tongue, spit out the husk
halves, move the smooth kernel to the left-side molars, and
munch there, while the next seed which in the meantime has
already been cracked on the right, is being processed in its
turn. Speaking of right, he admitted he was a staunch "monarchist" (of a romantic rather than political nature) and went
on to deplore my alleged (and perfectly abstract) "democra-
tism." He recited samples of his fluent album poetry and
proudly remarked that he had been complimented by Di-
lanov-Tomski, a fashionable poet (who favored Italian epi-
graphs and sectional titles, such as "Songs of Lost Love,"
"Nocturnal Urns," and so on), for the striking "long" rhyme
"vnemlyu múze ya" ("I hearken to the Muse") and *"lyubvi
kontúziya"* ("love's contusion"), which I countered with my
best (and still unused) find: *"zápoved' "* (commandment) and
"posápivat' " (to sniffle). He was boiling with anger over Tolstoy's dismissal of the art of war and burning with admiration
for Prince Andrey Bolkonski—for he had just discovered *War
and Peace* which I had read for the first time when I was
eleven (in Berlin, on a Turkish sofa, in our somberly rococo
Privatstrasse flat giving on a dark, damp back garden with
larches and gnomes that have remained in that book, like an
old postcard, forever).

I suddenly see myself in the uniform of an officers' training
school: we are strolling again villageward, in 1916, and (like
Maurice Gerald and doomed Henry Pointdexter) have exchanged clothes—Yuri is wearing my white flannels and
striped tie. During the short week he stayed that year we devised a singular entertainment which I have not seen described
anywhere. There was a swing in the center of a small circular
playground surrounded by jasmins, at the bottom of our garden. We adjusted the ropes in such a way as to have the green
swingboard pass just a couple of inches above one's forehead
and nose if one lay supine on the sand beneath. One of us
would start the fun by standing on the board and swinging
with increasing momentum; the other would lie down with
the back of his head on a marked spot, and from what seemed
an enormous height the swinger's board would swish swiftly

My mother and her brother, Vasiliy Ivanovich Rukavishnikov (1874–1916), on the terrace of his château at Pau, Basses Pyrenees, October 1913.

above the supine one's face. And three years later, as a cavalry
officer in Denikin's army, he was killed fighting the Reds in
northern Crimea. I saw him dead in Yalta, the whole front of
his skull pushed back by the impact of several bullets, which
had hit him like the iron board of a monstrous swing, when
having outstripped his detachment he was in the act of recklessly attacking alone a Red machine-gun nest. Thus was
quenched his lifelong thirst for intrepid conduct in battle, for
that ultimate gallant gallop with drawn pistol or unsheathed
sword. Had I been competent to write his epitaph, I might
have summed up matters by saying—in richer words than I
can muster here—that all emotions, all thoughts, were gov-
erned in Yuri by one gift: a sense of honor equivalent, morally,
to absolute pitch.

2

I have lately reread *The Headless Horseman* (in a drab edition, without pictures). It has its points. Take, for instance,
that barroom in a log-walled Texan hotel, in the year of our
Lord (as the captain would say) 1850, with its shirt-sleeved
"saloon-clerk"—a fop in his own right, since the shirt was a
ruffled one "of finest linen and lace." The colored decanters
(among which a Dutch clock "quaintly ticked") were like "an
iris sparkling behind his shoulders," like "an aureole surrounding his perfumed head." From glass to glass, the ice and
the wine and the monongahela passed. An odor of musk, ab-
sinthe, and lemon peel filled the saloon. The glare of its cam-
phine lamps brought out the dark asterisks produced on the
white sand of its floor "by expectoration." In another year of
our Lord—namely 1941—I caught some very good moths at
the neon lights of a gasoline station between Dallas and Fort
Worth.

Into the bar comes the villain, the "slave-whipping Missis-
sippian," ex-captain of Volunteers, handsome, swaggering,
scowling Cassius Calhoun. After toasting "America for Americans, and confusion to all foreign interlopers—especially the
d—d [an evasion that puzzled me sorely when I first stumbled
upon it: dead? detested?] Irish!" he intentionally collided with
Maurice the Mustanger (scarlet scarf, slashed velvet trousers,

hot Irish blood), a young horse trader who was really a bar-
onet, *Sir* Maurice Gerald, as his thrilled bride was to discover
at the end of the book. Wrong thrills, like this, may have been
one of the reasons that the Irish-born author's fame waned so
soon in his adopted country.

Immediately after the collision, Maurice performed several
actions in the following order: he deposited his glass upon the
counter, drew a silk handkerchief from his pocket, wiped from
his embroidered shirt-bosom "the defilement of the whiskey,"
transferred the handkerchief from his right hand to his left,
took the half-empty glass from the counter, swilled its remaining contents into Calhoun's face, quietly redeposited the
glass upon the counter. This sequence I still know by heart,
so often did my cousin and I enact it.

The duel took place there and then, in the emptied barroom, the men using Colt's six-shooters. Despite my interest
in the fight (. . . both were wounded . . . their blood spurted
all over the sanded floor . . .), I could not prevent myself
from leaving the saloon in my fancy to mingle with the hushed
crowd in front of the hotel, so as to make out (in the "scented
dark") certain señoritas "of questionable calling."

With still more excitement did I read of Louise Pointdexter,
Calhoun's fair cousin, daughter of a sugar planter, "the highest and haughtiest of his class" (though why an old man who
planted sugar should be high and haughty was a mystery to
me). She is revealed in the throes of jealousy (which I used
to feel so keenly at miserable parties when Mara Rzhevuski, a
pale child with a white silk bow in her black hair, suddenly
and inexplicably stopped noticing me) standing upon the edge
of her *azotea*, her white hand resting upon the copestone of
the parapet which is "still wet with the dews of night," her
twin breasts sinking and swelling in quick, spasmodic
breathing, her twin breasts, let me reread, sinking and swelling, her lorgnette directed . . .

That lorgnette I found afterward in the hands of Madame
Bovary, and later Anna Karenin had it, and then it passed into
the possession of Chekhov's Lady with the Lapdog and was
lost by her on the pier at Yalta. When Louise held it, it was
directed toward the speckled shadows under the mesquites,
where the horseman of her choice was having an innocent

conversation with the daughter of a wealthy *haciendado*, Doña Isidora Covarubio de los Llanos (whose "head of hair in luxuriance rivalled the tail of a wild steed").

"I had the opportunity," Maurice later explained to Louise, as one rider to another, "of being useful to Doña Isidora, in once rescuing her from some rude Indians." "A slight service, you call it!" the young Creole exclaimed. "A man who should do that much for *me*—" "What would you do for *him*?" asked Maurice eagerly. "*Pardieu!* I should *love* him!" "Then I would give half my life to see you in the hands of Wild Cat and his drunken comrades—and the other half to deliver you from the danger."

And here we find the gallant author interpolating a strange confession: "The sweetest kiss that I ever had in my life was when a woman—a fair creature, in the hunting field—leant over in her saddle and kissed me as I sate in mine."

The "sate," let us concede, gives duration and body to the kiss which the captain so comfortably "had," but I could not help feeling, even at the age of eleven, that centaurian lovemaking was not without its special limitations. Moreover, Yuri and I both knew a boy who had tried it, but the girl's horse had pushed his into a ditch. Exhausted by our adventures in the chaparral, we lay on the grass and discussed women. Our innocence seems to me now almost monstrous, in the light of various "sexual confessions" (to be found in Havelock Ellis and elsewhere), which involve tiny tots mating like mad. The slums of sex were unknown to us. Had we ever happened to hear about two normal lads idiotically masturbating in each other's presence (as described so sympathetically, with all the smells, in modern American novels), the mere notion of such an act would have seemed to us as comic and impossible as sleeping with an amelus. Our ideal was Queen Guinevere, Isolda, a not quite merciless *belle dame*, another man's wife, proud and docile, fashionable and fast, with slim ankles and narrow hands. The little girls in neat socks and pumps whom we and other little boys used to meet at dancing lessons or at Christmas Tree parties had all the enchantments, all the sweets and stars of the tree preserved in their flame-dotted iris, and they teased us, they glanced back, they delightfully participated in our vaguely festive dreams, but they belonged, those nymphets, to another class of creatures than the adolescent belles and large-hatted vamps for whom we actually yearned. After having made me sign an oath of secrecy with blood, Yuri told me about the married lady in Warsaw with whom at twelve or thirteen he was secretly in love and whom a couple of years later he made love to. By comparison it would have sounded jejune, I feared, to tell him about my seaside playmates, but I cannot recall what substitute I invented to match his romance. Around that time, though, a real romantic adventure did come my way. I am now going to do something quite difficult, a kind of double somersault with a Welsh waggle (old acrobats will know what I mean), and I want complete silence, please.

3

In August 1910, my brother and I were in Bad Kissingen with our parents and tutor (Lenski); after that my father and mother traveled to Munich and Paris, and back to St. Petersburg, and then to Berlin where we boys, with Lenski, were spending the autumn and the beginning of the winter, having our teeth fixed. An American dentist—Lowell or Lowen, I do not remember his name exactly—ripped some of our teeth out and trussed up others with twine before disfiguring us with braces. Even more hellish than the action of the rubber pear pumping hot pain into a cavity were the cotton pads—I could not endure their dry contact and squeak—which used to be thrust between gum and tongue for the operator's convenience; and there would be, in the windowpane before one's helpless eyes, a transparency, some dismal seascape or gray grapes, shuddering with the dull reverberations of distant trams under dull skies. *"In den Zelten achtzehn A"*—the address comes back to me dancing trochaically, immediately followed by the whispery motion of the cream-colored electric taxi that took us there. We expected every possible compensation in atonement for those dreadful mornings. My brother loved the museum of wax figures in the Arcade off the Unter den Linden—Friedrich's grenadiers, Bonaparte communing with a mummy, young Liszt, who composed a rhapsody in his sleep, and Marat, who died in a shoe; and for me (who did not know yet that Marat had been an ardent lepidopterist) there was, at the corner of that Arcade, Gruber's famous butterfly shop, a camphoraceous paradise at the top of a steep, narrow staircase which I climbed every other day to inquire if Chapman's new Hairstreak or Mann's recently rediscovered White had been obtained for me at last. We tried tennis on a public court; but a wintry gale kept chasing dead leaves across it, and, besides, Lenski could not really play, although insisting on joining us, without removing his overcoat, in a lopsided threesome. Subsequently, most of our afternoons were spent at a roller-skating rink in the Kurfürstendamm. I remember Lenski rolling inexorably toward a pillar which he attempted to embrace while collapsing with a dreadful clatter; and after persevering awhile he would content himself with sitting in one of the loges that flanked the plush parapet and consuming there wedges of slightly salty mokka *torte* with whipped cream, while I kept self-sufficiently overtaking poor gamely stumbling Sergey, one of those galling little pictures that revolve on and on in one's mind. A military band (Germany, at the time, was the land of music), manned by an uncommonly jerky conductor, came to life every ten minutes or so but could hardly drown the ceaseless, sweeping rumble of wheels.

There existed in Russia, and still exists no doubt, a special type of school-age boy who, without necessarily being athletic in appearance or outstanding in mental scope, often having, in fact, no energy in class, a rather scrawny physique, and even, perhaps, a touch of pulmonary consumption, excels quite phenomenally at soccer *and* chess, and learns with the utmost ease and grace any kind of sport or game of skill (Borya Shik, Kostya Buketov, the famous brothers Sharabanov—where are they now, my teammates and rivals?). I was a good skater on ice and switching to rollers was for me not more difficult than for a man to replace an ordinary razor by a safety one. Very quickly I learned two or three tricky steps on the wooden floor of the rink and in no ballroom have I danced with more zest or ability (we, Shiks and Buketovs, are poor ballroom dancers, as a rule). The several instructors wore scarlet uniforms, half hussar and half hotel page. They all spoke English, of one brand or another. Among the regular visitors, I soon noticed a group of American young ladies. At first, they all merged in a common spin of bright exotic beauty. The process of differentiation began when, during one of my lone dances (and a few seconds before I came the worst cropper that I ever came on a rink), somebody said something about me as I whirled by, and a wonderful, twangy feminine voice answered, "Yes, isn't he cunning?"

I can still see her tall figure in a navy-blue tailor-made suit. Her large velvet hat was transfixed by a dazzling pin. For obvious reasons, I decided her name was Louise. At night, I would lie awake and imagine all kinds of romantic situations, and think of her willowy waist and white throat, and worry over an odd discomfort that I had associated before only with chafing shorts. One afternoon, I saw her standing in the lobby of the rink, and the most dashing of the instructors, a sleek ruffian of the Calhoun type, was holding her by the wrist and interrogating her with a crooked grin, and she was looking away and childishly turning her wrist this way and that in his grasp, and the following night he was shot, lassoed, buried alive, shot again, throttled, bitingly insulted, coolly aimed at, spared, and left to drag a life of shame.

High-principled but rather simple Lenski, who was abroad for the first time, had some trouble keeping the delights of sightseeing in harmony with his pedagogical duties. We took advantage of this and guided him toward places where our parents might not have allowed us to go. He could not resist the Wintergarten, for instance, and so, one night, we found ourselves there, drinking ice-chocolate in an orchestra box. The show developed on the usual lines: a juggler in evening clothes; then a woman, with flashes of rhinestones on her bosom, trilling a concert aria in alternating effusions of green and red light; then a comic on roller skates. Between him and a bicycle act (of which more later) there was an item on the program called "The Gala Girls," and with something of the shattering and ignominious physical shock I had experienced when coming that cropper on the rink, I recognized my American ladies in the garland of linked, shrill-voiced, shameless "girls," all rippling from left to right, and then from right to left, with a rhythmic rising of ten identical legs that shot up from ten corollas of flounces. I located my Louise's face—

and knew at once that it was all over, that I had lost her, that I would never forgive her for singing so loudly, for smiling so redly, for disguising herself in that ridiculous way so unlike the charm of either "proud Creoles" or "questionable señoritas." I could not stop thinking of her altogether, of course, but the shock seems to have liberated in me a certain inductive process, for I soon noticed that *any* evocation of the feminine form would be accompanied by the puzzling discomfort already familiar to me. I asked my parents about it (they had come to Berlin to see how we were getting along) and my father ruffled the German newspaper he had just opened and replied in English (with the parody of a possible quotation—a manner of speech he often adopted in order to get going): "That, my boy, is just another of nature's absurd combinations, like shame and blushes, or grief and red eyes." *"Tolstoy vient de mourir,"* he suddenly added, in another, stunned voice, turning to my mother.

"*Da chto tï* [something like "good gracious"]!" she exclaimed in distress, clasping her hands in her lap. "*Pora domoy* [Time to go home]," she concluded, as if Tolstoy's death had been the portent of apocalyptic disasters.

4

And now comes that bicycle act—or at least my version of it. The following summer, Yuri did not visit us at Vyra, and I was left alone to cope with my romantic agitation. On rainy days, crouching at the foot of a little-used bookshelf, in a poor light that did all it could to discourage my furtive inquiry, I used to look up obscure, obscurely tantalizing and enervating terms in the Russian eighty-two-volume edition of Brockhaus' *Encyclopedia*, where, in order to save space, the title word of this or that article would be reduced, throughout a detailed discussion, to its capitalized initial, so that the columns of dense print in minion type, besides taxing one's attention, acquired the trumpery fascination of a masquerade, at which the abbreviation of a none too familiar word played hide and seek with one's avid eyes: "Moses tried to abolish P. but failed . . . In modern times, hospitable P. flourished in Austria under Maria Theresa . . . In many parts of Germany the profits

from P. went to the clergy . . . In Russia, P. has been officially
tolerated since 1843 . . . Seduced at the age of ten or twelve
by her master, his sons or one of his menials, an orphan almost
invariably ends in P.''—and so forth, all of which went to
enrich with mystery, rather than soberly elucidate, the allusions to meretricious love that I met with during my first im-
mersions in Chekhov or Andreev. Butterfly hunting and
various sports took care of the sunny hours, but no amount
of exercise could prevent the restlessness which, every evening,
launched me on vague voyages of discovery. After riding on
horseback most of the afternoon, bicycling in the colored dusk
was a curiously subtle, almost discarnate feeling. I had turned
upside down and lowered to subsaddle level the handlebars
of my Enfield bicycle, converting it into my conception of a
racing model. Along the paths of the park I would skim, following yesterday's patterned imprint of Dunlop tires; neatly
avoiding the ridges of tree roots; selecting a fallen twig and
snapping it with my sensitive front wheel; weaving between
two flat leaves and then between a small stone and the hole
from which it had been dislodged the evening before; enjoying the brief smoothness of a bridge over a brook; skirting
the wire fence of the tennis court; nuzzling open the little
whitewashed gate at the end of the park; and then, in a melancholy ecstasy of freedom, speeding along the hard-baked,
pleasantly agglutinate margins of long country roads.

   That summer I would always ride by a certain isba, golden
in the low sun, in the doorway of which Polenka, the daughter
of our head coachman Zahar, a girl of my age, would stand,
leaning against the jamb, her bare arms folded on her breast
in a soft, comfortable manner peculiar to rural Russia. She
would watch me approach with a wonderful welcoming radiance on her face, but as I rode nearer, this would dwindle
to a half smile, then to a faint light at the corners of her
compressed lips, and, finally, this, too, would fade, so that
when I reached her, there would be no expression at all on
her round, pretty face. As soon as I had passed, however, and
had turned my head for an instant to take a last look before
sprinting uphill, the dimple would be back, the enigmatic light
would be playing again on her dear features. I never spoke to
her, but long after I had stopped riding by at that hour, our

ocular relationship was renewed from time to time during two or three summers. She would appear from nowhere, always standing a little apart, always barefoot, rubbing her left instep against her right calf or scratching with her fourth finger the parting in her light brown hair, and always leaning against things—against the stable door while my horse was being saddled, against the trunk of a tree when the whole array of country servitors would be seeing us off to town for the winter on a crisp September morning. Every time, her bosom seemed a little softer, her forearms a little stronger, and once or twice I discerned, just before she drifted out of my ken (at sixteen she married a blacksmith in a distant village), a gleam of gentle mockery in her wide-set hazel eyes. Strange to say, she was the first to have the poignant power, by merely *not* letting her smile fade, of burning a hole in my sleep and jolting me into clammy consciousness, whenever I dreamed of her, although in real life I was even more afraid of being revolted by her dirt-caked feet and stale-smelling clothes than of insulting her by the triteness of quasi-seignioral advances.

5

There are two especially vivid aspects of her that I would like to hold up simultaneously before my eyes in conclusion of her haunting image. The first lived for a long while within me quite separately from the Polenka I associated with doorways and sunsets, as if I had glimpsed a nymphean incarnation of her pitiful beauty that were better left alone. One June day, the year when she and I were both thirteen, on the banks of the Oredezh, I was engaged in collecting some so-called Parnassians—*Parnassius mnemosyne*, to be exact—strange butterflies of ancient lineage, with rustling, glazed, semitransparent wings and catkin-like flossy abdomens. My quest had led me into a dense undergrowth of milky-white racemosa and dark alder at the very edge of the cold, blue river, when suddenly there was an outburst of splashes and shouts, and from behind a fragrant bush, I caught sight of Polenka and three or four other naked children bathing from the ruins of an old bathhouse a few feet away. Wet, gasping, one nostril of her snub nose running, the ribs of her adolescent body arched under her pale, goose-pimpled skin, her calves flecked with black mud, a curved comb burning in her damp-darkened hair, she was scrambling away from the swish and clack of water-lily stems that a drum-bellied girl with a shaven head and a shamelessly excited stripling wearing around the loins a kind of string, locally used against the evil eye, were yanking out of the water and harrying her with; and for a second or two—before I crept away in a dismal haze of disgust and desire—I saw a strange Polenka shiver and squat on the boards of the half-broken wharf, covering her breasts against the east wind with her crossed arms, while with the tip of her tongue she taunted her pursuers.

The other picture refers to a Sunday at Christmastide in 1916. From the silent, snow-blanketed platform of the little station of Siverski on the Warsaw line (it was the nearest to our country place), I was watching a distant silvery grove as it changed to lead under the evening sky and waiting for it to emit the dull-violet smoke of the train that would take me back to St. Petersburg after a day of skiing. The smoke duly appeared and at the same moment, she and another girl walked past me, heavily kerchiefed, in huge felt boots and horrible, shapeless, long quilted jackets, with the stuffing showing at the torn spots of the coarse black cloth, and as she passed, Polenka, a bruise under her eye and a puffed-up lip (did her husband beat her on Saturdays?) remarked in wistful and melodious tones to nobody in particular: "*A barchuk-to menya ne priznal* [Look, the young master does not know me]—" and that was the only time I ever heard her speak.

6

The summer evenings of my boyhood when I used to ride by her cottage speak to me in that voice of hers now. On a road among fields, where it met the desolate highway, I would dismount and prop my bicycle against a telegraph pole. A sunset, almost formidable in its splendor, would be lingering in the fully exposed sky. Among its imperceptibly changing amassments, one could pick out brightly stained structural details of celestial organisms, or glowing slits in dark banks, or flat, ethereal beaches that looked like mirages of desert islands.

I did not know then (as I know perfectly well now) what to do with such things—how to get rid of them, how to transform them into something that can be turned over to the reader in printed characters to have *him* cope with the blessed shiver—and this inability enhanced my oppression. A colossal shadow would begin to invade the fields, and the telegraph poles hummed in the stillness, and the night-feeders ascended the stems of their plants. Nibble, nibble, nibble—went a handsome striped caterpillar, not figured in Spuler, as he clung to a campanula stalk, working down with his mandibles along the edge of the nearest leaf out of which he was eating a leisurely hemicircle, then again extending his neck, and again bending it gradually, as he deepened the neat concave. Automatically, I might slip him, with a bit of his plantlet, into a matchbox to take home with me and have him produce next year a Splendid Surprise, but my thoughts were elsewhere: Zina and Colette, my seaside playmates; Louise, the prancer; all the flushed, low-sashed, silky-haired little girls at festive parties; languorous Countess G., my cousin's lady; Polenka smiling in the agony of my new dreams—all would merge to form somebody I did not know but was bound to know soon.

I recall one particular sunset. It lent an ember to my bicycle bell. Overhead, above the black music of telegraph wires, a number of long, dark-violet clouds lined with flamingo pink hung motionless in a fan-shaped arrangement; the whole thing was like some prodigious ovation in terms of color and form! It was dying, however, and everything else was darkening, too; but just above the horizon, in a lucid, turquoise space, beneath a black stratus, the eye found a vista that only a fool could mistake for the spare parts of this or any other sunset. It occupied a very small sector of the enormous sky and had the peculiar neatness of something seen through the wrong end of a telescope. There it lay in wait, a family of serene clouds in miniature, an accumulation of brilliant convolutions, anachronistic in their creaminess and extremely remote; remote but perfect in every detail; fantastically reduced but faultlessly shaped; my marvelous tomorrow ready to be delivered to me.

Eleven

IN ORDER to reconstruct the summer of 1914, when the numb fury of verse-making first came over me, all I really need is to visualize a certain pavilion. There the lank, fifteen-year-old lad I then was, sought shelter during a thunderstorm, of which there was an inordinate number that July. I dream of my pavilion at least twice a year. As a rule, it appears in my dreams quite independently of their subject matter, which, of course, may be anything, from abduction to zoolatry. It hangs around, so to speak, with the unobtrusiveness of an artist's signature. I find it clinging to a corner of the dream canvas or cunningly worked into some ornamental part of the picture. At times, however, it seems to be suspended in the middle distance, a trifle baroque, and yet in tune with the handsome trees, dark fir and bright birch, whose sap once ran through its timber. Wine-red and bottle-green and dark-blue lozenges of stained glass lend a chapel-like touch to the latticework of its casements. It is just as it was in my boyhood, a sturdy old wooden structure above a ferny ravine in the older, riverside part of our Vyra park. Just as it was, or perhaps a little more perfect. In the real thing some of the glass was missing, crumpled leaves had been swept in by the wind. The narrow little bridge that arched across the ghyll at its deepest part, with the pavilion rising midway like a coagulated rainbow, was as slippery after a rainy spell as if it had been coated with some dark and in a sense magic ointment. Etymologically, "pavilion" and "papilio" are closely related. Inside, there was nothing in the way of furniture except a folding table hinged rustily to the wall under the east window, through the two or three glassless or pale-glassed compartments of which, among the bloated blues and drunken reds, one could catch a glimpse of the river. On a floorboard at my feet a dead horsefly lay on its back near the brown remains of a birch ament. And the patches of disintegrating whitewash on the inside of the door had been used by various trespassers for such jottings as: "Dasha, Tamara and Lena have been here" or "Down with Austria!"

The storm passed quickly. The rain, which had been a mass of violently descending water wherein the trees writhed and rolled, was reduced all at once to oblique lines of silent gold breaking into short and long dashes against a background of subsiding vegetable agitation. Gulfs of voluptuous blue were expanding between great clouds—heap upon heap of pure white and purplish gray, *lepota* (Old Russian for "stately beauty"), moving myths, gouache and guano, among the curves of which one could distinguish a mammary allusion or the death mask of a poet.

The tennis court was a region of great lakes.

Beyond the park, above steaming fields, a rainbow slipped into view; the fields ended in the notched dark border of a remote fir wood; part of the rainbow went across it, and that section of the forest edge shimmered most magically through the pale green and pink of the iridescent veil drawn before it: a tenderness and a glory that made poor relatives of the rhomboidal, colored reflections which the return of the sun had brought forth on the pavilion floor.

A moment later my first poem began. What touched it off? I think I know. Without any wind blowing, the sheer weight of a raindrop, shining in parasitic luxury on a cordate leaf, caused its tip to dip, and what looked like a globule of quicksilver performed a sudden glissando down the center vein, and then, having shed its bright load, the relieved leaf unbent. Tip, leaf, dip, relief—the instant it all took to happen seemed to me not so much a fraction of time as a fissure in it, a missed heartbeat, which was refunded at once by a patter of rhymes: I say "patter" intentionally, for when a gust of wind did come, the trees would briskly start to drip all together in as crude an imitation of the recent downpour as the stanza I was already muttering resembled the shock of wonder I had experienced when for a moment heart and leaf had been one.

2

In the avid heat of the early afternoon, benches, bridges and boles (all things, in fact, save the tennis court) were drying with incredible rapidity, and soon little remained of my initial inspiration. Although the bright fissure had closed, I doggedly went on composing. My medium happened to be Russian but could have been just as well Ukrainian, or Basic English, or Volapük. The kind of poem I produced in those days was hardly anything more than a sign I made of being alive, of passing or having passed, or hoping to pass, through certain intense human emotions. It was a phenomenon of orientation rather than of art, thus comparable to stripes of paint on a roadside rock or to a pillared heap of stones marking a mountain trail.

But then, in a sense, all poetry is positional: to try to express one's position in regard to the universe embraced by consciousness, is an immemorial urge. The arms of consciousness reach out and grope, and the longer they are the better. Tentacles, not wings, are Apollo's natural members. Vivian Bloodmark, a philosophical friend of mine, in later years, used to say that while the scientist sees everything that happens in one point of space, the poet feels everything that happens in one point of time. Lost in thought, he taps his knee with his wandlike pencil, and at the same instant a car (New York license plate) passes along the road, a child bangs the screen door of a neighboring porch, an old man yawns in a misty Turkestan orchard, a granule of cinder-gray sand is rolled by the wind on Venus, a Docteur Jacques Hirsch in Grenoble puts on his reading glasses, and trillions of other such trifles occur—all forming an instantaneous and transparent organism of events, of which the poet (sitting in a lawn chair, at Ithaca, N.Y.) is the nucleus.

That summer I was still far too young to evolve any wealth of "cosmic synchronization" (to quote my philosopher again). But I did discover, at least, that a person hoping to become a poet must have the capacity of thinking of several things at a time. In the course of the languid rambles that accompanied the making of my first poem, I ran into the village schoolmaster, an ardent Socialist, a good man, intensely devoted to my father (I welcome this image again), always with a tight posy of wild flowers, always smiling, always perspiring. While politely discussing with him my father's sudden journey to town, I registered simultaneously and with equal clarity not only his wilting flowers, his flowing tie and the blackheads on the fleshy volutes of his nostrils, but also the

The author in 1915, St. Petersburg.

dull little voice of a cuckoo coming from afar, and the flash of a Queen of Spain settling on the road, and the remembered impression of the pictures (enlarged agricultural pests and bearded Russian writers) in the well-aerated classrooms of the village school which I had once or twice visited; and—to continue a tabulation that hardly does justice to the ethereal simplicity of the whole process—the throb of some utterly irrelevant recollection (a pedometer I had lost) was released from a neighboring brain cell, and the savor of the grass stalk I was chewing mingled with the cuckoo's note and the fritillary's takeoff, and all the while I was richly, serenely aware of my own manifold awareness.

He beamed and he bowed (in the effusive manner of a Russian radical), and took a couple of steps backward, and turned, and jauntily went on his way, and I picked up the thread of my poem. During the short time I had been otherwise engaged, something seemed to have happened to such words as I had already strung together: they did not look quite as lustrous as they had before the interruption. Some suspicion crossed my mind that I might be dealing in dummies. Fortunately, this cold twinkle of critical perception did not last. The fervor I had been trying to render took over again and brought its medium back to an illusory life. The ranks of words I reviewed were again so glowing, with their puffed-out little chests and trim uniforms, that I put down to mere fancy the sagging I had noticed out of the corner of my eye.

3

Apart from credulous inexperience, a young Russian versificator had to cope with a special handicap. In contrast to the rich vocabulary of satirical or narrative verse, the Russian elegy suffered from a bad case of verbal anemia. Only in very expert hands could it be made to transcend its humble origin—the pallid poetry of eighteenth-century France. True, in my day a new school was in the act of ripping up the old rhythms, but it was still to the latter that the conservative beginner turned in search of a neutral instrument—possibly because he did not wish to be diverted from the simple expression of simple emotions by adventures in hazardous form. Form, however, got its revenge. The rather monotonous designs into which early nineteenth-century Russian poets had twisted the pliant elegy resulted in certain words, or types of words (such as the Russian equivalents of *fol amour* or *langoureux et rêvant*) being coupled again and again, and this later lyricists could not shake off for a whole century.

In an especially obsessive arrangement, peculiar to the iambic of four to six feet, a long, wriggly adjective would occupy the first four or five syllables of the last three feet of the line. A good tetrametric example would be *ter-pi bes-chis-len-ni-e mu-ki* (en-dure in-cal-cu-la-ble tor-ments). The young Russian poet was liable to slide with fatal ease into this alluring abyss of syllables, for the illustration of which I have chosen *beschislennïe* only because it translates well; the real favorites were such typical elegiac components as *zadumchivïe* (pensive), *utrachennïe* (lost), *muchitel'nïe* (anguished), and so forth, all accented on the second syllable. Despite its great length, a word of that kind had but a single accent of its own, and, consequently, the penultimate metrical stress of the line encountered a normally unstressed syllable (*nï* in the Russian example, "la" in the English one). This produced a pleasant scud, which, however, was much too familiar an effect to redeem banality of meaning.

An innocent beginner, I fell into all the traps laid by the singing epithet. Not that I did not struggle. In fact, I was working at my elegy very hard, taking endless trouble over every line, choosing and rejecting, rolling the words on my tongue with the glazed-eyed solemnity of a tea-taster, and still it would come, that atrocious betrayal. The frame impelled the picture, the husk shaped the pulp. The hackneyed order of words (short verb or pronoun—long adjective—short noun) engendered the hackneyed disorder of thought, and some such line as *poeta gorestnïe gryozï*, translatable and accented as "the poet's melancholy daydreams," led fatally to a rhyming line ending in *rozï* (roses) or *beryozï* (birches) or *grozï* (thunderstorms), so that certain emotions were connected with certain surroundings not by a free act of one's will but by the faded ribbon of tradition. Nonetheless, the nearer my poem got to its completion, the more certain I became that whatever I saw before me would be seen by others. As I focused my eyes upon a kidney-shaped flower bed (and noted one pink petal lying on the loam and a small ant investigating its decayed edge) or considered the tanned midriff of a birch trunk where some hoodlum had stripped it of its papery, pepper-and-salt bark, I really believed that all this would be perceived by the reader through the magic veil of my words such as *utrachennïe rozï* or *zadumchivoy beryozï*. It did not occur to me then that far from being a veil, those poor words were so opaque that, in fact, they formed a wall in which all one could distinguish were the well-worn bits of the major and minor poets I imitated. Years later, in the squalid suburb of a foreign town, I remember seeing a paling, the boards of which had been brought from some other place where they had been used, apparently, as the inclosure of an itinerant circus. Animals had been painted on it by a versatile barker; but whoever had removed the boards, and then knocked them together again, must have been blind or insane, for now the fence showed only disjointed parts of animals (some of them, moreover, upside down)—a tawny haunch, a zebra's head, the leg of an elephant.

4

On the physical plane, my intense labors were marked by a number of dim actions or postures, such as walking, sitting, lying. Each of these broke again into fragments of no spatial importance: at the walking stage, for instance, I might be wandering one moment in the depths of the park and the next pacing the rooms of the house. Or, to take the sitting stage, I would suddenly become aware that a plate of something I could not even remember having sampled was being removed and that my mother, her left cheek twitching as it did whenever she worried, was narrowly observing from her place at the top of the long table my moodiness and lack of appetite. I would lift my head to explain—but the table had gone, and I was sitting alone on a roadside stump, the stick of my butterfly net, in metronomic motion, drawing arc after arc on the brownish sand; earthen rainbows, with variations in depth of stroke rendering the different colors.

When I was irrevocably committed to finish my poem or

die, there came the most trancelike state of all. With hardly a twinge of surprise, I found myself, of all places, on a leathern couch in the cold, musty, little-used room that had been my grandfather's study. On that couch I lay prone, in a kind of reptilian freeze, one arm dangling, so that my knuckles loosely touched the floral figures of the carpet. When next I came out of that trance, the greenish flora was still there, my arm was still dangling, but now I was prostrate on the edge of a rickety wharf, and the water lilies I touched were real, and the undulating plump shadows of alder foliage on the water—apotheosized inkblots, oversized amoebas—were rhythmically palpitating, extending and drawing in dark pseudopods, which, when contracted, would break at their rounded margins into elusive and fluid macules, and these would come together again to reshape the groping terminals. I relapsed into my private mist, and when I emerged again, the support of my extended body had become a low bench in the park, and the live shadows, among which my hand dipped, now moved on the ground, among violet tints instead of aqueous black and green. So little did ordinary measures of existence mean in that state that I would not have been surprised to come out of its tunnel right into the park of Versailles, or the Tiergarten, or Sequoia National Forest; and, inversely, when the old trance occurs nowadays, I am quite prepared to find myself, when I awaken from it, high up in a certain tree, above the dappled bench of my boyhood, my belly pressed against a thick, comfortable branch and one arm hanging down among the leaves upon which the shadows of other leaves move.

Various sounds reached me in my various situations. It might be the dinner gong, or something less usual, such as the foul music of a barrel organ. Somewhere near the stables the old tramp would grind, and on the strength of more direct impressions imbibed in earlier years, I would see him mentally from my perch. Painted on the front of his instrument were Balkan peasants of sorts dancing among palmoid willows. Every now and then he shifted the crank from one hand to the other. I saw the jersey and skirt of his little bald female monkey, her collar, the raw sore on her neck, the chain which she kept plucking at every time the man pulled it, hurting her badly, and the several servants standing around, gaping, grinning—simple folks terribly tickled by a monkey's "antics." Only the other day, near the place where I am recording these matters, I came across a farmer and his son (the kind of keen healthy kid you see in breakfast food ads), who were similarly diverted by the sight of a young cat torturing a baby chipmunk—letting him run a few inches and then pouncing upon him again. Most of his tail was gone, the stump was bleeding. As he could not escape by running, the game little fellow tried one last measure: he stopped and lay down on his side in order to merge with a bit of light and shade on the ground, but the too violent heaving of his flank gave him away.

The family phonograph, which the advent of the evening set in action, was another musical machine I could hear through my verse. On the veranda where our relatives and friends assembled, it emitted from its brass mouthpiece the so-called *tsïganskie romansï* beloved of my generation. These were more or less anonymous imitations of gypsy songs—or imitations of such imitations. What constituted their gypsiness was a deep monotonous moan broken by a kind of hiccup, the audible cracking of a lovesick heart. At their best, they were responsible for the raucous note vibrating here and there in the works of true poets (I am thinking especially of Alexander Blok). At their worst, they could be likened to the apache stuff composed by mild men of letters and delivered by thickset ladies in Parisian night clubs. Their natural environment was characterized by nightingales in tears, lilacs in bloom and the alleys of whispering trees that graced the parks of the landed gentry. Those nightingales trilled, and in a pine grove the setting sun banded the trunks at different levels with fiery red. A tambourine, still throbbing, seemed to lie on the darkening moss. For a spell, the last notes of the husky contralto pursued me through the dusk. When silence returned, my first poem was ready.

5

It was indeed a miserable concoction, containing many borrowings besides its pseudo-Pushkinian modulations. An echo of Tyutchev's thunder and a refracted sunbeam from Fet were alone excusable. For the rest, I vaguely remember the mention of "memory's sting"—*vospominan'ya zhalo* (which I had really visualized as the ovipositor of an ichneumon fly straddling a cabbage caterpillar, but had not dared say so)—and something about the old-world charm of a distant barrel organ. Worst of all were the shameful gleanings from Apuhtin's and Grand Duke Konstantin's lyrics of the *tsïganski* type. They used to be persistently pressed upon me by a youngish and rather attractive aunt, who could also spout Louis Bouilhet's famous piece (*À Une Femme*), in which a metaphorical violin bow is incongruously used to play on a metaphorical guitar, and lots of stuff by Ella Wheeler Wilcox—a tremendous hit with the empress and her ladies-in-waiting. It seems hardly worthwhile to add that, as themes go, my elegy dealt with the loss of a beloved mistress—Delia, Tamara or Lenore—whom I had never lost, never loved, never met but was all set to meet, love, lose.

In my foolish innocence, I believed that what I had written was a beautiful and wonderful thing. As I carried it homeward, still unwritten, but so complete that even its punctuation marks were impressed on my brain like a pillow crease on a sleeper's flesh, I did not doubt that my mother would greet my achievement with glad tears of pride. The possibility of her being much too engrossed, that particular night, in other events to listen to verse did not enter my mind at all. Never in my life had I craved more for her praise. Never had I been more vulnerable. My nerves were on edge because of the darkness of the earth, which I had not noticed muffling itself up, and the nakedness of the firmament, the disrobing of which I had not noticed either. Overhead, between the formless trees bordering my dissolving path, the night sky was pale with stars. In those years, that marvelous mess of constellations, nebulae, interstellar gaps and all the rest of the awesome show provoked in me an indescribable sense of nausea, of utter panic, as if I were hanging from earth upside down on the brink of infinite space, with terrestrial gravity still holding me by the heels but about to release me any moment.

Except for two corner windows in the upper story (my mother's sitting room), the house was already dark. The night watchman let me in, and slowly, carefully, so as not to disturb the arrangement of words in my aching head, I mounted the stairs. My mother reclined on the sofa with the St. Petersburg *Rech* in her hands and an unopened London *Times* in her lap. A white telephone gleamed on the glass-topped table near her. Late as it was, she still kept expecting my father to call from St. Petersburg where he was being detained by the tension of approaching war. An armchair stood by the sofa, but I always avoided it because of its golden satin, the mere sight of which caused a laciniate shiver to branch from my spine like nocturnal lightning. With a little cough, I sat down on a footstool and started my recitation. While thus engaged, I kept staring at the farther wall upon which I see so clearly in retrospect some small daguerreotypes and silhouettes in oval frames, a Somov aquarelle (young birch trees, the half of a rainbow—everything very melting and moist), a splendid Versailles autumn by Alexandre Benois, and a crayon drawing my mother's mother had made in her girlhood—that park pavilion again with its pretty windows partly screened by linked branches. The Somov and the Benois are now in some Soviet Museum but that pavilion will never be nationalized.

As my memory hesitated for a moment on the threshold of the last stanza, where so many opening words had been tried that the finally selected one was now somewhat camouflaged by an array of false entrances, I heard my mother sniff. Presently I finished reciting and looked up at her. She was smiling ecstatically through the tears that streamed down her face. "How wonderful, how beautiful," she said, and with the tenderness in her smile still growing, she passed me a hand mirror so that I might see the smear of blood on my cheekbone where at some indeterminable time I had crushed a gorged mosquito by the unconscious act of propping my cheek on my fist. But I saw more than that. Looking into my own eyes, I had the shocking sensation of finding the mere dregs of my usual self, odds and ends of an evaporated identity which it took my reason quite an effort to gather again in the glass.

Twelve

WHEN I first met Tamara—to give her a name concolorous with her real one—she was fifteen, and I was a year older. The place was the rugged but comely country (black fir, white birch, peatbogs, hayfields, and barrens) just south of St. Petersburg. A distant war was dragging on. Two years later, that trite *deus ex machina*, the Russian Revolution, came, causing my removal from the unforgettable scenery. In fact, already then, in July 1915, dim omens and backstage rumblings, the hot breath of fabulous upheavals, were affecting the so-called "Symbolist" school of Russian poetry—especially the verse of Alexander Blok.

During the beginning of that summer and all through the previous one, Tamara's name had kept cropping up (with the feigned naïveté so typical of Fate, when meaning business) here and there on our estate (Entry Forbidden) and on my uncle's land (Entry Strictly Forbidden) on the opposite bank of the Oredezh. I would find it written with a stick on the reddish sand of a park avenue, or penciled on a whitewashed wicket, or freshly carved (but not completed) in the wood of some ancient bench, as if Mother Nature were giving me mysterious advance notices of Tamara's existence. That hushed July afternoon, when I discovered her standing quite still (only her eyes were moving) in a birch grove, she seemed to have been spontaneously generated there, among those watchful trees, with the silent completeness of a mythological manifestation.

She slapped dead the horsefly that she had been waiting for to light and proceeded to catch up with two other, less pretty girls who were calling to her. Presently, from a vantage point above the river, I saw them walking over the bridge, clicking along on brisk high heels, all three with their hands tucked into the pockets of their navy-blue jackets and, because of the flies, every now and then tossing their beribboned and beflowered heads. Very soon I traced Tamara to the modest *dachka* (summer cottage) that her family rented in the village.

I would ride my horse or my bicycle in the vicinity, and with the sudden sensation of a dazzling explosion (after which my heart would take quite a time to get back from where it had landed) I used to come across Tamara at this or that bland bend of the road. Mother Nature eliminated first one of her girl companions, then the other, but not until August—August 9, 1915, to be Petrarchally exact, at half-past four of that season's fairest afternoon in the rainbow-windowed pavilion that I had noticed my trespasser enter—not until then, did I muster sufficient courage to speak to her.

Seen through the carefully wiped lenses of time, the beauty of her face is as near and as glowing as ever. She was short and a trifle on the plump side but very graceful, with her slim ankles and supple waist. A drop of Tatar or Circassian blood might have accounted for the slight slant of her merry dark eye and the duskiness of her blooming cheek. A light down, akin to that found on fruit of the almond group, lined her profile with a fine rim of radiance. She accused her rich-brown hair of being unruly and oppressive and threatened to have it bobbed, and did have it bobbed a year later, but I always recall it as it looked first, fiercely braided into a thick plait that was looped up at the back of her head and tied there with a big bow of black silk. Her lovely neck was always bare, even in winter in St. Petersburg, for she had managed to obtain permission to eschew the stifling collar of a Russian schoolgirl's uniform. Whenever she made a funny remark or produced a jingle from her vast store of minor poetry, she had a most winning way of dilating her nostrils with a little snort of amusement. Still, I was never quite sure when she was serious and when she was not. The rippling of her ready laughter, her rapid speech, the roll of her very uvular *r*, the tender, moist gleam on her lower eyelid—indeed, all her features were ecstatically fascinating to me, but somehow or other, instead of divulging her person, they tended to form a brilliant veil in which I got entangled every time I tried to learn more about her. When I used to tell her we would marry in the last days of 1917, as soon as I had finished school, she would quietly call me a fool. I visualized her home but vaguely. Her mother's first name and patronymic (which were all I knew of the

woman) had merchant-class or clerical connotations. Her father, who, I gathered, took hardly any interest in his family,
was the steward of a large estate somewhere in the south.

Autumn came early that year. Layers of fallen leaves piled
up ankle-deep by the end of August. Velvet-black Camberwell
Beauties with creamy borders sailed through the glades. The
tutor to whose erratic care my brother and I were entrusted
that season used to hide in the bushes in order to spy upon
Tamara and me with the aid of an old telescope he had found
in the attic; but in his turn, one day, the peeper was observed
by my uncle's purple-nosed old gardener Apostolski (incidentally, a great tumbler of weeding-girls) who very kindly reported it to my mother. She could not tolerate snooping, and
besides (though I never spoke to her about Tamara) she knew
all she cared to know of my romance from my poems which
I recited to her in a spirit of praiseworthy objectivity, and
which she lovingly copied out in a special album. My father
was away with his regiment; he did feel it his duty, after ac-
quainting himself with the stuff, to ask me some rather awkward questions when he returned from the front a month
later; but my mother's purity of heart had carried her, and was
to carry her, over worse difficulties. She contented herself with
shaking her head dubiously though not untenderly, and telling the butler to leave every night some fruit for me on the
lighted veranda.

I took my adorable girl to all those secret spots in the
woods, where I had daydreamed so ardently of meeting her,
of creating her. In one particular pine grove everything fell
into place, I parted the fabric of fancy, I tasted reality. As my
uncle was absent that year, we could also stray freely in his
huge, dense, two-century-old park with its classical cripples of
green-stained stone in the main avenue and labyrinthine paths
radiating from a central fountain. We walked "swinging
hands," country-fashion. I picked dahlias for her on the borders along the gravel drive, under the distant benevolent eye
of old Priapostolski. We felt less safe when I used to see her
home, or near-home, or at least to the village bridge. I remember the coarse graffiti linking our first names, in strange
diminutives, on a certain white gate and, a little apart from
that village-idiot scrawl, the adage "Prudence is the friend of

Passion," in a bristly hand well-known to me. Once, at sunset, near the orange and black river, a young *dachnik* (vacationist) with a riding crop in his hand bowed to her in passing; whereupon she blushed like a girl in a novel but only said, with a spirited sneer, that he had never ridden a horse in his life. And another time, as we emerged onto a turn of the highway, my two little sisters in their wild curiosity almost fell out of the red family "torpedo" swerving toward the bridge.

On dark rainy evenings I would load the lamp of my bicycle with magical lumps of calcium carbide, shield a match from the gusty wind and, having imprisoned a white flame in the glass, ride cautiously into the darkness. The circle of light cast by my lamp would pick out the damp, smooth shoulder of the road, between its central system of puddles and the long bordering grasses. Like a tottering ghost, the pale ray would weave across a clay bank at the turn as I began the downhill ride toward the river. Beyond the bridge the road sloped up again to meet the Rozhestveno–Luga highway, and just above that junction a footpath among dripping jasmin bushes ascended a steep escarpment. I had to dismount and push my bicycle. As I reached the top, my livid light flitted across the six-pillared white portico at the back of my uncle's mute, shuttered manor—as mute and shuttered as it may be today, half a century later. There, in a corner of that arched shelter, from where she had been following the zigzags of my ascending light, Tamara would be waiting, perched on the broad parapet with her back to a pillar. I would put out my lamp and grope my way toward her. One is moved to speak more eloquently about these things, about many other things that one always hopes might survive captivity in the zoo of words—but the ancient limes crowding close to the house drown Mnemosyne's monologue with their creaking and heaving in the restless night. Their sigh would subside. The rain pipe at one side of the porch, a small busybody of water, could be heard steadily bubbling. At times, some additional rustle, troubling the rhythm of the rain in the leaves, would cause Tamara to turn her head in the direction of an imagined footfall, and then, by a faint luminosity—now rising above the horizon of my memory despite all that rain—I could distinguish the outline of her face; but there was nothing and nobody to fear, and presently she would gently exhale the breath she had held for a moment and her eyes would close again.

2

With the coming of winter our reckless romance was transplanted to grim St. Petersburg. We found ourselves horribly deprived of the sylvan security we had grown accustomed to. Hotels disreputable enough to admit us stood beyond the limits of our daring, and the great era of parked amours was still remote. The secrecy that had been so pleasurable in the country now became a burden, yet neither of us could face the notion of chaperoned meetings at her home or mine. Consequently, we were forced to wander a good deal about the town (she, in her little gray-furred coat, I, white-spatted and karakul-collared, with a knuckle-duster in my velvet-lined pocket), and this permanent quest for some kind of refuge produced an odd sense of hopelessness, which, in its turn, foreshadowed other, much later and lonelier, roamings.

We skipped school: I forget what Tamara's procedure was; mine consisted of talking either of the two chauffeurs into dropping me at this or that corner on the way to school (both were good sports and actually refused to accept my gold—handy five-rouble pieces coming from the bank in appetizing, weighty sausages of ten or twenty shining pieces, in the aesthetic recollection of which I can freely indulge now that my proud émigré destitution is also a thing of the past). Nor had I any trouble with our wonderful, eminently bribable Ustin, who took the calls on our ground-floor telephone, the number of which was 24-43, *dvadtsat' chetïre sorok tri*; he briskly replied I had a sore throat. I wonder, by the way, what would happen if I put in a long-distance call from my desk right now? No answer? No such number? No such country? Or the voice of Ustin saying *"moyo pochtenietse!"* (the ingratiating diminutive of "my respects")? There exist, after all, well-publicized Slavs and Kurds who are well over one hundred and fifty. My father's telephone in his study (584-51) was not listed, and my form master in his attempts to learn the truth about my failing health never got anywhere, though sometimes I missed three days in a row.

The author aged nineteen, with his brothers and sisters, in Yalta, November 1918. Kirill is seven; Sergey (unfortunately disfigured by flaws in the picture), wearing a rimless pince-nez and the uniform of the Yalta Gymnasium, is eighteen; Olga is fifteen; Elena (firmly clasping Box II) is twelve.

We walked under the white lacery of berimed avenues in public parks. We huddled together on cold benches—after having removed first their tidy cover of snow, then our snow-incrusted mittens. We haunted museums. They were drowsy and deserted on weekday mornings, and very warm, in contrast to the glacial haze and its red sun that, like a flushed moon, hung in the eastern windows. There we would seek the quiet back rooms, the stopgap mythologies nobody looked at, the etchings, the medals, the paleographic items, the Story of Printing—poor things like that. Our best find, I think, was a small room where brooms and ladders were kept; but a batch of empty frames that suddenly started to slide and topple in the dark attracted an inquisitive art lover, and we fled. The Hermitage, St. Petersburg's Louvre, offered nice nooks, especially in a certain hall on the ground floor, among cabinets with scarabs, behind the sarcophagus of Nana, high priest of Ptah. In the Russian Museum of Emperor Alexander III, two halls (Nos. 30 and 31, in its northeastern corner), harboring repellently academic paintings by Shishkin ("Clearing in a Pine Forest") and by Harlamov ("Head of a Young Gypsy"), offered a bit of privacy because of some tall stands with drawings—until a foul-mouthed veteran of the Turkish campaign threatened to call the police. So from these great museums we graduated to smaller ones, such as the Suvorov, for instance, where I recall a most silent room full of old armor and tapestries, and torn silk banners, with several bewigged, heavily booted dummies in green uniforms standing guard over us. But wherever we went, invariably, after a few visits, this or that hoary, blear-eyed, felt-soled attendant would grow suspicious and we would have to transfer our furtive frenzy elsewhere—to the Pedagogical Museum, to the Museum of Court Carriages, or to a tiny museum of old maps, which guidebooks do not even list—and then out again into the cold, into some lane of great gates and green lions with rings in their jaws, into the stylized snowscape of the "Art World," *Mir Iskusstva*—Dobuzhinski, Alexandre Benois—so dear to me in those days.

On late afternoons, we got into the last row of seats in one of the two movie theatres (the Parisiana and the Piccadilly) on Nevski Avenue. The art was progressing. Sea waves were tinted a sickly blue and as they rode in and burst into foam

against a black, remembered rock (Rocher de la Vierge, Biarritz—funny, I thought, to see again the beach of my cosmopolitan childhood), there was a special machine that imitated
the sound of the surf, making a kind of washy swish that never
quite managed to stop short with the scene but for three or
four seconds accompanied the next feature—a brisk funeral,
say, or shabby prisoners of war with their dapper captors. As
often as not, the title of the main picture was a quotation from
some popular poem or song and might be quite long-winded,
such as *The Chrysanthemums Blossom No More in the Garden*
or *Her Heart Was a Toy in His Hands and Like a Toy It Got
Broken*. Female stars had low foreheads, magnificent eyebrows, lavishly shaded eyes. The favorite actor of the day was
Mozzhuhin. One famous director had acquired in the Moscow countryside a white-pillared mansion (not unlike that of
my uncle), and it appeared in all the pictures he made. Mozzhuhin would drive up to it in a smart sleigh and fix a steely
eye on a light in one window while a celebrated little muscle
twitched under the tight skin of his jaw.

When museums and movie houses failed us and the night
was young, we were reduced to exploring the wilderness of
the world's most gaunt and enigmatic city. Solitary street
lamps were metamorphosed into sea creatures with prismatic
spines by the icy moisture on our eyelashes. As we crossed the
vast squares, various architectural phantoms arose with silent
suddenness right before us. We felt a cold thrill, generally associated not with height but with depth—with an abyss opening at one's feet—when great, monolithic pillars of polished
granite (polished by slaves, repolished by the moon, and rotating smoothly in the polished vacuum of the night) zoomed
above us to support the mysterious rotundities of St. Isaac's
cathedral. We stopped on the brink, as it were, of these perilous massifs of stone and metal, and with linked hands, in
Lilliputian awe, craned our heads to watch new colossal visions rise in our way—the ten glossy-gray atlantes of a palace
portico, or a giant vase of porphyry near the iron gate of a
garden, or that enormous column with a black angel on its
summit that obsessed, rather than adorned, the moon-flooded
Palace Square, and went up and up, trying in vain to reach
the subbase of Pushkin's *"Exegi monumentum."*

She contended afterward, in her rare moments of moodiness, that our love had not withstood the strain of that winter; a flaw had appeared, she said. Through all those months, I had kept writing verse to her, for her, about her, two or three poems per week; in the spring of 1916 I published a collection of them—and was horrified when she drew my attention to something I had not noticed at all when concocting the book. There it was, the same ominous flaw, the banal hollow note, and glib suggestion that our love was doomed since it could never recapture the miracle of its initial moments, the rustle and rush of those limes in the rain, the compassion of the wild countryside. Moreover—but this neither of us saw at the time—my poems were juvenile stuff, quite devoid of merit and ought never to have been put on sale. The book (a copy of which still exists, alas, in the "closed stacks" of the Lenin Library, Moscow) deserved what it got at the tearing claws of the few critics who noticed it in obscure periodicals. My Russian literature teacher at school, Vladimir Hippius, a first-rate though somewhat esoteric poet whom I greatly admired (he surpassed in talent, I think, his much better known cousin, Zinaïda Hippius, woman poet and critic) brought a copy with him to class and provoked the delirious hilarity of the majority of my classmates by applying his fiery sarcasm (he was a fierce man with red hair) to my most romantic lines. His famous cousin at a session of the Literary Fund asked my father, its president, to tell me, please, that I would never, never be a writer. A well-meaning, needy and talentless journalist, who had reasons to be grateful to my father, wrote an impossibly enthusiastic piece about me, some five hundred lines dripping with fulsome praise; it was intercepted in time by my father, and I remember him and me, while we read it in manuscript, grinding our teeth and groaning—the ritual adopted by our family when faced by something in awful taste or by somebody's *gaffe*. The whole business cured me permanently of all interest in literary fame and was probably the cause of that almost pathological and not always justified indifference to reviews which in later years deprived me of the emotions most authors are said to experience.

That spring of 1916 is the one I see as the very type of a St. Petersburg spring, when I recall such specific images as

Tamara, wearing an unfamiliar white hat, among the spectators of a hard-fought interscholastic soccer game, in which,
that Sunday, the most sparkling luck helped me to make save
after save in goal; and a Camberwell Beauty, exactly as old as
our romance, sunning its bruised black wings, their borders
now bleached by hibernation, on the back of a bench in Alex-
androvski Garden; and the booming of cathedral bells in
the keen air, above the corrugated dark blue of the Neva,
voluptuously free of ice; and the fair in the confetti-studded
slush of the Horse Guard Boulevard during Catkin Week,
with its squeaking and popping din, its wooden toys, its loud
hawking of Turkish delight and Cartesian devils called *ameri-
kanskie zhiteli* ("American inhabitants")—minute goblins of
glass riding up and down in glass tubes filled with pink- or
lilac-tinted alcohol as real Americans do (though all the epithet meant was "outlandish") in the shafts of transparent
skyscrapers as the office lights go out in the greenish sky. The
excitement in the streets made one drunk with desire for the
woods and the fields. Tamara and I were especially eager to
return to our old haunts, but all through April her mother
kept wavering between renting the same cottage again and
economically staying in town. Finally, under a certain condition (accepted by Tamara with the fortitude of Hans Andersen's little mermaid), the cottage was rented, and a glorious
summer immediately enveloped us, and there she was, my
happy Tamara, on the points of her toes, trying to pull down
a racemosa branch in order to pick its puckered fruit, with all
the world and its trees wheeling in the orb of her laughing
eye, and a dark patch from her exertions in the sun forming
under her raised arm on the raw shantung of her yellow frock.
We lost ourselves in mossy woods and bathed in a fairy-tale
cove and swore eternal love by the crowns of flowers that, like
all little Russian mermaids, she was so fond of weaving, and
early in the fall she moved to town in search of a job (this was
the condition set by her mother), and in the course of the
following months I did not see her at all, engrossed as I was
in the kind of varied experience which I thought an elegant
littérateur should seek. I had already entered an extravagant
phase of sentiment and sensuality, that was to last about ten

years. In looking at it from my present tower I see myself as a hundred different young men at once, all pursuing one changeful girl in a series of simultaneous or overlapping love affairs, some delightful, some sordid, that ranged from one-night adventures to protracted involvements and dissimulations, with very meager artistic results. Not only is the experience in question, and the shadows of all those charming ladies useless to me now in recomposing my past, but it creates a bothersome defocalization, and no matter how I worry the screws of memory, I cannot recall the way Tamara and I parted. There is possibly another reason, too, for this blurring: we had parted too many times before. During that last summer in the country, we used to part forever after each secret meeting when, in the fluid blackness of the night, on that old wooden bridge between masked moon and misty river, I would kiss her warm, wet eyelids and rain-chilled face, and immediately after go back to her for yet another farewell—and then the long, dark, wobbly uphill ride, my slow, laboriously pedaling feet trying to press down the monstrously strong and resilient darkness that refused to stay under.

I do remember, however, with heartbreaking vividness, a certain evening in the summer of 1917 when, after a winter of incomprehensible separation, I chanced to meet Tamara on a suburban train. For a few minutes between two stops, in the vestibule of a rocking and rasping car, we stood next to each other, I in a state of intense embarrassment, of crushing regret, she consuming a bar of chocolate, methodically breaking off small, hard bits of the stuff, and talking of the office where she worked. On one side of the tracks, above bluish bogs, the dark smoke of burning peat was mingling with the smoldering wreck of a huge, amber sunset. It can be proved, I think, by published records that Alexander Blok was even then noting in his diary the very peat smoke I saw, and the wrecked sky. There was later a period in my life when I might have found this relevant to my last glimpse of Tamara as she turned on the steps to look back at me before descending into the jasmin-scented, cricket-mad dusk of a small station; but today no alien marginalia can dim the purity of the pain.

3

When, at the end of the year, Lenin took over, the Bolsheviks immediately subordinated everything to the retention of power, and a regime of bloodshed, concentration camps, and hostages entered upon its stupendous career. At the time many believed one could fight Lenin's gang and save the achievements of the March Revolution. My father, who had been elected to the Constituent Assembly which, in its preliminary phase, strove to prevent the entrenchment of the Soviets, decided to remain as long as possible in St. Petersburg but to send his large family to the Crimea, a region that was still free (this freedom was to last for only a few weeks longer). We traveled in two parties, my brother and I going separately from my mother and the three younger children. The Soviet era was a dull week old; liberal newspapers still came out; and while seeing us off at the Nikolaevski station and waiting with us, my imperturbable father settled down at a corner table in the buffet to write, in his flowing, "celestial" hand (as the typesetters said, marveling at the absence of corrections), a leading article for the moribund *Rech* (or perhaps some emergency publication) on those special long strips of ruled paper, which corresponded proportionally to columns of print. As far as I remember, the main reason for sending my brother and me off so promptly was the probability of our being inducted into the new "Red" army if we stayed in town. I was annoyed at going to a fascinating region in mid-November, long after the collecting season was over, having never been very good at digging for pupae (though, eventually, I did turn up a few beneath a big oak in our Crimean garden). Annoyance changed to distress, when after making a precise little cross over the face of each of us, my father rather casually added that very possibly, *ves'ma vozmozhno*, he would never see us again; whereupon, in trench coat and khaki cap, with his briefcase under his arm, he strode away into the steamy fog.

The long journey southward started tolerably well, with the heat still humming and the lamps still intact in the Petrograd–Simferopol first-class sleeper, and a passably famous singer in dramatic makeup, with a bouquet of chrysanthemums in brown paper pressed to her breast, stood in the corridor, tap-

ping upon the pane, along which somebody walked and
waved as the train started to glide, without one jolt to indicate
we were leaving that gray city forever. But soon after Moscow,
all comfort came to an end. At several points of our slow
dreary progression, the train, including our sleeping car, was
invaded by more or less Bolshevized soldiers who were returning to their homes from the front (one called them either
"deserters" or "Red Heroes," depending upon one's political
views). My brother and I thought it rather fun to lock ourselves up in our compartment and thwart every attempt to
disturb us. Several soldiers traveling on the roof of the car
added to the sport by trying to use, not unsuccessfully, the
ventilator of our room as a toilet. My brother, who was a first-
rate actor, managed to simulate all the symptoms of a bad
case of typhus, and this helped us out when the door finally
gave way. Early on the third morning, at a vague stop, I took
advantage of a lull in those merry proceedings to get a breath
of fresh air. I moved gingerly along the crowded corridor,
stepping over the bodies of snoring men, and got off. A milky
mist hung over the platform of an anonymous station—we
were somewhere not far from Kharkov. I wore spats and a
derby. The cane I carried, a collector's item that had belonged
to my uncle Ruka, was of a light-colored, beautifully freckled
wood, and the knob was a smooth pink globe of coral cupped
in a gold coronet. Had I been one of the tragic bums who
lurked in the mist of that station platform where a brittle
young fop was pacing back and forth, I would not have withstood the temptation to destroy him. As I was about to board
the train, it gave a jerk and started to move; my foot slipped
and my cane was sent flying under the wheels. I had no special
affection for the thing (in fact, I carelessly lost it a few years
later), but I was being watched, and the fire of adolescent
amour propre prompted me to do what I cannot imagine my
present self ever doing. I waited for one, two, three, four cars
to pass (Russian trains were notoriously slow in gaining momentum) and when, at last, the rails were revealed, I picked
up my cane from between them and raced after the night-
marishly receding bumpers. A sturdy proletarian arm conformed to the rules of sentimental fiction (rather than to those
of Marxism) by helping me to swarm up. Had I been left

behind, those rules might still have held good, since I would have been brought near Tamara, who by that time had also moved south and was living in a Ukrainian hamlet less than a hundred miles from the scene of that ridiculous occurrence.

4

Of her whereabouts I learned unexpectedly a month or so after my arrival in southern Crimea. My family settled in the vicinity of Yalta, at Gaspra, near the village of Koreiz. The whole place seemed completely foreign; the smells were not Russian, the sounds were not Russian, the donkey braying every evening just as the muezzin started to chant from the village minaret (a slim blue tower silhouetted against a peach-colored sky) was positively Baghdadian. And there was I standing on a chalky bridle path near a chalky stream bed where separate, serpentlike bands of water thinly glided over oval stones—there was I, holding a letter from Tamara. I looked at the abrupt Yayla Mountains, covered up to their rocky brows with the karakul of the dark Tauric pine; at the maquis-like stretch of evergreen vegetation between mountain and sea; at the translucent pink sky, where a self-conscious crescent shone, with a single humid star near it; and the whole artificial scene struck me as something in a prettily illustrated, albeit sadly abridged, edition of *The Arabian Nights.* Suddenly I felt all the pangs of exile. There had been the case of Pushkin, of course—Pushkin who had wandered in banishment here, among those naturalized cypresses and laurels—but though some prompting might have come from his elegies, I do not think my exaltation was a pose. Thenceforth for several years, until the writing of a novel relieved me of that fertile emotion, the loss of my country was equated for me with the loss of my love.

Meanwhile, the life of my family had completely changed. Except for a few jewels astutely buried in the normal filling of a talcum powder container, we were absolutely ruined. But this was a very minor matter. The local Tatar government had been swept away by a brand-new Soviet, and we were subjected to the preposterous and humiliating sense of utter insecurity. During the winter of 1917–18 and well into the windy and bright Crimean spring, idiotic death toddled by our side. Every other day, on the white Yalta pier (where, as you remember, the lady of Chekhov's "Lady with the Lapdog" lost her lorgnette among the vacational crowd), various harmless people had, in advance, weights attached to their feet and then were shot by tough Bolshevik sailors imported from Sebastopol for the purpose. My father, who was not harmless, had joined us by this time, after some dangerous adventures, and, in that region of lung specialists, had adopted the mimetic disguise of a doctor without changing his name ("simple and elegant," as a chess annotator would have said of a corresponding move on the board). We dwelt in an inconspicuous villa that a kind friend, Countess Sofia Panin, had placed at our disposal. On certain nights, when rumors of nearing assassins were especially strong, the men of our family took turns patrolling the house. The slender shadows of oleander leaves would cautiously move in the sea breeze along a pale wall, as if pointing at something, with a great show of stealth. We had a shotgun and a Belgian automatic, and did our best to pooh-pooh the decree which said that anyone unlawfully possessing firearms would be executed on the spot.

Chance treated us kindly; nothing happened beyond the shock we got in the middle of a January night, when a brigand-like figure, all swathed in leather and fur, crept into our midst—but it turned out to be only our former chauffeur, Tsiganov, who had thought nothing of riding all the way from St. Petersburg, on buffers and in freight cars, through the immense, frosty and savage expanse of Russia, for the mere purpose of bringing us a very welcome sum of money unexpectedly sent us by some good friends of ours. He also brought the mail received at our St. Petersburg address; among it was that letter from Tamara. After a month's stay, Tsiganov declared the Crimean scenery bored him and departed—to go all the way back north, with a big bag over his shoulder, containing various articles which we would have gladly given him had we thought he coveted them (such as a trouser press, tennis shoes, nightshirts, an alarm clock, a flat-iron, several other ridiculous things I have forgotten) and the absence of which only gradually came to light if not pointed out, with vindictive zeal, by an anemic servant girl whose pale charms he had also rifled. Curiously enough, he had prevailed upon us to transfer my mother's precious stones from the talcum powder container (that he had at once detected) to a hole dug in the garden under a versatile oak—and there they all were after his departure.

Then, one spring day in 1918, when the pink puffs of blossoming almond trees enlivened the dark mountainside, the Bolsheviks vanished and a singularly silent army of Germans replaced them. Patriotic Russians were torn between the animal relief of escaping native executioners and the necessity of owing their reprieve to a foreign invader—especially to the Germans. The latter, however, were losing their war in the west and came to Yalta on tiptoe, with diffident smiles, an army of gray apparitions easy for a patriot to ignore, and ignored it was, save for some rather ungrateful snickers at the halfhearted KEEP OFF THE GRASS signs that appeared on park lawns. A couple of months later, having nicely repaired the plumbing in various villas vacated by commissars, the Germans faded out in their turn; the Whites trickled in from the east and soon began fighting the Red Army, which was attacking the Crimea from the north. My father became Minister of Justice in the Regional Government located in Simferopol, and his family was lodged near Yalta on the Livadia grounds, the Tsar's former domain. A brash, hectic gaiety associated with White-held towns brought back, in a vulgarized version, the amenities of peaceful years. Cafés did a wonderful business. All kinds of theatres thrived. One morning, on a mountain trail, I suddenly met a strange cavalier, clad in a Circassian costume, with a tense, perspiring face painted a fantastic yellow. He kept furiously tugging at his horse, which, without heeding him, proceeded down the steep path at a curiously purposeful walk, like that of an offended person leaving a party. I had seen runaway horses, but I had never seen a walkaway one before, and my astonishment was given a still more pleasurable edge when I recognized the unfortunate rider as Mozzhuhin, whom Tamara and I had so often admired on the screen. The film *Haji Murad* (after Tolstoy's tale of that gallant, rough-riding mountain chief) was being rehearsed on the mountain pastures of the range. "Stop that brute [*Derzhite proklyatoe zhivotnoe*]," he said through his teeth as he saw me, but at the same moment, with a mighty sound of crunching and crashing stones, two authentic Tatars came running down to the rescue, and I trudged on, with my butterfly net, toward the upper crags where the Euxine race of the Hippolyte Grayling was expecting me.

In that summer of 1918, a poor little oasis of miraged youth, my brother and I used to frequent the amiable and eccentric family who owned the coastal estate Oleiz. A bantering friendship soon developed between my coeval Lidia T. and me. Many young people were always around, brown-limbed braceleted young beauties, a well-known painter called Sorin, actors, a male ballet dancer, merry White Army officers, some of whom were to die quite soon, and what with beach parties, blanket parties, bonfires, a moon-spangled sea and a fair supply of Crimean Muscat Lunel, a lot of amorous fun went on; and all the while, against this frivolous, decadent and somehow unreal background (which I was pleased to believe conjured up the atmosphere of Pushkin's visit to the Crimea a century earlier), Lidia and I played a little oasal game of our own invention. The idea consisted of parodizing a biographic approach projected, as it were, into the future and thus transforming the very specious present into a kind of paralyzed past as perceived by a doddering memoirist who recalls, through a helpless haze, his acquaintance with a great writer when both were young. For instance, either Lidia or I (it was a matter of chance inspiration) might say, on the terrace after supper: "The writer liked to go out on the terrace after supper," or "I shall always remember the remark V. V. made one warm night: 'It is,' he remarked, 'a warm night'"; or, still sillier: "He was in the habit of lighting his cigarette, before smoking it"—all this delivered with much pensive, reminiscent fervor which seemed hilarious and harmless to us at the time; but now—now I catch myself wondering if we did not disturb unwittingly some perverse and spiteful demon.

Through all those months, every time a bag of mail managed to get from the Ukraine to Yalta, there would be a letter for me from my Cynara. Nothing is more occult than the way letters, under the auspices of unimaginable carriers, circulate through the weird mess of civil wars; but whenever, owing to that mess, there was some break in our correspondence,

Tamara would act as if she ranked deliveries with ordinary natural phenomena such as the weather or tides, which human affairs could not affect, and she would accuse me of not answering her, when in fact I did nothing but write to her and think of her during those months—despite my many betrayals.

5

Happy is the novelist who manages to preserve an actual love letter that he received when he was young within a work of fiction, embedded in it like a clean bullet in flabby flesh and quite secure there, among spurious lives. I wish I had kept the whole of our correspondence that way. Tamara's letters were a sustained conjuration of the rural landscape we knew so well. They were, in a sense, a distant but wonderfully clear antiphonal response to the much less expressive lyrics I had once dedicated to her. By means of unpampered words, whose secret I fail to discover, her high-school-girlish prose could evoke with plangent strength every whiff of damp leaf, every autumn-rusted frond of fern in the St. Petersburg countryside. "Why did we feel so cheerful when it rained?" she asked in one of her last letters, reverting as it were to the pure source of rhetorics. *"Bozhe moy"* (*mon Dieu*—rather than "My God"), where has it gone, all that distant, bright, endearing (*Vsyo eto dalyokoe, svetloe, miloe*—in Russian no subject is needed here, since these are neuter adjectives that play the part of abstract nouns, on a bare stage, in a subdued light).

Tamara, Russia, the wildwood grading into old gardens, my northern birches and firs, the sight of my mother getting down on her hands and knees to kiss the earth every time we came back to the country from town for the summer, *et la montagne et le grand chêne*—these are things that fate one day bundled up pell-mell and tossed into the sea, completely severing me from my boyhood. I wonder, however, whether there is really much to be said for more anesthetic destinies, for, let us say, a smooth, safe, small-town continuity of time, with its primitive absence of perspective, when, at fifty, one is still dwelling in the clapboard house of one's childhood, so that every time one cleans the attic one comes across the same

pile of old brown schoolbooks, still together among later ac-
cumulations of dead objects, and where, on summery Sunday
mornings, one's wife stops on the sidewalk to endure for a
minute or two that terrible, garrulous, dyed, church-bound
McGee woman, who, way back in 1915, used to be pretty,
naughty Margaret Ann of the mint-flavored mouth and nimble fingers.

The break in my own destiny affords me in retrospect a
syncopal kick that I would not have missed for worlds. Ever
since that exchange of letters with Tamara, homesickness has
been with me a sensuous and particular matter. Nowadays,
the mental image of matted grass on the Yayla, of a canyon
in the Urals or of salt flats in the Aral Region, affects me
nostalgically and patriotically as little, or as much, as, say,
Utah; but give me anything on any continent resembling the
St. Petersburg countryside and my heart melts. What it would
be actually to see again my former surroundings, I can hardly
imagine. Sometimes I fancy myself revisiting them with a false
passport, under an assumed name. It could be done.

But I do not think I shall ever do it. I have been dreaming
of it too idly and too long. Similarly, during the latter half of
my sixteen-month stay in the Crimea, I planned for so long a
time to join Denikin's army, with the intention not so much
of clattering astride a chamfrained charger into the cobbled
outskirts of St. Petersburg (my poor Yuri's dream) as of reaching Tamara in her Ukrainian hamlet, that the army ceased to
exist by the time I had made up my mind. In March of 1919,
the Reds broke through in northern Crimea, and from various
ports a tumultuous evacuation of anti-Bolshevik groups began. Over a glassy sea in the bay of Sebastopol, under wild
machine-gun fire from the shore (the Bolshevik troops had
just taken the port), my family and I set out for Constantinople and Piraeus on a small and shoddy Greek ship *Nadezhda*
(Hope) carrying a cargo of dried fruit. I remember trying to
concentrate, as we were zigzagging out of the bay, on a game
of chess with my father—one of the knights had lost its head,
and a poker chip replaced a missing rook—and the sense of
leaving Russia was totally eclipsed by the agonizing thought
that Reds or no Reds, letters from Tamara would be still

coming, miraculously and needlessly, to southern Crimea, and would search there for a fugitive addressee, and weakly flap about like bewildered butterflies set loose in an alien zone, at the wrong altitude, among an unfamiliar flora.

Thirteen

I N 1919, by way of the Crimea and Greece, a flock of Nabokovs—three families in fact—fled from Russia to western
Europe. It was arranged that my brother and I would go up
to Cambridge, on a scholarship awarded more in atonement
for political tribulations than in acknowledgement of intellectual merit. The rest of my family expected to stay for a while
in London. Living expenses were to be paid by the handful
of jewels which Natasha, a farsighted old chambermaid, just
before my mother's departure from St. Petersburg in November 1917, had swept off a dresser into a *nécessaire* and which
for a brief spell had undergone interment or perhaps some
kind of mysterious maturation in a Crimean garden. We had
left our northern home for what we thought would be a brief
wait, a prudent perching pause on the southern ledge of Russia; but the fury of the new regime had refused to blow over.
In Greece, during two spring months, braving the constant
resentment of intolerant shepherd dogs, I searched in vain for
Gruner's Orange-tip, Heldreich's Sulphur, Krueper's White: I
was in the wrong part of the country. On the Cunard liner
Pannonia which left Greece on May 18, 1919 (twenty-one years
too soon as far as I was concerned) for New York, but let us
off at Marseilles, I learned to foxtrot. France rattled by in the
coal-black night. The pale Channel was still oscillating inside
us, when the Dover–London train quietly came to a stop.
Repetitive pictures of gray pears on the grimy walls of Victoria
Station advertised the bath soap English governesses had used
upon me in my childhood. A week later I was already shuffling
cheek-to-cheek at a charity ball with my first English sweetheart, a wayward willowy girl five years my senior.

My father had visited London before—the last time in February 1916, when, with five other prominent representatives of
the Russian press, he had been invited by the British Government to take a look at England's war effort (which, it was
hinted, did not meet with sufficient appreciation on the part
of Russia's public opinion). On the way there, being challenged by my father and Korney Chukovski to rhyme on

Afrika, the poet and novelist Aleksey Tolstoy (no relation to Count Lyov Nikolaevich) had supplied, though seasick, the charming couplet

> *Vizhu pal'mu i Kafrika.*
> *Eto—Afrika.*
> (I see a palm and a little Kaffir. That's Afrika.)

In England the visitors had been shown the Fleet. Dinners and speeches had followed in noble succession. The timely capture of Erzerum by the Russians and the pending introduction of conscription in England ("Will you march too or wait till March 2?" as the punning posters put it) had provided the speakers with easy topics. There had been an official banquet presided over by Sir Edward Grey, and a funny interview with George V whom Chukovski, the *enfant terrible* of the group, insisted on asking if he liked the works of Oscar Wilde—"dze ooarks of OOald." The king, who was baffled by his interrogator's accent and who, anyway, had never been a voracious reader, neatly countered by inquiring how his guests liked the London fog (later Chukovski used to cite this triumphantly as an example of British cant—tabooing a writer because of his morals).

A recent visit to the Public Library in New York has revealed that the above incident does not appear in my father's book *Iz Voyuyushchey Anglii*, Petrograd, 1916 (*A Report on England at War*)—and indeed there are not many samples therein of his habitual humor beyond, perhaps, a description of a game of badminton (or was it fives?) that he had with H. G. Wells, and an amusing account of a visit to some first-line trenches in Flanders, where hospitality went so far as to allow the explosion of a German grenade within a few feet of the visitors. Before publication in book form, this report appeared serially in a Russian daily. There, with a certain old-world naïveté, my father had mentioned making a present of his Swan fountain pen to Admiral Jellicoe, who at table had borrowed it to autograph a menu card and had praised its fluent and suave nib. This unfortunate disclosure of the pen's make was promptly echoed in the London papers by a Mabie, Todd and Co., Ltd., advertisement, which quoted a translation of the passage and depicted my father handing the firm's

The author in Cambridge, Spring 1920. It was not unnatural for a Russian, when gradually discovering the pleasures of the Cam, to prefer, at first, a rowboat to the more proper canoe or punt.

product to the Commander-in-Chief of the Grand Fleet, under the chaotic sky of a sea battle.

But now there were no banquets, no speeches, and even no fives with Wells whom it proved impossible to convince that Bolshevism was but an especially brutal and thorough form of barbaric oppression—in itself as old as the desert sands—and not at all the attractively new revolutionary experiment that so many foreign observers took it to be. After several expensive months in a rented house in Elm Park Gardens, my parents and the three younger children left London for Berlin (where, until his death in March, 1922, my father joined Iosif Hessen, a fellow member of the People's Freedom Party, in editing a Russian émigré newspaper), while my brother and I went to Cambridge—he to Christ College, I to Trinity.

2

I had two brothers, Sergey and Kirill. Kirill, the youngest child (1911–1964), was also my godson as happened in Russian families. At a certain stage of the baptismal ceremony, in our Vyra drawing room, I held him gingerly before handing him to his godmother, Ekaterina Dmitrievna Danzas (my father's first cousin and a grandniece of Colonel K. K. Danzas, Pushkin's second in his fatal duel). In his childhood Kirill belonged, with my two sisters, to the remote nurseries which were so distinctly separated from his elder brothers' apartments in town house and manor. I saw very little of him during my two decades of European expatriation, 1919–1940, and nothing at all after that, until my next visit to Europe, in 1960, when a brief period of very friendly and joyful meetings ensued.

Kirill went to school in London, Berlin and Prague, and to college at Louvain. He married Gilberte Barbanson, a Belgian girl, ran (humorously but not unsuccessfully) a travel agency in Brussels, and died of a heart attack in Munich.

He loved seaside resorts and rich food. He loathed, as much as I do, bullfighting. He spoke five languages. He was a dedicated practical joker. His one great reality in life was literature, especially Russian poetry. His own verse reflects the influence of Gumilyov and Hodasevich. He published sparsely and was always as reticent about his writing as he was about his persiflage-misted inner existence.

For various reasons I find it inordinately hard to speak about my other brother. That twisted quest for Sebastian Knight (1940), with its gloriettes and self-mate combinations, is really nothing in comparison to the task I balked in the first version of this memoir and am faced with now. Except for the two or three poor little adventures I have sketched in earlier chapters, his boyhood and mine seldom mingled. He is a mere shadow in the background of my richest and most detailed recollections. I was the coddled one; he, the witness of coddling. Born, caesareanally, ten and a half months after me, on March 12, 1900, he matured earlier than I and physically looked older. We seldom played together, he was indifferent to most of the things I was fond of—toy trains, toy pistols, Red Indians, Red Admirables. At six or seven he developed a passionate adulation, condoned by Mademoiselle, for Napoleon and took a little bronze bust of him to bed. As a child, I was rowdy, adventurous and something of a bully. He was quiet and listless, and spent much more time with our mentors than I. At ten, began his interest in music, and thenceforth he took innumerable lessons, went to concerts with our father, and spent hours on end playing snatches of operas, on an upstairs piano well within earshot. I would creep up behind and prod him in the ribs—a miserable memory.

We attended different schools; he went to my father's former *gimnasiya* and wore the regulation black uniform to which, at fifteen, he added an illegal touch: mouse-gray spats. About that time, a page from his diary that I found on his desk and read, and in stupid wonder showed to my tutor, who promptly showed it to my father, abruptly provided a retroactive clarification of certain oddities of behavior on his part.

The only game we both liked was tennis. We played a lot of it together, especially in England, on an erratic grass court in Kensington, on a good clay court in Cambridge. He was left-handed. He had a bad stammer that hampered discussions of doubtful points. Despite a weak service and an absence of any real backhand, he was not easy to beat, being the kind of player who never double-faults, and returns everything with the consistency of a banging wall. In Cambridge, we saw more of each other than anywhere before and had, for once, a few friends in common. We both graduated in the same subjects, with the same honors, after which he moved to Paris where, during the following years, he gave lessons of English and Russian, just as I did in Berlin.

We again met in the nineteen-thirties, and were on quite amiable terms in 1938–1940, in Paris. He often dropped in for a chat, rue Boileau where I lodged in two shabby rooms with you and our child, but it so happened (he had been away for a while) that he learned of our departure to America only after we had left. My bleakest recollections are associated with Paris, and the relief of leaving it was overwhelming, but I am sorry he had to stutter his astonishment to an indifferent concierge. I know little of his life during the war. At one time he was employed as translator at an office in Berlin. A frank and fearless man, he criticized the regime in front of colleagues, who denounced him. He was arrested, accused of being a "British spy" and sent to a Hamburg concentration camp where he died of inanition, on January 10, 1945. It is one of those lives that hopelessly claim a belated something—compassion, understanding, no matter what—which the mere recognition of such a want can neither replace nor redeem.

3

The beginning of my first term in Cambridge was inauspicious. Late in the afternoon of a dull and damp October day, with the sense of indulging in some weird theatricals, I put on my newly acquired, dark-bluish academic gown and black square cap for my first formal visit to E. Harrison, my college tutor. I went up a flight of stairs and knocked on a massive door that stood slightly ajar. "Come in," said a distant voice with hollow abruptness. I crossed a waiting room of sorts and entered my tutor's study. The brown dusk had forestalled me. There was no light in the study save for the glow of a large fireplace near which a dim figure sat in a dimmer chair. I advanced saying: "My name is—" and stepped into the tea things that stood on the rug beside Mr. Harrison's low wicker armchair. With a grunt, he bent sideways from his seat to right the pot, and then scooped up and dumped back into it the wet black mess of tea leaves it had disgorged. Thus the college period of my life began on a note of embarrassment, a note that was to recur rather persistently during my three years of residence.

Mr. Harrison thought it a fine idea to have one "White Russian" lodge with another, and so, at first, I shared an apartment in Trinity Lane with a puzzled compatriot. After a few months he left college, and I remained sole occupant of those lodgings. They seemed intolerably squalid in comparison with my remote and by now nonexistent home. Well do I remember the ornaments on the mantelpiece (a glass ashtray, with the Trinity crest, left by some former lodger; a seashell in which I found the imprisoned hum of one of my own seaside summers), and my landlady's old mechanical piano, a pathetic contraption, full of ruptured, crushed, knotted music, which one sampled once and no more. Narrow Trinity Lane was a staid and rather sad little street, with almost no traffic, but with a long, lurid past beginning in the sixteenth century, when it used to be Findsilver Lane, although commonly called at the time by a coarser name because of the then abominable state of its gutters. I suffered a good deal from the cold, but it is quite untrue, as some have it, that the polar temperature in Cambridge bedrooms caused the water to freeze solid in one's washstand jug. As a matter of fact, there would be hardly more than a thin layer of ice on the surface, and this was easily broken by means of one's toothbrush into tinkling bits, a sound which, in retrospect, has even a certain festive appeal to my Americanized ear. Otherwise, getting up was no fun at all. I still feel in my bones the bleakness of the morning walk up Trinity Lane to the Baths, as one shuffled along, exuding pallid puffs of breath, in a thin dressing gown over one's pajamas and with a cold, fat sponge-bag under one's arm. Nothing in the world could induce me to wear next to my skin the "woolies" that kept Englishmen secretly warm. Overcoats were considered sissy. The usual attire of the average Cambridge undergraduate, whether athlete or leftist poet, struck a sturdy and dingy note: his shoes had thick rubber soles, his flannel trousers were dark gray, and the buttoned sweater, called a "jumper," under his Norfolk jacket was a conservative brown. What I suppose might be termed the gay set wore old pumps, very light gray flannel trousers, a bright-yellow "jumper," and the coat part of a good suit. By that time my youthful preoccupation with clothes was on the wane, but it did seem rather a lark, after the formal fashions in Russia, to go about in slippers, eschew garters, and wear one's collar sewn onto one's shirt—a daring innovation in those days.

The mild masquerade in which I indolently joined has left such trifling impressions upon my mind that it would be tedious to continue in this strain. The story of my college years in England is really the story of my trying to become a Russian writer. I had the feeling that Cambridge and all its famed features—venerable elms, blazoned windows, loquacious tower clocks—were of no consequence in themselves but existed merely to frame and support my rich nostalgia. Emotionally, I was in the position of a man who, having just lost a fond kinswoman, realized—too late—that through some laziness of the routine-drugged human soul, he had neither troubled to know her as fully as she deserved, nor had shown her in full the marks of his not quite conscious then, but now unrelieved, affection. As with smarting eyes I meditated by the fire in my Cambridge room, all the potent banality of embers, solitude and distant chimes pressed against me, contorting the very folds of my face as an airman's face is disfigured by the fantastic speed of his flight. And I thought of all I had missed in my country, of the things I would not have omitted to note and treasure, had I suspected before that my life was to veer in such a violent way.

To some of the several fellow émigrés I met in Cambridge the general trend of my feelings was so obvious and familiar a thing that it would have fallen flat and seemed almost improper if put into words. With the whiter of those White Russians I soon found out that patriotism and politics boiled down to a snarling resentment which was directed more against Kerenski than against Lenin and which proceeded solely from material discomforts and losses. Then, too, I ran into some quite unexpected difficulties with such of my English acquaintances as were considered to be cultured and subtle, and humane, but who, for all their decency and refinement, would lapse into the most astonishing drivel when Russia was being discussed. I want to single out here a young

Socialist I knew, a lanky giant whose slow and multiple manipulations of a pipe were horribly aggravating when you did
not agree with him and delightfully soothing when you did.
With him, I had many political wrangles, the bitterness of
which invariably dissolved when we turned to the poets we
both cherished. Today he is not unknown among his peers,
which is, I readily admit, a pretty meaningless phrase, but
then, I am doing my best to obscure his identity; let me refer
to him by the name of "Nesbit" as I dubbed him (or affirm
now having dubbed him), not only because of his alleged resemblance to early portraits of Maxim Gorki, a regional mediocrity of that era, one of whose first stories ("My Fellow
Traveler"—another apt note) had been translated by a certain
R. Nesbit Bain, but also because "Nesbit" has the advantage
of entering into a voluptuous palindromic association with
"Ibsen," a name I shall have to evoke presently.

It is probably true, as some have argued, that sympathy for
Leninism on the part of English and American liberal opinion
in the twenties was swung by consideration of home politics.
But it was also due to simple misinformation. My friend knew
little of Russia's past and this little had come to him through
polluted Communist channels. When challenged to justify the
bestial terror that had been sanctioned by Lenin—the torture-
house, the blood-bespattered wall—Nesbit would tap the
ashes out of his pipe against the fender knob, recross sinistrally
his huge, heavily shod, dextrally crossed legs, and murmur
something about the "Allied Blockade." He lumped together
as "Czarist elements" Russian émigrés of all hues, from peasant Socialist to White general—much as today Soviet writers
wield the term "Fascist." He never realized that had he and
other foreign idealists been Russians in Russia, he and they
would have been destroyed by Lenin's regime as naturally as
rabbits are by ferrets and farmers. He maintained that the reason for what he demurely called "less variety of opinion" under the Bolsheviks than in the darkest Tsarist days was "the
want of any tradition of free speech in Russia," a statement
he got, I believe, from the sort of fatuous "Dawn in Russia"
stuff that eloquent English and American Leninists wrote in
those years. But the thing that irritated me perhaps most was
Nesbit's attitude toward Lenin himself. All cultured and dis-

criminating Russians knew that this astute politician had about as much taste and interest in aesthetic matters as an ordinary Russian bourgeois of the Flaubertian *épicier* sort (the type that admired Pushkin on the strength of Chaykovski's vile librettos, wept at the Italian opera, and was allured by any painting that told a story); but Nesbit and his highbrow friends saw in him a kind of sensitive, poetic-minded patron and promoter of the newest trends in art and would smile a superior smile when I tried to explain that the connection between advanced politics and advanced art was a purely verbal one (gleefully exploited by Soviet propaganda), and that the more radical a Russian was in politics, the more conservative he was on the artistic side.

I had at my disposal a number of such truths that I liked to air, but that Nesbit, firmly entrenched in his ignorance, regarded as mere fancies. The history of Russia (I might, for example, declare) could be considered from two points of view (both of which, for some reason, equally annoyed Nesbit): first, as the evolution of the police (a curiously impersonal and detached force, sometimes working in a kind of void, sometimes helpless, and at other times outdoing the government in brutal persecution); and second, as the development of a marvelous culture. Under the Tsars (I might go on), despite the fundamentally inept and ferocious character of their rule, a freedom-loving Russian had had incomparably more means of expressing himself, and used to run incomparably less risk in doing so, than under Lenin. Since the reforms of the eighteen-sixties, the country had possessed (though not always adhered to) a legislation of which any Western democracy might have been proud, a vigorous public opinion that held despots at bay, widely read periodicals of all shades of liberal political thought, and what was especially striking, fearless and independent judges ("Oh come . . ." Nesbit would interpose). When revolutionaries did get caught, banishment to Tomsk or Omsk (now Bombsk) was a restful vacation in comparison to the concentration camps that Lenin introduced. Political exiles escaped from Siberia with farcical ease, witness the famous flight of Trotsky—Santa Leo, Santa Claws Trotsky—merrily riding back in a Yuletide sleigh drawn by reindeer: On, Rocket, on, Stupid, on, Butcher and Blitzen!

I soon became aware that if my views, the not unusual views of Russian democrats abroad, were received with pained surprise or polite sneers by English democrats *in situ*, another group, the English ultraconservatives, rallied eagerly to my side but did so from such crude reactionary motivation that I was only embarrassed by their despicable support. Indeed, I pride myself with having discerned even then the symptoms of what is so clear today, when a kind of family circle has gradually been formed, linking representatives of all nations, jolly empire-builders in their jungle clearings, French policemen, the unmentionable German product, the good old churchgoing Russian or Polish *pogromshchik*, the lean American lyncher, the man with the bad teeth who squirts antiminority stories in the bar or the lavatory, and, at another point of the same subhuman circle, those ruthless, paste-faced automatons in opulent John Held trousers and high-shouldered jackets, those *Sitzriesen* looming at all our conference tables, whom—or shall I say which?—the Soviet State began to export around 1945 after more than two decades of selective breeding and tailoring, during which men's fashions abroad had had time to change, so that the symbol of infinitely available cloth could only provoke cruel derision (as occurred in postwar England when a famous Soviet team of professional soccer players happened to parade in mufti).

4

Very soon I turned away from politics and concentrated on literature. I invited to my Cambridge rooms the vermilion shields and blue lightning of the *Song of Igor's Campaign* (that incomparable and mysterious epic of the late twelfth or late eighteenth century), the poetry of Pushkin and Tyutchev, the prose of Gogol and Tolstoy, and also the wonderful works of the great Russian naturalists who had explored and described the wilds of Central Asia. At a bookstall in the Market Place, I unexpectedly came upon a Russian work, a secondhand copy of Dahl's *Interpretative Dictionary of the Living Russian Language* in four volumes. I bought it and resolved to read at least ten pages per day, jotting down such words and expressions as might especially please me, and I kept this up for a considerable time. My fear of losing or corrupting, through alien influence, the only thing I had salvaged from Russia—her language—became positively morbid and considerably more harassing than the fear I was to experience two decades later of my never being able to bring my English prose anywhere close to the level of my Russian. I used to sit up far into the night, surrounded by an almost Quixotic accumulation of unwieldy volumes, and make polished and rather sterile Russian poems not so much out of the live cells of some compelling emotion as around a vivid term or a verbal image that I wanted to use for its own sake. It would have horrified me at the time to discover what I see so clearly now, the direct influence upon my Russian structures of various contemporaneous ("Georgian") English verse patterns that were running about my room and all over me like tame mice. And to think of the labor I expended! Suddenly, in the small hours of a November morning, I would become conscious of the silence and chill (my second winter in Cambridge seems to have been the coldest, and most prolific one). The red and blue flames wherein I had been seeing a fabled battle had sunk to the lugubrious glow of an arctic sunset among hoary firs. Still I could not force myself to go to bed, dreading not so much insomnia as the inevitable double systole, abetted by the cold of the sheets, and also the curious affection called *anxietas tibiarum*, a painful condition of unrest, an excruciating increase of muscular sense, which leads to a continual change in the position of one's limbs. So I would heap on more coals and help revive the flames by spreading a sheet of the London *Times* over the smoking black jaws of the fireplace, thus screening completely its open recess. A humming noise would start behind the taut paper, which would acquire the smoothness of drumskin and the beauty of luminous parchment. Presently, as the hum turned into a roar, an orange-colored spot would appear in the middle of the sheet, and whatever patch of print happened to be there (for example, "The League does not command a guinea or a gun," or ". . . the revenges that Nemesis has had upon Allied hesitation and indecision in Eastern and Central Europe . . .") stood out with ominous clarity—until suddenly the orange spot burst. Then the flaming sheet, with the whirr of a liberated phoenix, would fly up the chimney to join the stars. It cost one a fine of twelve shillings if that firebird was observed.

The literary set, Nesbit and his friends, while commending my nocturnal labors, frowned upon various other things I went in for, such as entomology, practical jokes, girls, and, especially, athletics. Of the games I played at Cambridge, soccer has remained a wind-swept clearing in the middle of a rather muddled period. I was crazy about goal keeping. In Russia and the Latin countries, that gallant art had been always surrounded with a halo of singular glamour. Aloof, solitary, impassive, the crack goalie is followed in the streets by entranced small boys. He vies with the matador and the flying ace as an object of thrilled adulation. His sweater, his peaked cap, his kneeguards, the gloves protruding from the hip pocket of his shorts, set him apart from the rest of the team. He is the lone eagle, the man of mystery, the last defender. Photographers, reverently bending one knee, snap him in the act of making a spectacular dive across the goal mouth to deflect with his fingertips a low, lightning-like shot, and the stadium roars in approval as he remains for a moment or two lying full length where he fell, his goal still intact.

But in England, at least in the England of my youth, the national dread of showing off and a too grim preoccupation with solid teamwork were not conducive to the development of the goalie's eccentric art. This at least was the explanation I dug up for not being oversuccessful on the playing fields of Cambridge. Oh, to be sure, I had my bright, bracing days— the good smell of turf, that famous inter-Varsity forward, dribbling closer and closer to me with the new tawny ball at his twinkling toe, then the stinging shot, the lucky save, its protracted tingle. . . . But there were other, more memorable, more esoteric days, under dismal skies, with the goal area a mass of black mud, the ball as greasy as a plum pudding, and my head racked with neuralgia after a sleepless night of verse-making. I would fumble badly—and retrieve the ball from the net. Mercifully the game would swing to the opposite end of the sodden field. A weak, weary drizzle would start, hesitate, and go on again. With an almost cooing tenderness in their subdued croaking, dilapidated rooks would be flapping about a leafless elm. Mists would gather. Now the game would be a vague bobbing of heads near the remote goal of St. John's or Christ, or whatever college we were playing. The far, blurred sounds, a cry, a whistle, the thud of a kick, all that was perfectly unimportant and had no connection with me. I was less the keeper of a soccer goal than the keeper of a secret. As with folded arms I leant my back against the left goalpost, I enjoyed the luxury of closing my eyes, and thus I would listen to my heart knocking and feel the blind drizzle on my face and hear, in the distance, the broken sounds of the game, and think of myself as of a fabulous exotic being in an English footballer's disguise, composing verse in a tongue nobody understood about a remote country nobody knew. Small wonder I was not very popular with my teammates.

Not once in my three years of Cambridge—repeat: not once—did I visit the University Library, or even bother to locate it (I know its new place now), or find out if there existed a college library where books might be borrowed for reading in one's digs. I skipped lectures. I sneaked to London and elsewhere. I conducted several love affairs simultaneously. I had dreadful interviews with Mr. Harrison. I translated into Russian a score of poems by Rupert Brooke, *Alice in Wonderland*, and Romain Rolland's *Colas Breugnon*. Scholastically, I might as well have gone up to the Inst. M. M. of Tirana.

Such things as the hot muffins and crumpets one had with one's tea after games or the newsboys' cockneyish cries of "Piper, piper!" mingling with the bicycle bells in the darkening streets, seemed to me at the time more characteristic of Cambridge than they do now. I cannot help realizing that, aside from striking but more or less transient customs, and deeper than ritual or rule, there did exist the residual something about Cambridge that many a solemn alumnus has tried to define. I see this basic property as the constant awareness one had of an untrammeled extension of time. I do not know if anyone will ever go to Cambridge in search of the imprints which the teat-cleats on my soccer boots have left in the black mud before a gaping goal or follow the shadow of my cap across the quadrangle to my tutor's stairs; but I know that I thought of Milton, and Marvell, and Marlowe, with more than a tourist's thrill as I passed beside the reverend walls.

Nothing one looked at was shut off in terms of time, everything was a natural opening into it, so that one's mind grew accustomed to work in a particularly pure and ample environment, and because, in terms of space, the narrow lane, the cloistered lawn, the dark archway hampered one physically, that yielding diaphanous texture of time was, by contrast, especially welcome to the mind, just as a sea view from a window exhilarates one hugely, even though one does not care for sailing. I had no interest whatever in the history of the place, and was quite sure that Cambridge was in no way affecting my soul, although actually it was Cambridge that supplied not only the casual frame, but also the very colors and inner rhythms for my very special Russian thoughts. Environment, I suppose, does act upon a creature if there is, in that creature, already a certain responsive particle or strain (the English I had imbibed in my childhood). Of this I had my first inkling just before leaving Cambridge, during my last and saddest spring there, when I suddenly felt that something in me was as naturally in contact with my immediate surroundings as it was with my Russian past, and that this state of harmony had been reached at the very moment that the careful reconstruction of my artificial but beautifully exact Russian world had been at last completed. I think one of the very few "practical" actions I have ever been guilty of was to use part of that crystalline material to obtain an Honours degree.

5

I remember the dreamy flow of punts and canoes on the Cam, the Hawaiian whine of phonographs slowly passing through sunshine and shade and a girl's hand gently twirling this way and that the handle of her peacock-bright parasol as she reclined on the cushions of the punt which I dreamily navigated. The pink-coned chestnuts were in full fan; they made overlapping masses along the banks, they crowded the sky out of the river, and their special pattern of flowers and leaves produced a kind of *en escalier* effect, the angular figuration of some splendid green and old-rose tapestry. The air was as warm as in the Crimea, with the same sweet, fluffy smell of a certain flowering bush that I never could quite identify

(I later caught whiffs of it in the gardens of the southern States). The three arches of an Italianate bridge, spanning the narrow stream, combined to form, with the help of their almost perfect, almost unrippled replicas in the water, three lovely ovals. In its turn, the water cast a patch of lacy light on the stone of the intrados under which one's gliding craft passed. Now and then, shed by a blossoming tree, a petal would come down, down, down, and with the odd feeling of seeing something neither worshiper nor casual spectator ought to see, one would manage to glimpse its reflection which swiftly—more swiftly than the petal fell—rose to meet it; and, for the fraction of a second, one feared that the trick would not work, that the blessed oil would not catch fire, that the reflection might miss and the petal float away alone, but every time the delicate union did take place, with the magic precision of a poet's word meeting halfway his, or a reader's, recollection.

When, after an absence of almost seventeen years I revisited England, I made the dreadful mistake of going to see Cambridge again not at the glorious end of the Easter term but on a raw February day that reminded me only of my own confused old nostalgia. I was hopelessly trying to find an academic job in England (the ease with which I obtained that type of employment in the U.S.A. is to me, in backthought, a constant source of grateful wonder). In every way the visit was not a success. I had lunch with Nesbit at a little place, which ought to have been full of memories but which, owing to various changes, was not. He had given up smoking. Time had softened his features and he no longer resembled Gorki or Gorki's translator, but looked a little like Ibsen, minus the simian vegetation. An accidental worry (the cousin or maiden sister who kept house for him had just been removed to Binet's clinic or something) seemed to prevent him from concentrating on the very personal and urgent matter I wanted to speak to him about. Bound volumes of *Punch* were heaped on a table in a kind of small vestibule where a bowl of goldfish had formerly stood—and it all looked so different. Different too were the garish uniforms worn by the waitresses, of whom none was as pretty as the particular one I remembered so clearly. Rather desperately, as if struggling against boredom,

Ibsen launched into politics. I knew well what to expect—
denunciation of Stalinism. In the early twenties Nesbit had
mistaken his own ebullient idealism for a romantic and humane something in Lenin's ghastly rule. Ibsen, in the days of
the no less ghastly Stalin, was mistaking a quantitative increase
in his own knowledge for a qualitative change in the Soviet
regime. The thunderclap of purges that had affected "old Bolsheviks," the heroes of his youth, had given him a salutary
shock, something that in Lenin's day all the groans coming
from the Solovki forced labor camp or the Lubyanka dungeon
had not been able to do. With horror he pronounced the
names of Ezhov and Yagoda—but quite forgot their predecessors, Uritski and Dzerzhinski. While time had improved his
judgment regarding contemporaneous Soviet affairs, he did
not bother to reconsider the preconceived notions of his
youth, and still saw in Lenin's short reign a kind of glamorous
quinquennium Neronis.

He looked at his watch, and I looked at mine, and we
parted, and I wandered around the town in the rain, and then
visited the Backs, and for some time peered at the rooks in
the black network of the bare elms and at the first crocuses in
the mist-beaded turf. As I strolled under those sung trees, I
tried to put myself into the same ecstatically reminiscent mood
in regard to my student years as during those years I had
experienced in regard to my boyhood, but all I could evoke
were fragmentary little pictures: M. K., a Russian, dyspepti-
cally cursing the aftereffects of a College Hall dinner; N. R.,
another Russian, romping about like a child; P. M. storming
into my room with a copy of *Ulysses* freshly smuggled from
Paris; J. C. quietly dropping in to say that he, too, had just
lost his father; R. C. charmingly inviting me to join him on a
trip to the Swiss Alps; Christopher something or other, wriggling out of a proposed tennis double upon learning that his
partner was to be a Hindu; T., a very old and fragile waiter,
spilling the soup in Hall on Professor A. E. Housman, who
then abruptly stood up as one shooting out of a trance; S. S.,
who was in no way connected with Cambridge, but who, having dozed off in his chair at a literary party (in Berlin) and
being nudged by a neighbor, also stood up suddenly—in the
middle of a story someone was reading; Lewis Carroll's Dor-

mouse, unexpectedly starting to tell a tale; E. Harrison unexpectedly making me a present of *The Shropshire Lad*, a little volume of verse about young males and death.

The dull day had dwindled to a pale yellow streak in the gray west when, acting upon an impulse, I decided to visit my old tutor. Like a sleepwalker, I mounted the familiar steps and automatically knocked on the half-open door bearing his name. In a voice that was a jot less abrupt, and a trifle more hollow, he bade me come in. "I wonder if you remember me . . ." I started to say, as I crossed the dim room to where he sat near a comfortable fire. "Let me see," he said, slowly turning around in his low chair, "I do not quite seem . . ." There was a dismal crunch, a fatal clatter: I had stepped into the tea things that stood at the foot of his wicker chair. "Oh, yes, of course," he said, "I know who you are."

Fourteen

THE SPIRAL is a spiritualized circle. In the spiral form, the circle, uncoiled, unwound, has ceased to be vicious; it has been set free. I thought this up when I was a schoolboy, and I also discovered that Hegel's triadic series (so popular in old Russia) expressed merely the essential spirality of all things in their relation to time. Twirl follows twirl, and every synthesis is the thesis of the next series. If we consider the simplest spiral, three stages may be distinguished in it, corresponding to those of the triad: We can call "thetic" the small curve or arc that initiates the convolution centrally; "antithetic" the larger arc that faces the first in the process of continuing it; and "synthetic" the still ampler arc that continues the second while following the first along the outer side. And so on.

A colored spiral in a small ball of glass, this is how I see my own life. The twenty years I spent in my native Russia (1899–1919) take care of the thetic arc. Twenty-one years of voluntary exile in England, Germany and France (1919–1940) supply the obvious antithesis. The period spent in my adopted country (1940–1960) forms a synthesis—and a new thesis. For the moment I am concerned with my antithetic stage, and more particularly with my life in Continental Europe after I had graduated from Cambridge in 1922.

As I look back at those years of exile, I see myself, and thousands of other Russians, leading an odd but by no means unpleasant existence, in material indigence and intellectual luxury, among perfectly unimportant strangers, spectral Germans and Frenchmen in whose more or less illusory cities we, émigrés, happened to dwell. These aborigines were to the mind's eye as flat and transparent as figures cut out of cellophane, and although we used their gadgets, applauded their clowns, picked their roadside plums and apples, no real communication, of the rich human sort so widespread in our own midst, existed between us and them. It seemed at times that we ignored them the way an arrogant or very stupid invader ignores a formless and faceless mass of natives; but occasionally, quite often in fact, the spectral world through which we serenely paraded our sores and our arts would produce a kind of awful convulsion and show us who was the discarnate captive and who the true lord. Our utter physical dependence on this or that nation, which had coldly granted us political refuge, became painfully evident when some trashy "visa," some diabolical "identity card" had to be obtained or prolonged, for then an avid bureaucratic hell would attempt to close upon the petitioner and he might wilt while his dossier waxed fatter and fatter in the desks of rat-whiskered consuls and policemen. *Dokumentï*, it has been said, is a Russian's placenta. The League of Nations equipped émigrés who had lost their Russian citizenship with a so-called "Nansen" passport, a very inferior document of a sickly green hue. Its holder was little better than a criminal on parole and had to go through most hideous ordeals every time he wished to travel from one country to another, and the smaller the countries the worse the fuss they made. Somewhere at the back of their glands, the authorities secreted the notion that no matter how bad a state—say, Soviet Russia—might be, any fugitive from it was intrinsically despicable since he existed outside a national administration; and therefore he was viewed with the preposterous disapproval with which certain religious groups regard a child born out of wedlock. Not all of us consented to be bastards and ghosts. Sweet are the recollections some Russian émigrés treasure of how they insulted or fooled high officials at various ministries, *Préfectures* and *Polizeipraesidiums.*

In Berlin and Paris, the two capitals of exile, Russians formed compact colonies, with a coefficient of culture that greatly surpassed the cultural mean of the necessarily more diluted foreign communities among which they were placed. Within those colonies they kept to themselves. I have in view, of course, Russian intellectuals, mostly belonging to democratic groups, and not the flashier kind of person who "was, you know, adviser to the Tsar or something" that American clubwomen immediately think of whenever "White Russians" are mentioned. Life in those settlements was so full and intense that these Russian *"intelligenti"* (a word that had more socially idealistic and less highbrow connotations than "intellectuals" as used in America) had neither time nor reason to seek ties beyond their own circle. Today, in a new and beloved world, where I have learned to feel at home as easily as I have ceased barring my sevens, extroverts and cosmopolitans to whom I happen to mention these past matters think I am jesting, or accuse me of snobbery in reverse, when I maintain that in the course of almost one-fifth of a century spent in Western Europe I have not had, among the sprinkling of Germans and Frenchmen I knew (mostly landladies and literary people), more than two good friends all told.

Somehow, during my secluded years in Germany, I never came across those gentle musicians of yore who, in Turgenev's novels, played their rhapsodies far into the summer night; or those happy old hunters with their captures pinned to the crown of their hats, of whom the Age of Reason made such fun: La Bruyère's gentleman who sheds tears over a parasitized caterpillar, Gay's "philosophers more grave than wise" who, if you please, "hunt science down in butterflies," and, less insultingly, Pope's "curious Germans," who "hold so rare" those "insects fair"; or simply the so-called wholesome and kindly folks that during the last war homesick soldiers from the Middle West seem to have preferred so much to the cagey French farmer and to brisk Madelon II. On the contrary, the most vivid figure I find when sorting out in memory the meager stack of my non-Russian and non-Jewish acquaintances in the years between the two wars is the image of a young German university student, well-bred, quiet, bespectacled, whose hobby was capital punishment. At our second meeting he showed me a collection of photographs among which was a purchased series (*"Ein bischen retouchiert,"* he said wrinkling his freckled nose) that depicted the successive stages of a routine execution in China; he commented, very expertly, on the splendor of the lethal sword and on the spirit of perfect cooperation between headsman and victim, which culminated in a veritable geyser of mist-gray blood spouting from the very clearly photographed neck of the decapitated party. Being pretty well off, this young collector could afford to travel, and travel he did, in between the humanities he studied for his Ph.D. He complained, however, of continuous ill luck and added that if he did not see something really good soon, he might not stand the strain. He had attended a few passable hangings in the Balkans and a well-advertised, although rather

My wife took, unnoticed, this picture, unposed, of me in the act of writing a novel in our hotel room. The hotel is the Établissement Thermal at Le Boulou, in the East Pyrenees. The date (discernible on the captured calendar) is February 27, 1929. The novel, *Zashchita Luzhina* (*The Defense*), deals with the defense invented by an insane chess player. Note the pat pattern of the tablecloth. A half-empty package of Gauloises cigarettes can be made out between the ink bottle and an overful ashtray. Family photos are propped against the four volumes of Dahl's Russian dictionary. The end of my robust, dark-brown penholder (a beloved tool of young oak that I used during all my twenty years of literary labors in Europe and may rediscover yet in one of the trunks stored at Dean's, Ithaca, N. Y.) is already well chewed. My writing hand partly conceals a stack of setting boards. Spring moths would float in through the open window on overcast nights and settle upon the lighted wall on my left. In that way we collected a number of rare Pugs in perfect condition and spread them at once (they are now in an American museum). Seldom does a casual snapshot compendiate a life so precisely.

Many years ago, in St. Petersburg, I remember being amused by the Collected Poems of a tram conductor, and especially by his picture, in uniform, sturdily booted, with a pair of new rubbers on the floor beside him and his father's war medals on the photographer's console near which the author stood at attention. Wise conductor, farseeing photographer!

bleak and mechanical *guillotinade* (he liked to use what he thought was colloquial French) on the Boulevard Arago in Paris; but somehow he never was sufficiently close to observe everything in detail, and the highly expensive teeny-weeny camera in the sleeve of his raincoat did not work as well as he had hoped. Despite a bad cold, he had journeyed to Regensburg where beheading was violently performed with an axe; he had expected great things from that spectacle but, to his intense disappointment, the subject had apparently been drugged and had hardly reacted at all, beyond feebly flopping about on the ground while the masked executioner and his clumsy mate fell all over him. Dietrich (my acquaintance's first name) hoped some day to go to the States so as to witness a couple of electrocutions; from this word, in his innocence, he derived the adjective "cute," which he had learned from a cousin of his who had been to America, and with a little frown of wistful worry Dietrich wondered if it were really true that, during the performance, sensational puffs of smoke issued from the natural orifices of the body. At our third and last encounter (there still remained bits of him I wanted to file for possible use) he related to me, more in sorrow than in anger, that he had once spent a whole night patiently watching a good friend of his who had decided to shoot himself and had agreed to do so, in the roof of the mouth, facing the hobbyist in a good light, but having no ambition or sense of honor, had got hopelessly tight instead. Although I have lost track of Dietrich long ago, I can well imagine the look of calm satisfaction in his fish-blue eyes as he shows, nowadays (perhaps at the very minute I am writing this), a never-expected profusion of treasures to his thigh-clapping, guffawing coveterans—the absolutely *wunderbar* pictures he took during Hitler's reign.

2

I have sufficiently spoken of the gloom and the glory of exile in my Russian novels, and especially in the best of them, *Dar* (recently published in English as *The Gift*); but a quick recapitulation here may be convenient. With a very few exceptions, all liberal-minded creative forces—poets, novelists,

critics, historians, philosophers and so on—had left Lenin's
and Stalin's Russia. Those who had not were either withering
away there or adulterating their gifts by complying with the
political demands of the state. What the Tsars had never been
able to achieve, namely the complete curbing of minds to the
government's will, was achieved by the Bolsheviks in no time
after the main contingent of the intellectuals had escaped
abroad or had been destroyed. The lucky group of expatriates
could now follow their pursuits with such utter impunity that,
in fact, they sometimes asked themselves if the sense of enjoying absolute mental freedom was not due to their working
in an absolute void. True, there was among émigrés a sufficient number of good readers to warrant the publication, in
Berlin, Paris, and other towns, of Russian books and periodicals on a comparatively large scale; but since none of those
writings could circulate within the Soviet Union, the whole
thing acquired a certain air of fragile unreality. The number
of titles was more impressive than the number of copies any
given work sold, and the names of the publishing houses—
Orion, Cosmos, Logos, and so forth—had the hectic, unstable
and slightly illegal appearance that firms issuing astrological
or facts-of-life literature have. In serene retrospect, however,
and judged by artistic and scholarly standards alone, the books
produced *in vacuo* by émigré writers seem today, whatever
their individual faults, more permanent and more suitable for
human consumption than the slavish, singularly provincial and
conventional streams of political consciousness that came during those same years from the pens of young Soviet authors
whom a fatherly state provided with ink, pipes and pullovers.

The editor of the daily *Rul'* (and the publisher of my first
books), Iosif Vladimirovich Hessen, allowed me with great le-
niency to fill his poetry section with my unripe rhymes. Blue
evenings in Berlin, the corner chestnut in flower, light-head-
edness, poverty, love, the tangerine tinge of premature shop-
lights, and an animal aching yearn for the still fresh reek of
Russia—all this was put into meter, copied out in longhand and
carted off to the editor's office, where myopic I. V. would bring
the new poem close to his face and after this brief, more or less
tactual, act of cognition put it down on his desk. By 1928, my
novels were beginning to bring a little money in German trans-

lations, and in the spring of 1929, you and I went butterfly hunting in the Pyrenees. But only at the end of the nineteen-thirties did we leave Berlin for good, although long before that I used to take trips to Paris for public readings of my stuff.

Quite a feature of émigré life, in keeping with its itinerant and dramatic character, was the abnormal frequency of those literary readings in private houses or hired halls. The various types of performers stand out very distinctly in the puppet show going on in my mind. There was the faded actress, with eyes like precious stones, who having pressed for a moment a clenched handkerchief to a feverish mouth, proceeded to evoke nostalgic echoes of the Moscow Art Theatre by subjecting some famous piece of verse to the action, half dissection and half caress, of her slow limpid voice. There was the hopelessly second-rate author whose voice trudged through a fog of rhythmic prose, and one could watch the nervous trembling of his poor, clumsy but careful fingers every time he tucked the page he had finished under those to come, so that his manuscript retained throughout the reading its appalling and pitiful thickness. There was the young poet in whom his envious brethren could not help seeing a disturbing streak of genius as striking as the stripe of a skunk; erect on the stage, pale and glazed-eyed, with nothing in his hands to anchor him to this world, he would throw back his head and deliver his poem in a highly irritating, rolling chant and stop abruptly at the end, slamming the door of the last line and waiting for applause to fill the hush. And there was the old *cher maître* dropping pearl by pearl an admirable tale he had read innumerable times, and always in the same manner, wearing the expression of fastidious distaste that his nobly furrowed face had in the frontispiece of his collected works.

I suppose it would be easy for a detached observer to poke fun at all those hardly palpable people who imitated in foreign cities a dead civilization, the remote, almost legendary, almost Sumerian mirages of St. Petersburg and Moscow, 1900–1916 (which, even then, in the twenties and thirties, sounded like 1916–1900 B.C.). But at least they were rebels as most major Russian writers had been ever since Russian literature had existed, and true to this insurgent condition which their sense of justice and liberty craved for as strongly as it had done under the oppression of the Tsars, émigrés regarded as monstrously un-Russian and subhuman the behavior of pampered authors in the Soviet Union, the servile response on the part of those authors to every shade of every governmental decree; for the art of prostration was growing there in exact ratio to the increasing efficiency of first Lenin's, then Stalin's political police, and the successful Soviet writer was the one whose fine ear caught the soft whisper of an official suggestion long before it had become a blare.

Owing to the limited circulation of their works abroad, even the older generation of émigré writers, whose fame had been solidly established in pre-Revolution Russia, could not hope that their books would make a living for them. Writing a weekly column for an émigré paper was never quite sufficient to keep body and pen together. Now and then translations into other languages brought in an unexpected scoop; but, otherwise, grants from various émigré organizations, earnings from public readings and lavish private charity were responsible for prolonging elderly authors' lives. Younger, less known but more adaptable writers supplemented chance subsidies by engaging in various jobs. I remember teaching English and tennis. Patiently I thwarted the persistent knack Berlin businessmen had of pronouncing "business" so as to rhyme with "dizziness"; and like a slick automaton, under the slow-moving clouds of a long summer day, on dusty courts, I ladled ball after ball over the net to their tanned, bob-haired daughters. I got five dollars (quite a sum during the inflation in Germany) for my Russian *Alice in Wonderland*. I helped compile a Russian grammar for foreigners in which the first exercise began with the words *Madam, ya doktor, vot banan* (Madam, I am the doctor, here is a banana). Best of all, I used to compose for a daily émigré paper, the Berlin *Rul'*, the first Russian crossword puzzles, which I baptized *krestoslovitsï*. I find it strange to recall that freak existence. Deeply beloved of blurbists is the list of more or less earthy professions that a young author (writing about Life and Ideas—which are so much more important, of course, than mere "art") has followed: newspaper boy, soda jerk, monk, wrestler, foreman in a steel mill, bus driver and so on. Alas, none of these callings has been mine.

My passion for good writing put me in close contact with various Russian authors abroad. I was young in those days and much more keenly interested in literature than I am now. Current prose and poetry, brilliant planets and pale galaxies, flowed by the casement of my garret night after night. There were independent authors of diverse age and talent, and there were groupings and cliques within which a number of young or youngish writers, some of them very gifted, clustered around a philosophizing critic. The most important of these mystagogues combined intellectual talent and moral mediocrity, an uncanny sureness of taste in modern Russian poetry and a patchy knowledge of Russian classics. His group believed that neither a mere negation of Bolshevism nor the routine ideals of Western democracies were sufficient to build a philosophy upon which émigré literature could lean. They thirsted for a creed as a jailed drug addict thirsts for his pet heaven. Rather pathetically, they envied Parisian Catholic groups for the seasoned subtleties that Russian mysticism so obviously lacked. Dostoevskian drisk could not compete with neo-Thomist thought; but were there not other ways? The longing for a system of faith, a constant teetering on the brink of some accepted religion was found to provide a special satisfaction of its own. Only much later, in the forties, did some of those writers finally discover a definite slope down which to slide in a more or less genuflectory attitude. This slope was the enthusiastic nationalism that could call a state (Stalin's Russia, in this case) good and lovable for no other reason than because its army had won a war. In the early thirties, however, the nationalistic precipice was only faintly perceived and the mystagogues were still enjoying the thrills of slippery suspension. In their attitude toward literature they were curiously conservative; with them soul-saving came first, logrolling next, and art last. A retrospective glance nowadays notes the surprising fact of these free belles-lettrists abroad aping fettered thought at home by decreeing that to be a representative of a group or an epoch was more important than to be an individual writer.

Vladislav Hodasevich used to complain, in the twenties and thirties, that young émigré poets had borrowed their art form from him while following the leading cliques in modish *angoisse* and soul-reshaping. I developed a great liking for this bitter man, wrought of irony and metallic-like genius, whose poetry was as complex a marvel as that of Tyutchev or Blok. He was, physically, of a sickly aspect, with contemptuous nostrils and beetling brows, and when I conjure him up in my mind he never rises from the hard chair on which he sits, his thin legs crossed, his eyes glittering with malevolence and wit, his long fingers screwing into a holder the half of a *Caporal Vert* cigarette. There are few things in modern world poetry comparable to the poems of his *Heavy Lyre*, but unfortunately for his fame the perfect frankness he indulged in when voicing his dislikes made him some terrible enemies among the most powerful critical coteries. Not all the mystagogues were Dostoevskian Alyoshas; there were also a few Smerdyakovs in the group, and Hodasevich's poetry was played down with the thoroughness of a revengeful racket.

Another independent writer was Ivan Bunin. I had always preferred his little-known verse to his celebrated prose (their interrelation, within the frame of his work, recalls Hardy's case). At the time I found him tremendously perturbed by the personal problem of aging. The first thing he said to me was to remark with satisfaction that his posture was better than mine, despite his being some thirty years older than I. He was basking in the Nobel prize he had just received and invited me to some kind of expensive and fashionable eating place in Paris for a heart-to-heart talk. Unfortunately I happen to have a morbid dislike for restaurants and cafés, especially Parisian ones—I detest crowds, harried waiters, Bohemians, vermouth concoctions, coffee, *zakuski*, floor shows and so forth. I like to eat and drink in a recumbent position (preferably on a couch) and in silence. Heart-to-heart talks, confessions in the Dostoevskian manner, are also not in my line. Bunin, a spry old gentleman, with a rich and unchaste vocabulary, was puzzled by my irresponsiveness to the hazel grouse of which I had had enough in my childhood and exasperated by my refusal to discuss eschatological matters. Toward the end of the meal we were utterly bored with each other. "You will die in dreadful pain and complete isolation," remarked Bunin bitterly as we went toward the cloakroom. An attractive, frail-looking girl took the check for our heavy overcoats and

A snapshot taken by my wife of our three-year-old son Dmitri (born May 10, 1934) standing with me in front of our boardinghouse, Les Hesperides, in Mentone, at the beginning of December 1937. We looked it up twenty-two years later. Nothing had changed, except the management and the porch furniture. There is always, of course, the natural thrill of retrieved time; beyond that, however, I get no special kick out of revisiting old émigré haunts in those incidental countries. The winter mosquitoes, I remember, were terrible. Hardly had I extinguished the light in my room than it would come, that ominous whine whose unhurried, doleful, and wary rhythm contrasted so oddly with the actual mad speed of the satanic insect's gyrations. One waited for the touch in the dark, one freed a cautious arm from under the bedclothes—and mightily slapped one's own ear, whose sudden hum mingled with that of the receding mosquito. But then, next morning, how eagerly one reached for a butterfly net upon locating one's replete tormentor—a thick dark little bar on the white of the ceiling!

presently fell with them in her embrace upon the low counter. I wanted to help Bunin into his raglan but he stopped me with a proud gesture of his open hand. Still struggling per-functorily—*he* was now trying to help *me*—we emerged into the pallid bleakness of a Paris winter day. My companion was about to button his collar when a look of surprise and distress twisted his handsome features. Gingerly opening his overcoat, he began tugging at something under his armpit. I came to his assistance and together we finally dragged out of his sleeve my long woolen scarf which the girl had stuffed into the wrong coat. The thing came out inch by inch; it was like unwrapping a mummy and we kept slowly revolving around each other in the process, to the ribald amusement of three sidewalk whores. Then, when the operation was over, we walked on without a word to a street corner where we shook hands and separated. Subsequently we used to meet quite of-ten, but always in the midst of other people, generally in the house of I. I. Fondaminski (a saintly and heroic soul who did more for Russian émigré literature than any other man and who died in a German prison). Somehow Bunin and I adopted a bantering and rather depressing mode of conver-sation, a Russian variety of American "kidding," and this pre-cluded any real commerce between us.

I met many other émigré Russian authors. I did not meet Poplavski who died young, a far violin among near balalaikas.

Go to sleep, O Morella, how awful are aquiline lives

His plangent tonalities I shall never forget, nor shall I ever forgive myself the ill-tempered review in which I attacked him for trivial faults in his unfledged verse. I met wise, prim, charming Aldanov; decrepit Kuprin, carefully carrying a bottle of *vin ordinaire* through rainy streets; Ayhenvald—a Russian version of Walter Pater—later killed by a trolleycar; Marina Tsvetaev, wife of a double agent, and poet of genius, who, in the late thirties, returned to Russia and perished there. But the author that interested me most was naturally Sirin. He belonged to my generation. Among the young writers pro-duced in exile he was the loneliest and most arrogant one. Beginning with the appearance of his first novel in 1925 and throughout the next fifteen years, until he vanished as strangely as he had come, his work kept provoking an acute and rather morbid interest on the part of critics. Just as Marxist publicists of the eighties in old Russia would have denounced his lack of concern with the economic structure of society, so the mystagogues of émigré letters deplored his lack of religious insight and of moral preoccupation. Everything about him was bound to offend Russian conventions and especially that Russian sense of decorum which, for example, an American offends so dangerously today, when in the presence of Soviet military men of distinction he happens to lounge with both hands in his trouser pockets. Conversely, Sirin's admirers made much, perhaps too much, of his unusual style, brilliant precision, functional imagery and that sort of thing. Russian readers who had been raised on the sturdy straightforwardness of Russian realism and had called the bluff of decadent cheats, were impressed by the mirror-like angles of his clear but weirdly misleading sentences and by the fact that the real life of his books flowed in his figures of speech, which one critic has compared to "windows giving upon a contiguous world . . . a rolling corollary, the shadow of a train of thought." Across the dark sky of exile, Sirin passed, to use a simile of a more conservative nature, like a meteor, and disappeared, leaving nothing much else behind him than a vague sense of uneasiness.

3

In the course of my twenty years of exile I devoted a prodigious amount of time to the composing of chess problems. A certain position is elaborated on the board, and the problem to be solved is how to mate Black in a given number of moves, generally two or three. It is a beautiful, complex and sterile art related to the ordinary form of the game only insofar as, say, the properties of a sphere are made use of both by a juggler in weaving a new act and by a tennis player in winning a tournament. Most chess players, in fact, amateurs and masters alike, are only mildly interested in these highly specialized, fanciful, stylish riddles, and though appreciative of a catchy problem would be utterly baffled if asked to compose one.

Inspiration of a quasi-musical, quasi-poetical, or to be quite

exact, poetico-mathematical type, attends the process of thinking up a chess composition of that sort. Frequently, in the
friendly middle of the day, on the fringe of some trivial occupation, in the idle wake of a passing thought, I would experience, without warning, a twinge of mental pleasure as the
bud of a chess problem burst open in my brain, promising me
a night of labor and felicity. It might be a new way of blending
an unusual strategic device with an unusual line of defense; it
might be a glimpse of the actual configuration of men that
would render at last, with humor and grace, a difficult theme
that I had despaired of expressing before; or it might be a
mere gesture made in the mist of my mind by the various
units of force represented by chessmen—a kind of swift dumb
show, suggesting new harmonies and new conflicts; whatever
it was, it belonged to an especially exhilarating order of sensation, and my only quarrel with it today is that the maniacal
manipulation of carved figures, or of their mental counter-
parts, during my most ebullient and prolific years engulfed so
much of the time I could have devoted to verbal adventure.

Experts distinguish several schools of the chess-problem art:
the Anglo-American one that combines accurate construction
with dazzling thematic patterns, and refuses to be bound by
any conventional rules; the rugged splendor of the Teutonic
school; the highly finished but unpleasantly slick and insipid
products of the Czech style with its strict adherence to certain
artificial conditions; the old Russian end-game studies, which
attain the sparkling summits of the art, and the mechanical
Soviet problem of the so-called "task" type, which replaces
artistic strategy by the ponderous working of themes to their
utmost capacity. Themes in chess, it may be explained, are
such devices as forelaying, withdrawing, pinning, unpinning
and so forth; but it is only when they are combined in a certain
way that a problem is satisfying. Deceit, to the point of di-
abolism, and originality, verging upon the grotesque, were my
notions of strategy; and although in matters of construction
I tried to conform, whenever possible, to classical rules, such
as economy of force, unity, weeding out of loose ends, I was
always ready to sacrifice purity of form to the exigencies of
fantastic content, causing form to bulge and burst like a
sponge-bag containing a small furious devil.

It is one thing to conceive the main play of a composition and another to construct it. The strain on the mind is formidable; the element of time drops out of one's consciousness altogether: the building hand gropes for a pawn in the box, holds it, while the mind still ponders the need for a foil or a stopgap, and when the fist opens, a whole hour, perhaps, has gone by, has burned to ashes in the incandescent cerebration of the schemer. The chessboard before him is a magnetic field, a system of stresses and abysses, a starry firmament. The bishops move over it like searchlights. This or that knight is a lever adjusted and tried, and readjusted and tried again, till the problem is tuned up to the necessary level of beauty and surprise. How often I have struggled to bind the terrible force of White's queen so as to avoid a dual solution! It should be understood that competition in chess problems is not really between White and Black but between the composer and the hypothetical solver (just as in a first-rate work of fiction the real clash is not between the characters but between the author and the world), so that a great part of a problem's value is due to the number of "tries"—delusive opening moves, false scents, specious lines of play, astutely and lovingly prepared to lead the would-be solver astray. But whatever I can say about this matter of problem composing, I do not seem to convey sufficiently the ecstatic core of the process and its points of connection with various other, more overt and fruitful, operations of the creative mind, from the charting of dangerous seas to the writing of one of those incredible novels where the author, in a fit of lucid madness, has set himself certain unique rules that he observes, certain nightmare obstacles that he surmounts, with the zest of a deity building a live world from the most unlikely ingredients—rocks, and carbon, and blind throbbings. In the case of problem composition, the event is accompanied by a mellow physical satisfaction, especially when the chessmen are beginning to enact adequately, in a penultimate rehearsal, the composer's dream. There is a feeling of snugness (which goes back to one's childhood, to play-planning in bed, with parts of toys fitting into corners of one's brain); there is the nice way one piece is ambushed behind another, within the comfort and warmth of an out-of-the-way square; and there is the smooth motion of a well-oiled and polished machine that runs sweetly at the touch of two forked fingers lightly lifting and lightly lowering a piece.

I remember one particular problem I had been trying to compose for months. There came a night when I managed at last to express that particular theme. It was meant for the delectation of the very expert solver. The unsophisticated might miss the point of the problem entirely, and discover its fairly simple, "thetic" solution without having passed through the pleasurable torments prepared for the sophisticated one. The latter would start by falling for an illusory pattern of play based on a fashionable avant-garde theme (exposing White's King to checks), which the composer had taken the greatest pains to "plant" (with only one obscure little move by an inconspicuous pawn to upset it). Having passed through this "antithetic" inferno the by now ultrasophisticated solver would reach the simple key move (bishop to c2) as somebody on a wild goose chase might go from Albany to New York by way of Vancouver, Eurasia and the Azores. The pleasant experience of the roundabout route (strange landscapes, gongs, tigers, exotic customs, the thrice-repeated circuit of a newly married couple around the sacred fire of an earthen brazier) would amply reward him for the misery of the deceit, and after that, his arrival at the simple key move would provide him with a synthesis of poignant artistic delight.

I remember slowly emerging from a swoon of concentrated chess thought, and there, on a great English board of cream and cardinal leather, the flawless position was at last balanced like a constellation. It worked. It lived. My Staunton chessmen (a twenty-year-old set given to me by my father's Englished brother, Konstantin), splendidly massive pieces, of tawny or black wood, up to four and a quarter inches tall, displayed their shiny contours as if conscious of the part they played. Alas, if examined closely, some of the men were seen to be chipped (after traveling in their box through the fifty or sixty lodgings I had changed during those years); but the top of the king's rook and the brow of the king's knight still showed a small crimson crown painted upon them, recalling the round mark on a happy Hindu's forehead.

A brooklet of time in comparison to its frozen lake on the

chessboard, my watch showed half-past three. The season was
May—mid-May, 1940. The day before, after months of solic-
iting and cursing, the emetic of a bribe had been administered
to the right rat at the right office and had resulted finally in
a *visa de sortie* which, in its turn, conditioned the permission
to cross the Atlantic. All of a sudden, I felt that with the
completion of my chess problem a whole period of my life
had come to a satisfactory close. Everything around was very
quiet; faintly dimpled, as it were, by the quality of my relief.
Sleeping in the next room were you and our child. The lamp
on my table was bonneted with blue sugarloaf paper (an amusing military precaution) and the resulting light lent a lunar
tinge to the voluted air heavy with tobacco smoke. Opaque
curtains separated me from blacked-out Paris. The headline
of a newspaper drooping from the seat of a chair spoke of
Hitler's striking at the Low Countries.

I have before me the sheet of paper upon which, that night
in Paris, I drew the diagram of the problem's position. White:
King on a7 (meaning first file, seventh rank), Queen on b6,
Rooks on f4 and h5, Bishops on e4 and h8, Knights on d8
and e6, Pawns on b7 and g3; Black: King on e5, Rook on g7,
Bishop on h6, Knights on e2 and g5, Pawns on c3, c6 and d7.
White begins and mates in two moves. The false scent, the
irresistible "try" is: Pawn to b8, becoming a knight, with three
beautiful mates following in answer to disclosed checks by
Black; but Black can defeat the whole brilliant affair by *not*
checking White and making instead a modest dilatory move
elsewhere on the board. In one corner of the sheet with the
diagram, I notice a certain stamped mark that also adorns
other papers and books I took out of France to America in
May 1940. It is a circular imprint, in the ultimate tint of the
spectrum—*violet de bureau*. In its center there are two capital
letters of pica size, *R.F.*, meaning of course *République Fran-
çaise*. Other letters in lesser type, running peripherally, spell
Contrôle des Informations. However, it is only now, many
years later, that the information concealed in my chess symbols, which that control permitted to pass, may be, and in fact
is, divulged.

Fifteen

THEY ARE PASSING, posthaste, posthaste, the gliding years—to use a soul-rending Horatian inflection. The years are passing, my dear, and presently nobody will know what you and I know. Our child is growing; the roses of Paestum, of misty Paestum, are gone; mechanically minded idiots are tinkering and tampering with forces of nature that mild mathematicians, to their own secret surprise, appear to have foreshadowed; so perhaps it is time we examined ancient snapshots, cave drawings of trains and planes, strata of toys in the lumbered closet.

We shall go still further back, to a morning in May 1934, and plot with respect to this fixed point the graph of a section of Berlin. There I was walking home, at 5 A.M., from the maternity hospital near Bayerischer Platz, to which I had taken you a couple of hours earlier. Spring flowers adorned the portraits of Hindenburg and Hitler in the window of a shop that sold frames and colored photographs. Leftist groups of sparrows were holding loud morning sessions in lilacs and limes. A limpid dawn had completely unsheathed one side of the empty street. On the other side, the houses still looked blue with cold, and various long shadows were gradually being telescoped, in the matter-of-fact manner young day has when taking over from night in a well-groomed, well-watered city, where the tang of tarred pavements underlies the sappy smells of shade trees; but to me the optical part of the business seemed quite new, like some unusual way of laying the table, because I had never seen that particular street at daybreak before, although, on the other hand, I had often passed there, childless, on sunny evenings.

In the purity and vacuity of the less familiar hour, the shadows were on the wrong side of the street, investing it with a sense of not inelegant inversion, as when one sees reflected in the mirror of a barbershop the window toward which the melancholy barber, while stropping his razor, turns his gaze (as they all do at such times), and, framed in that reflected window, a stretch of sidewalk shunting a procession of uncon-

cerned pedestrians in the wrong direction, into an abstract
world that all at once stops being droll and loosens a torrent
of terror.

Whenever I start thinking of my love for a person, I am in
the habit of immediately drawing radii from my love—from
my heart, from the tender nucleus of a personal matter—to
monstrously remote points of the universe. Something impels
me to measure the consciousness of my love against such unimaginable and incalculable things as the behavior of nebulae
(whose very remoteness seems a form of insanity), the dreadful
pitfalls of eternity, the unknowledgeable beyond the unknown, the helplessness, the cold, the sickening involutions
and interpenetrations of space and time. It is a pernicious
habit, but I can do nothing about it. It can be compared to
the uncontrollable flick of an insomniac's tongue checking a
jagged tooth in the night of his mouth and bruising itself in
doing so but still persevering. I have known people who, upon
accidentally touching something—a doorpost, a wall—had to
go through a certain very rapid and systematic sequence of
manual contacts with various surfaces in the room before returning to a balanced existence. It cannot be helped; I must
know where I stand, where you and my son stand. When that
slow-motion, silent explosion of love takes place in me, unfolding its melting fringes and overwhelming me with the
sense of something much vaster, much more enduring and
powerful than the accumulation of matter or energy in any
imaginable cosmos, then my mind cannot but pinch itself to
see if it is really awake. I have to make a rapid inventory of
the universe, just as a man in a dream tries to condone the
absurdity of his position by making sure he is dreaming. I have
to have all space and all time participate in my emotion, in
my mortal love, so that the edge of its mortality is taken off,
thus helping me to fight the utter degradation, ridicule, and
horror of having developed an infinity of sensation and
thought within a finite existence.

Since, in my metaphysics, I am a confirmed non-unionist
and have no use for organized tours through anthropomorphic paradises, I am left to my own, not negligible devices
when I think of the best things in life; when, as now, I look
back upon my almost couvade-like concern with our baby.

The small butterfly, light blue above, grayish beneath, of which the two type specimens (male holotype on the left, both sides, one hindwing slightly damaged; and male paratype on the right, both sides), preserved in the American Museum of Natural History and figured now for the first time from photographs made by that institution, is *Plebejus* (*Lysandra*) *cormion* Nabokov. The first name is that of the genus, the second that of the subgenus, the third that of the species, and the fourth that of the author of the original description which I published in September 1941 (*Journal of the New York Entomological Society*, Vol. 49, p. 265), later figuring the genitalia of the paratype (October 26, 1945, *Psyche*, Vol. 52, Pl. 1). Possibly, as I pointed out, my butterfly owed its origin to hybridization between *Plebejus* (*Lysandra*) *coridon* Poda (in the large sense) and *Plebejus* (*Meleageria*) *daphnis* Schiffermüller. Live organisms are less conscious of specific or subgeneric differences than the taxonomist is. I took the two males figured, and saw at least two more (but no females) on July 20 (paratype) and 22 (holotype), 1938, at about 4,000 ft. near the village of Moulinet, Alpes Maritimes. It may not rank high enough to deserve a name, but whatever it be—a new species in the making, a striking sport, or a chance cross—it remains a great and delightful rarity.

You remember the discoveries we made (supposedly made by all parents): the perfect shape of the miniature fingernails of the hand you silently showed me as it lay, stranded starfish-wise, on your palm; the epidermic texture of limb and cheek, to which attention was drawn in dimmed, faraway tones, as if the softness of touch could be rendered only by the softness of distance; that swimming, sloping, elusive something about the dark-bluish tint of the iris which seemed still to retain the shadows it had absorbed of ancient, fabulous forests where there were more birds than tigers and more fruit than thorns, and where, in some dappled depth, man's mind had been born; and, above all, an infant's first journey into the next dimension, the newly established nexus between eye and reachable object, which the career boys in biometrics or in the rat-maze racket think they can explain. It occurs to me that the closet reproduction of the mind's birth obtainable is the stab of wonder that accompanies the precise moment when, gazing at a tangle of twigs and leaves, one suddenly realizes that what had seemed a natural component of that tangle is a marvelously disguised insect or bird.

There is also keen pleasure (and, after all, what else should the pursuit of science produce?) in meeting the riddle of the initial blossoming of man's mind by postulating a voluptuous pause in the growth of the rest of nature, a lolling and loafing which allowed first of all the formation of *Homo poeticus*—without which *sapiens* could not have been evolved. "Struggle for life" indeed! The curse of battle and toil leads man back to the boar, to the grunting beast's crazy obsession with the search for food. You and I have frequently remarked upon that maniacal glint in a housewife's scheming eye as it roves over food in a grocery or about the morgue of a butcher's shop. Toilers of the world, disband! Old books are wrong. The world was made on a Sunday.

2

Throughout the years of our boy's infancy, in Hitler's Germany and Maginot's France, we were more or less constantly hard up, but wonderful friends saw to his having the best things available. Although powerless to do much about it, you and I jointly kept a jealous eye on any possible rift between his childhood and our own incunabula in the opulent past, and this is where those friendly fates came in, doctoring the rift every time it threatened to open. Then, too, the science of building up babies had made the same kind of phenomenal, streamlined progress that flying or tilling had—*I*, when nine months old, did not get a pound of strained spinach at one feeding or the juice of a dozen oranges per day; and the pediatric hygiene you adopted was incomparably more artistic and scrupulous than anything old nurses could have dreamed up when we were babes.

I think bourgeois fathers—wing-collar workers in pencil-striped pants, dignified, office-tied fathers, so different from young American veterans of today or from a happy, jobless Russian-born expatriate of fifteen years ago—will not understand my attitude toward our child. Whenever you held him up, replete with his warm formula and grave as an idol, and waited for the postlactic all-clear signal before making a horizontal baby of the vertical one, I used to take part both in your wait and in the tightness of his surfeit, which I exaggerated, therefore rather resenting your cheerful faith in the speedy dissipation of what I felt to be a painful oppression; and when, at last, the blunt little bubble did rise and burst in his solemn mouth, I used to experience a lovely relief while you, with a congratulatory murmur, bent low to deposit him in the white-rimmed twilight of his crib.

You know, I still feel in my wrists certain echoes of the pram-pusher's knack, such as, for example, the glib downward pressure one applied to the handle in order to have the carriage tip up and climb the curb. First came an elaborate mouse-gray vehicle of Belgian make, with fat autoid tires and luxurious springs, so large that it could not enter our puny elevator. It rolled on sidewalks in slow stately mystery, with the trapped baby inside lying supine, well covered with down, silk and fur; only his eyes moved, warily, and sometimes they turned upward with one swift sweep of their showy lashes to follow the receding of branch-patterned blueness that flowed away from the edge of the half-cocked hood of the carriage, and presently he would dart a suspicious glance at my face to see if the teasing trees and sky did not belong, perhaps, to the same order of things as did rattles and parental humor. There followed a lighter carriage, and in this, as he spun along, he would tend to rise, straining at his straps; clutching at the edges; standing there less like the groggy passenger of a pleasure boat than like an entranced scientist in a spaceship; surveying the speckled skeins of a live, warm world; eyeing with philosophic interest the pillow he had managed to throw overboard; falling out himself when a strap burst one day. Still later he rode in one of those small contraptions called strollers; from initial springy and secure heights the child came lower and lower, until, when he was about one and a half, he touched ground in front of the moving stroller by slipping forward out of his seat and beating the sidewalk with his heels in anticipation of being set loose in some public garden. A new wave of evolution started to swell, gradually lifting him again from the ground, when, for his second birthday, he received a four-foot-long, silver-painted Mercedes racing car operated by inside pedals, like an organ, and in this he used to drive with a pumping, clanking noise up and down the sidewalk of the Kurfürstendamm while from open windows came the multiplied roar of a dictator still pounding his chest in the Neander valley we had left far behind.

It might be rewarding to go into the phylogenetic aspects of the passion male children have for things on wheels, particularly railway trains. Of course, we know what the Viennese Quack thought of the matter. We will leave him and his fellow travelers to jog on, in their third-class carriage of thought, through the police state of sexual myth (incidentally, what a great mistake on the part of dictators to ignore psychoanalysis—a whole generation might be so easily corrupted that way!). Rapid growth, quantum-quick thought, the roller coaster of the circulatory system—all forms of vitality are forms of velocity, and no wonder a growing child desires to out-Nature Nature by filling a minimum stretch of time with a maximum of spatial enjoyment. Innermost in man is the spiritual pleasure derivable from the possibilities of outtugging and outrunning gravity, of overcoming or re-enacting the earth's pull. The miraculous paradox of smooth round objects conquering space by simply tumbling over and over, instead of laboriously lifting heavy limbs in order to progress, must have given young mankind a most salutary shock. The bonfire into which the dreamy little savage peered as he squatted on naked haunches, or the unswerving advance of a forest fire— these have also affected, I suppose, a chromosome or two behind Lamarck's back, in the mysterious way which Western geneticists are as disinclined to elucidate as are professional physicists to discuss the outside of the inside, the whereabouts of the curvature; for every dimension presupposes a medium within which it can act, and if, in the spiral unwinding of things, space warps into something akin to time, and time, in its turn, warps into something akin to thought, then, surely, another dimension follows—a special Space maybe, not the old one, we trust, unless spirals become vicious circles again.

But whatever the truth may be, we shall never forget, you and I, we shall forever defend, on this or some other battleground, the bridges on which we spent hours waiting with our little son (aged anything from two to six) for a train to pass below. I have seen older and less happy children stop for a moment in order to lean over the railing and spit into the asthmatic stack of the engine that happened to pass under, but neither you nor I is ready to admit that the more normal of two children is the one who resolves pragmatically the aimless exaltation of an obscure trance. You did nothing to curtail or rationalize those hour-long stops on windy bridges when, with an optimism and a patience that knew no bounds, our child would hope for a semaphore to click and for a growing locomotive to take shape at a point where all the many tracks converged, in the distance, between the blank backs of houses. On cold days he wore a lambskin coat, with a similar cap, both a brownish color mottled with rime-like gray, and these, and mittens, and the fervency of his faith kept him glowing, and kept *you* warm too, since all you had to do to prevent your delicate fingers from freezing was to hold one of his hands alternately in your right and left, switching every minute or so, and marveling at the incredible amount of heat generated by a big baby's body.

3

Besides dreams of velocity, or in connection with them, there is in every child the essentially human urge to reshape the earth, to act upon a friable environment (unless he is a born Marxist or a corpse and meekly waits for the environment to fashion *him*). This explains a child's delight in digging, in making roads and tunnels for his favorite toys. Our son had a tiny model of Sir Malcolm Campbell's Bluebird, of painted steel and with detachable tires, and this he would play with endlessly on the ground, and the sun would make a kind of nimbus of his longish fair hair and turn to a toffee tint his bare back crisscrossed by the shoulder straps of his knitted navy-blue shorts (under which, when undressed, he was seen to be bottomed and haltered with natural white). Never in my life have I sat on so many benches and park chairs, stone slabs and stone steps, terrace parapets and brims of fountain basins as I did in those days. The popular pine barrens around the lake in Berlin's Grunewald we visited but seldom. You questioned the right of a place to call itself a forest when it was so full of refuse, so much more littered with rubbish than the glossy, self-conscious streets of the adjoining town. Curious things turned up in this Grunewald. The sight of an iron bedstead exhibiting the anatomy of its springs in the middle of a glade or the presence of a dressmaker's black dummy lying under a hawthorn bush in bloom made one wonder who, exactly, had troubled to carry these and other widely scattered articles to such remote points of a pathless forest. Once I came across a badly disfigured but still alert mirror, full of sylvan reflections—drunk, as it were, on a mixture of beer and chartreuse—leaning, with surrealistic jauntiness, against a tree trunk. Perhaps such intrusions on these burgherish pleasure grounds were a fragmentary vision of the mess to come, a prophetic bad dream of destructive explosions, something like the heap of dead heads the seer Cagliostro glimpsed in the ha-ha of a royal garden. And nearer to the lake, in summer, especially on Sundays, the place was infested with human bodies in various stages of nudity and solarization. Only the squirrels and certain caterpillars kept their coats on. Gray-footed goodwives sat on greasy gray sand in their slips; repulsive, seal-voiced males, in muddy swimming trunks, gamboled around; remarkably comely but poorly groomed girls, destined to bear a few years later—early in 1946, to be exact—a sudden crop of infants with Turkic or Mongol blood in their innocent veins, were chased and slapped on the rear (whereupon they would cry out, "Ow-wow!"); and the exhalations coming from these unfortunate frolickers, and their shed clothes (neatly spread out here and there on the ground) mingled with the stench of stagnant water to form an inferno of odors that, somehow, I have never found duplicated anywhere else. People in Berlin's public gardens and city parks were not permitted to undress; but shirts might be unbuttoned, and rows of young men, of a pronounced Nordic type, sat with closed eyes on benches and exposed their frontal and pectoral pimples to the nationally approved action of the sun. The squeamish and possibly exaggerated shudder that obtains in these notes may be attributed, I suppose, to the constant fear we lived in of some contamination affecting our child. You always considered abominably trite, and not devoid of a peculiar Philistine flavor, the notion that small boys, in order to be delightful, should hate to wash and love to kill.

I would like to remember every small park we visited; I would like to have the ability Professor Jack, of Harvard and the Arnold Arboretum, told his students he had of identifying twigs with his eyes shut, merely from the sound of their swish through the air ("Hornbeam, honeysuckle, Lombardy poplar. Ah—a folded *Transcript*"). Quite often, of course, I can determine the geographic position of this or that park by some particular trait or combination of traits: dwarf-box edgings along narrow gravel walks, all of which meet like people in plays; a low blue bench against a cuboid hedge of yew; a square bed of roses framed in a border of heliotrope—these features are obviously associated with small park areas at street intersections in suburban Berlin. Just as clearly, a chair of thin iron, with its spidery shadow lying beneath it a little to one side of center, or a pleasantly supercilious, although plainly psychopathic, rotatory sprinkler, with a private rainbow hanging in its spray above gemmed grass, spells a Parisian park; but, as you will well understand, the eye of memory is so firmly focused upon a small figure squatting on the ground

— 3 —

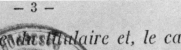

Photographie du titulaire et, le cas échéant, photographies des enfants qui l'accompagnent.

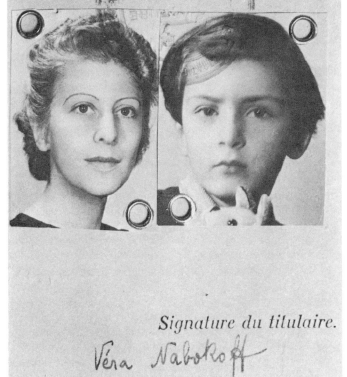

Signature du titulaire.

Véra Nabokoff

A Nansen passport picture taken in Paris in April 1940, of the author's wife, Véra, and son Dmitri, aged five. A few weeks later, in May, the last chapter of our European period was to end as it ends in this book.

(loading a toy truck with pebbles or contemplating the bright, wet rubber of a gardener's hose to which some of the gravel over which the hose has just slithered adheres) that the various loci—Berlin, Prague, Franzensbad, Paris, the Riviera, Paris again, Cap d'Antibes and so forth—lose all sovereignty, pool their petrified generals and fallen leaves, cement the friendship of their interlocked paths, and unite in a federation of light and shade through which bare-kneed, graceful children drift on whirring roller skates.

Now and then a recognized patch of historical background aids local identification—and substitutes other bonds for those a personal vision suggests. Our child must have been almost three on that breezy day in Berlin (where, of course, no one could escape familiarity with the ubiquitous picture of the Führer) when we stood, he and I, before a bed of pallid pansies, each of their upturned faces showing a dark mustache-like smudge, and had great fun, at my rather silly prompting, commenting on their resemblance to a crowd of bobbing little Hitlers. Likewise, I can name a blooming garden in Paris as the place where I noticed, in 1938 or 1939, a quiet girl of ten or so, with a deadpan white face, looking, in her dark, shabby, unseasonable clothes, as if she had escaped from an orphanage (congruously, I was granted a later glimpse of her being swept away by two flowing nuns), who had deftly tied a live butterfly to a thread and was promenading the pretty, weakly fluttering, slightly crippled insect on that elfish leash (the by-product, perhaps, of a good deal of dainty needlework in that orphanage). You have often accused me of unnecessary callousness in my matter-of-fact entomological investigations on our trips to the Pyrenees or the Alps; so, if I diverted our child's attention from that would-be Titania, it was not because I pitied her Red Admirable (Admiral, in vulgar parlance) but because there was some vaguely repulsive symbolism about her sullen sport. I may have been reminded, in fact, of the simple, old-fashioned trick a French policeman had—and no doubt still has—when leading a florid-nosed workman, a Sunday rowdy, away to jail, of turning him into a singularly docile and even alacritous satellite by catching a kind of small fishhook in the man's uncared-for but sensitive and responsive flesh. You and I did our best to encompass with vigilant tenderness the trustful tenderness of our child but were inevitably confronted by the fact that the filth left by hoodlums in a sandbox on a playground was the least serious of possible offenses, and that the horrors which former generations had mentally dismissed as anachronisms or things occurring only in remote khanates and mandarinates, were all around us.

As time went on and the shadow of fool-made history vitiated even the exactitude of sundials, we moved more restlessly over Europe, and it seemed as if not we but those gardens and parks traveled along. Le Nôtre's radiating avenues and complicated parterres were left behind, like sidetracked trains. In Prague, to which we journeyed to show our child to my mother in the spring of 1937, there was Stromovka Park, with its atmosphere of free undulating remoteness beyond man-trained arbors. You will also recall those rock gardens of Alpine plants—sedums and saxifrages—that escorted us, so to speak, into the Savoy Alps, joining us on a vacation (paid for by something my translators had sold), and then followed us back into the towns of the plains. Cuffed hands of wood nailed to boles in the old parks of curative resorts pointed in the direction whence came a subdued thumping of bandstand music. An intelligent walk accompanied the main driveway; not everywhere paralleling it but freely recognizing its guidance, and from duck pond or lily pool gamboling back to join the procession of plane trees at this or that point where the park had developed a city-father fixation and dreamed up a monument. Roots, roots of remembered greenery, roots of memory and pungent plants, roots, in a word, are enabled to traverse long distances by surmounting some obstacles, penetrating others and insinuating themselves into narrow cracks. So those gardens and parks traversed Central Europe with us. Graveled walks gathered and stopped at a *rond-point* to watch you or me bend and wince as we looked for a ball under a privet hedge where, on the dark, damp earth, nothing but a perforated mauve trolley ticket or a bit of soiled gauze and cotton wool could be detected. A circular seat would go around a thick oak trunk to see who was sitting on the other side and find there a dejected old man reading a foreign-language newspaper and picking his nose. Glossy-leaved evergreens enclosing a lawn where our child discovered his first live frog broke into a trimmed maze of topiary work, and you said you thought it was going to rain. At some farther stage, under less leaden skies, there was a great show of rose dells and pleached alleys, and trellises swinging their creepers, ready to turn into the vines of columned pergolas if given a chance, or, if not, to disclose the quaintest of quaint public toilets, a miserable chalet-like affair of doubtful cleanliness, with a woman attendant in black, black-knitting on its porch.

Down a slope, a flagged path stepped cautiously, putting the same foot first every time, through an iris garden; under beeches; and then was transformed into a fast-moving earthy trail patterned with rough imprints of horse hooves. The gardens and parks seemed to move ever faster as our child's legs grew longer, and when he was about four, the trees and flowering shrubs turned resolutely toward the sea. Like a bored stationmaster seen standing alone on the speed-clipped platform of some small station at which one's train does not stop, this or that gray park watchman receded as the park streamed on and on, carrying us south toward the orange trees and the arbutus and the chick-fluff of mimosas and the *pâte tendre* of an impeccable sky.

Graded gardens on hillsides, a succession of terraces whose every stone step ejected a gaudy grasshopper, dropped from ledge to ledge seaward, with the olives and the oleanders fairly toppling over each other in their haste to obtain a view of the beach. There our child kneeled motionless to be photographed in a quivering haze of sun against the scintillation of the sea, which is a milky blur in the snapshots we have preserved but was, in life, silvery blue, with great patches of purple-blue farther out, caused by warm currents in collaboration with and corroboration of (hear the pebbles rolled by the withdrawing wave?) eloquent old poets and their smiling similes. And among the candy-like blobs of sea-licked glass—lemon, cherry, peppermint—and the banded pebbles, and the little fluted shells with lustered insides, sometimes small bits of pottery, still beautiful in glaze and color, turned up. They were brought to you or me for inspection, and if they had indigo chevrons, or bands of leaf ornament, or any kind of gay emblemata, and were judged precious, down they went with a click into the toy pail, and, if not, a plop and a flash marked their return to the sea. I do not doubt that among those slightly convex chips of majolica ware found by our child there was one whose border of scrollwork fitted exactly, and continued, the pattern of a fragment I had found in 1903 on the same shore, and that the two tallied with a third my mother had found on that Mentone beach in 1882, and with a fourth piece of the same pottery that had been found by *her* mother a hundred years ago—and so on, until this assortment of parts, if all had been preserved, might have been put together to make the complete, the absolutely complete, bowl, broken by some Italian child, God knows where and when, and now mended by *these* rivets of bronze.

In the fall of 1939, we returned to Paris, and around May 20 of the following year we were again near the sea, this time on the western coast of France, at St. Nazaire. There, one last little garden surrounded us, as you and I, and our child, by now six, between us, walked through it on our way to the docks, where, behind the buildings facing us, the liner *Champlain* was waiting to take us to New York. That garden was what the French call, phonetically, *skwarr* and the Russians *skver*, perhaps because it is the kind of thing usually found in or near public squares in England. Laid out on the last limit of the past and on the verge of the present, it remains in my memory merely as a geometrical design which no doubt I could easily fill in with the colors of plausible flowers, if I were careless enough to break the hush of pure memory that (except, perhaps, for some chance tinnitus due to the pressure of my own tired blood) I have left undisturbed, and humbly listened to, from the beginning. What I really remember about this neutrally blooming design, is its clever thematic connection with transatlantic gardens and parks; for suddenly, as we came to the end of its path, you and I saw something that we did not immediately point out to our child, so as to enjoy in full the blissful shock, the enchantment and glee he would experience on discovering ahead the ungenuinely gigantic, the unrealistically real prototype of the various toy vessels he had doddled about in his bath. There, in front of us, where a broken row of houses stood between us and the harbor, and where the eye encountered all sorts of stratagems, such as pale-blue and pink underwear cakewalking on a clothesline, or a lady's bicycle and a striped cat oddly sharing a rudimentary balcony of cast iron, it was most satisfying to make out among the jumbled angles of roofs and walls, a splendid ship's funnel, showing from behind the clothesline as something in a scrambled picture—Find What the Sailor Has Hidden—that the finder cannot unsee once it has been seen.

Index

CHRONOLOGY

NOTE ON THE TEXTS

NOTES

Chronology

1899   Born Vladimir Vladimirovich Nabokov on April 23 (April 10 Old Style) at 47 Bolshaya Morskaya Street in St. Petersburg, first child of Vladimir Dmitrievich Nabokov, b. 1870, and Elena Ivanovna Nabokov, b. 1876. Christened in Orthodox ceremony in late spring. Father is a lecturer in criminal law at the Imperial School of Jurisprudence, and an editor of the liberal law journal *Pravo*. Family lives in plush Morskaya Street home with many servants and spends summer on the three neighboring estates of Rozhdestveno and Vyra (maternal grandfather's) and Batovo (paternal grandmother's), about 50 miles south of St. Petersburg. (Grandfather Dmitri Nikolaevich Nabokov, b. 1826, married Baroness Maria Ferdinandovna von Korff, b. 1842, in 1859. Grandfather became a member of the State Council and served as a liberal minister of justice from 1878 to 1885. Grandfather Ivan Vasilievich Rukavishnikov, b. 1841, a wealthy landowner and magistrate, married Olga Nikolaevna Kozlov, b. 1845, a daughter of the first president of the Royal Academy of Medicine. Mother was privately tutored in the natural sciences by a university professor. Parents were married in November 1897 and had a stillborn son in 1898.)

1900   Brother Sergey born in March. Nabokov speaks, and learns numbers, at an early age.

1901   Grandfather Rukavishnikov dies in March and grandmother Rukavishnikov dies in June, both of cancer. Mother inherits Vyra estate and uncle Vasiliy "Ruka" Rukavishnikov inherits Rozhdestveno. Doctors advise mother to go abroad for her health, and she takes Nabokov and Sergey to Pau and Biarritz in the south of France (father remains in St. Petersburg to teach).

1902   Nabokov and Sergey learn English from Rachel Home, first of a succession of British governesses. Spends summers at Vyra, enjoying the company of both sides of large extended family whose estates dot the area. Mother tells him to remember details they admire on walks in country, and reads him fairy tales and adventure stories in English at bedtime.

1903 Sister Olga born in January (brothers and sisters will be reared separately within household; Nabokov remains the favorite of parents). Father becomes a member of the St. Petersburg City Duma (council). After major pogrom at Kishinev in April, he writes article for *Pravo* charging government with tacitly encouraging pogroms. Family travels abroad in autumn and visits grandfather Nabokov, now senile, in Nice. In St. Petersburg Nabokov toboggans and takes long walks with new English governess; reads English juvenile magazines *Chatterbox* and *Little Folks* (has not yet learned to read Russian).

1904 Japan attacks Russia in February. Attends opera, which he does not enjoy, and theater with parents. Plays chess and cards with family. Grandfather Nabokov dies on March 28 in St. Petersburg. Father takes family to Rome and Naples for three weeks and then Beaulieu for the summer; there Nabokov falls in love with a Romanian girl. Family returns in fall to Russia, where setbacks in the Russo-Japanese War have increased pressure for political reform. Father plays active role in first national congress of zemstvos (local assemblies); congress, whose final session is held in the Nabokov home, calls for a written constitution, a national legislative assembly, and guaranteed civil rights, and effectively launches the 1905 (or First) Russian Revolution. Father, told his political activities are incompatible with his post at the Imperial School of Jurisprudence, resigns.

1905 Tsarist troops fire on a peaceful demonstration in St. Petersburg on January 22 ("Bloody Sunday"), killing more than a hundred people. Father denounces killings in the St. Petersburg Duma and is deprived of his court title. Advised to remove family from strife, father takes them in February to Abbazia (now Opatija, Croatia), where they stay with paternal aunt Natalia de Peterson and family. Nabokov misses Vyra and nostalgically traces details of the estate on his pillow with his finger. Father called back in October to Russia, where general strike spreads throughout country. Father goes to Moscow for founding sessions of Constitutional Democratic (CD) party; remainder of family moves to Wiesbaden, where Nabokov becomes friends with his cousin, Baron Yuri Rausch von Traubenburg, son of paternal aunt Nina.

1906   Family returns to Russia, but remains at Vyra through winter. Swiss governess Cécile Miauton arrives (she will be part of the household for seven years). Miauton tutors Nabokov and Sergey in mornings and in afternoons reads children her favorite French novels, poetry, and stories, beginning with Corneille and Hugo. Nabokov soon becomes fluent in French and memorizes passages from Racine. Sister Elena is born in March. Father, as leading speaker of the CDs, the largest party in the First State Duma, challenges Chief Minister Ivan Goremykin's rejection of the Duma's reform program in May: "Let the executive power submit to the legislative!" Nabokov is now taught to read and write in Russian over the summer by the village schoolmaster, Vasily Zhernosekov, a Socialist Revolutionary. Begins to catch butterflies (lepidopterology will become a lifelong passion). After Duma is unexpectedly dissolved by Tsar Nicholas II in July, father signs Vyborg manifesto (calling populace to civil disobedience) in protest and is stripped of his political rights; he becomes editor of *Rech'*, St. Petersburg's leading liberal daily and unofficial CD newspaper.

1907   Has severe bout of pneumonia, and loses his prodigious capacity for mathematical calculation. Studies books on Lepidoptera and specimens brought by mother while convalescing. Begins regular lessons with a succession of Russian-speaking tutors. Studies drawing and painting and learns tennis and boxing. Family travels to Biarritz in August, where Nabokov falls in love with Serbian girl, Zina.

1908   Father serves three-month prison sentence for signing Vyborg manifesto. Nabokov masters the known butterflies of Europe. Is permitted to stop going to church after telling father that he finds services boring.

1909   Sees father stop to chat with Leo Tolstoy during a walk. Becomes infatuated and spends much time with nine-year-old girl, Claude Deprès, during fall vacation at Biarritz. Though he still enjoys English juvenile magazines and *Punch*, Nabokov reads widely in his father's library, which contains 10,000 volumes. Early favorites include Jules Verne, Conan Doyle, Kipling, Conrad, Chesterton, Wilde, Pushkin, and Tolstoy.

1910   Continues friendship with cousin Yuri; they provoke each other to repeated tests of courage. Translates into French alexandrines Mayne Reid's *The Headless Horseman*, rears caterpillars, keeps notes in English on the butterflies he collects, reads entomological journals, and "dreams" his way through A. Seitz's *Macrolepidoptera of the World*. After fall family vacation in Germany, Nabokov and Sergey stay in Berlin with tutor for three months while undergoing orthodontic work; reads Tolstoy's *Voyna i mir* (*War and Peace*).

1911   Begins classes at elite but liberal Tenishev School, helped in studies by tutors at home. Rankles at conformity of school life but copes easily with courses, which include history, geography, geometry, algebra, physics, chemistry, Russian, French, German, Scripture, and woodworking. Plays soccer, always as goalkeeper. Closest school friends are Samuil Rosov and Samuil Kyandzhuntsev. Brother Kirill is born in June. Father publicly challenges editor of conservative newspaper to duel for personal insult in October; Nabokov, in agony of apprehension, imagines father's death, but an apology averts the duel.

1912–13   Miauton returns to Switzerland. Nabokov begins two years of drawing lessons with leading St. Petersburg artist Mstislav Dobuzhinsky (who will later call him his most hopeless pupil). Begins reading new Symbolist, Acmeist, and Futurist poetry along with works of Pushkin, Poe, Browning, Keats, Verlaine, Rimbaud, Gogol, Chekhov, Dostoevsky, Shakespeare, Tolstoy, Flaubert, and William James.

1914   H. G. Wells, whose work Nabokov admires, dines at Nabokovs' home during his tour of Russia. School report in spring describes Nabokov: "zealous football-player, excellent worker, respected as comrade of both flanks (Rosov-Popov), always modest, serious and restrained (though not adverse to a joke), Nabokov creates a most agreeable impression by his moral decency." Composes what he later calls his first poem in July and becomes prey to "the numb fury of versemaking." Germany declares war on Russia August 1; father, a reserve officer, is called up on August 3 and leaves with his regiment for Vyborg while mother volunteers as nurse in hospital for wounded soldiers. Nabokov continues to write poetry almost daily. Evgenia Hofeld, governess for Elena and Olga, arrives (will remain with family for many years and become closest companion of mother in her last years).

1915   Confined to bed with typhus in early summer. After recovering, begins love affair with Valentina "Lyussya" Shulgin, who is vacationing with her family near Vyra; writes many love poems to her. Father is transferred in September to the General Staff in Petrograd (as capital has been renamed). Nabokov is taught Russian literature by poet and critic Vladimir Gippius, whose verse he likes but whose pressure towards social concern he resists. Often skips classes throughout school year to meet with Lyussya. Smokes heavily. In November co-edits the school journal *Yunaya mysl'* (*Young Thought*), which contains his first publication, poem "Osen'" ("Autumn"). Translates Alfred de Musset's "La Nuit de décembre," dedicating it to Lyussya.

1916   Translation of "La Nuit de décembre" appears in *Yunaya mysl'*. Publishes at own expense *Stikhi* (*Poems*), collection of 68 love poems; another poem appears in leading literary journal *Vestnik Evropy* in July. Sees cousin Yuri, now in the army. Uncle "Ruka" Rukavishnikov dies in France in fall, leaving Nabokov 2,000-acre Rozhdestveno estate and manor. Is compelled to take extra lessons, having received "not satisfactory" grade in algebra at end of spring term. Affair with Lyussya ends and Nabokov begins what he later describes as "an extravagant phase of sentiment and sensuality." By end of year he is conducting affairs with three married women, including his cousin Tatiana Segerkranz, Yuri's 27-year-old sister.

1917   Sick with pneumonia, then measles. While recuperating at Imatra resort in Finland in January, begins romance with Eva Lubryjinksa. In Petrograd on March 12 soldiers refuse to fire on demonstrators and then mutiny, leading to the collapse of the Tsarist regime. Father becomes head of chancellery in the first Provisional Government. Nabokov has his appendix removed in May; writes "Dozhd' proletel" (later translated as "The Rain Has Flown"), the earliest poem he will include in his collected poems. Selects verses he will publish with schoolmate Andrey Balashov in *Dva puti* (*Two Paths*; printed 1918). Begins album of verses dedicated to Eva Lubryjinksa. Bolsheviks seize power in Petrograd in coup on November 7. Father sends family to Gaspra, estate outside Yalta in the Crimea, before being imprisoned by Bolsheviks for five days in December; after his release, he joins family in Crimea. Nabokov plays chess with him nightly and composes his first chess problems.

1918   After the Bolsheviks seize the Yalta area in late January, father adopts "disguise" of medical doctor. Nabokov writes first short verse play, "Vesnoy" ("In Spring"). German army occupies Crimea in April. Father begins to write his memoir *The Provisional Government.* Nabokov hunts butterflies, sees Yuri while he is on leave in Yalta. Family moves to Livadia, nearer Yalta, so that Sergey, Olga, and Elena can attend school. Nabokov studies Latin with tutor, continues writing poetry; publishes two poems in CD newspaper *Yaltinsky golos.* Meets poet Maximilian Voloshin, who suggests reading Andrey Bely on metrical patterns in Russian verse. Applies Bely's method to classics of Russian poetry and his own works; finds his poems metrically featureless and for about a year constructs his new verse to yield arresting Belian diagrams. Tutors favorite sister, Elena. After German troops withdraw in November, father becomes minister of justice in the Crimean Provisional Regional Government, civilian regime organized by CDs and Tatars.

1919   Writes "Dvoe" ("The Two"), 430-line riposte to Aleksandr Blok's "Dvenadstat" ("The Twelve"). Considers enlisting in White Army commanded by General Anton Denikin when cousin Yuri visits. Yuri is killed in battle soon after returning to the front; Nabokov serves as a pallbearer at his funeral in Yalta on March 14. Red Army begins advance into Crimea on April 3. Family sails from Sebastopol on April 15 aboard Greek freighter and arrives in Athens on April 23, then goes in late May to London, where they rent house in South Kensington with money from sale of mother's jewels. Nabokov spends time with other Russian emigrés including old schoolmate Samuil Rosov; renews romance with Eva Lubryjinksa. Enters Trinity College, Cambridge, on partial scholarship, in October. Studies Modern and Medieval Languages (French and Russian) and Natural Sciences (zoology). Shares room with Russian emigré Mikhail Kalashnikov. Writes poetry in Russian and plays goal for Trinity soccer team. Buys Dahl's four-volume Russian dictionary and reads in it every night, jotting down verbal finds. Writes first entomological paper, "A Few Notes on Crimean Lepidoptera" (published in *Entomologist*, Feb. 1920). Also reads Housman, Rupert Brooke, and Walter de la Mare and writes a few English poems.

1920   Spends time with brother Sergey, now at Christ's College, Cambridge, and becomes friends with Prince Nikita Romanov. Drops zoology to leave time for verse, women, soccer. Family moves to Berlin and father helps found liberal daily emigré newspaper *Rul'* (*The Rudder*). Nabokov receives advance from emigré publishing house Slovo for Russian translation of Romain Rolland's *Colas Breugnon*. Moves into lodgings next to Trinity with Kalashnikov in October. Argues with George Wells, son of H. G. Wells, about politics. Poem "Remembrance" published in *The English Review* (November).

1921   Three poems and story "Nezhit'" (later translated as "The Wood-Sprite") appear in *Rul'* on January 7 under name Vladimir Sirin, pseudonym adopted to distinguish himself from father (Nabokov will retain the Sirin pseudonym for his Russian writings into the 1960s). Begins regular contributions to *Rul'* of poems, plays, stories, chess problems, crossword puzzles, and reviews. Completes *Nikolka Persik*, translation of *Colas Breugnon* (published Nov. 1922). Spends summer in Berlin, where he falls in love with Svetlana Siewert, Kalashnikov's cousin. Visitors to family's house in Wilmersdorf include poet Sasha Chorny, Iosif Hessen, head of Slovo, cousin Nicolas Nabokov, Konstantin Stanislavsky, and actors from Stanislavsky's Moscow Art Theater. Returns to Cambridge and becomes friend of Count Robert de Calry, English student of Russian ancestry. During winter ski trip to Switzerland with de Calry visits Cécile Miauton in Lausanne.

1922   Father is shot and killed on March 28 while struggling with one of the monarchist gunmen attempting to assassinate fellow CD leader Pavel Milyukov. Nabokov attends funeral in Tegel, near Berlin, then returns to Cambridge to study for exams. Writes mother: "At times it's all so oppressive I could go out of my mind—but I have to hide. There are things and feelings no one will ever find out." Graduates with second-class honors B.A. degree in June. Returns to Berlin and becomes engaged to Svetlana Siewert. Takes job in bank but leaves after three hours. Receives advance of $5 from Gamayun publishers to translate *Alice's Adventures in Wonderland*. With several writers including friends Gleb Struve and Ivan Lukash, forms literary circle they name Bratstvo kruglogo stola (Brotherhood of the Round Table). *Grozd'* (*The Cluster*), collection of poems written 1921 to 1922, published by Gamayun in December.

1923   *Gorniy put'* (*Empyrean Path*), collection of poems written 1918 to 1921, published by Grani in January. Engagement to Svetlana is broken off by her parents, who object to Nabokov's not having steady job. *Anya v strane chudes* (translation of *Alice's Adventures in Wonderland*) published by Gamayun in March. At masquerade charity ball on May 8 Nabokov meets Véra Evseevna Slonim (b. 1902), formerly of St. Petersburg, daughter of a Russian Jewish emigré businessman. Works briefly as film extra, then for three months as agricultural laborer in south of France; writes verse plays. Returns in August to Berlin where he courts Véra Slonim; begins writing stories regularly. Hoping that theatrical work will earn more money, writes sketches with his good friend Ivan Lukash. Mother goes with Elena and Olga to find apartment in Prague, where she is eligible for a pension. Nabokov takes Kirill and Hofeld to join them in December; while in Prague, writes five-act verse play *Tragediya gospodina Morna* (*The Tragedy of Mr. Morn*; still unpublished). Evsey Slonim's businesses fail in hyperinflation.

1924   Meets Russian poet Marina Tsvetaeva. Returns to Berlin and takes room at 21 Lutherstrasse. Pantomime "Voda zhivaya" ("Living Water"), written with Lukash, is performed at emigré cabaret for more than a month. As center of Russian emigration shifts to Paris, Nabokov remains in Berlin (later attributes decision in part to his fear that his Russian would atrophy if he lived in a country whose language he knew well). Becomes engaged to Véra and begins to earn living tutoring in English, French, tennis, and boxing (tutoring will be his major source of income until 1929 and continue sporadically until 1941). Works on scenarios for cabarets and theater alone or with Lukash. Publishes nine stories in emigré journals and newspapers and begins contributing poems, chess problems, and crossword puzzles to new *Rul'* Sunday supplement, *Nash mir* (*Our World*).

1925   Marries Véra in civil ceremony on April 15. Nabokov acts as private tutor to two Russian Jewish schoolboys; he has them read and discuss Proust and Joyce's *Ulysses*. Increased income allows him to send more money to his mother. Often visits with Slonim family. Takes Véra to meet his family in Prague in August; they go to Konstanz, Germany, for a week before returning to Berlin, where they move into two rooms at 31 Motzstrasse. Writes novel *Mashen'ka* (later translated as *Mary*), September–November. Joins literary club organized by Raisa Tatarinov and critic Yuli Aykhenvald (will remain a member and contribute talks until 1933). Publishes six stories during year.

1926   Forms close friendships with George Hessen, son of *Rul'* editor Iosif Hessen, and Mikhail Kaminka, son of his father's CD and publishing colleague and best friend, Avgust Kaminka. Gives reading of *Mashen'ka* at local literary club where Aykhenvald proclaims: "A new Turgenev has appeared"; novel is published by Slovo in March to good reviews. Writes play *Chelovek iz SSSR* (later translated as *The Man from the USSR*) for new emigré Group Theater. Continues publishing stories. Composes 882-line Pushkinian poem, "Universitetskaya poema."

1927   *Chelovek iz SSSR*, performed in April, is well received. Poem "Bilet" (*Rul'*, June 26), about returning to a Russia freed from Communism, is printed in *Pravda* on July 17 along with a reply by Soviet poet Demyan Bedny ("Bilet" will be Nabokov's only work published in the Soviet Union in his lifetime). Has idea for *Korol', dama, valet* (later translated as *King, Queen, Knave*) while acting as chaperone with Véra for three boys at Baltic beach of Binz in summer. Goes with Véra to Misdroy, Germany, where he hunts moths; on return to Berlin they move into rented rooms at 12 Passauer Strasse. Nabokov becomes poetry reviewer for *Rul'*; continues publishing stories and poems, doing some translations with Véra, giving readings, and tutoring, though he has fewer pupils.

1928   Signs agreement in March with major newspaper *Vossische Zeitung* for serialization in German of *Mashen'ka*. With Véra begins attending Poets' Club, whose members include Raïsa Blokh and Vladimir Korvin-Piotrovsky. Véra's father dies in June and her mother dies in August; Véra takes job as secretary in French embassy to pay their medical bills. *Korol', dama, valet* (written January–June) published by Slovo in September to good reviews. Sells German rights to Ullstein publishing company for 7,500 marks. Aykhenvald, the first major critic to hail Nabokov, is killed by a streetcar as he returns from party at the Nabokovs' on December 16.

1929   Goes with Véra to the Pyrenees, February–June, where he hunts butterflies and begins novel *Zashchita Luzhina* (later translated as *The Defense*). Buys a small lakefront property in Kolberg with Anna Feigin, Véra's cousin; completes novel there in August and it is serialized in *Sovremennye zapiski* (*Contemporary Annals*), leading emigré literary review published in Paris, October 1929–April 1930. (All Nabokov's remaining Russian novels will be published serially in the journal, which pays better than emigré book publishers.) Moves with Véra into furnished rooms at 27 Luitpoldstrasse. *Vozvrashchenie Chorba* (*The Return of Chorb*), collection of stories and poems, published in December by Slovo.

1930   Completes novella *Soglyadatay* (later translated as *The Eye*) in February. Begins novel *Podvig* (later translated as *Glory*) in May; later that month goes to Prague, where he visits his family, counsels Kirill on his poetry, and gives public readings. Economic depression in Germany causes further decline in numbers of Berlin emigré community and viability of *Rul'*, but Nabokov's publication in *Sovremennye zapiski* provokes high praise from some writers like Vladislav Khodasevich and Nina Berberova, and attacks from others, like Georgy Adamovich and Georgy Ivanov, associated with new rival journal *Chisla* (*Numbers*). Véra takes job as secretary in a firm of German Jewish lawyers. *Zashchita Luzhina* is published as book in September and

Soglyadatay appears in *Sovremennye zapiski* in November. Completes *Podvig*.

1931 Writes novel *Kamera obskura* (later translated as *Camera Obscura* and as *Laughter in the Dark*) between January and May. *Podvig* is serialized in *Sovremennye zapiski* (Feb. 1931–Jan. 1932). Writes "Les Écrivains et l'époque" (*Le Mois*, June–July), his first French article. Continues publishing stories. *Rul'* fails in October. Joins soccer team of Russian sports club as goalkeeper.

1932 Writes appeal for assistance for the unemployed in emigré paper *Poslednie novosti* (*The Latest News*). In severe financial straits, Nabokov and Véra take a room in a crowded family apartment on 29 Westfälische Strasse. Meets Hollywood director Sergey Bertenson, a Russian emigré; offers him *Kamera obskura* but Bertenson pronounces it unsuitable for filming. Visits family in Prague; is delighted with nephew Rostislav Petkevitch, infant son of sister Olga. *Kamera obskura* appears in *Sovremennye zapiski* (May 1932–May 1933). Writes first draft of *Otchayanie* (later translated as *Despair*) between June and September. Moves with Véra into apartment of Anna Feigin on 22 Nestorstrasse in the Wilmersdorf district in July. Travels to Paris in fall where he gives highly successful public reading and explores opportunities for work. Sees brother Sergey and cousin Nicolas Nabokov, who live in France. Meets Vladislav Khodasevich, Nina Berberova, Mark Aldanov, Jean Paulhan, Gabriel Marcel, and Jules Supervielle. Visits with *Sovremennye zapiski* editors. Completes *Otchayanie*. Gives reading in Antwerp before returning to Berlin. *Podvig* is published in book form in November by Sovremennye zapiski.

1933 Adolf Hitler is appointed chancellor of Germany on January 30. Nabokov begins gathering materials on Nikolay Chernyshevsky and on Russian naturalist-explorers of Central Asia for projected novel *Dar* (later translated as *The Gift*). Is sick with neuralgia intercostalis for most of winter. Véra loses her secretarial job when law firm is forced to close in March and begins working as a free-lance stenographer, tourist guide, and interpreter. Nabokov writes Gleb Struve, now at the University of London, asking for help arranging English translations of his works. Applies for teaching position in Switzerland, but is rejected. Reads Virginia Woolf and Katherine Mansfield for story "Admiralteyskaya igla" ("The Admiralty Spire"). At invitation of emigré publisher, writes to James Joyce in November, offering to translate *Ulysses*: "the Russian language can be made to convey in a most subtle way the musical peculiarities and intricacies of the original." Sees Ivan Bunin, who has just been awarded the Nobel Prize, and speaks at meeting in his honor. *Kamera obskura* published as a book in December by Sovremennye zapiski.

1934   *Otchayanie* is serialized in *Sovremennye zapiski* (Jan.–Oct.). *La Course du fou*, translation of *Zashchita Luzhina*, is published in France. Continues working on Chernyshevsky chapter of *Dar*; writes Khodasevich that it is "monstrously difficult." Son, Dmitri Vladimirovich Nabokov, is born May 10. In June, begins anti-totalitarian novel *Priglashenie na kazn'* (later translated as *Invitation to a Beheading*), which he completes in December. Continues publishing stories in journals.

1935   Helps care for Dmitri; calls it "a mixture of hard labor and heaven." Continues publishing stories. In June, begins new chapter of *Dar*. *Priglashenie na kazn'* published serially in *Sovremennye zapiski* (June 1935–Feb. 1936). Writes in English autobiographical piece, "It Is Me" (later lost), about his English education. Contacts Gleb Struve about possibility of teaching Russian or French literature in England. Dissatisfied with Winifred Roy's translation, *Camera Obscura* (published in England by John Long in 1936), Nabokov translates *Otchayanie* into English as *Despair*, September–December.

1936   Makes successful reading tour of Brussels, Antwerp, and Paris in January and February; "Mademoiselle O," memoir in French of Cécile Miauton written for the tour, is especially well received. In Brussels, sees brother Kirill, who is studying at Louvain University. Shares a reading in Paris with Khodasevich, whom he considers the greatest contemporary Russian poet. *Otchayanie* published as book by Petropolis (Berlin) in February. Véra is fired in May from her job with an engineering firm because she is Jewish. Nabokov learns that one of his father's murderers,

Sergey Taboritsky, is deputy secretary in new Reich department of Russian emigré affairs and begins search for work in England or America. By August, begins final consecutive composition of *Dar*. Avoids government's registration of emigrés.

1937   Leaves Germany on January 18 for reading tour of Brussels, Paris, and London, planning to find employment in France or England, while Véra winds up their affairs in Berlin. Visits Kirill in Brussels. In Paris is pleased to see James Joyce in audience during a reading. Begins four-month affair with Russian emigré Irina Guadanini in February; plagued by guilt, develops severe psoriasis and comes near suicide. Goes to England late in February; gives readings in London, visits Cambridge, and unsuccessfully seeks work. Returns to France and obtains permits for him and Véra to stay there. In April *Despair* is published in London by John Long and first chapter of *Dar* appears in *Sovremennye zapiski*. Meets Sylvia Beach, Adrienne Monnier, and Henry Church. Receives free radiation treatments for psoriasis from emigré physician. Véra and Dmitri leave Germany for Prague in April to visit Nabokov's mother, who has not yet seen her grandson; Nabokov joins them in May (last time he sees mother) and on June 30 returns with them to Paris. Sells French rights to *Despair* to Gallimard, then settles with Véra and Dmitri in Cannes, where it is cheaper to live. Tells Véra of his affair with Guadanini. Cherynshevsky chapter of *Dar* is turned down by *Sovremennye zapiski* in August; Nabokov protests political censorship but, needing money, agrees to continue publishing novel in the journal (remaining chapters appear Sept. 1937–Oct. 1938). Signs contract with New York publisher Bobbs-Merrill for *Kamera obskura* and begins translating and rewriting it under title *Laughter in the Dark*. Moves with family to Menton in October; works on *Dar* and writes three-act play *Sobytie* (later translated as *The Event*) for new Russian theater in Paris.

1938   Completes *Dar* in January. *Sobytie* is successfully produced in March and appears in *Russkie zapiski* in April. *Laughter in the Dark*, published in New York by Bobbs-Merrill on April 22, receives some good reviews but does not sell well. Moves with family to Moulinet, above Menton, in July, and captures what seems to be his first new species of butterfly (after Nabokov's death it proves to be a hybrid). Redescends to Cap d'Antibes in late August where he writes play *Izobretenie Val'sa* (published by *Russkie zapiski* in November and later translated as *The Waltz Invention*). Receiving only small remuneration for his works, requests monthly support from Russian Literary Fund in the U.S.; they send him $20. *Soglyadatay* (*The Eye*), collection of 1930 novella and other stories, published by Russkie zapiski. After receiving official identity card, moves with family to Paris in October and rents small apartment at 8 rue de Saigon. Often sees friends, including Khodasevich, George Hessen, Mark Aldanov, and *Sovremennye zapiski* editors Ilya Fondaminsky and Vladimir Zenzinov. *Priglashenie na kazn'* published in book form by Dom Knigi, emigré house in Paris. Continues publishing stories in emigré papers and journals. In December begins novel in English, *The Real Life of Sebastian Knight*, completing it the following month.

1939   Asks Lucie Léon Noel to check his English in *The Real Life of Sebastian Knight*. At Paul Léon's home, meets James Joyce. Moves with family to larger apartment at 59 rue Boileau. Financially desperate without a work permit in France, travels to England in April in unsuccessful search for literary or academic work. Mother dies in Prague on May 2. Seeks work in England again in June. Khodasevich dies of cancer on June 14. Publishes "Poety" ("The Poets") over pseudonym "Vasily Shishkov" to catch out influential critic Georgy Adamovich, who has regularly condescended to Nabokov's and Khodasevich's work. Adamovich enthusiastically announces arrival of major new talent; Nabokov obliquely discloses hoax in story "Vasily Shishkov." Summers with family at Fréjus on the Riviera. Germany invades Poland on September 1 and France declares war on Germany September 3. Fearing Paris will be bombed, sends Dmitri to stay with Anna Feigin in Deauville. Fails to find publisher for *Sebastian Knight*, with no other work to sell, begins accepting 1,000 francs monthly from Samuil Kyandzhuntsev, old Tenishev friend, which he supplements by tutoring. Aldanov, who has been offered a job teaching summer course in Russian literature at Stanford University in California, recommends Nabokov in his place. Nabokov receives and accepts

Stanford offer and applies for U.S. visa. Writes novella *Volshebnik* (posthumously published as *The Enchanter*), October–November, about a man who desires a 12-year-old girl. Dmitri returns to Paris in December.

1940   Writes lectures on Russian literature over spring and summer in preparation for teaching in the U.S. Begins Russian novel, *Solus Rex* (never completed). Germans begin offensive against France and the Low Countries on May 10. With help of the Hebrew Immigrant Aid Society, given in appreciation of Nabokov's father's championing of Jews in pre-revolutionary Russia, Nabokov, Véra, and Dmitri sail for New York aboard the *Champlain*, arriving on May 27 with $600. Meets Sergei Rachmaninoff, who had twice sent him money in Europe. Unsuccessfully seeks employment and receives small grant from Russian Literary Fund. With Véra and Dmitri vacations at Vermont summer home of Harvard professor Mikhail Karpovich, then rents New York apartment at 35 West 87th Street; begins tutoring in Russian and seeking ways to bring Anna Feigin and other emigré friends to the U.S. Abandons *Solus Rex* after realizing his English prose style can develop only if he renounces composing in Russian. Through cousin Nicolas Nabokov, meets Edmund Wilson, acting literary editor of *The New Republic*, and is soon writing literary reviews for the journal; also writes reviews for New York *Sun* and *The New York Times*. Sees old friends including Roman Grynberg, Mstislav Dobuzhinsky, Aldanov, and Zenzinov, meets Max Eastman, and becomes friends with Wilson and his wife, Mary McCarthy, and Harry and Elena Levin. Receives final terms of offer from Stanford to teach Modern Russian Literature and Art of Writing in summer of 1941. Begins preparing full set of lectures on Russian literature in fall. Researches Lepidoptera at American Museum of Natural History. Receives advance from Wilson to translate Pushkin's "Mozart and Salieri" for *The New Republic* (published April 21, 1941).

1941   Tutors privately in Russian, writes two papers on Lepidoptera, and establishes himself on lecture roster of Institute of International Education. Has eight teeth extracted and dentures fitted. Receives $750 and bonus for two weeks of extremely successful lectures at Wellesley College in March. His frank anti-Sovietism particularly appeals to

Wellesley president Mildred McAfee. Begins translating
Pushkin and other Russian poets in April for Stanford
course. Through Wilson, meets Edmund Weeks, editor of
Atlantic Monthly; "Cloud, Castle, Lake," translation of
1937 story "Ozero, oblako, bashnya," appears in June (the
first of many Nabokov stories and poems published in
Atlantic over next two years). Is appointed to one-year
position at Wellesley College as Resident Lecturer in
Comparative Literature, with salary of $3,000. In late May
Dorothy Leuthold, whom Nabokov has tutored in Russian, drives Nabokov, Véra, and Dmitri to California for
Stanford course. During stops Nabokov hunts butterflies
and moths and on June 9 discovers new species on rim of
Grand Canyon; names it *Neonympha dorothea* in Leuthold's honor. Meets Yvor Winters and Henry Lanz over
summer. In July, learns that *The Real Life of Sebastian
Knight* has been accepted by James Laughlin for New Directions on recommendation of reader Delmore Schwartz.
Returns east by train to begin position at Wellesley College, renting house at 19 Appleby Road in Wellesley,
Massachusetts. Translates three poems of Khodasevich
(published in *New Directions in Prose and Poetry*) and
translates Gogol, Pushkin, Lermontov, and Tyutchev for
teaching. Begins traveling regularly to Harvard's Museum
of Comparative Zoology in Cambridge, where he volunteers to set the Lepidoptera collection in order. Writes
poem in English, "Softest of Tongues" (*Atlantic Monthly*,
Dec.). *The Real Life of Sebastian Knight*, published
by New Directions December 18, receives mostly good reviews but sells poorly. Begins writing a new novel (later
titled *Bend Sinister*).

1942   Commissioned by New Directions to write volume of
          verse translations of Pushkin and Tyutchev and critical
          book on Gogol. Despite faculty backing and student en-
          thusiasm, is not reappointed at Wellesley through oppo-
          sition of president Mildred McAfee, who now disapproves
          of Nabokov's hostility toward the Soviet government
          (U.S. is now allied with the Soviet Union in World War
          II and McAfee has entered government service as head of
          the Women's Naval Reserve, WAVES). Appointed in June
          to part-time position as Research Fellow in Entomology
          at the Museum of Comparative Zoology for 1942–43 ac-
          ademic year at salary of $1,000 (over next four years will

spend more time researching and writing on Lepidoptera than in writing fiction). "The Refrigerator Awakes," first of his poems published in *The New Yorker*, appears June 6. Long poem "Slava" (later translated as "Fame") published in New York emigré journal *Novy zhurnal*. Spends most of summer with Mikhail and Tatiana Karpovich in Vermont, where Nabokov works in attic for eight to ten hours a day on Gogol book. Rents apartment at 8 Craigie Circle, Cambridge, where he and his family remain until 1948; often sees Harry and Elena Levin, and Edmund Wilson and Mary McCarthy. Undertakes lecture and reading tour for Institute of International Education, traveling to colleges in South Carolina, Georgia, and Tennessee in October and in Illinois and Minnesota in November. Begins friendship with Florence Read, president of Spelman, college for black women in Atlanta. Gives Dmitri lessons in Russian grammar while Véra is hospitalized with pneumonia in December. Completes book on Gogol.

1943   Writes first story in English, "The Assistant Producer" (published *Atlantic Monthly*, May) and begins teaching noncredit course in elementary Russian at Wellesley College. Awarded Guggenheim Fellowship of $2,500 to complete new novel. Visits emigré friends in New York, including George Hessen and Anna Feigin, whom he helped bring to America; on return to Cambridge writes story "That in Aleppo Once . . . " (*Atlantic Monthly*, Nov.). Continues writing poems in Russian for *Novy zhurnal*. Dictates book tentatively titled *Gogol Through the Looking-Glass* to Véra (she types all Nabokov's works for publication) and sends it to New Directions. Travels with Véra and Dmitri to Wasatch Mountains in Utah, where he hunts butterflies and moths and captures several new species. In fall, resumes teaching noncredit course at Wellesley and receives $200 salary increase on new annual contract at Museum of Comparative Zoology (museum appointment will be renewed annually until 1948). Responding to Laughlin's complaint that the Gogol book needs more factual information, Nabokov adds a chronology. Publishes "The Nearctic Forms of *Lycaeides* Hüb." in *Psyche* (Sept.–Dec.). Has upper teeth removed and a dental plate fitted in November. Corresponds regularly with Wilson and often visits him.

1944   Persuaded by Véra to devote more time to new novel, soon completes four chapters under working title *The Person from Porlock* (later retitled *Bend Sinister*). Gives lecture on Russian literature at Yale in March and a reading at Cornell in May. Through Katharine White, an admirer of his *Atlantic* stories, signs first reading agreement with *The New Yorker* in June (agreement will be maintained over three decades); White also arranges a $500 advance, having been informed by Wilson that Nabokov is short of money. Devises system for studying butterfly markings and their evolution by counting rows of scales on wings, and writes major paper revising the neotropical Plebejinae. Vacations with Véra near Wilson and McCarthy in Wellfleet, Massachusetts, and, after Dmitri returns from summer camp, spends August with family in Wellesley, often playing tennis with poet Jorge Guillén. *Nikolai Gogol* published by New Directions August 15. Writes story "Time and Ebb" (*Atlantic Monthly*, Jan. 1945). Dmitri enters Dexter School in Brookline, Massachusetts, in fall and Nabokov begins appointment as lecturer in Russian at Wellesley College on year's contract for $800 salary, teaching elementary Russian.

1945   Lectures at St. Timothy's College in Maryland and Smith College in Massachusetts. *Three Russian Poets*, verse translations of Pushkin, Lermontov, and Tyutchev, published by New Directions in February. *The New Yorker* accepts first story from Nabokov, "Double Talk" (published July 23), paying $817.50, the most he has ever received for a story. After suffering heart palpitations, gives up smoking on doctor's advice in spring and begins "inhaling" molasses candies (gains 60 pounds over the summer). Nabokov and Véra become American citizens on July 12. Begins teaching a second course, intermediate Russian, at Wellesley, with salary increased to $2,000. In September learns in a letter from Kirill, who is working as an interpreter for American occupation forces in Germany and has traced him through *New Yorker* story, that Sergey died from malnutrition in a German concentration camp after being arrested as a "British spy" for criticizing Nazi Germany. Also hears from sister Elena Sikorski and Evgenia Hofeld, who is caring for nephew Rostislav Petkevich; sends them money and packages and seeks a way to bring them out of Czechoslovakia.

1946   Meets W. H. Auden; compliments him on work of Conrad Aiken, with whom he has confused him. Third course, on Russian literature in translation, is approved for the next academic year at Wellesley; anticipating its demands, Nabokov hurries to complete novel and submits it under provisional title *Solus Rex* to Allen Tate at Henry Holt in June. Suffering from exhaustion, goes with family to Newfound Lake in New Hampshire, then to town of Wellesley for August. Rereads Tolstoy and Dostoevsky in preparation for new lectures. Begins research for monograph on nearctic *Lycaeides* (completes research in spring 1947, having examined 2,000 specimens). Continues seeking a permanent job; is passed over for positions at the Voice of America, Harvard, and Vassar. Just before novel goes to printer in November, settles on title *Bend Sinister*. Earns extra money by speaking to women's clubs.

1947   Begins planning autobiography and a novel about "a man who likes little girls." Finishes first draft of *Lycaeides* monograph in May. *Bend Sinister* published June 12 to mixed reviews; since Tate has left Henry Holt, it is poorly promoted and does not sell well. Loses 20 pounds hunting butterflies and climbing with Dmitri and Véra in and around Estes Park in Colorado during summer. Writes autobiographical essay "Portrait of My Uncle" (*The New Yorker*, Jan. 3, 1948). Dmitri begins at St. Mark's boarding school in Southborough, Massachusetts, in fall. Nabokov resumes work at Museum of Comparative Zoology and Wellesley on new annual contracts. Receives offer of a permanent position teaching Russian literature at Cornell University at $5,000 salary, which he accepts after Wellesley refuses him a permanent appointment. Helps obtain position for Elena Sikorski at United Nations library in Geneva; continues sending money to Hofeld and Rostislav and writes affidavit in unsuccessful attempt to bring Rostislav to America. *Nine Stories* published by New Directions in December.

1948   Story "Signs and Symbols" published with minor editorial intervention by *The New Yorker* (May 15) after Nabokov tells Katharine White planned alterations are unnecessary and in some cases "murderous." Seriously ill throughout spring from broken blood vessel in lung. Véra reads his lectures at Wellesley and takes students through final exams while Nabokov writes in bed three additional chapters of autobiography (published in *The New Yorker* July 1948–Jan. 1949). Completes "The Nearctic Members of the Genus *Lycaeides Hübner*" in June (published as whole issue of *Bulletin of the Museum of Comparative Zoology*, Feb. 1949). Moves to Ithaca, New York, in July and settles with Véra and Dmitri into furnished house at 802 East Seneca Street. Still convalescing, prepares lectures and completes "First Poem" chapter of autobiography (published in *Partisan Review*, Sept. 1949). Becomes close friend of Morris Bishop, who initiated job offer from Cornell. Dmitri enters Holderness School in New Hampshire, with tuition costing about a third of Nabokov's salary. Buys eight-year-old Plymouth that Véra drives (Nabokov never learns to drive) and takes in lodger to help pay rent. Teaches two surveys of Russian literature (one in Russian). Translates medieval heroic poem *Slovo o polku Igoreve* (*The Song of Igor's Campaign*) for classes. Véra acts as his teaching assistant, drives him to school, continues typing up his writing, and begins conducting most of his business correspondence in her own name.

1949   Teaches seminar, Russian Poetry 1870–1925, in spring term, holding classes in his home, in addition to the two survey courses. Writes two more chapters of autobiography. Publishes negative review of Sartre's *La Nausée* and its English translation in *The New York Times Book Review*. Drives with Véra in May to New York City for reading from his Russian works and visits with emigré friends and relatives. Travels west in summer in newly purchased 1946 Oldsmobile. Conducts classes at University of Utah Writers' Workshop in July, where he enjoys company of Wallace Stegner and son Page, Theodore Geisel ("Dr. Seuss"), Martha Foley, and John Crowe Ransom. Hunts butterflies in Utah and Wyoming with Véra. Returns to Cornell where he teaches Russian literature surveys and seminar on Pushkin. Katharine and E. B. White visit in October. Submits "Student Days" chapter of autobiography to *The New Yorker*; cannot agree to changes suggested by White and withdraws it (published as "Lodgings in Trinity Lane," *Harper's Magazine*, Jan. 1951).

1950   Needing money, lectures at University of Toronto for $150 during semester break. Meets Harold Ross at *New Yorker* party in March and sees Edmund Wilson for first time since Wilson went to Europe in 1948. Hospitalized in April for two weeks with severe pain, eventually determined to be from intercostal neuralgia; has relapse and is unwell until May. Véra conducts classes during his absences. Finishes autobiography, *Conclusive Evidence*, in May and in June has his remaining six teeth extracted in Boston; while returning to Ithaca with Véra, captures specimens of rare *Lycaeides melissa samuelis*, which he had been the first to classify. Under pressure to teach larger classes, spends summer writing lectures for new Masterpieces of European Fiction course on Austen, Dickens, Flaubert, Tolstoy, Stevenson, Proust, Kafka, and Joyce. Begins novel under title *The Kingdom by the Sea* (later, *Lolita*). Dissatisfied, decides to burn the manuscript but is dissuaded by Véra.

1951   *Conclusive Evidence*, published in February by Harper and Brothers, receives excellent reviews but sells poorly (book is published in England as *Speak, Memory*). Receives National Institute of Arts and Letters award of $1,000 at ceremony in New York City on May 25. Dmitri is accepted by Harvard without scholarship. Nabokov borrows $1,000 from emigré friend Roman Grynberg, explaining: "I can't write stories for money . . . and something else has me, a novel . . ." He and Véra sell their furniture and piano and move out of rented house before going west for summer. Works on *Lolita* in car and motels; catches first female of *Lycaeides argyrognomon sublivens* in Telluride, Colorado, where Dmitri joins them, then hunts butterflies in Wyoming and Montana. Moves with Véra into a professor's home for fall semester at Cornell (will live in homes of absent professors throughout remaining time there). Does research on schoolgirls for *Lolita*. Suffers from severe insomnia while writing story "The Lance" (*The New Yorker*, Feb. 2, 1952). Reads and lectures at Nabokov evening staged by Russian emigré community in New York City.

1952   As visiting lecturer for second semester at Harvard, teaches courses on Russian modernism, on Pushkin, and on the novel, including *Don Quixote*. With Véra, often sees Dmitri, Harry and Elena Levin, Alice and William James (son of the philosopher), and old Wellesley friends, as well as

Edmund Wilson and his fourth wife, Elena. Meets Richard Wilbur and May Sarton. Reads in Morris Gray Poetry Series; gives reading at Wellesley and lectures on Gogol at Dartmouth. In April, *Dar* (*The Gift*) is published for the first time complete by Chekhov, Russian publishing house in New York. Agrees to do a Russian version of *Conclusive Evidence* for Chekhov and receives $1,500 advance. Receives second Guggenheim award, which he plans to use to write an annotated literal translation of Pushkin's *Evgeniy Onegin*. Goes to Wyoming with Véra to hunt butterflies in summer. Resumes Cornell teaching in fall and works on *Lolita*.

1953   Takes unpaid semester's leave from Cornell to do research for his *Eugene Onegin* in Cambridge. Hunts butterflies with Véra in Arizona in spring and Oregon in summer; writes story about Professor Pnin as first installment of novel he can publish as sketches (four chapters are published in *The New Yorker* April 23, 1953–Nov. 12, 1955). Chiefly through efforts of Morris Bishop, Nabokov's Cornell salary is increased to $6,000 in fall. Completes *Lolita* on December 6 and while in New York to record talk for BBC on translation gives typescript to Pascal Covici of Viking. Plans to have the novel published anonymously to avoid scandal that would endanger his position at Cornell.

1954   Viking turns down *Lolita* for fear of prosecution. Second chapter of *Pnin* is rejected by *The New Yorker* as "unpleasant." In February and March, rushes to complete *Drugie berega* (*Other Shores*), expanded and revised Russian translation of autobiography (published by Chekhov). Records reading in New York for BBC program and lectures for three days at University of Kansas. During summer in New Mexico with Véra and Dmitri, works on notes (never completed) for projected Simon and Schuster edition of *Anna Karenina*. Simon and Schuster rejects *Lolita* in July as "pure pornography." Returns to Cornell and works intensely on *Eugene Onegin*. Gives paper, "Problems of Translation: *Onegin* in English" (published in *Partisan Review*, Autumn 1955), at English Institute conference at Columbia University. Sends *Lolita* manuscript to Edmund Wilson, who reads half of it and responds that he likes it less than anything of Nabokov's that he has read (Nabokov later urges Wilson to read the whole work carefully; tells Wilson that it is "a highly moral affair"). *Lolita* is turned down by New Directions, Farrar, Straus, and in December by Doubleday, despite editor Jason Epstein's support of it. Philip Rahv of *Partisan Review* counsels Nabokov that publishing the book anonymously will destroy its best defense.

1955   Convinced that he will not find an American publisher for *Lolita*, Nabokov sends typescript to literary agent Doussia Ergaz in Paris. Maurice Girodias, founder of new Olympia Press, agrees to publish it on condition that it carry Nabokov's name. Dmitri graduates cum laude from Harvard and enrolls in Longy School of Music in Cambridge, where he concentrates on singing. Epstein visits in June and arranges for Nabokov and Dmitri to translate Lermontov's *Geroy nashego vremeni* (*A Hero of Our Time*) and for Nabokov to translate *Anna Karenina* (his translation is never completed). Nabokov is hospitalized for eight days during summer with attack of lumbago. *Lolita* is published in Paris in September in Olympia's Traveler's Edition, a line consisting mostly of pornographic books aimed at English-speaking tourist market. Nabokov receives copies of the book in October and discovers that copyright has been assigned to Olympia Press as well as to him. Pnin novel, provisionally titled *My Poor Pnin*, is rejected as too short by Viking and then by Harper and Brothers. Nabokov is distressed when Katharine White moves from editorial to general policy department at *The New Yorker*. Graham Greene names *Lolita* one of the three best books of 1955 in London *Sunday Times* Christmas issue.

1956   On sabbatical for spring semester, conducts final research for *Eugene Onegin* in Cambridge. Meets John Dos Passos. Scandal begins to break around *Lolita* when John Gordon attacks Greene for praising it and denounces the novel as "Sheer unrestrained pornography" in the London *Sunday Express*. After *The New York Times Book Review* reports on the dispute and cites letters praising the quality of *Lolita*, Nabokov receives offers for rights from several American publishers. *Vesna v Fial'te i drugie rasskazy* (*Spring in Fialta and Other Stories*) published by Chekhov in March. Nabokov records reading from his *Eugene Onegin* for BBC. In June U.S. Customs seizes, and then releases, copies of *Lolita* (it will do so again in November). Travels with Véra to Utah, Wyoming, Montana, Minnesota, and Michigan, hunting butterflies and working on translation, *A Hero of Our Time*. In New York in October discusses with Epstein, Fred Dupee, and Melvin Lasky, editor of *Anchor Review*, plans to publish excerpts from *Lolita* in the magazine to test public reaction to it. Writes afterword, "On a Book Entitled *Lolita*." The French Ministry of Interior bans *Lolita* and 24 other Olympia titles in December and Girodias sues to have the ban lifted (he wins the case in January 1958).

1957 Harvard University, seeking a new Russian professor, almost appoints Nabokov; opposition to him is led by Roman Jakobson, who comments during faculty meeting: "Gentlemen, even if one allows that he is an important writer, are we next to invite an elephant to be professor of zoology?" *Pnin*, published March 7 by Doubleday to extremely favorable reviews, goes into second printing in two weeks. Begins work on novel (later *Pale Fire*) but puts it aside to complete *Eugene Onegin* and stays in Ithaca over summer. *Anchor Review* publishes nearly a third of *Lolita* in June, with Nabokov's afterword and critical commentary by Dupee. Nabokov contracts with publishers in Italy, France, Germany, and Sweden for translation rights to *Lolita*. Doubleday and then MacDowell, Obolensky, withdraw their offers for American rights when Girodias demands up to 62.5 percent of Nabokov's royalties. In December completes revisions of *Eugene Onegin*.

1958 *A Hero of Our Time* published by Doubleday in March. Hunts butterflies in Montana, Alberta, and Wyoming with Véra in summer. Hears from George Weidenfeld in England and Gallimard in France that they want to publish as many Nabokov works as possible. Putnam's works out contract for *Lolita* in March, assigning to Nabokov royalties of 7.5 percent and the same to Girodias. Published on August 18, *Lolita* sells 100,000 copies in three weeks, the fastest sales for an American novel since *Gone With the Wind*. *Nabokov's Dozen*, collection of 13 stories, published in September by Doubleday. Nabokov contracts with Harris-Kubrick Pictures in November for film rights to *Lolita* for $150,000 plus share of profits. Is awarded a year's leave of absence from Cornell, and searches for replacement so that leave can commence in February; finds novelist Herbert Gold to fill the position.

1959   Delivers last Cornell lectures on January 19. Makes first notes for "Texture of Time" (later a part of *Ada*) and stores belongings before leaving with Véra for New York City on February 24. Is interviewed by major American and English publications, meets George Weidenfeld, and sees Anna Feigin and Dmitri. Reworks translation, *Song of Igor's Campaign*, and begins preparing annotations. Hunts butterflies in Tennessee and Texas in April, then in Arizona, where he revises *Invitation to a Beheading*, Dmitri's translation of *Priglashenie na kazn'*. Asked to write *Lolita* screenplay, travels to Los Angeles with Véra in late July for discussions with director Stanley Kubrick and producer James Harris; cannot agree to changes they propose and soon rejects offer. Persuaded by Véra that the combination of teaching and writing is too burdensome for him, resigns from Cornell and sails to Europe on September 29 to visit sister Elena and brother Kirill, planning to return in a few months. Spends two weeks in Geneva with Elena, a UNESCO librarian, and Kirill, a Brussels travel agent, then goes with Véra to Paris for reception at Gallimard where Nabokov encounters Girodias, but fails to realize who he is. Gives numerous press interviews. Asks to meet Alain Robbe-Grillet, whose work he admires, and is interviewed by him. In London, meets Graham Greene and appears on *The Bookman* television show. Delivers lecture in Cambridge, then returns to London for November 6 Weidenfeld and Nicolson publication of *Lolita*, which immediately sells out. For next two months travels with Véra in Italy and Sicily; when he can elude the press, works on *Letters to Terra* project (later a part of *Ada*). Begins giving interviews in groups. Kubrick cables request that Nabokov write *Lolita* screenplay, with more artistic freedom. In Milan for reception by Mondadori, arranges audition for Dmitri with singing teacher Maestro Campogalliani. Spends Christmas holidays in San Remo, joined by Dmitri and Elena and nephew Vladimir Sikorski. Dmitri begins translating *Dar* as *The Gift*.

1960   During stay in Menton, Nabokov accepts offer of $40,000 for writing *Lolita* screenplay, plus an additional $35,000 if script is credited solely to him. Dmitri begins studying with Campogalliani. Nabokov turns down membership in the American National Institute of Arts and Letters, writing "all my thinking life I have declined to 'belong' " (will continue to reject all offers of honorary degrees and memberships). Arrives in Los Angeles with Véra in early March. Finishes screenplay July 9; told that it would take seven hours to run, produces a shorter version by September 8. Rostislav Petkevich dies in Prague of the effects of alcoholism. *Song of Igor's Campaign* published by Vintage. Nabokov hears that Dmitri has won first prize among basses in international opera competition in Italy. Returns to Europe in November to be near him, settling with Véra in Nice; works intensively on *Pale Fire* over winter.

1961   Completes *Pale Fire* poem February 11 and begins work on prose portion of novel. Attends Dmitri's operatic debut in *La Bohème* in Reggio, in which Luciano Pavarotti also debuts, then sees Dmitri in *Lucia da Lammermoor* (Nabokov and Véra try to see each of his new roles). In Stresa in May, revises Dmitri's translation of the first chapter of *Dar* (*The Gift*). Hunts butterflies in Valais, Switzerland, in August, then goes to Montreux, where he finds atmosphere conducive to writing. On advice of Peter Ustinov, who lives in the Montreux Palace Hotel, Nabokov and Véra take rooms there in October, planning to stay until spring. Completes *Pale Fire* on December 4.

1962   Corrects French translation of *Pnin* and Michael Scammell's English translation of the last four chapters of *Dar* (*The Gift*). Regularly reads New York *Herald Tribune* and American magazines and literary journals. Hears from agent Irving Lazar in February that Harris and Kubrick have extensively reworked *Lolita* screenplay. *Pale Fire* published by Putnam's in April. Sails aboard *Queen Elizabeth* with Véra for premiere of *Lolita* in New York. Sees film at screening a few days before attending opening on June 13 and praises the director and cast; conceals his disappointment that little remains of his original screenplay. Gives numerous interviews before returning to Montreux in late June. Featured in cover story in *Newsweek* (June 25) and in July hears that *Pale Fire* has made the bestseller list. Visited by former schoolmate Samuil Rosoff, whom he has not seen since 1919, and Elena. Moves with Véra into sixth-floor apartment of Montreux Palace, facing Lake

Geneva. Dmitri becomes ill with painful swelling of joints; in October, while in remission, he begins racing car in competitions. During visit by George Weidenfeld, Nabokov plans reissue of *Speak, Memory* and projected *Butterflies of Europe*, complete illustrated catalog of all species and main subspecies with notes by Nabokov on classification, habitat, and behavior. Compiles index for *Eugene Onegin*. Dmitri's illness recurs and is diagnosed as Reiter's syndrome.

1963   Dmitri is hospitalized in January and February, and again in summer. Nabokov revises *Eugene Onegin*, begins translating *Lolita* into Russian, and goes over *The Eye*, Dmitri's translation of *Soglyadatay*. Interviewed by Alvin Toffler in March for *Playboy* (published Jan. 1964). *The Gift*, translation with Michael Scammell and Dmitri of *Dar*, published in May by Putnam's; reviews stress the extent and achievement of Nabokov's work. Hunts butterflies with Véra in Valais and in Vaud, Switzerland, where they are joined by Dmitri; visitors include George Hessen, Raisa Tatarinov, Elena, Anna Feigin, and Véra's sister Sonia Slonim. Writes introduction for Time-Life reissue of *Bend Sinister* (published 1964).

1964   With Dmitri well enough to resume singing lessons in March, leaves with Véra for publication of *Eugene Onegin* in New York. Goes to Ithaca to retrieve some papers from storage and to visit with Morris Bishop. Gives reading at Harvard (his last public reading), where he meets graduate student Andrew Field. Kirill dies of a heart attack in Munich on April 16. After April 21 reception for *Eugene Onegin* (published by Bollingen in June), returns to Switzerland. Véra is hospitalized for several weeks of tests in May and has appendix removed. Makes revisions in *The Eye* for *Playboy* (published March 1965). Hunts butterflies at Valais in summer. *The Defense*, translation with Michael Scammell of *Zaschita Luzhina*, published by Putnam's in September. Works on *The Texture of Time* while awaiting British Museum's response to his queries for *Butterflies of Europe*. Resumes translating *Lolita* into Russian in December.

1965   Begins extensively revising *Despair* (1936 translation of *Otchayanie*). Composes first chess problem in years. Completes Russian translation of *Lolita*. During construction work at Montreux Palace Hotel in spring, travels with Véra to Gardone, then St. Moritz, for butterflies, taking side trip to Milan to research paintings for projected work *Butterflies in Art* (never completed). Is relieved to learn that Dmitri will give up car racing to concentrate on singing. Reads Edmund Wilson's harshly critical review of *Eugene Onegin* for *New York Review of Books* (July 15) and writes immediate response (letter appears Aug. 26); the controversy draws in writers including Anthony Burgess, Robert Lowell, and George Steiner. Unable to endure publishing uncertainties about ever-expanding *Butterflies of Europe* and finding his creative energies being drained, cancels project despite Weidenfeld's offer of a $10,000 advance. *The Eye* published by Phaedra in early fall. Interviewed and filmed by Robert Hughes in and around Montreux in September for New York Educational Television. Writes new afterword for Russian *Lolita* about difficulties of translating from English to Russian. Extensively rewrites parts of *The Waltz Invention*, Dmitri's translation of *Izobretenie Val'sa*. Over winter revises autobiography as *Speak, Memory: An Autobiography Revisited*. Agrees to allow Radio Liberty to publish some of his works for free clandestine distribution in Soviet Union, under imprint Editions Victor (they will publish *Priglashenie na kazn'* in 1966 and *Zaschita Luzhina* in 1967). In December has first detailed flash of a section of *Ada*.

1966   Completes work on *Speak, Memory*. "Nabokov's Reply," article on *Eugene Onegin* controversy, appears in *Encounter* (Feb.). Writes "*Lolita* and Mr. Girodias" (*Evergreen Review*, Feb. 1967), refutation of Girodias' "*Lolita*, Nabokov, and I" (*Evergreen Review*, Sept. 1965). Begins composing *Ada* at a rapid rate. *The Waltz Invention* published by Phaedra in February. Visited by cartoonist Saul Steinberg. Revised *Despair* published by Putnam's in May. Explores Italian galleries for butterflies in art project in spring and summer; continues working on *Ada*. Véra flies to New York to discuss Nabokov's publishing future with Putnam. Dissatisfied with Putnam's response concerning advances and advertising, Nabokov seeks another publisher. Stops work on *Ada* in November to revise *Eugene Onegin*, making translation still more literal. Extensively revises *King, Queen, Knave*, Dmitri's translation of *Korol', dama, valet* (completes revisions in March 1967).

1967 *Speak, Memory: An Autobiography Revisited* published by Putnam's in January. French court rules agreement between Olympia Press and Nabokov canceled as of December 1964. Nabokov spends April to August with Véra in northern Italy, working intensively on *Ada*; they are joined in Camogli by Dmitri and Elena, and visited by Peter Kemeny of McGraw-Hill. Russian translation of *Lolita* published by Phaedra in August. Véra flies to New York in November to settle with McGraw-Hill final details of contract for 11 books at $250,000 advance. Andrew Field, who is updating and expanding Dieter Zimmer's Nabokov bibliography for McGraw-Hill, visits in December.

1968 Visited by Irving Lazar, who discusses film rights for *Ada* and a *Lolita* musical proposed by Harold Prince, and by Alfred Appel, who goes over notes for his *Annotated Lolita* with Nabokov. Véra brings Anna Feigin, now 80 years old and ailing, from New York to live near her and Nabokov in Montreux. *King, Queen, Knave* published by McGraw-Hill in April. Nabokov agrees to Andrew Field's request to undertake his biography. Hunts butterflies in Vaud and Valais, Switzerland, from May to July. Receives from sister Olga in Prague about 150 letters he had written to his mother. Completes *Ada* in October and begins choosing and translating Russian poems for collection (later titled *Poems and Problems*).

1969 Joseph Papp stages Russell McGrath's adaptation of *Invitation to a Beheading* at New York Shakespeare Festival in March. Film rights for *Ada* are bought by Columbia for $500,000 (film is not produced). *Ada* published by McGraw-Hill on May 5 to initial critical acclaim and strong sales. Summers with Véra in Ticino and Bernese Oberland, Switzerland; enjoys visit from Carl and Ellendea Proffer, who are setting up Ardis Press to publish Russian works. Writes "Notes to Ada by Vivian Darkbloom" (published in 1970 Penguin edition in England). Gives numerous interviews to Italian journalists in Montreux for Mondadori translation of *Ada*. In October, begins writing *Transparent Things*, but makes slow progress.

1970 Completes compilation of *Poems and Problems* in January. Drafts notes for inclusion in *Tri-Quarterly* issue devoted to his work (published Winter 1970). Visits Vatican Museum for *Butterflies in Art* project. Goes with Véra to Sicily in spring and Valais during summer for butterflies. *Transparent Things* "bursts into life" on June 30. Visited by Alan Jay Lerner to discuss musical of *Lolita*, and by Alfred and Nina Appel for five days in November. With Dmitri now singing in North and South America, Véra completes the translation of *Podvig* (*Glory*) while Nabokov revises the translations. *Mary*, translation by Nabokov with Michael Glenny of *Mashen'ka*, published in September by McGraw-Hill. Field arrives December 31 for month's stay in Montreux to discuss Nabokov biography.

1971 Musical *Lolita, My Love* staged unsuccessfully in Philadelphia and Boston. Nabokov starts translating Russian stories with Dmitri in spring for McGraw-Hill collections. *Poems and Problems*, collection of 39 Russian poems with translations, 14 English poems, and 18 chess problems, published by McGraw-Hill in March. Flies to Portugal with Véra for spring, but finds few butterflies and soon returns. Cuts short butterfly hunting in France in summer when Véra is hospitalized for reaction to antibiotics; reads her Solzhenitsyn's *Avgust chetyrnadtsatogo* (*August 1914*) while she recovers. Vacations near Gstaad with Véra, Dmitri, Anna Feigin, Elena, and Sonia Slonim in August; hunts butterflies and hikes with Dmitri. Receives reply to a recent letter to Wilson, first friendly exchange since their *Eugene Onegin* quarrel. Soon after, Nabokov receives copy of passage about him in Wilson's *Upstate* and writes letter to *The New York Times Book Review* (Nov. 7) refuting statements "on the brink of libel." After five-month pause, begins intensive work on *Transparent Things. Glory* published by McGraw-Hill in December.

1972 Completes *Transparent Things* on April 1; published by McGraw-Hill in November to mixed reviews, it sells poorly. In spring and summer hunts butterflies in France and Switzerland. Edmund Wilson dies on June 12. At request of Edmund White, Nabokov writes article, "On Inspiration," for *Saturday Review of the Arts* (Jan. 6, 1973) Nabokov issue. Revises Dmitri's translations of stories for collection *Tyrants Destroyed and Other Stories.*

1973   Anna Feigin dies on January 6. Véra is hospitalized in mid-
        January with two slipped discs; Nabokov writes that the
        "feeling of distress, désarroi, utter panic and dreadful pre-
        sentiment every time V. is away in hospital, is one of the
        greatest torments of my life." In January and February
        reads and corrects manuscript of Andrew Field's *Nabokov:
        His Life in Part*, distressed by its inaccuracies. Begins writ-
        ing *Look at the Harlequins!* In April, starts translating
        stories with Dmitri for *Details of a Sunset and Other Sto-
        ries. A Russian Beauty and Other Stories*, translations with
        Simon Karlinsky and Dmitri, published by McGraw-Hill
        in April. Gives Elena a list of details to check for his *Look
        at the Harlequins!* on her summer trip to Leningrad.
        Spends June and July with Véra in Italy hunting butter-
        flies. During August and September reads and corrects
        revised manuscript of Field's biography, strongly disap-
        proving of it; beyond a letter asking him to acknowledge
        corrections, will never communicate directly with Field
        again. Learns that he has won National Medal for Liter-
        ature prize of $10,000. *Strong Opinions*, collection of
        interviews and other public prose, published by McGraw-
        Hill in November.

1974   *Lolita: A Screenplay*, published by McGraw-Hill in Feb-
        ruary, sells very poorly. Writes letter welcoming Solzhe-
        nitsyn to West after his expulsion from the Soviet Union.
        Signs new agreement with McGraw-Hill for six books over
        next four years. Goes over Edmund Wilson's letters for his
        widow, Elena, who is preparing a book on Wilson's cor-
        respondence; writes her that it is "agony" to go over the
        exchanges from the "early radiant era of our correspon-
        dence." Spends eight days revising German translation of
        Ada. Composes chess problems in April. Begins writing
        letters on behalf of Soviet dissidents. Has new novel (even-
        tually called *The Original of Laura*) "mapped out rather
        clearly for next year." Works on revisions to French ed-
        ition of *Ada* during summer butterfly expedition to Zer-
        matt, then travels on with Véra for a week with Dmitri in
        Sarnico. Visited by Viktor Nekrasov and Vladimir Maxi-
        mov. Is distressed when Solzhenitsyn fails to arrive for visit
        due to a miscommunication. *Look at the Harlequins!*
        published by McGraw-Hill in August to mixed reviews.
        Mashen'ka and *Podvig* are reissued in November by Ardis

(Ardis will republish all of Nabokov's Russian fiction over next decade).

1975　*Tyrants Destroyed and Other Stories*, translated with Dmitri, published by McGraw-Hill in January. Names J. D. Salinger, John Updike, and Edmund White as his favorite American writers in interview for *Esquire*. After completing revisions to French *Ada ou l'ardeur* in February, exhausts himself checking proofs to meet May publication deadline. Goes to Davos in June for butterflies and in late July has severe fall on mountainside. Continues to feel unwell and has tests that disclose tumor on prostate, found to be benign after October operation. Returns to writing *The Original of Laura* in December. Revised translation of *Eugene Onegin* published by Princeton University Press.

1976　Suggests that McGraw-Hill bring out a volume of the Nabokov-Wilson correspondence with Simon Karlinsky as editor (*The Nabokov-Wilson Letters, 1940–1971*, is posthumously published in 1979). *Details of a Sunset and Other Stories* published by McGraw-Hill in March to good reviews. Suffers concussion from fall on May 1 and is hospitalized for ten days. Lumbago attack forces postponement of summer butterfly excursion and an infection causes fever. Readmitted to hospital, semi-conscious, in June and remains until September, delirious much of the time, then undergoes two weeks of convalescence and physiotherapy in Valmont Clinic with Véra, who had damaged her spine attempting to support him after fall. Selects poems for collection *Stikhi* (*Poems*) for Ardis in autumn; weak, with almost no sleep, can write out little of *The Original of Laura*.

1977　Has last interview with BBC Television in February. Develops high fever during bout of influenza and is hospitalized in Lausanne from March 17 to May 7. Reenters Nestlé Hospital in Lausanne when fever returns on June 5 and is placed in intensive care on June 30 with severe bronchial congestion. Dies at 6:50 P.M. on July 2, with Véra and Dmitri at bedside. After cremation at a non-religious funeral service in Vevey attended by a dozen family members and friends, ashes are interred in Clarens cemetery on July 8.

Note on the Texts

This volume presents three works by Vladimir Nabokov, *The Real Life of Sebastian Knight* (1941), *Bend Sinister* (1947), and *Speak, Memory: An Autobiography Revisited* (1966). The texts presented here incorporate revisions and corrections Nabokov noted in his own copies. *Speak, Memory: An Autobiography Revisited* is a substantially revised version of his autobiography, which was originally published in 1951 under the title *Conclusive Evidence* in America and *Speak, Memory* in England.

Nabokov began work on *The Real Life of Sebastian Knight*, his first novel written in English, in December 1938 and completed it in January 1939. He was unable to find a publisher for it until after his arrival in America in 1940, when Edmund Wilson and Harry Levin put him in touch with James Laughlin, publisher of New Directions in Norfolk, Connecticut. Delmore Schwartz, acting as reader for Laughlin, recommended publication of the novel. *The Real Life of Sebastian Knight* was published on December 18, 1941, and though it received good reviews, it did not sell well. Later editions and printings were based on the first American publication. The text printed here is that of the first edition, incorporating corrections subsequently made by Nabokov in his own copies, as well as his addition of the dedication to his wife, Véra.

Nabokov began working on his second novel in English, tentatively titled *The Person from Porlock*, late in 1941 but was not able to concentrate on the writing until early in 1944. On May 25, 1946, he wrote Edmund Wilson that he had completed the novel except for a few minor revisions. It was first sent to Doubleday in May 1946, under the title *Solus Rex*; Nabokov also allowed Allen Tate, then working for Henry Holt and Company, to read the book in typescript. Doubleday did not respond until late September 1946, by which time Holt had expressed interest. Nabokov decided to have Holt publish the book because, as he wrote Wilson in October 1946, "Holt advances 2000, Doubleday offered only 1000. Holt loved the book. Doubleday was cool." Just before the novel was sent to the printer in November, Nabokov changed the title to *Bend Sinister*. The book, published in New York on June 12, 1947, by Holt, received mixed reviews and sales were not good. An English edition was published by Weidenfeld and Nicolson in 1960, using the first American edition as setting copy and incorporating corrections made by Nabokov. In this edition, British spelling was used and chapter numbers were added (in the first edition the chapters were divided by symbols). The introduction was written by Nabokov in September 1963 for the Time Reading Program Special Edition, published in New York by Time Incorporated in 1964. Although published in New York and entirely reset, the Time Incorporated edition used the English edition as setting copy, probably because of the corrections made in that edition, and also retained its British spellings (the introduction does not have British spelling). When McGraw-Hill published its edition in 1973, it used the Time Incorporated edition, retained the British spelling, and because of the particular chapter opening design of the Time edition, made a few errors in paragraphing. The text printed here is that of the 1947 first American edition, incorporating revisions and corrections marked by Nabokov in his own copies, some of which were incorporated in later printings. The Introduction is from the 1964 Time edition, but includes the revisions and corrections marked in Nabokov's own copies. The chapter numbers have been accepted as Nabokov's revision, since they are referred to in the Introduction; the text presented in this volume also includes Nabokov's dedication of the novel to Véra, which he added after its initial publication in 1947.

Nabokov's autobiography was first published in America by Harper & Brothers on March 14, 1951, as *Conclusive Evidence*, although Nabokov was not satisfied with the title. Earlier he had considered using as titles "The Person in Question," "Speak, Mnemosyne," "Rainbow Edge," "Clues," "The Prismatic Edge," "The Moulted Feather" (from Browning's poem), "Nabokov's Opening" (alluding to chess), and "Emblemata." By June 1951, Nabokov had settled on *Speak, Memory*, and the English edition published by Victor Gollancz in November 1951 appeared under that title. All fifteen chapters were first published in magazines before they were revised for inclusion in the 1951 book edition. Chapter Five, originally published in French in the second issue of *Mesures*, Paris, 1936, was translated into English by Hilda Ward, with revisions made by Nabokov, and appeared under the French title, "Mademoiselle O," in the January 1943 issue of *The Atlantic Monthly*. Eleven chapters were published in *The New Yorker*: Chapter Three, titled "Portrait of My Uncle," on January 3, 1948; Chapter Four, "My English Education," March 27, 1948; Chapter Six, "Butterflies," June 12, 1948; Chapter Seven, "Colette," July 31, 1948; Chapter Nine, "My Russian Education," September 18, 1948; Chapter Ten, "Curtain-Raiser," January 1, 1949; Chapter Two, "Portrait of My Mother," April 9, 1949; Chapter Twelve, "Tamara," December 10, 1949; Chapter Eight, "Lantern Slides," February 11, 1950; Chapter One, "Perfect Past," April 15, 1950; and Chapter Fifteen, "Gardens and Parks," June 17, 1950. Two chapters were published in

Partisan Review: Chapter Eleven, "First Poem," September 1949; and Chapter Fourteen, "Exile," January–February 1951. *Harper's Magazine* published Chapter Thirteen, "Lodgings in Trinity Lane," in January 1951. Several chapters appeared in other Nabokov collections: "Mademoiselle O" was included in *Nine Stories* (1947) and *Nabokov's Dozen* (1958), which also included Chapter Seven under a new title, "First Love."

During his translation of *Conclusive Evidence* into Russian, Nabokov remembered some episodes and details that he had not recalled before and added these to the Russian edition. This version, published in the U.S. in the fall of 1954 by the Chekhov Publishing House, was titled *Drugie Berega* ("Other Shores"). Later, during visits to Europe, Nabokov had the opportunity to discuss his autobiography with family members for the first time; he began revising and expanding it in November 1965, and completed work on it in January 1966. He rewrote approximately one-fifth of the book, and also added a foreword and an index. The book was entirely reset, using the 1951 American edition as partial copy with new typed pages inserted where necessary, and was published by G. P. Putnam's Sons in January 1967 (dated 1966) under the title *Speak, Memory: An Autobiography Revisited*. The text printed here is that of the Putnam first edition, incorporating revisions and corrections marked in his own copies of the work.

This volume presents the texts of the original printings chosen for inclusion here, but it does not attempt to reproduce features of their typographic design, such as display capitalization of chapter openings. The texts are printed without change, except for the correction of typographical errors and the incorporation of revisions and corrections made by Nabokov. Spelling, punctuation, and capitalization are often expressive features, and they are not altered, even when inconsistent or irregular.

The following three lists record by page and line number, Nabokov's revisions and corrections (other than corrections of typographical errors) incorporated into the text of this volume; in each case the reading of the present text comes first, followed by that of the first edition.

The Real Life of Sebastian Knight
92.18, eye-ball] apple

Bend Sinister
163.5, middle 'Forties] winter and spring of 1945–1946   201.16, A score of] Some twenty   230.23, Ekwilism] "Ekwilism"   250.39, Shut up!] Be still.   271.24, sidewalk] pavement   301.30, lover and be-

loved] lower and belowed   308.7, notions] motions   355.22, operatic] Cavalleria Rusticana

Speak, Memory, An Autobiography Revisited
406.7, came] came my father; then   406.9–10, Smolensk . . . father.] Smolensk.   406.26, 1927] 1929   411.35 forelimb] forelimbs   451.19, bass] base   451.34, an Italianate] a stylish Italianate   480.33, Lavington . . . children),] Lavington,   481.1–2, companion . . . actor).] companion.   500.35, discern] make out   508.17–18, *morbus et passio aureliani*] *passio et morbo aureliana*   523.5, are] is

   The following is a list of typographical errors corrected, cited by page and line number: 5.32, war—; 26.18, magazine?; 43.32, city-flavour; 56.2, Café; 62.27, born; 67.37, said,; 68.3, beechwood; 77.1, tophat; 80.5, The *Funny*; 83.33, *Property*; 85.5, come).; 90.21, langour; 91.35, 1933,; 95.34, *beacoup*; 98.6, man, "is; 98.36, lightly,; 101.14, And pay; 105.26, She; 106.5, half-an hour; 107.33, midgets; 112.4, soon).; 113.15,, ago.; 114.10, said,; 117.1, Von; 119.10, strategem; 133.4, furcoat; 140.20, every one; 145.25, sanitorium; 151.12–13, Etat désespéré; 157.20, I'll; 174.21, bed; 178.9, lad; 185.12, instance; 188.7, unscrutable; 196.28, armchair,; 201.26, believed,; 208.29, President; 213.31, looking; 220.24, tunnel",; 225.38, that; 227.9, look; 234.3, Maximov's; 253.18, "why; 254.10, Wern; 262.19, provide.; 268.8, Hustav; 271.5, Padukrad; 292.6, fancy,; 292.29, MSS.; 295.5, eyes).; 305.9, "common-sense"; 305.38, mind; 308.2, ne; 309.2, "Escape."; 309.2, "Brikabrak,"; 310.11, Padukrad; 312.15, *"cette*; 312.16, *Ophilie."*; 315.5, near by; 320.20, Ignore,; 323.37, guess,; 333.9, heads); 333.16, A: [new paragraph} "I'll; 333.16, you," [new line flush left} then; 344.38, Night."; 345.12, Backofen; 355.12, wall; 356.20, queesy; 397.24, *floreat*; 401.35, *magazin*; 401.36, *péronelles*; 451.37, Peterburg; 581.21, undestanding; 585.18, views; 586.28, Song of; 615.8 *New Entomological.*

Notes

In the notes below, the reference numbers denote page and line of this volume (the line count includes titles and headings). No note is made for material included in standard desk-reference books such as Webster's *Collegiate*, *Biographical*, and *Geographical* dictionaries. Quotations from Shakespeare are keyed to *The Riverside Shakespeare*, ed. G. Blakemore Evans (Boston: Houghton Mifflin, 1974). For further background and references to other studies, see Brian Boyd, *Vladimir Nabokov, The Russian Years* and *Vladimir Nabokov, The American Years* (Princeton: Princeton University Press, 1990 and 1991); *The Nabokov-Wilson Letters, 1940–1971*, ed. Simon Karlinsky (New York: Harper & Row, Publishers, 1979); *Vladimir Nabokov: Selected Letters, 1940–1977*, ed. Dmitri Nabokov and Matthew J. Bruccoli (San Diego and New York: Harcourt, Brace, Jovanovich / Bruccoli Clark Layman, 1989); Vladimir Nabokov, *Strong Opinions* (New York: McGraw-Hill Book Company, 1973).

The publishers thank Dmitri Nabokov for his cooperation and assistance in the preparation of this volume and Glenn Horowitz for generous access to Vladimir Nabokov's personal copies of his books.

THE REAL LIFE OF SEBASTIAN KNIGHT

3.16   twelves degrees . . . zero]   5 degrees F.

3.20–21   Olga Olegovna Orlov]   Olga (c. 890–969, later beatified) was the first princess of Kievan Russia and regent for her son Svyatoslav, 945–964. Oleg (d. c. 912) was founder of the Kievan Rus state. *Orlov* means "eagle" (the two-headed eagle was the symbol of the Russian empire).

5.29   redheels]   In the 18th century fashionable fops wore red heels with their patches and periwigs.

5.32   Japanese war]   The Russo-Japanese War of 1904–5.

7.10   Hotel d'Europe]   One of the finest of St. Petersburg's hotels, built in 1873–75, on Ulitsa Mikhaylovskaya (later Ulitsa Brodskogo), just off the Nevsky Prospekt.

16.29–31   ("cette horrible . . . admirable")]   That horrible Englishwoman . . . that admirable woman.

20.8–9   blue remembered hills . . . highways]   A. E. Housman, *A Shropshire Lad* (1896), xl, st. 1–2: "Into my heart an air that kills / From yon far country blows: / What are those blue remembered hills, / What spires, what farms are those? // That is the land of lost content, / I see it shining plain, / The happy highways where I went / And cannot come again."

20.9   the hedge . . . unofficial rose]   In "The Old Vicarage, Grant-chester" (1912), Rupert Brooke pictures himself thinking of home from a Berlin café: "*there* the dews / Are soft beneath a morn of gold, / Here tulips bloom as they are told; / Unkempt about those hedges blows / An English unofficial rose" (lines 22–26).

20.10   the distant spire]   Thomas Gray, "Ode on a Distant Prospect of Eton College" (1742), line 1: "Ye distant spires, ye antique towers."

21.18   futurist poet]   The avant-garde futurist movement in Russian poetry began around 1910 and in 1912 several futurists including Vladimir Mayakovsky (1893–1930) and Velimir Khlebnikov (1885–1922) issued a manifesto in the pamphlet *A Slap in the Face of Public Taste* attacking classical writers and calling for Pushkin, Tolstoy, and Dostoevsky to be cast off the "ship" of modern life.

21.24   the "submental grunt"]   A number of futurist poets experimented with "trans-rational" language, notably Khlebnikov, who invented a "transsense" (*zaum'*) language; in 1916 Vasilisk Gnedov "composed" a poem without words.

22.2   Marcopolian journey]   Parody of Mayakovsky's lecture and reading tours.

22.14   the Greater Dog]   Canis Major.

22.16–17   mouse engendering mountains.]   Cf. Horace's *Ars poetica*, lines 138–39: "quid dignum tanto feret hic promissor hiatu? / parturient montes, nascetur ridiculus mus" ("what will this boaster produce in keeping with such mouthing? / Mountains will labor, a ridiculous mouse will be born").

24.5   Sore-bone]   The Sorbonne, the university of Paris.

27.23–24   imperfections . . . head]   In *Hamlet*, the revengeful ghost of King Hamlet laments to his son that, being murdered, he died without the chance of confessing his sins, was "sent to my account / With all my imperfections on my head" (I.5.78–79).

31.21–23   *La morte . . . Retrouvé*]   *Le morte d'Arthur* (1470) by Sir Thomas Malory; *The Bridge of San Luis Rey* (1927) by Thornton Wilder (1897–1975); *The Strange Case of Dr. Jekyll and Mr. Hyde* (1886), by Robert Louis Stevenson; *South Wind* (1917) by Norman Douglas (1868–1952); short story, "Dama s sobachkoy" ("The Lady with the Little Dog," 1899), by Anton Chekhov; *The Invisible Man* (1897) by H. G. Wells; and *Le Temps Retrouvé*, last volume (*Time Regained*, 1927) of Marcel Proust's novel *A la recherche du temps perdu* (*In Search of Lost Time*, 1913–27).

31.24   *The Author of Trixie*]   *The Author of "Trixie"* (1923), comic novel by William Caine (1873–1925).

31.25   *About Buying a Horse*]   Humorous autobiographical sketches (1875) by Sir Francis Cowley Burnand (1836–1917).

33.10   Large Copper]   The butterfly *Lycaena dispar* Haworth, which formerly occurred in the fens of Cambridgeshire and Huntingdonshire, but became extinct there due to drainage of the fens and over-collecting.

33.17   Great Court]   The large grassed main quadrangle in Trinity College.

35.30   the Pitt]   The Pitt Club (founded 1835), the select social club for Cambridge students, in Jesus Lane.

35.39   Henry the Eighth]   A 16th-century copy by Hans Eworth of Holbein's portrait of Henry VIII—the founder of Trinity College—dominates the north end of Trinity College's Hall.

39.17–18   the Backs]   At Cambridge, the picturesque stretch of the river Cam passing by the backs of the colleges from St. John's to Queen's.

42.22   Mrs. Grundy's]   Thomas Morton (1764–1838) introduced the character of Mrs. Grundy in his comedy *Speed the Plough* (1798); she subsequently became the stereotype of conventional moral rigidity.

46.28–29   face . . . cow's udder]   Cf. Nikolay Gumilov's poem "Zabludivshiysya tramvay" ("The Tram Off the Rails," c. 1919–20), lines 29–30: "V krasnoy rubashke, s litsom kak vymya, / Golovu srezal palach i mne" ("The executioner, in a red shirt, with a face like an udder, cut off my head too").

47.23–24   Goodman's . . . Goodrich's]   Godfrey Goodman (1583–1656), Bishop of Gloucester, and Samuel Goodrich (1793–1860) a writer and Boston publisher known by the pseudonym "Peter Parley."

49.30   Jerome K. Jerome book]   *Three Men in the Bummel* (1900), ch. 9.

49.32–35   fat . . . father.]   Cf. *Hamlet.*

50.1   story by Chekhov]   "Chyorniy monakh" ("The Black Monk," 1894).

52.30   New Forest]   Scenic area in southwest Hampshire, earning its name after being placed under forest laws by William the Conqueror in 1079.

54.7   the Etoile]   The Place de l'Etoile, later Place Charles de Gaulle, site of the Arc de Triomphe.

54.19   V.]   Nabokov wrote to Andrew Field (Feb. 3, 1967): "V stands for Victor."

55.25   "Gah-song,"]   *Garçon,* "waiter."

56.14   bongs-bongs]   *Bonbons,* "candy."

68.17   sinuses of Salva]   Probably the sinus of Valsalva, part of the venous draining of the heart.

80.17–18   "moving . . . arrased eavesdropper,"]   Polonius hides "Behind the arras" (*Hamlet*, III.iii.28) to eavesdrop on Hamlet's conversation with his mother, only to be killed there by Hamlet.

83.13   'pelmenies']   Small ravioli-like dumplings.

95.27–28   elenctic . . . Carroll's caterpillar] *Elenctic:* cross-examining, aiming to refute another's position. The caterpillar who dominates Ch. 5 of *Alice's Adventures in Wonderland* begins, "Who are *You*? . . . What do you mean by that? . . . Explain yourself!"

95.34   *"Nous avons . . . dames,"*] We have had many attractive women.

97.9–10   picture . . . side.] St. Sebastian, condemned to execution by archers, is commonly shown in Renaissance painting pierced by arrows.

99.1–2   *cigarette-étuis*] Cigarette-cases.

99.10   *Gavrit parussky?*] An attempt at *Vy govorite po-russki?* ("You speak Russian?"). Nabokov's spelling of Russian throughout *The Real Life of Sebastian Knight* departs slightly from strict transliteration to provide a syllable-by-syllable approximation to pronunciation.

100.3   her build] German, *Bild*, "picture."

103.38   depences] From French *dépense*, "expense."

108.6   in Byron's dream, . . . changes.] In "The Dream" (1816), "A change came o'er the spirit of my dream" becomes a refrain.

108.22   A Camberwell Beauty] The beautiful butterfly *Nymphalis antiopa* Linnaeus. Its upperside wings are maroon in the center, bordered with a row of blue spots and then cream-yellow margins.

115.8   *carte de travail*] Work permit.

117.15   *"Mais oui, . . . russe,"*] Certainly, she's as Russian as they come.

117.35   *Il va sans dire*] It goes without saying.

118.15   *Elle fait des passions.*] People fall in love with her.

120.5   *"Viens, mon vieux,"*] Here, old chap.

120.19   *j'ai . . . vous.*] I have a little surprise for you.

120.26–27   *tout . . . thé.*] All that you think reasonable to ask of a cup of tea.

121.32   *hors concours*] Beyond competition.

122.6   *Un coeur . . . jamais.*] A woman's heart never revives.

122.16–17   *Voyez vous ça!*] That's really something!

123.28–29   *Ah non . . . voudriez pas!*] Oh, no thank you, I'm not my friend's diary. You wouldn't!

124.19   *à l'improviste*] Without warning.

124.32–33   *des jeunes . . . rigoler*] Young people who like a good laugh.

125.14–16   *vitalité . . . vie.*] Joyful vitality which is, besides, in tune with an innate philosophy, a quasi-religious sense of the phenomena of life.

126.11–12   *Eh bien . . . d'accord?*]   Well, is that okay by you?

128.24   *"Enchanté . . . connaître,"*]   Delighted to meet you.

128.25   *Je suis navré*]   I am terribly sorry.

129.7   *"Ecoutez,"*]   Listen.

129.8–9   *Ce n'est . . . savez.*]   It's not very polite, you know.

129.12   *Monsieur l'entêté.*]   Mr. Stubborn.

129.31–32   *Vous devez mourir de faim*]   You must be starving.

130.20–21   *On . . . n'est-ce-pas?*]   The boredom there must drive you crazy, surely.

131.30   *alors vous . . . Monsieur.*]   Then you are ridiculous, my dear sir.

133.12–13   Maupassant story . . . book."]   In "Ce cochon de Marin" ("That Pig, Marin"; 1882), the narrator, Labarbe, who has ended up staying the night at the house of people he has just met, enters the bedroom of the young woman he has begun to seduce: " 'I have forgotten, mademoiselle, to ask for something to read.' She struggled with herself; but I soon opened the book I was looking for. I won't say its name. It was really the most wonderful of novels, and the most divine of poems. Once the first page was turned, she let me run through the rest as I liked; and I leafed through so many chapters that our candles burnt right down."

134.19   *"Vous . . . aimable,"*]   You're not being very pleasant.

134.30   *Ah-oo-neigh . . . pah-ook*]   *A u ney na sheiki pauk,* "Look, she has a spider on her neck."

135.4   *"Mais vous êtes fou,"*]   But you're mad.

144.24   the *Prattler*]   Cf. *The Tatler,* a society magazine for the upper class.

145.18–19   heard voices . . . *Dot chetu?*]   The narrator assumes this word, like the rest of the letter, is in Cyrillic; in fact the letters are Roman and spell "Domremy," the village where Joan of Arc first heard voices she believed to be of angels or God.

151.12–13   *Etat désespéré*]   State hopeless.

151.39–40   *Il est dangereux . . . E pericoloso*]   From the sign on European trains (in French, Italian, Spanish, and German) warning that "It is dangerous to lean out the windows."

152.34   *Cadran*]   *Dial.*

153.19   strapontin]   Folding seat.

153.29   cuirs, peaux]   Leathers, skins.

153.30   jongleur, humoriste]   Juggler, comedian.

154.20–21   *Vive le front populaire*]   Long live the Popular Front.

156.34   "K, n, i, g . . . "]   Also spells in Russian "of (the) books."

159.4–5   *Non, . . . le soigne*]   No, it's Doctor Guinet who's looking after him.

BEND SINISTER

164.11   symptoms . . . Soviet Russia]   Following Stalin's death in 1953.

166.33   Malheur]   French, "misfortune."

166.34   ancient Kuranian]   Invented blend of Ukranian and the old language of Kurland or Courland, a region of West and South Latvia between the Baltic Sea and the river Dvina once inhabited by the Baltic tribes the Letts and Kurs: in other words, the languages of the peoples between the Germans and the Russians.

167.32–33   *Gone . . . Roses*]   The title of the best-selling novel *Gone with the Wind* (1936) by Margaret Mitchell (1900–49) comes from stanza 3 of "Last night, ah, yesternight, betwtixt her lips and mine" (usually known as "Cynara," 1891) by English poet Ernest Dowson (1867–1900): "I have forgot much, Cynara! gone with the wind, / Flung roses, roses riotously with the throng, / Dancing, to put thy pale, lost lilies out of mind; / But I was desolate and sick of an old passion, / Yea, all the time, because the dance was long: / I have been faithful to thee, Cynara! in my fashion."

167.34   novels . . . Sholokhov)]   *All Quiet on the Western Front* (1929) by Erich Maria Remarque (1898–1970) and *Tikhiy Don* (*The Quiet Don*, known in English as *And Quiet Flows the Don*; 1928–40), by Mikhail Sholokhov (1905–84).

167.37   *L'Après-Midi d'un Faune*]   "The Afternoon of a Faun."

168.15   Tzikutin]   *Tzikuta*, Russian "hemlock."

168.21   Saul Steinberg]   Born 1914, cartoonist with *The New Yorker* from 1941.

169.8   bombinates]   Hums or booms.

176.13–15   brief love affair . . . mother]   The Russian vulgarism *eb tvoyu mat'* can mean "I have fucked your mother," "I would fuck your mother," or "Fuck your mother."

179.12   Flaubertian *farceurs.*]   In this sense, "humbugs." Gustave Flaubert liked to compile examples of human crassness, especially in his letters and his unfinished novel *Bouvard et Pecuchet* (1881) and the *Dictionnaire des idées reçues* (*Dictionary of Received Ideas*) that was to have formed part of it.

179.14–15   those who *are* . . . Cartesianism.] Alluding to the Cartesian maxim "Cogito, ergo sum" ("I think, therefore I am").

182.15   *Strekoza*] Russian, "dragonfly."

182.36   gammadion] A cross formed of four capital gammas (Γ), especially in the figure of a swastika.

183.6–7   *C'est . . . bonjour*] It's as simple as "Good day."

184.7   Cucumber] In German, *Gurke.*

186.24   gabberloon] Scottish *gaberlunzie,* "wandering beggar."

188.14–15   Da Vinci . . . monks)] Leonardo painted *The Last Supper* (1495–98; Santa Maria delle Grazie, Milan) on a wall of what was then the refectory of a Dominican monastery.

190.7–8   *Pourvu . . . atroce.*] So long as he doesn't ask the awful question.

191.24   Ember] Hungarian for "man," as *adam* is Hebrew for "man."

193.13–14   *Annunciata . . .* funnies.] See page 167.28–29. Franz Werfel's *Das Lied von Bernadette* (1941, trans. as *Song of Bernadette,* 1944) begins in the Cave of Massabielle at Lourdes; in the United States, the novel was serialized in newspapers near the comic strip section.

195.16–17   follow the pairtaunt . . . skeins-mate.] See Introduction, p. 167.12–13 in this volume. For *perttaunt* ("pair-taunt"), cf. *Love's Labour's Lost,* V.ii.67–68, for *jauncing, Romeo and Juliet,* II.v.51–52 and *Richard II,* V.v.94, and for *skeins-mate* ("skains-mates"), *Romeo and Juliet,* II.iv.153–54.

195.35–36   *Ce sont . . . trimbala.*] It's my colleagues and the old man and the whole dragging lot.

196.23–24   Gregoire, . . . beetle] Cf. Gregor Samsa, who finds himself turned into a beetle in Kafka's *Die Verwandlung* (*Metamorphosis,* 1915).

196.29   Chardin's "House of Cards"] Between 1735 and 1737 Jean Chardin painted a number of canvases known by this title; although different in composition, all feature a boy building a house of cards by himself.

197.5   paletoted] From French *paletot,* "overcoat."

197.24–26   emblem . . . red flaglet] Combines the Nazi flag with a hint of Paduk (*pauk* is Russian for "spider").

197.37–38   *"Bonsoir . . . vôtre?"*] Good evening, dear colleague. They pulled me from my bed, to the great displeasure of my wife. How is yours?

198.3–5   *'Les morts . . . souffle'*] "The dead, the poor dead, have great sorrows. And when October blows—"; from "La servante au grand coeur dont vous étiez jalouse" ("The great-hearted servant of whom you were jealous"), poem XV in the "Tableaux parisiens" ("Parisian pictures") section of the 1861 edition of *Les Fleurs du mal* (*Flowers of Evil*) by Charles Baudelaire (1821–67).

198.16   Skotoma]   A blind or dark spot in the visual field; from Greek *skotos*, darkness. The Russian *skot* or *skotina* means "livestock" but applied to an individual means "brute."

198.24   *terrains vagues*]   Waste lands.

198.28   *culotte bouffante*]   Knickerbockers.

198.30   *"On va . . . gaillard-là,"*]   That funster's going to get his backside wiped for him.

199.35   gardyloo]   From French *gardez l'eau*, "Watch out for the water," once a warning cried out by those emptying household slops from an upper window onto the street below.

200.21–35   having zoomed . . . quivering——]   Explaining that this was "a hard passage," Véra Nabokov wrote to Charles Timmer, the Dutch translator of *Bend Sinister* (Dec. 20, 1949): "It develops simultaneously on several planes. The word 'Keeweenawatin' is a telescopic combination of two terms 'Keewatin' (name of a schist of the Archaeozoic—the oldest—period) and 'Keewanawan' (subdivision of the Proterozoic). Laurentian belongs to the Archaeozoic, Permian to the Paleozoic. Through Early Recent etc.—further partly existent partly invented periods of geological development. In other words—from the dimmest past into the present, through all the phases of the earth's development, as he rides up in the elevator through the numerous floors of an American skyscraper. Some sideline additions: in 'ghoul-haunted Province of Perm' there are both a hint at the horrors of Soviet labor camps and a hint at the esoteric world of Edgar Poe's 'Ulalume' (brought in by means of similar rhythm—'ghoul-haunted region of Weir,' I believe it is [actually, line 7, 'In the misty mid region of Weir,' line 9, 'the ghoul-haunted woodland of Weir']) . . . this remote past of the world is actually still here with us, a few floors removed, with its savagery etc. . . . . The 'I' (*my* room, *my* hotel floor) tragically alone not only in the present world but in one still infinitely larger, with all the past actually still present. 'delicate hands' etc.— the elevators are mostly manned by Negro attendants ('my own in a negative picture'—the Negro's black hands) . . . Going through all these floors the Negro attendant never reaches paradise, or even a roof garden. And the world, by implication, though having reached from the Archaeozoic to the Present, and from cave dwellings to skyscrapers with roof-gardens, is just as far removed from true Paradise on earth. Incidentally a slight reflexion on the awful position of the Negroes. 'The depth of stag-headed hall' etc.—ever so slightly this covers the whole ground covered by the book: Professor Azureus with his flat materialistic world is a kind of Troglodite coming out of his cave. . . . The 'long, wrinkled upper lip' adds to the remote indication of his apishness."

200.37   circle in Krug] *Krug*, Russian, "circle."

201.22   *à ses heures*] In his spare time.

201.25   *bouchées*] Pasties.

202.20   *"Ils . . . pourtant,"*] All the same, they have some nerve.

202.39   *pauvres gosses*] Poor kids.

204.36   Paduk] Russian *upadok* means "decline, decay, breakdown"; it derives from the root *pad*, "fall."

205.36–38   bow tie . . . hindwing.] Véra Nabokov explained to Charles Timmer (Sept. 27, 1949): the "bow tie is treated as a butterfly and described in entomological terms, as a new species would have been described in an entomological journal: the interneural maculae, which would have been white in the typical species, are of Isabella color (dirty white, approaching very, very pale flesh color) in this particular form or subspecies."

208.14–15   *en fait . . . d'enfance*] In terms of childhood memories.

208.18   *Buxum biblioformis*] *Buxus* is the real genus boxwood, *biblioformis* an invented species, "book-shaped."

210.13–16   dove . . . fig leaf,"] Cf. Genesis 8:11 and 3:7.

211.8–9   ships of the desert] Camels.

211.9–10   collecting . . . orthopterist.] Specialist in Orthoptera, the insect order that includes grasshoppers and crickets; allusion to the biblical plagues of locusts (Exodus 10:4–19, etc.).

213.24   Nobody can touch our circles] During the sack of Syracuse in A.D. 212 the mathematician Archimedes, drawing geometric figures in the sand, is said to have told the Roman soldiers bursting upon him, " *Noli turbare circulos meos*" ("Don't disturb my circles"). A soldier who questioned him about what he was doing, and was dissatisfied with the answers, ran his body through.

216.35   *qui m'effrayent, Blaise*] "Which frighten me, Blaise." Cf. Blaise Pascal, *Pensées*, III ("De la Nécessité du Pari"), 206: "Le silence éternel de ces espaces infinis m'effraie" ("The eternal silence of these infinite spaces frightens me").

217.1–2   amphiphorical] Bearing (heaven) with both hands.

218.28   supes] Supernumeraries, stage extras.

220.33   *collier de chien*] Dog collar.

221.36   galatea] Boys' sailor suits made from galatea, a cloth like light denim.

221.37   *en laid*] In an uglier version.

232.19   afternoon with Mallarmé] See note 167.37.

234.3–4   Maximovs' *dacha* . . . cottage.]   During this country visit the national language is almost pure Russian, unlike in the remainder of the book.

235.14   velvetina]   Véra Nabokov to Charles Timmer (Sept. 27, 1949): "imaginary cereal, in line with the American commercial foods, such as 'Pablum' or 'Wheatina.' "

236.9–10   safety razor . . . signature]   Gillette blades once came in paper wrappings printed with the signature and face of Gillette.

236.19   (*Flung Roses . . . Don*)]   See notes 167.33–34.

239.23   *Ra*]   Symbol for radium.

239.29   *Je resterai coi*]   I will keep quiet.

252.4–5   three engravings]   After the three inset illustrations from the title page of Gustavus Selenus's study of cryptographic systems, *Cryptomenytices et Cryptographiae* (1624), reproduced in Sir Edwin Durning-Lawrence's *Bacon is Shakespeare* (London, 1910). Durning-Lawrence claims (p. 110) that "Bacon must have had a hand in" the production of this book, and (p. 129) that "the whole title page clearly shows that it is drawn to give a revelation about Shakespeare."

252.8–9   spear . . . sinistral detail]   Durning-Lawrence repeatedly (pp. 23, 29, 130, 133) stresses left-handedness as a "proof" that Bacon is Shakespeare.

252.9–10   Ah, "that . . . *d'hier*]   In Flaubert's *Madame Bovary* (1857), Homais, the pharmacist, says: "Ah! that is the question! Such indeed is the question. 'That is the question,' as I was lately reading in the newspaper." *Le journal d'hier:* "yesterday's paper."

252.12–14   legend: "Ink, a Drug."]   Invented by Nabokov.

252.14   numbered . . . "bacon"]   A parody of Durning-Lawrence's methods (cf. his p. 23).

252.18   shapska.]   *Shapka* is Russian for "cap, fur hat."

252.19   *Homelette au Lard*]   *Omelette au lard* means "bacon omelette." The inscription does not occur in Selenus or Durning-Lawrence.

252.21   road sign "To High Wycombe."]   The words on the road sign are Nabokov's invention. High Wycombe, in Buckinghamshire, lies between Stratford-on-Avon and London.

252.24–25   November 27, 1582]   The date of Shakespeare's marriage license.

252.27–28   cunningly composed . . . mask.]   Durning-Lawrence wrote of the engraving of Shakespeare's portrait used as the frontispiece in the 1623 First Folio: "in fact it is a cunningly drawn cryptographic picture, shewing two left arms and a mask" (p. 23).

252.28–30   The person . . . find it.]   Proverbs 25:2: "It is the glory of God to conceal a thing, but the honor of kings to search out a matter." Bacon reworked this several times, as in *The Advancement of Learning* (1605, Book 1: "Salomon . . . saith expressly, *The glory of God is to conceal a thing, but the glory of the king is to find it out*") and in *The Great Instauration* ("Of the sciences which regard nature, it is the glory of God to conceal a thing, but it is the glory of the King to find it out").

252.31–33   Warwickshire . . . primrose.]   Shakespeare came from the county of Warwickshire; scholars have shown how the plants he names reflect the locale of his early upbringing.

253.30–31   full habit of body]   Gertrude's remark concerning Hamlet, "He's fat, and scant of breath" (V.ii.287) caused Charles Cowden Clarke in his edition of 1864 to comment on his having "that full habit of body which is apt to be the result of sedentary occupation and a too sedulous addiction to scholarly pursuits" (Horace Howard Furness, ed., *Hamlet: A New Variorum Edition*, 10th ed., 1877, I, 446). Nabokov drew in detail on the notes throughout the two-volume Furness variorum edition of *Hamlet*.

254.4–5   the gibberish . . . (Kronberg's)]   The 1844 translation of *Hamlet* by Andrey Kroneberg (1814–55), although an inexact paraphrase, long held sway in Russia.

254.5   Wern]   Based on the sociologically minded critic H. A. Werner, "Über das Dunkel in der Hamlet-Tragödie" (*Jahrbuch der Deutschen Shakespeare-Gesellschaft*, 1870; in Furness, II); Nabokov paraphrases passages from Werner at 254.27–28 and 254.31–33.

254.15–16   Fortinbras (Ironside)]   An etymology taken from Robert Latham (*Athenaeum*, 1872) in Furness I, 14.

254.17–18   what is boded . . . eruption]   Cf. *Hamlet* I.i.69: "This bodes some strange eruption to our state."

254.26   Shakespeare's or Kyd's intentions]   An earlier version of *Hamlet*, known to have been performed on the English stage by 1589 (since its text and title are lost, it is now referred to as the Ur-*Hamlet*), has commonly been attributed to Thomas Kyd (1558–94).

254.29–30   a soldier . . . at heart!]   Francisco, at I.i.9.

254.35–255.7   The real hero . . . restored to power.]   Cf. Franz Horn, *Shakespeare Erläutert* (1823), in Furness, II, 282–83: "To quiet us, there comes forward a blooming young hero, beautiful and sound to the core—Fortinbras, Prince of Norway. . . . But why is this young hero represented so sparing of words, almost monosyllabic? I think there was a most excellent reason for it. Upon a closer study of this inexhaustible drama, almost all the persons in it appear to suffer from a plethora of words, and for this reason the spoken word loses for them its healing efficacy. If the State is to be saved and a new life begun, all this must be changed, and the simple word, accompanied by fit action, must regain its power." The "caviar": *Hamlet* II.ii.437.

255.7–15   Fortinbras possesses . . . historical significance.] Cf. Hermann Ulrici, *Shakespeares Dramatische Kunst* (1839), in Furness, II, 293: "Fortinbras, in whose favor Hamlet gives his dying voice, possesses an ancient claim and hereditary right to the throne of Denmark. Some deed of violence or injustice, by which his family were dispossessed of their just claims, hung in the dark background over the head of that royal house which has now become extinct. Of this crime its last successors have now paid the penalty. And thus, in this closing scene, that idea of the overruling justice of God, which pervades all the other tragedies of Shakespeare, impresses on the whole play its seal of historical significance."

255.16   Three thousand crowns]   *Hamlet* II.ii.73: "threescore thousand crowns."

255.26–27   "go softly on"]   *Hamlet* IV.iv.8.

255.39   *innerliche Unruhe*]   Inner unrest.

256.6–7   the "judgments" . . . Horatio the Recorder]   *Hamlet* V.ii.382.

256.9–10   this quarry cries on havoc]   Cf. *Hamlet* V.ii.364.

256.12   the rotten . . . Denmark]   Cf. *Hamlet* I.iv.90.

256.13   old mole]   *Hamlet* I.v.162: "Well said, old mole, canst work i' th' earth so fast?"

256.18–19   "Runs . . . head."]   Cf. *Hamlet* V.ii.185–86.

256.20–21   Mixing . . . ship,]   John Dover Wilson wrote in *Hamlet* (1936) of Osric at V.ii.104–11: "Osric . . . deserts the language of the shop for that of the ship. . . . Osric has mixed the metaphors of the shop and the ship."

256.22–24   fantastic courtier . . . doublet]   Cf. Wilson's stage direction for Osric's first entrance, V.ii.

256.33   Paduk or Paddock]   In *Hamlet*, "paddock" is used in the sense of "toad"; cf. III.iv.189–91.

256.33–34   *bref . . . en question*]   In short, the person in question.

257.15–17   Ghostly . . . mobled moon]   Cf. *Hamlet* I.i.115–16 ("The graves stood tenantless and the sheeted dead / Did squeak and gibber in the Roman streets") and II.ii.502 ("the mobled queen"); Nabokov explained to Edmund Wilson (Feb. 9, 1947): " 'Ghostly apes,' etc. is of course not supposed to sound like Shakespeare. The meter is not of his time."

257.18–22   ramparts . . . castle.]   Cf. E. W. Godwin, "Architecture and Costume of Shakespere's Plays," 1874, in Furness, II, 262–63.

257.23–24   an unweeded . . . seed.]   Hamlet calls the world "an un-weeded garden / That grows to seed" (I.ii.135–36).

257.28–31   The trunk . . . "self-slaughter."] Cf. *Hamlet*, I.ii.131–32: "Or that the Everlasting had not fix'd / His canon 'gainst self-slaughter!" In the Quartos and Folio, "canon" was spelt "cannon."

257.32–33   Wittenberg . . . Bruno's lectures] "Klein states, in his admirable *History of the Drama* . . . that Giordano Bruno delivered lectures at Wittenberg during the very year that Hamlet was a student there, and that Hamlet might have attended them, supposing that Hamlet, like most of Shakespeare's characters, was a contemporary of the poet's" (Furness, II, 332).

257.33–35   never using a watch . . . midnight.] Cf. *Hamlet* I.ii.251–2 and I.iv.3–5.

257.36–37   moonlight . . . steel,] Cf. *Hamlet* I.iv.51–53.

257.37   pauldron] Armor for the shoulder.

257.38   taces] Obsolete form of *tasses*, overlapping pieces of armor just below the waist.

257.39   Ratman] *Hamlet*, III.iv.24: Hamlet, hearing Polonius behind the arras: "How now! a rat? Dead, for a ducat, dead!" *Rat* is also German for "councillor," Polonius's position at Elsinore.

258.1   to stow . . . passage] *Hamlet* III.iv.212, IV.ii.1, IV.iii.16–37.

258.2   torch-bearing Switzers] *Hamlet* IV.v.98. "Switzers" are Swiss mercenaries employed as bodyguards.

258.3–4   sea-gowned] Cf. *Hamlet* V.ii.13.

258.6–7   Rosenstern and Guildenkranz, . . . twins] Cf. *Hamlet* II.ii.33–34.

258.9   sagebrush country] Sagebrush is a kind of wormwood (*Artemisia*): cf. Hamlet's "That's wormwood" (III.ii.181).

258.13–14   R. following young L.] Cf. *Hamlet* II.i.

258.14–15   Polonius . . . acting Caesar] Cf. *Hamlet* III.ii.98–106.

258.15–16   skull . . . live jester] Cf. *Hamlet* V.i.175–95.

258.18   poleaxe the Polacks] At *Hamlet* I.i.63 the Quarto phrase "sleaded pollax" and the Folio reading "sledded Pollax" have been interpreted as referring either to a leaded (or sledged) "poleaxe" or to "Polacks" (Poles) on sleds.

258.24   rivermaid's father] See Introduction, p. 168.22–23. In *Finnegans Wake* (1939), Anna Livia Plurabelle is in one sense the river Liffey.

258.25   salix.] Latin "willow."

258.26   glassy water] *Hamlet* IV.vii.167: "glassy stream."

258.28–29   trying . . . phallacious sliver]   "There on the pendent boughs
her crownet weeds / Clamb'ring to hang, an envious sliver broke" (*Hamlet*
IV.vii.172–73).

259.3–4   soaked, . . . bombast-quilted garments]   Cf. *Hamlet* IV.vii.181:
"her garments, heavy with their drink." "Bombast" originally meant cotton
or other soft material used as padding or stuffing.

259.4–5   hey non . . . old laud.]   Ophelia, before going to the brook,
sings, "Hey non nonny nonny" (IV.v.166); as she dies, Gertrude reports (in
the Second Folio's reading, adopted in some editions): "she chanted snatches
of old lauds" (IV.vii.177).

259.6–7   liberal shepherd . . . *Orchis mascula*]   Among the flowers Ophelia picked were "long purples, / That liberal shepherds give a grosser name
/ But our cold maids do dead men's fingers call them" (IV.vii.169–71). John
Dover Wilson identifies the "long purple" as the "early purple orchis, *Orchis
mascula*."

259.15–16   her name . . . shepherd in Arcadia.]   Cf. C. Eliot Browne,
"Notes on Shakespeare's Names" (*The Athenaeum*, 1876; in Furness, II, 242).

259.16–19   anagram of Alpheios . . . tee]   Alpheios or Alpheus, a river in
Greece and a river-god. He fell in love with and pursued the nymph Arethusa,
who fled from him and was changed by Artemis into a fountain; Alpheios
then flowed under the sea to be united with her. John Livingstone Lowes
points to Alpheus as a source for Coleridge's "Kubla Khan" (Nabokov's working title for *Bend Sinister* had been *The Person from Porlock*, after the person
who, Coleridge reports, interrupted him from a dream in which he had composed a longer version of "Kubla Khan.") Coleridge's "Alph, the sacred river,
ran," flowed in turn into the "riverrun" with which *Finnegans Wake* starts
and the ALP river that runs through Joyce's novel.

259.20   Vico Press]   *Finnegans Wake* was based on Giambattista Vico's
theory of cyclic history and was published in the U.S. by Viking Press.

259.21–22   Greek . . . Danske serpent name]   Cf. C. Elliot Browne, in
Furness, II, 242.

259.22   Lithe, lithping . . . Ophelia]   Cf. *Hamlet* III.i.144: "you jig and
amble, and you lisp."

259.22   Amleth's]   Amleth is the name of the hero in Saxo Grammaticus's
Historia Danica (written in the late 12th century), the source from which
Shakespeare (or the author of the Ur-*Hamlet*) derived the play.

259.23   mermaid of Lethe]   Cf. *Hamlet* IV.vii.176.

259.23–24   *Russalka letheana* of science]   Alluding to Pushkin's unfinished
playlet *Rusalka* ("The Mermaid," 1826–32).

259.25–26   in an embayed window]   Lucia Calhoun, describing a production with Edwin Booth as Hamlet, notes: "In a deep embayed window Ophelia kneels" (Furness, II, 256).

259.32–33   Ophelia, serviceableness]   John Ruskin (*Munera Pulveris*, 1872): "Ophelia, *serviceableness*, the true lost wife of Hamlet . . . " (Furness, II, 241).

260.2   the dead man's finger]   See note 259.6–7.

260.3   I loved . . . forty thousand brothers]   Cf. *Hamlet* V.i.269–71.

260.3–4   forty . . . moon)]   Cf. "Ali Baba and the Forty Thieves" in *The Thousand and One Nights* (also known as *The Arabian Nights*).

260.5   Lamord's pupils]   Lamord is the Norman soldier and horseman who praises Laertes' skill with his rapier (IV.vii.81–102).

260.6–8   caught a cold . . . sleazy lap]   While his head lay in Ophelia's lap as he watched the performance (III.ii). "Sleazy" means thin or flimsy, but the one other time Nabokov uses it, in the Foreword to *Pale Fire*, it is also associated with severe cold.

260.7–8   *l'aurore . . . verte.*]   "The shivering dawn in a pink and green dress," line 25 in Baudelaire's poem "Le Crépuscule du matin" ("Morning Twilight," 1852).

260.17   *Worte, worte, worte*]   German, "Words, words, words"; cf. Hamlet II.ii.192.

260.18   Tschischwitz]   Dr. Benno Tschischwitz's *Shakespeares Hamlet, vorzugsweise nach historischen Gesichtspuncten erläutert* (*Shakespeare's Hamlet Explained Chiefly From a Historical Point of View*, 1868), is cited in Furness, II, 331–32.

260.19   *soupir de petit chien*]   Little dog's sigh.

261.11–12   "her whole being . . . passion,"]   In Goethe's *Wilhelm Meisters Lehrjahre* (*Wilhelm Meister's Apprenticeship*), 4.14.

261.13   Oh, horrible.]   Cf. *Hamlet* I.v.80: "O, horrible, O, horrible, most horrible!"

261.22   *The World Waltzes*]   Metternich became prominent at the time (1810s) when the waltz began to dominate European ballrooms.

261.22–23   wise and wily statesman]   Cf. Ludwig Tieck, *Dramaturgische Blätter* (1824): "I see in Polonius a real statesman" (Furness, II, 285). When Tieck wrote this, Metternich was foreign minister and prime minister of the Austrian Empire and the foremost statesman in Europe.

261.27–28   Claudio . . . brought them]   *Hamlet* IV.vii.40–41.

261.34   German original (*Bestrafter Brudermord*)]   Through much of the 19th century this anonymous play (known from a manuscript of 1710) was thought to be a version of Shakespeare's presumed immediate source, the Ur-*Hamlet*, but scholars now agree it is in fact a corrupt version of Shakespeare's play, deriving from an English troupe's theatrical tour into Germany in the early 17th century. The title may be translated *Fratricide Punished*.

262.6–7   Polonius . . . 'father' of good news]   Cf. *Hamlet* II.ii.42.

262.17   'poor Yorick']   *Hamlet* V.i.184.

262.25–27   *Ubit' il' ne ubit'? . . . roka*—]   The first words (with their echo-reversal of the sound of "To be" and echo of the natural Russian translation ("Byt' ili ne byt'?")) mean "To kill or not to kill?"—alluding to "the well-known hypothesis that what Hamlet meant by the first words of his soliloquy was: 'Is my killing of the king to be or not to be?'" (Nabokov to Edmund Wilson, Feb. 9, 1947); cf. pp. 166.38–167.3 in this volume and Furness, II, 315: "v. Friesen adopts Tieck's and Ziegler's theory, that the soliloquy, 'To be or not to be,' refers not to suicide, but to the hazard of an attempt on the life of the King." Most of the translation is Russian, "except that *oprosen* is a non-existent noun derived from the verb *oprosit'*, 'to canvass,' 'to take a poll'; *vto bude* is a rather transparent distortion of *chto budet*, 'which would be' (*bude* is the Ukrainian equivalent of the Russian *budet*); *edler* is German for 'nobler': and *tzerpieren* is a quasi-Yiddish infinitive derived from the Russian *terpet'*, 'to endure,' 'to tolerate.'" (Simon Karlinsky, in *The Nabokov-Wilson Letters*, p. 186). Retranslated, the passage gives: "To kill or not to kill? There is the question. / What would be nobler: in the mind to endure / The fiery slings and arrows of evil fate . . . "

262.29–31   *L'égorgerai-je . . . destin*—]   "Shall I kill him or not? Here's the real problem. / Is it nobler in itself to support all the same / Both the darts and fire of a crushing destiny—" (*égorger* is literally "to cut the throat, to slaughter").

262.33–263.5   *Tam . . . crowflowers*—]   Translates *Hamlet* IV.vii.165–69 ("There is a willow grows aslant the brook / That shows his hoar leaves in the glassy stream; / There with fantastic garlands did she come / Of crow-flowers, nettles, daisies . . . "). The Russian is genuine, the English retranslation accurate, and as Nabokov notes in the Introduction there is a "built-in scholium": at IV.vii.169, the Second and Third Quartos have "Therewith fantastic garlands did she make," which Jennens interprets: "With the willow she made a garland, and stuck flowers in it" (Furness, I, 371), and Ember's genuine translation reflects both this text and commentary.

263.8–12   *Ne dumaete-li . . . sudar'?*]   Translates III.ii.275–78 ("Would not this, sir, and a forest of feathers—if the rest of my fortunes turn Turk with me—with two Provincial roses on my raz'd shoes, get me a fellowship in a cry of players?") as "Do you not think, sir, that this, and a forest of feathers on my hat, and two patterned roses on my razed shoes, would, if fortune posed me a Turk, get me a part in a theatre company, eh, sir?" "Patterned" in this retranslation of *kamchatye* does scant justice to Ember's find for "Provincial roses": a particular old style of silk pattern, and a play on remote Kamchatka province.

264.24   'russet'] *Hamlet* I.i.166: "But look, the morn in russet mantle clad . . . "

264.38   Several . . . zigzag profiles] See Introduction, p. 168.20–21, and note.

266.26   *Gott weiss was.*] God knows what.

268.12   *"Heraus, Mensch, marsch,"*] Out, man, move!

269.34–35   *Et voilà . . . prison.*] And there . . . and here I am. . . . A poor harmless critter they're dragging off to prison.

269.37–38   *Je suis . . . détresse*] I am ill, I'm in a bad way.

270.18   *Liebling*] Darling.

270.22   *Il est saoul*] He is drunk.

274.8   *chambre violette*] Violet room.

275.12   *Les Pensées*] Blaise Pascal's *Thoughts* (1670).

275.20–21   *à pas de loup*] Stealthily.

277.9   *"Mirokonzepsia"*] Almost "conception of the world" (*mira kontsepsia*) in Russian.

280.8   *ministr dvortza*] Russian, "Minister of the Court."

280.39–40   *pour . . . claire*] For good measure. To be precise, a large very light room.

284.31   *Erlkönig*] "The Elf King": a ballad by Goethe in which a little boy riding through the night with his father cries out at the threat of the elf king, who lusts after him. The father, thinking the boy only imagines danger, rides on, but when he reaches refuge he finds his son dead in his arms.

284.40   menstratum] Véra Nabokov glossed for Charles Timmer (Nov. 27, 1949): "a combination of 'stratum' (clouds) and 'menses' (blood), with just a touch of 'monstrosity.' "

286.39–287.2   Aldobrandini's "Wedding," . . . bride)] The fresco known as the "Aldobrandini Wedding" (formerly in the Villa of Cardinal Aldobrandini, now in the Vatican Gallery, Rome) was painted at the end of the first century B.C. for a Roman house on the Esquiline (the characters in it are jocularly misidentified here).

290.26–27   Victorian . . . ladies] Cf. for example Marie Corelli (1855–1924) whose works include *A Romance of Two Worlds* (1886), *Ardath: The*

Story of a Dead Self (1889), *The Soul of Lilith* (1892: in the author's words, "a strange and daring experiment . . . offered to those who are interested in the unseen 'possibilities' of the Hereafter"). At least five novels were written by persons claiming to have been guided by Corelli's spirit.

291.1   Miss Bidder]   Mary Bidder (later Mary Porter), a late Victorian novelist who also wrote on questions of spirituality.

291.13–14   papyrus . . . Rhind]   Once known as the Rhind papyrus, after its former owner, and now as the Ahmes papyrus, after its author. Dated between 1700 and 1550 B.C., it is the most important ancient Egyptian mathematical manuscript known, containing the first problems that can be called algebraic, as well as arithmetical and geometrical problems.

291.24–25   famous American poem]   The passages are from *Moby-Dick* (1871) by Herman Melville (see p. 167.17–18 in this volume).

292.1   Truganini . . . Tasmanian]   The aboriginals of Van Diemen's Land (later Tasmania) were hunted to extinction in the late 17th century; Truganini (1803–76), the Beauty of Bruny, nicknamed "Lallah Rookh" by Europeans, was the last survivor.

292.4–5   Raphael's . . . draught]   Raphael's cartoon for *The Miraculous Drought of Fishes* (c. 1515–16; Victoria and Albert Museum, London) for a tapestry now in the Vatican, rendering a scene from Luke 5:3–7.

292.27–28   "Civil War . . . youth."]   Cf. Horace, Epode 16, line 7.

292.29–30   Cruquius . . . Horace]   Jacobus Cruquius, professor at Bruges, used the four Horatian manuscripts housed in the monastery at Mount Blandin in preparing his edition of Horace (published 1578); the manuscripts were destroyed when the monastery was sacked, actually in 1566.

292.32–34   Appian Way . . . *rheda*?]   Allusion to Horace's *Satires*, Book I:V (for which there are important textual variants in the oldest of the Blandinian MSS), the only part where the raeda or rheda is explicitly used (line 86: "quattor hinc rapimur viginti et milia raedis," "From here we bowled along twenty-four miles in carriages").

292.34   Painted Ladies]   The Nymphalid butterfly *Vanessa cardui* Linnaeus.

292.40–293.2   Dr. Livingstone . . . Sakomi]   Sekgoma I (usually spelled Sekhomi or Sekhome by Livingstone), chief (1834–75, with two breaks) of the BaNgwato. When Livingstone met Sekgoma for the first time, in 1842, he was struck by the "state of both mental and moral degradation among his people. . . . Their conceptions of the Deity are of the most vague and contradictory nature, and his name conveys no more to their understanding than the idea of superiority. Hence they do not hesitate to apply the name of God to their chiefs, and I was every day shocked by being addressed by that title" (letter to J. J. Freeman, July 3, 1842).

293.7–10   eighteen thousand . . . Psalmanazar]   The story of the annual sacrifice demanded by "Psalmanaazaar," a "prophet" of the "Formosan religion" recurs throughout *An Historical and Geographical Description of Formosa* (1704) by George Psalmanazar (c. 1679–1763), real name unknown. A French-born literary impostor in London, Psalmanazar also published in 1704 a fraudulent autobiography in which he claimed to be a Formosan convert to Christianity.

293.37   *"petit éternuement intérieur"*]   Little inner sneeze.

294.3–4   Baron Munchausen's . . . story]   In Chapter 2 of *Baron Munchausen, Narrative of his Marvellous Travels* (1785), by Rudolph Eric Raspe (1737–94), the baron ties his horse up to what looks like a stump, and goes to sleep on the snow. He wakes up and the horse is nowhere to be seen, because in a sudden change of weather the snow has melted, the baron has sunk down to the level of the churchyard, and he finds that he had in fact tied his horse to the top of a steeple.

294.19–20   *Femineum . . . corpus.*]   From the *Epigrams* of Martial (c. 38–104), Bk. VIII, 68, line 7: "So a woman's body shines through silk."

294.26   *Sanglot*]   French, "sob"; see page 167.40–168.2.

297.37   Angliskii]   Russian, "English."

301.31   "Lacedaemonian"]   Spartan. Nabokov wrote to Edmund Wilson (Dec. 24, 1945): "I am working furiously at my novel (and very anxious to show you a couple of new chapters). I detest Plato, I loathe Lacedaemon and all Perfect States."

301.34   "Pankrat Tzikutin"]   See note 168.15.

303.1–2   *glockenmetall . . .* campane]]   Bell metal.

303.2–3   *geschützbronze . . .* cannoni]]   Gun metal.

303.4   *blasebalgen . . .* mekha]]   Blast furnace bellows.

303.9   *en escalier*]   Stepped down across the page. Such typography was typical of Vladimir Mayakovsky's pro-Bolshevik agitprop verse after the Russian Revolution.

304.13   *mouches volantes*]   Muscae volitantes, the floating specks in the vitreous humors of the eye.

304.24–25   FitzGerald contractions]   Irish physicist George FitzGerald (1851–1901) in 1892 proposed a contraction of distance along the direction of light's motion to explain why in the 1887 Michelson-Morley experiment no difference was found between the speed of light along lines parallel and perpendicular to the observer. Hendrik Lorentz elaborated on this when in 1895 he proposed that matter contracted along the direction of motion. The effect became known as the Fitzgerald-Lorentz contraction and was explained in Einstein's theory of relativity.

305.40   chess-Mephisto] Wolfgang Kempel's Automaton Chessplayer, built in Vienna in 1769 and exhibited around Europe and North America, contained a chess master ingeniously concealed within the cabinet who made the "automaton's" moves against its human challengers.

305.40–306.1   "I," . . . in the *cogito*!)] See note 179.14–15.

306.21   this Nile is settled)] Cf. the telegram sent by explorer John Speke (1827–64) to the Royal Geographic Society in 1862 after his visit to the point where the White Nile flows out of Lake Victoria: "Inform Sir Roderick Murchison that all is well, and that the Nile is settled." Speke first reached the lake in 1858, but his claim that it was the source of the Nile had been disputed.

308.8   [*Da mi basia mille*.]] From the fifth of the *Carmina* or lyrics of Catullus (c. 84–54 B.C.), lines 5–8: "nobis, cum semel occidit brevis lux, / nox est perpetua una dormienda. / da mi basia mille, deinde centum, / dein mille altera, dein secunda centum . . . " ("For us, when once the brief light has set, remains the sleeping of one perpetual night. Give me a thousand kisses, then a hundred, then another thousand, then a second hundred . . . ").

310.22   *que j'ai été veule*] How feeble I have been.

310.33   *voilette*] Veil.

312.15–16   '*cette petite . . . Ophélie.*'] "This little Phryne who thinks herself Ophelia." Phryne was a celebrated Greek courtesan, reputedly the model for Praxiteles's statue of Aphrodite.

314.28   *Gruss aus Padukbad*.] Greetings from Padukbad.

319.38   *dushka* [*animula*]] Russian then Latin: "little soul" (also "darling" in Russian).

320.16   *connu, mon vieux!*] That's old hat, old chap!

320.28   *néant*] Nothing(ness).

322.17   *puella*] Girl.

323.17–18   *Brevis . . . mille.*] See note 308.8.

327.29   *merzavtzy*] Russian *merzavets*, "scoundrel."

334.16–17   Kolokololiteishchikov] The name is Russian for "of bell-ringers."

335.18   *chinovnik*] Functionary.

337.24–25   *Stolitza i Usad'ba*] ´*Capital and Country*, a real pre-revolutionary Russian magazine.

337.25   *Die Woche*] *The Week*.

338.40   *même jeu*] Same again.

344.14–15   yarovization of the ego.] Yarovization or vernalization is the process of treating seeds in some way that will speed up flowering and fruiting. The Soviet agronomist Trofim Lysenko (1898–1976) falsely claimed that winter wheat could be made spring wheat by the inheritance of acquired characteristics. His belief that humans could radically transform the environment and his attacks on "bourgeois genetics" appealed to Stalin, who allowed Lysenko to gain control of Soviet biological science in the 1940s.

345.32–33   "*Yablochko . . .* rolling?"] Véra Nabokov to Dieter Ziemmer (Feb. 10, 1962): "A Bolshevik soldier song of the time of the revolution. The 'little apple' was meant to mean a bourgeois." The *chastushka* in full: "Hey, little apple, / Where are you rolling? / Bump into the Cheka [secret police], / And you won't come back!"

346.2   *Mezdhu tem . . .* themes?] "Meanwhile"; although *mezhdu temami* would mean "between the themes."

346.27–28   wrongly accented *piróshki*] *Piroshkí,* small pastry pies.

346.28   wrongly spelled *schtschi*] *Shchi,* cabbage soup.

347.15   morpho-blue] Any butterfly of the South American genus *Morpho,* with large, evenly colored metallic-blue wings.

356.19   *c'est . . . cabinets*] It's the tragedy of the toilets.

356.22   *C'est atroce.*] It's atrocious.

SPEAK, MEMORY

359.1   SPEAK, MEMORY . . . *Revisited*] Nabokov had considered inserting a motto at the beginning of the book but apparently changed his mind. In the setting copy of the 1966 edition appears the following:
Discarded motto to the First Edition, 1951
The house was there. Right there. I never imagined the place would have changed so completely. How dreadful—I don't recognize a thing. No use walking any farther. Sorry, Hopkinson, to have made you come such a long way. I had been looking forward to a perfect orgy of nostalgia and recognition! That man over there seems to be growing suspicious. Speak to him. Turistï. Amerikantsï. *Oh, wait a minute. Tell him I am a ghost. You surely know the Russian word for "ghost"?* Mechta. Prizrak. Metafizicheskiy kapitalist. *Run, Hopkinson!*

["Mechta. Prizrak. Metafizicheskiy kapitalist" means "Dream. Ghost. Metaphysical capitalist."]

361.15   Hilda Ward] One of Nabokov's three Russian-language tutees in his first winter in the U.S., in New York, 1940–41.

361.20   a short poem] "A Literary Dinner."

362.28   *Mnemosyne*] Greek goddess of memory and mother of the nine muses; also the name of a butterfly, *Parnassius mnemosyne,* which Nabokov drew for the 1966 edition (the drawing is reproduced on page 368 in this volume).

365.19   "Speak on, Memory,"]   Never written, apart from a few preparatory notes and fragments.

366.11   great cartoonist]   See page 547.24–25 and note.

366.22–23   ex Ponto]   After Ovid's *Epistulae ex Ponto* (*Letters from the Black Sea*), which records his sufferings in exile.

370.6–7   retired colonels]   Cf. Henry S. Olcott (1832–1907), a colonel in the U.S. Civil War who became a lawyer and writer on spiritualism. With Madame Blavatsky he founded the Theosophical Society in 1875 and was its first president; he lectured widely in India, Ceylon, and Japan.

370.13–15   bitter little embryos . . . parents.]   In "From the History of an Infantile Neurosis" (1918, revised 1923), popularly known as "The Case of the Wolf-Man," Freud analyzed a terrifying dream about wolves that his patient, a Russian aristocrat, had experienced immediately before his fourth birthday. Freud traced the source of the dream to his patient's unconscious memory, or perhaps fantasy, of having witnessed, at the age of eighteen months, "the primal scene" of his parents having sexual intercourse.

374.28   Abbazia]   Now Opatija, Croatia.

377.7   *Die Waffen Nieder!*]   (1889) *Down with Weapons!*

377.28   *Vozdushnïe puti*]   *Aerial Ways.*

378.19   *barin*]   Master, landowner.

379.2   *"Un jour . . . tomber,"*]   One day they are going to drop him.

380.36   *flou*]   Hazy, blurred.

382.15   *Ruslan . . . Pikovaya Dama*]   *Ruslan and Lyudmila* (1842), by Mikhail Glinka (1804–57) and *Pikovaya Dama* (1890; *The Queen of Spades*), by Pyotr Ilich Chaikovsky (1840–93), from a Pushkin poem (1820) and story (1834) respectively.

382.18   read over Pimen's shoulder]   Pimen, the monk writing his chronicle history of Russia in the opening scene of the opera *Boris Godunov* (1874) by Modest Mussorgsky (1839–81), as revised (1896) by Nikolay Rimsky-Korsakov (1844–1908). The opera is based on Pushkin's 1825 play.

382.20   Juliet's garden.]   In Act II of the opera *Roméo et Juliette* (1867) by Charles Gounod (1818–93).

388.2   *(bika za roga)*]   The bull by the horns.

393.20   *"Ah, que c'est beau!"*]   Oh, that's so beautiful!

394.17   *cul de jatte*]   Legless cripple.

394.35–38   little poem . . . *dïmnïy iris*]   "Florentsiya, ty iris nezhniy" ("Florence, you are a delicate iris," 1909), lines 11–12: "Tvoy dïmnïy iris budet snit'sya / Kak yunost' rannyaya moya" ("I will dream of your smoky iris, / As of my early youth").

398.1–6   Nikolay . . . "Nabokov's River"]   Nabokov was unaware that Nicolay Aleksandrovich Nabokov was not a participant in the expedition, although Wrangel and Litke did honor their friend by naming the river after him. Much of the action in Nabokov's *Pale Fire* takes place in Zembla, a location he chose without knowing about the Nabokov River on Nova Zembla.

398.14–15   *n'ayant . . . marin*]   Not having sea legs.

399.10–11   *pommettes*]   Cheekbones.

399.22   Nicolaus von Korff]   Nabokov intended to add a "genealogical note on Nicolaus von Korff" in later editions of *Speak, Memory*, taking it from an October 1971 interview with Kurt Hoffman of the *Bayerischer Rundfunk*, and published in *Strong Opinions* (New York: McGraw-Hill, 1973), page 188. Since he did not indicate exactly how this was to be done, the relevant passage from the interview is printed here: "My grandmother's paternal ancestors, the von Korffs, are traceable to the fourteenth century, while on their distaff side there is a long line of von Tiesenhausens, one of whose ancestors was Engelbrecht von Tiesenhausen of Livland who took part, around 1200, in the Third and Fourth Crusades. Another direct ancestor of mine was Can Grande della Scala, Prince of Verona, who sheltered the exiled Dante Alighieri, and whose blazon (two big dogs holding a ladder) adorns Boccaccio's *Decameron* (1353). Della Scala's granddaughter Beatrice married, in 1370, Wilhelm Count Oettingen, grandson of fat Bolko the Third, Duke of Silesia. Their daughter married a von Waldburg, and three Waldburgs, one Kittlitz, two Polenzes and ten Osten-Sackens later, Wilhelm Carl von Korff and Eleonor von der Osten-Sacken engendered my paternal grandmother's grandfather, Nicolaus, killed in battle on June 12, 1812."

399.30   *Justizrat*]   King's Counsel.

399.37   Wannsee]   Lake just west of Berlin.

400.7–8   *"Königlicher . . . Akziseneinnehmer"*]   Exciseman of the King of Poland and Elector of Saxony.

401.9   *vase de voyage*]   Traveler's toilet.

401.16   *"une noble . . . France"*]   A noblewoman that Russia has lent France this winter.

402.31   *"Encore un comte raté"*]   Another count lost.

405.22   *Qui . . . chassez-la!*]   Who is this woman—chase her away!

406.5   majorat]   An estate descending by primogeniture.

406.22   Sablin]   Evgeny Sablin (d. 1949).

406.27   Grand Duke Sergey]   Uncle of Tsar Nicholas II and governor-general of Moscow, assassinated February 17, 1905, by the Socialist Revolutionary Ivan Kalyaev.

407.5   Portsmouth Treaty]   Signed August 1905, in Portsmouth, New Hampshire, it brought a formal end to the Russo-Japanese War of 1904–5.

407.33–34   sang Prince Aleksey's castle]   In Rïleev's poem "Tsarevich Aleksey Petrovich v Rozhestvene" (1823).

407.36   my notes to *Onegin*]   In the commentary to IV.xix of his translation of Pushkin's *Eugene Onegin*.

408.14   platbands]   Grass borders, flower-beds.

408.19   Orange-tips]   Butterflies of the Pierid family whose white upper wings have orange tips.

409.2–3   *la Chambre du Revenant*]   The (bed)room of the ghost.

409.19–20   *on ne parle . . . pendu*]   You don't mention rope in the home of the hanged.

409.37   *escalier dérobé*]   Hidden staircase.

410.5–6   blackamoor . . . Pushkin]   Abram Gannibal (1693?–1781); Nabokov wrote about him in Appendix One to *Eugene Onegin*.

410.20   Schurmann]   Georg Caspar Schürmann (1672–1751).

412.12–13   Ayvazovski]   Ivan Ayvazovski (1817–1900).

415.3   "Ruka"]   Russian, "hand."

415.17–18   *"Basile, . . . attend."*]   Basil (Vasily), we are waiting for you.

415.25–26   *"l'audience . . . dire."*]   The audience is finished. I have nothing more to say to you.

416.2–3   "racemosa" . . . "Onegin"]   *Eugene Onegin*, commentary to VI.vii.

416.10–11   *"Pour . . . verte."*]   For my nephew, the most beautiful thing in the world—a green leaf.

416.38–417.1   *"Il sanglotait . . . rocher."*]   He was sobbing, sitting on a rock.

417.2–4   *"Ils . . . bois"*]   "They both look at each other, devouring each other with their eyes . . . " "She died in February, poor Colinette! . . . " "The sun was still shining, I wanted to see the great forests again . . . "

417.7–8   princely disregard . . . mute *e*'s.]   In French verse, a final *e* or -*ent*, normally unsounded, may optionally be given a slight sound and syllabic value depending on verbal and metrical context. Nabokov writes in his "Notes on Prosody" appendix to *Eugene Onegin*: "The *e muet*: the interplay between the theoretical or generic value of the unelided *e muet* (which is never heard as a full semeion, as all the other vowels in the line are) and its actual or specific value in a given line. The number of such incomplete semeia and their distribution allow endless varieties of melody. . . . "

418.20   The house, . . . 1940]   The house survived World War II and was still standing in 1996.

419.7–9   Beneath . . . Russia.]   Homage to Pushkin's *Eugene Onegin*, I.l.10–12: "I sred' poludennykh zybey, / Pod nebom Afriki moey, / Vzdykhat' o sumrachnoy Rossii" (translated by Nabokov as: "and 'mid meridian ripples / beneath the sky of my Africa / to sigh for somber Russia").

419.28   Noyer]   Real name Nussbaum.

419.34   *se débattant*]   Struggling.

419.36   *"chapelle . . . violents"*]   Ardent chapel of violent-toned leaves.

420.5   *"L'air . . . plaine*]   The clear air makes rise from the plain.

420.13–14   *Un vol . . . Toussaint*]   A flight of doves striates the tender sky, / The chrysanthemums deck themselves out for All Saints' Day.

421.24   *"Sophie . . . jolie*]   Sophie wasn't pretty.

421.28   *vie de château*]   Life in a castle.

431.5   Miss Rachel]   Rachel Home.

431.9   Miss Clayton]   Real surname, Sheldon.

431.35–36   Corelli's *The Mighty Atom*]   The novel (1896) warned against the dangers of atheism, as Nabokov notes in the Russian version of his autobiography, *Drugie berega*.

432.34–35   the instruction . . . *belle*)]   "Tell her that she is beautiful," from Siebel's song at the beginning of Act III of the opera *Faust* (1859) by Gounod.

432.35–36   Lenski's . . . *udalilis'*]   "Where, where, where have you gone," from Act II of Chaikovsky's opera *Eugene Onegin* (1879).

433.34   *shapka*]   Soft hat.

434.26   gutticles of the percha]   From "gutta percha."

435.17   Yaremich]   Stepan Yaremich (1860–1939), painter, draughtsman, and art historian close to the Mir Iskusstva group.

436.21–23   locomotive . . . in the sixties]   "In the famous photograph (1869) of the first two transcontinental trains meeting at Promontory Summit, Utah, the engine of the Central Pacific . . . is seen to have a great flaring funnel stack, while the engine of the Union Pacific . . . sports but a straight slender stack topped by a spark-arrester. Both types of chimneys were used on Russian locomotives." (Nabokov's *Lectures on Russian Literature*: "Commentary Notes" to part 1 of "*Anna Karenin*.")

436.29–37   Burness . . . poems]   Robert Burness translated Pushkin and Lermontov.

438.15–16   Mademoiselle]   Cécile Miauton.

440.32–33   *comme la Comtesse Karenine*]   Like Countess Karenin.

446.15   *bonne promenade*]   Lovely walk.

448.27–29   *Le Tour . . . Monte Cristo*]   Jules Verne's *Around the World in Eighty Days* (1873), Alphonse Daudet's *Little What's-His-Name* (1868), Victor Hugo's 1862 novel, and Alexandre Dumas the elder's *The Count of Monte Cristo* (1844–45).

449.38   *Votre tante, la Princesse*]   Your aunt, the princess.

450.18   *Mater Dolorosa*]   A common title for representations in art of the grieving mother of Jesus.

450.35   Racine's absurd play]   *Athélie* (1691).

451.31   *toquades anglaises*]   English fads.

452.19   Suchard]   A make of chocolates.

452.20–21   *La Revue des Deux Mondes*]   *Review of Two Worlds*.

453.3–4   *on allait . . . équipage*]   We would take carriage rides.

453.6   *polushubok*]   (Shortish) fur coat.

453.18   Brimstone]   A bright yellow Pierid butterfly, *Gonepteryx rhamni*.

454.9–10   *"Je suis . . . d'elle,"*]   I am a sylph beside her.

454.14–15   *"Excusez-moi, . . . pensées."*]   Sorry, I was smiling at my sad thoughts.

455.25   *"le comble."*]   The last straw.

457.22   *"Il pleut . . . Suisse"*]   It rains all the time in Switzerland.

458.29–31   *A celle . . . oublier*]   To her who has always known how to make others love her and will never know how to make herself forgotten.

459.26–460.3   Fra Angelico's . . . Swallowtail]   The only Fra Angelico *Annunciation* whose Gabriel rather resembles the Swallowtail, *Papilio machaon*, is on one of the door panels of the silver chest of the church of the Santissima Annunziata, Florence, now in the Museo di San Marco there.

461.5–7   Seba's *Locupletissimi . . . Descriptio*]   *An Accurate Description of the Richest Treasury of Natural Things*, in which Seba (1665–1736), a Dutch amateur naturalist, described the collection that was housed in his museum of natural history.

461.22   *Die Schmetterlinge*]   *The Butterflies.*

461.23–24   *Icones . . . Connus*]   *Historical Images of New or Little-Known Lepidoptera.*

461.26–27   *Die Gross-Schmetterlinge Europas*]   *The Macrolepidoptera of Europe.*

462.2   *le chemin . . . bruns*]   The brown butterfly path.

462.19–20   *Die Gross-Schmetterlinge der Erde*]   *The Macrolepidotera of the World.*

467.5   a schoolmate]   Nikolay Shustov.

467.35   Large White]   *Pieris brassicae.*

467.38   *Allons . . . potager!*]   Come on, they're only garden butterflies.

468.13   Urania moth]   Moth of the genus *Urania*, large, brightly colored, and with tailed hindwings.

468.20   Tortoiseshell butterflies]   Butterflies from the genera *Nymphalis*, *Aglais*, and *Vanessa* with mottled black, brown, red, and yellow wings.

468.30–31   Small White]   *Pieris rapae.*

468.35–38   And there . . . ceiling]   From lines 5–8 of Bunin's "Nastanet den'—ischeznu ya" ("The day will come—I will disappear," 1916).

468.39–469.4   Fet's "Butterfly" . . . respite.]   "Babochka" (1884), lines 5–8: "Ne sprashivay: otkuda poyavilas'? / Kuda speshu? / Zdes' na tsvetok ya legkiy opistilas' / I vot—dyshu."

469.5–8   Musset's . . . *embaumés*]   "The Willow" (1831–32), II, lines 164–65: "The golden moth in its light course / Crosses the embalmed meadows."

469.11–13   Fargue . . . *Sylvain*]   Léon Paul Fargue (1876–1947), "The Four Days": "frosts itself in blue like the wing of the Poplar Admirable," *Limenitis populi.*

470.19   Muromtsev]   Sergey Muromtsev (1850–1910).

471.13   Arran Browns]   The satyrid butterfly *Erebia ligea.*

471.17–18   Ringlet called Hero]   The satyrid *Ceononympha hero.*

471.21   Oak Eggar]   The lasiocampid moth *Lasiocampa quercus.*

471.24   Large Emerald]   The geometrid moth *Geometra papilionaria.*

471.25   Goat Moth]   *Cossus cossus.*

471.31   Sievers' Carmelite]   The notodontid moth *Odontosia sieversi.*

471.33   Silvius Skipper]   The hesperiid moth *Carterocephalus silvicolus.*

472.2–4   uncommon Hairstreak . . . white W]   The *Satyrium (Thecla) W-album.*

472.11–14   Wilhelm Edmundson . . . Dr. Schach]   *Schach* is German for "chess" or "check." Nabokov added this section to his autobiography after Edmund Wilson's harshly critical review (*New York Review of Books,* July 15, 1965) of Nabokov's 1964 translation of and commentary on *Eugene Onegin.* Wilson ended his first rejoinder to Nabokov's first reply (both in *New York Review of Books,* Aug. 26, 1965): "Nabokov's present advice [on a matter of Russian pronunciation] is quite at variance with that of his book on Gogol . . . [and] is a feature of ByeloRussian. Now, I have heard Mr. Nabokov insist on the superiority of the Petersburg pronunciation to that of Moscow, and am rather surprised to find him recommending the pronunciation of Minsk."

475.25   blind man . . . novel]   Albinus Kretschmar in *Kamera obskura* (*Laughter in the Dark*).

475.36   olive . . . Hummingbird moth]   The sphingid *Macroglossum stellatarum.*

476.15   Turgenevian benches]   From Turgenev's having his characters encounter one another in such settings so often in his fiction.

477.5   Pugs in England]   Small geometrids of the genera *Eupithecia* or *Chlorocystis.*

478.34   Fritillary . . . Norse goddess]   The Freya fritillary, *Boloria freija;* Freya is the goddess of love and beauty.

478.35   Cordigera]   The noctuid moth *Anarta cordigera.*

478.36–37   rose-margined Sulphurs]   The Pink Edged Sulphur, *Colias interior.*

479.6–9   Mariposa lilies . . . Longs Peak.]   The locale quietly shifts from Russia to the United States, from Vyra to Longs Peak, Colorado, and the vegetation changes accordingly.

480.2–3   Nevski Avenue]   Petersburg's main street.

481.25   *nécessaire de voyage*]   Travel bag.

481.26   "H.N."]   For "Hélène Nabokoff."

483.6   *omelette . . . fraises*]   Strawberry jam omelette.

483.36   Westinghousian]   Westinghouse, the manufacturer of the brakes.

484.22   *terrains à vendre*]   Land for sale.

484.37   Speckled Woods]   The satyrid butterfly *Pararge aegeria.*

484.38   Cleopatra]   The pierid butterfly *Gonepteryx cleopatra.*

485.14   Clouded Yellow] The pierid butterfly *Colias crocea*.

485.17   *cacahuètes*] Peanuts.

486.9–10   "butterfly" . . . *misericoletea*] In fact, *misirikote*.

486.19   Colette] Real name Claude Deprès.

486.35   *grain de beauté*] Mole.

487.34   *"Là-bas, . . . montagne,"*] "There, there, in the mountains." In Act II of *Carmen* (1875), by Georges Bizet (1838–75).

488.37   *tenue-de-ville-pour-fillettes*] Young girls' city wear.

490.31   Volgin] Real name Nikolay Sakharov.

491.22   *boules de gomme*] Gum, candy.

492.7   Ordo] Real name Ordyntsev.

492.18   Amur hawkmoth] The sphingid moth *Smerinthus tremulae amurensis*.

493.1   Sigismond Lejoyeux] See Foreword, page 366.9–10 (*Freude* is German for "joy").

493.3   a Ukrainian] Surname, Pedenko.

493.32   *pensums*] Impositions.

493.33–34   *Qui aime . . . bien*] Who loves well, punishes well.

493.36   a Pole] Borislav Okolokulak.

495.6   Lenski] Real name, Filip Zelenski.

496.20   *Schnellzugs*] Express trains.

499.35   poem by Lermontov] *Mtsyri* ("The Novice" in Georgian; 1840).

501.17–18   Rose in . . . altars,] *Mtsyri*, 6.18–19.

501.20–22   O, I . . . mine] *Mtsyri*, 18.11–12.

505.2   *poules*] Literally, "hens"; slang: "tarts."

505.3   fashionable lady] Ekaterina Danzas.

506.5   *diktantï*] Dictations.

508.17–18   *morbus . . . aureliani*] Butterfly sickness and passion.

509.13–17   This permission . . . court title] *Pravo* means "law, right." Nabokov relied on his cousin Sergey Sergeevich Nabokov for this guess at the reason for his father's being stripped of his court title. The *Pravo* article had been published on April 27, 1903; what actually provoked the court to take V.D. Nabokov's title was his denouncing in the St. Petersburg City Duma the slaughter of peaceful protesters on Bloody Sunday, 22 January 1905.

510.17   Cabbage Whites]   The members of the genus *Pieris*, especially *P. brassicae* and *P. rapae.*

511.20   *à fond*]   In depth.

512.26–27   *à l'âge . . . vozraste)*]   Of the most tender age.

513.16   "Ruslan" overture]   To Glinka's opera: see note 382.15.

514.34   (*"Battez!" "Rompez!"*)]   "Fight!" "Break!"

515.15   catalogue]   *Systematicheskii katalog biblioteki V.D. Nabokova* (St. Petersburg, 1904, supplement 1911).

519.24   Dzerzhinski's or Yagoda's men]   Feliks Dzerzhinski (1877–1926) led the Cheka, the first Soviet secret police organization, from its founding in 1917 until 1922, and then headed the Cheka's successors, the GPU (1922–23) and the OGPU (1923–26), until his death from a heart attack. Dzerzhinski was praised by Soviet propagandists for his merciless repression of opposition to Bolshevik rule; under his direction, the Cheka shot at least 140,000 persons and established scores of concentration camps. Genrikh Yagoda (1891–1938) was deputy head of the OGPU from 1926 to 1934, and head of its successor, the NKVD, from July 1934 to September 1936. As head of the NKVD Yagoda played a central role in the early stages of Stalin's purge of 1934–38. Yagoda was arrested in 1937 and shot in 1938 after a public show trial.

520.20   journalist . . . piece]   Snessarev's piece appeared in *Novoe Vremya* (*New Times*), October 16, 1911.

520.25   editor]   Aleksey Suvorin.

521.5–6   battle of Tsushima]   Decisive naval battle in the 1904–5 Russo-Japanese War, fought in the Tsushima Strait between Korea and Japan, May 27–29, 1905. The battle resulted in the destruction of the Russian Baltic Fleet.

521.21–22   *maître d'armes*]   Master of arms.

522.20–21   Pushkin . . . d'Anthès]   On January 27, 1837, Pushkin was killed in a duel by Georges d'Anthès (1812–95), an encounter Nabokov describes at length in *Eugene Onegin*, commentary to VI.xxix–xxx.

522.21–22   Lermontov . . . Martïnov]   Lermontov died in a duel with an old schoolmate in 1841.

522.22   Sobinov . . . part of Lenski]   The tenor Leonid Sabinov (1872–1934), in Chaikovsky's opera *Eugene Onegin.*

522.23–24   No Russian writer . . . *une rencontre*]   For Nabokov's own detailed explanation of the Russian duel, see *Eugene Onegin*, commentary to VI.xxix–xxx.

524.16–17   two Russian Fascists]   Sergey Tabortisky and Pyotr Shabelsky-Bork, extreme right-wing Monarchists who later became Fascists.

525.21–22   ranch you and I rented]   Nabokov and his wife, Véra, spent the spring of 1953 in Portal, Arizona.

528.11–12   Dilanov-Tomski]   Play on "Dylan Thomas."

531.25   monongahela]   Old name for American, especially rye, whiskey, originally made in Pennsylvania's Monongahela River region.

532.30   *azotea*]   Flat roof of a house.

533.9   *Pardieu!*]   Why of course!

533.32   amelus]   A limbless fetus.

534.30   *achtzehn A*]   18A.

534.38   Marat, who died in a shoe]   Jacques-Louis David's painting *Marat expirant* (1793) shows French revolutionary leader Jean-Paul Marat (1743–93) dying in the bathtub in which he was stabbed; a writing board resting on top of the tub makes it resemble a shoe.

535.5   Chapman's new Hairstreak]   The lycaenid butterfly *Callophrys avis* Chapman.

535.5–6   Mann's . . . White]   The pierid butterfly *Pieris manni.*

537.15–16   *"Tolstoy . . . mourir,"*]   "Tolstoy has just died" (Nov. 21, 1910).

542.26–27   Etymologically, "pavilion" . . . related.]   "Pavilion" derives from Latin *papilio,* "butterfly," since in its original meaning it was a large, often sumptuous tent, which could be unfolded and spread out like a butterfly.

544.14–15   Vivian Bloodmark]   Anagram of "Vladimir Nabokov."

547.24–25   puffed-out . . . trim uniforms]   A tribute to cartoonist Otto Soglow (1900–75), a frequent contributor to *The New Yorker* from 1925, this describes the characters in the series he created, *The Little King.*

548.4   *fol . . . rêvant*]   "Mad love" or "langorous and dreaming."

549.12   foreign town]   Prague.

550.23   Tiergarten]   In Berlin.

552.6–7   Apuhtin's . . . Konstantin's]   Aleksey Apukhtin (1840–93), minor poet, and Grand Duke Konstantin Konstantinovich Romanov (1858–1915), president of the Academy of Sciences, known for his melancholy verse.

552.7   *tsïganski*]   Gypsy.

553.19   Somov]   Konstantin Somov (1869–1939), painter in the Mir Iskusstva group.

555.5   Mother Nature eliminated]   Nabokov wrote to Katharine White (Sept. 4, 1949): "I meant that by the very nature of things (hence 'Mother Nature') the two other girls tacitly gave Tamara the right of way."

555.7   Petrarchally exact] Petrarch recorded in his autobiographical treatise *Secretum meum* the place, time, and date (April 6, 1327) when he first saw
the lady celebrated as Laura in his *Canzoniere*.

556.5–6   Camberwell Beauties] The nymphalid butterfly *Nymphalis (Vanessa) antiopa*.

561.19   Shishkin] Ivan Shishkin (1832–98).

562.14   Mozzhuhin] Ivan Mozzhuhin (1888–1939); he also became a star
in Berlin.

562.37   enormous column] The Alexander Column, erected by Nicholas
I in 1834 to the memory of Alexander I.

562.40   Pushkin's "*Exegi monumentum*"] "Ya pamyatnik sebe vozdvig
nerukotvorniy" ("I have erected a monument to myself not turned by
hand"), Pushkin's 1836 imitation of Horace's "Exegi monumentum" (*Odes*
III.xxx: "I have raised a monument"). Nabokov used the title for his translation of Pushkin's poem in *Three Russian Poets*.

563.18   Vladimir Hippius] Hippius (1876–1941) also wrote under the
names Vladimir Bestuzhev and Vladimir Neledinskiy.

564.23–24   Hans Andersen's little mermaid] In order to be with her human prince, the little mermaid accepts being severed from her family, having
her tongue cut out, and walking on new human legs even if it feels as if she
is stepping on sharp knives.

568.18   Tauric] Of the southern Crimea.

568.24–25   case of Pushkin] Expelled from St. Petersburg in May 1820,
Pushkin spent most of the summer in the Caucasus and three weeks in southern Crimea. He had to remain away from the capital until 1826. Nabokov
discusses his "exile" in *Eugene Onegin*, commentary to Chap. 8, IV.

569.13   Countess Sofia Panin] One of the leaders of the Constitutional
Democratic Party.

571.4–5   Euxine race . . . Hippolyte Grayling] The Black Sea race of the
satyrid butterfly *Pseudochazara hippolyte*.

571.9   Lidia T.] Lidia Tokmakov.

571.11   Sorin] Savely Sorin (1878–1953), portraitist.

571.37   Cynara] For Dowson's poem, see note 167.32–33.

572.7–9   Happy . . . fiction] Nabokov preserved some of Valentina Shulgin's letters to him in his first novel, *Mashen'ka* (*Mary*).

572.29–30   *et la montagne . . . chêne*] "And the mountain and the great
oak," line 26 of Chateubriand's poem "Romance à Hélène": "Combien j'ai
douce souvenance" ("Romance for Hélène": "How sweet a memory I

have"), composed in 1805 and later included in his novella *Aventures du dernier Abencérage* (1826; *Adventures of the Last Abencerage*).

575.11   *nécessaire*]   Small case, bag.

575.19   Gruner's Orange-tip, Heldreich's Sulphur, Krueper's White]   The pierid butterflies *Anthocaris gruneri, Colias aurorina heldreichi* and *Pieris krueperi.*

575.37   Korney Chukovski]   Children's writer and literary critic (1882–1969).

580.5   gloriettes]   Ornamented chambers.

581.28   E. Harrison]   Ernest Harrison (1877–1943).

582.7–8   puzzled compatriot . . . occupant]   Mikhail Kalashnikov; he and Nabokov actually remained as roommates, first in Great Court then in rented rooms at 2 Trinity Lane, for two years.

583.12–13   loquacious tower clocks]   Wordsworth, *The Prelude*, III.53: "Near me hung Trinity's loquacious clock" (1850 ed.; "Near me was," 1805 ed.).

585.3   *épicier*]   Grocer.

585.38   flight of Trotsky]   In 1907 Leon Trotsky (1879–1940) began his second escape from Siberian exile hidden under a load of hay in a reindeer sleigh. He described his escape in *There and Back* (1907) and *My Life* (1930).

586.12   *pogromshchik*]   Pogromist.

586.17   *Sitzriesen*]   People who look tall sitting down.

586.32   Russian naturalists]   Such as Grigoriy Grum-Grzhimaylo (1860–1936), Nikolay Przhevalksy (1839–88), and Grand-Duke Nikolay Romanov (1859–1918).

587.25   *anxietas tibiarum*]   Anxiety of the tibias.

589.20–21   I translated . . . Brooke]   In his article "Rupert Bruk" (1922).

590.35   *en escalier*]   Stepped, staircase.

592.12–13   Ezhov and Yagoda . . . Uritski and Dzerzhinski]   For Yagoda and Dzerzhinski, see note 519.24. Nikolai Ezhov (or Yezhov; 1895–1940) was head of the NKVD, the Soviet secret police, from September 1936 to December 1938. Under Stalin's orders, he directed the NKVD to carry out millions of arrests and executions in a reign of terror that became known as the "Yezhovshchina" ("time of Yezhov"). Yezhov was arrested in 1939 and shot in secret in 1940. Moisei Uritski (1873–1918) helped disperse the elected Constituent Assembly in January 1918 and became chairman of the Petrograd Cheka (secret police) in March 1918. He was assassinated on August 30, 1918, by the friend of an officer cadet who had been shot by the Cheka a few days earlier.

592.17   *quinquennium Neronis*] "Five years of Nero." The first five years of Nero's reign, A.D. 54–59, were relatively benevolent.

592.26   M. K.] Mikhail Kalashnikov.

592.27   N. R.] Nikita Romanov.

592.28   P. M.] Peter Mrosovski.

592.31   R. C.] Robert de Calry.

593.2   *The Shropshire Lad*] *A Shropshire Lad* (1896), by A. E. Housman (1859–1936).

595.26   *Préfectures* and *Polizeipraesidiums*] Police headquarters.

596.14–15   La Bruyère's . . . caterpillar] Jean La Bruyère (1645–96), in his *Les Caractères de Théophraste traduits du grec avec Les Caractères ou les Moeurs de ce siècle* (*The Characters of Theophrastus with the Characters or the Manners of This Century*), 6th ed. (1691), "De la Mode (Of Fashion)," 2: "This one likes insects; he buys new ones every day; he is above all the foremost man in Europe for butterflies; he has them in all sizes and colors. What time do you take to visit him? He is plunged in bitter grief; he is black in spirits, so upset that all the family suffers: for he has had an irreparable loss. Come closer, look what he is showing you on his finger, lifeless, just expired: a caterpillar, and what a caterpillar!"

596.15–16   Gay's "philosophers . . . butterflies,"] Lines 19–20 of "To a Lady on Her Passion for old China" (1725) by John Gay (1685–1732).

596.17–18   Pope's "curious . . . fair"] From his *Imitations of English Poets: Earl of Dorset*: II: "Phryne" (1709) which ends: "So have I known those Insects fair, / (Which curious *Germans* hold so rare,) / Still vary Shapes and Dyes; / Still gain new Titles with new Forms; / First Grubs obscene, then wriggling Worms, / Then painted Butterflies" (lines 19–24).

596.28   *Ein bischen retouchiert*] Slightly retouched.

601.12   Moscow Art Theatre] Russia's leading and first artistically innovative theater, founded in 1897 by Konstantin Stanislavsky and Vladimir Nemirovich-Danchenko.

602.29   a Russian grammar] Jakow Trachtenberg, *Lehrbuch der russischen Sprache in der neuen Orthographie zum Selbstunterricht* (*Teach Yourself Russian in the New Orthography*, Berlin, 1927). Lesson 12, the first with coherent sentences, has "I am a doctor" and "Where is the pineapple?" *Ananas* (pineapple), like *banan*, is almost the same in Russian and German.

602.33   *krestoslovitsï*] The word subsequently adopted in the Soviet Union was *krossvord*.

603.10–12   combined . . . His group] In *Conclusive Evidence*, this reads: "were the so-called Adamites, an appellation fancifully derived (by the poet

Hodasevich, I think) from the name of their leader, a talented critic who strove to combine the greenish twilight of a kind of catacumbal Christianity with the pagan mores of ancient Rome. The Adamites . . ." Georgy Adamovich (1892–1972) was a critic and minor poet.

604.10   *Heavy Lyre*]   *Tyazholaya lira* (1922).

604.13–14   Dostoevskian Alyoshas . . . Smerdyakovs]   Alyosha, the saintly, forgiving brother, and Smerdyakov, the murderer of Fyodor Karamazov, in *The Brothers Karamazov* (1880).

604.29   *zakuski*]   Snacks, nibbles.

605.2   Les Hesperides]   11 rue Partonneaux.

607.25–26   Poplavski . . . aquiline lives]   Boris Poplavski (1903–35); "Morella, I" (1930), line 19: "O, Morella, usni, kak uzhasny ogromnye zhizni" (*ogromnye zhizni*: literally, "enormous lives"). The rest of the poem justifies the eagle imagery in Nabokov's translation.

607.33   double agent]   Sergey Efron (1893–1940).

607.35   Sirin]   From 1921, pseudonym used by Nabokov in emigration (he continued to use the pseudonym for his Russian writings into the 1960s).

611.5   a night]   November 19, 1939, according to the manuscript.

612.5   *visa de sortie*]   Exit visa.

612.18   the problem's position]   See also the diagram and solution of the problem in Nabokov's *Poems and Problems* (1970).

612.32   *violet de bureau*]   Office purple.

613.2–3   THEY . . . Horatian inflection.]   "Eheu fugaces, Postume, Postume, labuntur anni" ("Alas, O Postumus, Postumus, the fleeting years slip by," *Odes* II.xiv.1–2).

613.5–6   roses of Paestum]   Paestum, south of modern Naples, was founded as the city-colony Poseidonia by the Greeks about 600 B.C. and conquered by the Romans three centuries later. Its roses were proverbial in Latin literature. Cf. Ovid, *Ex Ponto* IV.225–29 ("and sooner . . . shall the lily surpass in perfume the roses of Paestum than you shall forget what we share") and Virgil, *Georgics* IV.119 ("I might sing of the rose-beds of twice-blooming Paestum").

620.8–10   Lamarck's . . . physicists]   Nabokov explained to *The New Yorker* editor Katharine White (April 16, 1950): "Geneticists of the 'Western' school, when rejecting the oversimplification of Lamarck in regard to acquired characters, have trouble in explaining how this or that character (say, a missing tooth throughout the line of a given family) was acquired and inherited in the first place. The appeal to 'chance mutations' leads us back to Noah's Ark. Physicists of the 'Einstein' school (actually the idea was current before Einstein) have much the same trouble (i.e. a tendency to have the subject drift into almost metaphysical obscurities) when they maintain that the world is a finite curvature but are asked what exists on the *outside* of that curvature of that inside finite world, since no matter how ample a sphere you make, it must have some environment within which to *be* a sphere. I am afraid that it would take much too long to clarify things in the passage itself for readers who are unaware of the difficulties modern science encounters, especially when divorced from philosophy."

625.31   Titania]   In *A Midsummer Night's Dream*, the fairy queen Titania has Moth as one of her fairy servants.

627.20   *pâte tendre*]   Soft paste.

CATALOGING INFORMATION

Nabokov, Vladimir Vladimirovich, 1899–1977.
    [Selections. 1996]
    Novels and memoirs, 1941–1951 / Vladimir Nabokov.
       p. cm. — (The Library of America ; 87)
    Contents: The real life of Sebastian Knight — Bend
sinister — Speak, memory.

    1. Nabokov, Vladimir Vladimirovich, 1899–1977.
I. Title.   II. Series.
PS3527.A15A6   1996b
813'.54—dc20   96-15257
ISBN 1–883011–18–3 (alk. paper)   CIP

THE LIBRARY OF AMERICA SERIES

This book is set in 10 point Linotron Galliard,
a face designed for photocomposition by Matthew Carter
and based on the sixteenth-century face Granjon. The paper is
acid-free Ecusta Nyalite and meets the requirements for permanence
of the American National Standards Institute. The binding
material is Brillianta, a woven rayon cloth made by
Van Heek-Scholco Textielfabrieken, Holland.
The composition is by The Clarinda
Company. Printing and binding by
R.R.Donnelley & Sons Company.
Designed by Bruce Campbell.

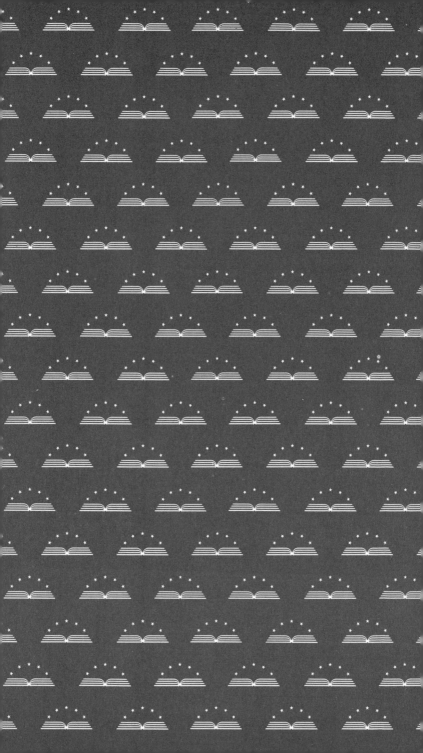